THOMAS HARRIS

RED DRAGON

THE SILENCE OF THE LAMBS

Red Dragon originally published in Great Britain in 1982
by The Bodley Head Ltd.

The Silence of the Lambs originally published in Great Britain in 1988
by William Heinemann Ltd.

This combined edition published in Great Britain in 1991 by
Peerage Books an imprint of
Reed International Books Limited
Michelin House
81 Fulham Road
London SW3 6RB

ISBN 1 85052 231 6

Printed and bound in Great Britain by The Bath Press

THOMAS HARRIS

CONTENTS

RED DRAGON

One can only see what one observes,
and one observes only things which are already
in the mind

ALPHONSE BERTILLON

. . . For Mercy has a human heart,
Pity a human face,
And Love, the human form divine,
And Peace, the human dress.
  WILLIAM BLAKE, *Songs of Innocence*,
  ('The Divine Image')

Cruelty has a Human Heart,
And Jealousy a Human Face,
Terror the Human Form Divine,
And Secrecy the Human Dress.

The Human Dress is forged Iron,
The Human Form a fiery Forge,
The Human Face a Furnace seal'd,
The Human Heart its hungry Gorge.
  WILLIAM BLAKE, *Songs of Experience*,
  ('A Divine Image')*

*After Blake's death, this poem was found with
prints from the plates of *Songs of Experience*.
It appears only in posthumous editions.

Chapter One

Will Graham sat Crawford down at a picnic table between the house and the ocean and gave him a glass of iced tea.

Jack Crawford looked at the pleasant old house, saltsilvered wood in the clear light. 'I should have caught you in Marathon when you got off work,' he said. 'You don't want to talk about it here.'

'I don't want to talk about it anywhere, Jack. You've got to talk about it, so let's have it. Just don't get out any pictures. If you brought pictures, leave them in the briefcase – Molly and Willy will be back soon.'

'How much do you know?'

'What was in the Miami *Herald* and the *Times*,' Graham said. 'Two families killed in their houses a month apart. Birmingham and Atlanta. The circumstances were similar.'

'Not similar. The same.'

'How many confessions so far?'

'Eighty-six when I called in this afternoon,' Crawford said. 'Cranks. None of them knew details. He smashes the mirrors and uses the pieces. None of them knew that.'

'What else did you keep out of the papers?'

'He's blond, right-handed and really strong, wears a size-eleven shoe. He can tie a bowline. The prints are all smooth gloves.'

'You said that in public.'

'He's not too comfortable with locks,' Crawford said. 'Used a glass cutter and a suction cup to get in the house last time. Oh, and his blood's AB positive.'

'Somebody hurt him?'

'Not that we know of. We typed him from semen and saliva. He's a secretor.' Crawford looked out at the flat sea. 'Will, I want to ask you something. You saw this in the papers. The second one was all over the TV. Did you ever think about giving me a call?'

'No.'

'Why not?'

'There weren't many details at first on the one in Birmingham. It could have been anything – revenge, a relative.'

'But after the second one, you knew what it was.'

'Yeah. A psychopath. I didn't call you because I didn't want to. I know who you have already to work on this. You've got the best lab. You'd have Heimlich at Harvard, Bloom at the University of Chicago –'

'And I've got you down here fixing fucking boat motors.'

'I don't think I'd be all that useful to you, Jack. I never think about it anymore.'

'Really? You caught two. The last two we had, you caught.'

'How? By doing the same things you and the rest of them are doing.'

'That's not entirely true, Will. It's the way you think.'

'I think there's been a lot of bullshit about the way I think.'

'You made some jumps you never explained.'

'The evidence was there,' Graham said.

'Sure. Sure there was. Plenty of it – afterward. Before the collar there was so damn little we couldn't get probable cause to go in.'

'You have the people you need, Jack. I don't think I'd be an improvement. I came down here to get away from that.'

'I know it. You got hurt last time. Now you look all right.'

'I'm all right. It's not getting cut. You've been cut.'

'I've been cut, but not like that.'

'It's not getting cut. I just decided to stop. I don't think I can explain it.'

'If you couldn't look at it anymore, God knows I'd understand that.'

'No. You know – having to look. It's always bad, but you get so you can function anyway, as long as they're dead. The hospital, interviews, that's worse. You have to shake it off and keep on thinking. I don't believe I could do it now. I could make myself look, but I'd shut down the thinking.'

'These are all dead, Will,' Crawford said as kindly as he could.

Jack Crawford heard the rhythm and syntax of his own speech in Graham's voice. He had heard Graham do that before, with other people. Often in intense conversation Graham took on the other person's speech patterns. At first, Crawford had thought he was doing it deliberately, that it was a gimmick to get the back-and-forth rhythm going.

Later Crawford realized that Graham did it involuntarily, that sometimes he tried to stop and couldn't.

Crawford dipped into his jacket pocket with two fingers. He flipped two photographs across the table, face up.

'All dead,' he said.

Graham stared at him a moment before picking up the pictures.

They were only snapshots: A woman, followed by three children and a duck, carried picnic items up the bank of a pond. A family stood behind a cake.

After half a minute he put the photographs down again. He pushed them into a stack with his finger and looked far down the beach where the boy hunkered, examining something in the sand. The woman stood watching, hand on her hip, spent waves creaming around her ankles. She leaned inland to swing her wet hair off her shoulders.

Graham, ignoring his guest, watched Molly and the boy for as long as he had looked at the pictures. Crawford was pleased. He kept the satisfaction out of his face with the same care he had used to choose the site of this conversation. He thought he had Graham. Let it cook.

Three remarkably ugly dogs wandered up and flopped to the ground around the table.

'My God,' Crawford said.

'These are probably dogs,' Graham explained. 'People dump small ones here all the time. I can give away the cute ones. The rest stay around and get to be big ones.'

'They're fat enough.'

'Molly's a sucker for strays.'

'You've got a nice life here, Will. Molly and the boy. How old is he?'

'Eleven.'

'Good-looking kid. He's going to be taller than you.'

Graham nodded. 'His father was. I'm lucky here. I know that.'

'I wanted to bring Phyllis down here. Florida. Get a place when I retire, and stop living like a cave fish. She says all her friends are in Arlington.'

'I meant to thank her for the books she brought me in the hospital, but I never did. Tell her for me.'

'I'll tell her.'

Two small bright birds lit on the table, hoping to find jelly. Crawford watched them hop around until they flew away.

'Will, this freak seems to be in phase with the moon. He killed the Jacobis in Birmingham on Saturday night, June 28, full moon. He killed the Leeds family in Atlanta night before last, July 26. That's one day short of a lunar month. So if we're lucky we may have a little over three weeks before he does it again.

'I don't think you want to wait here in the Keys and read about the next one in your Miami *Herald*. Hell, I'm not the pope, I'm not saying what you ought to do, but I want to ask you, do you respect my judgment, Will?'

'Yes.'

'I think we have a better chance to get him fast if you help. Hell, Will, saddle up and help us. Go to Atlanta and Birmingham and look, then come on to Washington. Just TDY.'

Graham did not reply.

Crawford waited while five waves lapped the beach. Then he got up and slung his suit coat over his shoulder. 'Let's talk after dinner.'

'Stay and eat.'

Crawford shook his head. 'I'll come back later. There'll be messages at the Holiday Inn and I'll be a while on the phone. Tell Molly thanks, though.'

Crawford's rented car raised thin dust that settled on the bushes beside the shell road.

Graham returned to the table. He was afraid that this was how he would remember the end of Sugarloaf Key – ice melting in two tea glasses and paper napkins fluttering off the redwood table in the breeze and Molly and Willy far down the beach.

Sunset on Sugarloaf, the herons still and the red sun swelling.

Will Graham and Molly Foster Graham sat on a bleached drift log, their faces orange in the sunset, backs in violet shadow. She picked up his hand.

'Crawford stopped by to see me at the shop before he came out here,' she said. 'He asked directions to the house. I tried to call you. You really ought to answer the phone once in a while. We saw the car when we got home and went around to the beach.'

'What else did he ask you?'

'How you are.'

'And you said?'

'I said you're fine and he should leave you the hell alone. What does he want you to do?'

'Look at evidence. I'm a forensic specialist, Molly. You've seen my diploma.'

'You mended a crack in the ceiling paper with your diploma, I saw that.' She straddled the log to face him. 'If you missed your other life, what you used to do, I think you'd talk about it. You never do. You're open and calm and easy now . . . I love that.'

'We have a good time, don't we?'

Her single styptic blink told him he should have said something better. Before he could fit it, she went on.

'What you did for Crawford was bad for you. He has a lot of other people – the whole damn government I guess – why can't he leave us alone?'

'Didn't Crawford tell you that? He was my supervisor the two times I left the FBI Academy to go back to the field. Those two cases were the only ones like this he ever had, and Jack's been working a long time. Now he's got a new one. This kind of psychopath is very rare. He knows I've had . . . experience.'

'Yes, you have,' Molly said. His shirt was unbuttoned and she could see the looping scar across his stomach. It was finger width and raised, and it never tanned. It ran down from his left hipbone and turned up to notch his rib cage on the other side.

Dr Hannibal Lecter did that with a linoleum knife. It happened a year before Molly met Graham, and it very nearly killed him. Dr Lecter, known in the tabloids as 'Hannibal the Cannibal,' was the second psychopath Graham had caught.

When he finally got out of the hospital, Graham resigned from the Federal Bureau of Investigation, left Washington and found a job as a diesel mechanic in the boatyard at Marathon in the Florida Keys. It was a trade he grew up with. He slept in a trailer at the boatyard until Molly and her good ramshackle house on Sugarloaf Key.

Now he straddled the drift log and held both her hands. Her feet burrowed under his.

'All right, Molly. Crawford thinks I have a knack for the monsters. It's like a superstition with him.'

'Do you believe it?'

Graham watched three pelicans fly in line across the tidal flats. 'Molly, an intelligent psychopath – particularly a sadist – is hard to catch for several reasons. First, there's no traceable motive. So you can't go that way. And most of the time you won't have any help from informants. See, there's a lot more stooling than sleuthing behind most arrests, but in a case like this there won't *be* any informants. *He* may not even know that he's doing it. So you have to take whatever evidence you have and extrapolate. You try to reconstruct his thinking. You try to find patterns.'

'And follow him and find him,' Molly said. 'I'm afraid if you go after this maniac, or whatever he is – I'm afraid he'll do you like the last one did. That's it. That's what scares me.'

'He'll never see me or know my name, Molly. The police, they'll have to take him down if they can find him, not me. Crawford just wants another point of view.'

She watched the red sun spread over the sea. High cirrus glowed above it.

Graham loved the way she turned her head, artlessly giving him her less perfect profile. He could see the pulse in her throat, and remembered suddenly and completely the taste of salt on her skin. He swallowed and said, 'What the hell can I do?'

'What you've already decided. If you stay here and there's more killing, maybe it would sour this place for you. *High Noon* and all that crap. If it's that way, you weren't really asking.'

'If I *were* asking, what would you say?'

'Stay here with me. Me. Me. Me. And Willy, I'd drag him in if it would do any good. I'm supposed to dry my eyes and wave my hanky. If things don't go so well, I'll have the satisfaction that you did the right thing. That'll last about as long as taps. Then I can go home and switch one side of the blanket on.'

'I'd be at the back of the pack.'

'Never in your life. I'm selfish, huh?'

'I don't care.'

'Neither do I. It's keen and sweet here. All the things that happen to you before make you know it. Value it, I mean.'

He nodded.

'Don't want to lose it either way,' she said.

'Nope. We won't, either.'

Darkness fell quickly and Jupiter appeared, low in the southwest.

They walked back to the house beside the rising gibbous moon. Far out past the tidal flats, bait fish leaped for their lives.

Crawford came back after dinner. He had taken off his coat and tie and rolled up his sleeves for the casual effect. Molly thought Crawford's thick pale forearms were repulsive. To her he looked like a damnably wise ape. She served him coffee under the porch fan and sat with him while Graham and Willy went out to feed the dogs. She said nothing. Moths batted softly at the screens.

RED DRAGON

'He looks good, Molly,' Crawford said. 'You both do – skinny and brown.'

'Whatever I say, you'll take him anyway, won't you?'

'Yeah. I have to. I have to do it. But I swear to God, Molly, I'll make it as easy on him as I can. He's changed. It's great you got married.'

'He's better and better. He doesn't dream so often now. He was really obsessed with the dogs for a while. Now he just takes care of them; he doesn't talk about them all the time. You're his friend, Jack. Why can't you leave him alone?'

'Because it's his bad luck to be the best. Because he doesn't think like other people. Somehow he never got in a rut.'

'He thinks you want him to look at evidence.'

'I do want him to look at evidence. There's nobody better with evidence. But he has the other thing too. Imagination, projection, whatever. He doesn't like that part of it .'

'You wouldn't like it either if you had it. Promise me something, Jack. Promise me you'll see to it he doesn't get too close. I think it would kill him to have to fight.'

'He won't have to fight. I can promise you that.'

When Graham finished with the dogs, Molly helped him pack.

Chapter Two

Will Graham drove slowly past the house where the Charles Leeds family had lived and died. The windows were dark. One yard light burned. He parked two blocks away and walked back through the warm night, carrying the Atlanta police detectives' report in a cardboard box.

Graham had insisted on coming alone. Anyone else in the house would distract him – that was the reason he gave Crawford. He had another, private reason: he was not sure how he would act. He didn't want a face aimed at him all the time.

He had been all right at the morgue.

The two-story brick home was set back from the street on a wooded lot. Graham stood under the trees for a long time looking at it. He tried to be still inside. In his mind a silver pendulum swung in darkness. He waited until the pendulum was still.

A few neighbors drove by, lookng at the house quickly and looking away. A murder house is ugly to the neighbors, like the face of someone who betrayed them. Only outsiders and children stare.

The shades were up. Graham was glad. That meant no relatives had been inside. Relatives always lower the shades.

He walked around the side of the house, moving carefully, not using his flashlight. He stopped twice to listen. The Atlanta police knew he was here, but the neighbors did not. They would be jumpy. They might shoot.

Looking in a rear window, he could see all the way through to the light in the front yard, past silhouettes of furniture. The scent of Cape jasmine was heavy in the air.

A latticed porch ran across most of the back. On the porch door was the seal of the Atlanta police department. Graham removed the seal and went in.

The door from the porch into the kitchen was patched with plywood where the police had taken out the glass. By flashlight he unlocked it with the key the police had given him. He wanted to turn on lights. He wanted to put on his shiny badge and make some official noises to justify himself to the silent house where five people had died. He did none of that. He went into the dark kitchen and sat down at the breakfast table.

Two pilot lights on the kitchen range glowed blue in the dark. He smelled furniture polish and apples.

The thermostat clicked and the air conditioning came on. Graham started at the noise, felt a trickle of fear. He was an old hand at fear. He could manage this one. He simply was afraid, and he could go on anyway.

He could see and hear better afraid; he could not speak as concisely, and fear sometimes made him rude. Here, there was nobody left to speak to, there was nobody to offend anymore.

Madness came into this house through that door into this kitchen, moving on size-eleven feet. Sitting in the dark, he sensed madness like a bloodhound sniffs a shirt.

Graham had studied the detectives' report at Atlanta Homicide for most of the day and early evening. He remembered that the light on the vent hood over the stove had been on when the police arrived. He turned it on now.

Two framed samplers hung on the wall beside the stove. One said

'Kissin' don't last, cookin' do.' The other was 'It's always to the kitchen that our friends best like to come, to hear the heartbeat of the house, take comfort in its hum.'

Graham looked at his watch. Eleven-thirty P.M. According to the pathologist, the deaths occurred between eleven P.M. and one A.M.

First there was the entry. He thought about that . . .

The madman slipped the hook on the outside screen door. Stood in the darkness of the porch and took something from his pocket. A suction cup, maybe the base of a pencil sharpener designed to stick to a desktop.

Crouched against the wooden lower half of the kitchen door, the madman raised his head to peer through the glass. He put out his tongue and licked the cup, pressed it to the glass and flicked the lever to make it stick. A small glass cutter was attached to the cup with string so that he could cut a circle.

Tiny squeal of the glass cutter and one solid tap to break the glass. One hand to tap, one hand to hold the suction cup. The glass must not fall. The loose piece of glass is slightly egg-shaped because the string wrapped around the shaft of the suction cup as he cut. A little grating noise as he pulls the piece of glass back outside. He does not care that he leaves AB saliva on the glass.

His hand in the tight glove snakes in through the hole, finds the lock. The door opens silently. He is inside. In the light of the vent hood he can see his body in this strange kitchen. It is pleasantly cool in the house.

Will Graham ate two Di-Gels. The crackle of the cellophane irritated him as he stuffed it in his pocket. He walked through the living room, holding his flashlight well away from him by habit. Though he had studied the floor plan, he made one wrong turn before he found the stairs. They did not creak.

Now he stood in the doorway of the master bedroom. He could see faintly without the flashlight. A digital clock on a nightstand projected the time on the ceiling and an orange night light burned above the baseboard by the bathroom. The coppery smell of blood was strong.

Eyes accustomed to the dark could see well enough. The madman could distinguish Mr Leeds from his wife. There was enough light for him to cross the room, grab Leeds's hair and cut his throat. What then? Back to the wall switch, a greeting to Mrs Leeds and then the gunshot that disabled her?

Graham switched on the lights and bloodstains shouted at him from the walls, from the mattress and the floor. The very air had screams smeared on it. He flinched from the noise in this silent room full of dark stains drying.

Graham sat on the floor until his head was quiet. Still, still, be still. The number and variety of the bloodstains had puzzled Atlanta detectives trying to reconstruct the crime. All the victims were found slain in their beds. This was not consistent with the locations of the stains.

At first they believed Charles Leeds was attacked in his daughter's room and his body dragged to the master bedroom. Close examination of the splash patterns made them reconsider.

The killer's exact movements in the rooms were not yet determined.

Now, with the advantage of the autopsy and lab reports, Will Graham began to see how it had happened.

The intruder cut Charles Leeds's throat as he lay asleep beside his wife, went back to the wall switch and turned on the light – hairs and oil from Mr Leeds's head were left on the switchplate by a smooth glove. He shot Mrs Leeds as she was rising, then went toward the children's rooms.

Leeds rose with his cut throat and tried to protect the children, losing great gouts of blood in an unmistakable arterial spray as he tried to fight. He was shoved away, fell and died with his daughter in her room.

One of the two boys was shot in bed. The other boy was also found in bed, but he had dust balls in his hair. Police believed he was dragged out from under his bed to be shot.

When all of them were dead, except possibly Mrs Leeds, the smashing of mirrors began, the selection of shards, the further attention to Mrs Leeds.

Graham had full copies of all the autopsy protocols in his box. Here was the one on Mrs Leeds. The bullet entered to the right of her navel and lodged in her lumbar spine, but she died of strangulation.

The increase in serotonin and free histamine levels in the gunshot wound indicated she had lived at least five minutes after she was shot. The histamine was much higher than the serotonin, so she had not lived more than fifteen minutes. Most of her other injuries were probably, but not conclusively, postmortem.

If the other injuries were postmortem, what was the killer doing in the interval while Mrs Leeds waited to die? Graham wondered. Struggling with Leeds and killing the others, yes, but that would have taken less than a minute. Smashing the mirrors. But what else?

The Atlanta detectives were thorough. They had measured and photographed exhaustively, had vacuumed and grid-searched and taken the traps from the drains. Still. Graham looked for himself.

From the police photographs and taped outlines on the mattresses,

Graham could see where the bodies had been found. The evidence – nitrate traces on bedclothes in the case of the gunshot wounds – indicated that they were found in positions approximating those in which they died.

But the profusion of bloodstains and matted sliding marks on the hall carpet remained unexplained. One detective had theorized that some of the victims tried to crawl away from the killer. Graham did not believe it – clearly the killer moved them after they were dead and then put them back the way they were when he killed them.

What he did with Mrs Leeds was obvious. But what about the others? He had not disfigured them further, as he did Mrs Leeds. The children each suffered a single gunshot wound in the head. Charles Leeds bled to death, with aspirated blood contributing. The only additional mark on him was a superficial ligature mark around his chest, believed to be postmortem. What did the killer do with them after they were dead?

From his box Graham took the police photographs, lab reports on the individual blood and organic stains in the room and standard comparison plates of blood-drop trajectories.

He went over the upstairs rooms minutely, trying to match injuries to stains, trying to work backward. He plotted each splash on a measured field sketch of the master bedroom, using the standard comparison plates to estimate the direction and velocity of the bloodfall. In this way he hoped to learn the positions the bodies were in at different times.

Here was a row of three bloodstains slanting up and around a corner of the bedroom wall. Here were three faint stains on the carpet beneath them. The wall above the headboard on Charles Leeds's side of the bed was bloodstained, and there were swipes along the baseboards. Graham's field sketch began to look like a join-the-dots puzzle with no numbers. He stared at it, looked up at the room and back to the sketch until his head ached.

He went into the bathroom and took his last two Bufferin, scooping up water in his hand from the faucet in the sink. He splashed water on his face and dried it with his shirttail. Water spilled on the floor. He had forgotten that the trap was gone from the drain. Otherwise the bathroom was undisturbed, except for the broken mirror and traces of the red fingerprint powder called Dragon's Blood. Toothbrushes, facial cream, razor, were all in place.

The bathroom looked as though a family still used it. Mrs Leeds's panty hose hung on the towel racks where she had left them to dry. He saw that she cut the leg off a pair when it had a runner so she could match two one-legged pairs, wear them at the same time, and save money. Mrs Leeds's small, homey economy pierced him; Molly did the same thing.

Graham climbed out a window onto the porch roof and sat on the gritty shingles. He hugged his knees, his damp shirt pressed cold across his back, and snorted the smell of slaughter out of his nose.

The lights of Atlanta rusted the night sky and the stars were hard to see. The night would be clear in the Keys. He could be watching shooting stars with Molly and Willy, listening for the whoosh they solemnly agreed a shooting star must make. The Delta Aquarid meteor shower was at its maximum, and Willy was up for it.

He shivered and snorted again. He did not want to think of Molly now. To do so was tasteless as well as distracting.

Graham had a lot of trouble with taste. Often his thoughts were not tasty. There were no effective partitions in his mind. What he saw and learned touched everything else he knew. Some of the combinations were hard to live with. But he could not anticipate them, could not block and repress. His learned values of decency and propriety tagged along, shocked at his associations, appalled at his dreams; sorry that in the bone arena of his skull there were no forts for what he loved. His associations came at the speed of light. His value judgments were at the pace of a responsive reading. They could never keep up and direct his thinking.

He viewed his own mentality as grotesque but useful, like a chair made of antlers. There was nothing he could do about it.

Graham turned off the lights in the Leeds house and went out through the kitchen. At the far end of the back porch, his flashlight revealed a bicycle and a wicker dog bed. There was a doghouse in the backyard, a dog bowl by the steps.

The evidence indicated the Leedses were surprised in their sleep.

Holding the flashlight between his chin and chest, he wrote a memo: *Jack – where was the dog?*

Graham drove back to his hotel. He had to concentrate on his driving, though there was little traffic at four-thirty A.M. His head still ached and he watched for an all-night pharmacy.

He found one on Peachtree. A slovenly rent-a-cop dozed near the door. A pharmacist in a jacket dingy enough to highlight his dandruff sold Graham Bufferin. The glare in the place was painful. Graham disliked young pharmacists. They had a middle-of-the-litter look about them. They were often smug and he suspected that they were unpleasant at home.

'What else?' the pharmacist said, his fingers poised above the cash register keys. 'What else?'

The Atlanta FBI office had booked him into an absurd hotel near the city's new Peachtree Center. It had glass elevators shaped like milkweed pods to let him know he was really in town now.

Graham rode up to his room with two conventioneers wearing name tags with the printed greeting 'Hi!' They held to the rail and looked over the lobby as they ascended.

'Looka yonder by the desk – that's Wilma and them just now coming in,' the larger one said. 'God damn, I'd love to tear off a piece of that.'

'Fuck her till her nose bleeds,' the other one said.

Fear and rut, and anger at the fear.

'Say, you know why a woman has legs?'

'Why?'

'So she won't leave a trail like a snail.'

The elevator doors opened.

'Is this it? This is it,' the larger one said. He lurched against the facing as he got off.

'This is the blind leading the blind,' the other one said.

Graham put his cardboard box on the dresser in his room. Then he put it in a drawer where he could not see it. He had had enough of the wide-eyed dead. He wanted to call Molly, but it was too early.

A meeting was scheduled for eight A.M. at the Atlanta police head-quarters. He'd have little enough to tell them.

He would try to sleep. His mind was a busy rooming house with arguments all around him, and they were fighting somewhere down the hall. He was numb and empty and he drank two fingers of whiskey from his bathroom glass before he lay down. The darkness pressed too closely on him. He turned on the bathroom light and went back to bed. He pretended Molly was in the bathroom brushing her hair.

Lines from the autopsy protocols sounded in his own voice, though he had never read them aloud: '. . . the feces was formed . . . a trace of talcum on the lower right leg. Fracture of the medial orbit wall owing to insertion of mirror shard . . .'

Graham tried to think about the beach at Sugarloaf Key, he tried to hear the waves. He pictured his workbench in his mind and thought about the escapement for the water clock he and Willy were building. He sang

'Whiskey River' under his breath and tried to run 'Black Mountain Rag' through his head from one end to the other. Molly's music. Doc Watson's guitar part was all right, but he always lost it in the fiddle break. Molly had tried to teach him clog dancing in the backyard and she was bouncing . . . and finally he dozed.

He woke in an hour, rigid and sweating, seeing the other pillow silhouetted against the bathroom light and it was Mrs Leeds lying beside him bitten and torn, mirrored eyes and blood like the legs of spectacles over her temples and ears. He could not turn his head to face her. Brain screaming like a smoke alarm, he put his hand over there and touched dry cloth.

Having acted, he felt some immediate relief. He rose, his heart pounding, and put on a dry T-shirt. He threw the wet one into the bathtub. He could not move over to the dry side of the bed. Instead he put a towel on the side where he had sweated and lay down on it, propped against the headboard with a stiff drink in his hand. He swallowed a third of it.

He reached for something to think about, anything. The pharmacy where he bought the Bufferin, then; perhaps because it was his only experience all day that was not related to death.

He could remember old drugstores with soda fountains. As a boy, he thought old drugstores had a slightly furtive air. When you went in, you always thought about buying rubbers whether you needed any or not. There were things on the shelves you shouldn't look at too long.

In the pharmacy where he bought the Bufferin, the contraceptives with their illustrated wrappings were in a lucite case on the wall behind the cash register, framed like art.

He preferred the drugstore and sundry of his childhood. Graham was nearly forty and just beginning to feel the tug of the way the world was then; it was a sea anchor streamed behind him in heavy weather.

He thought about Smoot. Old Smoot had been the soda jerk and manager for the pharmacist who owned the local drugstore when Graham was a child. Smoot, who drank on the job, forgot to unroll the awning and the sneakers melted in the window. Smoot forgot to unplug the coffeepot, and the fire department was summoned. Smoot sold ice cream cones to children on credit.

His principal outrage was ordering fifty Kewpie dolls from a detail man while the store owner was on vacation. On his return, the owner fired Smoot for a week. Then they held a Kewpie doll sale. Fifty of the Kewpie dolls were arranged in a semicircle in the front window so that they all stared at whoever was looking in.

They had wide eyes of cornflower blue. It was a striking display and Graham had looked at it for some time. He knew they were only Kewpie dolls, but he could feel the focus of their attention. So many of them looking. A number of people stopped to look at them. Plaster dolls, all with the same silly spit curl, yet their concentrated gaze had made his face tingle.

Graham began to relax a little on the bed. Kewpie dolls staring. He started to take a drink, gasped, and choked it onto his chest. He fumbled for the bedside lamp and fetched his box from the dresser drawer. He took out the autopsy protocols of the three Leeds children and his measured field sketches of the master bedroom and spread them on the bed.

Here were the three bloodstains slanting up the corner, and here were the matching stains on the carpet. Here were the dimensions of the three children. Brother, sister, big brother. Match. Match. Match.

They had been in a row, seated along the wall facing the bed. An audience. A dead audience. And Leeds. Tied around the chest to the headboard. Composed to look as though he were sitting up in bed. Getting the ligature mark, staining the wall above the headboard.

What were they watching? Nothing; they were all dead. But their eyes were open. They were watching a performance starring the madman and the body of Mrs Leeds, beside Mr Leeds in the bed. An audience. The crazy could look around at their faces.

Graham wondered if he had lit a candle. The flickering light would simulate expression on their faces. No candle was found. Maybe he would think to do that next time . . .

This first small bond to the killer itched and stung like a leech. Graham bit the sheet, thinking.

Why did you move them again? Why didn't you leave them that way? Graham asked. *There's something you don't want me to know about you. Why, there's something you're ashamed of. Or is it something you can't afford for me to know?*

Did you open their eyes?

Mrs Leeds was lovely, wasn't she? You turned on the light after you cut his throat so Mrs Leeds could watch him flop, didn't you? It was maddening to have to wear gloves when you touched her, wasn't it?

There was talcum on her leg.

There was no talcum in the bathroom.

Someone else seemed to speak those two facts in a flat voice.

You took off your gloves, didn't you? The powder came out of a rubber glove as you pulled it off to touch her, DIDN'T IT, YOU SON OF A BITCH? You touched her with your bare hands and then you put the gloves back on and you wiped her down. But while the gloves were off, DID YOU OPEN THEIR EYES?

Jack Crawford answered his telephone on the fifth ring. He had answered the telephone in the night many times and he was not confused.

'Jack, this is Will.'

'Yes, Will.'

'Is Price still in Latent Prints?'

'Yeah. He doesn't go out much anymore. He's working on the single-print index.'

'I think he ought to come to Atlanta.'

'Why? You said yourself the guy down here is good.'

'He *is* good, but not as good as Price.'

'What do you want him to do? Where would he look?'

'Mrs Leeds's fingernails and toenails. They're painted, it's a slick surface. And the corneas of all their eyes. I think he took his gloves off, Jack.'

'Jesus, Price'll have to gun it,' Crawford said. 'The funeral's this afternoon.'

Chapter Three

'I think he had to touch her,' Graham said in greeting.

Crawford handed him a Coke from the machine in Atlanta police headquarters. It was seven-fifty A.M.

'Sure, he moved her around,' Crawford said. 'There were grip marks on her wrists and behind her knees. But every print in the place is from nonporous gloves. Don't worry, Price is here. Grouchy old bastard. He's on his way to the funeral home now. The morgue released the bodies last night, but the funeral home's not doing anything yet. You look bushed. Did you get any sleep?'

'Maybe an hour. I think he had to touch her with his hands.'

'I hope you're right, but the Atlanta lab swears he wore like surgeon's gloves the whole time,' Crawford said. 'The mirror pieces had those smooth prints. Forefinger on the back of the piece wedged in the labia, smudged thumb on the front.'

'He polished it after he placed it, so he could see his damn face in there probably,' Graham said.

'The one in her mouth was obscured with blood. Same with the eyes. He never took the gloves off.'

'Mrs Leeds was a good-looking woman,' Graham said. 'You've seen the family pictures, right? I'd want to touch her skin in an intimate situation, .wouldn't you?'

'*Intimate?*' Distaste sounded in Crawford's voice before he could stop it. Suddenly he was busy rummaging his pockets for change.

'Intimate – they had privacy. Everybody else was dead. He could have their eyes open or shut, however he liked.'

'Any way he liked,' Crawford said. 'They tried her skin for prints, of course. Nothing. They did get a hand spread off her neck.'

'The report didn't say anything about dusting nails.'

'I expect her fingernails were smudged when they took scrapings. The scrapings were just where she cut her palms with them. She never scratched him.'

'She had pretty feet,' Graham said.

'Umm-hmm. Let's head upstairs,' Crawford said. 'The troops are about to muster.'

Jimmy Price had a lot of equipment – two heavy cases plus his camera bag and tripod. He made a clatter coming through the front door of the Lombard Funeral Home in Atlanta. He was a frail old man and his humor had not been improved by a long taxi ride from the airport in the morning rush.

An officious young fellow with styled hair hustled him into an office decorated in apricot and cream. The desk was bare except for a sculpture called *The Praying Hands*.

Price was examining the fingertips of the praying hands when Mr Lombard himself came in. Lombard cheeked Price's credentials with extreme care.

'Your Atlanta office or agency or whatever called me, of course, Mr Price. But last night we had to get the police to remove an obnoxious fellow who was trying to take pictures for *The National Tattler*, so I'm being very careful. I'm sure you understand. Mr Price, the bodies were only released to us about one o'clock this morning, and the funeral is this afternoon at five. We simply can't delay it.'

'This won't take a lot of time,' Price said. 'I need one reasonably intelligent assistant, if you have one. Have you touched the bodies, Mr Lombard?'

'No.'

'Find out who has. I'll have to print them all.'

The morning briefing of police detectives on the Leeds case was concerned mostly with teeth.

Atlanta Chief of Detectives R. J. (Buddy) Springfield, a burly man in shirtsleeves, stood by the door with Dr Dominic Princi as the twenty-three detectives filed in.

'All right, boys, let's have the big grin as you come by,' Springfield said. 'Show Dr Princi your teeth. That's right, let's see 'em all. Christ, Sparks, is that your tongue or are you swallowing a squirrel? Keep moving.'

A large frontal view of a set of teeth, upper and lower, was tacked to the bulletin board at the front of the squad room. It reminded Graham of the celluloid strip of printed teeth in a dime-store jack-o'lantern. He and Crawford sat down at the back of the room while the detectives took their places at schoolroom desks.

Atlanta Public Safety Commissioner Gilbert Lewis and his public-relations officer sat apart from them in folding chairs. Lewis had to face a news conference in an hour.

Chief of Detectives Springfield took charge.

'All right. Let's cease fire with the bullshit. If you read up this morning, you saw zero progress.

'House-to-house interviews will continue for a radius of four additional blocks around the scene. R & I has loaned us two clerks to help cross-matching airline reservations and car rentals in Birmingham and Atlanta.

'Airport and hotel details will make the rounds again today. Yes, again today. Catch every maid and attendant as well as the desk people. He had to clean up somewhere and he may have left a mess. If you find somebody who cleaned up a mess, roust out whoever's in the room, seal it, and get on the horn to the laundry double quick. This time we've got something for you to show around. Dr Princi?'

Dr Dominic Princi, chief medical examiner for Fulton County, walked to the front and stood under the drawing of the teeth. He held up a dental cast.

'Gentlemen, this is what the subject's teeth look like. The Smithsonian in Washington reconstructed them from the impressions we took of bite marks on Mrs Leeds and a clear bite mark in a piece of cheese from the Leedses' refrigerator,' Princi said.

'As you can see, he has pegged lateral incisors – the teeth here and here.' Princi pointed to the cast in his hand, then to the chart above him. 'The teeth are crooked in alignment and a corner is missing from this central incisor. The other incisor is grooved, here. It looks like a "tailor's notch," the kind of wear you get biting thread.'

'Snaggletoothed son of a bitch,' somebody mumbled.

'How do you know for sure it was the perpetrator that bit the cheese, Doc?' a tall detective in the front row asked.

Princi disliked being called 'Doc,' but he swallowed it. 'Saliva washes from the cheese and from the bite wounds matched for blood type,' he said. 'The victims' teeth and blood type didn't match.'

'Fine, Doctor,' Springfield said. 'We'll pass out pictures of the teeth to show around.'

'What about giving it to the papers?' The public-relations officer, Simpkins, was speaking. 'A "have-you-seen-these-teeth" sort of thing.'

'I see no objection to that,' Springfield said. 'What about it, Commissioner?'

Lewis nodded.

Simpkins was not through. 'Dr Princi, the press is going to ask why it took four days to get this dental representation you have here. And why it all had to be done in Washington.'

Special Agent Crawford studied the button on his ballpoint pen.

Princi reddened but his voice was calm. 'Bite marks on flesh are distorted when a body is moved, Mr Simpson –'

'Simpkins.'

'Simpkins, then. We couldn't make this using only the bite marks on the victims. That is the importance of the cheese. Cheese is relatively solid, but tricky to cast. You have to oil it first to keep the moisture out of the casting medium. Usually you get one shot at it. The Smithsonian has done it for the FBI crime lab before. They're better equipped to do a face bow registration and they have an anatomical articulator. They have a consulting forensic odontologist. We don't. Anything else?'

'Would it be fair to say that the delay was caused by the FBI lab and not here?'

Princi turned on him. 'What it would be fair to say, Mr Simpkins, is that a federal investigator, Special Agent Crawford, found the cheese in the refrigerator two days ago – after your people had been through the place. He expedited the lab work at my request. It would be fair to say I'm relieved that it wasn't one of you that bit the goddamned thing.'

Commissioner Lewis broke in, his heavy voice booming in the squad room. 'Nobody's questioning your judgment, Dr Princi. Simpkins, the last thing we need is to start a pissing contest with the FBI. Let's get on with it.'

'We're all after the same thing,' Springfield said. 'Jack, do you fellows want to add anything?'

Crawford took the floor. The faces he saw were not entirely friendly. He had to do something about that.

'I just want to clear the air, Chief. Years ago there was a lot of rivalry about who got the collar. Each side, federal and local, held out on the other. It made a gap that crooks slipped through. That's not Bureau policy now, and it's not my policy. I don't give a damn who gets the collar. Neither does Investigator Graham. That's him sitting back there, if some of you are wondering. If the man who did this is run over by a garbage truck, it would suit me just fine as long as it puts him off the street. I think you feel the same way.'

Crawford looked over the detectives and hoped they were mollified. He hoped they wouldn't hoard leads. Commissioner Lewis was talking to him.

'Investigator Graham has worked on this kind of thing before.'

'Yes, sir.'

'Can you add anything, Mr Graham, suggest anything?'

Crawford raised his eyebrows at Graham.

'Would you come up to the front?' Springfield said.

Graham wished he had been given the chance to talk to Springfield in private. He didn't want to go to the front.

He went, though.

Rumpled and sun-blasted, Graham didn't look like a federal investigator. Springfield thought he looked more like a house painter who had put on a suit to appear in court.

The detectives shifted from one buttock to the other.

When Graham turned to face the room, the ice-blue eyes were startling in his brown face.

'Just a couple of things,' he said. 'We can't assume he's a former mental patient or somebody with a record of sex offenses. There's a high probability that he doesn't have any kind of record. If he does, it's more likely to be breaking and entering than a minor sex offense.

'He may have a history of biting in lesser assaults – bar fights or child abuse. The biggest help we'll have on that will come from emergency-room personnel and the child-welfare people.

'Any bad bite they can remember is worth checking, regardless of who was bitten or how they said it happened. That's all I have.'

The tall detective on the front row raised his hand and spoke at the same time.

'But he only bit women so far, right?'

'That's all we know about. He bites a lot, though. Six bad ones in Mrs Leeds, eight in Mrs Jacobi. That's way above average.'

'What's average?'

'In a sex murder, three. He likes to bite.'

'Women.'

'Most of the time in sex assaults the bite mark has a livid spot in the center, a suck mark. These don't. Dr Princi mentioned it in his autopsy report, and I saw it at the morgue. No suck marks. For him biting may be a fighting pattern as much as sexual behavior.'

'Pretty thin,' the detective said.

'It's worth checking,' Graham said. 'Any bite is worth checking. People lie about how it happened. Parents of a bitten child will claim an animal did it and let the child take rabies shots to cover for a snapper in the family – you've all seen that. It's worth asking at the hospitals – who's been referred for rabies shots.

'That's all I have.' Graham's thigh muscles fluttered with fatigue when he sat down.

'It's worth asking, and we'll ask,' Chief of Detectives Springfield said. 'Now. The Safe and Loft Squad works the neighborhood along with Larceny. Work the dog angle. You'll see the update and the picture in the file. Find out if any stranger was seen with the dog. Vice and Narcotics, take the K-Y cowboys and the leather bars after you finish the day tour. Marcus and Whitman – heads up at the funeral. Do you have relatives, friends of the family, lined up to spot for you? Good. What about the photographer? All right. Turn in the funeral guest book to R & I. They've got the one from Birmingham already. The rest of the assignments are on the sheet. Let's go.'

'One other thing,' Commissioner Lewis said. The detectives sank back in their seats. 'I have heard officers in this command referring to the killer as the "Tooth Fairy." I don't care what you call him among yourselves, I realize you have to call him something. But I had better not hear any police officer refer to him as the Tooth Fairy in public. It sounds flippant. Neither will you use that name on any internal memoranda.

'That's all.'

Crawford and Graham followed Springfield back to his office. The chief of detectives gave them coffee while Crawford checked in with the switchboard and jotted down his messages.

'I didn't get a chance to talk to you when you got here yesterday,' Springfield said to Graham. 'This place has been a fucking madhouse. It's Will, right? Did the boys give you everything you need?'

'Yeah, they were fine.'

'We don't have shit and we know it,' Springfield said. 'Oh, we developed a walking picture from the footprints in the flowerbed. He was walking around bushes and stuff, so you can't tell much more than his shoe size, maybe his height. The left print's a little deeper, so he may have been carrying something. It's busy work. We did get a burglar, though, a couple of years ago, off a walking picture. Showed Parkinson's disease. Princi picked it up. No luck this time.'

'You have a good crew,' Graham said.

'They are. But this kind of thing is out of our usual line, thank God. Let me get it straight, do you fellows work together all the time – you and Jack and Dr Bloom – or do you just get together for one of these?'

'Just for these,' Graham said.

'Some reunion. The commissioner was saying you were the one who nailed Lecter three years ago.'

'We were all there with the Maryland police,' Graham said. 'The Maryland state troopers arrested him.'

Springfield was bluff, not stupid. He could see that Graham was uncomfortable. He swiveled in his chair and picked up some notes.

'You asked about the dog. Here's the sheet on it. Last night a vet here called Leeds's brother. He had the dog. Leeds and his oldest boy brought it in to the vet the afternoon before they were killed. It had a puncture wound in the abdomen. The vet operated and it's all right. He thought it was shot at first, but he didn't find a bullet. He thinks it was stabbed with something like an ice pick or an awl. We're asking the neighbors if they saw anybody fooling with the dog, and we're working the phones today checking local vets for other animal mutilations.'

'Was the dog wearing a collar with the Leeds name on it?'

'No '

'Did the Jacobis in Birmingham have a dog?' Graham asked.

'We're supposed to be finding that out,' Springfield said. 'Hold on, let me see.' He dialed an inside number. 'Lieutenant Flatt is our liaison with Birmingham . . . yeah, Flatt. What about the Jacobis' dog? Uh-huh . . . uh-huh. Just a minute.' He put his hand over the phone. 'No dog. They found a litter box in the downstairs bathroom with cat droppings in it. They didn't find any cat. The neighbors are watching for it.'

'Could you ask Birmingham to check around in the yard and behind any outbuildings,' Grabam said. 'If the cat was hurt, the children might not have found it in time and they might have buried it. You know how cats do. They hide to die. Dogs come home. And would you ask if it's wearing a collar?'

'Tell them if they need a methane probe, we'll send one,' Crawford said. 'Save a lot of digging.'

Springfield relayed the request. The telephone rang as soon as he hung it up. The call was for Jack Crawford. It was Jimmy Price at the Lombard Funeral Home. Crawford punched on from the other phone.

'Jack, I got a partial that's probably a thumb and a fragment of a palm.'

'Jimmy, you're the light of my life.'

'I know. The partial's a tented arch, but it's smudged. I'll have to see what I can do with it when I get back. Came off the oldest kid's left eye. I never did that before. Never would have seen it, but it stood out against an eight-ball hemorrhage from the gunshot wound.'

'Can you make an identification off it?'

'It's a very long shot, Jack. If he's in the single-print index, maybe, but that's like the Irish Sweepstakes, you know that. The palm came off the nail of Mrs Leeds's left big toe. It's only good for comparison. We'll be lucky to get six points off it. The assistant SAC witnessed, and so did Lombard. He's a notary. I've got pictures *in situ*. Will that do it?'

'What about elimination prints on the funeral-home employees?'

'I inked up Lombard and all his Merry Men, major case prints whether they said they had touched her or not. They're scrubbing their hands and bitching now. Let me go home, Jack. I want to work these up in my own darkroom. Who knows what's in the water here – turtles – who knows?'

'I can catch a plane to Washington in an hour and fax the prints down to you by early afternoon.'

Crawford thought a moment. 'Okay, Jimmy, but step on it. Copies to Atlanta and Birmingham PD's and Bureau offices.'

'You got it. Now, something else we've got to get straight on your end.'

Crawford rolled his eyes to the ceiling. 'Gonna piss in my ear about the per diem, aren't you?'

'Right.'

'Today, Jimmy my lad, nothing's too good for you.'

Graham stared out the window while Crawford told them about the prints.

'That's by God remarkable,' was all Springfield said.

Graham's face was blank; closed like a lifer's face, Springfield thought. He watched Graham all the way to the door.

The public-safety commissioner's news conference was breaking up in the foyer as Crawford and Graham left Springfield's office. The print reporters headed for the phones. Television reporters were doing 'cutaways,' standing alone before their cameras asking the best questions they had heard at the news conference and extending their microphones to thin air for a reply that would be spliced in later from film of the commissioner.

Crawford and Graham had started down the front steps when a small man darted ahead of them, spun and took a picture. His face popped up behind his camera.

'Will Graham!' he said. 'Remember me – Freddy Lounds? I covered the Lecter case for the *Tattler*. I did the paperback.'

'I remember,' Graham said. He and Crawford continued down the steps, Lounds walking sideways ahead of them.

'When did they call you in, Will? What have you got?'

'I won't talk to you, Lounds.'

'How does this guy compare with Lecter? Does he do them – ?'

'Lounds.' Graham's voice was loud and Crawford got in front of him fast. 'Lounds, you write lying shit and *The National Tattler* is an asswipe. Keep away from me.'

Crawford gripped Graham's arm. 'Get away, Lounds. *Go on*. Will, let's get some breakfast. Come on, Will.' They rounded the corner, walking swiftly.

'I'm sorry, Jack. I can't stand that bastard. When I was in the hospital, he came in and – '

'I know it,' Crawford said. 'I reamed him out, much good it did.' Crawford remembered the picture in *The National Tattler* at the end of the Lecter case. Lounds had come into the hospital room while Graham was asleep. He flipped back the sheet and shot a picture of Graham's temporary colostomy. The paper ran it retouched with a black square covering Graham's groin. The caption said 'Crazy Guts Cop.'

The diner was bright and clean. Graham's hands trembled and he slopped coffee in his saucer.

He saw Crawford's cigarette smoke bothering a couple in the next booth. The couple ate in a peptic silence, their resentment hanging in the smoke.

Two women, apparently mother and daughter, argued at a table near the door. They spoke in low voices, anger ugly in their faces. Graham could feel their anger on his face and neck.

Crawford was griping about having to testify at a trial in Washington in the morning. He was afraid the trial could tie him up for several days. As he lit another cigarette, he peered across the flame at Graham's hands and his color.

'Atlanta and Birmingham can run the thumbprint against their known sex offenders,' Crawford said. 'So can we. And Price has dug a single print out of the files before. He'll program the FINDER with it – we've come a long way with that just since you left.'

FINDER, the FBI's automated fingerprint reader and processor, might recognize the thumbprint on an incoming fingerprint card from some unrelated case.

'When we get him, that print and his teeth will put him away,' Crawford said. 'What we have to do, we have to figure on what he *could* be. We have to swing a wide loop. Indulge me, now. Say we've arrested a good suspect. You walk in and see him. What is there about him that doesn't surprise you?'

'I don't know, Jack. Goddammit, he's got no face for me. We could spend a lot of time looking for people we've invented. Have you talked to Bloom?'

'On the phone last night. Bloom doubts he's suicidal, and so does Heimlich. Bloom was only here a couple of hours the first day, but he and

Heimlich have the whole file. Bloom's examining PhD candidates this week. He said tell you hello. Do you have his number in Chicago?'

'I have it.'

Graham liked Dr Alan Bloom, a small round man with sad eyes, a good forensic psychiatrist – maybe the best. Graham appreciated the fact that Dr Bloom had never displayed professional interest in him. That was not always the case with psychiatrists.

'Bloom says he wouldn't be surprised if we heard from the Tooth Fairy. He might write us a note,' Crawford said.

'On a bedroom wall.'

'Bloom thinks he might be disfigured or he may believe he's disfigured. He told me not to give that a lot of weight. "I won't set up a straw man to chase, Jack," is what he told me. "That would be a distraction and would diffuse the effort." Said they taught him to talk like that in graduate school.'

'He's right,' Graham said.

'You could tell something about him or you wouldn't have found that fingerprint,' Crawford said.

'That was the evidence on the damn wall, Jack. Don't put this on me. Look, don't expect too much from me, all right?'

'Oh, we'll get him. You know we'll get him, don't you?'

'I know it. One way or the other.'

'What's one way?'

'We'll find evidence we've overlooked.'

'What's the other?'

'He'll do it and do it until one night he makes too much noise going in and the husband gets to a gun in time.'

'No other possibilities?'

'You think I'm going to spot him across a crowded room? No, that's Ezio Pinza you're thinking about, does that. The Tooth Fairy will go on and on until we get smart or get lucky. He won't stop.'

'Why?'

'Because he's got a genuine taste for it.'

'See, you do know something about him,' Crawford said.

Graham did not speak again until they were on the sidewalk. 'Wait until the next full moon,' he told Crawford. 'Then tell me how much I know about him.'

Graham went back to his hotel and slept for two and a half hours. He woke at noon, showered, and ordered a pot of coffee and a sandwich. It was time to make a close study of the Jacobi file from Birmingham. He scrubbed his reading glasses with hotel soap and settled in by the window with the file. For the first few minutes he looked up at every sound, footsteps in the hall, the distant thud of the elevator door. Then he knew nothing but the file.

The waiter with the tray knocked and waited, knocked and waited. Finally he left the lunch on the floor outside the door and signed the bill himself.

Chapter Four

Hoyt Lewis, meter reader for Georgia Power Company, parked his truck under a big tree in the alley and settled back with his lunch box. It was no fun opening his lunch now that he packed it himself. No little notes in there anymore, no surprise Twinkie.

He was halfway through his sandwich when a loud voice at his ear made him jump.

'I guess I used a thousand dollars' worth of electricity this month, is that right?'

Lewis turned and saw at the truck window the red face of H. G. Parsons. Parsons wore Bermuda shorts and carried a yard broom.

'I didn't understand what you said.'

'I guess you'll say I used a thousand dollars' worth of electricity this month. Did you hear me that time?'

'I don't know what you've used because I haven't read your meter yet, Mr Parsons. When I do read it, I'll put it down on this piece of paper right here.'

Parsons was bitter about the size of the bill. He had complained to the power company that he was being prorated.

'I'm keeping up with what I use,' Parsons said. 'I'm going to the Public Service Commission with it, too.'

'You want to read your meter with me? Let's go over there right now and –'

'I know how to read a meter. I guess you could read one too if it wasn't so much trouble.'

'Just be quiet a minute, Parsons.' Lewis got out of his truck. 'Just be quiet a minute now, dammit. Last year you put a magnet on your meter. Your wife said you was in the hospital, so I just took it off and didn't say anything. When you poured molasses in it last winter, I reported it. I notice you paid up when we charged you for it.

'Your bill went up after you did all that wiring yourself. I've told you until I'm blue in the face: something in that house is draining off current. Do you hire an electrician to find it? No, you call down to the office and bitch about me. I've about got a bait of you.' Lewis was pale with anger.

'I'll get to the bottom of this,' Parsons said, retreating down the alley toward his yard. 'They're checking up on you, Mr Lewis. I saw somebody reading your route ahead of you,' he said across the fence. 'Pretty soon you'll have to go to work like everybody else.'

Lewis cranked his truck and drove on down the alley. Now he would have to find another place to finish his lunch. He was sorry. The big shade tree had been a good lunch place for years.

It was directly behind Charles Leeds's house.

At five-thirty P.M. Hoyt Lewis drove in his own automobile to the Cloud Nine Lounge, where he had several boilermakers to ease his mind.

When he called his estranged wife, all he could think of to say was 'I wish you was still fixing my lunch.'

'You ought to have thought about that, Mr Smarty,' she said, and hung up.

He played a gloomy game of shuffleboard with some linemen and a dispatcher from Georgia Power and looked over the crowd. Goddamned airline clerks had started coming in the Cloud Nine. All had the same little mustache and pinkie ring. Pretty soon they'd be fixing the Cloud Nine English with a damned dart board. You can't depend on nothing.

'Hey, Hoyt. I'll match you for a bottle of beer.' It was his supervisor, Billy Meeks.

'Say, Billy, I need to talk to you.'

'What's up?'

'You know that old son of a bitch Parsons that's all the time calling up?'

'Called me last week, as a matter of fact,' Meeks said. 'What about him?'

'He said somebody was reading my route ahead of me, like maybe somebody thought I wasn't making the rounds. You don't think I'm reading meters at home, do you?'

'Nope.'

'You don't think that, do you? I mean, if I'm on a man's shit list I want him to come right out and say it.'

'If you was on my shit list, you think I'd be scared to say so to your face?'

'No.'

'All right, then. If anybody was checking your route, I'd know it. Your executives is always aware of a situation like that. Nobody's checking up on you, Hoyt. You can't pay any attention to Parsons, he's just old and contrary. He called me up last week and said, "Congratulations on getting wise to that Hoyt Lewis." I didn't pay him any mind.'

'I wish we'd put the law on him about that meter,' Lewis said. 'I was just setting back there in the alley under a tree trying to eat my lunch today and he jumped me. What he needs is a good ass-kicking.'

'I used to set back there myself when I had the route,' Meeks said. 'Boy, I tell you one time I seen Mrs Leeds – well, it don't seem right to talk about it now she's dead – but one or two times she was out there sunning herself in the backyard in her swimming suit. Whooee. Had a cute little peter belly. That was a damn shame about them. She was a nice lady.'

'Did they catch anybody yet?'

'Naw.'

'Too bad he got the Leedses when old Parsons was right down the street convenient,' Lewis observed.

'I'll tell you what, I don't let my old lady lay around out in the yard in no swimming suit. She goes "Silly Billy, who's gonna see me?" I told her, I said you can't tell what kind of a insane bastard might jump over that hedge with his private out. Did the cops talk to you? Ast you had you seen anybody?'

'Yeah, I think they got everybody that has a route out there. Mailmen, everybody. I was working Laurelwood on the other side of Betty Jane Drive the whole week until today, though.' Lewis picked at the label on his beer. 'You say Parsons called you up last week?'

'Yep.'

'Then he must have saw somebody reading his meter. He wouldn't have called in if he'd just made it up today to bother me. You say you didn't send nobody, and it sure wasn't me he saw.'

'Might have been Southeastern Ben checking something.'

'Might have been.'

'We don't share poles out there, though.'

'Reckon I ought to call the cops?'

'Wouldn't hurt nothing,' Meeks said.

'Naw, it might do Parsons some good, talk with the law. Scare the shit out of him when they drive up, anyhow.'

Chapter Five

Graham went back to the Leeds house in the late afternoon. He entered through the front door and tried not to look at the ruin the killer had left. So far he had seen files, a killing floor and meat – all aftermath. He knew a fair amount about how they died. How they lived was on his mind today.

A survey, then. The garage contained a good ski boat, well used and well maintained, and a station wagon. Golf clubs were there, and a trail bike. The power tools were almost unused. Adult toys.

Graham took a wedge from the golf bag and had to choke up on the long shaft as he made a jerky swing. The bag puffed a smell of leather at him as he leaned it back against the wall. Charles Leeds's things.

Graham pursued Charles Leeds through the house. His hunting prints hung in the den. His set of the Great Books were all in a row. Sewanee annuals. H. Allen Smith and Perelman and Max Shulman on the bookshelves. Vonnegut and Evelyn Waugh. C. S. Forrester's *Beat to Quarters* was open on a table.

In the den closet a good skeet gun, a Nikon camera, a Bolex Super Eight movie camera and projector.

Graham, who owned almost nothing except basic fishing equipment, a third-hand Volkswagen, and two cases of Montrachet, felt a mild animosity toward the adult toys and wondered why.

Who was Leeds? A successful tax attorney, a Sewanee footballer, a rangy man who liked to laugh, a man who got up and fought with his throat cut.

Graham followed him through the house out of an odd sense of obligation. Learning about him first was a way of asking permission to look at his wife.

Graham felt that it was she who drew the monster, as surely as a singing cricket attracts death from the redeyed fly.

Mrs Leeds, then.

She had a small dressing room upstairs. Graham managed to reach it without looking around the bedroom. The room was yellow and appeared undisturbed except for the smashed mirror above the dressing table. A pair of L. L. Bean moccasins was on the floor in front of the closet, as though she had just stepped out of them. Her dressing gown appeared to have been flung on its peg, and the closet revealed the mild disorder of a woman who had many other closets to organize.

Mrs Leeds's diary was in a plum velvet box on the dressing table. The key was taped to the lid along with a check tag from the police property room.

Graham sat on a spindly white chair and opened the diary at random:

December 23rd, Tuesday, Mama's house. The children are still asleep. When Mama glassed in the sun porch, I hated the way it changed the looks of the house, but it's very pleasant and I can sit here warm looking out at the snow. How many more Christmases can she manage a houseful of grandchildren? A lot, I hope.

A hard drive yesterday up from Atlanta, snowing after Raleigh. We had to creep. I was tired anyway from getting everyone ready. Outside Chapel Hill, Charlie stopped the car and got out. He snapped some icicles off a branch to make me a martini. He came back to the car, long legs lifting high in the snow, and there was snow in his hair and on his eyelashes and I remembered that I love him. It felt like something breaking with a little pain and spilling warm.

I hope the parka fits him. If he got me that tacky dinner ring, I'll die. I could kick Madelyn's big cellulite behind for showing hers and carrying on. Four ridiculously big diamonds the color of dirty ice. Icicle ice is so clear. The sun came through the car window and where the icicle was broken off it stuck up out of the glass and made a little prism. It made a spot of red and green on my hand holding the glass. I could feel the colors on my hand.

He asked me what I want for Christmas and I cupped my hands around his ear and whispered: Your big prick, silly, in as far as it will go.

The bald spot on the back of his head turned red. He's always afraid the children will hear. Men have no confidence in whispers.

The page was flecked with detective's cigar ash.

Graham read on as the light faded, through the daughter's tonsillectomy, and a scare in June when Mrs Leeds found a small lump in her breast. (*Dear God, the children are so small.*)

Three pages later the lump was a small benign cyst, easily removed.

Dr Ianovich turned me loose this afternoon. We left the hospital and drove to the pond. We hadn't been there in a long while. There never seems to be enough time. Charlie had two bottles of champagne on ice and we drank them and fed the ducks while the sun went down. He stood at edge of the water with his back to me for a while and I think he cried a little.

Susan said she was afraid we were coming home from the hospital with another brother for her. Home!

Graham heard the telephone ring in the bedroom. A click and the hum of an answering machine. 'Hello, this is Valerie Leeds. I'm sorry I can't come to the phone right now, but if you'll leave your name and number after the tone, we'll get back to you. Thank you.'

Graham half-expected to hear Crawford's voice after the beep, but there was only the dial tone. The caller had hung up.

He had heard her voice; now he wanted to see her. He went down to the den.

He had in his pocket a reel of Super Eight movie film belonging to Charles Leeds. Three weeks before his death, Leeds had left the film with a druggist who sent it away for processing. He never picked it up. Police found the receipt in Leeds's wallet and got the film from the druggist. Detectives viewed the home movie along with family snapshots developed at the same time and found nothing of interest.

Graham wanted to see the Leedses alive. At the police station, the detectives had offered Graham their projector. He wanted to watch the movie at the house. Reluctantly they let him check it out of the property room.

Graham found the screen and projector in the den closet, set them up, and sat down in Charles Leeds's big leather armchair to watch. He felt something tacky on the chair arm under his palm – a child's sticky fingerprints fuzzed with lint. Graham's hand smelled like candy.

It was a pleasant little silent home movie, more imaginative than most. It opened with a dog, a gray Scotty, asleep on the den rug The dog was disturbed momentarily by the moviemaking and raised his head to look at the camera. Then he went to sleep again. A jumpy cut to the dog still asleep. Then the Scotty's ears perked up. He rose and barked, and the camera followed him into the kitchen as he ran to the door and stood expectantly, shivering and wagging his stumpy tail.

Graham bit his lower lip and waited too. On the screen, the door opened and Mrs Leeds came in carrying groceries. She blinked and laughed in surprise and touched her tousled hair with her free hand. Her lips moved as she walked out of the picture, and the children came in behind her carrying smaller sacks. The girl was six, the boys eight and ten.

The younger boy, apparently a veteran of home movies, pointed to his ears and wiggled them. The camera was positioned fairly high. Leeds was seventy-five inches tall, according to the coroner's report.

Graham believed that this part of the movie must have been made in the early spring. The children wore wind-breakers and Mrs Leeds appeared pale. At the morgue she had a good tan and bathing-suit marks.

Brief scenes followed of the boys playing Ping-Pong in the basement and the girl, Susan, wrapping a present in her room, tongue curled over her upper lip in concentration and a wisp of hair down over her forehead. She brushed her hair back with her plump hand, as her mother had done in the kitchen.

A subsequent scene showed Susan in a bubble bath, crouched like a small frog. She wore a large shower cap. The camera angle was lower and the focus uncertain, clearly the work of a brother. The scene ended with her shouting soundlessly at the camera and covering her six-year-old chest as her shower cap slipped down over her eyes.

Not to be outdone, Leeds had surprised Mrs Leeds in the shower. The shower curtain bumped and bulged as the curtain does before a grade-school theatrical. Mrs Leeds's arm appeared around the curtain. In her hand was a large bath sponge. The scene closed with the lens obscured in soapsuds.

The film ended with a shot of Norman Vincent Peale speaking on television and a pan to Charles Leeds snoring in the chair where Graham now sat.

Graham stared at the blank square of light on the screen. He liked the Leedses. He was sorry that he had been to the morgue. He thought the madman who visited them might have liked them too. But the madman would like them better the way they were now.

Graham's head felt stuffed and stupid. He swam in the pool at his hotel until he was rubber-legged, and came out of the water thinking of two things at once – a Tanqueray martini and the taste of Molly's mouth.

He made the martini himself in a plastic glass and telephoned Molly.

'Hello, hotshot.'

'Hey, baby! Where are you?'

'In this damned hotel in Atlanta.'

'Doing some good?'

'None you'd notice. I'm lonesome.'

'Me too.'

'Horny.'

'Me too.'

'Tell me about yourself.'

'Well, I had a run-in with Mrs Holper today. She wanted to return a dress with a huge big whiskey stain on the seat. I mean, obviously she had worn it to the Jaycee thing.'

'And what did *you* say?'

'I told her I didn't sell it to her like that.'

'And what did *she* say?'

'She said she never had any trouble returning dresses before, which was one reason she shopped at my place rather than some others that she knew about.'

'And then what did *you* say?'

'Oh, I said I was upset because Will talks like a jackass on the phone.'

'I see.'

'Willy's fine. He's covering some turtle eggs the dogs dug up. Tell me what you're doing.'

'Reading reports. Eating junk food.'

'Thinking a good bit, I expect.'

'Yep.'

'Can I help you?'

'I just don't have a lock on anything, Molly. There's not enough information. Well, there's a lot of information, but I haven't done enough with it.'

'Will you be in Atlanta for a while? I'm not bugging you about coming home, I just wonder.'

'I don't know. I'll be here a few more days at least. I miss you.'

'Want to talk about fucking?'

'I don't think I could stand it. I think maybe we better not do that.'

'Do what?'

'Talk about fucking.'
'Okay. You don't mind if I think about it, though?'
'Absolutely not.'
'We've got a new dog.'
'Oh hell.'
'Looks like a cross between a basset hound and a Pekingese.'
'Lovely.'
'He's got big balls.'
'Never mind about his balls.'
'They almost drag the ground. He has to retract them when he runs.'
'He can't do that.'
'Yes he can. *You* don't know.'
'Yes I do know.'
'Can you retract yours?'
'I thought we were coming to that.'
'Well?'
'If you must know, I retracted them once.'
'When was that?'
'In my youth. I had to clear a barbed-wire fence in a hurry.'
'Why?'
'I was carrying this watermelon that I had not cultivated.'
'You were fleeing? From whom?'
'A swineherd of my acquaintance. Alerted by his dogs, he burst from his dwelling in his BVD's, waving a fowling piece. Fortunately, he tripped over a butterbean trellis and gave me a running start.'
'Did he shoot at you?'
'I thought so at the time, yes. But the reports I heard might have issued from my behind. I've never been entirely clear on that.'
'Did you clear the fence?'
'Handily.'
'A criminal mind, even at that age.'
'I don't have a criminal mind.'
'Of course you don't. I'm thinking about painting the kitchen. What color do you like? Will? What color do you like? Are you there?'
'Yeah, uh, yellow. Let's paint it yellow.'
'Yellow is a bad color for me. I'll look green at breakfast.'
'Blue, then.'
'Blue is cold.'

'Well goddammit, paint it baby-shit tan for all I care . . . . No, look, I'll probably be home before long and we'll go to the paint store and get some chips and stuff, okay? And maybe some new handles and that.'

'Let's do, let's get some handles. I don't know why I'm talking about this stuff. Look, I love you and I miss you and you're doing the right thing. It's costing you too, I know that. I'm here and I'll be here whenever you come home, or I'll meet you anywhere, anytime. That's what.'

'Dear Molly. Dear Molly. Go to bed now.'

'All right.'

'Good night.'

Graham lay with his hands behind his head and conjured dinners with Molly. Stone crab and Sancerre, the salt breeze mixed with the wine.

But it was his curse to pick at conversations, and he began to do it now. He had snapped at her after a harmless remark about his 'criminal mind.' Stupid.

Graham found Molly's interest in him largely inexplicable.

He called police headquarters and left word for Springfield that he wanted to start helping with the legwork in the morning. There was nothing else to do.

The gin helped him sleep.

Chapter Six

Flimsy copies of the notes on all calls about the Leeds case were placed on Buddy Springfield's desk. Tuesday morning at seven o'clock when Springfield arrived at his office, there were sixty-three of them. The top one was red-flagged.

It said Birmingham police had found a cat buried in a shoebox behind the Jacobis' garage. The cat had a flower between its paws and was wrapped in a dish towel. The cat's name was written on the lid in a childish hand. It wore no collar. A string tied in a granny knot held the lid on.

The Birmingham medical examiner said the cat was strangled. He had shaved it and found no puncture wound.

Springfield tapped the earpiece of his glasses against his teeth.

They had found soft ground and dug it up with a shovel. Didn't need any damned methane probe. Still, Graham had been right.

The chief of detectives licked his thumb and started through the rest of the stack of flimsies. Most were reports of suspicious vehicles in the neighborhood during the past week, vague descriptions giving only vehicle type or color. Four anonymous telephone callers had told Atlanta residents: 'I'm gonna do you like the Leedses.'

Hoyt Lewis' report was in the middle of the pile.

Springfield called the overnight watch commander.

'What about the meter reader's report on this Parsons? Number forty-eight.'

'We tried to check with the utilities last night, Chief, to see if they had anybody in that alley,' the watch commander said.

'They'll have to get back to us this morning.'

'You have somebody get back to them now,' Springfield said. 'Check sanitation, the city engineer, check for construction permits along the alley and catch me in my car.'

He dialed Will Graham's number. 'Will? Meet me in front of your hotel in ten minutes and let's take a little ride.'

At 7:45 A.M. Springfield parked near the end of the alley. He and Graham walked abreast in wheel tracks pressed in the gravel. Even this early the sun was hot.

'You need to get you a hat,' Springfield said. His own snappy straw was tilted down over his eyes.

The chain-link fence at the rear of the Leeds property was covered with vines. They paused by the light meter on the pole.

'If he came down this way, he could see the whole back end of the house,' Springfield said.

In only five days the Leeds property had begun to look neglected. The lawn was uneven, and wild onions sprouted above the grass. Small branches had fallen in the yard. Graham wanted to pick them up. The house seemed asleep, the latticed porch striped and dappled with the long morning shadows of the trees. Standing with Springfield in the alley, Graham could see himself looking in the back window, opening the porch door. Oddly, his reconstruction of the entry by the killer seemed to elude him now, in the sunlight. He watched a child's swing move gently in the breeze.

'That looks like Parsons,' Springfield said.

H. G. Parsons was out early, grubbing in a flowerbed in his backyard, two houses down. Springfield and Graham went to Parsons' back gate and stood beside his garbage cans. The lids were chained to the fence.

Springfield measured the height of the light meter with a tape.

He had notes on all the Leedses' neighbors. His notes said Parsons had taken early retirement from the post office at his supervisor's request. The supervisor had reported Parsons to be 'increasingly absent-minded.'

Springfield's notes contained gossip, too. The neighbors said Parsons' wife stayed with her sister in Macon as much as she could, and that his son never called him anymore.

'Mr Parsons. Mr Parsons,' Springfield called.

Parsons leaned his tilling fork against the house and came to the fence. He wore sandals and white socks. Dirt and grass had stained the toes of his socks. His face was shiny pink.

Arteriosclerosis, Graham thought. He's taken his pill.

'Yes?'

'Mr Parsons, could we talk to you for a minute? We were hoping you could help us,' Springfield said.

'Are you from the power company?'

'No, I'm Buddy Springfield from the police department.'

'It's about the murder, then. My wife and I were in Macon, as I told the officer –'

'I know, Mr Parsons. We wanted to ask about your light meter. Did –'

'If that . . . meter reader said I did anything improper, he's just –'

'No, no. Mr Parsons, did you see a stranger reading your meter last week?'

'No.'

'Are you sure? I believe you told Hoyt Lewis that someone else read your meter ahead of him.'

'I did. And it's about time. I'm keeping up with this, and the Public Service Commission will get a full report from me.'

'Yes, sir. I'm sure they'll take care of it. Who did you see reading your meter?'

'It wasn't a stranger, it was somebody from Georgia Power.'

'How do you know?'

'Well, he looked like a meter reader.'

'What was he wearing?'

'What they all wear, I guess. What is it? A brown outfit and the cap.'

'Did you see his face?'

'I can't remember if I did. I was looking out the kitchen window when I saw him. I wanted to talk to him, but I had to put on my robe, and by the time I got outside, he was gone.'

'Did he have a truck?'

'I don't remember seeing one. What's going on? Why do you want to know?'

'We're checking everybody who was in this neighborhood last week. It's really important, Mr Parsons. Try hard to remember.'

'So it is about the murder. You haven't arrested anybody yet, have you?'

'No.'

'I watched the street last night, and *fifteen minutes* went by without a single squad car passing. It was horrible, what happened to the Leedses. My wife has been beside herself. I wonder who'll buy their house. I saw some Negroes looking at it the other day. You know, I had to speak to Leeds a few times about his children, but they were all right. Of course, he wouldn't do anything I suggested about his lawn. The Department of Agriculture has some *excellent* pamphlets on the control of nuisance grasses. Finally I just put them in his mailbox. Honestly, when he mowed the wild onions were suffocating.'

'Mr Parsons, exactly when did you see this fellow in the alley?' Springfield asked.

'I'm not sure, I was trying to think.'

'Do you recall the time of day? Morning? Noon? Afternoon?'

'I know the times of day, you don't have to name them. Afternoon, maybe. I don't remember.'

Springfield rubbed the back of his neck. 'Excuse me, Mr Parsons, but I have to get this just right. Could we go in your kitchen and you show us just where you saw him from?'

'Let me see your credentials. Both of you.'

In the house, silence, shiny surfaces, and dead air. Neat. Neat. The desperate order of an aging couple who see their lives begin to blur.

Graham wished he had stayed outside. He was sure the drawers held polished silver with egg between the tines.

Stop it and let's pump the old fart.

The window over the kitchen sink gave a good view of the backyard.

'There. Are you satisfied?' Parsons asked. 'You *can* see out there from here. I never talked to him, I don't remember what he looked like. If that's all, I have a lot to do.'

Graham spoke for the first time. 'You said you went to get your robe, and when you came back he was gone. You weren't dressed, then?'

'No.'

'In the middle of the afternoon? Were you not feeling well, Mr Parsons?'

'What I do in my own house is my business. I can wear a kangaroo suit in here if I want to. Why aren't you out looking for the killer? Probably because it's cool in here.'

'I understand you're retired, Mr Parsons, so I guess it doesn't matter if you put on your clothes every day or not. A lot of days you just don't get dressed at all, am I right?'

Veins stood out in Parsons' temples. 'Just because I'm retired doesn't mean I don't put my clothes on and get busy every day. I just got hot and I came in and took a shower. I was working. I was mulching, and I had done a day's work by afternoon, which is more than you'll do today.'

'You were what?'

'Mulching.'

'What day did you mulch?'

'Friday. It was last Friday. They delivered it in the morning, a big load, and I had . . . I had it all spread by afternoon. You can ask at the Garden Center how much it was.'

'And you got hot and came in and took a shower. What were you doing in the kitchen?'

'Fixing a glass of iced tea.'

'And you got out some ice? But the refrigerator is over there, away from the window.'

Parsons looked from the window to the refrigerator, lost and confused. His eyes were dull, like the eyes of a fish in the market toward the end of the day. Then they brightened in triumph. He went to the cabinet by the sink.

'I was right here, getting some Sweet 'N Low when I saw him. That's it. That's all. Now, if you're through prying . . .'

'I think he saw Hoyt Lewis,' Graham said.

'So do I,' Springfield said.

'It was not Hoyt Lewis. It was not.' Parsons' eyes were watering.

'How do you know?' Springfield said. 'It might have been Hoyt Lewis, and you just *thought* —'

'Lewis is brown from the sun. He's got old greasy hair and those peckerwood sideburns.' Parsons' voice had risen and he was talking so fast it was hard to understand him. 'That's how I knew. Of course it wasn't Lewis. This fellow was paler and his hair was blond. He turned to write on his clipboard and I could see under the back of his hat. Blond. Cut off square on the back of his neck.'

Springfield stood absolutely still and when he spoke his voice was still skeptical. 'What about his face?'

'I don't know. He may have had a mustache.'

'Like Lewis?'

'Lewis doesn't have a mustache.'

'Oh,' Springfield said. 'Was he at eye level with the meter? Did he have to look up at it?'

'Eye level, I guess.'

'Would you know him if you saw him again?'

'No.'

'What age was he?'

'Not old. I don't know.'

'Did you see the Leedses' dog anywhere around him?'

'No.'

'Look, Mr Parsons, I can see I was wrong,' Springfield said. 'You're a real big help to us. If you don't mind, I'm going to send our artist out here, and if you'd just let him sit right here at your kitchen table, maybe you could give him an idea of what this fellow looked like. It sure wasn't Lewis.'

'I don't want my name in any newspapers.'

'It won't be.'

Parsons followed them outside.

'You've done a hell of a fine job on this yard, Mr Parsons,' Springfield said. 'It ought to win some kind of a prize.

Parsons said nothing. His face was red and working, his eyes wet. He stood there in his baggy shorts and sandals and glared at them. As they left the yard, he grabbed his fork and began to grub furiously in the ground, hacking blindly through the flowers, scattering mulch on the grass.

Springfield checked in on his car radio. None of the utilities or city agencies could account for the man in the alley on the day before the murders. Springfield reported Parsons' description and gave instructions for the artist. 'Tell him to draw the pole and the meter first and go from there. He'll have to ease the witness along.

'Our artist doesn't much like to make house calls,' the chief of detectives told Graham as he slid the stripline Ford through the traffic. 'He likes for the secretaries to see him work, with the witness standing on one foot and then the other, looking over his shoulder. A police station is a damn poor place to question anybody that you don't need to scare. Soon as we get the picture, we'll door-to-door the neighborhood with it.

'I feel like we just got a whiff, Will. Just faint, but a whiff, don't you? Look, we did it to the poor old devil and he came through. Now let's do something with it.'

'If the man in the alley is the one we want, it's the best news yet,' Graham said. He was sick of himself.

'Right. It means he's not just getting off a bus and going whichever way his peter points. He's got a plan. He stayed in town overnight. He knows where he's going a day or two ahead. He's got some kind of an idea. Case the place, kill the pet, then the family. What the hell kind of an idea is that?' Springfield paused. 'That's kind of your territory, isn't it?'

'It is, yes. If it's anybody's, I suppose it's mine.'

'I know you've seen this kind of thing before. You didn't like it the other day when I asked you about Lecter, but I need to talk to you about it.'

'All right.'

'He killed nine people, didn't he, in all?'

'Nine that we know of. Two others didn't die.'

'What happened to them?'

'One is on a respirator at a hospital in Baltimore. The other is in a private mental hospital in Denver.'

'What made him do it, how was he crazy?'

Graham looked out the car window at the people on the sidewalk. His voice sounded detached, as though he were dictating a letter.

'He did it because he liked it. Still does. Dr Lecter is not crazy, in any common way we think of being crazy. He did some hideous things because he enjoyed them. But he can function perfectly when he wants to.'

'What did the psychologists call it – what was wrong with him.'

'They say he's a sociopath, because they don't know what else to call him. He has some of the characteristics of what they call a sociopath. He has no remorse or guilt at all. And he had the first and worst sign – sadism to animals as a child.'

Springfield grunted.'But he doesn't have any of the other marks,'

Graham said. 'He wasn't a drifter, he had no history of trouble with the law. He wasn't shallow and exploitive in small things, like most sociopaths are. He's not insensitive. They don't know what to call him. His electroencephalograms show some odd patterns, but they haven't been able to tell much from them.'

'What would you call him?' Springfield asked.

Graham hesitated.

'Just to yourself, what do you call him?'

'He's a monster. I think of him as one of those pitiful things that are born in hospitals from time to time. They feed it, and keep it warm, but they don't put it on the machines and it dies. Lecter is the same way in his head, but he looks normal and nobody could tell.'

'A couple of friends of mine in the chiefs' association are from Baltimore. I asked them how you spotted Lecter. They said they didn't know. How did you do it? What was the first indication, the first thing you felt?'

'It was a coincidence,' Graham said. 'The sixth victim was killed in his workshop. He had woodworking equipment and he kept his hunting stuff out there. He was laced to a pegboard where the tools hung, and he was really torn up, cut and stabbed, and he had arrows in him. The wounds reminded me of something. I couldn't think what it was.'

'And you had to go on to the next ones.'

'Yes. Lecter was very hot – he did the next three in nine days. But this sixth one, he had two old scars on his thigh. The pathologist checked with the local hospital and found he had fallen out of a tree blind five years before while he was bow hunting and stuck an arrow through his leg.

'The doctor of record was a resident surgeon, but Lecter had treated him first – he was on duty in the emergency room. His name was on the admissions log. It had been a long time since the accident, but I thought Lecter might remember if anything had seemed fishy about the arrow wound, so I went to his office to see him. We were grabbing at anything then.

'He was practicing psychiatry by that time. He had a nice office. Antiques. He said he didn't remember much about the arrow wound, that one of the victim's hunting buddies had brought him in, and that was it.

'Something bothered me, though. I thought it was something Lecter said, or something in the office. Crawford and I hashed it over. We checked the files, and Lecter had no record. I wanted some time in his office by myself, but we couldn't get a warrant. We had nothing to show. So I went back to see him.

'It was Sunday, he saw patients on Sunday. The building was empty except for a couple of people in his waiting room. He saw me right away. We were talking and he was making this polite effort to help me and I looked up at some very old medical books on the shelf above his head. And I knew it was him.

'When I looked at him again, maybe my face changed, I don't know. I knew it and *he knew* I knew it. I still couldn't think of the reason, though. I didn't trust it. I had to figure it out. So I mumbled something and got out of there, into the hall. There was a pay phone in the hall. I didn't want to stir him up until I had some help. I was talking to the police switchboard when he came out a service door behind me in his socks. I never heard him coming. I felt his breath was all, and then . . . there was the rest of it.'

'How did you know, though?'

'I think it was maybe a week later in the hospital I finally figured it out. It was *Wound Man* – an illustration they used in a lot of the early medical books like the ones Lecter had. It shows different kinds of battle injuries, all in one figure. I had seen it in a survey course a pathologist was teaching at GWU. The sixth victim's position and his injuries were a close match to *Wound Man.*'

'*Wound Man,* you say? That's all you had?'

'Well, yeah. It was a coincidence that I had seen it. A piece of luck.'

'That's some luck.'

'If you don't believe me, what the fuck did you ask me for?'

'I didn't hear that.'

'Good. I didn't mean to say it. That's the way it happened, though.'

'Okay,' Springfield said. 'Okay. Thank you for telling me. I need to know things like that.'

Parsons' description of the man in the alley and the information on the cat and the dog were possible indications of the killer's methods: it seemed likely that he scouted as a meter reader and felt compelled to hurt the victims' pets before he came to kill the family.

The immediate problem the police faced was whether or not to publicize their theory.

With the public aware of the danger signals and watching, police might get advance warning of the killer's next attack – but the killer probably followed the news too.

He might change his habits.

There was strong feeling in the police department that the slender leads should be kept secret except for a special bulletin to veterinarians and animal shelters throughout the Southeast asking for immediate reports on pet mutilations.

That meant not giving the public the best possible warning. It was a moral question, and the police were not comfortable with it.

They consulted Dr Alan Bloom in Chicago. Dr Bloom said that if the killer read a warning in the newspapers, he would probably change his method of casing a house. Dr Bloom doubted that the man could stop attacking the pets, regardless of the risk. The psychiatrist told the police that they should by no means assume they had twenty-five days to work the period before the next full moon on August 25.

On the morning of July 31, three hours after Parsons gave his description, a decision was reached in a telephone conference among Birmingham and Atlanta police and Crawford in Washington: they would send the private bulletin to veterinarians, canvass for three days in the neighborhood with the artist's sketch, then release the information to the news media.

For those three days Graham and the Atlanta detectives pounded the sidewalks showing the sketch to householders in the area of the Leeds home. There was only a suggestion of a face in the sketch, but they hoped to find someone who could improve it.

Graham's copy of the sketch grew soft around the edges from the sweat of his hands. Often it was difficult to get residents to answer the door. At night he lay in his room with powder on his heat rash, his mind circling the problem as though it were a hologram. He courted the feeling that precedes an idea. It would not come.

Meanwhile, there were four accidental injuries and one fatality in Atlanta as householders shot at relatives coming home late. Prowler calls multiplied and useless tips stacked up in the In baskets at police headquarters. Despair went around like the flu.

Crawford returned from Washington at the end of the third day and dropped in on Graham as he sat peeling off his wet socks.

'Hot work?'

'Grab a sketch in the morning and see,' Graham said.

'No, it'll all be on the news tonight. Did you walk all day?'

'I can't drive through their yards.'

'I didn't think anything would come of this canvass,' Crawford said.

'Well, what the hell did you expect me to do?'

'The best you can, that's all.' Crawford rose to leave. 'Busywork's been a narcotic for me sometimes, especially after I quit the booze. For you too, I think.'

Graham was angry. Crawford was right, of course.

Graham was a natural procrastinator, and he knew it. Long ago in school he had made up for it with speed. He was not in school now.

There was something else he could do, and he had known it for days. He could wait until he was driven to it by desperation in the last days before the full moon. Or he could do it now, while it might be of some use.

There was an opinion he wanted. A very strange view he needed to share; a mindset he had to recover after his warm round years in the Keys.

The reasons clacked like roller-coaster cogs pulling up to the first long plunge, and at the top, unaware that he clutched his belly, Graham said it aloud.

'I have to see Lecter.'

Chapter Seven

Dr Frederick Chilton, chief of staff at the Chesapeake State Hospital for the Criminally Insane, came around his desk to shake Will Graham's hand.

'Dr Bloom called me yesterday, Mr Graham – or should I call you Dr Graham?'

'I'm not a doctor.'

'I was delighted to hear from Dr Bloom, we've known each other for *years*. Take that chair.'

'We appreciate your help, Dr Chilton.'

'Frankly, I sometimes feel like Lecter's secretary rather than his keeper,' Chilton said. 'The volume of his mail alone is a nuisance. I think among some researchers it's considered chic to correspond with him – I've seen his letters *framed* in psychology departments – and for a while it seemed that every PhD candidate in the field wanted to interview him. Glad to cooperate with you, of course, and Dr Bloom.'

'I need to see Dr Lecter in as much privacy as possible,' Graham said. 'I may need to see him again or telephone him after today.'

Chilton nodded. 'To begin with, Dr Lecter will stay in his room. That is absolutely the only place where he is not put in restraints. One wall of his room is a double barrier which opens on the hall. I'll have a chair put there, and screens if you like.

'I must ask you not to pass him any objects whatever, other than paper free of clips or staples. No ring binders, pencils, or pens. He has his own felt-tipped pens.'

'I might have to show him some material that could stimulate him,' Graham said.

'You can show him what you like as long as it's on soft paper. Pass him documents through the sliding food tray. Don't hand anything through the barrier and do not accept anything he might extend through the barrier. He can return papers in the food tray. I insist on that. Dr Bloom and Mr Crawford assured me that you would cooperate on procedure.'

'I will,' Graham said. He started to rise.

'I know you're anxious to get on with it, Mr Graham, but I want to tell you something first. This will interest you.

'It may seem gratuitous to warn you, of all people, about Lecter. But he's very disarming. For a year after he was brought here, he behaved perfectly and gave the appearance of cooperating with attempts at therapy. As a result – this was under the previous administrator – security around him was slightly relaxed.

'On the afternoon of July 8, 1976, he complained of chest pain. His restraints were removed in the examining room to make it easier to give him an electrocardiogram. One of his attendants left the room to smoke, and the other turned away for a second. The nurse was very quick and strong. She managed to save one of her eyes.

'You may find this curious.' Chilton took a strip of EKG tape from a drawer and unrolled it on his desk. He traced the spiky line with his forefinger. 'Here, he's resting on the examining table. Pulse seventy-two. Here, he grabs the nurse's head and pulls her down to him. Here, he is subdued by the attendant. He didn't resist, by the way, though the attendant dislocated his shoulder. Do you notice the strange thing. His pulse never got over eighty-five. Even when he tore out her tongue.'

Chilton could read nothing in Graham's face. He leaned back in his chair and steepled his fingers under his chin. His hands were dry and shiny.

'You know, when Lecter was first captured we thought he might provide us with a singular opportunity to study a pure sociopath,' Chilton said. 'It's so rare to get one alive. Lecter is so lucid, so perceptive; he's trained in psychiatry . . . and he's a mass murderer. He seemed cooperative, and we thought that he could be a window on this kind of aberration. We thought we'd be like Beaumont studying digestion through the opening in St. Martin's stomach.

'As it turned out, I don't think we're any closer to understanding him now than the day he came in. Have you ever talked with Lecter for any length of time?'

'No. I just saw him when . . . I saw him mainly in court. Dr Bloom showed me his articles in the journals,' Graham said.

'He's very familiar with *you*. He's given you a lot of thought.'

'You had some sessions with him?'

'Yes. Twelve. He's impenetrable. Too sophisticated about the tests for them to register anything. Edwards, Fabré, even Dr Bloom himself had a crack at him. I have their notes. He was an enigma to them too. It's impossible, of course, to tell what he's holding back or whether he understands more than he'll say. Oh, since his commitment he's done some brilliant pieces for *The American Journal of Psychiatry* and *The General Archives*. But they're always about problems he doesn't have. I think he's afraid that if we "solve" him, nobody will be interested in him anymore and he'll be stuck in a back ward somewhere for the rest of his life.'

Chilton paused. He had practiced using his peripheral vision to watch his subject in interviews. He believed that he would watch Graham this way undetected.

'The consensus around here is that the only person who has demonstrated any practical understanding of Hannibal Lecter is you, Mr Graham. Can you tell me anything about him?'

'No.'

'Some of the staff are curious about this: when you saw Dr Lecter's murders, their "style," so to speak, were you able perhaps to reconstruct his fantasies? And did that help you identify him?'

Graham did not answer.

'We're woefully short of material on that sort of thing. There's one single piece in *The Journal of Abnormal Psychology*. Would you mind talking with some of the staff – no, no, not this trip – Dr Bloom was very severe with me on that point. We're to leave you alone. Next trip, perhaps.'

Dr Chilton had seen a lot of hostility. He was seeing some at the moment.

Graham stood up. 'Thank you, doctor. I want to see Lecter now.'

The steel door of the maximum-security section closed behind Graham. He heard the bolt slide home.

Graham knew that Lecter slept most of the morning. He looked down the corridor. At that angle he could not see into Lecter's cell, but he could tell that the lights inside were dimmed.

Graham wanted to see Dr Lecter asleep. He wanted time to brace himself. If he felt Lecter's madness in his head, he had to contain it quickly, like a spill.

To cover the sound of his footsteps, he followed an orderly pushing a linen cart. Dr Lecter is very difficult to slip up on.

Graham paused partway down the hall. Steel bars covered the entire front of the cell. Behind the bars, farther than arm's reach, was a stout nylon net stretched ceiling to floor and wall to wall. Through the barrier, Graham could see a table and chair bolted to the floor. The table was stacked with softcover books and correspondence. He walked up to the bars, put his hands on them, took his hands away.

Dr Hannibal Lecter lay on his cot asleep, his head propped on a pillow against the wall. Alexandre Dumas' *Le Grand Dictionnaire de Cuisine* was open on his chest.

Graham had stared through the bars for about five seconds when Lecter opened his eyes and said, 'That's the same atrocious aftershave you wore in court.'

'I keep getting it for Christmas.'

Dr Lecter's eyes are maroon and they reflect the light redly in tiny points. Graham felt each hair bristle on his nape. He put his hand on the back of his neck.

'Christmas, yes,' Lecter said. 'Did you get my card?'

'I got it. Thank you.'

Dr Lecter's Christmas card had been forwarded to Graham from the FBI crime laboratory in Washington. He took it into the backyard, burned it, and washed his hands before touching Molly.

Lecter rose and walked over to his table. He is a small, lithe man. Very neat. 'Why don't you have a seat, Will? I think there are some folding chairs in a closet just down that way. At least, that's where it sounds like they come from.'

'The orderly's bringing one.'

Lecter stood until Graham was seated in the hall. 'And how is Officer Stewart?' he asked.

'Stewart's fine.' Officer Stewart left law enforcement after he saw Dr Lecter's basement. He managed a motel now. Graham did not mention this. He didn't think Stewart would appreciate any mail from Lecter.

'Unfortunate that his emotional problems got the better of him. I thought he was a very promising young officer. Do you ever have any problems, Will?'

'No.'

'Of course you don't.'

Graham felt that Lecter was looking through to the back of his skull. His attention felt like a fly walking around in there.

'I'm glad you came. It's been what now, three years? My callers are all professional. Banal clinical psychiatrists and grasping second-rate *doctors* of psychology from silo colleges somewhere. Pencil lickers trying to protect their tenure with pieces in the journals.'

'Dr Bloom showed me your article on surgical addiction in *The Journal of Clinical Psychiatry*.'

'And?'

'Very interesting, even to a layman.'

'A layman . . . layman – layman. Interesting term,' Lecter said. 'So many learned fellows going about. So many experts on government grants. And you say you're a layman. But it was you who caught me, wasn't it, Will? Do you know how you did it?'

'I'm sure you've read the transcript. It's all in there.'

'No it's not. Do you know how you did it, Will?'

'It's in the transcript. What does it matter now?'

'It doesn't matter to me, Will.'

'I want you to help me, Dr Lecter.'

'Yes, I thought so.'

'It's about Atlanta and Birmingham.'

'Yes.'

'You read about it, I'm sure.'

'I've read the papers. I can't clip them. They won't let me have scissors, of course. Sometimes they threaten me with loss of books, you know. I wouldn't want them to think I was dwelling on anything morbid.' He laughed. Dr Lecter has small white teeth. 'You want to know how he's choosing them, don't you?'

'I thought you would have some ideas. I'm asking you to tell me what they are.'

'Why should I?'

Graham had anticipated the question. A reason to stop multiple murders would not occur readily to Dr Lecter.

'There are things you don't have,' Graham said. 'Research materials, filmstrips even. I'd speak to the chief of staff.'

'Chilton. You must have seen him when you came in. Gruesome, isn't it? Tell me the truth, he fumbles at your head like a freshman pulling at a panty girdle, doesn't he? Watched you out of the corner of his eye. Picked *that* up, didn't you? You may not believe this, but he actually tried to give *me* a Thematic Apperception Test. He was sitting there just like the Cheshire cat waiting for Mf 13 to come up. Ha. Forgive me, I forget that you're not among the anointed. It's a card with a woman in bed and a man in the foreground. I was supposed to avoid a sexual interpretation. I laughed. He puffed up and told everybody I avoided prison with a Ganser syndrome – never mind, it's boring.'

'You'd have access to the AMA filmstrip library.'

'I don't think you'd get me the things I want.'

'Try me.'

'I have quite enough to read as it is.'

'You'd get to see the file on this case. There's another reason.'

'Pray.'

'I thought you might be curious to find out if you're smarter than the person I'm looking for.'

'Then, by implication, you think you are smarter than I am, since you caught me.'

'No. I know I'm not smarter than you are.'

'Then how did you catch me, Will?'

'You had disadvantages.'

'What disadvantages?'

'Passion. And you're insane.'

'You're very tan, Will.'

Graham did not answer.

'Your hands are rough. They don't look like a cop's hands anymore. That shaving lotion is something a child would select. It has a ship on the bottle, doesn't it?' Dr Lecter seldom holds his head upright. He tilts it as he asks a question, as though he were screwing an auger of curiosity into your face. Another silence, and Lecter said, 'Don't think you can persuade me with appeals to my intellectual vanity.'

'I don't think I'll persuade you. You'll do it or you won't. Dr Bloom is working on it anyway, and he's the most – '

'Do you have the file with you?'

'Yes.'

'And pictures?'

'Let me have them, and I might consider it.'

'No.'

'Do you dream much, Will?'

'Goodbye, Dr Lecter.'

'You haven't threatened to take away my books yet.'

Graham walked away.

'Let me have the file, then. I'll tell you what I think.'

Graham had to pack the abridged file tightly into the sliding tray. Lecter pulled it through.

'There's a summary on top. You can read that now,' Graham said.

'Do you mind if I do it privately? Give me an hour.'

Graham waited on a tired plastic couch in a grim lounge. Orderlies came in for coffee. He did not speak to them. He stared at small objects in the room and was glad they held still in his vision. He had to go to the rest room twice. He was numb.

The turnkey admitted him to the maximum-security section again.

Lecter sat at his table, his eyes filmed with thought. Graham knew he had spent most of the hour with the pictures.

'This is a very shy boy, Will. I'd love to meet him. . . . Have you considered the possibility that he's disfigured? Or that he may believe he's disfigured?'

'The mirrors.'

'Yes. You notice he smashed all the mirrors in the houses, not just enough to get the pieces he wanted. He doesn't just put the shards in place for the damage they cause. They're set so he can see himself. In their eyes – Mrs Jacobi and . . . What was the other name?'

'Mrs Leeds.'

'Yes.'

'That's interesting,' Graham said.

'It's not "interesting." You'd thought of that before.'

'I had considered it.'

'You just came here to look at me. Just to get the old scent again, didn't you? Why don't you just smell yourself?'

'I want your opinion.'

'I don't have one right now.'

'When you do have one, I'd like to hear it.'

'May I keep the file?'

'I haven't decided yet,' Graham said.

'Why are there no descriptions of the grounds? Here we have frontal views of the houses, floor plans, diagrams of the rooms where the deaths occurred, and little mention of the grounds. What were the yards like?'

'Big backyards, fenced, with some hedges. Why?'

'Because, my dear Will, if this pilgrim feels a special relationship with the moon, he might like to go outside and look at it. Before he tidies himself up, you understand. Have you seen blood in the moonlight, Will? It appears quite black. Of course, it keeps the distinctive sheen. If one were nude, say, it would be better to have outdoor privacy for that sort of thing. One must show some consideration for the neighbors, hmmmm?'

'You think the yard might be a factor when he selects victims?'

'Oh yes. And there will be more victims, of course. Let me keep the file, Will. I'll study it. When you get more files, I'd like to see them, too. You can call me. On the rare occasions when my lawyer calls, they bring me a telephone. They used to patch him through on the intercom, but everyone listened of course. Would you like to give me your home number?'

'No.'

'Do you know how you caught me, Will?'

'Good-bye, Dr Lecter. You can leave messages for me at the number on the file.' Graham walked away.

'Do you know how you caught me?'

Graham was out of Lecter's sight now, and he walked faster toward the far steel door.

'The reason you caught me is that we're *just alike*' was the last thing Graham heard as the steel door closed behind him.

He was numb except for dreading the loss of numbness. Walking with his head down, speaking to no one, he could hear his blood like a hollow drumming of wings. It seemed a very short distance to the outside. This was only a building; there were only five doors between Lecter and the outside. He had the absurd feeling that Lecter had walked out with him. He stopped outside the entrance and looked around him, assuring himself that he was alone.

From a car across the street, his long lens propped on the window sill, Freddy Lounds got a nice profile shot of Graham in the doorway and the words in stone above him: 'Chesapeake State Hospital for the Criminally Insane.'

As it turned out, *The National Tattler* cropped the picture to just Graham's face and the last two words in the stone.

Chapter Eight

Dr Hannibal Lecter lay on his cot with the cell lights down after Graham left him. Several hours passed.

For a while he had textures; the weave of the pillowcase against his hands clasped behind his head, the smooth membrane that lined his cheek.

Then he had odors and let his mind play over them. Some were real, some were not. They had put Clorox in the drains; semen. They were serving chili down the hall; sweat-stiffened khaki. Graham would not give him his home telephone number; the bitter green smell of cut cocklebur and teaweed.

Lecter sat up. The man might have been civil. His thoughts had the warm brass smell of an electric clock.

Lecter blinked several times, and his eyebrows rose. He turned up the lights and wrote a note to Chilton asking for a telephone to call his counsel.

Lecter was entitled by law to speak with his lawyer in privacy and he hadn't abused the right. Since Chilton would never allow him to go to the telephone, the telephone was brought to him.

Two guards brought it, unrolling a long cord from the telephone jack at their desk. One of the guards had the keys. The other held a can of Mace.

'Go to the back of the cell, Dr Lecter. Face the wall.' If you turn around or approach the barrier before you hear the lock snap, I'll Mace you in the face. Understand?'

'Yes, indeed,' Lecter said. 'Thank you so much for bringing the telephone.'

He had to reach through the nylon net to dial. Chicago information gave him numbers for the University of Chicago Department of Psychiatry and Dr Alan Bloom's office number. He dialed the psychiatry department switchboard.

'I'm trying to reach Dr Alan Bloom.'

'I'm not sure he's in today, but I'll connect you.'

'Just a second, I'm supposed to know his secretary's name and I'm embarrassed to say I've forgotten it.'

'Linda King. Just a moment.'

'Thank you.'

The telephone rang eight times before it was picked up.

'Linda King's desk.'

'Hi, Linda?'

'Linda doesn't come in on Saturday.'

Dr Lecter had counted on that. 'Maybe you could help me, if you don't mind. This is Bob Greer at Blaine and Edwards Publishing Company. Dr Bloom asked me to send a copy of the Overholser book, *The Psychiatrist and the Law*, to Will Graham, and Linda was supposed to send me the address and phone number, but she never did.'

'I'm just a graduate assistant, she'll be in on Mon –'

'I have to catch Federal Express with it in about five minutes, and I hate to bother Dr Bloom about it at home because he told Linda to send it and I don't want to get her in hot water. It's right there in her Rolodex or whatever. I'll dance at your wedding if you'll read it to me.'

'She doesn't have a Rolodex.'

'How about a Call Caddy with the slide on the side?'

'Yes.'

'Be a darling and slide that rascal and I won't take up any more of your time.'

'What was the name?'

'Graham. Will Graham.'

'All right, his home number is 305 JL5-7002.'

'I'm supposed to mail it to his house.'

'It doesn't give the address of his house.'

'What does it have?'

'Federal Bureau of Investigation, Tenth and Pennsylvania, Washington,

D.C. Oh, and Post Office Box 3680, Marathon, Florida.'

'That's fine, you're an angel.'

'You're welcome.'

Lecter felt much better. He thought he might surprise Graham with a call sometime, or if the man couldn't be civil, he might have a hospital-supply house mail Graham a colostomy bag for old times' sake.

Chapter Nine

Seven hundred miles to the southwest, in the cafeteria at Gateway Film Laboratory of St. Louis, Francis Dolarhyde was waiting for a hamburger. The entrées offered in the steam table were filmed over. He stood beside the cash register and sipped coffee from a paper cup.

A red-haired young woman wearing a laboratory smock came into the cafeteria and studied the candy machine. She looked at Francis Dolarhyde's back several times and pursed her lips. Finally she walked over to him and said, 'Mr D.?'

Dolarhyde turned. He always wore red goggles outside the darkroom. She kept her eyes on the nosepiece of the goggles.

'Will you sit down with me a minute? I want to tell you something.'

'What can you tell me, Eileen?'

'That I'm really sorry. Bob was just really drunk and, you know, clowning around. He didn't mean anything. Please come sit down. Just for a minute. Will you do that?'

'Mmmm-hmmm.' Dolarhyde never said 'yes,' as he had trouble with the sibilant /s/.

They sat. She twisted a napkin in her hands.

'Everybody was having a good time at the party and we were glad you came by,' she said. 'Real glad, and surprised, too. You know how Bob is, he does voices all the time – he ought to be on the radio. He did two or three accents, telling jokes and all – he can talk just like a Negro. When he did that other voice, he didn't mean to make you feel bad. He was too drunk to know who was there.'

'They were all laughing and then they . . . didn't laugh.' Dolarhyde never said 'stopped' because of the fricative /s/.

'That's when Bob realized what he had done.'

'He went on, though.'

'I know it,' she said, managing to look from her napkin to his goggles without lingering on the way. 'I got on his case about it, too. He said he didn't mean anything, he just saw he was into it and tried to keep up the joke. You saw how red his face got.'

'He invited me to . . . perform a duet with him.'

'He hugged you and tried to put his arm around you. He wanted you to laugh it off, Mr D.'

'I've laughed it off, Eileen.'

'Bob feels terrible.'

'Well, I don't want him to feel terrible. I don't want that. Tell him for me. And it won't make it any different here at the plant. Golly, if I had talent like Bob I'd make jo . . . a joke all the time.' Dolarhyde avoided plurals whenever he could. 'We'll all get together before long and he'll know how I feel.'

'Good, Mr D. You know he's really, under all the fun, he's a sensitive guy.'

'I'll bet. Tender, I imagine.' Dolarhyde's voice was muffled by his hand. When seated, he always pressed the knuckle of his forefinger under his nose.

'Pardon?'

'I think you're good for him, Eileen.'

'I think so, I really do. He's not drinking but just on weekends. He just starts to relax and his wife calls the house. He makes faces while I talk to her, but I can tell he's upset after. A woman knows.' She tapped Dolarhyde on the wrist and, despite the goggles, saw the touch register in his eyes. 'Take it easy, Mr D. I'm glad we had this talk.'

'I am too, Eileen.'

Dolarhyde watched her walk away. She had a suck mark on the back of her knee. He thought, correctly, that Eileen did not appreciate him. No one did, actually.

The great darkroom was cool and smelled of chemicals. Francis Dolarhyde checked the developer in the A tank. Hundreds of feet of home-movie film from all over the country moved through the tank hourly. Temperature and freshness of the chemicals were critical. This was his responsibility, along with all the other operations until the film had passed through the dryer. Many times a day he lifted samples of film from the tank and checked them frame by frame. The darkroom was quiet. Dolarhyde discouraged chatter among his assistants and communicated with them largely in gestures.

When the evening shift ended, he remained alone in the darkroom to develop, dry, and splice some film of his own.

Dolarhyde got home about ten P.M. He lived alone in a big house his grandparents had left him. It stood at the end of a gravel drive that runs through an apple orchard north of St. Charles, Missouri, across the Missouri River from St. Louis. The orchard's absentee owner did not take care of it. Dead and twisted trees stood among the green ones. Now, in late July, the smell of rotting apples hung over the orchard. There were many bees in the daytime. The nearest neighbor was a half-mile away.

Dolarhyde always made an inspection tour of the house as soon as he got home; there had been an abortive burglary attempt some years before. He flicked on the lights in each room and looked around. A visitor would not think he lived alone. His grandparents' clothes still hung in the closets, his grandmother's brushes were on her dresser with combings of hair in them. Her teeth were in a glass on the bedside table. The water had long since evaporated. His grandmother had been dead for ten years.

(The funeral director had asked him, 'Mr Dolarhyde, wouldn't you like to bring me your grandmother's teeth?' He replied, 'Just drop the lid.')

Satisfied that he was alone in the house, Dolarhyde went upstairs, took a long shower, and washed his hair.

He put on a kimono of a synthetic material that felt like silk and lay down on his narrow bed in the room he had occupied since childhood. His grandmother's hair dryer had a plastic cap and hose. He put on the cap and, while he dried, he thumbed through a new high-fashion magazine. The hatred and brutishness in some of the photographs were remarkable.

He began to feel excited. He swiveled the metal shade of his reading lamp to light a print on the wall at the foot of the bed. It was William Blake's *The Great Red Dragon and the Woman Clothed with the Sun*.

The picture had stunned him the first time he saw it. Never before had he seen anything that approached his graphic thought. He felt that Blake must have peeked in his ear and seen the Red Dragon. For weeks Dolarhyde had worried that his thoughts might glow out his ears, might be visible in the darkroom, might fog the film. He put cotton balls in his ears. Then, fearing that cotton was too flammable, he tried steel wool. That made his ears bleed. Finally he cut small pieces of asbestos cloth from an ironing-board cover and rolled them into little pills that would fit in his ears.

The Red Dragon was all he had for a long time. It was not all he had now. He felt the beginnings of an erection.

He had wanted to go through this slowly, but now he could not wait.

Dolarhyde closed the heavy draperies over windows in the downstairs parlor. He set up his screen and projector. His grandfather had put a La-Z-Boy recliner in the parlor, over his grandmother's objections. (She had put a doily on the headrest.) Now Dolarhyde was glad. It was very comfortable. He draped a towel over the arm of the chair.

He turned out the lamps. Lying back in the dark room, he might have been anywhere. Over the ceiling fixture he had a good light machine which rotated, making varicolored dots of light crawl over the walls, the floor, his skin. He might have been reclining on the acceleration couch of a space vehicle, in a glass bubble out among the stars. When he closed his eyes he thought he could feel the points of light move over him, and when he opened them, those might be the lights of cities above or beneath him. There was no more down or up. The light machine turned faster as it got warm, and the dots swarmed over him, flowed over furniture in angular streams, fell in meteor showers down the walls. He might have been a comet plunging through the Crab Nebula.

There was one place shielded from the light. He had placed a piece of cardboard near the machine, and it cast a shadow over the movie screen.

Sometimes, in the future, he would smoke first to heighten the effect, but he did not need it now, this time.

He thumbed the drop switch at his side to start the projector. A white rectangle sprang on the screen, grayed and streaked as the leader moved past the lens, and then the gray Scotty perked up his ears and ran to the kitchen door, shivering and wagging his stump of a tail. A cut to the Scotty running beside a curb, turning to snap at his side as he ran.

Now Mrs Leeds came into the kitchen carrying groceries. She laughed and touched her hair. The children came in behind her.

A cut to a badly lit shot in Dolarhyde's own bedroom upstairs. He is standing nude before the print of *The Great Red Dragon and the Woman Clothed with the Sun*. He is wearing 'combat glasses,' the close-fitting wrap-around plastic glasses favored by hockey players. He has an erection, which he improves with his hand.

The focus blurs as he approaches the camera with stylized movements, hand reaching to change the focus as his face fills the frame. The picture quivers and sharpens suddenly to a close-up of his mouth, his disfigured upper lip rolled back, tongue out through the teeth, one rolling eye still in the frame. The mouth fills the screen, writhing lips pulled back from jagged teeth and darkness as his mouth engulfs the lens.

The difficulty of the next part was evident.

A bouncing blur in a harsh movie light became a bed and Charles Leeds thrashing, Mrs Leeds sitting up, shielding her eyes, turning to Leeds and putting her hands on him, rolling toward the edge of the bed, legs tangled in the covers, trying to rise. The camera jerked toward the ceiling, molding whipping across the screen like a stave, and then the picture steadied, Mrs Leeds back down on the mattress, a dark spot on her nightdress spreading and Leeds, hands to his neck and eyes wild rising. The screen went black for five beats, then the tic of a splice.

The camera was steady now, on a tripod. They were all dead now. Arranged. Two children seated against the wall facing the bed, one seated across the corner from them facing the camera. Mr and Mrs Leeds in bed with the covers over them. Leeds propped up against the headboard, the sheet covering the rope around his chest and his head lolled to the side. Dolarhyde came into the picture from the left with the stylized movements of a Balinese dancer. Blood-smeared and naked except for his glasses and gloves, he mugged and capered among the dead. He approached the far side of the bed, Mrs Leeds's side, took the corner of the covers, whipped them off the bed and held the pose as though he had executed a veronica.

Now, watching in the parlor of his grandparents' house, Dolarhyde was covered with a sheen of sweat. His thick tongue ran out constantly, the scar on his upper lip wet and shiny and he moaned as he stimulated himself.

Even at the height of his pleasure he was sorry to see that in the film's ensuing scene he lost all his grace and elegance of motion, rooting piglike with his bottom turned carelessly to the camera. There were no dramatic pauses, no sense of pace or climax, just brutish frenzy.

It was wonderful anyway. Watching the film was wonderful. But not as wonderful as the acts themselves.

Two major flaws, Dolarhyde felt, were that the film did not actually show the deaths of the Leedses and that his own performance was poor toward the end. He seemed to lose all his values. That was not how the Red Dragon would do it.

Well. He had many films to make and, with experience, he hoped he could maintain some aesthetic distance, even in the most intimate moments.

He must bear down. This was his life's work, a magnificent thing. It would live forever.

He must press on soon. He must select his fellow performers. Already he had copied several films of Fourth of July family outings. The end of summer always brought a rush of business at the film-processing plant as vacation movies came in. Thanksgiving would bring another rush.

Families were mailing their applications to him every day.

Chapter Ten

The plane from Washington to Birmingham was half-empty. Graham took a window seat with no one beside him.

He declined the tired sandwich the stewardess offered and put his Jacobi file on the tray table. At the front he had listed the similarities between the Jacobis and the Leedses.

Both couples were in their late thirties, both had children – two boys and a girl. Edward Jacobi had another son, by a previous marriage, who was away at college when the family was killed.

Both parents in each case had college degrees, and both families lived in two-story houses in pleasant suburbs. Mrs Jacobi and Mrs Leeds were attractive women. The families had some of the same credit cards and they subscribed to some of the same popular magazines.

There the similarities ended. Charles Leeds was a tax attorney, while Edward Jacobi was an engineer and metallurgist. The Atlanta family were Presbyterian; the Jacobis were Catholic. The Leedses were lifelong Atlanta residents, while the Jacobis had lived in Birmingham only three months, transferred there from Detroit.

The word 'random' sounded in Graham's head like a dripping faucet.

'Random selection of victims,' 'no apparent motive' – newspapers used those terms, and detectives spat them out in anger and frustration in homicide squad rooms.

'Random' wasn't accurate, though. Graham knew that mass murderers and serial murderers do not select their victims at random.

The man who killed the Jacobis and the Leedses saw something in them that drew him and drove him to do it. He might have known them well – Graham hoped so – or he might not have known them at all. But Graham was sure the killer saw them at some time before he killed them. He chose them because *something* in them spoke to him, and the women were at the core of it. What was it?

There were some differences in the crimes.

Edward Jacobi was shot as he came down the stairs carrying a flashlight – probably he was awakened by a noise.

Mrs Jacobi and her children were shot in the head, Mrs Leeds in the abdomen. The weapon was a nine-millimeter automatic pistol in all the shootings. Traces of steel wool from a homemade silencer were found in the wounds. The cartridge cases bore no fingerprints.

The knife had been used only on Charles Leeds. Dr Princi believed it was thin-bladed and very keen, possibly a fileting knife.

The methods of entry were different too; a patio door pried open at the Jacobis', the glass cutter at the Leedses'.

Photographs of the crime in Birmingham did not show the quantity of blood found at the Leedses', but there were stains on the bedroom walls about two and one-half feet above the floor. So the killer had an audience in Birmingham too. The Birmingham police checked the bodies for fingerprints, including the fingernails, and found nothing. Burial for a summer month in Birmingham would destroy any prints like the one on the Leeds child.

In both places were the same blond hairs, same spit, same semen.

Graham propped photographs of the two smiling families against the seat back in front of him and stared at them for a long time in the hanging quiet of the airplane.

What could have attracted the murderer specifically to *them?* Graham wanted very much to believe there was a common factor and that he would find it soon.

Otherwise he would have to enter more houses and see what the Tooth Fairy had left for him.

● ● ●

Graham got directions from the Birmingham field office and checked in with the police by telephone from the airport. The compact car he rented spit water from the air conditioner vents onto his hands and arms.

His first stop was the Geehan Realty office on Dennison Avenue.

Geehan, tall and bald, made haste across his turquoise shag to greet Graham. His smile faded when Graham showed his identification and asked for the key to the Jacobi house.

'Will there be some cops in uniform out there today?' he asked, his hand on the top of his head.

'I don't know.'

'I hope to God not. I've got a chance to show it twice this afternoon. It's a nice house. People see it and they forget this other. Last Thursday I had a couple from Duluth, substantial retired people hot on the Sun Belt. I had them down to the short rows – talking mortgages – I mean that man could have fronted a *third*, when the squad car rode up and in they came. Couple asked them questions and, boy, did they get some answers. These good officers gave 'em the whole tour – who was laying where. Then it was Goodbye, Geehan, much obliged for your trouble. I try to show 'em how safe we've fixed it, but they don't listen. There they go, jake-legged through the gravel, climbing back in their Sedan de Ville.'

'Have any single men asked to look at it?'

'They haven't asked me. It's a multiple listing. I don't think so, though. Police wouldn't let us start painting until, I don't know, we just got finished inside last Tuesday. Took two coats of interior latex, three in places. We're still working outside. It'll be a genuine showplace.'

'How can you sell it before the estate's probated?'

'I can't *close* until probate, but that doesn't mean I can't be ready. People could move in on a memorandum of understanding. I need to do something. A business associate of mine is holding the paper, and that interest just works all day and all night while you're asleep.'

'Who is Mr Jacobi's executor?'

'Byron Metcalf, firm of Metcalf and Barnes. How long you figure on being out there?'

'I don't know. Until I've finished.'

'You can drop that key in the mail. You don't have to come back by.'

Graham had the flat feeling of a cold trail as he drove out to the Jacobi house. It was barely within the city limits in an area newly annexed. He stopped beside the highway once to check his map before he found the turnoff onto an asphalt secondary road.

More than a month had passed since they were killed. What had he been doing then? Putting a pair of diesels in a sixty-five foot Rybovich hull, signaling to Ariaga in the crane to come down another half-inch. Molly came over in the late afternoon and he and Molly and Ariaga sat under an awning in the cockpit of the half-finished boat and ate the big prawns Molly brought and drank cold Dos Equis beer. Ariaga explained the best way to clean crayfish, drawing the tail fan in sawdust on the deck, and the sunlight, broken on the water, played on the undersides of the wheeling gulls.

Water from the air conditioner squirted on the front of Graham's shirt and he was in Birmingham now and there were no prawns or gulls. He was driving, and pastures and wooded lots were on his right with goats and horses in them, and on his left was Stonebridge, a long-established residential area with a few elegant homes and a number of rich people's houses.

He saw the realtor's sign a hundred yards before he reached it. The Jacobi house was the only one on the right side of the road. Sap from the pecan trees beside the drive had made the gravel sticky, and it rattled inside the fenders of the car. A carpenter on a ladder was installing window guards. The workman raised a hand to Graham as he walked around the house.

A flagged patio at the side was shaded by a large oak tree. At night the tree would block out the floodlight in the side yard as well. This was where the Tooth Fairy had entered, through sliding glass doors. The doors had been replaced with new ones, the aluminum frames still bright and bearing the manufacturer's sticker. Covering the sliding doors was a new wrought-iron security gate. The basement door was new too – flush steel and secured by deadbolts. The components of a hot tub stood in crates on the flagstones.

Graham went inside. Bare floors and dead air. His footsteps echoed in the empty house.

The new mirrors in the bathrooms had never reflected the Jacobis' faces or the killer's. On each was a fuzzy white spot where the price had been torn off. A folded dropcloth lay in a corner of the master bedroom. Graham sat on it long enough for the sunlight through the bare windows to move one board-width across the floor.

There was nothing here. Nothing anymore.

If he had come here immediately after the Jacobis were killed, would the Leedses still be alive? Graham wondered. He tested the weight of that burden.

It did not lift when he was out of the house and under the sky again.

Graham stood in the shade of a pecan tree, shoulders hunched, hands in his pockets, and looked down the long drive to the road that passed in front of the Jacobi house.

How had the Tooth Fairy come to the Jacobi house? He had to drive. Where did he park? The gravel driveway was too noisy for a midnight visit, Graham thought. The Birmingham police did not agree.

He walked down the drive to the roadside. The asphalt road was bordered with ditches as far as he could see. It might be possible to pull across the ditch and hide a vehicle in the brush on the Jacobis' side of the road if the ground were hard and dry.

Facing the Jacobi house across the road was the single entrance to Stonebridge. The sign said that Stonebridge had a private patrol service. A strange vehicle would be noticed there. So would a man walking late at night. Scratch parking in Stonebridge.

Graham went back into the house and was surprised to find the telephone working. He called the Weather Bureau and learned that three inches of rain fell on the day before the Jacobis were killed. The ditches were full, then. The Tooth Fairy did not hide his vehicle beside the asphalt road.

A horse in the pasture beside the yard kept pace with Graham as he walked along the whitewashed fence toward the rear of the property. He gave the horse a Life-Saver and left him at the corner as he turned along the back fence behind the outbuildings.

He stopped when he saw the depression in the ground where the Jacobi children had buried their cat. Thinking about it in the Atlanta police station with Springfield, he had pictured the outbuildings as white. Actually they were dark green.

The children had wrapped the cat in a dish towel and buried it in a shoebox with a flower between its paws.

Graham rested his forearm on top of the fence and leaned his forehead against it.

A pet funeral, solemn rite of childhood. Parents going back into the house, ashamed to pray. The children looking at one another, discovering new nerves in the place loss pierces. One bows her head, then they all do, the shovel taller than any of them. Afterward a discussion of whether or not the cat is in heaven with God and Jesus, and the children don't shout for a while.

A certainty came to Graham as he stood, sun hot on the back of his neck: as surely as the Tooth Fairy killed the cat, he had watched the children bury it. He had to see that if he possibly could.

He did not make two trips out here, one to kill the cat and the second for the Jacobis. He came and killed the cat and waited for the children to find it.

There was no way to determine exactly where the children found the cat. The police had located no one who spoke to the Jacobis after noon, ten hours or so before they died.

How had the Tooth Fairy come, and where had he waited?

Behind the back fence the brush began, running head-high for thirty yards to the trees. Graham dug his wrinkled map out of his back pocket and spread it on the fence. It showed an unbroken strip of woods a quarter-mile deep running across the back of the Jacobi property and continuing in both directions. Beyond the woods, bounding them on the south, was a section line road that paralleled the one in front of the Jacobi house.

Graham drove from the house back to the highway, measuring the distance on his odometer. He went south on the highway and turned onto the section line road he had seen on the map. Measuring again, he drove slowly along it until the odometer showed him he was behind the Jacobi house on the other side of the woods.

Here the pavement ended at a low-income housing project so new it did not show on his map. He pulled into the parking lot. Most of the cars were old and sagging on their springs. Two were up on blocks.

Black children played basketball on the bare earth around a single netless goal. Graham sat on his fender to watch the game for a moment.

He wanted to take off his jacket, but he knew the .44 Special and the flat camera on his belt would attract attention. He always felt a curious embarrassment when people looked at his pistol.

There were eight players on the team wearing shirts. The skins had eleven, all playing at once. Refereeing was by acclamation.

A small skin, shoved down in the rebounding, stalked home mad. He came back fortified with a cookie and dived into the pack again.

The yelling and the thump of the ball lifted Graham's spirits.

One goal, one basketball. It struck him again how many *things* the Leedses had. The Jacobis too, according to the Birmingham police when they ruled out burglary. Boats and sporting equipment, camping equipment, cameras and guns and rods. It was another thing the families had in common.

And with the thought of the Leedses and the Jacobis alive came the thought of how they were afterward, and Graham couldn't watch basketball anymore. He took a deep breath and headed for the dark woods across the road.

The underbrush, heavy at the edge of the pine woods, thinned when Graham reached the deep shade and he had easy going over the pine needles. The air was warm and still. Blue jays in the trees ahead announced his coming.

The ground sloped gently to a dry streambed where a few cypresses grew and the tracks of raccoons and field mice were pressed into the red clay. A number of human footprints marked the streambed, some of them left by children. All were caved in and rounded, left several rains ago.

Past the streambed the land rose again, changing to sandy loam that supported ferns beneath the pines. Graham worked his way uphill in the heat until he saw the light beneath the trees at the edge of the woods.

Between the trunks he could see the upper story of the Jacobi house.

Undergrowth again, head-high from the edge of the woods to the Jacobis' back fence. Graham worked his way through it and stood at the fence looking into the yard.

The Tooth Fairy could have parked at the housing development and come through the woods to the brush behind the house.

He could have lured the cat into the brush and choked it, the body limp in one hand as he crawled on his knees and other hand to the fence. Graham could see the cat in the air, never twisting to land on its feet, but hitting on its back with a thump in the yard.

The Tooth Fairy did that in daylight – the children would not have found or buried the cat at night.

And he waited to see them find it. Did he wait for the rest of the day in the heat of the underbrush? At the fence he would be visible through the rails. In order to see the yard from farther back in the brush, he would have to stand and face the windows of the house with the sun beating on him. Clearly he would go back to the trees. So did Graham.

The Birmingham police were not stupid. He could see where they had pushed through the brush, searching the area as a matter of course. But that was before the cat was found. They were looking for clues, dropped objects, tracks – not for a vantage point.

He went a few yards into the forest behind the Jacobi house and worked back and forth in the dappled shade. First he took the high ground that afforded a partial view of the yard and then worked his way down the tree line.

He had searched for more than an hour when a wink of light from the ground caught his eye. He lost it, found it again. It was the ring-pull tab from a soft-drink can half-buried in the leaves beneath an elm tree, one of the few elms among the pines.

He spotted it from eight feet away and went no closer for five minutes while he scanned the ground around the tree. He squatted and brushed the leaves away ahead of him as he approached the tree, duck-walking in the path he made to avoid ruining any impressions. Working slowly, he cleared the leaves all around the trunk. No footprints had pressed through the mat of last year's leaves.

Near the aluminum tab he found a dried apple core eaten thin by ants. Birds had pecked out the seeds. He studied the ground for ten more minutes. Finally he sat on the ground, stretched out his aching legs, and leaned back against the tree.

A cone of gnats swarmed in a column of sunlight. A caterpillar rippled along the underside of a leaf.

There was a wedge of red creek mud from the instep of a boot on the limb above his head.

Graham hung his coat on a branch and began to climb carefully on the opposite side of the tree, peering around the trunk at the limbs above the wedge of mud. At thirty feet he looked around the trunk, and there was the Jacobi house 175 yards away. It looked different from this height, the roof color dominant. He could see the backyard and the ground behind the outbuildings very well. A decent pair of field glasses would pick up the expression on a face easily at this distance.

Graham could hear traffic in the distance, and far away he heard a beagle on a case. A cicada started its numbing handsaw buzz and drowned out the other sounds.

A thick limb just above him joined the trunk at a right angle to the Jacobi house. He pulled himself up until he could see, and leaned around the trunk to look at it.

Close by his cheek a soft drink can was wedged between the limb and the trunk.

'I love it,' Graham whispered into the bark. 'Oh, sweet Jesus, yes. Come on, can.'

Still, a child might have left it.

He climbed higher on his side of the tree, dicey work on small branches, and moved around until he could look down on the big limb.

A patch of outer bark on the upper side of the limb was shaved away, leaving a field of green inner bark the size of a playing card. Centered in the green rectangle, carved through to the white wood, Graham saw this:

It was done carefully and cleanly with a very sharp knife. It was not the work of a child.

Graham photographed the mark, carefully bracketing his exposures.

The view from the big limb was good, and it had been improved: the stub of a small branch jutted down from the limb above. It had been clipped off to clear the view. The fibers were compressed and the end slightly flattened in the cutting.

Graham looked for the severed branch. If it had been on the ground, he would have seen it. There, tangled in the limbs below, brown withered leaves amid the green foliage.

The laboratory would need both sides of the cut in order to measure the pitch of the cutting edges. That meant coming back here with a saw. He made several photographs of the stub. All the while he mumbled to himself.

I think that after you killed the cat and threw it into the yard, my man, you climbed up here and waited. I think you watched the children and passed the time whistling and dreaming. When night came, you saw them passing their bright windows and you watched the shades go down, and you saw the lights go out one by one. And after a while you climbed down and went in to them. Didn't you? It wouldn't be too hard a climb straight down from the big limb with a flashlight and the bright moon rising.

It was a hard enough climb for Graham. He stuck a twig into the opening of the soft-drink can, gently lifted it from the crotch of the tree, and descended, holding the twig in his teeth when he had to use both hands.

Back at the housing project, Graham found that someone had written 'Levon is a doo-doo head' in the dust on the side of his car. The height of the writing indicated that even the youngest residents were well along in literacy.

He wondered if they had written on the Tooth Fairy's car.

Graham sat for a few minutes looking up at the rows of windows. There appeared to be about a hundred units. It was possible that someone might remember a white stranger in the parking lot late at night. Even though a month had passed, it was well worth trying. To ask every resident, and get it done quickly, he would need the help of the Birmingham police.

He fought the temptation to send the drink can straight to Jimmy Price in Washington. He had to ask the Birmingham police for manpower. It would be better to give them what he had. Dusting the can would be a straightforward job. Trying for fingerprints etched by acid sweat was another matter. Price could still do it after Birmingham dusted, as long as the can wasn't handled with bare fingers. Better give it to the police. He knew the FBI document section would fall on the carving like a rabid mongoose. Pictures of that for everybody, nothing lost there.

He called Birmingham Homicide from the Jacobi house. The detectives arrived just as the realtor, Geehan, was ushering in his prospective buyers.

Chapter Eleven

Eileen was reading a *National Tattler* article called 'Filth in Your Bread!' when Dolarhyde came into the cafeteria. She had eaten only the filling in her tuna-salad sandwich.

Behind the red goggles Dolarhyde's eyes zigged down the front page of the *Tattler*. Cover lines in addition to 'Filth in Your Bread!' included 'Elvis at Secret Love Retreat – Exclusive Pix!!' 'Stunning Breakthrough for Cancer Victims!' and the big banner line 'Hannibal the Cannibal Helps Lawmen – Cops Consult Fiend in "Tooth Fairy" Murders.'

He stood at the window absently stirring his coffee until he heard Eileen get up. She dumped her tray in the trash container and was about to throw in the *Tattler* when Dolarhyde touched her shoulder.

'May I have that paper, Eileen?'

'Sure, Mr D. I just get it for the horoscopes.'

Dolarhyde read it in his office with the door closed.

Freddy Lounds had two bylines in the same double-page center spread. The main story was a breathless reconstruction of the Jacobi and Leeds murders. Since the police had not divulged many of the specifics, Lounds consulted his imagination for lurid details.

Dolarhyde found them banal.

The sidebar was more interesting:

Insane Fiend Consulted in Mass Murders by Cop He Tried to Kill
by
Freddy Lounds

CHESAPEAKE, MD. – Federal manhunters, stymied in their search for the 'Tooth Fairy,' psychopathic slayer of entire families in Birmingham and Atlanta, have turned to the most savage killer in captivity for help.

Dr Hannibal Lecter, whose unspeakable practices were reported in these pages three years ago, was consulted this week in his maximum-security-asylum cell by ace investigator William (Will) Graham.

Graham suffered a near-fatal slashing at Lecter's hands when he unmasked the mass murderer.

He was brought back from early retirement to spearhead the hunt for the 'Tooth Fairy.'

What went on in this bizarre meeting of two mortal enemies? What was Graham after?

'It takes one to catch one,' a high federal official told this reporter. He was referring to Lecter, known as 'Hannibal the Cannibal,' who is both a psychiatrist and a mass murderer.

OR WAS HE REFERRING TO GRAHAM???

The *Tattler* has learned that Graham, former instructor in forensics at the FBI Academy in Quantico, Va., was once confined to a mental institution for a period of four weeks. . . .

Federal officials refused to say why they placed a man with a history of mental instability at the forefront of a desperate manhunt.

The nature of Graham's mental problem was not revealed, but one former psychiatric worker called it 'deep depression.'

Garmon Evans, a paraprofessional formerly employed at Bethesda Naval Hospital, said Graham was admitted to the psychiatric wing soon after he killed Garrett Jacob Hobbs, the 'Minnesota Shrike.' Graham shot Hobbs to death in 1975, ending Hobbs' eight-month reign of terror in Minneapolis.

Evans said Graham was withdrawn and refused to eat or speak during the first weeks of his stay.

Graham has never been an FBI agent. Veteran observers attribute this to the Bureau's strict screening procedures, designed to detect instability.

Federal sources would reveal only that Graham originally worked in the FBI crime laboratory and was assigned teaching duties at the FBI Academy after outstanding work both in the laboratory and in the field, where he served as a 'special investigator.'

The *Tattler* learned that before his federal service, Graham was in the homicide division of the New Orleans police department, a post he left to attend graduate school in forensics at George Washington University.

One New Orleans officer who served with Graham commented, 'Well, you can call him retired, but the feds like to know he's around. It's like having a king snake under the house. They may not see him much, but it's nice to know he's there to eat the moccasins.'

Dr Lecter is confined for the rest of his life. If he is ever declared sane, he will have to stand trial on nine counts of first-degree murder.

Lecter's attorney says the mass murderer spends his time writing useful articles for the scientific journals and has an 'ongoing dialogue' by mail with some of the most respected figures in psychiatry.

Dolarhyde stopped reading and looked at the pictures. There were two of them above the sidebar. One showed Lecter pinned against the side of a state trooper's car. The other was the picture of Will Graham taken by Freddy Lounds outside the Chesapeake State Hospital. A small photograph of Lounds ran beside each of his bylines.

Dolarhyde looked at the pictures for a long time. He ran the tip of his forefinger over them slowly, back and forth, his touch exquisitely sensitive to the rough newsprint. Ink left a smudge on his fingertip. He wet the smudge with his tongue and wiped it off on a Kleenex. Then he cut out the sidebar and put it in his pocket.

On his way home from the plant, Dolarhyde bought toilet paper of the quick-dissolving kind used in boats and campers, and a nasal inhaler.

He felt good despite his hay fever; like many people who have undergone extensive rhinoplasty, Dolarhyde had no hair in his nose and hay fever plagued him. So did upper respiratory infections.

When a stalled truck held him up for ten minutes on the Missouri River bridge to St. Charles, he sat patiently. His black van was carpeted, cool and quiet. Handel's Water Music played on the stereo.

He rippled his fingers on the steering wheel in time with the music and dabbed at his nose.

Two women in a convertible were in the lane beside him. They wore shorts and blouses tied across the midriff. Dolarhyde looked down into the convertible from his van. They seemed tired and bored squinting into the lowering sun. The woman on the passenger side had her head against the seat back and her feet on the dash. Her slumped posture made two creases across her bare stomach. Dolarhyde could see a suck mark on the inside of her thigh. She caught him looking, sat up and crossed her legs. He saw weary distaste in her face.

She said something to the woman at the wheel. Both looked straight ahead. He knew they were talking about him. He was *so* glad it did not make him angry. Few things made him angry anymore. He knew that he was developing a becoming dignity.

The music was very pleasant.

The traffic in front of Dolarhyde began to move. The lane beside him was still stalled. He looked forward to getting home. He tapped the wheel in time with the music and rolled down the window with his other hand.

He hawked and spit a blob of green phlegm into the lap of the woman beside him, hitting her just beside the navel. Her curses sounded high and thin over the Handel as he drove away.

Dolarhyde's great ledger was at least a hundred years old. Bound in black leather with brass corners, it was so heavy a sturdy machine table supported it in the locked closet at the top of the stairs.

From the moment he saw it at the bankruptcy sale of an old St. Louis printing company, Dolarhyde knew it should be his.

Now, bathed and in his kimono, he unlocked the closet and rolled it out. When the book was centered beneath the painting of the Great Red Dragon, he settled himself in a chair and opened it. The smell of foxed paper rose to his face.

Across the first page, in large letters he had illuminated himself, were the words from Revelation: 'And There Came a Great Red Dragon Also . . .'

The first item in the book was the only one not neatly mounted. Loose between the pages was a yellowed photograph of Dolarhyde as a small child with his grandmother on the steps of the big house. He is holding on to Grandmother's skirt. Her arms are folded and her back is straight.

Dolarhyde turned past it. He ignored it as though it had been left there by mistake.

There were many clippings in the ledger, the earliest ones about the disappearances of elderly women in St. Louis and Toledo. Pages between the clippings were covered with Dolarhyde's writing – black ink in a fine copperplate script not unlike William Blake's own handwriting.

Fastened in the margins, ragged bites of scalp trailed their tails of hair like comets pressed in God's scrapbook.

The Jacobi clippings from Birmingham were there, along with film cartridges and slides set in pockets glued to the pages.

So were stories on the Leedses, with film beside them.

The term 'Tooth Fairy' had not appeared in the press until Atlanta. The name was marked out in all the Leeds stories.

Now Dolarhyde did the same with his *Tattler* clipping, obliterating 'Tooth Fairy' with angry slashes of a red marker pen.

He turned to a new, blank page in his ledger and trimmed the *Tattler* clipping to fit. Should Graham's picture go in? The words 'Criminally Insane' carved in the stone above Graham offended Dolarhyde. He hated the sight of any place of confinement. Graham's face was closed to him. He set it aside for the time being.

But Lecter . . . Lecter. This was not a good picture of the doctor. Dolarhyde had a better one, which he fetched from a box in his closet. It was published upon Lecter's committal and showed the fine eyes. Still, it was not satisfactory. In Dolarhyde's mind, Lecter's likeness should be the dark portrait of a Renaissance prince. For Lecter, alone among all men, might have the sensitivity and experience to understand the glory, the majesty of Dolarhyde's Becoming.

Dolarhyde felt that Lecter knew the unreality of the people who die to help you in these things – understood that they are not flesh, but light and air and color and quick sounds quickly ended when you change them. Like balloons of color bursting. That they are more important for the changing, more important than the lives they scrabble after, pleading.

Dolarhyde bore screams as a sculptor bears dust from the beaten stone.

Lecter was capable of understanding that blood and breath were only elements undergoing change to fuel his Radiance. Just as the source of light is burning.

He would like to meet Lecter, talk and share with him, rejoice with him in their shared vision, be recognized by him as John the Baptist recognized the One who came after, sit on him as the Dragon sat on 666 in Blake's Revelation series, and film his death as, dying, he melded with the strength of the Dragon.

Dolarhyde pulled on a new pair of rubber gloves and went to his desk. He unrolled and discarded the outer layer of the toilet paper he had bought. Then he unrolled a strip of seven sheets and tore it off.

Printing carefully on the tissue with his left hand, he wrote a letter to Lecter.

Speech is never a reliable indicator of how a person writes; you never know. Dolarhyde's speech was bent and pruned by disabilities real and imagined, and the difference between his speech and his writing was startling. Still, he found he could not say the most important things he felt.

He wanted to hear from Lecter. He needed a personal response before he could tell Dr Lecter the important things.

How could he manage that? He rummaged through his box of Lecter clippings, read them all again.

Finally a simple way occurred to him and he wrote again.

The letter seemed too diffident and shy when he read it over. He had signed it 'Avid Fan.'

He brooded over the signature for several minutes.

'Avid Fan' indeed. His chin rose an imperious fraction.

He put his gloved thumb in his mouth, removed his dentures, and placed them on the blotter.

The upper plate was unusual. The teeth were normal, straight and white, but the pink acrylic upper part was a tortuous shape cast to fit the twists and fissures of his gums. Attached to the plate was a soft plastic prosthesis with an obturator on top, which helped him close off his soft palate in speech.

He took a small case from his desk. It held another set of teeth. The upper casting was the same, but there was no prosthesis. The crooked teeth had dark stains between them and gave off a faint stench.

They were identical to Grandmother's teeth in the bedside glass downstairs.

Dolarhyde's nostrils flared at the odor. He opened his sunken smile and put them in place and wet them with his tongue.

He folded the letter across the signature and bit down hard on it. When he opened the letter again, the signature was enclosed in an oval bite mark; his notary seal, an imprimatur flecked with old blood.

Chapter Twelve

Attorney Byron Metcalf took off his tie at five o'clock, made himself a drink, and put his feet up on his desk.

'Sure you won't have one?'

'Another time.' Graham, picking the cockleburs off his cuffs, was grateful for the air conditioning.

'I didn't know the Jacobis very well,' Metcalf said. 'They'd only been here three months. My wife and I were there for drinks a couple of times. Ed Jacobi came to me for a new will soon after he was transferred here, that's how I met him.'

'But you're his executor.'

'Yes. His wife was listed first as executor, then me as alternate in case she was deceased or infirm. He has a brother in Philadelphia, but I gather they weren't close.'

'You were an assistant district attorney.'

'Yeah, 1968 to '72. I ran for DA in '72. It was close, but I lost. I'm not sorry now.'

'How do you see what happened here, Mr Metcalf?'

'The first thing I thought about was Joseph Yablonski, the labor leader?'

Graham nodded.

'A crime with a motive, power in that case, disguised as an insane attack. We went over Ed Jacobi's papers with a fine-tooth comb – Jerry Estridge from the DA's office and I.

'Nothing. Nobody stood to make much money off Ed Jacobi's death. He made a big salary and he had some patents paying off, but he spent it almost as fast as it came in. Everything was to go to the wife, with a little land in California entailed to the kids and their descendants. He had a small spendthrift trust set up for the surviving son. It'll pay his way through three more years of college. I'm sure he'll still be a freshman by then.'

'Niles Jacobi.'

'Yeah. The kid gave Ed a big pain in the ass. He lived with his mother in California. Went to Chino for theft. I gather his mother's a flake. Ed went out there to see about him last year. Brought him back to Birmingham and put him in school at Bardwell Community College. Tried to keep him at home, but he dumped on the other kids and made it unpleasant for everybody. Mrs Jacobi put up with it for a while, but finally they moved him to a dorm.'

'Where was he?'

'On the night of June 28?' Metcalf's eyes were hooded as he looked at Graham. 'The police wondered about that, and so did I. He went to a movie and then back to school. It's verified. Besides, he has type-O blood. Mr Graham, I have to pick up my wife in half an hour. We can talk tomorrow if you like. Tell me how I can help you.'

'I'd like to see the Jacobis' personal effects. Diaries, pictures, whatever.'

'There's not much of that – they lost about everything in a fire in Detroit before they moved down here. Nothing suspicious – Ed was welding in the basement and the sparks got into some paint he had stored down there and the house went up.

'There's some personal correspondence. I have it in the lockboxes with the small valuables. I don't remember any diaries. Everything else is in storage. Niles may have some pictures, but I doubt it. Tell you what – I'm going to court at nine-thirty in the morning, but I could get you into the bank to look at the stuff and come back by for you afterward.'

'Fine,' Graham said. 'One other thing. I could use copies of everything to do with the probate: claims against the estate, any contest of the will, correspondence. I'd like to have all the paper.'

'The Atlanta DA's office asked me for that already. They're comparing with the Leeds estate in Atlanta, I know,' Metcalf said.

'Still, I'd like copies for myself.'

'Okay, copies to you. You don't really think it's money, though, do you?'

'No. I just keep hoping the same name will come up here and in Atlanta.'

'So do I.'

Student housing at Bardwell Community College was four small dormitory buildings set around a littered quadrangle of beaten earth. A stereo war was in progress when Graham got there.

Opposing sets of speakers on the motel-style balconies blared at each other across the quad. It was Kiss versus the *1812 Overture*. A water balloon arched high in the air and burst on the ground ten feet from Graham.

He ducked under a clothesline and stepped over a bicycle to get through the sitting room of the suite Niles Jacobi shared. The door to Jacobi's bedroom was ajar and music blasted through the crack. Graham knocked.

No response.

He pushed open the door. A tall boy with a spotty face sat on one of the twin beds sucking on a four-foot bong pipe. A girl in dungarees lay on the other bed.

The boy's head jerked around to face Graham. He was struggling to think.

'I'm looking for Niles Jacobi.'

The boy appeared stupefied. Graham switched off the stereo.

'I'm looking for Niles Jacobi.'

'Just some stuff for my asthma, man. Don't you ever knock?'

'Where's Niles Jacobi?'

'Fuck if I know. What do you want him for?'

Graham showed him the tin. 'Try real hard to remember.'

'Oh, shit,' the girl said.

'Narc, goddammit. I ain't worth it, look, let's talk about this a minute, man.'

'Let's talk about where Jacobi is.'

'I think I can find out for you,' the girl said.

Graham waited while she asked in the other rooms. Everywhere she went, commodes flushed.

There were few traces of Niles Jacobi in the room-one photograph of the Jacobi family lay on a dresser. Graham lifted a glass of melting ice off it and wiped away the wet ring with his sleeve.

The girl returned. 'Try the Hateful Snake,' she said.

● ● ●

The Hateful Snake bar was in a storefront with the windows painted dark green. The vehicles parked outside were an odd assortment, big trucks looking bobtailed without their trailers, compact cars, a lilac convertible, old Dodges and Chevrolets crippled with high rear ends for the drag-strip look, four full-dress Harley-Davidsons.

An air conditioner, mounted in the transom over the door, dripped steadily onto the sidewalk.

Graham ducked around the dribble and went inside.

The place was crowded and smelled of disinfectant and stale Canoe. The bartender, a husky woman in overalls, reached over heads at the service bar to hand Graham his Coke. She was the only woman there.

Niles Jacobi, dark and razor-thin, was at the jukebox. He put the money in the machine, but the man beside him pushed the buttons. Jacobi looked like a dissolute schoolboy, but the one selecting the music did not.

Jacobi's companion was a strange mixture; he had a boyish face on a knobby, muscular body. He wore a T-shirt and jeans, worn white over the objects in his pockets. His arms were knotty with muscle, and he had large, ugly hands. One professional tattoo on his left forearm said 'Born to Fuck.' A crude jailhouse tattoo on his other arm said 'Randy.' His short jail haircut had grown out unevenly. As he reached for a button on the lighted jukebox, Graham saw a small shaved patch on his forearm.

Graham felt a cold place in his stomach. He followed Niles Jacobi and 'Randy' through the crowd to the back of the room. They sat in a booth.

Graham stopped two feet from the table.

'Niles, my name is Will Graham. I need to talk with you for a few minutes.'

Randy looked up with a bright false smile. One of his front teeth was dead. 'Do I know you?'

'No. Niles, I want to talk to you.'

Niles arched a quizzical eyebrow. Graham wondered what had happened to him in Chino.

'We were having a private conversation here. Butt out,' Randy said.

Graham looked thoughtfully at the marred muscular forearms, the dot of adhesive in the crook of the elbow, the shaved patch where Randy had tested the edge of his knife. Knife fighter's mange.

I'm afraid of Randy. Fire or fall back.

'Did you hear me?' Randy said. 'Butt out.'

Graham unbuttoned his jacket and put his identification on the table.

'Sit still, Randy. If you try to get up, you're gonna have two navels.'

'I'm sorry, sir.' Instant inmate sincerity.

'Randy, I want you to do something for me. I want you to reach in your left back pocket. Just use two fingers. You'll find a five-inch knife in there with a Flicket clamped to the blade. Put it on the table. . . . Thank you.'

Graham dropped the knife into his pocket. It felt greasy.

'Now, in your other pocket is your wallet. Get it out. You sold some blood today, didn't you?'

'So what?'

'So hand me the slip they gave you, the one you show next time at the blood bank. Spread it out on the table.'

Randy had type-O blood. Scratch Randy.

'How long have you been out of jail?'

'Three weeks.'

'Who's your parole officer?'

'I'm not on parole.'

'That's probably a lie.' Graham wanted to roust Randy. He could get him for carrying a knife over the legal length. Being in a place with a liquor license was a parole violation. Graham knew he was angry at Randy because he had feared him.

'Randy.'

'Yeah.'

'Get out.'

'I don't know what I can tell you, I didn't know my father very well,' Niles Jacobi said as Graham drove him to the school. 'He left Mother when I was three, and I didn't see him after that – Mother wouldn't *have* it.'

'He came to see you last spring.'

'Yes.'

'At Chino.'

'You know about that.'

'I'm just trying to get it straight. What happened?'

'Well, there he was in Visitors, uptight and trying not to look around – so many people treat it like the *zoo*. I'd heard a lot about him from Mother, but he didn't look so bad. He was just a man standing there in a tacky sport coat.'

'What did he say?'

'Well, I *expected* him either to jump right in my shit or to be real guilty, that's the way it goes mostly in Visitors. But he just asked me if I thought I could go to school. He said he'd go custody if I'd go to school. And try. "You have to help *yourself* a little. Try and help yourself, and I'll see you get in school," and like that.'

'How long before you got out?'

'Two weeks.'

'Niles, did you ever talk about your family while you were in Chino? To your cellmates or anybody?'

Niles Jacobi looked at Graham quickly. 'Oh. Oh, I see. No. Not about my *father*. I hadn't *thought* about him in years, why would I talk about him?'

'How about here? Did you ever take any of your friends over to your parents' house?'

'*Parent*, not parents. She was not my mother.'

'Did you ever take anybody over there? School friends or . . .'

'Or rough trade, Officer Graham?'

'That's right.'

'No.'

'Never?'

'Not once.'

'Did he ever mention any kind of threat, was he ever disturbed about anything in the last month or two before it happened?'

'He was disturbed the last time I talked to him, but it was just my grades. I had a lot of cuts. He bought me two alarm clocks. There wasn't anything else that I know of.'

'Do you have any personal papers of his, correspondence, photographs, anything?'

'No.'

'You have a picture of the family. It's on the dresser in your room. Near the bong.'

'That's not my bong. I wouldn't put that filthy thing in my mouth.'

'I need the picture. I'll have it copied and send it back to you. What else do you have?'

Jacobi shook a cigarette out of his pack and patted his pockets for matches. 'That's all. I can't imagine why they gave *that* to me. My father smiling at *Mrs* Jacobi and all the little Munchkins. You can have it. He never looked like that to me.'

● ● ●

Graham needed to know the Jacobis. Their new acquaintances in Birmingham were little help.

Byron Metcalf gave him the run of the lockboxes. He read the thin stack of letters, mostly business, and poked through the jewelry and the silver.

For three hot days he worked in the warehouse where the Jacobis' household goods were stored. Metcalf helped him at night. Every crate on every pallet was opened and their contents examined. Police photographs helped Graham see where things had been in the house.

Most of the furnishings were new, bought with the insurance from the Detroit fire. The Jacobis hardly had time to leave their marks on their possessions.

One item, a bedside table with traces of fingerprint powder still on it, held Graham's attention. In the center of the tabletop was a blob of green wax.

For the second time he wondered if the killer liked candlelight.

The Birmingham forensics unit was good about sharing.

The blurred print of the end of a nose was the best Birmingham and Jimmy Price in Washington could do with the soft-drink can from the tree.

The FBI laboratory's Firearms and Toolmarks section reported on the severed branch. The blades that clipped it were thick, with a shallow pitch; it had been done with a bolt cutter.

Document section had referred the mark cut in the bark to the Asian Studies department at Langley.

Graham sat on a packing case at the warehouse and read the long report. Asian Studies advised that the mark was a Chinese character which meant 'You hit it' or 'You hit it on the head' – an expression sometimes used in gambling. It was considered a 'positive' or 'lucky' sign. The character also appeared on a Mah-Jongg piece, the Asian scholars said. It marked the Red Dragon.

Chapter Thirteen

Crawford at FBI headquarters in Washington was on the telephone with Graham at the Birmingham airport when his secretary leaned into the office and flagged his attention.

'Dr Chilton at Chesapeake Hospital on 2706. He says it's urgent.'

Crawford nodded. 'Hang on, Will.' He punched the telephone. 'Crawford.'

'Frederick Chilton, Mr Crawford, at the –'

'Yes, Doctor.'

'I have a note here, or two pieces of a note, that appears to be from the man who killed those people in Atlanta and –'

'Where did you get it?'

'From Hannibal Lecter's cell. It's written on toilet tissue, of all things, and it has teeth marks pressed in it.'

'Can you read it to me without handling it any more?'

Straining to sound calm, Chilton read it:

My dear Dr Lecter,

I wanted to tell you I'm delighted that you have taken an interest in me. And when I learned of your vast correspondence I thought *Dare I?* Of course I do. I don't believe you'd tell them who I am, even if you knew. Besides, what particular body I currently occupy is trivia.

The important thing is what I am *Becoming*. I know that you alone can understand this. I have some things I'd love to show you. Someday, perhaps, if circumstances permit. I hope we can correspond . . .

'Mr Crawford, there's a hole torn and punched out. Then it says:

I have admired you for *years* and have a complete collection of your press notices. Actually, I think of them as unfair reviews. As unfair as mine. They like to sling demeaning nicknames, don't they? The *Tooth Fairy*. What could be more inappropriate? It would shame me for you to see that if I didn't know you had suffered the same distortions in the press.

Investigator Graham interests me. Odd-looking for a flatfoot, isn't he? Not very handsome, but purposeful-looking.

You should have taught him not to meddle.

Forgive the stationery. I chose it because it will dissolve very quickly if you should have to swallow it.

'There's a piece missing here, Mr Crawford. I'll read the bottom part:

If I hear from you, next time I might send you something wet. Until then I remain your

Avid Fan

Silence after Chilton finished reading. 'Are you there?'

'Yes. Does Lecter know you have the note?'

'Not yet. This morning he was moved to a holding cell while his quarters were cleaned. Instead of using a proper rag, the cleaning man was pulling handfuls of toilet paper off the roll to wipe down the sink. He found the note wound up in the roll and brought it to me. They bring me anything they find hidden.'

'Where's Lecter now?'

'Still in the holding cell.'

'Can he see his quarters at all from there?'

'Let me think . . . No, no, he can't.'

'Wait a second, Doctor.' Crawford put Chilton on hold. He stared at the two winking buttons on his telephone for several seconds without seeing them. Crawford, fisher of men, was watching his cork move against the current. He got Graham again.

'Will . . . a note, maybe from the Tooth Fairy, hidden in Lecter's cell at Chesapeake. Sounds like a fan letter. He wants Lecter's approval, he's curious about you. He's asking questions.'

'How was Lecter supposed to answer?'

'Don't know yet. Part's torn out, part's scratched out. Looks like there's a chance of correspondence as long as Lecter's not aware that we know. I want the note for the lab and I want to toss his cell, but it'll be risky. If Lecter gets wise, who knows how he could warn the bastard? We need the link but we need the note too.'

Crawford told Graham where Lecter was held, how the note was found. 'It's eighty miles over to Chesapeake. I can't wait for you, buddy. What do you think?'

'Ten people dead in a month – we can't play a long mail game. I say go for it.'

'I am,' Crawford said.

'See you in two hours.'

Crawford hailed his secretary. 'Sarah, order a helicopter. I want the next thing smoking and I don't care whose it is – ours, DCPD or Marines. I'll be on the roof in five minutes. Call Documents, tell them to have a document case up there. Tell Herbert to scramble a search team. On the roof. Five minutes.'

He picked up Chilton's line.

'Dr Chilton, we have to search Lecter's cell without his knowledge and we need your help. Have you mentioned this to anybody else?'

'No.'

'Where's the cleaning man who found the note?'

'He's here in my office.'

'Keep him there, please, and tell him to keep quiet. How long has Lecter been out of his cell?'

'About half an hour.'

'Is that unusually long?'

'No, not yet. But it takes only about a half-hour to clean it. Soon he'll begin to wonder what's wrong.'

'Okay, do this for me: Call your building superintendent or engineer, whoever's in charge. Tell him to shut off the water in the building and to pull the circuit breakers on Lecter's hall. Have the super walk down the hall past the holding cell carrying tools. He'll be in a hurry, pissed off, too busy to answer any questions – got it? Tell him he'll get an explanation from me. Have the garbage pickup canceled for today if they haven't already come. Don't touch the note, okay? We're coming.'

Crawford called the section chief, Scientific Analysis. 'Brian, I have a note coming in on the fly, possibly from the Tooth Fairy. Number-one priority. It has to go back where it came from within the hour and unmarked. It'll go to Hair and Fiber, Latent Prints, and Documents, then to you, so coordinate with them, will you? . . . Yes. I'll walk it through. I'll deliver it to you myself.'

It was warm – the federally mandated eighty degrees – in the elevator when Crawford came down from the roof with the note, his hair blown silly by the helicopter blast. He was mopping his face by the time he reached the Hair and Fiber section of the laboratory.

Hair and Fiber is a small section, calm and busy. The common room is stacked with boxes of evidence sent by police departments all over the country; swatches of tape that have sealed mouths and bound wrists, torn and stained clothing, deathbed sheets.

Crawford spotted Beverly Katz through the window of an examining room as he wove his way between the boxes. She had a pair of child's coveralls suspended from a hanger over a table covered with white paper. Working under bright lights in the draft-free room, she brushed the overalls with a metal spatula, carefully working with the wale and across it, with the nap and against it. A sprinkle of dirt and sand fell to the paper. With it, falling through the still air more slowly than sand but faster than lint, came a tightly coiled hair. She cocked her head and looked at it with her bright robin's eye.

Crawford could see her lips moving. He knew what she was saying.

'Gotcha.'

That's what she always said.

Crawford pecked on the glass and she came out fast, stripping off her white gloves.

'It hasn't been printed yet, right?'

'No.'

'I'm set up in the next examining room.' She put on a fresh pair of gloves while Crawford opened the document case.

The note, in two pieces, was contained gently between two sheets of plastic film. Beverly Katz saw the tooth impressions and glanced up at Crawford, not wasting time with the question.

He nodded: the impressions matched the clear overlay of the killer's bite he had carried with him to Chesapeake.

Crawford watched through the window as she lifted the note on a slender dowel and hung it over white paper. She looked it over with a power glass, then fanned it gently. She tapped the dowel with the edge of a spatula and went over the paper beneath it with the magnifying glass.

Crawford looked at his watch.

Katz flipped the note over another dowel to get the reverse side up. She removed one tiny object from its surface with tweezers almost as fine as a hair.

She photographed the torn ends of the note under high magnification and returned it to its case. She put a clean pair of white gloves in the case with it. The white gloves – the signal not to touch – would always be beside the evidence until it was checked for fingerprints.

'That's it,' she said, handing the case back to Crawford. 'One hair, maybe a thirty-second of an inch. A couple of blue grains. I'll work it up. What else have you got?'

Crawford gave her three marked envelopes. 'Hair from Lecter's comb. Whiskers from the electric razor they let him use. This is hair from the cleaning man. Gotta go.'

'See you later,' Katz said. 'Love *your* hair.'

Jimmy Price in Latent Fingerprints winced at the sight of the porous toilet paper. He squinted fiercely over the shoulder of his technician operating the helium-cadmium laser as they tried to find a fingerprint and make it fluoresce. Glowing smudges appeared on the paper, perspiration stains, nothing.

Crawford started to ask him a question, thought better of it, waited with the blue light reflecting off his glasses.

'We know three guys handled this without gloves, right?' Price said.

'Yeah, the cleanup man, Lecter, and Chilton.'

'The fellow scrubbing sinks probably had washed the oil off his fingers. But the others – this stuff is terrible.' Price held the paper to the light, forceps steady in his mottled old hand. 'I could fume it, Jack, but I couldn't guarantee the iodine stains would fade out in the time you've got.'

'Ninhydrin? Boost it with heat?' Ordinarily, Crawford would not have ventured a technical suggestion to Price, but he was floundering for anything. He expected a huffy reply, but the old man sounded rueful and sad.

'No. We couldn't wash it after. I can't get you a print off this, Jack. There isn't one.'

'Fuck,' Crawford said.

The old man turned away. Crawford put his hand on Price's bony shoulder. 'Hell, Jimmy. If there was one, you'd have found it.'

Price didn't answer. He was unpacking a pair of hands that had arrived in another matter. Dry ice smoked in his wastebasket. Crawford dropped the white gloves into the smoke.

Disappointment growling in his stomach, Crawford hurried on to Documents where Lloyd Bowman was waiting. Bowman had been called out of court and the abrupt shear in his concentration left him blinking like a man just wakened.

'I congratulate you on your hairstyle. A brave departure,' Bowman said, his hands quick and careful as he transferred the note to his work surface 'How long do I have?'

'Twenty minutes max.'

The two pieces of the note seemed to glow under Bowman's lights. His blotter showed dark green through a jagged oblong hole in the upper piece.

'The main thing, the first thing, is how Lecter was to reply,' Crawford said when Bowman had finished reading.

'Instructions for answering were probably in the part torn out.' Bowman worked steadily with his lights and filters and copy camera as he talked. 'Here in the top piece he says "I hope we can correspond . . ." and then the hole begins. Lecter scratched over that with a felt-tip pen and then folded it and pinched most of it out.'

'He doesn't have anything to cut with.'

Bowman photographed the tooth impressions and the back of the note under extremely oblique light, his shadow leaping from wall to wall as he moved the light through 360 degrees around the paper and his hands made phantom folding motions in the air.

'Now we can mash just a little.' Bowman put the note between two panes of glass to flatten the jagged edges of the hole. The tatters were smeared with vermilion ink. He was chanting under his breath.

On the third repetition Crawford made out what he was saying. 'You're so sly, but so am I.'

Bowman switched filters on his small television camera and focused it on the note. He darkened the room until there was only the dull red glow of a lamp and the blue-green of his monitor screen.

The words 'I hope we can correspond' and the jagged hole appeared enlarged on the screen. The ink smear was gone, and on the tattered edges appeared fragments of writing.

'Aniline dyes in colored inks are transparent to infrared,' Bowman said. 'These could be the tips of T's here and here. On the end is the tail of what could be an M or N, or possibly an R.' Bowman took a photograph and turned the lights on. 'Jack, there are just two common ways of carrying on a communication that's one-way blind – the phone and publication. Could Lecter take a fast phone call?'

'He can take calls, but it's slow and they have to come in through the hospital switchboard.'

'Publication is the only safe way, then.'

'We know this sweetheart reads the *Tattler*. The stuff about Graham and Lecter was in the *Tattler*. I don't know of any other paper that carried it.'

'Three T's and an R in *Tattler*. Personal column, you think? It's a place to look.'

Crawford checked with the FBI library, then telephoned instructions to the Chicago field office.

Bowman handed him the case as he finished.

'The *Tattler* comes out this evening,' Crawford said. 'It's printed in Chicago on Mondays and Thursdays. We'll get proofs of the classified pages.'

'I'll have some more stuff – minor, I think,' Bowman said.

'Anything useful, fire it straight to Chicago. Fill me in when I get back from the asylum,' Crawford said on his way out the door.

Chapter Fourteen

The turnstile at Washington's Metro Central spit Graham's fare card back to him and he came out into the hot afternoon carrying his flight bag.

The J. Edgar Hoover Building looked like a great concrete cage above the heat shimmer on Tenth Street. The FBI's move to the new headquarters had been under way when Graham left Washington. He had never worked there.

Crawford met him at the escort desk off the underground driveway to augment Graham's hastily issued credentials with his own. Graham looked tired and he was impatient with the signing-in. Crawford wondered how he felt, knowing that the killer was thinking about him.

Graham was issued a magnetically encoded tag like the one on Crawford's vest. He plugged it into the gate and passed into the long white corridors. Crawford carried his flight bag.

'I forgot to tell Sarah to send a car for you.'

'Probably quicker this way. Did you get the note back to Lecter all right?'

'Yeah,' Crawford said. 'I just got back. We poured water on the hall floor. Faked a broken pipe and electrical short. We had Simmons – he's the assistant SAC Baltimore now – we had him mopping when Lecter was brought back to his cell. Simmons thinks he bought it.'

'I kept wondering on the plane if Lecter wrote it himself.'

'That bothered me too until I looked at it. Bite mark in the paper matches the ones on the women. Also it's ball-point, which Lecter doesn't have. The person who wrote it had read the *Tattler*, and Lecter hasn't had a *Tattler*. Rankin and Willingham tossed the cell. Beautiful job, but they didn't find diddly. They took Polaroids first to get everything back just right. Then the cleaning man went in and did what he always does.'

'So what do you think?'

'As far as physical evidence toward an ID, the note is pretty much dreck,' Crawford said. 'Some way we've got to make the contact work for us, but damn if I know how yet. We'll get the rest of the lab results in a few minutes.'

'You've got the mail and phone covered at the hospital?'

'Standing trace-and-tape order for any time Lecter's on the phone. He made a call Saturday afternoon. He told Chilton he was calling his lawyer. It's a damn WATS line, and I can't be sure.'

'What did his lawyer say?'

'Nothing. We got a leased line to the hospital switchboard for Lecter's convenience in the future, so that won't get by us again. We'll fiddle with his mail both ways, starting next delivery. No problem with warrants, thank God.'

Crawford bellied up to a door and stuck the tag on his vest into the lock slot. 'My new office. Come on in. Decorator had some paint left over from a battleship he was doing. Here's the note. This print is exactly the size.'

Graham read it twice. Seeing the spidery lines spell his name started a high tone ringing in his head.

'The library confirms the *Tattler* is the only paper that carried a story about Lecter and you,' Crawford said, fixing himself an Alka-Seltzer. 'Want one of these? Good for you. It was published Monday night a week ago. It was on the stands Tuesday nationwide – some areas not till Wednesday – Alaska and Maine and places. The Tooth Fairy got one – couldn't have done it before Tuesday. He reads it, writes to Lecter. Rankin and Willingham are still sifting the hospital trash for the envelope. Bad job. They don't separate the papers from the diapers at Chesapeake.'

'All right, Lecter gets the note from the Tooth Fairy no sooner than Wednesday. He tears out the part about how to reply and scratches over and pokes out one earlier reference – I don't know why he didn't tear that out too.'

'It was in the middle of a paragraph full of compliments,' Graham said. 'He couldn't stand to ruin them. That's why he didn't throw the whole thing away.' He rubbed his temples with his knuckles.

'Bowman thinks Lecter will use the *Tattler* to answer the Tooth Fairy. He says that's probably the setup. You think he'd answer this thing?'

'Sure. He's a great correspondent. Pen pals all over.'

'If they're using the *Tattler*, Lecter would barely have time to get his answer in the issue they'll print tonight, even if he sent it special delivery to the paper the same day he got the Tooth Fairy's note. Chester from the Chicago office is down at the *Tattler* checking the ads. The printers are putting the paper together right now.'

'Please God don't stir the *Tattler* up,' Graham said.

'The shop foreman thinks Chester's a realtor trying to get a jump on the ads. He's selling him the proof sheets under the table, one by one as they come off. We're getting everything, all the classifieds, just to blow some smoke. All right, say we find out how Lecter was to answer and we can duplicate the method. Then we can fake a message to the Tooth Fairy – but what do we say? How do we use it?'

'The obvious thing is to try to get him to come to a mail drop,' Graham said. 'Bait him with something he'd like to see. "Important evidence" that Lecter knows about from talking to me. Some mistake he made that we're waiting for him to repeat.'

'He'd be an idiot to go for it.'

'I know. Want to hear what the best bait would be?'

'I'm not sure I do.'

'Lecter would be the best bait,' Graham said.

'Set up how?'

'It would be hell to do, I know that. We'd take Lecter into federal custody – Chilton would never sit still for this at Chesapeake – and we stash him in maximum security at a VA psychiatric hospital. We fake an escape.'

'Oh, Jesus.'

'We send the Tooth Fairy a message in next week's Tattler, after the big "escape." It would be Lecter asking him for a rendezvous.'

'Why in God's name would anybody want to meet Lecter? I mean, even the Tooth Fairy?'

'To kill him, Jack.' Graham got up. There was no window to look out of as he talked. He stood in front of the 'Ten Most Wanted,' Crawford's only wall decoration. 'See, the Tooth Fairy could absorb him that way, engulf him, become more than he is.'

'You sound pretty sure.'

'I'm not sure. Who's sure? What he said in the note was "I have some things I'd love to show you. Someday, perhaps, if circumstances permit." Maybe it was a serious invitation. I don't think he was just being polite.'

'Wonder what he's got to show? The victims were intact. Nothing missing but a little skin and hair, and that was probably . . . How did Bloom put it?'

'Ingested,' Graham said. 'God knows what he's got. Tremont, remember Tremont's costumes in Spokane? While he was strapped to a stretcher he was pointing with his chin, still trying to show them to the Spokane PD. I'm not sure Lecter would draw the Tooth Fairy, Jack. I say it's the best shot.'

'We'd have a goddamn *stampede* if people thought Lecter was out. Papers all over us screaming. Best shot, maybe, but we'll save it for last.'

'He probably wouldn't come near a mail drop, but he might be curious enough to *look* at a mail drop to see if Lecter had sold him. If he could do it from a distance. We could pick a drop that could be watched from only a few places a long way off and stake out the observation points.' It sounded weak to Graham even as he said it.

'Secret Service has a setup they've never used. They'd let us have it. But if we don't put an ad in today, we'll have to wait until Monday before the next issue comes out. Presses roll at five our time. That gives Chicago another hour and fifteen minutes to come up with Lecter's ad, if there *is* one.'

'What about Lecter's ad *order*, the letter he'd have sent the *Tattler* ordering the ad – could we get to that quicker?'

'Chicago put out some general feelers to the shop foreman,' Crawford said. 'The mail stays in the classified advertising manager's office. They sell the names and return addresses to mailing lists – outfits that sell products for lonely people, love charms, rooster pills, squack dealers, "meet beautiful Asian girls," personality courses, that sort of stuff.

'We might appeal to the ad manager's citizenship and all and get a look, request him to be quiet, but I don't want to chance it and risk the *Tattler* slobbering all over us. It would take a warrant to go in there and Bogart the mail. I'm thinking about it.'

'If Chicago turns up nothing, we could put an ad in anyway. If we're wrong about the *Tattler*, we wouldn't lose anything,' Graham said.

'And if we're right that the *Tattler* is the medium and we make up a reply based on what we have in this note and serew it up – if it doesn't look right to him we're down the tubes. I didn't ask you about Birmingham. Anything?'

'Birmingham's shut down and over with. The Jacobi house has been painted and redecorated and it's on the market. Their stuff is in storage waiting for probate. I went through the crates. The people I talked to didn't know the Jacobis very well. The one thing they always mentioned was how affectionate the Jacobis were to each other. Always patting. Nothing left of them now but five pallet loads of stuff in a warehouse. I wish I had –'

'Quit wishing, you're on it now.'

'What about the mark on the tree?'

' "You hit it on the head"? Means nothing to me,' Crawford said. 'The Red Dragon either. Beverly knows Mah-Jongg. She's sharp, and she can't see it. We know from his hair he's not Chinese.'

'He cut the limb with a bolt cutter. I don't see –'

Crawford's telephone rang. He spoke into it briefly.

'Lab's ready on the note, Will. Let's go up to Zeller's office. It's bigger and not so gray.'

Lloyd Bowman, dry as a document in spite of the heat, caught up with them in the corridor. He was flapping damp photographs in each hand and held a sheaf of Datafax sheets under his arm. 'Jack, I have to be in court at four-fifteen,' he said as he flapped ahead. 'It's that paper hanger Nilton Eskew and his sweetheart Nan. She could draw a Treasury note freehand. They've been driving me crazy for two years making their own traveler's checks on a color Xerox. Won't leave home without them. Will I make it in time, or should I call the prosecutor?'

'You'll make it,' Crawford said. 'Here we are.'

Beverly Katz smiled at Graham from the couch in Zeller's office, making up for the scowl of Price beside her.

Scientific Analysis Section Chief Brian Zeller was young for his job, but already his hair was thinning and he wore bifocals. On the shelf behind Zeller's desk Graham saw H. J. Walls's forensic science text, Tedeschi's great *Forensic Medicine* in three volumes, and an antique edition of Hopkins' *The Wreck of the Deutschland*.

'Will, we met once at GWU I think,' he said. 'Do you know everybody? . . . Fine.'

Crawford leaned against the corner of Zeller's desk, his arms folded. 'Anybody got a blockbuster? Okay, does anything you found indicate the note did not come from the Tooth Fairy?'

'No,' Bowman said. 'I talked to Chicago a few minutes ago to give them some numerals I picked up from an impression on the back of the note. Six-six-six. I'll show you when we get to it. Chicago has over two hundred personal ads so far.' He handed Graham a sheaf of Datafax copies. 'I've read them and they're all the usual stuff – marriage offers, appeals to runaways. I'm not sure how we'd recognize the ad if it's here.'

Crawford shook his head. 'I don't know either. Let's break down the physical. Now, Jimmy Price did everything we could do and there was no print. What about you, Bev?'

'I got one whisker. Scale count and core size match samples from Hannibal Lecter. So does color. The color's markedly different from samples taken in Birmingham and Atlanta. Three blue grains and some dark flecks went to Brian's end.' She raised her eyebrows at Brian Zeller.

'The grains were commercial granulated cleaner with chlorine,' he said. 'It must have come off the cleaning man's hands. There were several very minute particles of dried blood. It's definitely blood, but there's not enough to type.'

'The tears at the end of the pieces wandered off the perforations,' Beverly Katz continued. 'If we find the roll in somebody's possession and he hasn't torn it again, we can get a definite match. I recommend issuing an advisory now, so the arresting officers will be sure to search for the roll.'

Crawford nodded. 'Bowman?'

'Sharon from my office went after the paper and got samples to match. It's toilet tissue for marine heads and motor homes. The texture matches brand name Wedeker manufactured in Minneapolis. It has nationwide distribution.'

Bowman set up his photographs on an easel near the windows. His voice was surprisingly deep for his slight stature, and his bow tie moved slightly when he talked. 'On the handwriting itself, this is a right-handed person using his left hand and printing in a deliberate block pattern. You can see the unsteadiness in the strokes and varying letter sizes.

'The proportions make me think our man has a touch of uncorrected astigmatism.

'The inks on both pieces of the note look like the same standard ball-point royal blue in natural light, but a slight difference appears under colored filters. He used two pens, changing somewhere in the missing section of the note. You can see where the first one began to skip. The first pen is not used frequently – see the blob it starts with? It might have been stored point-down and uncapped in a pencil jar or canister, which suggests a desk situation. Also the surface the paper lay on was soft enough to be a blotter. A blotter might retain impressions if you find it. I want to add the blotter to Beverly's advisory.'

Bowman flipped to a photograph of the back of the note. The extreme enlargement made the paper look fuzzy. It was grooved with shadowed impressions. 'He folded the note to write the bottom part, including what was later torn out. In this enlargement of the back side, oblique light reveals a few impressions. We can make out "666 an." Maybe that's where he had pen trouble and had to bear down and overwrite. I didn't spot it until I had this high-contrast print. There's no 666 in any ad so far.

'The sentence structure is orderly, and there's no rambling. The folds suggest it was delivered in a standard letter-size envelope. These two dark places are printing-ink smudges. The note was probably folded inside some innocuous printed matter in the envelope.

'That's about it,' Bowman said. 'Unless you have questions, Jack, I'd better go to the courthouse. I'll check in after I testify.'

'Sink 'em deep,' Crawford said.

Graham studied the *Tattler* personals column. ('Attractive queen-size lady, young 52, seeks Christian Leo nonsmoker 40-70. No children please. Artificial limb welcomed. No phonies. Send photo first letter.')

Lost in the pain and desperation of the ads, he didn't notice that the others were leaving until Beverly Katz spoke to him.

'I'm sorry, Beverly. What did you say?' He looked at her bright eyes and kindly, well-worn face.

'I just said I'm glad to see you back, Champ. You're looking good.'

'Thanks, Beverly.'

'Saul's going to cooking school. He's still hit-or-miss, but when the dust settles come over and let him practice on you.'

'I'll do it.'

Zeller went away to prowl his laboratory. Only Crawford and Graham were left, looking at the clock.

'Forty minutes to *Tattler* press time,' Crawford said. 'I'm going after their mail. What do you say?'

'I think you have to.'

Crawford passed the word to Chicago on Zeller's telephone. 'Will, we need to be ready with a substitute ad if Chicago bingoes.'

'I'll work on it.'

'I'll set up the drop.' Crawford called the Secret Service and talked at some length. Graham was still scribbling when he finished.

'Okay, the mail drop's a beauty,' Crawford said at last. 'It's an outside message box on a fire-extinguisher service outfit in Annapolis. That's Lecter territory. The Tooth Fairy will see that it's something Lecter could know about. Alphabetical pigeonholes. The service people drive up to it and get assignments and mail. Our boy can check it out from a park across the street. Secret Service swears it looks good. They set it up to catch a counterfeiter, but it turned out they didn't need it. Here's the address. What about the message?'

'We have to use two messages in the same edition. The first one warns the Tooth Fairy that his enemies are closer than he thinks. It tells him he made a bad mistake in Atlanta and if he repeats the mistake he's doomed. It tells him Lecter has mailed "secret information" I showed Lecter about what we're doing, how close we are, the leads we have. It directs the Tooth Fairy to a second message that begins with "your signature."

'The second message begins "Avid Fan . . ." and contains the address of the mail drop. We have to do it that way. Even in roundabout language, the warning in the first message is going to excite some casual nuts. If they can't find out the address, they can't come to the drop and screw things up.'

'Good. Damn good. Want to wait it out in my office?'

'I'd rather be doing something. I need to see Brian Zeller.'

'Go ahead, I can get you in a hurry if I have to.'

Graham found the section chief in Serology.

'Brian, could you show me a couple of things?'

'Sure, what?'

'The samples you used to type the Tooth Fairy.'

Zeller looked at Graham through the close-range section of his bifocals. 'Was there something in the report you didn't understand?'

'No.'

'Was something unclear?'

'No.'

'Something *incomplete*?' Zeller mouthed the word as if it had an unpleasant taste.

'Your report was fine, couldn't ask for better. I just want to hold the evidence in my hand.'

'*Ah*, certainly. We can do that.' Zeller believed that all field men retain the superstitions of the hunt. He was glad to humor Graham. 'It's all together down at that end.'

Graham followed him between the long counters of apparatus. 'You're reading Tedeschi.'

'Yes,' Zeller said over his shoulder. 'We don't do any forensic medicine here, as you know, but Tedeschi has a lot of useful things in there. Graham. Will Graham. You wrote the standard monograph on determining time of death by insect activity, didn't you. Or do I have the right Graham?'

'I did it.' A pause. 'You're right, Mant and Nuorteva in the Tedeschi are better on insects.'

Zeller was surprised to hear his thought spoken. 'Well, it does have more pictures and a table of invasion waves. No offense.'

'Of course not. They're better. I told them so.'

Zeller gathered vials and slides from a cabinet and a refrigerator and set them on the laboratory counter. 'If you want to ask me anything, I'll be where you found me. The stage light on this microscope is on the side here.'

Graham did not want the microscope. He doubted none of Zeller's findings. He didn't know what he wanted. He raised the vials and slides to the light, and a glassine envelope with two blond hairs found in Birmingham. A second envelope held three hairs found on Mrs Leeds.

There were spit and hair and semen on the table in front of Graham and empty air where he tried to see an image, a face, something to replace the shapeless dread he carried.

A woman's voice came from a speaker in the ceiling. 'Graham, Will Graham, to Special Agent Crawford's office. On Red.'

He found Sarah in her headset typing, with Crawford looking over her shoulder.

'Chicago's got an ad order with 666 in it,' Crawford said out of the side of his mouth. 'They're dictating it to Sarah now. They said part of it looks like code.'

The lines were climbing out of Sarah's typewriter.

Dear Pilgrim,

You honor me . . .

'That's it. That's it,' Graham said. 'Lecter called him a pilgrim when he was talking to me.'

you're very beautiful . . .'

'Christ,' Crawford said.

> *I offer 100 prayers for your safety.*
> *Find help in John 6:22, 8:16, 9:1; Luke 1:7, 3:1; Galatians 6:11, 15:2; Acts 3.3; Revelation 18:7; Jonah 6:8 . . .*

The typing slowed as Sarah read back each pair of numbers to the agent in Chicago. When she had finished, the list of scriptural references covered a quarter of a page. It was signed 'Bless you, 666.'

'That's it,' Sarah said.

Crawford picked up the phone. 'Okay, Chester, how did it go down with the ad manager? . . . No, you did right . . . A complete clam, right. Stand by at that phone, I'll get back to you.'

'Code,' Graham said.

'Has to be. We've got twenty-two minutes to get a message in if we can break it. Shop foreman needs ten minutes' notice and three hundred dollars to shoehorn one in this edition. Bowman's in his office, he got a recess. If you'll get him cracking, I'll talk to Cryptography at Langley. Sarah, shoot a telex of the ad to CIA cryptography section. I'll tell 'em it's coming.'

Bowman put the message on his desk and aligned it precisely with the corners of his blotter. He polished his rimless spectacles for what seemed to Graham a very long time.

Bowman had a reputation for being quick. Even the explosives section forgave him for not being an ex-Marine and granted him that.

'We have twenty minutes,' Graham said.

'I understand. You called Langley?'

'Crawford did.'

Bowman read the message many times, looked at it upside down and sideways, ran down the margins with his finger. He took a Bible from his shelves. For five minutes the only sounds were the two men breathing and the crackle of onionskin pages.

'No,' he said. 'We won't make it in time. Better use what's left for whatever else you can do.'

Graham showed him an empty hand.

Bowman swiveled around to face Graham and took off his glasses. He had a pink spot on each side of his nose. 'Do you feel fairly confident the note to Lecter is the only communication he's had from your Tooth Fairy?'

'Right.'

'The code is something simple then. They only needed cover against casual readers. Measuring by the perforations in the note to Lecter only about three inches is missing. That's not much room for instructions. The numbers aren't right for a jailhouse alphabet grid – the tap code. I'm guessing it's a book code.'

Crawford joined them. 'Book code?'

'Looks like it. The first numeral, that "100 prayers," could be the page number. The paired numbers in the scriptural references could be line and letter. But what book?'

'Not the Bible?' Crawford said.

'No, not the Bible. I thought it might be at first. Galatians 6:11 threw me off. "Ye see how large a letter I have written unto you with mine own hand." That's appropriate, but it's coincidence because next he has Galatians 15:2. Galatians has only six chapters. Same with Jonah 6:8 – Jonah has four chapters. He wasn't using a Bible.'

'Maybe the book title could be concealed in the clear part of Lecter's message,' Crawford said.

Bowman shook his head. 'I don't think so.'

'Then the Tooth Fairy named the book to use. He specified it in his note to Lecter,' Graham said.

'It would appear so,' Bowman said. 'What about sweating Lecter? In a mental hospital I would think drugs –'

'They tried sodium amytal on him three years ago trying to find out where he buried a Princeton student,' Graham said. 'He gave them a recipe for dip. Besides, if we sweat him we lose the connection. If the Tooth Fairy picked the book, it's something he knew Lecter would have in his cell.'

'I know for sure he didn't order one or borrow one from Chilton,' Crawford said.

'What have the papers carried about that, Jack? About Lecter's books.'

'That he has medical books, psychology books, cookbooks.'

'Then it could be one of the standards in those areas, something so basic the Tooth Fairy knew Lecter would definitely have it,' Bowman said. 'We need a list of Lecter's books. Do you have one?'

'No.' Graham stared at his shoes. 'I could get Chilton . . . Wait. Rankin and Willingham, when they tossed his cell, they took Polaroids so they could get everything back in place.'

'Would you ask them to meet me with the pictures of the books?' Bowman said, packing his briefcase.

'Where?'

'The Library of Congress.'

Crawford checked with the CIA cryptography section one last time. The computer at Langley was trying consistent and progressive number-letter substitutions and a staggering variety of alphabet grids. No progress. The cryptographer agreed with Bowman that it was probably a book code.

Crawford looked at his watch. 'Will, we're left with three choices and we've got to decide right now. We can pull Lecter's message out of the paper and run nothing. We can substitute our messages in plain language, inviting the Tooth Fairy to the mail drop. Or we can let Lecter's ad run as is.'

'Are you sure we can still get Lecter's message out of the *Tattler*?'

'Chester thinks the shop foreman would chisel it for about five hundred dollars.'

'I hate to put in a plain-language message, Jack. Lecter would probably never hear from him again.'

'Yeah, but I'm leery of letting Lecter's message run without knowing what it says,' Crawford said. 'What could Lecter tell him that he doesn't know already? If he found out we have a partial thumbprint and his prints aren't on file anywhere, he could whittle his thumb and pull his teeth and give us a big gummy laugh in court.

'The thumbprint wasn't in the case summary Lecter saw. We better let Lecter's message run. At least it'll encourage the Tooth Fairy to contact him again.'

'What if it encourages him to do something besides write?'

'We'll feel sick for a long time,' Graham said. 'We have to do it.'

Fifteen minutes later in Chicago the *Tattler's* big presses rolled, gathering speed until their thunder raised the dust in the pressroom. The FBI agent waiting in the smell of ink and hot newsprint took one of the first ones.

The cover lines included 'Head Transplant!' and 'Astronomers Glimpse God!'

The agent checked to see that Lecter's personal ad was in place and slipped the paper into an express pouch for Washington. He would see that paper again and remember his thumb smudge on the front page, but it would be years later, when he took his children through the special exhibits on a tour of FBI headquarters.

Chapter Fifteen

In the hour before dawn Crawford woke from a deep sleep. He saw the room dark, felt his wife's ample bottom comfortably settled against the small of his back. He did not know why he had awakened until the telephone rang a second time. He found it with no fumbling.

'Jack, this is Lloyd Bowman. I solved the code. You need to know what it says right now.'

'Okay, Lloyd.' Crawford's feet searched for his slippers.

'It says: *Graham home Marathon, Florida. Save yourself. Kill them all.*'

'Goddammit. Gotta go.'

'I know.'

Crawford went to his den without stopping for his robe. He called Florida twice, the airport once, then called Graham at his hotel.

'Will, Bowman just broke the code.'

'What did it say?'

'I'll tell you in a second. Now listen to me. Everything is okay. I've taken care of it, so stay on the phone when I tell you.'

'Tell me now.'

'It's your home address. Lecter gave the bastard your home address. Wait, Will. Sheriff's department has two cars on the way to Sugarloaf right now. Customs launch from Marathon is taking the ocean side. The Tooth Fairy couldn't have done anything in this short time. Hold on. You can move faster with me helping you. Now, listen to this.

'The deputies aren't going to scare Molly. The sheriff's cars are just closing the road to the house. Two deputies will move up close enough to watch the house. You can call her when she wakes up. I'll pick you up in half an hour.'

'I won't be here.'

'The next plane in that direction doesn't go until eight. It'll be quicker to bring them up here. My brother's house on the Chesapeake is available to them. I've got a good plan, Will, wait and hear it. If you don't like it I'll put you on the plane myself.'

'I need some things from the armory.'

'We'll get it soon as I pick you up.'

Molly and Willy were among the first off the plane at National Airport in Washington. She spotted Graham in the crowd, did not smile, but turned to Willy and said something as they walked swiftly ahead of the stream of tourists returning from Florida.

She looked Graham up and down and came to him with a light kiss. Her brown fingers were cold on his cheek.

Graham felt the boy watching. Willy shook hands from a full arm's length away.

Graham made a joke about the weight of Molly's suitcase as they walked to the car.

'I'll carry it,' Willy said.

A brown Chevrolet with Maryland plates moved in behind them as they pulled out of the parking lot.

Graham crossed the bridge at Arlington and pointed out the Lincoln and Jefferson memorials and the Washington Monument before heading east toward the Chesapeake Bay. Ten miles outside Washington the brown Chevrolet pulled up beside in the inside lane. The driver looked across with his hand to his mouth and a voice from nowhere crackled in the car.

'Fox Edward, you're clean as a whistle. Have a nice trip.'

Graham reached under the dash for the concealed microphone. 'Roger, Bobby. Much obliged.'

The Chevrolet dropped behind them and its turn signal came on.

'Just making sure no press cars or anything were following,' Graham said.

'I see,' Molly said.

They stopped in the late afternoon and ate crabs at a roadside restaurant. Willy went to look at the lobster tank.

'I hate it, Molly. I'm sorry,' Graham said.

'Is he after you now?'

'We've had no reason to think so. Lecter just suggested it to him, urged him to do it.'

'It's a clammy, sick feeling.'

'I know it is. You and Willy are safe at Crawford's brother's house.

Nobody in the world knows you're there but me and Crawford.'

'I'd just as soon not talk about Crawford.'

'It's a nice place, you'll see.'

She took a deep breath and when she let it out the anger seemed to go with it, leaving her tired and calm. She gave him a crooked smile. 'Hell, I just got mad there for a while. Do we have to put up with any Crawfords?'

'Nope.' He moved the cracker basket to take her hand. 'How much does Willy know?'

'Plenty. His buddy Tommy's mother had a trash newspaper from the supermarket at their house. Tommy showed it to Willy. It had a lot of stuff about you, apparently pretty distorted. About Hobbs, the place you were after that, Lecter, everything. It upset him. I asked him if he wanted to talk about it. He just asked me if I knew it all along. I said yes, that you and I talked about it once, that you told me everything before we got married. I asked him if he wanted me to tell him about it, the way it really was. He said he'd ask you to your face.'

'Damn good. Good for him. What was it, the *Tattler*?'

'I don't know, I think so.'

'Thanks a lot, Freddy.' A swell of anger at Freddy Lounds lifted him from his seat. He washed his face with cold water in the rest room.

Sarah was saying good night to Crawford in the office when the telephone rang. She put down her purse and umbrella to answer it.

'Special Agent Crawford's office . . . No, Mr Graham is not in the office, but let me . . . Wait, I'll be glad to . . . Yes, he'll be in tomorrow afternoon, but let me . . .'

The tone of her voice brought Crawford around his desk.

She held the receiver as though it had died in her hand. 'He asked for Will and said he might call back tomorrow afternoon. I tried to hold him.'

'Who?'

'He said, ''Just tell Graham it's the Pilgrim.'' ' That's what Dr Lecter called –'

'The Tooth Fairy,' Crawford said.

Graham went to the grocery store while Molly and Willy unpacked. He found canary melons at the market and a ripe cranshaw. He parked across the street from the house and sat for a few minutes, still gripping the wheel. He was ashamed that because of him Molly was rooted out of the house she loved and put among strangers.

Crawford had done his best. This was no faceless federal safe house with chair arms bleached by palm sweat. It was a pleasant cottage, freshly whitewashed, with impatiens blooming around the steps. It was the product of careful hands and a sense of order. The rear yard sloped down to the Chesapeake Bay and there was a swimming raft.

Blue-green television light pulsed behind the curtains. Molly and Willy were watching baseball, Graham knew.

Willy's father had been a baseball player, and a good one. He and Molly met on the school bus, married in college.

They trooped around the Florida State League where he was in the Cardinals' farm system. They took Willy with them and had a terrific time. Spam and spirit. He got a tryout with the Cardinals and hit safely in his first two games. Then he began to have difficulty swallowing. The surgeon tried to get it all, but it metastasized and ate him up. He died five months later, when Willy was six.

Willy still watched baseball whenever he could. Molly watched baseball when she was upset.

Graham had no key. He knocked.

'I'll get it.' Willy's voice.

'Wait.' Molly's face between the curtains. 'All right.'

Willy opened the door. In his fist, held close to his leg, was a fish billy.

Graham's eyes stung at the sight. The boy must have brought it in his suitcase.

Molly took the bag from him. 'Want some coffee? There's gin, but not the kind you like.'

When she was in the kitchen, Willy asked Graham to come outside.

From the back porch they could see the riding lights of boats anchored in the bay.

'Will, is there any stuff I need to know to see about Mom?'

'You're both safe here, Willy. Remember the car that followed us from the airport making sure nobody saw where we went? Nobody can find out where you and your mother are.'

'This crazy guy wants to kill you, does he?'

'We don't know that. I just didn't feel easy with him knowing where the house is.'

'You gonna kill him?'

Graham closed his eyes for a moment. 'No. It's just my job to find him. They'll put him in a mental hospital so they can treat him and keep him from hurting anybody.'

'Tommy's mother had this little newspaper, Will. It said you killed a guy in Minnesota and you were in a mental hospital. I never knew that. Is it true?'

'Yes.'

'I started to ask Mom, but I figured I'd ask you.'

'I appreciate your asking me straight out. It wasn't just a mental hospital; they treat everything.' The distinction seemed important. 'I was in the psychiatric wing. It bothers you, finding out I was in there. Because I'm married to your mom.'

'I told my dad I'd take care of her. I'll do it, too.'

Graham felt he had to tell Willy enough. He didn't want to tell him too much.

The lights went out in the kitchen. He could see Molly's dim outline inside the screen door and he felt the weight of her judgment. Dealing with Willy he was handling her heart.

Willy clearly did not know what to ask next. Graham did it for him.

'The hospital part was after the business with Hobbs.'

'You shot him?'

'Yes.'

'How'd it happen?'

'To begin with, Garrett Hobbs was insane. He was attacking college girls and he . . . killed them.'

'How?'

'With a knife; anyway I found a little curly piece of metal in the clothes one of the girls had on. It was the kind of shred a pipe threader makes – remember when we fixed the shower outside?

'I was taking a look at a lot of steamfitters, plumbers and people. It took a long time. Hobbs had left this resignation letter at a construction job I was checking. I saw it and it was . . . peculiar. He wasn't working anywhere, and I had to find him at home.

'I was going up the stairs in Hobbs's apartment house. A uniformed officer was with me. Hobbs must have seen us coming. I was halfway up to his landing when he shoved his wife out the door and she came falling down the stairs dead.'

'He had killed her?'

'Yeah. So I asked the officer I was with to call for SWAT, to get some help. But then I could hear kids in there and some screaming. I wanted to wait, but I couldn't.'

'You went in the apartment?'

'I did. Hobbs had caught this girl from behind and he had a knife. He was cutting her with it. And I shot him.'

'Did the girl die?'

'No.'

'She got all right?'

'After a while, yes. She's all right now.'

Willy digested this silently. Faint music came from an anchored sailboat.

Graham could leave things out for Willy, but he couldn't help seeing them again himself.

He left out Mrs Hobbs on the landing clutching at him, stabbed so many times. Seeing she was gone, hearing the screaming from the apartment, prying the slick red fingers off and cracking his shoulder before the door gave in. Hobbs holding his own daughter busy cutting her neck when he could get to it, her struggling with her chin tucked down, the .38 knocking chunks out of him and he still cutting and he wouldn't go down. Hobbs sitting on the floor crying and the girl rasping. Holding her down and seeing Hobbs had gotten through the windpipe, but not the arteries. The daughter looked at him with wide glazed eyes and at her father sitting on the floor crying 'See? See?' until he fell over dead.

That was where Graham lost his faith in .38's.

'Willy, the business with Hobbs, it bothered me a lot. You know, I kept it on my mind and I saw it over and over. I got so I couldn't think about much else. I kept thinking there must be some way I could have handled it better. And then I quit feeling anything. I couldn't eat and I stopped talking to anybody. I got really depressed. So a doctor asked me to go into the hospital, and I did. After a while I got some distance on it. The girl that got hurt in Hobbs's apartment came to see me. She was okay and we talked a lot. Finally I put it aside and went back to work.'

'Killing somebody, even if you have to do it, it feels that bad?'

'Willy, it's one of the ugliest things in the world.'

'Say, I'm going in the kitchen for a minute. You want something, a Coke?' Willy liked to bring Graham things, but he always made it a casual adjunct to something he was going to do anyway. No special trip or anything.

'Sure, a Coke.'

'Mom ought to come out and look at the lights.'

● ● ●

Late in the night Graham and Molly sat in the back-porch swing. Light rain fell and the boat lights cast grainy halos on the mist. The breeze off the bay raised goose bumps on their arms.

'This could take a while, couldn't it?' Molly said.

'I hope it won't, but it might.'

'Will, Evelyn said she could keep the shop for this week and four days next week. But I've got to go back to Marathon, at least for a day or two when my buyers come. I could stay with Evelyn and Sam. I should go to market in Atlanta myself. I need to be ready for September.'

'Does Evelyn know where you are?'

'I just told her Washington.'

'Good.'

'It's hard to have anything, isn't it? Rare to get it, hard to keep it. This is a damn slippery planet.'

'Slick as hell.'

'We'll be back in Sugarloaf, won't we?'

'Yes we will.'

'Don't get in a hurry and hang it out too far. You won't do that?'

'No.'

'Are you going back early?'

He had talked to Crawford half an hour on the phone.

'A little before lunch. If you're going to Marathon at all, there's something we need to tend to in the morning. Willy can fish.'

'He had to ask you about the other.'

'I know, I don't blame him.'

'Damn that reporter, what's his name?'

'Lounds. Freddy Lounds.'

'I think maybe you hate him. And I wish I hadn't brought it up. Let's go to bed and I'll rub your back.'

Resentment raised a minute blister in Graham. He had justified himself to an eleven-year-old. The kid said it was okay that he had been in the rubber Ramada. Now she was going to rub his back. Let's go to bed – it's okay with Willy.

When you feel strain, keep your mouth shut if you can.

'If you want to think awhile, I'll let you alone,' she said.

He didn't want to think. He definitely did not. 'You rub my back and I'll rub your front,' he said.

'Go to it, Buster.'

Winds aloft carried the thin rain out over the bay and by nine A.M. the ground steamed. The far targets on the sheriff's department range seemed to flinch in the wavy air.

The rangemaster watched through his binoculars until he was sure the man and woman at the far end of the firing line were observing the safety rules.

The Justice Department credentials the man showed when he asked to use the range said 'Investigator.' That could be anything. The rangemaster did not approve of anyone other than a qualified instructor teaching pistolcraft.

Still, he had to admit the fed knew what he was doing.

They were only using a .22-caliber revolver but he was teaching the woman combat shooting from the Weaver stance, left foot slightly forward, a good two-handed grip on the revolver with isometric tension in the arms. She was firing at the silhouette target seven yards in front of her. Again and again she brought the weapon up from the outside pocket of her shoulderbag. It went on until the rangemaster was bored with it.

A change in the sound brought the rangemaster's glasses up again. They had the earmuffs on now and she was working with a short, chunky revolver. The rangemaster recognized the pop of the light target loads.

He could see the pistol extended in her hands and it interested him. He strolled along the firing line and stood a few yards behind them.

He wanted to examine the pistol, but this was not a good time to interrupt. He got a good look at it as she shucked out the empties and popped in five from a speedloader.

Odd arm for a fed. It was a Bulldog .44 Special, short and ugly with its startling big bore. It had been extensively modified by Mag Na Port. The barrel was vented near the muzzle to help keep the muzzle down on recoil, the hammer was bobbed and it had a good set of fat grips. He suspected it was throated for the speedloader. One hell of a mean pistol when it was loaded with what the fed had waiting. He wondered how the woman would stand up to it.

The ammunition on the stand beside them was an interesting progression. First there was a box of lightly loaded wadcutters. Then came regular service hardball, and last was something the rangemaster had read much about but had rarely seen. A row of Glaser Safety Slugs. The tips looked like pencil erasers. Behind each tip was a copper jacket containing number-twelve shot suspended in liquid Teflon.

The light projectile was designed to fly at tremendous velocity, smash into the target and release the shot. In meat the results were devastating. The rangemaster even recalled the figures. Ninety Glasers had been fired at men so far. All ninety were instant one-shot stops. In eighty-nine of the cases immediate death resulted. One man survived, surprising the doctors. The Glaser round had a safety advantage, too – no ricochets,and it would not go through a wall and kill someone in the next room.

The man was very gentle with her and encouraging, but he seemed sad about something.

The woman had worked up to the full service loads now and the rangemaster was pleased to see she handled the recoil very well, both eyes open and no flinch. True, it took her maybe four seconds to get the first one off, coming up from the bag, but three were in the X ring. Not bad for a beginner. She had some talent.

He had been back in the tower for some time when he heard the hellish racket of the Glasers going off.

She was pumping all five. It was not standard federal practice.

The rangemaster wondered what in God's name they saw in the silhouette that it would take five Glasers to kill.

Graham came to the tower to turn in the earmuffs, leaving his pupil sitting on a bench, head down, her elbows on her knees.

The rangemaster thought he should be pleased with her, and told him so. She had come a long way in one day. Graham thanked him absently. His expression puzzled the rangemaster. He looked like a man who had witnessed an irrevocable loss.

Chapter Sixteen

The caller, 'Mr Pilgrim,' had said to Sarah that he might call again on the following afternoon. At FBI headquarters certain arrangements were made to receive the call.

Who was Mr Pilgrim? Not Lecter – Crawford had made sure of that. Was Mr Pilgrim the Tooth Fairy? Maybe so, Crawford thought.

The desks and telephones from Crawford's office had been moved overnight to a larger room across the hall.

Graham stood in the open doorway of a soundproof booth. Behind him in the booth was Crawford's telephone. Sarah had cleaned it with Windex. With the voiceprint spectrograph, tape recorders, and stress evaluator taking up most of her desk and another table beside it, and Beverly Katz sitting in her chair, Sarah needed something to do.

The big clock on the wall showed ten minutes before noon.

Dr Alan Bloom and Crawford stood with Graham. They had adopted a sidelines stance, hands in their pockets.

A technician seated across from Beverly Katz drummed his fingers on the desk until a frown from Crawford stopped him.

Crawford's desk was cluttered with two new telephones, an open line to the Bell System's electronic switching center (ESS) and a hot line to the FBI communications room.

'How much time do you need for a trace?' Dr Bloom asked.

'With the new switching it's a lot quicker than most people think,' Crawford said. 'Maybe a minute if it comes through all-electronic switching. More if it's from someplace where they have to swarm the flame.'

Crawford raised his voice to the room. 'If he calls at all, it'll be short, so let's play him perfect. Want to go over the drill, Will?'

'Sure. When we get to the point where I talk, I want to ask you a couple of things, Doctor.'

Bloom had arrived after the others. He was scheduled to speak to the behavioral-science section at Quantico later in the day. Bloom could smell cordite on Graham's clothes.

'Okay,' Graham said. 'The phone rings. The circuit's completed immediately and the trace starts at ESS, but the tone generator continues the ringing noise so he doesn't know we've picked up. That gives us about twenty seconds on him.' He pointed to the technician. 'Tone generator to "off" at the end of the fourth ring, got it?'

The technician nodded. 'End of the fourth ring.'

'Now, Beverly picks up the phone. Her voice is different from the one he heard yesterday. No recognition in the voice. Beverly sounds bored. He asks for me. Bev says, "I'll have to page him, may I put you on hold?"'

Ready with that, Bev?' Graham thought it would be better not to rehearse the lines. They might sound flat by rote.

'All right, the line is open to us, dead to him. I think he'll hold longer than he'll talk.'

'Sure you don't want to give him the hold music?' the technician asked.

'Hell no,' Crawford said.

'We give him about twenty seconds of hold, then Beverly comes back on and tells him, "Mr Graham's coming to the phone. I'll connect you now." I pick up.' Graham turned to Dr Bloom. 'How would you play him, Doctor?'

'He'll expect you to be skeptical about it really being him. I'd give him some polite skepticism. I'd make a strong distinction between the nuisance of fake callers, and the significance, the importance, of a call from the real person. The fakes are easy to recognize because they lack the *capacity* to understand what has happened, that sort of thing.'

'Make him tell something to prove who he is.' Dr Bloom looked at the floor and kneaded the back of his neck.

'You don't know what he wants. Maybe he wants understanding, maybe he's fixed on you as the adversary and wants to gloat – we'll see. Try to pick up his mood and give him what he's after, a little at a time. I'd be very leery of appealing to him to come to us for help, unless you sense he's asking for that.

'If he's paranoid you'll pick it up fast. In that case I'd play into his suspicion or grievance. Let him air it. If he gets rolling on that, he may forget how long he's talked. That's all I know to tell you.' Bloom put his hand on Graham's shoulder and spoke quietly. 'Listen, this is not a pep talk or any bullshit; you can take him over the jumps. Never mind advice, do what seems right to you.'

Waiting. Half an hour of silence was enough.

'Call or no call, we've got to decide where to go from here,' Crawford said. 'Want to try the mail drop?'

'I can't see anything better,' Graham said.

'That would give us two baits, a stakeout at your house in the Keys and the drop.'

The telephone was ringing.

Tone generator on. At ESS the trace began. Four rings. The technician hit the switch and Beverly picked up. Sarah was listening.

'Special Agent Crawford's office.'

Sarah shook her head. She knew the caller, one of Crawford's cronies at

Alcohol, Tobacco, and Firearms. Beverly got him off in a hurry and stopped the trace. Everyone in the FBI building knew to keep the line clear.

Crawford went over the details of the mail drop again. They were bored and tense at the same time. Lloyd Bowman came around to show them how the number pairs in Lecter's Scriptures fit page 100 of the softcover *Joy of Cooking*. Sarah passed around coffee in paper cups.

The telephone was ringing.

The tone generator took over and at ESS the trace began. Four rings. The technician hit the switch. Beverly picked up.

'Special Agent Crawford's office.'

Sarah was nodding her head. Big nods.

Graham went into his booth and closed the door. He could see Beverly's lips moving. She punched 'Hold' and watched the second hand on the wall clock.

Graham could see his face in the polished receiver. Two bloated faces in the earpiece and mouthpiece. He could smell cordite from the firing range in his shirt. *Don't hang up. Sweet Jesus, don't hang up.* Forty seconds had elapsed.

The telephone moved slightly on his table when it rang. *Let it ring. Once more.* Forty-five seconds. *Now.*

'This is Will Graham, can I help you?'

Low laughter. A muffled voice: 'I expect you can.'

'Could I ask who's calling please?'

'Didn't your secretary tell you?'

'No, but she did call me out of a meeting, sir, and –'

'If you tell me you won't talk to Mr Pilgrim, I'll hang up right now. Yes or no?'

'Mr Pilgrim, if you have some problem I'm equipped to deal with, I'll be glad to talk with you.'

'I think you have the problem, Mr Graham.'

'I'm sorry, I didn't understand you.'

The second hand crawled toward one minute.

'You've been a busy boy, haven't you?' the caller said.

'Too busy to stay on the phone unless you state your business.'

'My business is in the same place yours is. Atlanta and Birmingham.'

'Do you know something about that?'

Soft laughter. 'Know something about it? Are you interested in Mr Pilgrim? Yes or No. I'll hang up if you lie.'

Graham could see Crawford through the glass. He had a telephone receiver in each hand.

'Yes. But, see, I get a lot of calls, and most of them are from people who say they know things.' *One minute.*

Crawford put one receiver down and scrawled on a piece of paper.

'You'd be surprised how many pretenders there are,' Graham said. 'Talk to them a few minutes and you can tell they don't have the capacity to even understand what's going on. Do you?'

Sarah held a sheet of paper to the glass for Graham to see. It said, 'Chicago phone booth. PD scrambling.'

'I'll tell you what, you tell me one thing you know about Mr Pilgrim and maybe I'll tell you whether you're right or not,' the muffled voice said.

'Let's get straight who we're talking about,' Graham said.

'We're talking about Mr Pilgrim.'

'How do I know Mr Pilgrim has done anything I'm interested in. Has he?'

'Let's say, yes.'

'Are you Mr Pilgrim?'

'I don't think I'll tell you that.'

'Are you his friend?'

'Sort of.'

'Well, prove it then. Tell me something that shows me how well you know him.'

'You first. You show me yours.' A nervous giggle. 'First time you're wrong, I hang up.'

'All right, Mr Pilgrim is right-handed.'

'That's a safe guess. Most people are.'

'Mr Pilgrim is misunderstood.'

'No general crap, please.'

'Mr Pilgrim is really strong physically.'

'Yes, you could say that.'

Graham looked at the clock. A minute and a half. Crawford nodded encouragement.

Don't tell him anything that he could change.

'Mr Pilgrim is white and about, say, five-feet-eleven. You haven't told me anything, you know. I'm not so sure you even know him at all.'

'Want to stop talking?'

'No, but you said we'd trade. I was just going along with you.'

'Do you think Mr Pilgrim is crazy?'

Bloom was shaking his head.

'I don't think anybody who is as careful as he is could be crazy. I think he's different. I think a lot of people do believe he's crazy, and the reason for that is, he hasn't let people understand much about him.'

'Describe exactly what you think he did to Mrs Leeds and maybe I'll tell you if you're right or not.'

'I don't want to do that.'

'Goodbye.'

Graham's heart jumped, but he could still hear breathing on the other end.

'I can't go into that until I know –'

Graham heard the telephone-booth door slam open in Chicago and the receiver fall with a clang. Faint voices and bangs as the receiver swung on its cord. Everyone in the office heard it on the speaker phone.

'Freeze. Don't even twitch. Now lock your fingers behind your head and back out of the booth slowly. Slowly. Hands on the glass and spread 'em.'

Sweet relief was flooding Graham.

'I'm not armed, Stan. You'll find my ID in my breast pocket. That tickles.'

A confused voice loud on the telephone. 'Who am I speaking to?'

'Will Graham, FBI.'

'This is Sergeant Stanley Riddle, Chicago police department.' Irritated now. 'Would you tell me what the hell's going on?'

'You tell me. You have a man in custody?'

'Damn right. Freddy Lounds, the reporter. I've known him for ten years . . . Here's your notebook, Freddy . . . Are you preferring charges against him?

Graham's face was pale. Crawford's was red. Dr Bloom watched the tape reels go around.

'Can you hear me?'

'Yes, I'm preferring charges.' Graham's voice was strangled. 'Obstruction of justice. Please take him in and hold him for the US attorney.'

Suddenly Lounds was on the telephone. He spoke fast and clearly with the cotton wads out of his cheeks.

'Will, listen –'

'Tell it to the US attorney. Put Sergeant Riddle on the phone.'

'I know something –'

'Put Riddle on the goddamned telephone.'

Crawford's voice came on the line. 'Let me have it, Will.'

Graham slammed his receiver down with a bang that made everyone in range of the speakerphone flinch. He came out of the booth and left the room without looking at anyone.

'Lounds, you have hubbed hell, my man,' Crawford said.

'You want to catch him or not? I can help you. Let me talk one minute.' Lounds hurried into Crawford's silence. 'Listen, you just showed me how bad you need the *Tattler*. Before, I wasn't sure – now I am. That ad's part of the Tooth Fairy case or you wouldn't have gone balls-out to nail this call. Great. The *Tattler's* here for you. Anything you want.'

'How did you find out?'

'The ad manager came to me. Said your Chicago office sent this suit-of-clothes over to check the ads. Your guy took five letters from the incoming ads. Said it was "pursuant to mail fraud." Mail fraud nothing. The ad manager made Xerox copies of the letters and envelopes before he let your guy have them.

'I looked them over. I knew he took five letters to smokescreen the one he really wanted. Took a day or two to check them all out. The answer was on the envelope. Chesapeake postmark. The postage meter number was for Chesapeake State Hospital. I was over there you know, behind your friend with the wild hair up his ass. What else could it be?

'I had to be sure, though. That's why I called, to see if you'd come down on "Mr Pilgrim" with both feet, and you did.'

'You made a large mistake, Freddy.'

'You need the *Tattler* and I can open it up for you. Ads, editorial, monitoring incoming mail, anything. You name it. I can be discreet. I can. Cut me in, Crawford.'

'There's nothing to cut you in on.'

'Okay, then it won't make any difference if somebody happened to put in six personal ads next issue. All to "Mr Pilgrim" and signed the same way.'

'I'll get an injunction slapped on you and a sealed indictment for obstruction of justice.'

'And it might leak to every paper in the country.' Lounds knew he was talking on tape. He didn't care anymore. 'I swear to God, I'll do it, Crawford. I'll tear up your chance before I lose mine.'

'Add interstate transmission of a threatening message to what I just said.'

'Let me *help* you, Jack. I can, believe me.'

'Run along to the police station, Freddy. Now put the sergeant back on the phone.'

Freddy Lounds's Lincoln Versailles smelled of hair tonic and aftershave, socks and cigars, and the police sergeant was glad to get out of it when they reached the station house.

Lounds knew the captain commanding the precinct and many of the patrolmen. The captain gave Lounds coffee and called the US attorney's office to 'try and clear this shit up.'

No federal marshal came for Lounds. In half an hour he took a call from Crawford in the precinct commander's office. Then he was free to go. The captain walked him to his car.

Lounds was keyed up and his driving was fast and jerky as he crossed the Loop eastward to his apartment overlooking Lake Michigan. There were several things he wanted out of this story and he knew that he could get them. Money was one, and most of that would come from the paperback. He would have an instant paperback on the stands thirty-six hours after the capture. An exclusive story in the daily press would be a news coup. He would have the satisfaction of seeing the straight press – the Chicago *Tribune*, the Los Angeles *Times*, the sanctified Washington *Post* and the holy New York *Times* – run his copyrighted material under his byline with his picture credits.

And then the correspondents of those august journals, who looked down on him, who would not drink with him, could eat their fucking hearts out.

Lounds was a pariah to them because he had taken a different faith. Had he been incompetent, a fool with no other resource, the veterans of the straight press could have forgiven him for working on the *Tattler*, as one forgives a retarded geek. But Lounds was good. He had the qualities of a good reporter – intelligence, guts, and the good eye. He had great energy and patience.

Against him were the fact that he was obnoxious and therefore disliked by news executives, and his inability to keep himself out of his stories.

In Lounds was the lunging need to be noticed that is often miscalled ego. Lounds was lumpy and ugly and small. He had buck teeth and his rat eyes had the sheen of spit on asphalt.

He had worked in straight journalism for ten years when he realized that no one would ever send him to the White House. He saw that his publishers would wear his legs out, use him until it was time for him to become a broken-down old drunk manning a dead-end desk, drifting inevitably toward cirrhosis or a mattress fire.

They wanted the information he could get, but they didn't want Freddy. They paid him top scale, which is not very much money if you have to buy women. They patted his back and told him he had a lot of balls and they refused to put his name on a parking place.

One evening in 1969 while in the office working rewrite, Freddy had an epiphany.

Frank Larkin was seated near him taking dictation on the telephone. Dictation was the glue factory for old reporters on the paper where Freddy worked. Frank Larkin was fifty-five, but he looked seventy. He was oyster-eyed and he went to his locker every half-hour for a drink. Freddy could smell him from where he sat.

Larkin got up and shuffled over to the slot and spoke in a hoarse whisper to the news editor, a woman. Freddy always listened to other people's conversations.

Larkin asked the woman to get him a Kotex from the machine in the ladies' room. He had to use them on his bleeding behind.

Freddy stopped typing. He took the story out of his typewriter, replaced the paper and wrote a letter of resignation.

A week later he was working for the *Tattler*.

He started as cancer editor at a salary nearly double what he had earned before. Management was impressed with his attitude.

The *Tattler* could afford to pay him well because the paper found cancer very lucrative.

One in five Americans dies of it. The relatives of the dying, worn out, prayed out, trying to fight a raging carcinoma with pats and banana pudding and copper-tasting jokes, are desperate for anything hopeful.

Marketing surveys showed that a bold 'New Cure for Cancer' or 'Cancer Miracle Drug' cover line boosted supermarket sales of any *Tattler* issue by 22.3 percent. There was a six-percentile drop in those sales when the story ran on page one beneath the cover line, as the reader had time to scan the empty text while the groceries were being totaled.

Marketing experts discovered it was better to have the big cover line in color on the front and play the story in the middle pages, where it was difficult to hold the paper open and manage a purse and grocery cart at the same time.

The standard story featured an optimistic five paragraphs in ten point type, then a drop to eight point, then to six point before mentioning that the 'miracle drug' was unavailable or that animal research was just beginning.

Freddy earned his money turning them out, and the stories sold a lot of *Tattlers*.

In addition to increased readership there were many spinoff sales of miracle medallions and healing cloths. Manufacturers of these paid a premium to get their ads located close to the weekly cancer story.

Many readers wrote to the paper for more information. Some additional revenue was realized by selling their names to a radio 'evangelist,' a screaming sociopath who wrote to them for money, using envelopes stamped 'Someone You Love Will Die Unless . . .'

Freddy Lounds was good for the *Tattler*, and the *Tattler* was good to him. Now, after eleven years with the paper, he earned $72,000 a year. He covered pretty much what he pleased and spent the money trying to have a good time. He lived as well as he knew how to live.

The way things were developing, he believed he could raise the ante on his paperback deal, and there was movie interest. He had heard that Hollywood was a fine place for obnoxious fellows with money.

Freddy felt good. He shot down the ramp to the underground garage in his building and wheeled into his parking place with a spirited squeal of rubber. There on the wall was his name in letters a foot high, marking his private spot. Mr Frederick Lounds.

Wendy was here already – her Datsun was parked next to his space. Good. He wished he could take her to Washington with him. That would make those flatfeets' eyes pop. He whistled in the elevator on his way upstairs.

Wendy was packing for him. She had lived out of suitcases and she did a good job.

Neat in her jeans and plaid shirt, her brown hair gathered in a chipmunk tail on her neck, she might have been a farm girl except for her pallor and her shape. Wendy's figure was almost a caricature of puberty.

She looked at Lounds with eyes that had not registered surprise in years. She saw that he was trembling.

'You're working too hard, Roscoe.' She liked to call him Roscoe, and it pleased him for some reason. 'What are you taking, the six-o'clock shuttle?' She brought him a drink and moved her sequined jump suit and wig case off the bed so he could lie down. 'I can take you to the airport. I'm not going to the club 'til six.'

'Wendy City' was her own topless bar, and she didn't have to dance anymore. Lounds had cosigned the note.

'You sounded like Morocco Mole when you called me,' she said.

'Who?'

'You know, on television Saturday morning, he's real mysterious and he helps Secret Squirrel. We watched it when you had the flu . . . You really pulled one off today, didn't you? You're really pleased with yourself.'

'Damn straight. I took a chance today, baby, and it paid off. I've got a chance at something sweet.'

'You've got time for a nap before you go. You're running yourself in the ground.'

Lounds lit a cigarette. He already had one burning in the ashtray.

'You know what?' she said. 'I bet if you drink your drink and get it off, you could go to sleep.'

Lounds's face, like a fist pressed against her neck, relaxed at last, became mobile as suddenly as a fist becomes a hand. His trembling stopped. He told her all about it, whispering into the buck jut of her augmented breasts; she tracing eights on the back of his neck with a finger.

'That is some kind of smart, Roscoe,' she said. 'You go to sleep now. I'll get you up for the plane. It'll be all right, all of it. And then we'll have a high old time.'

They whispered about the places they would go. He went to sleep.

Chapter Seventeen

Dr Alan Bloom and Jack Crawford sat on folding chairs, the only furniture left in Crawford's office.

'The cupboard is bare, Doctor.'

Dr Bloom studied Crawford's simian face and wondered what was coming. Behind Crawford's grousing and his Alka-Seltzers the doctor saw an intelligence as cold as an X-ray table.

'Where did Will go?'

'He'll walk around and cool off,' Crawford said. 'He hates Lounds.'

'Did you think you might lose Will after Lecter published his home address? That he might go back to his family?'

'For a minute, I did. It shook him.'

'Understandably,' Dr Bloom said.

'Then I realized – he can't go home, and neither can Molly and Willy, never, until the Tooth Fairy is out of the way.'

'You've met Molly?'

'Yeah. She's great, I like her. She'd be glad to see me in hell with my back broken, of course. I'm having to duck her right now.'

'She thinks you use Will?'

Crawford looked at Dr Bloom sharply. 'I've got some things I have to talk to him about. We'll need to check with you. When do you have to be at Quantico?'

'Not until Tuesday morning. I put it off.' Dr Bloom was a guest lecturer at the behavioral-science section of the FBI Academy.

'Graham likes you. He doesn't think you run any mind games on him,' Crawford said. Bloom's remark about using Graham stuck in his craw.

'I don't. I wouldn't try,' Dr Bloom said. 'I'm as honest with him as I'd be with a patient.'

'Exactly.'

'No, I want to be his friend, and I am. Jack, I owe it to my field of study to observe. Remember, though, when you asked me to give you a study on him, I refused.'

'That was Petersen, upstairs, wanted the study.'

'You were the one who asked for it. No matter, if I ever did anything on Graham, if there were ever anything that might be of therapeutic benefit to others, I'd abstract it in a form that would be totally unrecognizable. If I ever do anything in a scholarly way, it'll only be published posthumously.'

'After you or after Graham?'

Dr Bloom didn't answer.

'One thing I've noticed – I'm curious about this: you're never alone in a room with Graham, are you? You're smooth about it, but you're never one-on-one with him. Why's that? Do you think he's psychic, is that it?'

'No. He's an *eideteker* – he has a remarkable visual memory – but I don't think he's psychic. He wouldn't let Duke test him – that doesn't mean anything, though. He hates to be prodded and poked. So do I.'

'But –'

'Will wants to think of this as purely an intellectual exercise, and in the narrow definition of forensics, that's what it is. He's good at that, but there are other people just as good, I imagine.'

'Not many,' Crawford said.

'What he has in addition is pure empathy and projection,' Dr Bloom said. 'He can assume your point of view, or mine – and maybe some other points of view that scare and sicken him. It's an uncomfortable gift, Jack. Perception's a tool that's pointed on both ends.'

'Why aren't you ever alone with him?'

'Because I have some professional curiosity about him and he'd pick that up in a hurry. He's fast.'

'If he caught you peeking, he'd snatch down the shades.'

'An unpleasant analogy, but accurate, yes. You've had sufficient revenge now, Jack. We can get to the point. Let's make it short. I don't feel very well.'

'A psychosomatic manifestation, probably,' Crawford said.

'Actually it's my gall bladder. What do you want?'

'I have a medium where I can speak to the Tooth Fairy.'

'The *Tattler*,' Dr Bloom said.

'Right. Do you think there's any way to push him in a self-destructive way by what we say to him?'

'Push him toward suicide?'

'Suicide would suit me fine.'

'I doubt it. In certain kinds of mental illness that might be possible. Here, I doubt it. If he were self-destructive, he wouldn't be so careful. He wouldn't protect himself so well. If he were a classic paranoid schizophrenic, you might be able to influence him to blow up and become visible. You might even get him to hurt himself. I wouldn't help you though.' Suicide was Bloom's mortal enemy.

'No, I suppose you wouldn't,' Crawford said. 'Could we enrage him?'

'Why do you want to know? To what purpose?'

'Let me ask you this: could we enrage him and focus his attention?'

'He's already fixed on Graham as his adversary, and you know it. Don't fool around. You've decided to stick Graham's neck out, haven't you?'

'I think I have to do it. It's that or he gets his feet sticky on the twenty-fifth. Help me.'

'I'm not sure you know what you're asking'

'Advice – that's what I'm asking.'

'I don't mean from me,' Dr Bloom said. 'What you're asking from

Graham. I don't want you to misinterpret this, and normally I wouldn't say it, but you ought to know: what do you think one of Will's strongest drives is?'

Crawford shook his head.

'It's fear, Jack. The man deals with a huge amount of fear.'

'Because he got hurt?'

'No, not entirely. Fear comes with imagination, it's a penalty, it's the price of imagination.'

Crawford stared at his blunt hands folded on his stomach. He reddened. It was embarrassing to talk about it. 'Sure. It's what you don't even mention on the big boys' side of the playground, right? Don't worry about telling me he's afraid. I won't think he's not a "stand-up guy." I'm not a total asshole, Doctor.'

'I never thought you were, Jack.'

'I wouldn't put him out there if I couldn't cover him. Okay, if I couldn't cover him eighty percent. He's not bad himself. Not the best, but he's quick. Will you help us stir up the Tooth Fairy, Doctor? A lot of people are dead.'

'Only if Graham knows the entire risk ahead of time and assumes it voluntarily. I have to hear him say that.'

'I'm like you, Doctor. I never bullshit him. No more than we all bullshit each other.'

Crawford found Graham in the small workroom near Zeller's lab which he had commandeered and filled with photographs and personal papers belonging to the victims.

Crawford waited until Graham put down the *Law Enforcement Bulletin* he was reading.

'Let me fill you in on what's up for the twenty-fifth.' He did not have to tell Graham that the twenty-fifth would bring the next full moon.

'When he does it again?'

'Yeah, if we have a problem on the twenty-fifth.'

'Not if. When.'

'Both times it's been on Saturday night. Birmingham, June 28, a full moon falling on a Saturday night. It was July 26 in Atlanta, that's one day short of a full moon, but also Saturday night. This time the full moon falls on Monday, August 25. He likes the weekend, though, so we're ready from Friday on.'

'Ready? We're *ready*?'

'Correct. You know how it is in the textbooks – the ideal way to investigate a homicide?'

'I never saw it done that way,' Graham said. 'It never works out like that.'

'No. Hardly ever. It would be great to be able to do it, though: Send one guy in. Just one. Let him go over the place. He's wired and dictating all the time. He gets the place absolutely cherry for as long as he needs. Just him . . . just you.'

A long pause.

'What are you telling me?'

'Starting the night of Friday, the twenty-second, we have a Grumman Gulfstream standing by at Andrews Air Force Base. I borrowed it from Interior. The basic lab stuff will be on it. We stand by – me, you, Zeller, Jimmy Price, a photographer, and two people to do interrogations. Soon as the call comes in, we're on our way. Anywhere in the East or South, we can be there in an hour and fifteen minutes.'

'What about the locals? They don't have to cooperate. They won't wait.'

'We're blanketing the chiefs of police and sheriff's departments. Every one of them. We're asking orders to be posted on the dispatchers' consoles and the duty officers' desks.'

Graham shook his head. 'Balls. They'd never hold off. They couldn't.'

'This is what we're asking – it's not so much. We're asking that when a report comes in, the first officers at the scene go in and look. Medical personnel go in and make sure nobody's left alive. They come back out. Roadblocks, interrogations, go on any way they like, but the *scene,* that's sealed off until we get there. We drive up, you go in. You're wired. You talk it out to us when you feel like it, don't say anything when you don't feel like it. Take as long as you want. Then we'll come in.'

'The locals won't wait.'

'Of course they won't. They'll send in some guys from Homicide. But the request will have *some* effect. It'll cut down on traffic in there, and you'll get it fresh.'

Fresh. Graham tilted his head back against his chair and stared at the ceiling.

'Of course,' Crawford said, 'we've still got thirteen days before that weekend.'

'Aw, Jack.'

' "Jack" what?' Crawford said.

'You kill me, you really do.'

'I don't follow you.'

'Yes you do. What you've done, you've decided to use me for bait because you don't have anything else. So before you pop the question, you pump me up about how bad next time will be. Not bad psychology. To use on a fucking idiot. What did you think I'd say? You worried I don't have the onions for it since that with Lecter?'

'No.'

'I wouldn't blame you for wondering. We both know people it happened to. I don't like walking around in a Kevlar vest with my butt puckered up. But hell, I'm in it now. We can't go home as long as he's loose.'

'I never doubted you'd do it.'

Graham saw that this was true. 'It's something more then, isn't it?'

Crawford said nothing.

'No Molly. *No way.*'

'Jesus, Will, even *I* wouldn't ask you that.'

Graham stared at him for a moment. 'Oh, for Christ's sake, Jack. You've decided to play ball with Freddy Lounds, haven't you? You and little Freddy have cut a deal.'

Crawford frowned at a spot on his tie. He looked up at Graham. 'You know yourself it's the best way to bait him. The Tooth Fairy's gonna watch the *Tattler*. What else have we got?'

'It has to be Lounds doing it?'

'He's got the corner on the *Tattler*.'

'So I really bad-mouth the Tooth Fairy in the *Tattler* and then we give him a shot. You think it's better than the mail drop? Don't answer that, I know it is. Have you talked to Bloom about it?'

'Just in passing. We'll both get together with him. And Lounds. We'll run the mail drop on him at the same time.'

'What about the setup? I think we'll have to give him a pretty good shot at it. Something open. Someplace where he can get close. I don't think he'd snipe. He might fool me, but I can't see him with a rifle.'

'We'll have stillwatches on the high places.'

They were both thinking the same thing. Kevlar body armor would stop the Tooth Fairy's nine-millimeter and his knife unless Graham got hit in the face. There was no way to protect him against a head shot if a hidden rifleman got the chance to fire.

'You talk to Lounds. I don't have to do that.'

'He needs to interview you, Will,' Crawford said gently. 'He has to take your picture.'

Bloom had warned Crawford he'd have trouble on that point.

Chapter Eighteen

When the time came, Graham surprised both Crawford and Bloom. He seemed willing to meet Lounds halfway and his expression was affable beneath the cold blue eyes.

Being inside FBI headquarters had a salutary effect on Lounds's manners. He was polite when he remembered to be, and he was quick and quiet with his equipment.

Graham balked only once: he flatly refused to let Lounds see Mrs Leeds's diary or any of the families' private correspondence.

When the interview began, he answered Lounds's questions in a civil tone. Both men consulted notes taken in conference with Dr Bloom. The questions and answers were often rephrased.

Alan Bloom had found it difficult to scheme toward hurt. In the end, he simply laid out his theories about the Tooth Fairy. The others listened like karate students at an anatomy lecture.

Dr Bloom said the Tooth Fairy's acts and his letter indicated a projective delusional scheme which compensated for intolerable feelings of inadequacy. Smashing the mirrors tied these feelings to his appearance.

The killer's objection to the name 'Tooth Fairy' was grounded in the homosexual implications of the word 'fairy.' Bloom believed he had an unconscious homosexual conflict, a terrible fear of being gay. Dr Bloom's opinion was reinforced by one curious observation at the Leeds house: fold marks and covered bloodstains indicated the Tooth Fairy put a pair of shorts on Charles Leeds after he was dead Dr Bloom believed he did this to emphasize his lack of interest in Leeds.

The psychiatrist talked about the strong bonding of aggressive and sexual drives that occurs in sadists at a very early age.

The savage attacks aimed primarily at the women and performed in the presence of their families were clearly strikes at a maternal figure. Bloom, pacing, talking half to himself, called his subject 'the child of a nightmare.' Crawford's eyelids drooped at the compassion in his voice.

In the interview with Lounds, Graham made statements no investigator would make and no straight newspaper would credit.

He speculated that the Tooth Fairy was ugly, impotent with persons of the opposite sex, and he claimed falsely that the killer had sexually molested his male victims. Graham said that the Tooth Fairy doubtless was the laughingstock of his acquaintances and the product of an incestuous home.

He emphasized that the Tooth Fairy obviously was not as intelligent as Hannibal Lecter. He promised to provide the *Tattler* with more observations and insights about the killer as they occurred to him. Many law-enforcement people disagreed with him, he said, but as long as he was heading the investigation, the *Tattler* could count on getting the straight stuff from him.

Lounds took a lot of pictures.

The key shot was taken in Graham's 'Washington hideaway,' an apartment he had 'borrowed to use until he squashed the Fairy.' It was the only place where he could 'find solitude' in the 'carnival atmosphere' of the investigation.

The photograph showed Graham in a bathrobe at a desk, studying late into the night. He was poring over a grotesque 'artist's conception' of 'the Fairy.'

Behind him a slice of the floodlit Capitol dome could be seen through the window. Most importantly, in the lower-left corner of the window, blurred but readable, was the sign of a popular motel across the street.

The Tooth Fairy could find the apartment if he wanted to.

At FBI headquarters, Graham was photographed in front of a mass spectrometer. It had nothing to do with the case, but Lounds thought it looked impressive.

Graham even consented to have his picture taken with Lounds interviewing him. They did it in front of the vast gun racks in Firearms and Toolmarks. Lounds held a nine-millimeter automatic of the same type as the Tooth Fairy's weapon. Graham pointed to the homemade silencer, fashioned from a length of television-antenna mast.

Dr Bloom was surprised to see Graham put a comradely hand on

Lounds's shoulder just before Crawford clicked the shutter.

The interview and pictures were set to appear in the *Tattler* published the next day, Monday, August 11. As soon as he had the material, Lounds left for Chicago. He said he wanted to supervise the layout himself. He made arrangements to meet Crawford on Tuesday afternoon five blocks from the trap.

Starting Tuesday, when the *Tattler* became generally available, two traps would be baited for the monster.

Graham would go each evening to his 'temporary residence' shown in the *Tattler* picture.

A coded personal notice in the same issue invited the Tooth Fairy to a mail drop in Annapolis watched around the clock. If he were suspicious of the mail drop, he might think the effort to catch him was concentrated there. Then Graham would be a more appealing target, the FBI reasoned.

Florida authorities provided a stillwatch at Sugarloaf Key.

There was an air of dissatisfaction among the hunters – two major stake-outs took manpower that could be used elsewhere, and Graham's presence at the trap each night would limit his movement to the Washington area.

Though Crawford's judgment told him this was the best move, the whole procedure was too passive for his taste. He felt they were playing games with themselves in the dark of the moon with less than two weeks to go before it rose full again.

Sunday and Monday passed in curiously jerky time. The minutes dragged and the hours flew.

Spurgen, chief SWAT instructor at Quantico, circled the apartment block on Monday afternoon. Graham rode beside him. Crawford was in the back seat.

'The pedestrian traffic falls off around seven-fifteen. Everybody's settled in for dinner,' Spurgen said. With his wiry, compact body and his baseball cap tipped back on his head, he looked like an infielder. 'Give us a toot on the clear band tomorrow night when you cross the B&O railroad tracks. You ought to try to make it about eight-thirty, eight-forty or so.'

He pulled into the apartment parking lot. 'This setup ain't heaven, but it could be worse. You'll park here tomorrow night. We'll change the space you use every night after that, but it'll always be on this side. It's seventy-five yards to the apartment entrance. Let's walk it.'

Spurgen, short and bandy-legged, went ahead of Graham and Crawford.

He's looking for places where he could get the bad hop, Graham thought.

'The walk is probably where it'll happen, *if it* happens,' the SWAT leader said. 'See, from here the direct line from your car to the entrance, the natural route, is across the center of the lot. It's as far as you can get from the line of cars that are here all day. He'll have to come across open asphalt to get close. How well do you hear?'

'Pretty well,' Graham said. 'Damn well on this parking lot.'

Spurgen looked for something in Graham's face, found nothing he could recognize.

He stopped in the middle of the lot. 'We're reducing the wattage on these streetlights a little to make it tougher on a rifleman.'

'Tougher on your people too,' Crawford said.

'Two of ours have Startron night scopes,' Spurgen said. 'I've got some clear spray I'll ask you to use on your suitjackets, Will. By the way, I don't care how hot it is, you will wear body armor each and every time. Correct?'

'Yes.'

'What is it?'

'It's Kevlar – what, Jack? – Second Chance?'

'Second Chance,' Crawford said.

'It's pretty likely he'll come up to you, probably from behind, or he may figure on meeting you and then turning around to shoot when he's passed you,' Spurgen said. 'Seven times he's gone for the head shot, right? He's seen that work. He'll do it with you too if you give him the time. *Don't give him the time.* After I show you a couple of things in the lobby and the flop, let's go to the range. Can you do that?'

'He can do that,' Crawford said.

Spurgen was high priest on the range. He made Graham wear earplugs under the earmuffs and flashed targets at him from every angle. He was relieved to see that Graham did not carry the regulation .38, but he worried about the flash from the ported barrel. They worked for two hours. The man insisted on checking the cylinder crane and cylinder latch screws on Graham's .44 when he had finished firing.

Graham showered and changed clothes to get the smell of gunsmoke off him before he drove to the bay for his last free night with Molly and Willy.

He took his wife and stepson to the grocery store after dinner and made a considerable to-do over selecting melons. He made sure they bought plenty of groceries – the old *Tattler* was still on the racks beside the checkout stands and he hoped Molly would not see the new issue coming in the morning. He didn't want to tell her what was happening.

When she asked him what he wanted for dinner in the coming week, he had to say he'd be away, that he was going back to Birmingham. It was the first real lie he had ever told her and telling it made him feel as greasy as old currency.

He watched her in the aisles: Molly, his pretty baseball wife, with her ceaseless vigilance for lumps, her insistence on quarterly medical checkups for him and Willy, her controlled fear of the dark; her hard-bought knowledge that time is luck. She knew the value of their days. She could hold a moment by its stem. She had taught him to relish.

Pachelbel's Canon filled the sun-drowned room where they learned each other and there was the exhilaration too big to hold and even then the fear flickered across him like an osprey's shadow: this is too good to live for long.

Molly switched her bag often from shoulder to shoulder in the grocery aisles, as though the gun in it weighed much more than its nineteen ounces.

Graham would have been offended had he heard the ugly thing he mumbled to the melons: 'I have to put that bastard in a rubber sack, that's all. I have to do that.'

Variously weighted with lies, guns, and groceries, the three of them were a small and solemn troop.

Molly smelled a rat. She and Graham did not speak after the lights were out. Molly dreamed of heavy crazy footsteps coming in a house of changing rooms.

Chapter Nineteen

There is a newsstand in Lambert St. Louis International Airport which carries many of the major newspapers from all over the United States. The New York, Washington, Chicago, and Los Angeles papers come in by air freight and you can buy them on the same day they are published.

Like many newsstands, this one is owned by a chain and, along with the standard magazines and papers, the operator is required to take a certain amount of trash.

When the Chicago *Tribune* was delivered to the stand at ten o'clock on

Monday night, a bundle of *Tattlers* thumped to the floor beside it. The bundle was still warm in the center.

The newsstand operator squatted in front of his shelves arranging the *Tribunes*. He had enough else to do. The day guys never did their share of straightening.

A pair of black zippered boots came into the corner of his vision. A browser. No, the boots were pointed at him. Somebody wanted some damn thing. The newsie wanted to finish arranging his *Tribunes* but the insistent attention made the back of his head pricke.

His trade was transient. He didn't have to be nice. 'What is it?' he said to the knees.

'A *Tattler*.'

'You'll have to wait until I bust the bundle.'

The boots did not go away. They were too close.

'I said you'll have to wait until I bust the bundle. Understand? See I'm working here?'

A hand and a flash of bright steel and the twine on the bundle beside him parted with a pop. A Susan B. Anthony dollar rang on the floor in front of him. A clean copy of the *Tattler*, jerked from the center of the bundle, spilled the top ones to the floor.

The newsstand operator got to his feet. His cheeks were flushed. The man was leaving with the paper under his arm.

'Hey. Hey, you.'

The man turned to face him. 'Me?'

'Yeah, you. I told you –'

'You told me what?' He was coming back. He stood too close. 'You told me what?'

Usually a rude merchant can fluster his customers. There was something awful in this one's calm.

The newsie looked at the floor. 'You got a quarter coming back.'

Dolarhyde turned his back and walked out. The newsstand operator's cheeks burned for half an hour. *Yeah, that guy was in here last week too. He comes in here again, I'll tell him where to fuckin' get off. I got somethin' under the counter for wise-asses.*

Dolarhyde did not look at the *Tattler* in the airport. Last Thursday's message from Lecter had left him with mixed feelings. Dr Lecter had been right, of course, in saying that he was beautiful and it was thrilling to read. He *was* beautiful. He felt some contempt for the doctor's fear of the policeman. Lecter did not understand much better than the public.

Still, he was on fire to know if Lecter had sent him another message. He would wait until he got home to look. Dolarhyde was proud of his self-control.

He mused about the newsstand operator as he drove.

There was a time when he would have apologized for disturbing the man and never come back to the newsstand. For years he had taken shit unlimited from people. Not anymore. The man could have insulted Francis Dolarhyde: he could not face the Dragon. It was all part of Becoming.

At midnight, the light above his desk still burned. The message from the *Tattler* was decoded and wadded on the floor. Pieces of the *Tattler* were scattered where Dolarhyde had clipped it for his journal. The great journal stood open beneath the painting of the Dragon, glue still drying where the new clippings were fastened. Beneath them, freshly attached, was a small plastic bag, empty as yet.

The legend beside the bag said: 'With These He Offended Me.'

But Dolarhyde had left his desk.

He was sitting on the basement stairs in the cool must of earth and mildew. The beam from his electric lantern moved over draped furniture, the dusty backs of the great mirrors that once hung in the house and now leaned against the walls, the trunk containing his case of dynamite.

The beam stopped on a tall draped shape, one of several in the far corner of the cellar. Cobwebs touched his face as he went to it. Dust made him sneeze when he pulled off the cloth cover.

He blinked back the tears and shone his light on the old oak wheelchair he had uncovered. It was high-backed, heavy, and strong, one of the three in the basement. The county had provided them to Grandmother in the 1940s when she ran her nursing home here.

The wheels squeaked as he rolled the chair across the floor. Despite its weight, he carried it easily up the stairs. In the kitchen he oiled the wheels. The small front wheels still squeaked, but the back ones had good bearings and spun freely at a flip of his finger.

The searing anger in him was eased by the wheel's soothing hum. As he spun them, Dolarhyde hummed too.

Chapter Twenty

When Freddy Lounds left the *Tattler* office at noon on Tuesday he was tired and high. He had put together the *Tattler* story on the plane to Chicago and laid it out in the composing room in thirty minutes flat.

The rest of the time he had worked steadily on his paperback, brushing off all callers. He was a good organizer and now he had fifty thousand words of solid background.

When the Tooth Fairy was caught, he'd do a whammo lead and an account of the capture. The background material would fit in neatly. He had arranged to have three of the *Tattler's* better reporters ready to go on short notice. Within hours of the capture they could be digging for details wherever the Tooth Fairy lived.

His agent talked very big numbers. Discussing the project with the agent ahead of time was, strictly speaking, a violation of his agreement with Crawford. All contracts and memos would be postdated after the capture to cover that up.

Crawford held a big stick – he had Lounds's threat on tape. Interstate transmission of a threatening message was an indictable offense outside any protection Lounds enjoyed under the First Amendment. Lounds also knew that Crawford, with one phone call, could give him a permanent problem with the Internal Revenue Service.

There were polyps of honesty in Lounds; he had few illusions about the nature of his work. But he had developed a near-religious fervor about his project.

He was possessed with a vision of a better life on the other side of the money. Buried under all the dirt he had ever done, his old hopes still faced east. Now they stirred and strained to rise.

Satisfied that his cameras and recording equipment were ready, he drove home to sleep for three hours before the flight to Washington, where he would meet Crawford near the trap.

A damned nuisance in the underground garage. The black van, parked in the space next to his, was over the line. It crowded into the space clearly marked 'Mr Frederick Lounds.'

Lounds opened his door hard, banging the side of the van and leaving a dent and a mark. That would teach the inconsiderate bastard.

Lounds was locking his car when the van door opened behind him. He was turning, had half-turned when the flat sap thocked over his ear. He got his hands up, but his knees were going and there was tremendous pressure around his neck and the air was shut off. When his heaving chest could fill again it sucked chloroform.

Dolarhyde parked the van behind his house, climbed out and stretched. He had fought a crosswind all the way from Chicago and his arms were tired. He studied the night sky. The Perseid meteor shower was due soon, and he must not miss it.

Revelation: And his tail drew the third part of the stars of heaven, and did cast them down to the earth . . .

His doing in another time. He must see it and remember.

Dolarhyde unlocked the back door and made his routine search of the house. When he came outside again he wore a stocking mask.

He opened the van and attached a ramp. Then he rolled out Freddy Lounds. Lounds wore nothing but his shorts and a gag and blindfold. Though he was only semiconscious, he did not slump. He sat up very straight, his head against the high back of the old oak wheelchair. From the back of his head to the soles of his feet he was bonded to the chair with epoxy glue.

Dolarhyde rolled him into the house and parked him in a corner of the parlor with his back to the room, as though he had misbehaved.

'Are you too cool? Would you like a blanket?'

Dolarhyde peeled off the sanitary napkins covering Lounds's eyes and mouth. Lounds didn't answer. The odor of chloroform hung on him.

'I'll get you a blanket.' Dolarhyde took an afghan from the sofa and tucked it around Lounds up to the chin, then pressed an ammonia bottle under his nose.

Lounds's eyes opened wide on a blurred joining of walls. He coughed and started talking.

'Accident? Am I hurt bad?'

The voice behind him: 'No, Mr Lounds. You'll be just fine.'

'My back hurts. My skin. Did I get burned? I hope to God I'm not burned.'

'Burned? Burned. No. You just rest there. I'll be with you in a little while.'

'Let me lie down. Listen, I want you to call my office. My God, I'm in a Striker frame. My back's broken – tell me the truth!'

Footsteps going away.

'What am I doing here?' The question shrill at the end.

The answer came from far behind him. 'Atoning, Mr Lounds.'

Lounds heard footsteps mounting stairs. He heard a shower running. His head was clearer now. He remembered leaving the office and driving, but he couldn't remember after that. The side of his head throbbed and the smell of chloroform made him gag. Held rigidly erect, he was afraid he would vomit and drown. He opened his mouth wide and breathed deep. He could hear his heart.

Lounds hoped he was asleep. He tried to raise his arm from the armrest, increasing the pull deliberately until the pain in his palm and arm was enough to wake him from any dream. He was not asleep. His mind gathered speed.

By straining he could turn his eyes enough to see his arm for seconds at a time. He saw how he was fastened.

This was no device to protect broken backs. This was no hospital. Someone had him.

Lounds thought he heard footsteps on the floor above, but they might have been his heartbeats.

He tried to think. Strained to think. *Keep cool and think*, he whispered. Cool and think.

The stairs creaked as Dolarhyde came down.

Lounds felt the weight of him in every step. A presence behind him now.

Lounds spoke several words before he could adjust the volume of his voice.

'I haven't seen your face. I couldn't identify you. I don't know what you look like. The *Tattler*, I work for *The National Tattler*, would pay a reward . . . a big reward for me. Half a million, a million maybe. A million dollars.'

Silence behind him. Then a squeak of couch springs. He was sitting down, then.

'What do you think, Mr Lounds?'

Put the pain and fear away and think. Now. For all time. To have some time. To have years. He hasn't decided to kill me. He hasn't let me see his face.

'What do you think, Mr Lounds?'

'I don't know what's happened to me.'

'Do you know Who I Am, Mr Lounds?'

'No. I don't want to know, believe me.'

'According to you, I'm a vicious, perverted sexual failure. An animal, you said. Probably turned loose from an asylum by a do-good judge.'

Ordinarily, Dolarhyde would have avoided the sibilant in 'sexual.' In the presence of this audience, very far from laughter, he was freed. 'You know now, don't you?'

Don't lie. Think fast. 'Yes.'

'Why do you write lies, Mr Lounds? Why do you say I'm crazy? Answer now.'

'When a person . . . when a person does things that most people can't understand, they call him . . .'

'Crazy.'

'They called, like . . . The Wright brothers. All through history –'

'History. Do you understand what I'm doing, Mr Lounds?'

Understand. There it was. A chance. Swing hard. 'No, but I think I've got an opportunity to understand, and then *all my readers could understand too.*'

'Do you feel privileged?'

'It's a privilege. But I have to tell you, man to man, that I'm scared. It's hard to concentrate when you're scared. If you have a great idea, you wouldn't have to scare me for me to really be impressed.'

'Man to man. Man to man. You use that expression to imply frankness, Mr Lounds, I appreciate that. But you see, I am not a man. I began as one but by the Grace of God and my own Will, I have become Other and More than a man. You say you're frightened. Do you believe that God is in attendance here, Mr Lounds?'

'I don't know.'

'Are you praying to Him now?'

'Sometimes I pray. I have to tell you, I just pray mostly when I'm scared.'

'And does God help you?'

'I don't know. I don't think about it after. I ought to.'

'You ought to. Um-hmmmm. There are so many things you ought to understand. In a little while I'll help you understand. Will you excuse me now?'

'Certainly.'

Footsteps out of the room. The slide and rattle of a kitchen drawer. Lounds had covered many murders committed in kitchens where things are handy. Police reporting can change forever your view of kitchens. Water running now.

Lounds thought it must be night. Crawford and Graham were expecting him. Certainly he had been missed by now. A great, hollow sadness pulsed briefly with his fear.

Breathing behind him, a flash of white caught by his rolling eye. A hand, powerful and pale. It held a cup of tea with honey. Lounds sipped it through a straw.

'I'd do a big story,' he said between sips. 'Anything you want to say. Describe you any way you want, or no description, no description.

'Shhhh.' A single finger tapped the top of his head. The lights brightened. The chair began to turn.

'No. I don't want to see you.'

'Oh, but you must, Mr Lounds. You're a reporter. You're here to report. When I turn you around, open your eyes and look at me. If you won't open them yourself, I'll staple your eyelids to your forehead.'

A wet mouth noise, a snapping click and the chair spun. Lounds faced the room, his eyes tight shut. A finger tapped insistently on his chest. A touch on his eyelids. He looked.

To Lounds, seated, he seemed very tall standing in his kimono. A stocking mask was rolled up to his nose. He turned his back to Lounds and dropped the robe. The great back muscles flexed above the brilliant tattoo of the tail that ran down his lower back and wrapped around the leg.

The Dragon turned his head slowly, looked over his shoulder at Lounds and smiled, all jags and stains.

'Oh my dear God Jesus,' Lounds said.

Lounds now in the center of the room where he can see the screen. Dolarhyde, behind him, has put on his robe and put in the teeth that allow him to speak.

'Do you want to know What I Am?'

Lounds tried to nod; the chair jerked his scalp. 'More than anything. I was afraid to ask.'

'Look.'

The first slide was Blake's painting, the great Man-Dragon, wings flared and tail lashing, poised above the Woman Clothed with the Sun.

'Do you see now?'

'I see.'

Rapidly Dolarhyde ran through his other slides.

Click. Mrs Jacobi alive. 'Do you see?'

'Yes.'

Click. Mrs Leeds alive. 'Do you see?'

'Yes.'

Click. Dolarhyde, the Dragon rampant, muscles flexed and tail tattoo above the Jacobis' bed. 'Do you see?'

'Yes.'

Click. Mrs Jacobi waiting. 'Do you see?'

'Yes.'

Click. Mrs Jacobi after. 'Do you see?'

'Yes.'

Click. The Dragon rampant. 'Do you see?'

'Yes '

Click. Mrs Leeds waiting, her husband slack beside her. 'Do you see?'

'Yes.'

Click. Mrs Leeds after, harlequined with blood. 'Do you see?'

'Yes.' Click. Freddy Lounds, a copy of a *Tattler* photograph. 'Do you see?'

'Oh God.'

'Do you see?'

'Oh my God.' The words *drawn* out, as a child speaks crying.

'Do you see?'

'Please no.'

'No what?'

'Not me.'

'No what? You're a man, Mr Lounds. Are you a man?'

'Yes.'

'Do you imply that I'm some kind of queer?'

'God no.'

'Are you a queer, Mr Lounds?'

'No.'

'Are you going to write more lies about me, Mr Lounds?'

'Oh no, no.'

'Why did you write lies, Mr Lounds?'

'The police told me. It was what they said.'

'You quote Will Graham.'

'Graham told me the lies. Graham.'

'Will you tell the truth now? About Me. My Work. My Becoming. My *Art*, Mr Lounds. Is this Art?'

'Art.'

The fear in Lounds's face freed Dolarhyde to speak and he could fly on sibilants and fricatives; plosives were his great webbed wings.

'You said that I, who see more than you, am insane. I, who pushed the world so much further than you, am insane. I have dared more than you. I have pressed my unique seal so much deeper in the earth, where it will last longer than your dust. Your life to mine is a slug track on stone. A thin silver mucus track in and out of the letters on my monument.' The words Dolarhyde had written in his journal swarmed in him now.

'I am the Dragon and you call me *insane?* My movements are followed and recorded as avidly as those of a mighty guest star. Do you know about the guest star in 1054? Of course not. Your readers follow you like a child follows a slug track with his finger, and in the same tired loops of reason. Back to your shallow skull and potato face as a slug follows his own slime back home.

'Before Me you are a slug in the sun. You are privy to a great Becoming and you recognize nothing. You are an ant in the afterbirth.

'It is in your nature to do one thing correctly: before Me you rightly tremble. Fear is not what you owe Me, Lounds, you and the other pismires. *You owe Me awe.'*

Dolarhyde stood with his head down, his thumb and forefinger against the bridge of his nose. Then he left the room.

He didn't take off the mask, Lounds thought. *He didn't take off the mask. If he comes back with it off, I'm dead. God, I'm wet all over.* He rolled his eyes toward the doorway and waited through the sounds from the back of the house.

When Dolarhyde returned, he still wore the mask. He carried a lunch box and two thermoses. 'For your trip back home.' He held up a thermos. 'Ice, we'll need that. Before we go, we'll tape a little while.'

He clipped a microphone to the afghan near Lounds's face. 'Repeat after me.'

They taped for half an hour. Finally, 'That's all, Mr Lounds. You did very well.'

'You'll let me go now?'

'I will. There's one way, though, that I can help you better understand and remember.' Dolarhyde turned away.

'I want to understand. I want you to know I appreciate you turning me loose. I'm really going to be fair from now on, you know that.'

Dolarhyde could not answer. He had changed his teeth.

The tape recorder was running again.

He smiled at Lounds, a brown-stained smile. He placed his hand on Lounds's heart and, leaning to him intimately as though to kiss him, he bit Lounds's lips off and spit them on the floor.

Chapter Twenty-one

Dawn in Chicago, heavy air and the gray sky low.

A security guard came out of the lobby of the *Tattler* building and stood at the curb smoking a cigarette and rubbing the small of his back. He was alone on the street and in the quiet he could hear the clack of the traffic light changing at the top of the hill, a long block away.

Half a block north of the light, out of the guard's sight, Francis Dolarhyde squatted beside Lounds in the back of the van. He arranged the blanket in a deep cowl that hid Lounds's head.

Lounds was in great pain. He appeared stuporous, but his mind was racing. There were things he must remember. The blindfold was tented across his nose and he could see Dolarhyde's fingers checking the crusted gag.

Dolarhyde put on the white jacket of a medical orderly, laid a thermos in Lounds's lap and rolled him out of the van. When he locked the wheels of the chair and turned to put the ramp back in the van, Lounds could see the end of the van's bumper beneath his blindfold.

Turning now, seeing the bumper guard . . . Yes! the license plate. Only a flash, but Lounds burned it into his mind.

Rolling now. Sidewalk seams. Around a corner and down a curb. Paper crackled under the wheels.

Dolarhyde stopped the wheelchair in a bit of littered shelter between a garbage dumpster and a parked truck. He pulled at the blindfold. Lounds closed his eyes. An ammonia bottle under his nose.

The soft voice close beside him.

'Can you hear me? You're almost there.' The blindfold off now. 'Blink if you can hear me.'

Dolarhyde opened his eye with a thumb and forefinger. Lounds was looking at Dolarhyde's face.

'I told you one fib.' Dolarhyde tapped the thermos. 'I don't *really* have your lips on ice.' He whipped off the blanket and opened the thermos.

Lounds strained hard when he smelled the gasoline, separating the skin from under his forearms and making the stout chair groan. The gas was cold all over him, fumes filling his throat and they were rolling toward the center of the street.

'Do you like being Graham's pet, Freeeeedeeeee?'

Lit with a whump and shoved, sent rolling down on the *Tattler*, eeek, eeek, eeekeeekeeek the wheels.

The guard looked up as a scream blew the burning gag away. He saw the fireball coming, bouncing on the potholes, trailing smoke and sparks and the flames blown back like wings, disjointed reflections leaping along the shop windows.

It veered, struck a parked car and overturned in front of the building, one wheel spinning and flames through the spokes, blazing arms rising in the fighting posture of the burned.

The guard ran back into the lobby. He wondered if it would blow up, if he should get away from the windows. He pulled the fire alarm. What else? He grabbed the fire extinguisher off the wall and looked outside. It hadn't blown up yet.

The guard approached cautiously through the greasy smoke spreading low over the pavement and, at last, sprayed foam on Freddy Lounds.

Chapter Twenty-two

The schedule called for Graham to leave the staked-out apartment in Washington at 5:45 A.M., well ahead of the morning rush.

Crawford called while he was shaving.

'Good morning.'

'Not so good,' Crawford said. 'The Tooth Fairy got Lounds in Chicago.'

'Oh hell no.'

'He's not dead yet and he's asking for you. He can't wait long.'

'I'll go.'

'Meet me at the airport. United 245. It leaves in forty minutes. You can be back for the stakeout, if it's still on.'

Special Agent Chester from the Chicago FBI office met them at O'Hare in a downpour. Chicago is a city used to sirens. The traffic parted reluctantly in front of them as Chester howled down the expressway, his red light flashing pink on the driving rain.

He raised his voice above the siren. 'Chicago PD says he was jumped in his garage. My stuff is secondhand. We're not popular around here today.'

'How much is out?' Crawford said.

'The whole thing, trap, all of it.'

'Did Lounds get a look at him?'

'I haven't heard a description. Chicago PD put out an all-points bulletin for a license number about six-twenty.'

'Did you get hold of Dr Bloom for me?'

'I got his wife, Jack. Dr Bloom had his gall bladder taken out this morning.'

'Glorious,' Crawford said.

Chester pulled under the dripping hospital portico. He turned in his seat. 'Jack, Will, before you go up . . . I hear this fruit really trashed Lounds. You ought to be ready for that.'

Graham nodded. All the way to Chicago he had tried to choke his hope that Lounds would die before he had to see him.

The corridor of Paege Burn Center was a tube of spotless tile. A tall doctor with a curiously old-young face beckoned Graham and Crawford away from the knot of people at Lounds's door.

'Mr Lounds's burns are fatal,' the doctor said. 'I *can* help him with the pain, and I intend to do it. He breathed flames and his throat and lungs are damaged. He may not regain consciousness. In his condition, that would be a blessing.

'In the event that he does regain consciousness, the city police have asked me to take the airway out of his throat so that he might possibly answer questions. I've agreed to try that – briefly.

'At the moment his nerve endings are anesthetized by fire. A lot of pain is coming, if he lives that long. I made this clear to the police and I want to make it clear to you: I'll interrupt any attempted questioning to sedate him if he wants me to. Do you understand me?'

'Yes,' Crawford said.

With a nod to the patrolman in front of the door, the doctor clasped his hands behind his white lab coat and moved away like a wading egret.

Crawford glanced at Graham. 'You okay?'

'I'm okay. *I* had the SWAT team.'

Lounds's head was elevated in the bed. His hair and ears were gone and compresses over his sightless eyes replaced the burned-off lids. His gums were puffed with blisters.

The nurse beside him moved an IV stand so Graham could come close. Lounds smelled like a stable fire.

'Freddy, it's Will Graham.'

Lounds arched his neck against the pillow.

'The movement's just reflex, he's not conscious,' the nurse said.

The plastic airway holding open his scorched and swollen throat hissed in time with the respirator.

A pale detective sergeant sat in the corner with a tape recorder and a clipboard on his lap. Graham didn't notice him until he spoke.

'Lounds said your name in the emergency room before they put the airway in.'

'You were there?'

'Later I was there. But I've got what he said on tape. He gave the firemen a license number when they first got to him. He passed out, and he was out in the ambulance, but he came around for a minute in the emergency room when they gave him a shot in the chest. Some *Tattler* people had followed the ambulance – they were there. I have a copy of their tape.'

'Let me hear it.'

The detective fiddled with his tape recorder. 'I think you want to use the earphone,' he said, his face carefully blank. He pushed the button.

Graham heard voices, the rattle of casters, '. . . put him in three,' the bump of a litter on a swinging door, a retching cough and a voice croaking, speaking without lips.

'*Tooth Hairy.*'

'Freddy, did you see him? What did he look like, Freddy?'

'*Wendy? Hlease Wendy. Grahan set ne uh. The cunt knew it. Graham set ne uh. Cunt tut his hand on ne in the ticture like a hucking tet. Wendy?*'

A noise like a drain sucking. A doctor's voice: 'That's it. Let me get there. Get out of the way. *Now.*'

That was all.

Graham stood over Lounds while Crawford listened to the tape.

'We're running down the license number,' the detective said. 'Could you understand what he was saying?'

'Who's Wendy?' Crawford asked.

'That hooker in the hall. The blonde with the chest. She's been trying to see him. She doesn't know anything.'

'Why don't you let her in?' Graham said from the bedside. His back was to them.

'No visitors.'

'The man's dying.'

'Think I don't know it? I've been here since a quarter to fucking six o'clock – excuse me, Nurse.'

'Take a few minutes,' Crawford said. 'Get some coffee, put some water on your face. He can't say anything. If he does, I'll be here with the recorder.'

'Okay, I could use it.'

When the detective was gone, Graham left Crawford at the bedside and approached the woman in the hall.

'Wendy?'

'Yeah.'

'If you're sure you want to go in there, I'll take you.'

'I want to. Maybe I ought to comb my hair.'

'It doesn't matter,' Graham said.

When the policeman returned, he didn't try to put her out.

Wendy of Wendy City held Lounds's blackened claw and looked straight at him. He stirred once, a little before noon.

'It's gonna be just fine, Roscoe,' she said. 'We'll have us some high old times.'

Lounds stirred again and died.

Chapter Twenty-three

Captain Osborne of Chicago Homicide had the gray, pointed face of a stone fox. Copies of the *Tattler* were all over the police station. One was on his desk.

He didn't ask Crawford and Graham to sit down.

'You had nothing at all working with Lounds in the city of Chicago?'

'No, he was coming to Washington,' Crawford said. 'He had a plane reservation. I'm sure you've checked it.'

'Yeah, I got it. He left his office about one-thirty yesterday. Got jumped in the garage of his building, must have been about ten of two.'

'Anything in the garage?'

'His keys got kicked under his car. There's no garage attendant – they had a radio-operated door but it came down on a couple of cars and they took it out. Nobody saw it happen. That's getting to be the refrain today. We're working on his car.'

'Can we help you there?'

'You can have the results when I get 'em. You haven't said much, Graham. You had plenty to say in the paper.'

'I haven't heard much either, listening to you.'

'You pissed off, Captain?' Crawford said.

'Me? Why should I be? We run down a phone trace for you and collar a fucking news reporter. Then you've got no charges against him. You *have* got some deal with him, gets him cooked in front of this scandal sheet. Now the other papers adopt him like he was their own.

'Now we've got our own Tooth Fairy murder right here in Chicago. That's great. "Tooth Fairy in Chicago," boy. Before midnight we'll have six accidental domestic shootings, guy trying to sneak in his own house drunk, wife hears him, bang. The Tooth Fairy may like Chicago, decide to stick around, have some fun.'

'We can do like this,' Crawford said. 'Butt heads, get the police commissioner and the US attorney all stirred up, get all the assholes stirred up, yours and mine. Or we can settle down and try to catch the bastard. This was my operation and it went to shit, I know that. You ever have that happen right here in Chicago? I don't want to fight you, Captain. We want to catch him and go home. What do you want?'

Osborne moved a couple of items on his desk, a penholder, a picture of a fox-faced child in band uniform. He leaned back in his chair, pursed his lips and blew out some air.

'Right now I want some coffee. You guys want some?'

'I'd like some,' Crawford said.

'So would I,' Graham said.

Osborne passed around the Styrofoam cups. He pointed to some chairs.

'The Tooth Fairy had to have a van or a panel truck to move Lounds around in that wheelchair,' Graham said.

Osborne nodded. 'The license plate Lounds saw was stolen off a TV repair truck in Oak Park. He took a commercial plate, so he was getting it for a truck or a van. He *replaced* the plate on the TV truck with another stolen plate so it wouldn't be noticed so fast. Very sly, this boy. One thing we do know – he got the plate off the TV truck sometime after eight-thirty yesterday morning. The TV repair guy bought gas first thing yesterday and he used a credit card. The attendant copied the correct license number on the slip, so the plate was stolen after that.'

'Nobody saw any kind of truck or van?' Crawford said.

'Nothing. The guard at the *Tattler* saw zip. He could referee wrestling he sees so little. The fire department responded first to the *Tattler*. They were just looking for fire. We're canvassing the overnight workers in the *Tattler* neighborhood and the neighborhoods where the TV guy worked Tuesday morning. We hope somebody saw him cop the plate.'

'I'd like to see the chair again,' Graham said.

'It's in our lab. I'll call them for you.' Osborne paused. 'Lounds was a ballsy little guy, you have to give him that. Remembering the license number and spitting it out, the shape he was in. You listened to what Lounds said at the hospital?'

Graham nodded.

'I don't mean to rub this in, but I want to know if we heard it the same way. What does it sound like to you?'

Graham quoted in a monotone: ' "Tooth Fairy. Graham set me up. The cunt knew it. Graham set me up. Cunt put his hand on me in the picture like a fucking pet." '

Osborne could not tell how Graham felt about it. He asked another question.

'He was talking about the picture of you and him in the *Tattler*?'

'Had to be.'

'Where would he get that idea?'

'Lounds and I had a few run-ins.'

'But you looked friendly towards Lounds in the picture. The Tooth Fairy kills the pet first, is that it?'

'That's it.' The stone fox was pretty fast, Graham thought.

'Too bad you didn't stake him out.'

Graham said nothing.

'Lounds was supposed to be with us by the time the Tooth Fairy saw the Tattler,' Crawford said.

'Does what he said mean anything else to you, anything we can use?'

Graham came back from somewhere and had to repeat Osborne's question in his mind before he answered. 'We know from what Lounds said that the Tooth Fairy saw the *Tattler* before he hit Lounds, right?'

'Right.'

'If you start with the idea that the *Tattler* set him off, does it strike you that he set this up in a hell of a hurry? The thing came off the press Monday night, he's in Chicago stealing license plates sometime Tuesday, probably Tuesday morning, and he's on top of Lounds Tuesday afternoon. What does that say to you?'

'That he saw it early or he didn't have far to come,' Crawford said. 'Either he saw it here in Chicago or he saw it someplace else Monday night. Bear in mind, he'd be watching for it to get the personal column.'

'Either he was already here, or he came from driving distance,' Graham said. 'He was on top of Lounds too fast with a big old wheelchair you couldn't carry on a plane – it doesn't even fold. And he didn't fly here, steal a van, steal plates for it, and go around looking for an antique wheelchair to use. He had to have an old wheelchair – a new one wouldn't work for what he did.' Graham was up, fiddling with the cord on the venetian blinds, staring at the brick wall across the airshaft. 'He already had the wheelchair or he saw it all the time.'

Osborne started to ask a question, but Crawford's expression cautioned him to wait.

Graham was tying knots in the blind cord. His hands were not steady.

'He saw it all the time . . .' Crawford prompted.

'Um-hmm,' Graham said. 'You can see how . . . the idea starts with the wheelchair. From the sight and thought of the wheelchair. That's where the idea would come from when he's thinking what he'll do to those fuckers. Freddy rolling down the street on fire, it must have been quite a sight.'

'Do you think he watched it?'

'Maybe. He certainly saw it before he did it, when he was making up his mind what he'd do.'

Osborne watched Crawford. Crawford was solid. Osborne knew Crawford was solid, and Crawford was going along with this.

'If he had the chair, or he saw it all the time . . . we can check around the nursing homes, the VA,' Osborne said.

'It was perfect to hold Freddy still,' Graham said.

'For a long time. He was gone fifteen hours and twenty-five minutes, more or less,' Osborne said.

'If he had just wanted to snuff Freddy, he could have done that in the garage,' Graham said. 'He could have burned him in his car. He wanted to talk to Freddy, or hurt him for a while.'

'Either he did it in the back of the van or he took him somewhere,'

Crawford said. 'That length of time, I'd say he took him somewhere.'

'It had to be somewhere safe. If he bundled him up good, he wouldn't attract much notice around a nursing home, going in and out,' Osborne said.

'He'd have the racket, though,' Crawford said. 'A certain amount of cleaning up to do. Assume he had the chair, and he had access to the van, and he had a safe place to take him to work on him. Does that sound like . . . home?'

Osborne's telephone rang. He growled into it.

'What? . . . No, I don't want to talk to the *Tattler* . . . Well, it better not be bullshit. Put her on . . . Captain Osborne, yes . . . What time? Who answered the phone initially at the switchboard? Take her off the switchboard, please. Tell me again what he said . . . I'll have an officer there in five minutes.'

Osborne looked at his telephone thoughtfully after he hung up.

'Lounds's secretary got a call about five minutes ago,' he said. 'She swears it was Lounds's voice. He said something, something she didn't get, ''. . . strength of the Great Red Dragon.' That's what she thought he said.'' '

Chapter Twenty-four

Dr Frederick Chilton stood in the corridor outside Hannibal Lecter's cell. With Chilton were three large orderlies. One carried a straightjacket and leg restraints and another held a can of Mace. The third loaded a tranquilizer dart into his air rifle.

Lecter was reading an actuarial chart at his table and taking notes. He had heard the footsteps coming. He heard the rifle breech close behind him, but he continued to read and gave no sign that he knew Chilton was there.

Chilton had sent him the newspapers at noon and let him wait until night to find out his punishment for helping the Dragon.

'Dr Lecter,' Chilton said.

Lecter turned around. 'Good evening, Dr Chilton.' He didn't acknowledge the presence of the guards. He looked only at Chilton.

'I've come for your books. *All* your books.'

'I see. May I ask how long you intend to keep them?'

'That depends on your attitude.'

'Is this *your* decision?'

'I decide the punitive measures here.'

'Of course you do. It's not the sort of thing Will Graham would request.'

'Back up to the net and slip these on, Dr Lecter. I won't ask you twice.'

'Certainly, Dr Chilton. I hope that's a thirty-nine – the thirty-sevens are snug around the chest.'

Dr Lecter put on the restraints as though they were dinner clothes. An orderly reached through the barrier and fastened them from the back.

'Help him to his cot,' Chilton said.

While the orderlies stripped the bookshelves, Chilton polished his glasses and stirred Lecter's personal papers with a pen.

Lecter watched from the shadowed corner of his cell. There was a curious grace about him, even in restraints.

'Beneath the yellow folder,' Lecter said quietly, 'you'll find a rejection slip the *Archives* sent you. It was brought to me by mistake with some of my *Archives* mail, and I'm afraid I opened it without looking at the envelope. Sorry.'

Chilton reddened. He spoke to an orderly. 'I think you'd better take the seat off Dr Lecter's toilet.'

Chilton looked at the actuarial table. Lecter had written his age at the top: forty-one. 'And what do you have here?' Chilton asked.

'Time,' Dr Lecter said.

Section Chief Brian Zeller took the courier's case and the wheelchair wheels into Instrumental Analysis, walking at a rate that made his gabardine pants whistle.

The staff, held over from the day shift, knew that whistling sound very well: Zeller in a hurry.

There had been enough delays. The weary courier, his flight from Chicago delayed by weather and then diverted to Philadelphia, had rented a car and driven down to the FBI laboratory in Washington.

The Chicago police laboratory is efficient, but there are things it is not equipped to do. Zeller prepared to do them now.

At the mass spectrometer he dropped off the paint flecks from Lounds's car door.

Beverly Katz in Hair and Fiber got the wheels to share with others in the section.

Zeller's last stop was the small hot room where Liza Lake bent over her gas chromatograph. She was testing ashes from a Florida arson case, watching the stylus trace its spiky line on the moving graph.

'Ace lighter fluid,' she said. 'That's what he lit it with.' She had looked at so many samples that she could distinguish brands without searching through the manual.

Zeller took his eyes off Liza Lake and rebuked himself severely for feeling pleasure in the office. He cleared his throat and held up the two shiny paint cans.

'Chicago?' she said.

Zeller nodded.

She checked the condition of the cans and the seal of the lids. One can contained ashes from the wheelchair; the other, charred material from Lounds.

'How long has it been in the cans?'

'Six hours anyway,' Zeller said.

'I'll headspace it.'

She pierced the lid with a heavy-duty syringe, extracted air that had been confined with the ashes, and injected the air directly into the gas chromatograph. She made minute adjustments. As the sample moved along the machine's five-hundred-foot column, the stylus jiggled on the wide graph paper.

'Unleaded . . .' she said. 'It's gasohol, unleaded gasohol. Don't see much of that.' She flipped quickly through a looseleaf file of sample graphs. 'I can't give you a brand yet. Let me do it with pentane and I'll get back to you.'

'Good,' Zeller said. Pentane would dissolve the fluids in the ashes, then fractionate early in the chromatograph, leaving the fluids for fine analysis.

By one A.M. Zeller had all he could get.

Liza Lake succeeded in naming the gasohol: Freddy Lounds was burned with a 'Servco Supreme' blend.

Patient brushing in the grooves of the wheelchair treads yielded two kinds of carpet fiber – wool and synthetic. Mold in dirt from the treads indicated the chair had been stored in a cool, dark place.

The other results were less satisfactory. The paint flecks were not original factory paint. Blasted in the mass spectrometer and compared with the national automotive paint file, the paint proved to be high-quality Duco enamel manufactured in a lot of 186,000 gallons during the first quarter of 1978 for sale to several auto-paintshop chains.

Zeller had hoped to pinpoint a make of vehicle and the approximate time of manufacture.

He telexed the results to Chicago.

The Chicago police department wanted its wheels back. The wheels made an awkward package for the courier. Zeller put written lab reports in his pouch along with mail and a package that had come for Graham.

'Federal express I'm not,' the courier said when he was sure Zeller couldn't hear him.

The Justice Department maintains several small apartments near Seventh District Court in Chicago for the use of jurists and favored expert witnesses when court is in session. Graham stayed in one of these, with Crawford across the hall.

He came in at nine P.M., tired and wet. He had not eaten since breakfast on the plane from Washington and the thought of food repelled him.

Rainy Wednesday was over at last. It was as bad a day as he could remember.

With Lounds dead, it seemed likely that he was next and all day Chester had watched his back; while he was in Lounds's garage, while he stood in the rain on the scorched pavement where Lounds was burned. With strobe lights flashing in his face, he told the press he was 'grieved at the loss of his friend Frederick Lounds.'

He was going to the funeral, too. So were a number of federal agents and police, in the hope that the killer would come to see Graham grieve.

Actually he felt nothing he could name, just cold nausea and an occasional wave of sickly exhilaration that he had not burned to death instead of Lounds.

It seemed to Graham that he had learned nothing in forty years: he had just gotten tired.

He made a big martini and drank it while he undressed. He had another after his shower while he watched the news.

('An FBI trap to catch the Tooth Fairy backfires and a veteran reporter is dead. We'll be back with details on Eyewitness News after this.')

They were referring to the killer as 'the Dragon' before the newscast was over. The *Tattler* had spilled it all to the networks. Graham wasn't surprised. Thursday's edition should sell well.

He made a third martini and called Molly.

She had seen the television news at six and ten o'clock and she had seen a *Tattler*. She knew that Graham had been the bait in a trap.

'You should have told me, Will.'

'Maybe. I don't think so.'

'Will he try to kill you now?'

'Sooner or later. It would be hard for him now, since I'm moving around. I'm covered all the time, Molly, and he knows it. I'll be okay.'

'You sound a little slurry, have you been to see your friend in the fridge?'

'I had a couple.'

'How do you feel?'

'Fairly rotten.'

'The news said the FBI didn't have any protection for the reporter.'

'He was supposed to be with Crawford by the time the Tooth Fairy got the paper.'

'The news is calling him the Dragon now.'

'That's what he calls himself.'

'Will, there's something . . . I want to take Willy and leave here.'

'And go where?'

'His grandparents'. They haven't seen him in a while, they'd like to see him.'

'Oh, um-hmm.'

Willy's father's parents had a ranch on the Oregon coast.

'It's creepy here. I know it's supposed to be safe – but we're not sleeping a whole lot. Maybe the shooting lessons spooked me, I don't know.'

'I'm sorry, Molly.' I wish I could tell you how sorry.

'I'll miss you. We both will.'

So she had made up her mind.

'When are you going?'

'In the morning.'

'What about the shop?'

'Evelyn wants to take it. I'll underwrite the fan stuff with the whole-salers, just for the interest, and she can keep what she makes.'

'The dogs?'

'I asked her to call the county, Will. I'm sorry, but maybe somebody will take some of them.'

'Molly, I –'

'If staying here I could keep something bad from happening to you, I'd stay. But you can't save anybody, Will, I'm not helping you here. With us up there, you can just think about taking care of yourself. I'm not carrying this damned pistol the rest of my life, Will.'

'Maybe you can get down to Oakland and watch the A's.' Didn't mean to say that. Oh boy, this silence is getting pretty long.

'Well, look, I'll call you,' she said, 'or I guess you'll have to call me up there.'

Graham felt something tearing. He felt short of breath.

'Let me get the office to make the arrangements. Have you made a reservation already?'

'I didn't use my name. I thought maybe the newspapers . . .'

'Good. Good. Let me get somebody to see you off. You wouldn't have to board through the gate, and you'd get out of Washington absolutely clean. Can I do that? Let me do that. What time does the plane go?'

'Nine-forty. American 118.'

'Okay, eight-thirty . . . behind the Smithsonian. There's a Park-Rite. Leave the car there. Somebody'll meet you. He'll listen to his watch, put it to his ear when he gets out of his car, okay?'

'That's fine.'

'Say, do you change at O'Hare? I could come out – '

'No. Change in Minneapolis.'

'Oh, Molly. Maybe I could come up there and get you when it's over?'

'That would be very nice.'

Very nice.

'Do you have enough money?'

'The bank's wiring me some.'

'What?'

'To Barclay's at the airport. Don't worry.'

'I'll miss you.'

'Me too, but that'll be the same as now. Same distance by phone. Willy says hi.'

'Hi to Willy.

'Be careful, darling.'

She had never called him darling before. He didn't care for it. He didn't care for new names; darling, Red Dragon.

The night-duty officer in Washington was glad to make the arrangements for Molly. Graham pressed his face to the cool window and watched sheets of rain whip over the muffled traffic below him, the street leaping from gray to sudden color in the lightning flashes. His face left a print of forehead, nose, lips, and chin on the glass.

Molly was gone.

The day was over and there was only the night to face, and the lipless voice accusing him.

Lounds's woman held what was left of his hand until it was over.

'Hello, this is Valerie Leeds. I'm sorry I can't come to the phone right now . . .'

'I'm sorry too,' Graham said.

Graham filled his glass again and sat at the table by the window, staring at the empty chair across from him. He stared until the space in the opposite chair assumed a man-shape filled with dark and swarming motes, a presence like a shadow on suspended dust. He tried to make the image coalesce, to see a face. It would not move, had no countenance but, faceless, faced him with palpable attention.

'I know it's tough,' Graham said. He was intensely drunk. 'You've got to try to stop, just hold off until we find you. If you've got to do something, fuck, come after me. I don't give a shit. It'll be better after that. They've got some things now to help you make it stop. To help you stop *wanting to* so bad. Help me. Help me a little. Molly's gone, old Freddy's dead. It's you and me now, sport.' He leaned across the table, his hand extended to touch, and the presence was gone.

Graham put his head down on the table, his cheek on his arm. He could see the print of his forehead, nose, mouth, and chin on the window as the lightning flashed behind it; a face with drops crawling through it down the glass. Eyeless. A face full of rain.

Graham had tried hard to understand the Dragon.

At times, in the breathing silence of the victims' houses, the very spaces the Dragon had moved through tried to speak.

Sometimes Graham felt close to him. A feeling he remembered from other investigations had settled over him in recent days: the taunting sense that he and the Dragon were doing the same things at various times of the day, that there were parallels in the quotidian details of their lives. Somewhere the Dragon was eating, or showering, or sleeping at the same time he did.

Graham tried hard to know him. He tried to see him past the blinding glint of slides and vials, beneath the lines of police reports, tried to see his face through the louvers of print. He tried as hard as he knew how.

But to begin to understand the Dragon, to hear the cold drips in his darkness, to watch the world through his red haze, Graham would have had to see things he could never see, and he would have had to fly through time . . .

Chapter Twenty-five

Springfield, Missouri, June 14, 1938.

Marian Dolarhyde Trevane, tired and in pain, got out of a taxi at City Hospital. Hot wind whipped grit against her ankles as she climbed the steps. The suitcase she lugged was better than her loose wash dress, and so was the mesh evening bag she pressed to her swollen belly. She had two quarters and a dime in her bag. She had Francis Dolarhyde in her belly.

She told the admitting officer her name was Betty Johnson, a lie. She said her husband was a musician, but she did not know his whereabouts, which was true.

They put her in the charity section of the maternity ward. She did not look at the patients on either side of her. She looked across the aisle at the soles of feet.

In four hours she was taken to the delivery room, where Francis Dolarhyde was born. The obstetrician remarked that he looked 'more like a leaf-nosed bat than a baby,' another truth. He was born with bilateral fissures in his upper lip and in his hard and soft palates. The center section of his mouth was unanchored and protruded. His nose was flat.

The hospital supervisors decided not to show him to his mother immediately. They waited to see if the infant could survive without oxygen. They put him in a bed at the rear of the infant ward and faced him away from the viewing window. He could breathe, but he could not feed. With his palate cleft, he could not suck.

His crying on the first day was not as continuous as that of a heroin-addicted baby, but it was as piercing.

By the afternoon of the second day a thin keening was all he could produce.

When the shifts changed at three P.M., a wide shadow fell across his bed. Prince Easter Mize, 260 pounds, cleaning woman and aide in the maternity ward, stood looking at him, her arms folded on top of her bosom. In twenty-six years in the nursery she had seen about thirty-nine thousand infants. This one would live if he ate.

Prince Easter had received no instructions from the Lord about letting this infant die. She doubted that the hospital had received any either. She took from her pocket a rubber stopper pierced with a curved glass drinking straw. She pushed the stopper into a bottle of milk. She could hold the baby and support his head in one great hand. She held him to her breast until she knew he felt her heartbeat. Then she flipped him over and popped the tube down his throat. He took about two ounces and went to sleep.

'Um-hum,' she said. She put him down and went about her assigned duties with the diaper pails.

On the fourth day the nurses moved Marian Dolarhyde Trevane to a private room. Hollyhocks left over from a previous occupant were in an enamel pitcher on the washstand. They had held up pretty well.

Marian was a handsome girl and the puffiness was leaving her face. She looked at the doctor when he started talking to her, his hand on her shoulder. She could smell strong soap on his hand and she thought about the crinkles at the corners of his eyes until she realized what he was saying. Then she closed her eyes and did not open them while they brought the baby in.

Finally she looked. They shut the door when she screamed. Then they gave her a shot.

On the fifth day she left the hospital alone. She didn't know where to go. She could never go home again; her mother had made that clear.

Marian Dolarhyde Trevane counted the steps between the light poles. Each time she passed three poles, she sat on the suitcase to rest. At least she had the suitcase. In every town there was a pawn shop near the bus station. She had learned that traveling with her husband.

Springfield in 1938 was not a center for plastic surgery. In Springfield, you wore your face as it was.

A surgeon at City Hospital did the best he could for Francis Dolarhyde, first retracting the front section of his mouth with an elastic band, then closing the clefts in his lip by a rectangular flap technique that is now outmoded. The cosmetic results were not good.

The surgeon had troubled to read up on the problem and decided, correctly, that repair of the infant's hard palate should wait until he was five. To operate sooner would distort the growth of his face.

A local dentist volunteered to make an obturator, which plugged the baby's palate and permitted him to feed without flooding his nose.

The infant went to the Springfield Foundling Home for a year and a half and then to Morgan Lee Memorial Orphanage.

Reverend S. B. 'Buddy' Lomax was head of the orphanage. Brother Buddy called the other boys and girls together and told them that Francis was a harelip but they must be careful never to call him a harelip.

Brother Buddy suggested they pray for him.

Francis Dolarhyde's mother learned to take care of herself in the years following his birth.

Marian Dolarhyde first found a job typing in the office of a ward boss in the St. Louis Democratic machine. With his help she had her marriage to the absent Mr Trevane annulled.

There was no mention of a child in the annulment proceedings.

She had nothing to do with her mother. ('I didn't raise you to slut for that Irish trash' were Mrs Dolarhyde's parting words to Marian when she left home with Trevane.)

Marian's ex-husband called her once at the office. Sober and pious, he told her he had been saved and wanted to know if he, Marian, and the child he 'never had the joy of knowing' might make a new life together. He sounded broke.

Marian told him the child was born dead and she hung up.

He showed up drunk at her boardinghouse with his suitcase. When she told him to go away, he observed that it was her fault the marriage failed and the child was stillborn. He expressed doubt that the child was his.

In a rage Marian Dolarhyde told Michael Trevane exactly what he had fathered and told him he was welcome to it. She reminded him that there were two cleft palates in the Trevane family.

She put him in the street and told him never to call her again. He didn't. But years later, drunk and brooding over Marian's rich new husband and her fine life, he did call Marian's mother.

He told Mrs Dolarhyde about the deformed child and said her snag teeth proved the hereditary fault lay with the Dolarhydes.

A week later a Kansas City streetcar cut Michael Trevane in two.

When Trevane told Mrs Dolarhyde that Marian had a hidden son, she sat up most of the night. Tall and lean in her rocker, Grandmother Dolarhyde stared into the fire. Toward dawn she began a slow and purposeful rocking.

Somewhere upstairs in the big house, a cracked voice called out of sleep. The floor above Grandmother Dolarhyde creaked as someone shuffled toward the bathroom.

A heavy thump on the ceiling – someone falling – and the cracked voice called in pain.

Grandmother Dolarhyde never took her eyes off the fire. She rocked faster and, in time, the calling stopped.

Near the end of his fifth year, Francis Dolarhyde had his first and only visitor at the orphanage.

He was sitting in the thick reek of the cafeteria when an older boy came for him and took him to Brother Buddy's office.

The lady waiting with Brother Buddy was tall and middle-aged, dredged in powder, her hair in a tight bun. Her face was stark white. There were touches of yellow in the gray hair and in the eyes and teeth.

What struck Francis, what he would always remember: she smiled with pleasure when she saw his face. That had never happened before. No one would ever do it again.

'This is your grandmother,' Brother Buddy said.

'Hello,' she said.

Brother Buddy wiped his own mouth with a long hand. 'Say "hello." Go ahead.'

Francis had learned to say some things by occluding his nostrils with his upper lip, but he did not have much occasion for 'hello.' 'Lhho' was the best he could do.

Grandmother seemed even more pleased with him. 'Can you say "grandmother"?'

'Try to say "grandmother," ' Brother Buddy said.

The plosive G defeated him. Francis strangled easily on tears.

A red wasp buzzed and tapped against the ceiling.

'Never mind,' his grandmother said. 'I'll just bet you can say your name. I just know a big boy like you can say his name. Say it for me.'

The child's face brightened. The big boys had helped him with this. He wanted to please. He collected himself.

'Cunt Face,' he said.

Three days later Grandmother Dolarhyde called for Francis at the orphanage and took him home with her. She began at once to help him with his speech. They concentrated on a single word. It was 'Mother.'

Within two years of the annulment, Marian Dolarhyde met and married Howard Vogt, a successful lawyer with solid connections to the St. Louis machine and what was left of the old Pendergast machine in Kansas City.

Vogt was a widower with three young children, an affable ambitious man fifteen years older than Marian Dolarhyde. He hated nothing in the world except the St. Louis *Post-Dispatch*, which had singed his feathers in the voter-registration scandal of 1936 and blasted the attempt in 1940 by the St. Louis machine to steal the governorship.

By 1943 Vogt's star was rising again. He was a brewery candidate for the state legislature and was mentioned as a possible delegate to the upcoming state constitutional convention.

Marian was a useful and attractive hostess and Vogt bought her a handsome, half-timbered house on Olive Street that was perfect for entertaining.

Francis Dolarhyde had lived with his grandmother for a week when she took him there.

Grandmother had never seen her daughter's house. The maid who answered the door did not know her.

'I'm Mrs Dolarhyde,' she said, barging past the servant. Her slip was showing three inches in the back. She led Francis into a big living room with a pleasant fire.

'Who is it, Viola?' A woman's voice from upstairs.

Grandmother cupped Francis' face in her hand. He could smell the cold leather glove. An urgent whisper. 'Go see Mother, Francis. Go see Mother. Run!'

He shrank from her, twisting on the tines of her eyes.

'Go see Mother. Run!' She gripped his shoulders and marched him toward the stairs. He trotted up to the landing and looked back down at her. She motioned upward with her chin.

Up to the strange hallway toward the open bedroom door.

Mother was seated at her dressing table checking her makeup in a mirror framed with lights. She was getting ready for a political rally, and too much rouge wouldn't do. Her back was to the door.

'Muhner,' Francis piped, as he had been taught. He tried hard to get it right. 'Muhner.'

She saw him in the mirror then. 'If you're looking for Ned, he isn't home from . . .'

'Muhner.' He came into the heartless light.

Marian heard her mother's voice downstairs demanding tea. Her eyes widened and she sat very still. She did not turn around. She turned out the makeup lights and vanished from the mirror. In the darkened room she gave a single low keening that ended in a sob. It might have been for herself, or it might have been for him.

Grandmother took Francis to all the political rallies after that and explained who he was and where he came from. She had him say hello to everyone. They did not work on 'hello' at home.

Mr Vogt lost the election by eighteen hundred votes.

Chapter Twenty-six

At Grandmother's house, Francis Dolarhyde's new world was a forest of blue-veined legs.

Grandmother Dolarhyde had been running her nursing home for three years when he came to live with her. Money had been a problem since her husband's death in 1936; she had been brought up a lady and she had no marketable skills.

What she had was a big house and her late husband's debts. Taking in boarders was out. The place was too isolated to be a successful boarding house. She was threatened with eviction.

The announcement in the newspaper of Marian's marriage to the affluent Mr Howard Vogt had seemed a godsend to Grandmother. She wrote to Marian repeatedly for help, but received no answer. Every time she telephoned, a servant told her Mrs Vogt was out.

Finally, bitterly, Grandmother Dolarhyde made an arrangement with the county and began to take in elderly indigent persons. For each one she received a sum from the county and erratic payments from such relatives as the county could locate. It was hard until she began to get some private patients from middle-class families.

No help from Marian all this time – and Marian could have helped.

Now Francis Dolarhyde played on the floor in the forest of legs. He played cars with Grandmother's Mah-Jongg pieces, pushing them among feet twisted like gnarled roots.

Mrs Dolarhyde could keep clean wash dresses on her residents, but she despaired at trying to make them keep on their shoes.

The old people sat all day in the living room listening to the radio. Mrs Dolarhyde had put in a small aquarium for them to watch as well, and a private contributor had helped her cover her parquet floors with linoleum against the inevitable incontinence.

They sat in a row on the couches and in wheelchairs listening to the radio, their faded eyes fixed on the fish or on nothing or something they saw long ago.

Francis would always remember the shuffle of feet on linoleum in the hot and buzzing day, and the smell of stewed tomatoes and cabbage from the kitchen, the smell of old people like meat wrappers dried in the sun, and always the radio.

> *Happy little washday song.*
> *Rinso white, Rinso bright*

Francis spent as much time as he could in the kitchen, because his friend was there. The cook, Queen Mother Bailey, had grown up in the service of the late Mr Dolarhyde's family. She sometimes brought Francis a plum in her apron pocket, and she called him 'Little Possum, always dreamin'.' The kitchen was warm and safe. But Queen Mother Bailey went home at night . . .

December 1943.

Francis Dolarhyde, five years old, lay in bed in his upstairs room in Grandmother's house. The room was pitch dark with its blackout curtains against the Japanese. He could not say 'Japanese.' He needed to pee. He was afraid to get up in the dark.

He called to his grandmother in bed downstairs.

'Aayma. Aayma.' He sounded like an infant goat. He called until he was tired. 'Mleedse Aayma'

It got away from him then, hot on his legs and under his seat, and then cold, his nightdress sticking to him. He didn't know what to do. He took a deep breath and rolled over to face the door. Nothing happened to him. He put his foot on the floor. He stood up in the dark, nightdress plastered to his legs, face burning. He ran for the door. The doorknob caught him over the eye and he sat down in wetness, jumped up and ran down the stairs, fingers squealing on the banister. To his grandmother's room. Crawling across her in the dark and under the covers, warm against her now.

Grandmother stirred, tensed, her back hardened against his cheek, voice hissing. 'I've never sheen . . .' A clatter on the bedside table as she found her teeth, clacket as she put them in. 'I've never seen a child as disgusting and dirty as you. Get *out*, get out of this bed.'

She turned on the bedside lamp. He stood on the carpet shivering. She wiped her thumb across his eyebrow. Her thumb came away bloody.

'Did you break something?'

He shook his head so fast droplets of blood fell on Grandmother's nightgown.

'Upstairs. Go on.'

The dark came down over him as he climbed the stairs. He couldn't turn on the lights because Grandmother had cut the cords off short so only she could reach them. He did not want to get back in the wet bed. He stood in the dark holding on to the footboard for a long time. He thought she wasn't coming. The blackest corners in the room knew she wasn't coming.

She came, snatching the short cord on the ceiling light, her arms full of sheets. She did not speak to him as she changed the bed.

She gripped his upper arm and pulled him down the hall to the bathroom. The light was over the mirror and she had to stand on tiptoe to reach it. She gave him a washcloth, wet and cold.

'Take off your nightshirt and wipe yourself off.'

Smell of adhesive tape and the bright sewing scissors clicking. She snipped out a butterfly of tape, stood him on the toilet lid and closed the cut over his eye.

'Now,' she said. She held the sewing scissors under his round belly and he felt cold down there.

'Look,' she said. She grabbed the back of his head and bent him over to see his little penis lying across the bottom blade of the open scissors. She closed the scissors until they began to pinch him.

'Do you want me to cut it off?'

He tried to look up at her, but she gripped his head. He sobbed and spit fell on his stomach.

'*Do* you?'

'No, Aayma. No, Aayma.'

'I pledge you my word, if you ever make your bed dirty again I'll cut it off. Do you understand?'

'Yehn, Aayma.'

'You can find the toilet in the dark and you can sit on it like a good boy. You don't have to stand up. Now go back to bed.'

At two A.M. the wind rose, gusting warm out of the southeast, clacking together the branches of the dead apple trees, rustling the leaves of the live ones. The wind drove warm rain against the side of the house where Francis Dolarhyde, forty-two years old, lay sleeping.

He lay on his side sucking his thumb, his hair damp and flat on his forehead and his neck.

Now he awakes. He listens to his breathing in the dark and the tiny clicks of his blinking eyes. His fingers smell faintly of gasoline. His bladder is full.

He feels on the bedside table for the glass containing his teeth.

Dolarhyde always puts in his teeth before he rises. Now he walks to the bathroom. He does not turn on the light. He finds the toilet in the dark and sits down on it like a good boy.

Chapter Twenty-seven

The change in Grandmother first became apparent in the winter of 1947, when Francis was eight.

She stopped taking meals in her room with Francis. They moved to the common table in the dining room, where she presided over meals with the elderly residents.

Grandmother had been trained as a girl to be a charming hostess, and now she unpacked and polished her silver bell and put it beside her plate.

Keeping a luncheon table going, pacing the service, managing conversation, batting easy conversational lobs to the strong points of the shy ones, turning the best facets of the bright ones in the light of the other guests' attention is a considerable skill and one now sadly in decline.

Grandmother had been good at it in her time. Her efforts at this table did brighten meals initially for the two or three among the residents who were capable of linear conversation.

Francis sat in the host's chair at the other end of the avenue of nodding heads as Grandmother drew out the recollections of those who could remember. She expressed keen interest in Mrs Floder's honeymoon trip to Kansas City, went through the yellow fever with Mr Eaton a number of times, and listened brightly to the random unintelligible sounds of the others.

'Isn't that interesting, Francis?' she said, and rang the bell for the next course. The food was a variety of vegetable and meat mushes, but she divided it into courses, greatly inconveniencing the kitchen help.

Mishaps at the table were never mentioned. A ring of the bell and a gesture in mid-sentence took care of those who had spilled or gone to sleep or forgotten why they were at the table. Grandmother always kept as large a staff as she could pay.

As Grandmother's general health declined, she lost weight and was able to wear dresses that had long been packed away. Some of them were elegant. In the cast of her features and her hairstyle, she bore a marked resemblance to George Washington on the dollar bill.

Her manners had slipped somewhat by spring. She ruled the table and permitted no interruptions as she told of her girlhood in St. Charles, even revealing personal matters to inspire and edify Francis and the others.

It was true that Grandmother had enjoyed a season as a belle in 1907 and was invited to some of the better balls across the river in St. Louis.

There was an 'object lesson' in this for everyone, she said. She looked pointedly at Francis, who crossed his legs beneath the table.

'I came up at a time when little could be done medically to overcome the little accidents of nature,' she said. 'I had lovely skin and hair and I took full advantage of them. I overcame my teeth with force of personality and bright spirits so successfully, in fact, that they became my "beauty spot." I think you might even call them my "charming trademark." I wouldn't have traded them for the world.'

trusted doctors, she explained at length, but when it became clear problems would cost her her teeth, she sought out one of the most reno... .ed dentists in the Midwest, Dr Felix Bertl, a Swiss. Dr Bertl's 'Swiss teeth' were very popular with a certain class of people, Grandmother said, and he had a remarkable practice.

Opera singers fearing that new shapes in their mouths would affect their tone, actors and others in public life came from as far away as San Francisco to be fitted.

Dr Bertl could reproduce a patient's natural teeth exactly and had experimented with various compounds and their effect on resonance.

When Dr Bertl had completed her dentures, her teeth appeared just as they had before. She overcame them with personality and lost none of her unique charm, she said with a spiky smile.

If there was an object lesson in all this, Francis did not appreciate it until later; there would be no further surgery for him until he could pay for it himself.

Francis could make it through dinner because there was something he looked forward to afterward.

Queen Mother Bailey's husband came for her each evening in the mule-drawn wagon he used to haul firewood. If Grandmother was occupied upstairs, Francis could ride with them down the lane to the main road.

He waited all day for the evening ride: sitting on the wagon seat beside Queen Mother, her tall flat husband silent and almost invisible in the dark, the iron tires of the wagon loud in the gravel behind the jingle of the bits. Two mules, brown and sometimes muddy, their cropped manes standing up like brushes, swishing their tails across their rumps. The smell of sweat and boiled cotton cloth, snuff and warm harness. There was the smell of woodsmoke when Mr Bailey had been clearing new ground and sometimes, when he took his shotgun to the new ground, a couple of rabbits or squirrels lay in the wagon box, stretched long as though they were running.

They did not talk on the ride down the lane; Mr Bailey spoke only to the mules. The wagon motion bumped the boy pleasantly against the Baileys. Dropped off at the end of the lane, he gave his nightly promise to walk straight back to the house and watched the lantern on the wagon move away. He could hear them talking down the road. Sometimes Queen Mother made her husband laugh and she laughed with him. Standing in the dark, it was pleasant to hear them and know they were not laughing at him.

Later he would change his mind about that . . .

Francis Dolarhyde's occasional playmate was the daughter of a sharecropper who lived three fields away. Grandmother let her come to play because it amused her now and then to dress the child in the clothing Marian had worn when she was small.

She was a red-haired listless child and she was too tired to play much of the time.

One hot June afternoon, bored with fishing for doodlebugs in the chicken yard with straws, she asked to see Francis' private parts.

In a corner between the chicken house and a low hedge that shielded them from the lower windows of the house, he showed her. She reciprocated by showing him her own, standing with her pilled cotton underwear around her ankles. As he squatted on his heels to see, a headless chicken flapped around the corner, traveling on its back, flapping up the dust. The hobbled girl hopped backwards as it spattered blood on her feet and legs.

Francis jumped to his feet, his trousers still down, as Queen Mother Bailey came around the corner after the chicken and saw them.

'Look here, boy,' she said calmly, 'you want to see what's what, well now you see, so go on and find yourselves something else to do. Occupy yourself with children's doings and keep your clothes on. You and that child help me catch that rooster.'

The children's embarrassment quickly passed as the rooster eluded them. But Grandmother was watching from the upstairs window . . .

Grandmother watched Queen Mother come back inside. The children went into the chicken house. Grandmother waited five minutes, then came up on them silently. She flung open the door and found them gathering feathers for headdresses.

She sent the girl home and led Francis into the house.

She told him he was going back to Brother Buddy's orphanage after she had punished him. 'Go upstairs. Go to your room and take your trousers off and wait for me while I get my scissors.'

He waited for hours in his room, lying on the bed with his trousers off, clutching the bedspread and waiting for the scissors. He waited through the sounds of supper downstairs and he heard the creak and clop of the firewood wagon and the snort of the mules as Queen Mother's husband came for her.

Sometime toward morning he slept, and woke in starts to wait.

Grandmother never came. Perhaps she had forgotten.

He waited through the routine of the days that followed, remembering many times a day in a rush of freezing dread. He would never cease from waiting.

He avoided Queen Mother Bailey, would not speak to her and wouldn't tell her why: he mistakenly believed that she had told Grandmother what she saw in the chicken yard. Now he was convinced that the laughter he heard while he watched the wagon lantern diminish down the road was about him. Clearly he could trust no one.

It was hard to lie still and go to sleep when it was there to think about. It was hard to lie still on such a bright night.

Francis knew that Grandmother was right. He had hurt her so. He had shamed her. Everyone must know what he had done – even as far away as St. Charles. He was not angry at Grandmother. He knew that he Loved her very much. He wanted to do right.

He imagined that burglars were breaking in and he protected Grandmother and she took back what she said. 'You're not a Child of the Devil after all, Francis. You are my good boy.'

He thought about a burglar breaking in. Coming in the house determined to show Grandmother his private parts.

How would Francis protect her? He was too small to fight a big burglar.

He thought about it. There was Queen Mother's hatchet in the pantry. She wiped it with newspaper after she killed a chicken. He should see about the hatchet. It was his responsibility. He would fight his fear of the dark. If he really Loved Grandmother, he should be the thing to be afraid of in the dark. The thing for the *burglar* to be afraid of.

He crept downstairs and found the hatchet hanging on its nail. It had a strange smell, like the smell at the sink when they were drawing a chicken. It was sharp and its weight was reassuring in his hand.

He carried the hatchet to Grandmother's room to be sure there were no burglars.

Grandmother was asleep. It was very dark but he knew exactly where she was. If there was a burglar, he would hear him breathing just as he could hear Grandmother breathing. He would know where his neck was just as surely as he knew where Grandmother's neck was. It was just below the breathing.

If there was a burglar, he would come up on him quietly like this. He would raise the hatchet over his head with both hands like this.

Francis stepped on Grandmother's slipper beside the bed. The hatchet swayed in the dizzy dark and pinged against the metal shade of her reading lamp.

Grandmother rolled over and made a wet noise with her mouth. Francis stood still. His arms trembled from the effort of holding up the hatchet. Grandmother began to snore.

The Love Francis felt almost burst him. He crept out of the room. He was frantic to be ready to protect her. He must do something. He did not fear the dark house now, but it was choking him.

He went out the back door and stood in the brilliant night, face upturned, gasping as though he could breathe the light. A tiny disk of moon, distorted on the whites of his rolled-back eyes, rounded as the eyes rolled down and was centered at last in his pupils.

The Love swelled in him unbearably tight and he could not gasp it out. He walked toward the chicken house, hurrying now, the ground cold under his feet, the hatchet bumping cold against his leg, running now before he burst . . .

Francis, scrubbing himself at the chicken-yard pump, had never felt such sweet and easy peace. He felt his way cautiously into it and found that the peace was endless and all around him.

What Grandmother kindly had not cut off was still there like a prize when he washed the blood off his belly and legs. His mind was clear and calm.

He should do something about the nightshirt. Better hide it under the sacks in the smokehouse.

Discovery of the dead chicken puzzled Grandmother. She said it didn't look like a fox job.

A month later Queen Mother found another one when she went to gather eggs. This time the head had been wrung off.

Grandmother said at the dinner table that she was convinced it was done for spite by some 'sorry help I ran off.' She said she had called the sheriff about it.

Francis sat silent at his place, opening and closing his hand on the memory of an eye blinking against his palm. Sometimes in bed he held himself to be sure he hadn't been cut. Sometimes when he held himself he thought he felt a blink.

Grandmother was changing rapidly. She was increasingly contentious and could not keep household help. Though she was short of housekeepers, it was the kitchen where she took personal charge, directing Queen Mother Bailey to the detriment of the food. Queen Mother, who had worked for the Dolarhydes all her life, was the only constant on the staff.

Red-faced in the kitchen heat, Grandmother moved restlessly from one task to the next, often leaving dishes half-made, never to be served. She made casseroles of leftovers while vegetables wilted in the pantry.

At the same time, she became fanatical about waste. She reduced the soap and bleach in the wash until the sheets were dingy gray.

In the month of November she hired five different black women to help in the house. They would not stay.

Grandmother was furious the evening the last one left. She went through the house yelling. She came into the kitchen and saw that Queen Mother Bailey had left a teaspoonful of flour on the board after rolling out some dough.

In the steam and heat of the kitchen a half-hour before dinner she walked up to Queen Mother and slapped her face.

Queen Mother dropped her ladle, shocked. Tears sprang into her eyes. Grandmother drew back her hand again. A big pink palm pushed her away.

'Don't you *ever* do that. You're not yourself, Mrs Dolarhyde, but don't you *ever* do that.'

Screaming insults, Grandmother with her bare hand shoved over a kettle of soup to slop and hiss down through the stove. She went to her room and slammed the door. Francis heard her cursing in her room and objects thrown against the walls. She didn't come out again all evening.

Queen Mother cleaned up the soup and fed the old people. She got her few things together in a basket and put on her old sweater and stocking cap. She looked for Francis but couldn't find him.

She was in the wagon when she saw the boy sitting in the corner of the porch. He watched her climb down heavily and come back to him.

'Possum, I'm going now. I won't be back here. Sironia at the feed store, she'll call your mama for me. You need me before your mama get here, you come to my house.'

He twisted away from the touch on his cheek.

Mr Bailey clucked to the mules. Francis watched the wagon lantern move away. He had watched it before, with a sad and empty feeling since he understood that Queen Mother betrayed him. Now he didn't care. He was glad. A feeble kerosene wagon light fading down the road. It was nothing to the moon.

He wondered how it feels to kill a mule.

Marian Dolarhyde Vogt did not come when Queen Mother Bailey called her.

She came two weeks later after a call from the sheriff in St. Charles. She arrived in midafternoon, driving herself in a prewar Packard. She wore gloves and a hat.

A deputy sheriff met her at the end of the lane and stooped to the car window.

'Mrs Vogt, your mother called our office around noon, saying something about the help stealing. When I come out here, you'll excuse me but she was talking out of her head and it looked like things wasn't tended to. Sheriff thought he ought to get ahold of y'all first, if you understand me. Mr Vogt being before the public and all.'

Marian understood him. Mr Vogt was commissioner of public works in St. Louis now and was not in the party's best graces.

'To my knowledge, nobody else has saw the place,' the deputy said.

Marian found her mother asleep. Two of the old people were still sitting at the table waiting for lunch One woman was out in the backyard in her slip.

Marian telephoned her husband. 'How often do they inspeet these places? . . . They must not have seen anything . . . I don't know if any relatives have complained, I don't think these people have any relatives . . . No. You stay away. I need some Negroes. Get me some Negroes . . . and Dr Waters. I'll take care of it.'

The doctor with an orderly in white arrived in forty-five minutes, followed by a panel truck bringing Marian's maid and five other domestics.

Marian, the doctor, and the orderly were in Grandmother's room when Francis came home from sehool. Francis could hear his grandmother cursing. When they rolled her out in one of the nursing-home wheelchairs, she was glassy-eyed and a piece of cotton was taped to her arm. Her face looked sunken and strange without her teeth. Marian's arm was bandaged too; she had been bitten.

Grandmother rode away in the doctor's car, sitting in the backseat with the orderly. Francis watched her go. He started to wave, but let his hand fall back to his side.

Marian's cleaning crew scrubbed and aired the house, did a tremendous wash, and bathed the old people.

Marian worked alongside them and supervised a sketchy meal.

She spoke to Francis only to ask where things were.

Then she sent the crew away and called the county authorities. Mrs Dolarhyde had suffered a stroke, she explained.

It was dark when the welfare workers came for the patients in a school bus. Francis thought they would take him too. He was not discussed.

Only Marian and Francis remained at the house. She sat at the dining-room table with her head in her hands. He went outside and climbed the crabapple tree.

Finally Marian called him. She had packed a small suitcase with his clothes.

'You'll have to come with me,' she said, walking to the car. 'Get in. Don't put your feet on the seat.'

They drove away in the Packard and left the empty wheelchair standing in the yard.

There was no scandal. The county authorities said it was sure a shame about Mrs Dolarhyde, she sure kept things nice. The Vogts remained untarnished.

Grandmother was confined to a private nerve sanatorium. It would be fourteen years before Francis went home to her again.

'Francis, here are your stepsisters and stepbrother,' his mother said. They were in the Vogts' library.

Ned Vogt was twelve, Victoria thirteen, and Margaret nine. Ned and Victoria looked at each other. Margaret looked at the floor.

Francis was given a room at the top of the servants' stairs. Since the disastrous election of 1944 the Vogts no longer employed an upstairs maid.

He was enrolled in Potter Gerard Elementary School, within walking distance of the house and far from the Episcopal private school the other children attended.

The Vogt children ignored him as much as possible during the first few days, but at the end of the first week Ned and Victoria came up the servants' stairs to call.

Francis heard them whispering for minutes before the knob turned on his door. When they found it bolted, they didn't knock. Ned said, 'Open this door.'

Francis opened it. They did not speak to him again while they looked through his clothes in the wardrobe. Ned Vogt opened the drawer in the small dressing table and picked up the things he found with two fingers: birthday handkerchiefs with F.D. embroidered on them, a capo for a guitar, a bright beetle in a pill bottle, a copy of *Baseball Joe in the World Series* which had once been wet, and a get-well card signed 'Your classmate, Sarah Hughes.'

'What's this?' Ned asked.

'A capo.'

'What's it for?'

'A guitar.'

'Do you have a guitar?'

'No.'

'What do you have it for?' Victoria asked.

'My father used it.'

'I can't understand you. What did you say? Make him say it again, Ned.'

'He said it belonged to his father.' Ned blew his nose on one of the handkerchiefs and dropped it back in the drawer.

'They came for the ponies today,' Victoria said. She sat on the narrow bed. Ned joined her, his back against the wall, his feet on the quilt.

'No more ponies,' Ned said. 'No more lake house for the summer. Do you know why? Speak up, you little bastard.'

'Father is sick a lot and doesn't make as much money,' Victoria said. 'Some days he doesn't go to the office at all.'

'Know why he's sick, you little bastard?' Ned asked. 'Talk where I can understand you.'

'Grandmother said he's a drunk. Understand that all right?'

'He's sick because of your ugly face,' Ned said.

'That's why people didn't vote for him, too,' Victoria said.

'Get out,' Francis said. When he turned to open the door, Ned kicked him in the back. Francis tried to reach his kidney with both hands, which saved his fingers as Ned kicked him in the stomach.

'Oh, Ned,' Victoria said. 'Oh, Ned.'

Ned grabbed Francis by the ears and held him close to the mirror over the dressing table.

'That's why he's sick!' Ned slammed his face into the mirror. 'That's why he's sick!' Slam. 'That's why he's sick!' Slam. The mirror was smeared with blood and mucus. Ned let him go and he sat on the floor. Victoria looked at him, her eyes wide, holding her lower lip between her teeth. They left him there. His face was wet with blood and spit. His eyes watered from the pain, but he did not cry.

Chapter Twenty-eight

Rain in Chicago drums through the night on the canopy over the open grave of Freddy Lounds.

Thunder jars Will Graham's pounding head as he weaves from the table to a bed where dreams coil beneath the pillow.

The old house above St. Charles, shouldering the wind, repeats its long sigh over the hiss of rain against the windows and the bump of thunder.

The stairs are creaking in the dark. Mr Dolarhyde is coming down them, his kimono whispering over the treads, his eyes wide with recent sleep.

His hair is wet and neatly combed. He has brushed his nails. He moves smoothly and slowly, carrying his concentration like a brimming cup.

Film beside his projector. Two subjects. Other reels are piled in the wastebasket for burning. Two left, chosen from the dozens of home movies he has copied at the plant and brought home to audition.

Comfortable in his reclining chair with a tray of cheese and fruit beside him, Dolarhyde settles in to watch.

The first film is a picnic from the Fourth of July weekend. A handsome family; three children, the father bullnecked, dipping into the pickle jar with his thick fingers. And the mother.

The best view of her is in the softball game with the neighbors' children. Only about fifteen seconds of her; she takes a lead off second base, faces the pitcher and the plate, feet apart ready to dash either way, her breasts swaying beneath her pullover as she leans forward from the waist. An annoying interruption as a child swings a bat. The woman again, walking back to tag up. She puts one foot on the boat cushion they use for a base and stands hip-shot, the thigh muscle tightening in her locked leg.

Over and over Dolarhyde watches the frames of the woman. Foot on the base, pelvis tilts, thigh muscle tightens under the cutoff jeans.

He freezes that last frame. The woman and her children. They are dirty and tired. They hug, and a dog wags among their legs.

A terrific crash of thunder clinks the cut crystal in Grandmother's tan cabinet. Dolarhyde reaches for a pear.

The second film is in several segments. The title, *The New House,* is spelled out in pennies on a shirt cardboard above a broken piggy bank. It opens with Father pulling up the 'For Sale' sign in the yard. He holds it up and faces the camera with an embarrassed grin. His pockets are turned out.

An unsteady long shot of Mother and three children on the front steps. It is a handsome house. A cut to the swimming pool. A child, sleek-headed and small, pads around to the diving board, leaving wet footprints on the tile. Heads bob in the water. A small dog paddles toward a daughter, his ears back, chin high, and the whites of his eyes showing

Mother in the water holds to the ladder and looks up at the camera. Her curly black hair has the gloss of pelt, her bosom swelling shining wet above her suit, her legs wavy below the surface, scissoring.

Night. A badly exposed shot across the pool to the lighted house, the lights reflected in the water.

Indoors and family fun. Boxes everywhere, and packing materials. An old trunk, not yet stored in the attic.

A small daughter is trying on Grandmother's clothes. She has on a big garden-party hat. Father is on the sofa. He looks a little drunk. Now Father must have the camera. It is not quite level. Mother is at the mirror in the hat.

The children jostle around her, the boys laughing and plucking at the old finery. The girl watches her mother coolly, appraising herself in time to come.

A close-up. Mother turns and strikes a pose for the camera with an arch smile, her hand at the back of her neck. She is quite lovely. There is a cameo at her throat.

Dolarhyde freezes the frame. He backs up the film. Again and again she turns from the mirror and smiles.

Absently Dolarhyde picks up the film of the softball game and drops it in the wastebasket.

He takes the reel from the projector and looks at the Gateway label on the box: *Bob Sherman, Star Route 7, Box 603, Tulsa, Okla.*

An easy drive, too.

Dolarhyde holds the film in his palm and covers it with his other hand as though it were a small living thing that might struggle to escape. It seems to jump against his palm like a cricket.

He remembers the jerkiness, the haste at the Leeds house when the lights came on. He had to deal with Mr Leeds before turning on his movie lights.

This time he wants a smoother progression. It would be wonderful to crawl in between the sleepers with the camera going and snuggle up a little while. Then he could strike in the dark and sit up between them happily getting wet.

He can do that with infrared film, and he knows where to get some.

The projector is still on. Dolarhyde sits holding the film between his hands while on the bright blank screen other images move for him to the long sigh of the wind.

There is no sense of vengeance in him, only Love and thoughts of the Glory to come; hearts becoming faint and fast, like footsteps fleeing into silence.

Him rampant. Him rampant, filled with Love, the Shermans opening to him.

The past does not occur to him at all; only the Glory to come. He does not think of his mother's house. In fact, his conscious memories of that time are remarkably few and indistinct.

Sometime in his twenties Dolarhyde's memories of his mother's house sank out of sight, leaving a slick on the surface of his mind.

He knew that he had lived there only a month. He did not recall that he was sent away at the age of nine for hanging Victoria's cat.

One of the few images he retained was the house itself, lighted, viewed from the street in winter twilight as he passed it going from Potter Gerard Elementary School to the house where he was boarded a mile away.

He could remember the smell of the Vogt library, like a piano just opened, when his mother received him there to give him holiday things. He did not remember the faces at the upstairs windows as he walked away, down the frozen sidewalk, the practical gifts burning hateful under his arm; hurrying home to a place inside his head that was quite different from St. Louis.

At the age of eleven his fantasy life was active and intense and when the pressure of his Love grew too great, he relieved it. He preyed on pets, carefully, with a cool eye to consequence. They were so tame that it was easy. The authorities never linked him with the sad little bloodstains soaked into the dirt floors of garages.

At forty-two he did not remember that. Nor did he ever think about the people in his mother's house – his mother, stepsisters, or stepbrother.

Sometimes he saw them in his sleep, in the brilliant fragments of a fever dream; altered and tall, faces and bodies in bright parrot colors, they poised over him in a mantis stance.

When he chose to reflect, which was seldom, he had many satisfactory memories. They were of his military service.

Caught at seventeen entering the window of a woman's house for a purpose never established, he was given the choice of enlisting in the Army or facing charges. He took the Army.

After basic training he was sent to specialist school in darkroom operation and shipped to San Antonio, where he worked on medical-corps training films at Brooke Army Hospital.

Surgeons at Brooke took an interest in him and decided to improve his face.

They performed a Z-plasty on his nose, using ear cartilage to lengthen the columella, and repaired his lip with an interesting Abbé flap procedure that drew an audience of doctors to the operating theater.

The surgeons were proud of the result. Dolarhyde declined the mirror and looked out the window.

Records at the film library show Dolarhyde checked out many films, mainly on trauma, and kept them overnight.

He reenlisted in 1958 and in his second hitch he found Hong Kong. Stationed at Seoul, Korea, developing film from the tiny spotter planes the Army floated over the thirty-eighth parallel in the late 1950's, he was able to go to Hong Kong twice on leave. Hong Kong and Kowloon could satisfy any appetite in 1959.

Grandmother was released from the sanatorium in 1961 in a vague Thorazine peace. Dolarhyde asked for and received a hardship discharge two months before his scheduled separation date and went home to take care of her.

It was a curiously peaceful time for him as well. With his new job at Gateway, Dolarhyde could hire a woman to stay with Grandmother in the daytime. At night they sat in the parlor together, not speaking. The tick of the old clock and its chimes were all that broke the silence.

He saw his mother once, at Grandmother's funeral in 1970. He looked through her, past her, with his yellow eyes so startlingly like her own. She might have been a stranger.

His appearance surprised his mother. He was deep-chested and sleek, with her fine coloring and a neat mustache which she suspected was hair transplanted from his head.

She called him once in the next week and heard the receiver slowly replaced.

For nine years after Grandmother's death Dolarhyde was untroubled and he troubled no one. His forehead was as smooth as a seed. He knew that he was waiting. For what, he didn't know.

One small event, which occurs to everyone, told the seed in his skull it was Time: standing by a north window, examining some film, he noticed aging in his hands. It was as though his hands, holding the film, had suddenly appeared before him and he saw in that good north light that the skin had slackened over the bones and tendons and his hands were creased in diamonds as small as lizard scales.

As he turned them in the light, an intense odor of cabbage and stewed tomatoes washed over him. He shivered though the room was warm. That evening he worked out harder than usual.

A full-length mirror was mounted on the wall of Dolarhyde's attic gym beside his barbells and weight bench. It was the only mirror hanging in his house, and he could admire his body in it comfortably because he always worked out in a mask.

He examined himself carefully while his muscles were pumped up. At forty, he could have competed successfully in regional body-building competition. He was not satisfied.

Within the week he came upon the Blake painting. It seized him instantly.

He saw it in a large, full-color photograph in *Time* magazine illustrating a report on the Blake retrospective at the Tate Museum in London. The Brooklyn Museum had sent *The Great Red Dragon and the Woman Clothed with the Sun* to London for the show.

Time's critic said: 'Few demonic images in Western art radiate such a nightmarish charge of sexual energy . . .' Dolarhyde didn't have to read the text to find that out.

He carried the picture with him for days, photographed and enlarged it in the darkroom late at night. He was agitated much of the time. He posted the painting beside his mirror in the weight room and stared at it while he pumped. He could sleep only when he had worked out to exhaustion and watched his medical films to aid him in sexual relief.

He had known since the age of nine that essentially he was alone and that he would always be alone, a conclusion more common to the forties.

Now, in his forties, he was seized by a fantasy life with the brilliance and freshness and immediacy of childhood. It took him a step beyond Alone.

At a time when other men first see and fear their isolation, Dolarhyde's became understandable to him: he was alone because he was Unique. With the fervor of conversion he saw that if he worked at it, if he followed the true urges he had kept down for so long – cultivated them as the inspirations they truly were – he could Become.

The Dragon's face is not visible in the painting, but increasingly Dolarhyde came to know how it looked.

Watching his medical films in the parlor, pumped up from lifting, he stretched his jaw wide to hold in Grandmother's teeth. They did not fit his distorted gums and his jaw cramped quickly.

He worked on his jaw in private moments, biting on a hard rubber block until the muscles stood out in his cheeks like walnuts.

In the fall of 1979, Francis Dolarhyde withdrew part of his considerable savings and took a three-month leave of absence from Gateway. He went to Hong Kong and he took with him his grandmother's teeth.

When he returned, red-haired Eileen and his other fellow workers agreed that the vacation had done him good. He was calm. They hardly noticed that he never used the employee's locker room or shower anymore – he had never done that often anyway.

His grandmother's teeth were back in the glass beside her bed. His own new ones were locked in his desk upstairs.

If Eileen could have seen him before his mirror, teeth in place, new tattoo brilliant in the harsh gym light, she would have screamed. Once.

There was time now; he did not have to hurry now. He had forever. It was five months before he selected the Jacobis.

The Jacobis were the first to help him, the first to lift him into the Glory of his Becoming. The Jacobis were better than anything, better than anything he ever knew.

Until the Leedses.

And now, as he grew in strength and Glory, there were the Shermans to come and the new intimacy of infrared. Most promising.

Chapter Twenty-nine

Francis Dolarhyde had to leave his own territory at Gateway Film Processing to get what he wanted.

Dolarhyde was production chief of Gateway's largest division home – movie processing – but there were four other divisions.

The recessions of the 1970s cut deeply into home moviemaking, and there was increasing competition from home video recorders. Gateway had to diversify.

The company added departments which transferred film to videotape, printed aerial survey maps, and offered custom services to small-format commercial filmmakers.

In 1979 a plum fell to Gateway. The company contracted jointly with the Department of Defense and the Department of Energy to develop and test new emulsions for infrared photography.

The Department of Energy wanted sensitive infrared film for its heat-conservation studies. Defense wanted it for night reconnaissance.

Gateway bought a small company next door, Baeder Chemical, in late 1979 and set up the project there.

Dolarhyde walked across to Baeder on his lunch hour under a scrubbed blue sky, carefully avoiding the reflecting puddles on the asphalt. Lounds's death had put him in an excellent humor.

Everyone at Baeder seemed to be out for lunch.

He found the door he wanted at the end of a labyrinth of halls. The sign beside the door said 'Infrared Sensitive Materials in Use. NO Safelights, NO Smoking, NO hot beverages.' The red light was on above the sign.

Dolarhyde pushed a button and, in a moment, the light turned green. He entered the light trap and rapped on the inner door.

'Come.' A woman's voice.

Cool, absolute darkness. The gurgle of water, the familiar smell of D-76 developer, and a trace of perfume.

'I'm Francis Dolarhyde. I came about the dryer.'

'Oh, good. Excuse me, my mouth's full. I was just finishing lunch.'

He heard papers wadded and dropped in a wastebasket.

'Actually, Ferguson wanted the dryer,' said the voice in the dark. 'He's on vacation, but I know where it goes. You have one over at Gateway?'

'I have two. One is larger. He didn't say how much room he has.' Dolarhyde had seen a memo about the dryer problem weeks ago.

'I'll show you, if you don't mind a short wait.'

'All right.'

'Put your back against the door' – her voice took on a touch of the lecturer's practiced tone – 'come forward three steps, until you feel the tile under your feet, and there'll be a stool just to your left.'

He found it. He was closer to her now. He could hear the rustle of her lab apron.

'Thanks for coming down,' she said. Her voice was clear, with a faint ring of iron in it. 'You're head of processing over in the big building, right?'

'Um-humm.'

'The same "Mr D." who sends the rockets when the requisitions are filed wrong?'

'The very one.'

'I'm Reba McClane. Hope there's nothing wrong over here.'

'Not my project anymore. I just planned the darkroom construction when we bought this place. I haven't been over here in six months.' A long speech for him, easier in the dark.

'Just a minute more and we'll get you some light. Do you need a tape measure?'

'I have one.'

Dolarhyde found it rather pleasant, talking to the woman in the dark. He heard the rattle of a purse being rummaged, the click of a compact.

He was sorry when the timer rang.

'There we go. I'll put this stuff in the Black Hole,' she said.

He felt a breath of cold air, heard a cabinet close on rubber seals and the hiss of a vacuum lock. A puff of air, and fragrance touched him as she passed.

Dolarhyde pressed his knuckle under his nose, put on his thoughtful expression and waited for the light.

The lights came on. She stood by the door smiling in his approximate direction. Her eyes made small random movements behind the closed lids.

He saw her white cane propped in the corner. He took his hand away from his face and smiled.

'Do you think I could have a plum?' he said. There were several on the counter where she had been sitting.

'Sure, they're really good.'

Reba McClane was about thirty, with a handsome prairie face shaped by good bones and resolution. She had a small star-shaped scar on the bridge of her nose. Her hair was a mixture of wheat and red-gold, cut in a pageboy that looked slightly out-of-date, and her face and hands were pleasantly freckled by the sun. Against the tile and stainless steel of the darkroom she was as bright as Fall.

He was free to look at her. His gaze could move over her as freely as the air. She had no way to parry eyes.

Dolarhyde often felt warm spots, stinging spots on his skin when he talked to a woman. They moved over him to wherever he thought the woman was looking. Even when a woman looked away from him, he suspected that she saw his reflection. He was always aware of reflective surfaces, knew the angles of reflection as a pool shark knows the banks.

His skin was now cool. Hers was freckled, pearly on her throat and the insides of her wrists.

'I'll show you the room where he wants to put it,' she said. 'We can get the measuring done.'

They measured.

'Now, I want to ask a favor,' Dolarhyde said.

'Okay.'

'I need some infrared movie film. Hot film, sensitive up around one thousand nanometers.'

'You'll have to keep it in the freezer and put it back in the cold after you shoot.'

'I know.'

'Could you give me an idea of the conditions, maybe I –'

'Shooting at maybe eight feet, with a pair of Wratten filters over the lights.' It sounded too much like a surveillance rig. 'At the zoo,' he said. 'In the World of Darkness. They want to photograph the nocturnal animals.'

'They must really be spooky if you can't use commercial infrared.'

'Ummm-hmmmm.'

'I'm sure we can fix you up. One thing, though. You know a lot of our stuff is under the DD contract. Anything that goes out of here, you have to sign for.'

'Right.'

'When do you need it?'

'About the twentieth. No later.'

'I don't have to tell you the more sensitive it is, the meaner it is to handle. You get into coolers, dry ice, all that. They're screening some samples about four o'clock, if you want to look. You can pick the tamest emulsion that'll do what you want.'

'I'll come.'

Reba McClane counted her plums after Dolarhyde left. He had taken one.

Strange man, Mr Dolarhyde. There had been no awkward pause of sympathy and concern in his voice when she turned on the lights. Maybe he already knew she was blind. Better yet, maybe he didn't give a damn.

That would be refreshing.

Chapter Thirty

In Chicago, Freddy Lounds's funeral was under way. The *National Tattler* paid for the elaborate service, rushing the arrangements so that it could be held on Thursday, the day after his death. Then the pictures would be available for the *Tattler* edition published Thursday night.

The funeral was long in the chapel and it was long at the graveside.

A radio evangelist went on and on in fulsome eulogy. Graham rode the greasy swells of his hangover and tried to study the crowd.

The hired choir at graveside gave full measure for the money while the *Tattler* photographers' motor-driven cameras whizzed. Two TV crews were present with fixed cameras and creepy-peepies. Police photographers with press credentials photographed the crowd.

Graham recognized several plainclothes officers from Chicago Homicide. Theirs were the only faces that meant anything to him.

And there was Wendy of Wendy City, Lounds's girlfriend. She was seated beneath the canopy, nearest the coffin. Graham hardly recognized her. Her blonde wig was drawn back in a bun and she wore a black tailored suit.

During the last hymn she rose, went forward unsteadily, knelt and laid her head on the casket, her arms outstretched in the pall of chrysanthemums as the strobe lights flashed.

The crowd made little noise moving over the spongy grass to the cemetery gates.

Graham walked beside Wendy. A crowd of the uninvited stared at them through the bars of the high iron fence.

'Are you all right?' Graham asked.

They stopped among the tombstones. Her eyes were dry, her gaze level.

'Better than you,' she said. 'Got drunk, didn't you?'

'Yep. Is somebody keeping an eye on you?'

'The precinct sent some people over. They've got plainclothes in the club. Lot of business now. More weirdos than usual.'

'I'm sorry you had this. You did . . . I thought you were fine at the hospital. I admired that.'

She nodded. 'Freddy was a sport. He shouldn't have to go out that hard. Thanks for getting me in the room.' She looked into the distance, blinking, thinking, eye shadow like stone dust on her lids. She faced Graham. 'Look, the *Tattler*'s giving me some money, you figured that, right? For an interview and the dive at the graveside. I don't think Freddy would mind.'

'He'd have been mad if you passed it up.'

'That's what I thought. They're jerks, but they pay. What it is, they tried to get me to say that I think you deliberately turned this freak on to Freddy, chumming with him in that picture. I didn't say it. If they print that I did say it, well that's bullshit.'

Graham said nothing as she scanned his face.

'You didn't like him, maybe – it doesn't matter. But if you thought this could happen, you wouldn't have missed the shot at the Fairy, right?'

'Yeah, Wendy, I'd have staked him out.'

'Do you have anything at all? I hear noise from these people and that's about it.'

'We don't have much. A few things from the lab we're following up. It was a clean job and he's lucky.'

'Are you?'

'What?'

'Lucky.'

'Off and on.'

'Freddy was never lucky. He told me he'd clean up on this. Big deals everywhere.'

'He probably would have, too.'

'Well look, Graham, if you ever, you know, feel like a drink, I've got one.'

'Thanks.'

'But stay sober on the street.'

'Oh yes.'

Two policemen cleared a path for Wendy through the crowd of curiosity-seekers outside the gate. One of the gawkers wore a printed T-shirt reading 'The Tooth Fairy Is a One-Night Stand.' He whistled at Wendy. The woman beside him slapped his face.

A big policeman squeezed into the 280ZX beside Wendy and she pulled into the traffic. A second policeman followed in an unmarked car.

Chicago smelled like a spent skyrocket in the hot afternoon.

Graham was lonely, and he knew why; funerals often make us want sex – it's one in the eye for death.

The wind rattled the dry stalks of a funeral arrangement near his feet. For a hard second he remembered palm fronds rustling in the sea wind. He wanted very much to go home, knowing that he would not, could not, until the Dragon was dead.

Chapter Thirty-one

The projection room at Baeder Chemical was small – five rows of folding chairs with an aisle in the middle.

Dolarhyde arrived late. He stood at the back with his arms folded while they screened gray cards, color cards, and cubes variously lighted, filmed on a variety of infrared emulsions.

His presence disturbed Dandridge, the young man in charge. Dolarhyde carried an air of authority at work. He was the recognized darkroom expert from the parent company next door, and he was known to be a perfectionist.

Dandridge had not consulted him in months, a petty rivalry that had gone on since Gateway bought Baeder Chemical.

'Reba, give us the development dope on sample . . . eight,' Dandridge said.

Reba McClane sat at the end of a row, a clipboard in her lap. Speaking in a clear voice, her fingers moving over the clipboard in the semidarkness, she outlined the mechanics of the development – chemicals, temperature and time, and storage procedures before and after filming.

Infrared-sensitive film must be handled in total darkness. She had done all the darkroom work, keeping the many samples straight by touch code and keeping a running record in the dark. It was easy to see her value to Baeder.

The screening ran through quitting time.

Reba McClane kept her seat as the others were filing out. Dolarhyde approached her carefully. He spoke to her at a distance while there were others in the room. He didn't want her to feel watched.

'I thought you hadn't made it,' she said.

'I had a machine down. It made me late.'

The lights were on. Her clean scalp glistened in the part of her hair as he stood over her.

'Did you get to see the 1000C sample?'

'I did.'

'They said it looked all right. It's a lot easier to handle than the 1200 series. Think it'll do?'

'It will.'

She had her purse with her, and a light raincoat. He stood back when she came into the aisle behind her searching cane. She didn't seem to expect any help. He didn't offer any.

Dandridge stuck his head back into the room.

'Reba, dear, Marcia had to fly. Can you manage?'

Spots of color appeared in her cheeks. 'I can manage very well, thank you, Danny.'

'I'd drop you, love, but I'm late already. Say, Mr Dolarhyde, if it wouldn't be too much trouble, could you –'

'Danny, I have a ride home.' She held in her anger. The nuances of expression were denied her, so she kept her face relaxed. She couldn't control her color, though.

Watching with his cold yellow eyes, Dolarhyde understood her anger perfectly; he knew that Dandridge's limp sympathy felt like spit on her cheek.

'I'll take you,' he said, rather late.

'No, but thank you.' She had thought he might offer and had intended to accept. She wouldn't have anybody forced into it. Damn Dandridge, damn his fumbling, she'd ride the damned bus, dammit. She had the fare and she knew the way and she could go anywhere she fucking pleased.

She stayed in the women's room long enough for the others to leave the building. The janitor let her out.

She followed the edge of a dividing strip across the parking lot toward the bus stop, her raincoat over her shoulders, tapping the edge with her cane and feeling for the slight resistance of the puddles when the cane swished through them.

Dolarhyde watched her from his van. His feelings made him uneasy; they were dangerous in daylight.

For a moment under the lowering sun, windshields, puddles, high steel wires splintered the sunlight into the glint of scissors.

Her white cane comforted him. It swept the light of scissors, swept scissors away, and the memory of her harmlessness eased him. He was starting the engine.

Reba McClane heard the van behind her. It was beside her now.

'Thank you for inviting me.'

She nodded, smiled, tapped along.

'Ride with me.'

'Thanks, but I take the bus all the time.'

'Dandridge is a fool. Ride with me . . .' – *what would someone say?* – 'for my pleasure.'

She stopped. She heard him get out of the van.

People usually grasped her upper arm, not knowing what else to do. Blind people do not like to have their balance disturbed by a firm hold on their triceps. It is as unpleasant for them as standing on wiggly scales to weigh. Like anyone else, they don't like to be propelled.

He didn't touch her. In a moment she said, 'It's better if *I* take *your* arm.'

She had wide experience of forearms, but his surprised her fingers. It was as hard as an oak banister.

She could not know the amount of nerve he summoned to let her touch him.

The van felt big and high. Surrounded by resonances and echoes unlike those of a car, she held to the edges of the bucket seat until Dolarhyde fastened her safety belt. The diagonal shoulder belt pressed one of her breasts. She moved it until it lay between them.

They said little during the drive. Waiting at the red lights, he could look at her.

She lived in the left side of a duplex on a quiet street near Washington University.

'Come in and I'll give you a drink.'

In his life, Dolarhyde had been in fewer than a dozen private homes. In the past ten years he had been in four; his own, Eileen's briefly, the Leedses', and the Jacobis'. Other people's houses were exotic to him.

She felt the van rock as he got out. Her door opened. It was a long step down from the van. She bumped into him lightly. It was like bumping into a tree. He was much heavier, more solid than she would have judged from his voice and his footfalls. Solid and light on his feet. She had known a Bronco linebacker once in Denver who came out to film a United Way appeal with some blind kids . . .

Once inside her front door, Reba McClane stood her cane in the corner and was suddenly free. She moved effortlessly, turning on music, hanging up her coat.

Dolarhyde had to reassure himself that she was blind. Being in a home excited him.

'How about a gin and tonic?'

'Tonic will be fine.'

'Would you rather have juice?'

'Tonic.'

'You're not a drinker, are you?'

'No.'

'Come on in the kitchen.' She opened the refrigerator. 'How about . . .' She made a quick inventory with her hands – 'a piece of pie, then? Karo pecan, it's dynamite.'

'Fine.'

She took a whole pie from the icebox and put it on the counter.

Hands pointing straight down, she spread her fingers along the edge of the pie tin until its circumference told her that her middle fingers were at nine and three o'clock. Then she touched her thumbtips together and brought them down to the surface of the pie to locate its exact center. She marked the center with a toothpick.

Dolarhyde tried to make conversation to keep her from feeling his stare. 'How long have you been at Baeder?' No S's in that one.

'Three months. Didn't you know?'

'They tell me the minimum.'

She grinned. 'You probably stepped on some toes when you laid out the darkrooms. Listen, the techs love you for it. The plumbing works and there are plenty of outlets. Two-twenty wherever you need it.'

She put the middle finger of her left hand on the toothpick, her thumb on the edge of the tin and cut him a slice of pie, guiding the knife with her left index finger.

He watched her handle the bright knife. Strange to look at the front of a woman as much as he liked. How often in company can one look where he wants to look?

She made herself a stiff gin and tonic and they went into the living room. She passed her hand over a floor lamp, felt no heat, switched it on.

Dolarhyde ate his pie in three bites and sat stiffly on the couch, his sleek hair shining under the lamp, his powerful hands on his knees.

She put her head back in her chair and propped her feet on an ottoman.

'When will they film at the zoo?'

'Maybe next week.' He was glad he had called the zoo and offered the infrared film: Dandridge might check.

'It's a great zoo. I went with my sister and my niece when they came to help me move in. They have the contact area, you know. I hugged this llama. It felt nice, but talk about *aroma,* boy . . . I thought I was being followed by a llama until I changed my shirt.'

This was Having a Conversation. He had to say something or leave. 'How did you come to Baeder?'

'They advertised at the Reiker Institute in Denver where I was working. I was checking the bulletin board one day and just happened to come across this job. Actually, what happened, Baeder had to shape up their employment practices to keep this Defense contract. They managed to pick six women, two blacks, two chicanos, an oriental, a paraplegic, and me into a total of eight hirings. We all count in at least two categories, you see.'

'You worked out well for Baeder.'

'The others did too. Baeder's not giving anything away.'

'Before that?' He was sweating a little. Conversation was hard. Looking was good, though. She had good legs.

She had nicked an ankle shaving. Along his arms a sense of the weight of her legs, limp.

'I trained newly blind people at the Reiker Institute in Denver for ten years after I finished school. This is my first job on the outside.'

'Outside of what?'

'Out in the big world. It was really insular at Reiker. I mean, we were training people to live in the sighted world and we didn't live in it ourselves. We talked to each other too much. I thought I'd get out and knock around a little. Actually, I had intended to go into speech therapy, for speech-and-hearing-impaired children. I expect I'll go back to that, one of these days.' She drained her glass. 'Say, I've got some Mrs Paul's crab-ball miniatures in here. They're pretty good. I shouldn't have served dessert first. Want some?'

'Um-hmmm.'

'Do you cook?'

'Um-hmmm.'

A tiny crease appeared in her forehead. She went into the kitchen. 'How about coffee?' she called.

'Uh-huh.'

She made small talk about grocery prices and got no reply. She came back into the living room and sat on the ottoman, her elbows on her knees.

'Let's talk about something for a minute and get it out of the way, okay?'

Silence.

'You haven't said anything lately. In fact, you haven't said anything since I mentioned speech therapy.' Her voice was kind, but firm. It carried no taint of sympathy. 'I understand you fine because you speak very well and because I listen. People don't pay attention. They ask me *what? what?* all the time. If you don't want to talk, okay. But I hope you will talk. Because you can, and I'm interested in what you have to say.'

'Ummm. That's good,' Dolarhyde said softly. Clearly this little speech was very important to her. Was she inviting him into the two-category club with her and the Chinese paraplegic? He wondered what his second category was.

Her next statement was incredible to him.

'May I touch your face? I want to know if you're smiling or frowning.' Wryly, now. 'I want to know whether to just shut up or not.'

She raised her hand and waited.

How well would she get around with her fingers bitten off? Dolarhyde mused. Even in street teeth he could do it as easily as biting off breadsticks.

If he braced his heels on the floor, his weight back on the couch, and locked both hands on her wrist, she could never pull away from him in time. Crunch, crunch, crunch, crunch, maybe leave the thumb. For measuring pies.

He took her wrist between his thumb and forefinger and turned her shapely, hard-used hand in the light. There were many small scars on it, and several new nicks and abrasions. A smooth scar on the back might have been a burn.

Too close to home. Too early in his Becoming. She wouldn't be there to look at anymore.

To ask this incredible thing, she could know nothing personal about him. She had not gossiped.

'Take my word that I'm smiling,' he said. Okay on the S. It was true that he had a sort of smile which exposed his handsome public teeth.

He held her wrist above her lap and released it. Her hand settled to her thigh and half-closed, fingers trailing on the cloth like an averted glance.

'I think the coffee's ready,' she said.

'I'm going.' Had to go. Home for relief.

She nodded. 'If I offended you, I didn't mean to.'

'No.'

She stayed on the ottoman, listened to be sure the lock clicked as he left.

Reba McClane made herself another gin and tonic. She put on some Segovia records and curled up on the couch. Dolarhyde had left a warm dent in the cushion. Traces of him remained in the air – shoe polish, a new leather belt, good shaving lotion.

What an intensely private man. She had heard only a few references to him at the office – Dandridge saying 'that son of a bitch Dolarhyde' to one of his toadies.

Privacy was important to Reba. As a child, learning to cope after she lost her sight, she had had no privacy at all.

Now, in public, she could never be sure that she was not watched. So Francis Dolarhyde's sense of privacy appealed to her. She had not felt one ion of sympathy from him, and that was good.

So was this gin.

Suddenly the Segovia sounded busy. She put on her whale songs.

Three tough months in a new town. The winter to face, finding curbs in the snow. Reba McClane, leggy and brave, damned self-pity. She would not have it. She was aware of a deep vein of cripple's anger in her and, while she could not get rid of it, she made it work for her, fueling her drive for independence, strengthening her determination to wring all she could from every day.

In her way, she was a hard one. Faith in any sort of natural justice was nothing but a night-light; she knew that. Whatever she did, she would end the same way everyone does: flat on her back with a tube in her nose, wondering 'Is this all?'

She knew that she would never have the light, but there were things she could have. There were things to enjoy. She had gotten pleasure from helping her students, and the pleasure was oddly intensified by the knowledge that she would be neither rewarded nor punished for helping them.

In making friends she was ever wary of people who foster dependency and feed on it. She had been involved with a few – the blind attract them, and they are the enemy.

Involved. Reba knew that she was physically attractive to men – God knows enough of them copped a feel with their knuckles when they grabbed her upper arm.

She liked sex very much, but years ago she had learned something basic about men; most of them are terrified of entailing a burden. Their fear was augmented in her case.

She did not like for a man to creep in and out of her bed as though he were stealing chickens.

Ralph Mandy was coming to take her to dinner. He had a particularly cowardly mew about being so scarred by life that he was incapable of love. Careful Ralph told her that too often, and it scalded her. Ralph was amusing, but she didn't want to own him.

She didn't want to see Ralph. She didn't feel like making conversation and hearing the hitches in conversations around them as people watched her eat.

It would be so nice to be wanted by someone with the courage to get his hat or stay as he damn pleased, and who gave her credit for the same. Someone who didn't *worry* about her.

Francis Dolarhyde – shy, with a linebacker's body and no bullshit.

She had never seen or touched a cleft lip and had no visual associations with the sound. She wondered if Dolarhyde thought she understood him easily because 'blind people hear so much better than we do.' That was a common myth. Maybe she should have explained to him that it was not true, that blind people simply pay more attention to what they hear.

There were so many misconceptions about the blind. She wondered if Dolarhyde shared the popular belief that the blind are 'purer in spirit' than most people, that they are somehow sanctified by their affliction. She smiled to herself. That one wasn't true either.

Chapter Thirty-two

The Chicago police worked under a media blitz, a nightly news 'countdown' to the next full moon. Eleven days were left.

Chicago families were frightened.

At the same time, attendance rose at horror movies that should have died at the drive-ins in a week. Fascination and horror. The entrepreneur who hit the punk-rock market with 'Tooth Fairy' T-shirts came out with an alternate line that said 'The Red Dragon Is a One-Night Stand.' Sales were divided about equally between the two.

Jack Crawford himself had to appear at a news conference with police officials after the funeral. He had received orders from Above to make the federal presence more visible; he did not make it more audible, as he said nothing.

When heavily manned investigations have little to feed on, they tend to turn upon themselves, covering the same ground over and over, beating it flat. They take on the circular shape of a hurricane or a zero.

Everywhere Graham went he found detectives, cameras, a rush of uniformed men and the incessant crackle of radios. He needed to be still.

Crawford, ruffled from his news conference, found Graham at nightfall in the quiet of an unused jury room on the floor above the US prosecutor's office.

Good lights hung low over the green felt jury table where Graham spread out his papers and photographs. He had taken off his coat and tie and he was slumped in a chair staring at two photographs. The Leedses' framed picture stood before him and beside it, on a clipboard propped against a carafe, was a picture of the Jacobis.

Graham's pictures reminded Crawford of a bullfighter's folding shrine, ready to be set up in any hotel room. There was no photograph of Lounds. He suspected that Graham had not been thinking about the Lounds case at all. He didn't need trouble with Graham.

'Looks like a poolroom in here,' Crawford said.

'Did you knock 'em dead?' Graham was pale but sober. He had a quart of orange juice in his fist.

'Jesus.' Crawford collapsed in a chair. 'You try to think out there, it's like trying to take a piss on a train.'

'Any news?'

'The commissioner was popping sweat over a question and scratched his balls on television, that's the only notable thing I saw. Watch at six and eleven if you don't believe it.'

'Want some orange juice?'

'I'd just as soon swallow barbed wire.'

'Good. More for me.' Graham's face was drawn. His eyes were too bright. 'How about the gas?'

'God bless Liza Lake. There're forty-one Servco Supreme franchise stations in greater Chicago. Captain Osborne's boys swarmed those, checking sales in containers to people driving vans and trucks. Nothing yet, but they haven't seen all shifts. Servco has 186 other stations – they're scattered over eight states. We've asked for help from the local jurisdictions. It'll take a while. If God loves me, he used a credit card. There's a chance.'

'Not if he can suck a siphon hose, there isn't.'

'I asked the commissioner not to say anything about the Tooth Fairy maybe living in this area. These people are spooked enough. If he told them that, this place would sound like Korea tonight when the drunks come home.'

'You still think he's close?'

'Don't you? It figures, Will.' Crawford picked up the Lounds autopsy report and peered at it through his halfglasses.

'The bruise on his head was older than the mouth injuries. Five to eight hours older, they're not sure. Now, the mouth injuries were hours old when they got Lounds to the hospital. They were burned over too, but inside his mouth they could tell. He retained some chloroform in his . . . hell, someplace in his wheeze. You think he was unconscious when the Tooth Fairy bit him?'

'No. He'd want him awake.'

'That's what I figure. All right, he takes him out with a lick on the head – that's in the garage. He has to keep him quiet with chloroform until he gets him someplace where the noise won't matter. Brings him back and gets here hours after the bite.'

'He could have done it all in the back of the van, parked way out somewhere,' Graham said.

Crawford massaged the sides of his nose with his fingers, giving his voice a megaphone effect. 'You're forgetting about the wheels on the chair. Bev got two kinds of carpet fuzz, wool and synthetic. Synthetic's from a van, maybe, but when have you ever seen a wool rug in a van? How many wool rugs have you seen in someplace you can rent? Damn few. Wool rug is a house, Will. And the dirt and mold were from a dark place where the chair was stored, a dirt-floored cellar.'

'Maybe.'

'Now, look at this.' Crawford pulled a Rand McNally road atlas out of his briefcase. He had drawn a circle on the 'United States mileage and driving time' map. 'Freddy was gone a little over fifteen hours, and his injuries are spaced over that time. I'm going to make a couple of assumptions. I don't like to do that, but here goes . . . What are you laughing at?'

'I just remembered when you ran those field exercises at Quantico – when the trainee told you he *assumed* something.'

'I don't remember that. Here's –'

'You made him write "assume" on the blackboard. You took the chalk and started underlining and yelling in his face. "When you assume, you make an *ASS* out of *U* and *ME* both," that's what you told him, as I recall.'

'He needed a boot in the ass to shape up. Now, look at this. Figure he had Chicago traffic on Tuesday afternoon, going out of town with Lounds. Allow a couple of hours to fool with Lounds at the location where he took him, and then the time driving back. He couldn't have gone much farther than six hours' driving time out of Chicago. Okay, this circle around Chicago is six hours' driving time. See, it's wavy because some roads are faster than others.'

'Maybe he just stayed here.'

'Sure, but this is the farthest away he *could* be.'

'So you've narrowed it down to Chicago, or inside a circle covering Milwaukee, Madison, Dubuque, Peoria, St. Louis, Indianapolis, Cincinnati, Toledo, and Detroit, to name a few.'

'Better than that. We know he got a *Tattler* very fast. Monday night, probably.'

'He could have done that in Chicago.'

'I know it, but once you get out of town the *Tattlers* aren't available on Monday night in a lot of locations. Here's a list from the *Tattler* circulation department – places *Tattlers* are air-freighted or trucked inside the circle on Monday night. See, that leaves Milwaukee, St. Louis, Cincinnati, Indianapolis, and Detroit. They go to the airports and maybe ninety newsstands that stay open all night, not counting the ones in Chicago. I'm using the field offices to check them. Some newsie might remember an odd customer on Monday night.'

'Maybe. That's a good move, Jack.'

Clearly Graham's mind was elsewhere.

If Graham were a regular agent, Crawford would have threatened him with a lifetime appointment to the Aleutians. Instead he said, 'My brother called this afternoon. Molly left his house, he said.'

'Yeah.'

'Someplace safe, I guess?'

Graham was confident Crawford knew exactly where she went.

'Willy's grandparents'.'

'Well, they'll be glad to see the kid.' Crawford waited.

No comment from Graham.

'Everything's okay, I hope.'

'I'm working, Jack. Don't worry about it. No, look, it's just that she got jumpy over there.'

Graham pulled a flat package tied with string from beneath a stack of funeral pictures and began to pick at the knot.

'What's that?'

'It's from Byron Metcalf, the Jacobis' lawyer. Brian Zeller sent it on. It's okay.'

'Wait a minute, let me see.' Crawford turned the package in his hairy fingers until he found the stamp and signature of S.F. 'Semper Fidelis' Aynesworth, head of the FBI's explosives section, certifying that the package had been fluoroscoped.

'Always check. Always check.'

'I always check, Jack.'

'Did Chester bring you this?'

'Yes.'

'Did he show you the stamp before he handed it to you?'

'He checked it and showed me.'

Graham cut the string. 'It's copies of all the probate business in the Jacobi estate. I asked Metcalf to send it to me – we can compare with the Leeds stuff when it comes in.'

'We have a lawyer doing that.'

'*I* need it. I don't know the Jacobis, Jack. They were new in town. I got to Birmingham a month late, and their stuff was scattered to shit and gone. I've got a feel for the Leedses. I don't for the Jacobis. I need to know them. I want to talk to people they knew in Detroit, and I want a couple of days more in Birmingham.'

'I need you here.'

'Listen, Lounds was a straight snuff. We made him mad at Lounds. The only connection to Lounds is one *we* made. There's a little hard evidence with Lounds, and the police are handling it. Lounds was just an annoyance to him, but the Leedses and the Jacobis are *what he needs*. We've got to have the connection between them. If we ever get him, that's how we'll do it.'

'So you have the Jacobi paper to use here,' Crawford said. 'What are you looking for? What kind of thing?'

'Any damn thing, Jack. Right now, a medical deduction.' Graham pulled the IRS estate-tax form from the package. 'Lounds was in a wheelchair. Medical. Valerie Leeds had surgery about six weeks before she died – remember in her diary? A small cyst in her breast. Medical again. I was wondering if Mrs Jacobi had surgery too.'

'I don't remember anything about surgery in the autopsy report.'

'No, but it might have been something they didn't show. Her medical history was split between Detroit and Birmingham. Something might have gotten lost there. If she had anything done, there'll be a deduction claimed and maybe an insurance claim.'

'Some itinerant orderly, you're thinking? Worked both places – Detroit or Birmingham and Atlanta?'

'If you spend time in a mental hospital you pick up the drill. You could pass as an orderly, get a job doing it when you got out,' Graham said.

'Want some dinner?'

'I'll wait till later. I get dumb after I eat.'

Leaving, Crawford looked back at Graham from the gloom of the doorway. He didn't care for what he saw. The hanging lights deepened the hollows in Graham's face as he studied with the victims staring at him from the photographs. The room smelled of desperation.

Would it be better for the case to put Graham back on the street? Crawford couldn't afford to let him burn himself out in here for nothing. But for something?

Crawford's excellent administrative instincts were not tempered by mercy. They told him to leave Graham alone.

Chapter Thirty-three

By ten P.M. Dolarhyde had worked out to near-exhaustion with the weights, had watched his films and tried to satisfy himself. Still he was restless.

Excitement bumped his chest like a cold medallion when he thought of Reba McClane. He should not think of Reba McClane.

Stretched out in his recliner, his torso pumped up and reddened by the workout, he watched the television news to see how the police were coming along with Freddy Lounds.

There was Will Graham standing near the casket with the choir howling away. Graham was slender. It would be easy to break his back. Better than killing him. Break his back and twist it just to be sure. They could roll him to the next investigation.

There was no hurry. Let Graham dread it.

Dolarhyde felt a quiet sense of power all the time now.

The Chicago police department made some noise at a news conference. Behind the racket about how hard they were working, the essense was: no progress on Freddy. Jack Crawford was in the group behind the microphones. Dolarhyde recognized him from a *Tattler* picture.

A spokesman from the *Tattler*, flanked by two bodyguards, said, 'This savage and senseless act will only make the *Tattler's* voice ring louder.'

Dolarhyde snorted. Maybe so. It had certainly shut Freddy up.

The news readers were calling him 'the Dragon' now. His acts were 'what the police *had* termed the "Tooth Fairy murders."'

Definite progress.

Nothing but local news left. Some prognathous lout was reporting from the zoo. Clearly they'd send him anywhere to keep him out of the office.

Dolarhyde had reached for his remote control when he saw on the screen someone he had talked with only hours ago on the telephone: Zoo Director Dr Frank Warfield, who had been so pleased to have the film Dolarhyde offered.

Dr Warfield and a dentist were working on a tiger with a broken tooth. Dolarhyde wanted to see the tiger, but the reporter was in the way. Finally the newsman moved.

Rocked back in his recliner, looking along his own powerful torso at the screen, Dolarhyde saw the great tiger stretched unconscious on a heavy work table.

Today they were preparing the tooth. In a few days they would cap it, the oaf reported.

Dolarhyde watched them calmly working between the jaws of the tiger's terrible striped face.

'May I touch your face?' said Miss Reba McClane.

He wanted to tell Reba McClane something. He wished she had one inkling of what she had almost done. He wished she had one flash of his Glory. But she could not have that and live. She must live: he had been seen with her and she was too close to home.

He had tried to share with Lecter, and Lecter had betrayed him.

Still, he would like to share. He would like to share with her a little, in a way she could survive.

Chapter Thirty-four

'I know it's political, *you* know it's political, but it's pretty much what you're doing anyway,' Crawford told Graham. They were walking down the State Street Mall toward the federal office building in the late afternoon. 'Do what you're doing, just write out the parallels and I'll do the rest.'

The Chicago police department had asked the FBI's Behavioral Science section for a detailed victim profile. Police officials said they would use it in planning disposition of extra patrols during the period of the full moon.

'Covering their ass is what they're doing,' Crawford said, waving his bag of Tater Tots. 'The victims have been affluent people, they need to stack the patrols in affluent neighborhoods. They know there'll be a squawk about that – the ward bosses have been fighting over the extra manpower ever since Freddy lit off. If they patrol the upper-middle-class neighborhoods and he hits the South Side, God help the city fathers. But if it happens, they can point at the damned feds. I can hear it now – "They told us to do it that way. That's what *they* said do."'

'I don't think he's any more likely to hit Chicago than anywhere else,' Graham said. 'There's no reason to think so. It's a jerkoff. Why can't Bloom do the profile? He's a consultant to Behavioral Science.'

'They don't want it from Bloom, they want it from us. It wouldn't do them any good to blame Bloom. Besides, he's still in the hospital. I'm instructed to do this. Somebody on the Hill has been on the phone with Justice. Above says do it. Will you just do it?'

'I'll do it. It's what I'm doing anyway.'

'That's what I know,' Crawford said. 'Just keep doing it.'

'I'd rather go back to Birmingham.'

'No,' Crawford said. 'Stay with me on this.'

The last of Friday burned down the west.

Ten days to go.

Chapter Thirty-five

'Ready to tell me what kind of an "outing" this is?' Reba McClane asked Dolarhyde on Saturday morning when they had ridden in silence for ten minutes. She hoped it was a picnic.

The van stopped. She heard Dolarhyde roll down his window.

'Dolarhyde,' he said. 'Dr Warfield left my name.'

'Yes, sir. Would you put this under your wiper when you leave the vehicle?'

They moved forward slowly. Reba felt a gentle curve in the road. Strange and heavy odors on the wind. An elephant trumpeted.

'The zoo,' she said. 'Terrific.' She would have preferred a picnic. What the hell, this was okay. 'Who's Dr Warfield?'

'The zoo director.'

'Is he a friend of yours?'

'No. We did the zoo a favor with the film. They're paying back.'

'How?'

'You get to touch the tiger.'

'Don't surprise me too much!'

'Did you ever look at a tiger?'

She was glad he could ask the question. 'No. I remember a puma when I was little. That's all they had at the zoo in Red Deer. I think we better talk about this.'

'They're working on the tiger's tooth. They have to put him to . . . sleep. If you want to, you can touch him.'

'Will there be a crowd, people waiting?'

'No. No audience. Warfield, me, a couple of people. TV's coming in after we leave. Want to do it?' An odd urgency in the question.

'Hell fuzzy yes, I do! Thank you . . . that's a fine surprise.'

The van stopped.

'Uh, how do I know he's sound asleep?'

'Tickle him. If he laughs, run for it.'

The floor of the treatment room felt like linoleum under Reba's shoes. The room was cool with large echoes. Radiant heat was coming from the far side.

A rhythmic shuffling of burdened feet and Dolarhyde guided her to one side until she felt the forked pressure of a corner.

It was in here now, she could smell it.

A voice. 'Up, now. Easy. Down. Can we leave the sling under him, Dr Warfield?'

'Yeah, wrap that cushion in one of the green towels and put it under his head. I'll send John for you when we've finished.'

Footsteps leaving.

She waited for Dolarhyde to tell her something. He didn't.

'It's in here,' she said.

'Ten men carried it in on a sling. It's big. Ten feet. Dr Warfield's listening to its heart. Now he's looking under one eyelid. Here he comes.'

A body damped the noise in front of her.

'Dr Warfield, Reba McClane,' Dolarhyde said.

She held out her hand. A large, soft hand took it.

'Thanks for letting me come,' she said. 'It's a treat.'

'Glad you *could* come. Enlivens my day. We appreciate the film, by the way.'

Dr Warfield's voice was middle-aged, deep, cultured, black. Virginia, she guessed.

'We're waiting to be sure his respiration and heartbeat are strong and steady before Dr Hassler starts. Hassler's over there adjusting his head mirror. Just between us, he only wears it to hold down his toupee. Come meet him. Mr Dolarhyde?'

'You go ahead.'

She put out her hand to Dolarhyde. The pat was slow in coming, light when it came. His palm left sweat on her knuckles.

Dr Warfield placed her hand on his arm and they walked forward slowly.

'He's sound asleep. Do you have a general impression . . . ? I'll describe as much as you like.' He stopped, uncertain how to put it.

'I remember pictures in books when I was a child, and I saw a puma once in the zoo near home.'

'This tiger is like a super puma,' he said. 'Deeper chest, more massive head, and a heavier frame and musculature. He's a four-year-old male Bengal. He's about ten feet long, from his nose to the tip of his tail, and he weighs eight hundred and fifteen pounds. He's lying on his right side under bright lights.'

'I can feel the lights.'

'He's striking, orange and black stripes, the orange is so bright it seems almost to bleed into the air around him.' Suddenly Dr Warfield feared that it was cruel to talk of colors. A glance at her face reassured him.

'He's six feet away, can you smell him?'

'Yes.'

'Mr Dolarhyde may have told you, some dimwit poked at him through the barrier with one of our gardener's spades. He snapped off the long fang on the upper left side on the blade. Okay, Dr Hassler?'

'He's fine. We'll give it another minute or two.'

Warfield introduced the dentist to Reba.

'My dear, you're the first *pleasant* surprise I've ever had from Frank Warfield,' Hassler said. 'You might like to examine this. It's a gold tooth, fang actually.' He put it in her hand. 'Heavy, isn't it? I cleaned up the broken tooth and took an impression several days ago, and today I'll cap it with this one. I could have done it in white of course, but I thought this would be more fun. Dr Warfield will tell you I never pass up an opportunity to show off. He's too inconsiderate to let me put an advertisement on the cage.'

She felt the taper, curve, and point with her sensitive battered fingers. 'What a nice piece of work!' She heard deep, slow breathing nearby.

'It'll give the kids a start when he yawns,' Hassler said. 'And I don't think it'll tempt any thieves. Now for the fun. You're not apprehensive, are you? Your muscular gentleman over there is watching us like a ferret. He's not making you do this?'

'No! No, I want to.'

'We're facing his back,' Dr Warfield said. 'He's just sleeping away about two and a half feet from you, waist-high on a work table. Tell you what: I'll put your left hand – you're right-handed aren't you? – I'll put your left hand on the edge of the table and you can explore with your right. Take your time. I'll be right here beside you.'

'So will I,' Dr Hassler said. They were enjoying this. Under the hot lights her hair smelled like fresh sawdust in the sun.

Reba could feel the heat on the top of her head. It made her scalp tingle. She could smell her warm hair, Warfield's soap, alcohol and disinfectant, and the cat. She felt a touch of faintness, quickly over.

She gripped the edge of the table and reached out tentatively until her fingers touched tips of fur, warm from the lights, a cooler layer and then a deep steady warmth from below. She flattened her hand on the thick coat and moved it gently, feeling the fur slide across her palm, with and against the lay, felt the hide slide over the wide ribs as they rose and fell.

She gripped the pelt and fur sprang between her fingers. In the very presence of the tiger her face grew pink and she lapsed into blindisms, inappropriate facial movements she had schooled herself against.

Warfield and Hassler saw her forget herself and were glad. They saw her through a wavy window, a pane of new sensation she pressed her face against.

As he watched from the shadows, the great muscles in Dolarhyde's back quivered. A drop of sweat bounced down his ribs.

'The other side's all business,' Dr Warfield said close to her ear.

He led her around the table, her hand trailing down the tail.

A sudden constriction in Dolarhyde's chest as her fingers trailed over the furry testicles. She cupped them and moved on.

Warfield lifted a great paw and put it in her hand. She felt the roughness of the pads and smelled faintly the cage floor. He pressed a toe to make the claw slide out. The heavy, supple muscles of the shoulders filled her hands.

She felt the tiger's ears, the width of its head and, carefully, the veterinarian guiding her, touched the roughness of its tongue. Hot breath stirred the hair on her forearms.

Last, Dr Warfield put the stethoscope in her ears. Her hands on the rhythmic chest, her face upturned, she was filled with the tiger heart's bright thunder.

Reba McClane was quiet, flushed, elated as they drove away. She turned to Dolarhyde once and said slowly, 'Thank you . . . very much. If you don't mind, I would dearly love a martini.'

'Wait here a minute,' Dolarhyde said as he parked in his yard.

She was glad they hadn't gone back to her apartment. It was stale and safe. 'Don't tidy up. Take me in and tell me it's neat.'

'Wait here.'

He carried in the sack from the liquor store and made a fast inspection tour. He stopped in the kitchen and stood for a moment with his hands over his face. He wasn't sure what he was doing. He felt danger, but not from the woman. He couldn't look up the stairs. He had to do something and he didn't know how. He should take her back home.

Before his Becoming, he would not have dared any of this.

Now he realized he could do anything. Anything. Anything.

He came outside, into the sunset, into the long blue shadow of the van. Reba McClane held on to his shoulders until her foot touched the ground.

She felt the loom of the house. She sensed its height in the echo of the van door closing.

'Four steps on the grass. Then there's a ramp,' he said.

She took his arm. A tremor through him. Clean perspiration in cotton.

'You *do* have a ramp. What for?'

'Old people were here.'

'Not now, though.'

'No.'

'It feels cool and tall,' she said in the parlor. Museum air. And was that incense? A clock ticked far away. 'Its a big house, isn't it? How many rooms?'

'Fourteen.'

'It's old. The things in here are old.' She brushed against a fringed lampshade and touched it with her fingers.

Shy Mr Dolarhyde. She was perfectly aware that it had excited him to see her with the tiger; he had shuddered like a horse when she took his arm leaving the treatment room.

An elegant gesture, his arranging that. Maybe eloquent as well, she wasn't sure.

'Martini?'

'Let me go with you and do it,' she said, taking off her shoes.

She flicked vermouth from her finger into the glass. Two and a half ounces of gin on top, and two olives. She picked up points of reference quickly in the house – the ticking clock, the hum of the window air conditioner. There was a warm place on the floor near the kitchen door where the sunlight had fallen through the afternoon.

He took her to his big chair. He sat on the couch.

There was a charge in the air. Like fluorescence in the sea, it limned movement; she found a place for her drink on the stand beside her, he put on music.

To Dolarhyde the room seemed changed. She was the first voluntary company he ever had in the house, and now the room was divided into her part and his.

There was the music, Debussy as the light failed.

He asked her about Denver and she told him a little, absently, as though she thought of something else. He described the house and the big hedged yard. There wasn't much need to talk.

In the silence while he changed records, she said, 'That wonderful tiger, this house, you're just full of surprises, D. I don't think anybody knows you at all.'

'Did you ask them?'

'Who?'

'Anybody.'

'No.'

'Then how do you know that nobody knows me?' His concentration on the tongue-twister kept the tone of the question neutral.

'Oh, some of the women from Gateway saw us getting into your van the other day. Boy, were they curious. All of a sudden I have company at the Coke machine.'

'What do they want to know?'

'They just wanted some juicy gossip. When they found out there isn't any, they went away. They were just fishing.'

'And what did they say?'

She had meant to make the women's avid curiosity into humor directed at herself. It was not working out that way.

'They wonder about everything,' she said. 'They find you very mysterious and interesting. Come on, it's a compliment.'

'Did they tell you how I look?'

The question was spoken lightly, very well done, but Reba knew that nobody is ever kidding. She met it head-on.

'I didn't ask them. But, yes, they told me how they think you look. Want to hear it? Verbatim? Don't ask if you don't.' She was sure he would ask.

No reply.

Suddenly Reba felt that she was alone in the room, that the place where he had stood was emptier than empty, a black hole swallowing everything and emanating nothing. She knew he could not have left without her hearing him.

'I think I'll tell you,' she said. 'You have a kind of hard clean neatness that they like. They said you have a remarkable body.' Clearly she couldn't leave it at that. 'They say you're very sensitive about your face and that you shouldn't be. Okay, here's the dippy one with the Dentine, is it Eileen?'

'Eileen.'

Ah, a return signal. She felt like a radio astronomer.

Reba was an excellent mimic. She could have reproduced Eileen's speech with startling fidelity, but she was too wise to mimic anyone's speech for Dolarhyde. She quoted Eileen as though she read from a transcript.

'"He's not a bad-looking guy. Honest to God I've gone out with lots of guys didn't look that good. I went out with a hockey player one time – played for the Blues? – had a little dip in his lip where his gum shrank back from his bridge? They all have that, hockey players. It's kind of, you know, *macho*, I think. Mr D.'s got the nicest skin, and what I wouldn't give for his hair." Satisfied? Oh, and she asked me if you're as strong as you look.'

'And?'

'I said I didn't know.' She drained her glass and got up. 'Where the hell are you anyway, D.?' She knew when he moved between her and a stereo speaker. 'Aha. Here you are. Do you want to know what I think about it?'

She found his mouth with her fingers and kissed it, lightly pressing his lips against his clenched teeth. She registered instantly that it was shyness and not distaste that held him rigid.

He was astonished.

'Now, would you show me where the bathroom is?'

She took his arm and went with him down the hall.

'I can find my own way back.'

In the bathroom she patted her hair and ran her fingers along the top of the basin, hunting toothpaste or mouthwash. She tried to find the door of the medicine cabinet and found there was no door, only hinges and exposed shelves. She touched the objects on them carefully, leery of a razor, until she found a bottle. She took off the cap, smelled to verify mouthwash, and swished some around.

When she returned to the parlor, she heard a familiar sound – the whir of a projector rewinding.

'I have to do a little homework,' Dolarhyde said, handing her a fresh martini.

'Sure,' she said. She didn't know how to take it. 'If I'm keeping you from working, I'll go. Will a cab come up here?'

'No. I want you to be here. I do. It's just some film I need to check. It won't take long.'

He started to take her to the big chair. She knew where the couch was. She went to it instead.

'Does it have a soundtrack?'

'No.'

'May I keep the music?'

'Um-hmmm.'

She felt his attention. He wanted her to stay, he was just frightened. He shouldn't be. All right. She sat down.

The martini was wonderfully cold and crisp.

He sat on the other end of the couch, his weight clinking the ice in her glass. The projector was still rewinding.

'I think I'll stretch out for a few minutes if you don't mind,' she said. 'No, don't move, I have plenty of room. Wake me up if I drop off, okay?'

She lay on the couch, holding the glass on her stomach; the tips of her hair just touched his hand beside his thigh.

He flicked the remote switch and the film began.

Dolarhyde had wanted to watch his Leeds film or his Jacobi film with this woman in the room. He wanted to look back and forth from the screen to Reba. He knew she would never survive that. The women saw her getting into his van. Don't even think about that. The women saw her getting into his van.

He would watch his film of the Shermans, the people he would visit next. He would see the promise of relief to come, and do it in Reba's presence, looking at her all he liked.

On the screen, *The New House* spelled in pennies on a shirt cardboard. A long shot of Mrs Sherman and the children. Fun in the pool. Mrs Sherman holds to the ladder and looks up at the camera, bosom swelling shining wet above her suit, pale legs scissoring.

Dolarhyde was proud of his self-control. He would think of this film, not the other one. But in his mind he began to speak to Mrs Sherman as he had spoken to Valerie Leeds in Atlanta.

You see me now, yes
That's how you feel to see me, yes

Fun with old clothes. Mrs Sherman has the wide hat on. She is before the mirror. She turns with an arch smile and strikes a pose for the camera, her hand at the back of her neck. There is a cameo at her throat.

Reba McClane stirs on the couch. She sets her glass on the floor. Dolarhyde feels a weight and warmth. She has rested her head on his thigh. The nape of her neck is pale and the movie light plays on it.

He sits very still, moves only his thumb to stop the film, back it up. On the screen, Mrs Sherman poses before the mirror in the hat. She turns to the camera and smiles.

You see me now, yes
That's how you feel to see me, yes
Do you feel me now? yes

Dolarhyde is trembling. His trousers are mashing him so hard. He feels heat. He feels warm breath through the cloth. Reba has made a discovery.

Convulsively his thumb works the switch.

You see me now, yes
That's how you feel to see me, yes
Do you feel this? yes

Reba has unzipped his trousers.

A stab of fear in him; he has never been erect before in the presence of a living woman. He is the Dragon, he doesn't have to be afraid.

Busy fingers spring him free.

OH.

Do you feel me now? yes
Do you feel this yes
You do I know it yes

Your heart is loud yes

He must keep his hands off Reba's neck. Keep them off. The women saw them in the van. His hand is squeezing the arm of the couch. His fingers pop through the upholstery.

Your heart is loud yes
And fluttering now
It's fluttering now
It's trying to get out yes
And now it's quick and light and quicker and light and . . .
Gone.
Oh, gone.

Reba rests her head on his thigh and turns her gleaming cheek to him. She runs her hand inside his shirt and rests it warm on his chest.

'I hope I didn't shock you,' she said.

It was the sound of her living voice that shocked him, and he felt to see if her heart was going and it was. She held his hand there gently.

'My goodness, you're not through yet, are you?'

A living woman. How bizarre. Filled with power, the Dragon's or his own, he lifted her from the couch easily. She weighed nothing, so much easier to carry because she wasn't limp. Not upstairs. Not upstairs. Hurrying now. Somewhere. Quick. Grandmother's bed, the satin comforter sliding under them.

'Oh, wait, I'll get them off. Oh, now it's torn. I don't care. Come on. My God, man. That's so sweeeet. Don't please hold me down, let me come up to you and take it.'

With Reba, his only living woman, held with her in this one bubbleskin of time, he felt for the first time that it was all right: it was his life he was releasing, himself past all mortality that he was sending into her starry darkness, away from this pain planet, ringing harmonic distances away to peace and the promise of rest.

Beside her in the dark, he put his hand on her and pressed her together gently to seal the way back. As she slept, Dolarhyde, damned murderer of eleven, listened time and again to her heart.

Images. Baroque pearls flying through the friendly dark. A Very pistol he had fired at the moon. A great firework he saw in Hong Kong called 'The Dragon Sows His Pearls.'

The Dragon.

He felt stunned, cloven. And all the long night beside her he listened, fearful, for himself coming down the stairs in the kimono.

She stirred once in the night, searching sleepily until she found the bedside glass. Grandmother's teeth rattled in it.

Dolarhyde brought her water. She held him in the dark. When she slept again, he took her hand off his great tattoo and put it on his face.

He slept hard at dawn.

Reba McClane woke at nine and heard his steady breathing. She stretched lazily in the big bed. He didn't stir. She reviewed the layout of the house, the order of rugs and floor, the direction of the ticking clock. When she had it straight, she rose quietly and found the bathroom.

After her long shower, he was still asleep. Her torn underclothes were on the floor. She found them with her feet and stuffed them in her purse. She pulled her cotton dress on over her head, picked up her cane and walked outside.

He had told her the yard was large and level, bounded by hedges grown wild, but she was cautious at first.

The morning breeze was cool, the sun warm. She stood in the yard and let the wind toss the seed heads of the elderberry through her hands. The wind found the creases of her body, fresh from the shower. She raised her arms to it and the wind blew cool beneath her breasts and arms and between her legs. Bees went by. She was not afraid of them and they left her alone.

Dolarhyde woke, puzzled for an instant because he was not in his room upstairs. His yellow eyes grew wide as he remembered. An owlish turn of his head to the other pillow. Empty.

Was she wandering around the house? What might she find? Or had something happened in the night? Something to clean up. He would be suspected. He might have to run.

He looked in the bathroom, in the kitchen. Down in the basement where his other wheelchair stood. The upper floor. He didn't want to go upstairs. He had to look. His tattoo flexed as he climbed the stairs. The Dragon glowed at him from the picture in his bedroom. He could not stay in the room with the Dragon.

From an upstairs window he spotted her in the yard.

'FRANCIS.' He knew the voice came from his room. He knew it was the voice of the Dragon. This new twoness with the Dragon disoriented him. He first felt it when he put his hand on Reba's heart.

The Dragon had never spoken *to* him before. It was frightening.

'FRANCIS, COME HERE.'

He tried to shut out the voice calling him, calling him as he hurried down the stairs.

What could she have found? Grandmother's teeth had rattled in the glass, but he put them away when he brought her water. She couldn't see anything.

Freddy's tape. It was in a cassette recorder in the parlor. He checked it. The cassette was rewound to the beginning. He couldn't remember if he had rewound it after he played it on the telephone to the *Tattler*.

She must not come back in the house. He didn't know what might happen in the house. She might get a surprise. The Dragon might come down. He knew how easily she would tear.

The women saw her getting in his van. Warfield would remember them together. Hurriedly he dressed.

Reba McClane felt the cool bar of a tree trunk's shadow, and then the sun again as she wandered across the yard. She could always tell where she was by the heat of the sun and the hum of the window air conditioner. Navigation, her life's discipline, was easy here. She turned around and around, trailing her hands on the shrubs and overgrown flowers.

A cloud blocked the sun and she stopped, not knowing in which direction she faced. She listened for the air conditioner. It was off. She felt a moment of uneasiness, then clapped her hands and heard the reassuring echo from the house. Reba flipped up her watch crystal and felt the time. She'd have to wake D. soon. She needed to go home.

The screen door slammed.

'Good morning,' she said.

His keys tinkled as he came across the grass.

He approached her cautiously, as though the wind of his coming might blow her down, and saw that she was not afraid of him.

She didn't seem embarrassed or ashamed of what they had done in the night. She didn't seem angry. She didn't run from him or threaten him. He wondered if it was because she had not seen his private parts.

Reba put her arms around him and laid her head on his hard chest. His heart was going fast.

He managed to say good morning.

'I've had a really terrific time, D.'

Really? What would someone say back? 'Good. Me too.' *That seemed all right.*

Get her away from here.

'But I need to go home now,' she was saying. 'My sister's coming by to pick me up for lunch. You could come too if you like.'

'I have to go to the plant,' he said, modifying the lie he had ready.

'I'll get my purse.'

Oh no. 'I'll get it.'

Almost blind to his own true feelings, no more able to express them than a scar can blush, Dolarhyde did not know what had happened to him with Reba McClane, or why. He was confused, spiked with new fright of being Two.

She threatened him, she did not threaten him.

There was the matter of her startling live movements of acceptance in Grandmother's bed.

Often Dolarhyde did not find out what he felt until he acted. He didn't know how he felt toward Reba McClane.

An ugly incident as he drove her home enlightened him a little.

Just past the Lindbergh Boulevard exit off Interstate 70, Dolarhyde pulled into a Servco Supreme station to fill his van.

The attendant was a heavyset, sullen man with muscatel on his breath. He made a face when Dolarhyde asked him to check the oil.

The van was a quart low. The attendant jammed the oil spout into the can and stuck the spout into the engine.

Dolarhyde climbed out to pay.

The attendant seemed enthusiastic about wiping the windshield; the passenger side of the windshield. He wiped and wiped.

Reba McClane sat in the high bucket seat, her legs crossed, her skirt riding up over her knee. Her white cane lay between the seats.

The attendant started over on the windshield. He was looking up her dress.

Dolarhyde glanced up from his wallet and caught him. He reached in through the window of the van and turned the wipers on high speed, batting the attendant's fingers.

'Hey, watch that.' The attendant got busy removing the oil can from the engine compartment. He knew he was caught and he wore a sly grin until Dolarhyde came around the van to him.

'You son of a bitch.' Fast over the /s/.

'What the hell's the matter with you?' The attendant was about Dolarhyde's height and weight, but he had nowhere near the muscle. He was young to have dentures, and he didn't take care of them.

Their greenness disgusted Dolarhyde. 'What happened to your teeth?' he asked softly.

'What's it to you?'

'Did you pull them for your boyfriend, you rotten prick?' Dolarhyde stood too close.

'Get the hell away from me.'

Quietly, 'Pig. Idiot. Trash. Fool.'

With a one-hand shove Dolarhyde sent him flying back to slam against the van. The oil can and spout clattered on the asphalt.

Dolarhyde picked it up.

'Don't run. I can catch you.' He pulled the spout from the can and looked at its sharp end.

The attendant was pale. There was something in Dolarhyde's face that he had never seen before, anywhere.

For a red instant Dolarhyde saw the spout jammed in the man's chest, draining his heart. He saw Reba's face through the windshield. She was shaking her head, saying something. She was trying to find the handle to roll her window down.

'Ever had anything broken, ass-eyes?'

The attendant shook his head fast. 'I didn't mean no offense, now. Honest to God.'

Dolarhyde held the curved metal spout in front of the man's face. He held it in both hands and his chest muscles bunched as he bent it double. He pulled out the man's waistband and dropped the spout down the front of his pants.

'Keep your pig eyes to yourself.' He stuffed money for the gas in the man's shirt pocket. 'You can run now,' he said. 'But I could catch you anytime.'

Chapter Thirty-six

The tape came on Saturday in a small package addressed to Will Graham, c/o FBI Headquarters, Washington. It had been mailed in Chicago on the day Lounds was killed.

The laboratory and Latent Prints found nothing useful on the cassette case or the wrapper.

A copy of the tape went to Chicago in the afternoon pouch. Special Agent Chester brought it to Graham in the jury room at midafternoon. A memo from Lloyd Bowman was attached:

> Voiceprints verify this is Lounds. Obviously he was repeating dictation. It's a new tape, manufactured in the last three months and never used before. Behavioral Science is picking at the content. Dr Bloom should hear it when he's well enough – you decide about that.
>
> Clearly the killer's trying to rattle you.
>
> He'll do that once too often, I think.

A dry vote of confidence, much appreciated.

Graham knew he had to listen to the tape. He waited until Chester left.

He didn't want to be closed up in the jury room with it. The empty courtroom was better – some sun came in the tall windows. The cleaning women had been in and dust still hung in the sunlight.

The tape recorder was small and gray. Graham put it on a counsel table and pushed the button.

A technician's monotone: 'Case number 426238, item 814, tagged and logged, a tape cassette. This is a rerecording.'

A shift in the quality of the sound.

Graham held on to the railing of the jury box with both hands.

Freddy Lounds sounded tired and frightened.

'I have had a great privilege. I have seen . . . I have seen with wonder. . . wonder and awe . . . awe . . . the strength of the Great Red Dragon.'

The original recording had been interrupted frequently as it was made. The machine caught the clack of the stop key each time. Graham saw the finger on the key. Dragon finger.

'I lied about Him. All I wrote was lies from Will Graham. He made me write them. I have . . . I have blasphemed against the Dragon. Even so . . . the Dragon is merciful. Now I want to serve Him. He . . . has helped me understand . . . His Splendor and I will praise Him. Newspapers, when you print this, always capitalize the H in "Him".

'He knows you made me lie, Will Graham. Because I was forced to lie, He will be more . . . more merciful to me than to you, Will Graham.

'Reach behind you, Will Graham . . . and feel for the small . . . knobs on the top of your pelvis. Feel your spine between them . . . that is the precise spot . . . where the Dragon will snap your spine.'

Graham kept his hands on the railing. Damn if I'll feel. Did the Dragon not know the nomenclature of the iliac spine, or did he choose not to use it?

'There's much . . . for you to dread. From . . . from my own lips you'll learn a little more to dread.'

A pause before the awful screaming. Worse, the blubbering lipless cry, 'You goddanned astard you romised.'

Graham put his head between his knees until the bright spots stopped dancing in front of his eyes. He opened his mouth and breathed deep.

An hour passed before he could listen to it again.

He took the recorder into the jury room and tried to listen there. Too close. He left the tape recorder turning and went back into the courtroom. He could hear through the open door.

'I have had a great privilege . . .'

Someone was at the courtroom door. Graham recognized the young clerk from the Chicago FBI office and motioned for him to come in.

'A letter came for you,' the clerk said. 'Mr Chester sent me with it. He told me to be sure and say the postal inspector fluoroscoped it.'

The clerk pulled the letter out of his breast pocket. Heavy mauve stationery. Graham hoped it was from Molly.

'It's stamped, see?'

'Thank you.'

'Also it's payday.' The clerk handed him his check.

On the tape, Freddy screamed.

The young man flinched.

'Sorry,' Graham said.

'I don't see how you stand it,' the young man said.

'Go home,' Graham said.

He sat in the jury box to read his letter. He wanted some relief. The letter was from Dr Hannibal Lecter.

Dear Will,

A brief note of congratulations for the job you did on Mr Lounds. I admired it enormously. What a cunning boy you are!

Mr Lounds often offended me with his ignorant drivel, but he did enlighten me on one thing – your confinement in the mental hospital.

My inept attorney should have brought that out in court, but never mind.

You know, Will, you worry too much. You'd be so much more comfortable if you relaxed with yourself.

We don't invent our natures, Will; they're issued to us along with our lungs and pancreas and everything else. Why fight it?

I want to help you, Will, and I'd like to start by asking you this: When you were so depressed after you shot Mr Garrett Jacob Hobbs to death, it wasn't the *act* that got you down, was it? Really, didn't you feel so bad *because killing him felt so good?*

Think about it, but don't worry about it. Why shouldn't it feel good? It must feel good to God – He does it all the time, and are we not made in His image?

You may have noticed in the paper yesterday, God dropped a church roof on thirty-four of His worshipers in Texas Wednesday night – just as they were groveling through a hymn. Don't you think that felt good?

Thirty-four. He'd let you have Hobbs.

He got 160 Filipinos in one plane crash last week – He'll let you have measly Hobbs. He won't begrudge you one measly murder. Two now. That's all right.

Watch the papers. God always stays ahead.

Best,

Hannibal Lecter, MD

Graham knew that Lecter was dead wrong about Hobbs, but for a half-second he wondered if Lecter might be a little bit right in the case of Freddy Lounds. The enemy inside Graham agreed with any accusation.

He had put his hand on Freddy's shoulder in the *Tattler* photograph to establish that he really had told Freddy those insulting things about the Dragon. Or had he wanted to put Freddy at risk, just a little? He wondered.

The certain knowledge that he would not knowingly miss a chance at the Dragon reprieved him.

'I'm just about worn out with you crazy sons of bitches,' Graham said aloud.

He wanted a break. He called Molly, but no one answered the telephone at Willy's grandparents' house. 'Probably out in their damned motorhome,' he mumbled.

He went out for coffee, partly to assure himself that he was not hiding in the jury room.

In the window of a jewelry store he saw a delicate antique gold bracelet. It cost him most of his paycheck. He had it wrapped and stamped for mailing. Only when he was sure he was alone at the mail drop did he address it to Molly in Oregon. Graham did not realize, as Molly did, that he gave presents when he was angry.

He didn't want to go back to his jury room and work, but he had to. The thought of Valerie Leeds spurred him.

I'm sorry I can't come to the phone right now, Valerie Leeds had said.

He wished that he had known her. He wished . . . Useless, childish thought.

Graham was tired, selfish, resentful, fatigued to a child-minded state in which his standards of measurement were the first ones he learned; where the direction 'north' was Highway 61 and 'six feet' was forever the length of his father.

He made himself settle down to the minutely detailed victim profile he was putting together from a fan of reports and his own observations.

Affluence. That was one parallel. Both families were affluent. Odd that Valerie Leeds saved money on panty hose.

Graham wondered if she had been a poor child. He thought so; her own children were a little too well turned out.

Graham had been a poor child, following his father from the boatyards in Biloxi and Greenville to the lake boats on Erie. Always the new boy at school, always the stranger. He had a half-buried grudge against the rich.

Valerie Leeds might have been a poor child. He was tempted to watch his film of her again. He could do it in the courtroom. No. The Leedses were not his immediate problem. He knew the Leedses. He did not know the Jacobis.

His lack of intimate knowledge about the Jacobis plagued him. The house fire in Detroit had taken everything – family albums, probably diaries too.

Graham tried to know them through the objects they wanted, bought and used. That was all he had.

The Jacobi probate file was three inches thick, and a lot of it was lists of possessions – a new household outfitted since the move to Birmingham. *Look at all this shit.* It was all insured, listed with serial numbers as the insurance companies required. Trust a man who has been burned out to buy plenty of insurance for the next time.

The attorney, Byron Metcalf, had sent him carbons instead of Xerox copies of the insurance declarations. The carbons were fuzzy and hard to read.

Jacobi had a ski boat, Leeds had a ski boat. Jacobi had a three-wheeler, Leeds had a trail bike. Graham licked his thumb and turned the page.

The fourth item on the second page was a Chinon Pacific movie projector.

Graham stopped. How had he missed it? He had looked through every crate on every pallet in the Birmingham warehouse, alert for anything that would give him an intimate view of the Jacobis.

Where was the projector? He could crosscheck this insurance declaration against the inventory Byron Metcalf had prepared as executor when he stored the Jacobis' things. The items had been checked off by the warehouse supervisor who signed the storage contract.

It took fifteen minutes to go down the list of stored items. No projector, no camera, no film.

Graham leaned back in his chair and stared at the Jacobis smiling from the picture propped before him.

What the hell did you do with it?

Was it stolen?

Did the killer steal it?

If the killer stole it, did he fence it?

Dear God, give me a traceable fence.

Graham wasn't tired anymore. He wanted to know if anything else was missing. He looked for an hour, comparing the warehouse storage inventory with the insurance declarations. Everything was accounted for except the small precious items. They should all be on Byron Metcalf's own lockbox list of things he had put in the bank vault in Birmingham.

All of them were on the list. Except two.

'Crystal oddment box, 4" x 3", sterling silver lid' appeared on the insurance declaration, but was not in the lockbox. 'Sterling picture frame, 9 x 11 inches, worked with vines and flowers' wasn't in the vault either.

Stolen? Mislaid? They were small items, easily concealed. Usually fenced silver is melted down immediately. It would be hard to trace. But movie equipment had serial numbers inside and out. It could be traced.

Was the killer the thief?

As he stared at his stained photograph of the Jacobis, Graham felt the sweet jolt of a new connection. But when he saw the answer whole it was seedy and disappointing and small.

There was a telephone in the jury room. Graham called Birmingham Homicide. He got the three-to-eleven watch commander.

'In the Jacobi case I noticed you kept an in-and-out log at the house after it was sealed off, right?'

'Let me get somebody to look,' the watch commander said.

Graham knew they kept one. It was good procedure to record every person entering or leaving a murder scene, and Graham had been pleased to see that Birmingham did it. He waited five minutes before a clerk picked up the telephone.

'Okay, in-and-out, what do you want to know?'

'Is Niles Jacobi, son of the deceased – is he on it?'

'Umm-hmmm, yep. July 2, 7 P.M. He had permission to get personal items.'

'Did he have a suitcase, does it say?'

'Nope. Sorry.'

Byron Metcalf's voice was husky and his breathing heavy when he answered the telephone. Graham wondered what he was doing.

'Hope I didn't disturb you.'

'What can I do for you, Will?'

'I need a little help with Niles Jacobi.'

'What's he done now?'

'I think he lifted a few things out of the Jacobi house after they were killed.'

'Ummm.'

'There's a sterling picture frame missing from your lockbox inventory. When I was in Birmingham I picked up a loose photograph of the family in Niles's dormitory room. It used to be in a frame – I can see the impression the mat left on it.'

'The little bastard. I gave permission for him to get his clothes and some books he needed,' Metcalf said.

'Niles has expensive friendships. This is mainly what I'm after, though – a movie projector and a movie camera are missing too. I want to know if he got them. Probably he did, but if he *didn't*, maybe the killer got them. In that case we need to get the serial numbers out to the hock shops. We need to put 'em on the national hot sheet. The frame's probably melted down by now.'

'He'll think "frame" when I get through with him.'

'One thing – if Niles took the projector, he might have kept the film. He couldn't get anything for it. I want the film. I need to see it. If you come at him from the front, he'll deny everything and flush the film if he has any.'

'Okay,' Metcalf said. 'His car title reverted to the estate. I'm executor, so I can search it without a warrant. My friend the judge won't mind papering his room for me. I'll call you.'

Graham went back to work.

Affluence. Put affluence in the profile the police would use.

Graham wondered if Mrs Leeds and Mrs Jacobi ever did their marketing in tennis clothes. That was a fashionable thing to do in some areas. It was a dumb thing to do in some areas because it was double provocative – arousing class resentment and lust at the same time.

Graham imagined them pushing grocery carts, short pleated skirts brushing the brown thighs, the little balls on their sweat socks winking – passing the husky man with the barracuda eyes who was buying cold lunch meat to gnaw in his car.

How many families were there with three children and a pet, and only common locks between them and the Dragon as they slept?

When Graham pictured possible victims, he saw clever, successful people in graceful houses.

But the next person to confront the Dragon did not have children or a pet, and there was no grace in his house. The next person to confront the Dragon was Francis Dolarhyde.

Chapter Thirty-seven

The thump of weights on the attic floor carried through the old house.

Dolarhyde was lifting, straining, pumping more weight than he had ever lifted. His costume was different; sweatpants covered his tattoo. The sweatshirt hung over *The Great Red Dragon and the Woman Clothed with the Sun*. The kimono hung on the wall like the shed skin of a tree snake. It covered the mirror.

Dolarhyde wore no mask.

Up. Two hundred and eighty pounds from the floor to his chest in one heave. Now over his head.

'WHOM ARE YOU THINKING ABOUT?'

Startled by the voice, he nearly dropped the weight, swayed beneath it. Down. The plates thudded and clanked on the floor.

He turned, his great arms hanging, and stared in the direction of the voice.

'WHOM ARE YOU THINKING ABOUT?'

It seemed to come from behind the sweatshirt, but its rasp and volume hurt his throat.

'WHOM ARE YOU THINKING ABOUT?'

He knew who spoke and he was frightened. From the beginning, he and the Dragon had been one. He was Becoming and the Dragon was his higher self. Their bodies, voices, wills were one.

Not now. Not since Reba. Don't think Reba.

'WHO IS ACCEPTABLE?' the Dragon asked.

'Mrs . . . erhman – herman.' It was hard for Dolarhyde to say.

'SPEAK UP. I CAN'T UNDERSTAND YOU. WHOM ARE YOU THINK-ING ABOUT?'

Dolarhyde, his face set, turned to the barbell. Up. Over his head. Much harder this time.

'Mrs . . . erhman wet in the water.'

'YOU THINK ABOUT YOUR LITTLE BUDDY, DON'T YOU? YOU WANT HER TO BE YOUR LITTLE BUDDY, DON'T YOU?'

The weight came down with a thud.

'I on't have a li'l . . . huddy.' With the fear his speech was failing. He had to occlude his nostrils with his upper lip.

'A STUPID LIE.' The Dragon's voice was strong and clear. He said the /s/ without effort. 'YOU FORGET THE BECOMING. PREPARE FOR THE SHERMANS. LIFT THE WEIGHT.'

Dolarhyde seized the barbell and strained. His mind strained with his body. Desperately he tried to think of the Shermans. He forced himself to think of the weight of Mrs Sherman in his arms. Mrs Sherman was next. It was Mrs Sherman. He was fighting Mr Sherman in the dark. Holding him down until loss of blood made Sherman's heart quiver like a bird. It was the only heart he heard. He didn't hear Reba's heart. He didn't.

Fear leeched his strength. He got the weight up to his thighs, could not make the turn up to his chest. He thought of the Shermans ranged around him, eyes wide, as he took the Dragon's due. It was no good. It was hollow, empty. The weight thudded down.

'NOT ACCEPTABLE.'

'Mrs . . .'

'YOU CAN'T EVEN SAY "MRS SHERMAN." YOU NEVER INTEND TO TAKE THE SHERMANS. YOU WANT REBA MCCLANE. YOU WANT HER TO BE YOUR LITTLE BUDDY, DON'T YOU? YOU WANT TO BE "FRIENDS."'

'No.'

'LIE!'

'Nyus mhor a niddow wyow.'

'JUST FOR A LITTLE WHILE? YOU SNIVELING HARELIP, WHO WOULD BE FRIENDS WITH YOU? COME HERE. I'LL SHOW YOU WHAT YOU ARE.'

Dolarhyde did not move.

'I'VE NEVER SEEN A CHILD AS DISGUSTING AND DIRTY AS YOU. COME HERE.'

He went.

'TAKE DOWN THE SWEATSHIRT.'

He took it down.

'LOOK AT ME.'

The Dragon glowed from the wall.

'TAKE DOWN THE KIMONO. LOOK IN THE MIRROR.'

He looked. He could not help himself or turn his face from the scalding light. He saw himself drool.

'LOOK AT YOURSELF. I'M GOING TO GIVE YOU A SURPRISE FOR YOUR LITTLE BUDDY. TAKE OFF THAT RAG.'

Dolarhyde's hands fought each other at the waistband of his sweatpants. The sweatpants tore. He stripped them away from him with his right hand, held the rags to him with his left.

His right hand snatched the rags away from his trembling, failing left. He threw them into the corner and fell back on the mat, curling on himself like a lobster split live. He hugged himself and groaned, breathing hard, his tattoo brilliant in the harsh gym lights.

'I'VE NEVER SEEN A CHILD AS DISGUSTING AND DIRTY AS YOU. GO GET THEM.'

'aaaymah.'

'GET THEM.'

He padded from the room and returned with the Dragon's teeth.

'PUT THEM IN YOUR PALMS. LOCK YOUR FINGERS AND SQUEEZE MY TEETH TOGETHER.'

Dolarhyde's pectoral muscles bunched.

'YOU KNOW HOW THEY CAN SNAP. NOW HOLD THEM UNDER YOUR BELLY. HOLD YOURSELF BETWEEN THE TEETH.'

'no.'

'DO IT . . . NOW LOOK.'

The teeth were beginning to hurt him. Spit and tears fell on his chest.

'mleadse.'

'YOU ARE OFFAL LEFT BEHIND IN THE BECOMING. YOU ARE OFFAL AND I WILL NAME YOU. YOU ARE CUNT FACE. SAY IT.'

'i am cunt face.' He occluded his nostrils with his lips to say the words.

'SOON I WILL BE CLEANSED OF YOU,' the Dragon said effortlessly. 'WILL THAT BE GOOD?'

'good.'

'WHO WILL BE NEXT WHEN IT IS TIME?'

'mrs . . . ehrman . . .'

Sharp pain shot through Dolarhyde, pain and terrible fear.

'I'LL TEAR IT OFF.'

'reba. reba. i'll give you reba.' Already his speech was improving.

'YOU'LL GIVE ME NOTHNG. SHE IS MINE. THEY ARE ALL MINE. REBA MCCLANE AND THE SHERMANS.'

'reba and then the Shermans. the law will know.'

'I HAVE PROVIDED FOR THAT DAY. DO YOU DOUBT IT?'

'no .'

'WHO ARE YOU?'

'cunt face.'

'YOU MAY PUT AWAY MY TEETH. YOU PITIFUL WEAK HARELIP, YOU'D KEEP OUR LITTLE BUDDY FROM ME, WOULD YOU? I'LL TEAR HER APART AND RUB THE PIECES IN YOUR UGLY FACE. I'LL HANG YOU WITH HER LARGE INTESTINE IF YOU OPPOSE ME. YOU KNOW I CAN. PUT THREE HUNDRED POUNDS ON THE BAR.'

Dolarhyde added the plates to the bar. He had never lifted as much as 280 until today.

'LIFT IT.'

If he were not as strong as the Dragon, Reba would die. He knew it. He strained until the room turned red before his bulging eyes.

'i can't.'

'NO YOU CAN'T. BUT I CAN.'

Dolarhyde gripped the bar. It bowed as the weight rose to his shoulders. UP. Above his head easily. 'GOODBYE, CUNT FACE,' he said, proud Dragon, quivering in the light.

Chapter Thirty-eight

Francis Dolarhyde never got to work on Monday morning.

He started from his house exactly on time, as he always did. His appearance was impeccable, his driving precise. He put on his dark glasses when he made the turn at the Missouri River bridge and drove into the morning sun.

His Styrofoam cooler squeaked as it jiggled against the passenger seat. He leaned across and set it on the floor, remembering that he must pick up the dry ice and get the film from . . .

Crossing the Missouri channel now, moving water under him. He looked at the whitecaps on the sliding river and suddenly felt that he was sliding and the river was still. A strange, disjointed, collapsing feeling flooded him. He let up on the accelerator.

The van slowed in the outside lane and stopped. Traffic behind him was stacking up, honking. He didn't hear it.

He sat, sliding slowly northward over the still river, facing the morning sun. Tears leaked from beneath his sunglasses and fell hot on his forearms.

Someone was pecking on the window. A driver, face early-morning pale and puffed with sleep, had gotten out of a car behind him. The driver was yelling something through the window.

Dolarhyde looked at the man. Flashing blue lights were coming from the other end of the bridge. He knew he should drive. He asked his body to step on the gas, and it did. The man beside the van skipped backward to save his feet.

Dolarhyde pulled into the parking lot of a big motel near the US 270 interchange. A school bus was parked in the lot, the bell of a tuba leaning against its back window.

Dolarhyde wondered if he was supposed to get on the bus with the old people.

No, that wasn't it. He looked around for his mother's Packard.

'Get in. Don't put your feet on the seat,' his mother said.

That wasn't it either.

He was in a motel parking lot on the west side of St. Louis and he wanted to be able to Choose and he couldn't.

In six days, if he could wait that long, he would kill Reba McClane. He made a sudden high sound through his nose.

Maybe the Dragon would be willing to take the Shermans first and wait another moon.

No. He wouldn't.

Reba McClane didn't know about the Dragon. She thought she was with Francis Dolarhyde. She wanted to put her body on Francis Dolarhyde. She welcomed Francis Dolarhyde in Grandmother's bed.

'I've had a really terrific time, D.,' Reba McClane said in the yard.

Maybe she liked Francis Dolarhyde. That was a perverted, despicable thing for a woman to do. He understood that he should despise her for it, but oh God it was good.

Reba McClane was guilty of liking Francis Dolarhyde. Demonstrably guilty.

If it weren't for the power of his Becoming, if it weren't for the Dragon, he could never have taken her to his house. He would not have been capable of sex. Or would he?

'My God, man. That's so sweeeet.'

That's what she said. She said 'man.'

The breakfast crowd was coming out of the motel, passing his van. Their idle glances walked on him with many tiny feet.

He needed to think. He couldn't go home. He checked into the motel, called his office and reported himself sick. The room he got was bland and quiet. The only decorations were bad steamboat prints. Nothing glowed from the walls.

Dolarhyde lay down in his clothes. The ceiling had sparkling flecks in the plaster. Every few minutes he had to get up and urinate. He shivered, then he sweated. An hour passed.

He did not want to give Reba McClane to the Dragon. He thought about what the Dragon would do to him if he didn't serve her up.

Intense fear comes in waves; the body can't stand it for long at a time. In the heavy calm between the waves, Dolarhyde could think.

How could he keep from giving her to the Dragon? One way kept nudging him. He got up.

The light switch clacked loud in the tiled bathroom. Dolarhyde looked at the shower-curtain rod, a solid piece of one-inch pipe bolted to the bathroom walls. He took down the shower curtain and hung it over the mirror.

Grasping the pipe, he chinned himself with one arm, his toes dragging up the side of the bathtub. It was stout enough. His belt was stout enough too. He could make himself do it. He wasn't afraid of *that*.

He tied the end of his belt around the pipe in a bowline knot. The buckle end formed a noose. The thick belt didn't swing, it hung down in a stiff noose.

He sat on the toilet lid and looked at it. He wouldn't get any drop, but he could stand it. He could keep his hands off the noose until he was too weak to raise his arms.

But how could he be positive that his death would affect the Dragon, now that he and the Dragon were Two? Maybe it wouldn't. How could he be sure the Dragon then would leave her alone?

It might be days before they found his body. She would wonder where he was. In that time would she go to his house and feel around for him? Go upstairs and feel around for him and get a surprise?

The Great Red Dragon would take an hour spitting her down the stairs.

Should he call her and warn her? What could she do against Him, even warned? Nothing. She could hope to die quickly, hope that in His rage He would quickly bite deep enough.

Upstairs in Dolarhyde's house, the Dragon waited in pictures he had framed with his own hands. The Dragon waited in art books and magazines beyond number, reborn every time a photographer . . . did what?

Dolarhyde could hear in his mind the Dragon's powerful voice cursing Reba. He would curse her first, before he bit. He would curse Dolarhyde too – tell her he was nothing.

'Don't do that. Don't . . . do that,' Dolarhyde said to the echoing tile. He listened to his voice, the voice of Francis Dolarhyde, the voice that Reba McClane understood easily, his own voice. He had been ashamed of it all his life, had said bitter and vicious things to others with it.

But he had never heard the voice of Francis Dolarhyde curse him.

'Don't do that.'

The voice he heard now had never, ever cursed him. It had repeated the Dragon's abuse. The memory shamed him.

He probably was not much of a man, he thought. It occurred to him that he had never really found out about that, and now he was curious.

He had one rag of pride that Reba McClane had given him. It told him dying in a bathroom was a sorry end.

What else? What other way was there?

There was a way and when it came to him it was blasphemy, he knew. But it was a way.

He paced the motel room, paced between the beds and from the door to the windows. As he walked he practiced speaking. The words came out all right if he breathed deep between the sentences and didn't hurry.

He could talk very well between the rushes of fear. Now he had a bad one, he had one that made him retch. A calm was coming after. He waited for it and when it came he hurried to the telephone and placed a call to Brooklyn.

A junior high school band was getting on the bus in the motel parking lot. The children saw Dolarhyde coming. He had to go through them to get to his van.

A fat, round-faced boy with his Sam Browne belt all crooked put on a scowl, puffed up his chest and flexed his biceps after Dolarhyde passed. Two girls giggled. The tuba blatted out the bus window as Dolarhyde went by, and he never heard the laughter behind him.

In twenty minutes he stopped the van in the lane three hundred yards from Grandmother's house.

He mopped his face, inhaled deeply three or four times. He gripped the house key in his left hand, the steering wheel with his right.

A high keening sounded through his nose. And again, louder. Louder, louder again. Go.

Gravel showered behind the van as it shot forward, the house bouncing bigger in the windshield. The van slid sideways into the yard and Dolarhyde was out of it, running.

Inside, not looking left or right, pounding down the basement stairs, fumbling at the padlocked trunk in the basement, looking at his keys.

The trunk keys were upstairs. He didn't give himself time to think. A high humming through his nose as loud as he could to numb thought, drown out voices as he climbed the stairs at a run.

At the bureau now, fumbling in the drawer for the keys, not looking at the picture of the Dragon at the foot of the bed.

'WHAT ARE YOU DOING?'

Where were the keys, where were the keys?

'WHAT ARE YOU DOING? STOP. I'VE NEVER SEEN A CHILD AS DISGUSTING AND DIRTY AS YOU. STOP.'

His searching hands slowed.

'LOOK . . . LOOK AT ME.'

He gripped the edge of the bureau – tried not to turn to the wall. He cut his eyes painfully away as his head turned in spite of him.

'WHAT ARE YOU DOING? '

'nothing.'

The telephone was ringing, telephone ringing, telephone ringing. He picked it up, his back to the picture.

'Hey, D., how are you feeling?' Reba McClane's voice.

He cleared his throat. 'Okay' – hardly a whisper.

'I tried to call you down here. Your office said you were sick – you sound terrible.'

'Talk to me.'

'Of course I'll talk to you. What do you think I called you for? What's wrong?'

'Flu,' he said.

'Are you going to the doctor? . . . Hello? I said, are you going to the doctor?'

'Talk loud.' He scrabbled in the drawer, tried the drawer next to it.

'Have we got a bad connection? D., you shouldn't be there sick by yourself.'

'TELL HER TO COME OVER TONIGHT AND TAKE CARE OF YOU.'

Dolarhyde almost got his hand over the mouthpiece in time.

'My God, what was that? Is somebody with you?'

'The radio, I grabbed the wrong knob.'

'Hey, D., do you want me to send somebody? You don't sound so hot. I'll come myself. I'll get Marcia to bring me at lunch.'

'No.' The keys were under a belt coiled in the drawer. He had them now. He backed into the hall, carrying the telephone. 'I'm okay. I'll see you soon.' The /s/s nearly foundered him. He ran down the stairs. The phone cord jerked out of the wall and the telephone tumbled down the stairs behind him.

A scream of savage rage. 'COME HERE CUNT FACE.'

Down to the basement. In the trunk beside his case of dynamite was a small valise packed with cash, credit cards and driver's licenses in various names, his pistol, knife, and blackjack.

He grabbed the valise and ran up to the ground floor, quickly past the stairs, ready to fight if the Dragon came down them. Into the van and driving hard, fishtailing in the gravel lane.

He slowed on the highway and pulled over to the shoulder to heave yellow bile. Some of the fear went away.

Proceeding at legal speed, using his flashers well ahead of turns, carefully he drove to the airport.

Chapter Thirty-nine

Dolarhyde paid his taxi fare in front of an apartment house on Eastern Parkway two blocks from the Brooklyn Museum. He walked the rest of the way. Joggers passed him, heading for Prospect Park.

Standing on the traffic island near the IRT subway station, he got a good view of the Greek Revival building. He had never seen the Brooklyn Museum before, though he had read its guidebook – he had ordered the book when he first saw 'Brooklyn Museum' in tiny letters beneath photographs of *The Great Red Dragon and the Woman Clothed with the Sun*.

The names of the great thinkers from Confucius to Demosthenes were carved in stone above the entrance. It was an imposing building with botanical gardens beside it, a fitting house for the Dragon.

The subway rumbled beneath the street, tingling the soles of his feet. Stale air puffed from the gratings and mixed with the smell of the dye in his mustache.

Only an hour left before closing time. He crossed the street and went inside. The checkroom attendant took his valise.

'Will the checkroom be open tomorrow?' he asked.

'The museum's closed tomorrow.' The attendant was a wizened woman in a blue smock. She turned away from him.

'The people who come in tomorrow, do they use the checkroom?'

'No. The museum's closed, the checkroom's closed.'

Good. 'Thank you.'

'Don't mention it.'

Dolarhyde cruised among the great glass cases in the Oceanic Hall and the Hall of the Americas on the ground floor – Andes pottery, primitive edged weapons, artifacts and powerful masks from the Indians of the Northwest coast.

Now there were only forty minutes left before the museum closed. There was no more time to learn the ground floor. He knew where the exits and the public elevators were.

He rode up to the fifth floor. He could feel that he was closer to the Dragon now, but it was all right – he wouldn't turn a corner and run into Him.

The Dragon was not on public display; the painting had been locked away in the dark since its return from the Tate Gallery in London.

Dolarhyde had learned on the telephone that *The Great Red Dragon and the Woman Clothed with the Sun* was rarely displayed. It was almost two hundred years old and a watercolor – light would fade it.

Dolarhyde stopped in front of Albert Bierstadt's *A Storm in the Rocky Mountains – Mt Rosalie 1866*. From there he could see the locked doors of the Painting Study and Storage Department. That's where the Dragon was. Not a copy, not a photograph: the Dragon. This is where he would come tomorrow when he had his appointment.

He walked around the perimeter of the fifth floor, past the corridor of portraits, seeing nothing of the paintings. The exits were what interested him. He found the fire exits and the main stairs, and marked the location of the public elevators.

The guards were polite middle-aged men in thick-soled shoes, years of standing in the set of their legs. None was armed, Dolarhyde noted; one of the guards in the lobby was armed. Maybe he was a moonlighting cop.

The announcement of closing time came over the public-address system.

Dolarhyde stood on the pavement under the allegorical figure of Brooklyn and watched the crowd come out into the pleasant summer evening.

Joggers ran in place, waiting while the stream of people crossed the sidewalk toward the subway.

Dolarhyde spent a few minutes in the botanical gardens. Then he flagged a taxi and gave the driver the address of a store he had found in the Yellow Pages.

Chapter Forty

At 9 P.M. Monday Graham set his briefcase on the floor outside the Chicago apartment he was using and rooted in his pocket for the keys.

He had spent a long day in Detroit interviewing staff and checking employment records at a hospital where Mrs Jacobi did volunteer work before the family moved to Birmingham. He was looking for a drifter, someone who might have worked in both Detroit and Atlanta or in Birmingham and Atlanta; someone with access to a van and a wheelchair who saw Mrs Jacobi and Mrs Leeds before he broke into their houses.

Crawford thought the trip was a waste of time, but humored him. Crawford had been right. Damn Crawford. He was right too much.

Graham could hear the telephone ringing in the apartment. The keys caught in the lining of his pocket. When he jerked them out, a long thread came with them. Change spilled down the inside of his trouser leg and scattered on the floor.

'Son of a bitch.'

He made it halfway across the room before the phone stopped ringing. Maybe that was Molly trying to reach him.

He called her in Oregon.

Willy's grandfather answered the telephone with his mouth full. It was suppertime in Oregon.

'Just ask Molly to call me when she's finished,' Graham told him.

He was in the shower with shampoo in his eyes when the telephone rang again. He sluiced his head and went dripping to grab the receiver. 'Hello, Hotlips.'

'You silver-tongued devil, this is Byron Metcalf in Birmingham.'

'Sorry.'

'I've got good news and bad news. You were right about Niles Jacobi. He took the stuff out of the house. He'd gotten rid of it, but I squeezed him with some hash that was in his room and he owned up. That's the bad news – I know you hoped the Tooth Fairy stole it and fenced it.

'The good news is there's some film. I don't have it yet. Niles says there are two reels stuffed under the seat in his car. You still want it, right?'

'Sure, sure I do.'

'Well, his intimate friend Randy's using the car and we haven't caught up with him yet, but it won't be long. Want me to put the film on the first plane to Chicago and call you when it's coming?'

'Please do. That's good, Byron, thanks.'

'Nothing to it.'

Molly called just as Graham was drifting off to sleep. After they assured each other that they were all right, there didn't seem to be much to say.

Willy was having a real good time, Molly said. She let Willy say good night.

Willy had plenty more to say than just good night – he told Will the exciting news: Grandpa bought him a pony.

Molly hadn't mentioned it.

Chapter Forty-one

The Brooklyn Museum is closed to the general public on Tuesdays, but art classes and researchers are admitted.

The museum is an excellent facility for serious scholarship. The staff members are knowledgeable and accommodating; often they allow researchers to come by appointment on Tuesdays to see items not on public display.

Francis Dolarhyde came out of the IRT subway station shortly after 2 P.M. carrying his scholarly materials. He had a notebook, a Tate Gallery catalog, and a biography of William Blake under his arm.

He had a flat 9-mm pistol, a leather sap and his razor-edged fileting knife under his shirt. An elastic bandage held the weapons against his flat belly. His sport coat would button over them. A cloth soaked in chloroform and sealed in a plastic bag was in his coat pocket.

In his hand he carried a new guitar case.

Three pay telephones stand near the subway exit in the center of Eastern Parkway. One of the telephones has been ripped out. One of the others works.

Dolarhyde fed it quarters until Reba said, 'Hello.'

He could hear darkroom noises over her voice.

'Hello, Reba,' he said.

'Hey, D. How're you feeling?'

Traffic passing on both sides made it hard for him to hear. 'Okay.'

'Sounds like you're at a pay phone. I thought you were home sick.'

'I want to talk to you later.'

'Okay. Call me late, all right?'

'I need to . . . see you.'

'I want you to see me, but I can't tonight. I have to work. Will you call me?'

'Yeah. If nothing . . .'

'Excuse me?'

'I'll call.'

'I do want you to come soon, D.'

'Yeah. Good-bye . . . Reba.'

All right. Fear trickled from his breastbone to his belly. He squeezed it and crossed the street.

Entrance to the Brooklyn Museum on Tuesdays is through a single door on the extreme right. Dolarhyde went in behind four art students. The students piled their knapsacks and satchels against the wall and got out their passes. The guard behind the desk checked them.

He came to Dolarhyde.

'Do you have an appointment?'

Dolarhyde nodded. 'Painting Study, Miss Harper.'

'Sign the register, please.' The guard offered a pen.

Dolarhyde had his own pen ready. He signed 'Paul Crane.'

The guard dialed an upstairs extension. Dolarhyde turned his back to the desk and studied Robert Blum's *Vintage Festival* over the entrance while the guard confirmed his appointment. From the corner of his eye he could see one more security guard in the lobby. Yes, that was the one with the gun.

'Back of the lobby by the shop there's a bench next to the main elevators,' the desk officer said. 'Wait there. Miss Harper's coming down for you.' He handed Dolarhyde a pink-on-white plastic badge.

'Okay if I leave my guitar here?'

'I'll keep an eye on it.'

The museum was different with the lights turned down. There was twilight among the great glass cases.

Dolarhyde waited on the bench for three minutes before Miss Harper got off the public elevator.

'Mr Crane? I'm Paula Harper.'

She was younger than she had sounded on the telephone when he called from St. Louis; a sensible-looking woman, severely pretty. She wore her blouse and skirt like a uniform.

'You called about the Blake watercolor,' she said. 'Let's go upstairs and I'll show it to you. We'll take the staff elevator – this way.'

She led him past the dark museum shop and through a small room lined with primitive weapons. He looked around fast to keep his bearings. In the corner of the Americas section was a corridor which led to the small elevator.

Miss Harper pushed the button. She hugged her elbows and waited. The clear blue eyes fell on the pass, pink on white, clipped to Dolarhyde's lapel.

'That's a sixth-floor pass he gave you,' she said. 'It doesn't matter – there aren't any guards on five today. What kind of research are you doing?'

Dolarhyde had made it on smiles and nods until now. 'A paper on Butts,' he said.

'On William Butts?'

He nodded.

'I've never read much on him. You only see him in footnotes as a patron of Blake's. Is he interesting?'

'I'm just beginning. I'll have to go to England.'

'I think the National Gallery has two watercolors he did for Butts. Have you seen them yet?'

'Not yet.'

'Better write ahead of time.'

He nodded. The elevator came.

Fifth floor. He was tingling a little, but he had blood in his arms and legs. Soon it would be just yes or no. If it went wrong, he wouldn't let them take him.

She led him down the corridor of American portraits. This wasn't the way he came before. He could tell where he was. It was all right.

But something waited in the corridor for him, and when he saw it he stopped dead still.

Paula Harper realized he wasn't following and turned around.

He was rigid before a niche in the wall of portraits.

She came back to him and saw what he was staring at.

'That's a Gilbert Stuart portrait of George Washington,' she said.

No it wasn't.

'You see a similar one on the dollar bill. They call it a Lansdowne portrait because Stuart did one for the Marquis of Lansdowne to thank him for his support in the American Revolution . . . Are you all right, Mr Crane?'

Dolarhyde was pale. This was worse than all the dollar bills he had ever seen. Washington with his hooded eyes and bad false teeth stared out of the frame. My God he looked like Grandmother. Dolarhyde felt like a child with a rubber knife.

'Mr Crane, are you okay?'

Answer or blow it all. Get past this. *My God, man, that's so sweeeet.* YOU'RE THE DIRTIEST . . . No.

Say something.

'I'm taking cobalt,' he said.

'Would you like to sit down for a few minutes?' There *was* a faint medicinal smell about him.

'No. Go ahead. I'm coming.'

And you are not going to cut me, Grandmother. God damn you, I'd kill you if you weren't already dead. Already dead. Already dead. Grandmother was already dead! Dead now, dead for always. My God, man, that's so sweeeet.

The other wasn't dead though, and Dolarhyde knew it.

He followed Miss Harper through thickets of fear.

They went through double doors into the Painting Study and Storage Department. Dolarhyde looked around quickly. It was a long, peaceful room, well-lighted and filled with carousel racks of draped paintings. A row of small office cubicles were partitioned off along the wall. The door to the cubicle on the far end was ajar, and he heard typing.

He saw no one but Paula Harper.

She took him to a counter-height work table and brought him a stool.

'Wait here. I'll bring the painting to you.'

She disappeared behind the racks.

Dolarhyde undid a button at his belly.

Miss Harper was coming. She carried a flat black case no bigger than a briefcase. It was in there. How did she have the strength to carry the picture? He had never thought of it as flat. He had seen the dimensions in the catalogs – 17$^1/_8$ by 13$^1/_2$ inches – but he had paid no attention to them. He expected it to be immense. But it was small. It was small and it was *here* in a quiet room. He had never realized how much strength the Dragon drew from the old house in the orchard.

Miss Harper was saying something '. . . have to keep it in this solander box because light will fade it. That's why it's not on display very often.'

She put the case on the table and unclasped it. A noise at the double doors. 'Excuse me, I have to get the door for Julio.' She refastened the case and carried it with her to the glass doors. A man with a wheeled dolly waited outside. She held the doors open while he rolled it in.

'Over here okay?'

'Yes, thank you, Julio.'

The man went out.

Here came Miss Harper with the solander box.

'I'm sorry, Mr Crane. Julio's dusting today and getting the tarnish off some frames.' She opened the case and took out a white cardboard folder. 'You understand that you aren't allowed to touch it. I'll display it for you – that's the rule. Okay?'

Dolarhyde nodded. He couldn't speak.

She opened the folder and removed the covering plastic sheet and mat.

There it was. *The Great Red Dragon and the Woman Clothed with the Sun* – the Man-Dragon rampant over the prostrate pleading woman caught in a coil of his tail.

It was small all right, but it was powerful. Stunning. The best reproductions didn't do justice to the details and the colors.

Dolarhyde saw it clear, saw it all in an instant – Blake's handwriting on the borders, two brown spots at the right edge of the paper. It seized him hard. It was too much . . . the colors were so much stronger.

Look at the woman wrapped in the Dragon's tail. Look.

He saw that her hair was the exact color of Reba McClane's. He saw that he was twenty feet from the door. He held in voices.

I hope I didn't shock you, said Reba McClane.

'It appears that he used chalk as well as watercolor,' Paula Harper was saying. She stood at an angle so that she could see what he was doing. Her eyes never left the painting.

Dolarhyde put his hand inside his shirt.

Somewhere a telephone was ringing. The typing stopped. A woman stuck her head out of the far cubicle.

'Paula, telephone for you. It's your mother.'

Miss Harper did not turn her head. Her eyes never left Dolarhyde or the painting. 'Would you take a message?' she said. 'Tell her I'll call her back.'

The woman disappeared into the office. In a moment the typing started again.

Dolarhyde couldn't hold it anymore. Play for it all, right now.

But the Dragon moved first. 'I'VE NEVER SEEN –'

'What?' Miss Harper's eyes were wide.

' – a rat that big!' Dolarhyde said, pointing. 'Climbing that frame!'

Miss Harper was turning. 'Where?'

The blackjack slid out of his shirt. With his wrist more than his arm, he tapped the back of her skull. She sagged as Dolarhyde grabbed a handful of her blouse and clapped the chloroform rag over her face. She made a high sound once, not overloud, and went limp.

He eased her to the floor between the table and the racks of paintings, pulled the folder with the watercolor to the floor, and squatted over her. Rustling, wadding, hoarse breathing and a telephone ringing.

The woman came out of the far office.

'Paula?' She looked around the room. 'It's your mother,' she called. 'She needs to talk to you *now*.'

She walked behind the table. 'I'll take care of the visitor if you . . .' She saw them then. Paula Harper on the floor, her hair across her face, and squatting over her, his pistol in his hand, Dolarhyde stuffing the last bite of the watercolor in his mouth. Rising, chewing, running. Toward her.

She ran for her office, slammed the flimsy door, grabbed at the phone and knocked it to the floor, scrambled for it on her hands and knees and tried to dial on the busy line as her door caved in. The lighted dial burst in bright colors at the impact behind her ear. The receiver fell quacking to the floor.

Dolarhyde in the staff elevator watched the indicator lights blink down, his gun held flat across his stomach, covered by his books.

First floor.

Out into the deserted galleries. He walked fast, his running shoes whispering on the terrazzo. A wrong turn and he was passing the whale masks, the great mask of Sisuit, losing seconds, running now into the presence of the Haida high totems and lost. He ran to the totems, looked left, saw the primitive edged weapons and knew where he was.

He peered around the corner at the lobby.

The desk officer stood at the bulletin board, thirty feet from the reception desk.

The armed guard was closer to the door. His holster creaked as he bent to rub a spot on the toe of his shoe.

If they fight, drop him first. Dolarhyde put the gun under his belt and buttoned his coat over it. He walked across the lobby, unclipping his pass.

The desk officer turned when he heard the footsteps.

'Thank you,' Dolarhyde said. He held up his pass by the edges, then dropped it on the desk.

The guard nodded. 'Would you put it through the slot there, please?'

The reception desk telephone rang.

The pass was hard to pick up off the glass top.

The telephone rang again. Hurry.

Dolarhyde got hold of the pass, dropped it through the slot. He picked up his guitar case from the pile of knapsacks.

The guard was coming to the telephone.

Out the door now, walking fast for the botanical gardens, he was ready to turn and fire if he heard pursuit.

Inside the gardens and to the left, Dolarhyde ducked into a space between a small shed and a hedge. He opened the guitar case and dumped out a tennis racket, a tennis ball, a towel, a folded grocery sack and a big bunch of leafy celery.

Buttons flew as he tore off his coat and shirt in one move and stepped out of his trousers. Underneath he wore a Brooklyn College T-shirt and warm-up pants. He stuffed his books and clothing into the grocery bag, then the weapons. The celery stuck out the top. He wiped the handle and clasps of the case and shoved it under the hedge.

Cutting across the gardens now toward Prospect Park, the towel around his neck, he came out onto Empire Boulevard. Joggers were ahead of him. As he followed the joggers into the park, the first police cruisers screamed past. None of the joggers paid any attention to them. Neither did Dolarhyde.

He alternated jogging and walking, carrying his grocery bag and racket and bouncing his tennis ball, a man cooling off from a hard workout who had stopped by the store on the way home.

He made himself slow down; he shouldn't run on a full stomach. He could choose his pace now.

He could choose anything.

Chapter Forty-two

Crawford sat in the back row of the jury box eating Redskin peanuts while Graham closed the courtroom blinds.

'You'll have the profile for me later this afternoon, I take it,' Crawford said. 'You told me Tuesday; this is Tuesday.'

'I'll finish it. I want to watch this first.'

Graham opened the express envelope from Byron Metcalf and dumped out the contents – two dusty rolls of home-movie film, each in a plastic sandwich bag.

'Is Metcalf pressing charges against Niles Jacobi?'

'Not for theft – he'll probably inherit anyway – he and Jacobi's brother,' Graham said. 'On the hash, I don't know. Birmingham DA's inclined to break his chops.'

'Good,' Crawford said.

The movie screen swung down from the courtroom ceiling to face the jury box, an arrangement which made it easy to show jurors filmed evidence.

Graham threaded the projector.

'On checking the newsstands where the Tooth Fairy could have gotten a *Tattler* – so fast I've had reports back from Cincinnati, Detroit, and a bunch from Chicago,' Crawford said. 'Various weirdos to run down.'

Graham started the film. It was a fishing movie.

The Jacobi children hunkered on the bank of a pond with cane poles and bobbers.

Graham tried not to think of them in their small boxes in the ground. He tried to think of them just fishing.

The girl's cork bobbed and disappeared. She had a bite.

Crawford crackled his peanut sack. 'Indianapolis is dragging ass on questioning newsies and checking the Servco Supreme stations,' he said.

'Do you want to watch this or what?' Graham said.

Crawford was silent until the end of the two-minute film. 'Terrific, she caught a perch,' he said. 'Now the profile –'

'Jack, you were in Birmingham right after it happened. I didn't get there for a month. You saw the house while it was still their house – I didn't. It was stripped and remodeled when I got there. Now, for Christ's sake let me look at these people and then I'll finish the profile.'

He started the second film.

A birthday party appeared on the screen in the courtroom. The Jacobis were seated around a dining table. They were singing.

Graham lip-read 'Haaappy Birth-day to you.'

Eleven-year-old Donald Jacobi faced the camera. He was seated at the end of the table with the cake in front of him. The candles reflected in his glasses.

Around the corner of the table, his brother and sister were side by side watching him as he blew out the candles.

Graham shifted in his seat.

Mrs Jacobi leaned over, her dark hair swinging, to catch the cat and dump it off the table.

Now Mrs Jacobi brought a large envelope to her son. A long ribbon trailed from it. Donald Jacobi opened the envelope and took out a big birthday card. He looked up at the camera and turned the card around. It said 'Happy Birthday – follow the ribbon.'

Bouncing progress as the camera followed the procession to the kitchen. A door there, fastened with a hook. Down the basement stairs, Donald first, then the others, following the ribbon down the steps. The end of the ribbon was tied around the handlebars of a ten-speed bicycle.

Graham wondered why they hadn't given him the bike outdoors.

A jumpy cut to the next scene, and his question was answered. Outdoors now, and clearly it had been raining hard. Water stood in the yard. The house looked different. Realtor Geehan had changed the color when he did it over after the murders. The outside basement door opened and Mr Jacobi emerged carrying the bicycle. This was the first view of him in the movie. A breeze lifted the hair combed across his bald spot. He set the bicycle ceremoniously on the ground.

The film ended with Donald's cautious first ride.

'Sad damn thing,' Crawford said, 'but we already knew that.'

Graham started the birthday film over.

Crawford shook his head and began to read something from his briefcase with the aid of a penlight.

On the screen Mr Jacobi brought the bicycle out of the basement. The basement door swung closed behind him. A padlock hung from it.

Graham froze the frame.

'There. That's what he wanted the bolt cutter for, Jack – to cut that padlock and go in through the basement. Why didn't he go in that way?'

Crawford clicked off his penlight and looked over his glasses at the screen. 'What's that?'

'I know he had a bolt cutter – he used it to trim that branch out of his way when he was watching from the woods. Why didn't he use it and go in through the basement door?'

'He couldn't.' With a small crocodile smile, Crawford waited. He loved to catch people in assumptions.

'Did he try? Did he mark it up? I never even saw that door – Geehan had put in a steel one with deadbolts by the time I got there.'

Crawford opened his jaws. 'You *assume* Geehan put it in. Geehan didn't put it in. The steel door was there when they were killed. Jacobi must have put it in – he was a Detroit guy, he'd favor deadbolts.'

'*When* did Jacobi put it in?'

'I don't know. Obviously it was after the kid's birthday – when was that? It'll be in the autopsy if you've got it here.'

'His birthday was April 14, a Monday,' Graham said, staring at the screen, his chin in his hand. 'I want to know when Jacobi changed the door.'

Crawford's scalp wrinkled. It smoothed out again as he saw the point. 'You think the Tooth Fairy cased the Jacobi house while the old door with the padlock was still there,' he said.

'He brought a bolt cutter, didn't he? How do you break in someplace with a bolt cutter?' Graham said. 'You cut padlocks, bars, or chain. Jacobi didn't have any bars or chained gates, did he?'

'No.'

'Then he went there expecting a padlock. A bolt cutter's fairly heavy and it's long. He was moving in daylight, and from where he parked he had to hike a long way to the Jacobi house. For all he knew, he might be coming back in one hell of a hurry if something went wrong. He wouldn't have carried a bolt cutter unless he knew he'd need it. He was expecting a padlock.'

'You figure he cased the place *before* Jacobi changed the door. Then he shows up to kill them, waits in the woods –'

'You can't see this side of the house from the woods.'

Crawford nodded. 'He waits in the woods. They go to bed and he moves in with his bolt cutter and finds the new door with the deadbolts.'

'Say he finds the new door. He had it all worked out, and now this,' Graham said, throwing up his hands. 'He's really pissed off, frustrated, he's hot to get in there. So he does a fast, loud pry job on the patio door. It was messy the way he went in – he woke Jacobi up and had to blow him away on the stairs. That's not like the Dragon. He's not messy that way. He's careful and he leaves nothing behind. He did a neat job at the Leedses' going in.'

'Okay, all right,' Crawford said. 'If we find out when Jacobi changed his door, maybe we'll establish the interval between when he cased it and when he killed them. The *minimum* time that elapsed, anyway. That seems like a useful thing to know. Maybe it'll match some interval the Birmingham convention and visitors bureau could show us. We can check car rentals again. This time we'll do vans too. I'll have a word with the Birmingham field office.'

Crawford's word must have been emphatic: in forty minues flat a Birmingham FBI agent, with realter Geehan in tow, was shouting to a carpenter working in the rafters of a new house. The carpenter's information was relayed in a radio patch to Chicago.

'Last week in April,' Crawford said, putting down the telephone. 'That's when they put in the new door. My God, that's two months before the Jacobis were hit. Why would he case it two months in advance?'

'I don't know, but I promise you he saw Mrs Jacobi or saw the whole family before he checked out their house. Unless he followed them down there from Detroit, he spotted Mrs Jacobi sometime between April 10, when they moved to Birmingham, and the end of April, when the door was changed. Sometime in that period he was in Birmingham. The bureau's going on with it down there?'

'Cops too,' Crawford said. 'Tell me this: how did he know there was an inside door from the basement into the house? You couldn't count on that – not in the South.'

'He saw the inside of the house, no question.'

'Has your buddy Metcalf got the Jacobi bank statements?'

'I'm sure he does.'

'Let's see what service calls they paid for between April 10 and the end of the month. I know the service calls have been checked for a couple of weeks back from the killings, but maybe we aren't looking back far enough. Same for the Leedses.'

'We always figured he looked around inside the *Leeds* house,' Graham said. 'From the alley he couldn't have seen the glass in the kitchen door. There's a latticed porch back there. But he was ready with his glass cutter. And they didn't have any service calls for three months before they were killed.'

'If he's casing this far ahead, maybe we didn't check back far enough. We will now. At the Leedses' though – when he was in the alley reading meters behind the Leeds house two days before he killed them – maybe he saw them going in the house. He could have looked in there while the porch door was open.'

'No, the doors don't line up – remember? Look here.'

Graham threaded the projector with the Leeds home movie.

The Leedses' gray Scotty perked up his ears and ran to the kitchen door. Valerie Leeds and the children came in carrying groceries. Through the kitchen door nothing but lattice was visible.

'All right, you want to get Byron Metcalf busy on the bank statement for April? Any kind of service call or purchase that a door-to-door salesman might handle. No – I'll do that while you wind up the profile. Have you got Metcalf's number?'

Seeing the Leedses preoccupied Graham. Absently he told Crawford three numbers for Byron Metcalf.

He ran the films again while Crawford used the phone in the jury room.

The Leeds film first.

There was the Leedses' dog. It wore no collar, and the neighborhood was full of dogs, but the Dragon knew which dog was theirs.

Here was Valerie Leeds. The sight of her tugged at Graham. There was the door behind her, vulnerable with its big glass pane. Her children played on the courtroom screen.

Graham had never felt as close to the Jacobis as he did to the Leedses. Their movie disturbed him now. It bothered him that he had thought of the Jacobis as chalk marks on a bloody floor.

There were the Jacobi children, ranged around the corner of the table, the birthday candles flickering on their faces.

For a flash Graham saw the blob of candle wax on the Jacobis' bedside table, the bloodstains around the corner of the bedroom at the Leedses'. Something . . .

Crawford was coming back. 'Metcalf said to ask you –'

'Don't talk to me!'

Crawford wasn't offended. He waited stock-still and his little eyes grew narrow and bright.

The film ran on, its light and shadows playing over Graham's face.

There was the Jacobis' cat. The Dragon knew it was the Jacobis' cat.

There was the inside basement door.

There was the outside basement door with its padlock. The Dragon had brought a bolt cutter.

The film ended. Finally it came off the reel and the end flapped around and around.

Everything the Dragon needed to know was on the two films.

They hadn't been shown in public, there wasn't any film club, film festi . . .

Graham looked at the familiar green box the Leeds movie came in. Their name and address were on it. And Gateway Film Laboratory, St. Louis, Mo. 63102.

His mind retrieved 'St. Louis' just as it would retrieve any telephone number he had ever seen. What about St. Louis? It was one of the places where the *Tattler* was available on Monday night, the same day it was printed – the day before Lounds was abducted.

'Oh me,' Graham said. 'Oh Jesus.'

He clamped his hands on the sides of his head to keep the thought from getting away.

'Do you still have Metcalf on the phone?'

Crawford handed him the receiver.

'Byron, it's Graham. Listen, did those reels of Jacobi film you sent – were they in any containers? . . . Sure, sure I know you would have sent 'em along. I need help bad on something. Do you have the Jacobi bank statements there? Okay, I want to know where they got movie film developed. Probably a store sent it off for them. If there're any checks to pharmacies or camera stores, we can find out where they did business. It's urgent, Byron. I'll tell you about it first chance. Birmingham FBI will start now checking the stores. If you find something, shoot it straight to them, then to us. Will you do that? Great. What? *No*, I will *not* introduce you to Hotlips.'

Birmingham FBI agents checked four camera stores before they found the one where the Jacobis traded. The manager said all customers' film was sent to one place for processing.

Crawford had watched the films twelve times before Birmingham called back. He took the message.

Curiously formal, he held out his hand to Graham. 'It's Gateway,' he said.

Chapter Forty-three

Crawford was stirring an Alka-Seltzer in a plastic glass when the stewardess's voice came over the 727's public-address system.

'Passenger Crawford, please?'

When he waved from his aisle seat, she came aft to him. 'Mr Crawford, would you go to the cockpit, please?'

Crawford was gone for four minutes. He slid back into the seat beside Graham.

'Tooth Fairy was in New York today.'

Graham winced and his teeth clicked together.

'No. He just tapped a couple of women on the head at the Brooklyn Museum and, listen to this, he *ate* a painting.'

'Ate it?'

'Ate it. The Art Squad in New York snapped to it when they found out what he ate. They got two partial prints off the plastic pass he used and they flashed them down to Price a little while ago. When Price put 'em together on the screen, he rang the cherries. No ID, but it's the same thumb that was on the Leeds kid's eye.'

'New York,' Graham said.

'Means nothing, he was in New York today. He could still work at Gateway. If he does, he was off the job today. Makes it easier.'

'What did he eat?'

'It was a thing called *The Great Red Dragon and the Woman Clothed with the Sun*. William Blake drew it, they said.'

'What about the women?'

'He's got a sweet touch with the sap. Younger one's just at the hospital for observation. The older one had to have four stitches. Mild concussion.'

'Could they give a description?'

'The younger one did. Quiet, husky, dark mustache and hair – a wig, I think. The guard at the door said the same thing. The older woman – he could've been in a rabbit suit for all she saw.'

'But he didn't kill anybody.'

'Odd,' Crawford said. 'He'd have been better off to wax 'em both – he could have been sure of his lead time leaving and saved himself a description or two. Behavioral Science called Bloom in the hospital about it. You know what he said? Bloom said maybe he's trying to stop.'

Chapter Forty-four

Dolarhyde heard the flaps moan down. The lights of St. Louis wheeled slowly beneath the black wing. Under his feet the landing gear rumbled into a rush of air and locked down with a thud.

He rolled his head on his shoulders to ease the stiffness in his powerful neck.

Coming home.

He had taken a great risk, and the prize he brought back was the power to choose. He could choose to have Reba McClane alive. He could have her to talk to, and he could have her startling and harmless mobility in his bed.

He did not have to dread his house. He had the Dragon in his belly now. He could go into his house, walk up to a copy Dragon on the wall and wad him up if he wanted to.

He did not have to worry about feeling Love for Reba. If he felt Love for her, he could toss the Shermans to the Dragon and ease it that way, go back to Reba calm and easy, and treat her well.

From the terminal Dolarhyde telephoned her apartment. Not home yet. He tried Baeder Chemical. The night line was busy. He thought of Reba walking toward the bus stop after work, tapping along with her cane, her raincoat over her shoulders.

He drove to the film laboratory through the light evening traffic in less than fifteen minutes.

She wasn't at the bus stop. He parked on the street behind Baeder

Chemical, near the entrance closest to the darkrooms. He'd tell her he was here, wait until she had finished working, and drive her home. He was proud of his new power to choose. He wanted to use it.

There were things he could catch up on in his office while he waited.

Only a few lights were on in Baeder Chemical.

Reba's darkroom was locked. The light above the door was neither red nor green. It was off. He pressed the buzzer. No response.

Maybe she had left a message in his office.

He heard footsteps in the corridor.

The Baeder supervisor, Dandridge, passed the darkroom area and never looked up. He was walking fast carrying a thick bundle of buff personnel files under his arm.

A small crease appeared in Dolarhyde's forehead.

Dandridge was halfway across the parking lot, heading for the Gateway building, when Dolarhyde came out of Baeder behind him.

Two delivery vans and half a dozen cars were on the lot. That Buick belonged to Fisk, Gateway's personnel director. What were they doing?

There was no night shift at Gateway. Much of the building was dark. Dolarhyde could see by the red exit signs in the corridor as he went toward his office. The lights were on behind the frosted glass door of the personnel department. Dolarhyde heard voices in there, Dandridge's for one, and Fisk's.

A woman's footsteps coming. Fisk's secretary turned the corner into the corridor ahead of Dolarhyde. She had a scarf tied over her curlers and she carried ledgers from Accounting. She was in a hurry. The ledgers were heavy, a big armload. She pecked on Fisk's office door with her toe.

Will Graham opened it for her.

Dolarhyde froze in the dark hall. His gun was in his van.

The office door closed again.

Dolarhyde moved fast, his running shoes quiet on the smooth floor. He put his face close to the glass of the exit door and scanned the parking lot. Movement now under the floodlights. A man moving. He was beside one of the delivery vans and he had a flashlight. Flicking something. He was dusting the outside mirror for fingerprints.

Behind Dolarhyde, somewhere in the corridors, a man was walking. Get away from the door. He ducked around the corner and down the stairs to the basement and the furnace room on the opposite side of the building.

By standing on a workbench he could reach the high windows that opened at ground level behind the shrubbery. He rolled over the sill and came up on his hands and knees in the bushes, ready to run or fight.

Nothing moved on this side of the building. He stood up, put a hand in his pocket and strolled across the street. Running when the sidewalk was dark, walking as cars went by, he made a long loop around Gateway and Baeder Chemical.

His van stood at the curb behind Baeder. There was no place to hide close to it. All right. He sprinted across the street and leaped in, clawing at his valise.

Full clip in the automatic. He jacked a round into the chamber and laid the pistol on the console, covering it with a T-shirt.

Slowly he drove away – don't catch the light red – slowly around the corner and into the scattered traffic.

He had to think now and it was hard to think.

It had to be the films. Graham knew about the films somehow. Graham knew *where*. He didn't know *who*. If he knew who, he wouldn't need personnel records. Why accounting records too? Absences, that's why. Match absences against the dates when the Dragon struck. No, those were Saturdays, except for Lounds. Absences on the days before those Saturdays; he'd look for those. Fool him there – no workmen's compensation slips were kept for management.

Dolarhyde drove slowly up Lindberg Boulevard, gesturing with his free hand as he ticked off the points.

They were looking for fingerprints. He'd given them no chance for fingerprints – except maybe on the plastic pass at Brooklyn Museum. He'd picked it up in a hurry, mostly by the edges.

They must have a print. Why fingerprint if they didn't have something to match it to?

They were checking that van for prints. No time to see if they were checking cars too.

Van. Carrying the wheelchair with Lounds in it – that tipped them. Or maybe somebody in Chicago saw the van. There were a lot of vans at Gateway, private vans, delivery vans.

No, Graham just knew he had a van. Graham knew because he knew. Graham knew. Graham knew. The son of a bitch was a monster.

They'd fingerprint everyone at Gateway and Baeder too. If they didn't spot him tonight, they'd do it tomorrow. He had to run forever with his *face* on every bulletin board in every post office and police station. It was all coming to pieces. He was puny and small before them.

'Reba,' he said aloud. Reba couldn't save him now. They were closing in on him, and he was nothing but a puny hareli–

'ARE YOU SORRY NOW THAT YOU BETRAYED ME?'

The Dragon's voice rumbled from deep within him, deep as the shredded painting in his bowels.

'I didn't. I just wanted to choose. You called me –'

'GIVE ME WHAT I WANT AND I'LL SAVE YOU.'

'No. I'll run.'

'GIVE ME WHAT I WANT AND YOU'LL HEAR GRAHAM'S SPINE SNAP.'

'No.'

'NOW ADMIRE WHAT YOU DID TODAY. WE'RE CLOSE NOW. WE CAN BE ONE AGAIN. DO YOU FEEL ME INSIDE YOU? YOU DO, DON'T YOU?'

'Yes.'

'AND YOU KNOW I CAN SAVE YOU. YOU KNOW THEY'LL SEND YOU TO A PLACE WORSE THAN BROTHER BUDDY'S. GIVE ME WHAT I WANT AND YOU'LL BE FREE.'

'No.'

'THEY'LL KILL YOU. YOU'LL JERK ON THE GROUND.'

'No '

'WHEN YOU'RE GONE SHE'LL FUCK OTHER PEOPLE, SHE'LL – '

'No! Shut up.'

'SHE'LL FUCK OTHER PEOPLE, PRETTY PEOPLE, SHE'LL PUT THEIR – '

'Stop it. Shut up.'

'SLOW DOWN AND I WON'T SAY IT.'

Dolarhyde's foot lifted on the accelerator.

'THAT'S GOOD. GIVE ME WHAT I WANT AND IT CAN'T HAPPEN. GIVE IT TO ME AND THEN I'LL ALWAYS LET YOU CHOOSE, YOU CAN ALWAYS CHOOSE, AND YOU'LL SPEAK WELL, I WANT YOU TO SPEAK WELL, SLOW DOWN, THAT'S RIGHT, SEE THE SERVICE STATION? PULL OVER THERE AND LET ME TALK TO YOU . . .'

Chapter Forty-five

Graham came out of the office suite and rested his eyes for a moment in the dim hallway. He was restive, uneasy. This was taking too long.

Crawford was sifting the 380 Gateway and Baeder employees as fast and well as it could be done – the man was a marvel at this kind of job – but time was passing and secrecy could be maintained only so long.

Crawford had kept the working group at Gateway to a minimum. ('We want to find him, not spook him,' Crawford had told them. 'If we can spot him tonight, we can take him outside the plant, maybe at his house or on the lot.')

The St. Louis police department was cooperating. Lieutenant Fogel of St. Louis homicide and one sergeant came quietly in an unmarked car, bringing a Datafax.

Wired to a Gateway telephone, in minutes the Datafax was transmitting the employment roll simultaneously to the FBI identification section in Washington and the Missouri Department of Motor Vehicles.

In Washington, the names would be checked against both the civil and criminal fingerprint records. Names of Baeder employees with security clearances were flagged for faster handling.

The Department of Motor Vehicles would check for ownership of vans.

Only four employees were brought in – the personnel manager, Fisk; Fisk's secretary; Dandridge from Baeder Chemical; and Gateway's chief accountant.

No telephones were used to summon the employees to this late-night meeting at the plant. Agents called at their houses and stated their business privately. ('Look 'em over before you tell 'em why you want 'em,' Crawford said. 'And don't let them use the telephone after. This kind of news travels fast.')

They had hoped for a quick identification from the teeth. None of the four employees recognized them.

Graham looked down the long corridors lit with red exit signs. Damn it felt right.

What else could they do tonight?

Crawford had requested that the woman from the Brooklyn Museum – Miss Harper – be flown out as soon as she could travel. Probably that would be in the morning. The St. Louis police department had a good surveillance van. She could sit in it and watch the employees go in.

If they didn't hit it tonight, all traces of the operation would be removed from Gateway before work started in the morning. Graham didn't kid himself – they'd be lucky to have a whole day to work before the word got out at Gateway. The Dragon would be watching for anything suspicious. He would fly.

Chapter Forty-six

A late supper with Ralph Mandy had seemed all right. Reba McClane knew she had to tell him sometime, and she didn't believe in leaving things hanging.

Actually, she thought Mandy knew what was coming when she insisted on going dutch.

She told him in the car as he took her home; that it was no big deal, she'd had a lot of fun with him and wanted to be his friend, but she was involved with somebody now.

Maybe he was hurt a little, but she knew he was relieved a little too. He was pretty good about it, she thought.

At her door he didn't ask to come in. He did ask to kiss her goodbye, and she responded gladly. He opened her door and gave her the keys. He waited until she was inside and had closed the door and locked it.

When he turned around Dolarhyde shot him in the throat and twice in the chest. Three putts from the silenced pistol. A scooter is louder.

Dolarhyde lifted Mandy's body easily, laid him between the shrubs and the house and left him there.

Seeing Reba kiss Mandy had stabbed Dolarhyde deep. Then the pain left him for good.

He still looked and sounded like Francis Dolarhyde – the Dragon was a very good actor; he played Dolarhyde well.

Reba was washing her face when she heard the doorbell. It rang four times before she got there. She touched the chain, but didn't take it off.

'Who is it?'

'Francis Dolarhyde.'

She eased the door open, still on the chain. 'Tell me again.'

'Dolarhyde. It's me.'

She knew it was. She took off the chain.

Reba did not like surprises. 'I thought you said you'd call me, D.'

'I would have. But this is an emergency, really,' he said, clapping the chloroformed cloth over her face as he stepped inside.

The street was empty. Most of the houses were dark. He carried her to the van. Ralph Mandy's feet stuck out of the shrubbery into the yard. Dolarhyde didn't bother with him anymore.

She woke on the ride. She was on her side, her cheek in the dusty carpet of the van, transmission whine loud in her ear.

She tried to bring her hands to her face. The movement mashed her bosom. Her forearms were stuck together.

She felt them with her face. They were bound together from her elbows to her wrists with what felt like soft strips of cloth. Her legs were tied the same way from knees to ankles. Something was across her mouth.

What . . . what . . . ? D. was at the door, and then . . . She remembered twisting her face away and the terrible strength of him. Oh Lord . . . what was it . . . ? D. was at the door and then she was choking something cold and she tried to twist her face away but there was a terrible grip on her head.

She was in D.'s van now. She recognized the resonances. The van was going. Fear ballooned in her. Her instinct said be quiet, but the fumes were in her throat, chloroform and gasoline. She retched against the gag.

D.'s voice. 'It won't be long now.'

She felt a turn and they were on gravel now, rocks pinging under the fenders and floorboard.

He's crazy. All right. That's it: Crazy.

'Crazy' is a fearsome word.

What was it? Ralph Mandy. He must have seen them at her house. It set him off.

Christ Jesus, get it all ready. A man had tried to slap her once at Reiker Institute. She was quiet and he couldn't find her – he couldn't see either. This one could fucking well see. Get it all ready. Get ready to talk. God he could kill me with this gag in my mouth. God he could be killing me and not understand what I was saying.

Be ready. Have it all ready and don't say 'Huh?' Tell him he can back out, no damage. I won't tell. Be passive as long as you can. If you can't be passive, wait until you can find his eyes.

The van stopped. The van rocked as he got out. Side door sliding open. Grass and hot tires on the air. Crickets. He came in the van.

In spite of herself she squealed into the gag and twisted her face away from him when he touched her.

Soft pats on the shoulder didn't stop her writhing. A stinging slap across the face did.

She tried to talk into the gag. She was lifted, carried. His footsteps hollow on the ramp. She was sure where she was now. His house. Where in his house? Clock ticking to the right. Rug, then floor. The bedroom where they did it. She was sinking in his arms, felt the bed under her.

She tried to talk into the gag. He was leaving. Noise outside. Van door slammed. Here he comes. Setting something on the floor – metal cans.

She smelled gasoline.

'Reba.' D.'s voice all right, but so calm. So terribly calm and strange. 'Reba. I don't know what to . . . say to you. You felt so good, and you don't know what I did for you. And I was wrong, Reba. You made me weak and then you hurt me.'

She tried to talk into the gag.

'If I untie you and let you sit up, will you be good? Don't try to run. I can catch you. Will you be good?'

She twisted her head toward the voice to nod.

A touch of cold steel against her skin, whisper of a knife through cloth and her arms were free. Now her legs. Her cheeks were wet where the gag came off.

Carefully and slowly she sat up in the bed. Take your best shot.

'D.,' she said, 'I didn't know you cared this much about me. I'm glad you feel that way but, see, you scared me with this.'

No answer. She knew he was there.

'D., was it old dumb Ralph Mandy that made you mad? Did you see him at my house? That's it, isn't it? I was telling him I don't want to see him anymore. Because I want to see you. I'm never going to see Ralph again.'

'Ralph died,' Dolarhyde said. 'I don't think he liked it very much.'

Fantasy. He's making it up Jesus do I hope. I've never hurt you, D. I never wanted to. Let's just be friends and fuck and have a good time and forget about this.'

'Shut up,' he said calmly. 'I'll tell you something. The most important thing you'll ever hear. Sermon-on-the-Mount important. Ten-Commandments important. Got it?'

'Yes, D. I – '

'Shut up. Reba, some remarkable events have happened in Birmingham and Atlanta. Do you know what I'm talking about?'

She shook her head.

'It's been on the news a lot. Two groups of people were changed. Leeds. And Jacobi. The police think they were murdered. Do you know now?'

She started to shake her head. Then she did know and slowly she nodded.

'Do you know what they call the Being that visited those people? You can say.'

'The Tooth – '

A hand gripped her face, shutting off the sound.

'Think carefully and answer correctly.'

'It's Dragon something. Dragon . . . Red Dragon.'

He was close to her. She could feel his breath on her face.

'I AM THE DRAGON.'

Leaping back, driven by the volume and terrible timbre of the voice, she slammed against the headboard.

'The Dragon wants you, Reba. He always has. I didn't want to give you to Him. I did a thing for you today so He couldn't have you. And I was wrong.'

This was D., she could talk to D. 'Please. Please don't let him have me. You won't, please don't, you wouldn't – I'm for *you*. Keep me with you. You like me, I know you do.'

'I haven't made up my mind yet. Maybe I can't help giving you to Him. I don't know. I'm going to see if you do as I tell you. Will you? Can I depend on you?'

'I'll try. I will try. Don't scare me too much or I can't.'

'Get up, Reba. Stand by the bed. Do you know where you are in the room?'

She nodded.

'You know where you are in the house, don't you? You wandered around in the house while I was asleep, didn't you?'

'Asleep?'

'Don't be stupid. When we spent the night here. You went through the house, didn't you? Did you find something odd? Did you take it and show it to somebody? Did you do that, Reba?'

'I just went outside. You were asleep and I went outside. I promise.'

'Then you know where the front door is, don't you?'

She nodded.

'Reba, feel on my chest. Bring your hands up slowly.'

Try for his eyes?

His thumb and fingers touched lightly on each side of her windpipe. 'Don't do what you're thinking, or I'll squeeze. Just feel on my chest. Just at my throat. Feel the key on the chain? Take it off over my head. Careful . . . that's right. Now I'm going to see if I can trust you. Go close the front door and lock it and bring me back the key. Go ahead. I'll wait right here. Don't try to run. I can catch you.'

She held the key in her hand, the chain tapping against her thigh. It was harder navigating in her shoes, but she kept them on. The ticking clock helped.

Rug, then floor, rug again. Loom of the sofa. Go to the right.

What's my best shot? Which? Fool along with him or go for it? Did the others fool along with him? She felt dizzy from deep breathing. Don't be dizzy. Don't be dead.

It depends on whether the door is open. Find out where he is.

'Am I going right?' She knew she was.

'It's about five more steps.' The voice was from the bedroom all right.

She felt air on her face. The door was half-open. She kept her body between the door and the voice behind her. She slipped the key in the keyhole below the knob. On the outside.

Now. Through the door fast making herself pull it to and turn the key. Down the ramp, no cane, trying to remember where the van was, running. Running. Into what – a bush – screaming now. Screaming 'Help me. Help me. Help me, help me.' On gravel running. A truck horn far away. Highway that way, a fast walk and trot and run, fast as she could, veering when she felt grass instead of gravel, zigging down the lane.

Behind her footsteps coming fast and hard, running in the gravel. She stopped and picked up a handful of rocks, waited until he was close and flung them, heard them thump on him.

A shove on the shoulder spun her, a big arm under her chin, around her neck, squeezing, squeezing, blood roared in her ears. She kicked backward, hit a shin as it became increasingly quiet.

Chapter Forty-seven

In two hours, the list of white male employees twenty to fifty years old who owned vans was completed. There were twenty-six names on it.

Missouri DMV provided hair color from driver's-license information, but it was not used as an exclusionary factor; the Dragon might wear a wig.

Fisk's secretary, Miss Trillman, made copies of the list and passed them around.

Lieutenant Fogel was going down the list of names when his beeper went off.

Fogel spoke to his headquarters briefly on the telephone, then put his hand over the receiver. 'Mr Crawford . . . Jack, one Ralph Mandy, white male, thirty-eight, was found shot to death a few minutes ago in University City – that's in the middle of town, close to Washington University – he was in the front yard of a house occupied by a woman named Reba McClane. The neighbors said she works for Baeder. Her door's unlocked, she's not home.'

'Dandridge!' Crawford called. 'Reba McClane, what about her?'

'She works in the darkroom. She's blind. She's from someplace in Colorado – '

'You know a Ralph Mandy?'

'Mandy?' Dandridge said. 'Randy Mandy?'

'*Ralph* Mandy, he work here?'

A check of the roll showed he didn't.

'Coincidence maybe,' Fogel said.

'Maybe,' Crawford said.

'I hope nothing's happened to Reba,' Miss Trillman said.

'You know her?' Graham said.

'I've talked with her several times.'

'What about Mandy?'

'I don't know him. The only man I've seen her with, I saw her getting into Mr Dolarhyde's van.'

'Mr Dolarhyde's van, Miss Trillman? What color is Mr Dolarhyde's van?'

'Let's see. Dark brown, or maybe black.'

'Where does Mr Dolarhyde work?' Crawford asked.

'He's production supervisor,' Fisk said.

'Where's his office?'

'Right down the hall.'

Crawford turned to speak to Graham, but he was already moving.

Mr Dolarhyde's office was locked. A passkey from Maintenance worked.

Graham reached in and flipped on the light. He stood still in the doorway while his eyes went over the room. It was extremely neat. No personal items were anywhere in sight. The bookshelf held only technical manuals.

The desk lamp was on the left side of the chair, so he was right-handed. Need a left thumbprint fast off a right-handed man.

'Let's toss it for a clipboard,' he said to Crawford, behind him in the hall. 'He'll use his left thumb on the clip.'

They had started on the drawers when the desk appointment calendar caught Graham's eye. He flipped back through the scribbled pages to Saturday, June 28, the date of the Jacobi killings.

The calendar was unmarked on the Thursday and Friday before that weekend.

He flipped forward to the last week in July. The Thursday and Friday were blank. There was a note on Wednesday. It said: 'Am 552 3:45-6:15.'

Graham copied the entry. 'I want to find out where this flight goes.'

'Let me do it, you go ahead here,' Crawford said. He went to a telephone across the hall.

Graham was looking at a tube of denture adhesive in the bottom desk drawer when Crawford called from the door.

'It goes to Atlanta, Will. Let's take him out.'

Chapter Forty-eight

Water cold on Reba's face, running in her hair. Dizzy. Something hard under her, sloping. She turned her head. Wood under her. A cold wet towel wiped her face.

'Are you all right, Reba?' Dolarhyde's calm voice.

She shied from the sound. 'Uhh-hh.'

'Breathe deeply.'

A minute passed.

'Do you think you can stand up? Try to stand up.'

She could stand with his arm around her. Her stomach heaved. He waited until the spasm passed.

'Up the ramp. Do you remember where you are?'

She nodded.

'Take the key out of the door, Reba. Come inside. Now lock it and put the key around my neck. Hang it around my neck. Good. Let's just be sure it's locked.'

She heard the knob rattle.

'That's good. Now go in the bedroom, you know the way.'

She stumbled and went down on her knees, her head bowed. He lifted her by the arms and supported her into the bedroom.

'Sit in this chair.'

She sat.

'GIVE HER TO ME NOW.'

She struggled to rise; big hands on her shoulders held her down.

'Sit still or I can't keep Him off you,' Dolarhyde said.

Her mind was coming back. It didn't want to.

'Please try,' she said.

'Reba, it's all over for me.'

He was up, doing something. The odor of gasoline was very strong.

'Put out your hand. Feel this. Don't grab it, feel it.'

She felt something like steel nostrils, slick inside. The muzzle of a gun.

'That's a shotgun, Reba. A twelve-gauge magnum. Do you know what it will do?'

She nodded.

'Take your hand down.' The cold muzzle rested in the hollow of her throat.

'Reba, I wish I could have trusted you. I wanted to trust you.'

He sounded like he was crying.

'You felt so good.'

He *was* crying.

'So did you, D. I love it. Please don't hurt me now.'

'It's all over for me. I can't leave you to Him. You know what He'll do?'

Bawling now.

'Do you know what He'll do? He'll bite you to death. Better you go with me.'

She heard a match struck, smelled sulfur, heard a whoosh. Heat in the room. Smoke. Fire. The thing she feared most in the world. Fire. Anything was better than that. She hoped the first shot killed her. She tensed her legs to run.

Blubbering.

'Oh, Reba, I can't stand to watch you burn.'

The muzzle left her throat.

Both barrels of the shotgun went off at once as she came to her feet.

Ears numbed, she thought she was shot, thought she was dead, felt the heavy thump on the floor more than she heard it.

Smoke now and the crackle of flames. Fire. Fire brought her to herself. She felt heat on her arms and face. Out. She stepped on legs, stumbled choking into the foot of the bed.

Stoop low, they said, under the smoke. Don't run, you'll bump into things and die.

She was locked in. Locked in. Walking, stooping low, fingers trailing on the floor, she found legs – other end – she found hair, a hairy flap, put her hand in something soft below the hair. Only pulp, sharp bone splinters and a loose eye in it.

Key around his neck . . . hurry. Both hands on the chain, legs under her, snatch. The chain broke and she fell backward, scrambling up again. Turned around, confused. Trying to feel, trying to listen with her numbed ears over the crackle of the flames. Side of the bed . . . which side? She stumbled on the body, tried to listen.

BONG, BONG, the clock striking. BONG, BONG, into the living room, BONG, BONG, take a right.

Throat seared with smoke. BONG, BONG. Door here. Under the knob. Don't drop it. Click the lock. Snatch it open. Air. Down the ramp. Air. Collapsed in the grass. Up again on hands and knees, crawling.

She came up on her knees to clap, picked up the house echo and crawled away from it, breathing deep until she could stand, walk, run until she hit something, run again.

Chapter Forty-nine

Locating Francis Dolarhyde's house was not so easy. The address listed at Gateway was a post-office box in St. Charles.

Even the St. Charles sheriff's department had to check a service map at the power-company office to be sure.

The sheriff's department welcomed St. Louis SWAT to the other side of the river, and the caravan moved quietly up State Highway 94. A deputy beside Graham in the lead car showed the way. Crawford leaned between them from the back seat and sucked at something in his teeth. They met light traffic at the north end of St. Charles, a pickup full of children, a Greyhound bus, a tow truck.

They saw the glow as they cleared the northern city limits.

'That's *it*!' the deputy said. 'That's where it is!'

Graham put his foot down. The glow brightened and swelled as they roared up the highway.

Crawford snapped his fingers for the microphone.

'All units, that's his house burning. Watch it now. He may be coming out. Sheriff, let us have a roadblock here, if you will.'

A thick column of sparks and smoke leaned southeast over the fields, hanging over them now.

'Here,' the deputy said, 'turn in on this gravel.'

They saw the woman then, silhouetted black against the fire, saw her as she heard them and raised her arms to them.

And then the great fire blasted upward, outward, burning beams and window frames describing slow high arcs into the night sky, the blazing van rocked over on its side, orange tracery of the burning trees suddenly blown out and dark. The ground shuddered as the explosion whump rocked the police cars.

The woman was face down in the road. Crawford and Graham and the deputies out, running to her as fire rained in the road, some running past her with their weapons drawn.

Crawford took Reba from a deputy batting sparks from her hair.

He held her arms, face close to her, red in the firelight.

'Francis Dolarhyde,' he said. He shook her gently. 'Francis Dolarhyde, where is he?'

'He's in there,' she said, raising her stained hand toward the heat, letting it fall. 'He's dead in there.'

'You *know* that?' Crawford peered into her sightless eyes.

'I was with him.'

'Tell me, please.'

'He shot himself in the face. I put my hand on it. He set fire to the house. He shot himself. I put my hand on it. He was on the floor. I put my hand in it – can I sit down?'

'Yes,' Crawford said. He got into the back of the police car with her. He put his arms around her and let her cry into his jowl.

Graham stood in the road and watched the flames until his face was red and sore.

The winds aloft whipped smoke across the moon.

Chapter Fifty

The wind in the morning was warm and wet. It blew wisps of clouds over the blackened chimneys where Dolarhyde's house had stood. Thin smoke blew flat across the fields.

A few raindrops struck coals and exploded in tiny puffs of steam and ashes.

A fire truck stood by, its light revolving.

S.F. Aynesworth, FBI section chief, Explosives, stood with Graham upwind of the ruins, pouring coffee from a thermos.

Aynesworth winced as the local fire marshal reached into the ashes with a rake.

'Thank God it's still too hot for him in there,' he said out of the side of his mouth. He had been carefully cordial to the local authorities. To Graham, he spoke his mind. 'I got to wade it, hell. This place'll look like a fucking turkey farm soon as all the special deputies and constables finish their pancakes and take a crap. They'll be right on down to help.'

Until Aynesworth's beloved bomb van arrived from Washington, he had to make do with what he could bring on the plane. He pulled a faded Marine Corps duffel bag out of the trunk of a patrol car and unpacked his Nomex underwear and asbestos boots and coveralls.

'What did it look like when it went up, Will?'

'A flash of intense light that died down. Then it looked darker at the base. A lot of stuff was going up, window frames, flat pieces of the roof, and chunks flying sideways, tumbling in the fields. There was a shock wave, and the wind after. It blew out and sucked back in again. It looked like it almost blew the fire out.'

'The fire was going good when it blew?'

'Yeah, it was through the roof and out the windows upstairs and down. The trees were burning.'

Aynesworth recruited two local firemen to stand by with a hose, and a third dressed in asbestos stood by with a winch line in case something fell on him.

He cleared the basement steps, now open to the sky, and went down into the tangle of black timbers. He could stay only a few minutes at a time. He made eight trips.

All he got for his effort was one flat piece of torn metal, but it seemed to make him happy.

Red-faced and wet with sweat, he stripped off his asbestos clothing and sat on the running board of the fire truck with a fireman's raincoat over his shoulders.

He laid the flat piece of metal on the ground and blew away a film of ash.

'Dynamite,' he told Graham. 'Look here, see the fern pattern in the metal? This stuff's the right gauge for a trunk or a footlocker. That's probably it. Dynamite in a footlocker. It didn't go off in the basement, though. Looks like the ground floor to me. See where the tree's cut there where that marble tabletop hit it? Blown out sideways. The dynamite was in something that kept the fire off of it for a while.'

'How about remains?'

'There may not be a lot, but there's always something. We've got a lot of sifting to do. We'll find him. I'll give him to you in a small sack.'

A sedative had finally put Reba McClane to sleep at DePaul Hospital shortly after dawn. She wanted the policewoman to sit close beside her bed. Several times through the morning she woke and reached out for the officer's hand.

When she asked for breakfast, Graham brought it in.

Which way to go? Sometimes it was easier for them if you were impersonal. With Reba McClane, he didn't think so.

He told her who he was.

'Do you know him?' she asked the policewoman.

Graham passed the officer his credentials. She didn't need them.

'I know he's a federal officer, Miss McClane.'

She told him everything, finally. All about her time with Francis Dolarhyde. Her throat was sore, and she stopped frequently to suck cracked ice.

He asked her the unpleasant questions and she took him through it, once waving him out the door while the policewoman held the basin to catch her breakfast.

She was pale and her face was scrubbed and shiny when he came back into the room.

He asked the last of it and closed his notebook.

'I won't put you through this again,' he said, 'but I'd like to come back by. Just to say hi and see how you're doing.'

'How could you help it? – a charmer like me.'

For the first time he saw tears and realized where it ate her.

'Would you excuse us for a minute, officer?' Graham said. He took Reba's hand.

'Look here. There was plenty wrong with Dolarhyde, but there's nothing wrong with you. You said he was kind and thoughtful to you. I believe it. That's what you brought out in him. At the end, he couldn't kill you and he couldn't watch you die. People who study this kind of thing say he was trying to stop. Why? Because you helped him. That probably saved some lives. You didn't draw a freak. You drew a man with a freak on his back. Nothing wrong with you, kid. If you let yourself believe there is, you're a sap. I'm coming back to see you in a day or so. I have to look at cops all the time, and I need relief – try to do something about your hair there.'

She shook her head and waved him toward the door. Maybe she grinned a little, he couldn't be sure.

Graham called Molly from the St. Louis FBI office. Willy's grandfather answered the telephone.

'It's Will Graham, Mama,' he said. 'Hello, Mr Graham.'

Willy's grandparents always called him 'Mr Graham.'

'Mama said he killed himself. She was looking at Donahue and they broke in with it. Damn lucky thing. Saved you fellows a lot of trouble catching him. Saves us taxpayers footing any more bills for this thing too. Was he really white?'

'Yes sir. Blond. Looked Scandinavian.'

Willy's grandparents were Scandinavian.

'May I speak to Molly, please?'

'Are you going back down to Florida now?'

'Soon. Is Molly there?'

'Mama, he wants to speak to Molly. She's in the bathroom, Mr Graham. My grandboy's eating breakfast again. Been out riding in that good air. You ought to see that little booger eat. I bet he's gained ten pounds. Here she is.'

'Hello.'

'Hi, hotshot.'

'Good news, huh?'

'Looks like it.'

'I was out in the garden. Mamamma came out and told me when she saw it on TV. When did you find out?'

'Late last night.'

'Why didn't you call me?'

'Mamamma was probably asleep.'

'No, she was watching Johnny Carson. I can't tell you, Will. I'm so glad you didn't have to catch him.'

'I'll be here a little longer.'

'Four or five days?'

'I'm not sure. Maybe not that long. I want to see you, kid.'

'I want to see you too, when you get through with everything you need to do.'

'Today's Wednesday. By Friday I ought to – '

'Will, Mamamma has all Willy's uncles and aunts coming down from Seattle next week, and –'

'Fuck Mamamma. What is this "Mamamma" anyway?'

'When Willy was real little, he couldn't say – '

'Come home with me.'

'Will, I've waited for you. They never get to see Willy and a few more days –'

'Come yourself. Leave Willy there, and your ex-mother-in-law can stick him on a plane next week. Tell you what – let's stop in New Orleans. There's a place called –'

'I don't think so. I've been working – just part-time – at this western store in town, and I have to give them a little notice.'

'What's wrong, Molly?'

'Nothing. Nothing's wrong . . . I got so sad, Will. You know I came up here after Willy's father died.' She always said 'Willy's father' as though it were an office. She never used his name. 'And we were all together – I got myself together, I got calm. I've gotten myself together now, too, and I –'

'Small difference: I'm not dead.'

'Don't be that way.'

'What way? Don't be what way?'

'You're mad.'

Graham closed his eyes for a moment.

'Hello.'

'I'm not mad, Molly. You do what you want to. I'll call you when things wind up here.'

'You could come up here.'

'I don't think so.'

'Why not? There's plenty of room. Mamamma would – '

'Molly, they don't like me and you know why. Every time they look at me, I remind them.'

'That's not fair and it's not true either.'

Graham was very tired.

'Okay. They're full of shit and they make me sick – try that one.'

'Don't say that.'

'They want the boy. Maybe they like you all right, probably they do, if they ever think about it. But they want the boy and they'll take you. They don't want me and I could care less. *I* want *you*. In Florida. Willy too, when he gets tired of his pony.'

'You'll feel better when you get some sleep.'

'I doubt it. Look, I'll call you when I know something here.'

'Sure.' She hung up.

'*Ape* shit,' Graham said. '*Ape* shit.'

Crawford stuck his head in the door. 'Did I hear you say "ape shit"?'

'You did.'

'Well, cheer up. Aynesworth called in from the site. He has something for you. He said we ought to come on out, he's got some static from the locals.'

Chapter Fifty-one

Aynesworth was pouring ashes carefully into new paint cans when Graham and Crawford got to the black ruin where Dolarhyde's house had stood.

He was covered with soot and a large blister puffed under his ear. Special Agent Janowitz from Explosives was working down in the cellar.

A tall sack of a man fidgeted beside a dusty Oldsmobile in the drive. He intercepted Crawford and Graham as they crossed the yard.

'Are you Crawford?'

'That's right.'

'I'm Robert L. Dulaney. I'm the coroner and this is my jurisdiction.' He showed them his card. It said 'Vote for Robert L. Dulaney.'

Crawford waited.

'Your man here has some evidence that should have been turned over to me. He's kept me waiting for nearly an hour.'

'Sorry for the inconvenience, Mr Dulaney. He was following my instructions. Why don't you have a seat in your car and I'll clear this up.'

Dulaney started after them.

Crawford turned around. 'You'll excuse us, Mr Dulaney. Have a seat in your car.'

Section Chief Aynesworth was grinning, his teeth white in his sooty face. He had been sieving ashes all morning.

'As section chief, it gives me great pleasure –'

'To pull your prong, we all know that,' Janowitz said, climbing from the black tangle of the cellar.

'Silence in the ranks, Indian Janowitz. Fetch the items of interest.' He tossed Janowitz a set of car keys.

From the trunk of an FBI sedan Janowitz brought a long cardboard box. A shotgun, the stock burned off and barrels twisted by the heat, was wired to the bottom of the box. A smaller box contained a blackened automatic pistol.

'The pistol came out better,' Aynesworth said. 'Ballistics may be able to make a match with it. Come on, Janowitz, get to it.'

Aynesworth took three plastic freezer bags from him.

'Front and center, Graham.' For a moment the humor left Aynesworth's face. This was a hunter's ritual, like smearing Graham's forehead with blood.

'That was a real sly show, podna.' Aynesworth put the bags in Graham's hands.

One bag contained five inches of a charred human femur and the ball of a hip. Another contained a wristwatch. The third held the teeth.

The plate was black and broken and only half was there, but that half contained the unmistakable pegged lateral incisor.

Graham supposed he should say something. 'Thanks. Thanks a lot.'

His head swam briefly and he relaxed all over.

'. . . museum piece,' Aynesworth was saying 'We have to turn it over to the turkey, don't we, Jack?'

'Yeah. But there're some pros in the St. Louis coroner's office. They'll come over and make good impressions. We'll have those.'

Crawford and the others huddled with the coroner beside his car.

Graham was alone with the house. He listened to the wind in the chimneys. He hoped Bloom would come here when he was well. Probably he would.

Graham wanted to know about Dolarhyde. He wanted to know what happened here, what bred the Dragon. But he had had enough for now.

A mockingbird lit on the top of a chimney and whistled.

Graham whistled back.

He was going home.

Chapter Fifty-two

Graham smiled when he felt the jet's big push rocket him up and away from St. Louis, turning across the sun's path south and east at last toward home.

Molly and Willy would be there.

'Let's don't jack around about who's sorry for what. I'll pick you up in Marathon, kiddo,' she said on the phone.

In time he hoped he could remember the few good moments – the satisfaction of seeing people at work who were deeply committed to their skills. He supposed you could find that anywhere if you knew enough about what you were watching.

It would have been presumptuous to thank Lloyd Bowman and Beverly Katz, so he just told them on the telephone that he was glad to have worked with them again.

One thing bothered him a little: the way he felt when Crawford turned from the telephone in Chicago and said, 'It's Gateway.'

Possibly that was the most intense and savage joy that had ever burst in him. It was unsettling to know that the happiest moment of his life had come then, in that stuffy jury room in the city of Chicago. *When even before he knew, he knew.*

He didn't tell Lloyd Bowman how it felt; he didn't have to.

'You know, when his theorem rang the cherries, Pythagoras gave one hundred oxen to the Muse,' Bowman said. 'Nothing sweeter, is there? Don't answer – it lasts better if you don't spend it talking.'

Graham grew more impatient the closer he got to home and to Molly. In Miami he had to go out on the apron to board *Aunt Lula*, the old DC-3 that flew to Marathon.

He liked DC-3's. He liked everything today.

Aunt Lula was built when Graham was five years old and her wings were always dirty with a film of oil that blew back from the engines. He had great confidence in her. He ran to her as though she had landed in a jungle clearing to rescue him.

Islamorada's lights were coming on as the island passed under the wing. Graham could still see whitecaps on the Atlantic side. In minutes they were descending to Marathon.

It was like the first time he came to Marathon. He had come aboard *Aunt Lula* that time too, and often afterward he went to the airfield at dusk to watch her coming in, slow and steady, flaps down, fire flickering out her exhausts and all the passengers safe behind their lighted windows.

The takeoffs were good to watch as well, but when the old airplane made her great arc to the north it left him sad and empty and the air was acrid with good-byes. He learned to watch only the landings and hellos.

That was before Molly.

With a final grunt, the airplane swung onto the apron. Graham saw Molly and Willy standing behind the fence, under the floodlights.

Willy was solidly planted in front of her. He'd stay there until Graham joined them. Only then would he wander along, examining whatever interested him. Graham liked him for that.

Molly was the same height as Graham, five feet ten inches. A level kiss in public carries a pleasant jolt, possibly because level kisses usually are exchanged in bed.

Willy offered to carry his suitcase. Graham gave him the suit bag instead.

Riding home to Sugarloaf Key, Molly driving, Graham remembered the things picked out by the headlights, imagined the rest.

When he opened the car door in the yard, he could hear the sea.

Willy went into the house, holding the suit bag on top of his head, the bottom flapping against the backs of his legs.

Graham stood in the yard absently brushing mosquitoes away from his face.

Molly put her hand on his cheek. 'What you ought to do is come on in the house before you get eaten up.'

He nodded. His eyes were wet.

She waited a moment longer, tucked her head and peered up at him, wiggling her eyebrows. 'Tanqueray martinis, steaks, hugging and stuff. Right this way . . . and the light bill and the water bill and lengthy conversations with my child,' she added out of the side of her mouth.

Chapter Fifty-three

Graham and Molly wanted very much for it to be the same again between them, to go on as they had before.

When they saw that it was not the same, the unspoken knowledge lived with them like unwanted company in the house. The mutual assurances they tried to exchange in the dark and in the day passed through some refraction that made them miss the mark.

Molly had never looked better to him. From a painful distance, he admired her unconscious grace.

She tried to be good to him, but she had been to Oregon and she had raised the dead.

Willy felt it and he was cool to Graham, maddeningly polite.

A letter came from Crawford. Molly brought it in the mail and did not mention it.

It contained a picture of the Sherman family, printed from movie film.

Not everything had burned, Crawford's note explained. A search of the fields around the house had turned this picture up, along with a few other things the explosion had blown far from the fire.

'These people were probably on his itinerary,' Crawford wrote. 'Safe now. Thought you'd like to know.'

Graham showed it to Molly.

'See? That's why,' he said. 'That's why it was worth it.'

'I know,' she said. 'I understand that, really I do.'

The bluefish were running under the moon. Molly packed suppers and they fished and they built fires, and none of it was any good.

Grandpa and Mamamma sent Willy a picture of his pony and he tacked it to the wall in his room.

The fifth day home was the last day before Graham and Molly would go back to work in Marathon. They fished in the surf, walking a quarter-mile around the curving beach to a place where they had luck before.

Graham had decided to talk to both of them together.

The expedition did not begin well. Willy pointedly put aside the rod Graham had rigged for him and brought the new surf-casting rod his grandfather sent home with him.

They fished for three hours in silence. Graham opened his mouth to speak several times, but it didn't seem right.

He was tired of being disliked.

Graham caught four snappers, using sand fleas for bait. Willy caught nothing. He was casting a big Rapala with three treble hooks which his grandfather had given him. He was fishing too fast, casting again and again, retrieving too fast, until he was red-faced and his T-shirt stuck to him.

Graham waded into the water, scooped sand in the backwash of a wave, and came up with two sand fleas, their legs waving from their shells.

'How about one of these, partner?' He held out a sand flea to Willy.

'I'll use the Rapala. It was my father's, did you know that?'

'No,' Graham said. He glanced at Molly.

She hugged her knees and looked far off at a frigate bird sailing high.

She got up and brushed off the sand. 'I'll go fix some sandwiches,' she said.

When Molly had gone, Graham was tempted to talk to the boy by himself. No. Willy would feel whatever his mother felt. He'd wait and get them both together when she came back. He'd do it this time.

She wasn't gone long and she came back without the sandwiches, walking swiftly on the packed sand above the surf.

'Jack Crawford's on the phone. I told him you'd call him back, but he said it's urgent,' she said, examining a fingernail. 'Better hurry.'

Graham blushed. He stuck the butt of his rod in the sand and trotted toward the dunes. It was quicker than going around the beach if you carried nothing to catch in the brush.

He heard a low whirring sound carried on the wind and, wary of a rattler, he scanned the ground as he went into the scrub cedar.

He saw boots beneath the brush, the glint of a lens and a flash of khaki rising.

He looked into the yellow eyes of Francis Dolarhyde and fear raised the hammers of his heart.

Snick of a pistol action working, an automatic coming up and Graham kicked at it, struck it as the muzzle bloomed pale yellow in the sun, and the pistol flew into the brush. Graham on his back, something burning in the left side of his chest, slid headfirst down the dune onto the beach.

Dolarhyde leaped high to land on Graham's stomach with both feet and he had the knife out now and never looked up at the thin screaming from the water's edge. He pinned Graham with his knees, raised the knife high and grunted as he brought it down. The blade missed Graham's eye and crunched deep into his cheek.

Dolarhyde rocked forward and put his weight on the handle of the knife to shove it through Graham's head.

The rod whistled as Molly swung it hard at Dolarhyde's face. The big Rapala's hooks sank solidly in his cheek and the reel screamed, paying out line as she drew back to strike again.

He growled, grabbed at his face as she hit him, and the treble hooks jammed into his hand as well. One hand free, one hand hooked to his face, he tugged the knife out and started after her.

Graham rolled over, got to his knees, then his feet, eyes wild and choking blood he ran, ran from Dolarhyde, ran until he collapsed.

Molly ran for the dunes, Willy ahead of her. Dolarhyde was coming, dragging the rod. It caught on a bush and pulled him howling to a stop before he thought to cut the line.

'Run baby, run baby, run baby! Don't look back,' she gasped. Her legs were long and she shoved the boy ahead of her, the crashing ever closer in the brush behind them.

They had one hundred yards on him when they left the dunes, seventy yards when they reached the house. Scrambling up the stairs. Clawing in Will's closet.

To Willy, 'Stay here.'

Down again to meet him. Down to the kitchen, not ready, fumbling with the speedloader.

She forgot the stance and she forgot the front sight but she got a good two-handed grip on the pistol and as the door exploded inward she blew a rat hole through his thigh – 'Muhner!' – and she shot him in the face as he slid down the door facing and she shot him in the face as he sat on the floor and she ran to him and shot him twice in the face as he sprawled against the wall, scalp down to his chin and his hair on fire.

Willy tore up a sheet and went to look for Will. His legs were shaking and he fell several times crossing the yard.

The sheriff's deputies and ambulances came before Molly ever thought to call them. She was taking a shower when they came in the house behind their pistols. She was scrubbing hard at the flecks of blood and bone on her face and hair and she couldn't answer when a deputy tried to talk to her through the shower curtain.

One of the deputies finally picked up the dangling telephone receiver and talked to Crawford in Washington, who had heard the shots and summoned them.

'I don't know, they're bringing him in now,' the deputy said. He looked out the window as the litter passed. 'It don't look good to me,' he said.

Chapter Fifty-four

On the wall at the foot of the bed there was a clock with numbers large enough to read through the drugs and the pain.

When Will Graham could open his right eye, he saw the clock and knew where he was – an intensive-care unit. He knew to watch the clock. Its movement assured him that this was passing, would pass.

That's what it was there for.

It said four o'clock. He had no idea which four o'clock and he didn't care, as long as the hands were moving. He drifted away.

The clock said eight when he opened his eye again.

Someone was to the side of him. Cautiously he turned his eye. It was Molly, looking out the window. She was thin. He tried to speak, but a great ache filled the left side of his head when he moved his jaw. His head and his chest did not throb together. It was more of a syncopation. He made a noise as she left the room.

The window was light when they pulled and tugged at him and did things that made the cords in his neck stand out.

Yellow light when he saw Crawford's face over him.

Graham managed to wink. When Crawford grinned, Graham could see a piece of spinach between his teeth.

Odd. Crawford eschewed most vegetables.

Graham made writing motions on the sheet beneath his hand.

Crawford slid his notebook under Graham's hand and put a pen between his fingers.

'Willy OK,' he wrote.

'Yeah, he's fine,' Crawford said. 'Molly too. She's been in here while you were asleep. Dolarhyde's dead. Will. I promise you, he's dead. I took the prints myself and had Price match them. There's no question. He's dead.'

Graham drew a question mark on the pad.

'We'll get into it. I'll be here, I can tell you the whole thing when you feel good. They only give me five minutes.'

'Now,' Graham wrote.

'Has the doctor talked to you? No? About you first – you'll be okay. Your eye's just swollen shut from a deep stab wound in the face. They've got it fixed, but it'll take time. They took out your spleen. But who needs a spleen? Price left his in Burma in '41.'

A nurse pecked on the glass.

'I've got to go. They don't respect credentials, nothing, around here. They just throw you out when the time's up. See you later.'

Molly was in the ICU waiting room. A lot of tired people were.

Crawford went to her. 'Molly . . .'

'Hello, Jack,' she said. '*You're* looking really well. Want to give him a face transplant?'

'Don't, Molly.'

'Did you look at him?'

'Yes.'

'I didn't think I could look at him, but I did.'

'They'll fix him up. The doctor told me. They can do it. You want somebody to stay with you, Molly? I brought Phyllis down, she – '

'No. Don't do anything else for me.'

She turned away, fumbling for a tissue. He saw the letter when she opened her purse; expensive mauve stationery that he had seen before.

Crawford hated this. He had to do it.

'Molly.'

'What is it?'

'Will got a letter?'

'Yes.'

'Did the nurse give it to you?'

'Yes, she *gave* it to me. They're holding some flowers from all his *friends* in Washington, too.'

'May I see the letter?'

'I'll give it to him when he feels like it.'

'Please let me see it.'

'Why?'

'Because he doesn't need to hear from . . . that particular person.'

Something was wrong with the expression on his face and she looked down at the letter and dropped it, purse and all. A lipstick rolled across the floor.

Stooping to pick up Molly's things, Crawford heard her heels tap fast as she left him, abandoning her purse.

He gave the purse to the charge nurse.

Crawford knew it would be nearly impossible for Lecter to get what he would need, but with Lecter he took no chances.

He had an intern fluoroscope the letter in the X-ray department. Crawford slit the envelope on all sides with a penknife and examined its inside surface and the note for any stain or dust – they would have lye for scrubbing at Chesapeake Hospital, and there was a pharmacy.

Satisfied at last, he read it:

Dear Will,

Here we are, you and I, languishing in our hospitals. You have your pain and I am without my books – the learned Dr Chilton has seen to that.

We live in a primitive time – don't we, Will? – neither savage nor wise. Half measures are the curse of it. Any rational society would either kill me or give me my books.

I wish you a speedy convalescence and hope you won't be very ugly.

I think of you often.

Hannibal Lecter

The intern looked at his watch, 'Do you need me anymore?'

'No.' Crawford said. 'Where's the incinerator?'

When Crawford returned in four hours for the next visiting period, Molly wasn't in the waiting room and she wasn't in the intensive-care unit.

Graham was awake. He drew a question mark on the pad at once. 'D. dead how?' he wrote under it.

Crawford told him. Graham lay still for a full minute. Then he wrote, 'Lammed how?'

'Okay,' Crawford said. 'St. Louis. Dolarhyde must have been looking for Reba McClane. He came in the lab while we were there and spotted us. His prints were on an open furnace-room window – it wasn't reported until yesterday.'

Graham tapped the pad. 'Body?'

'We think it was a guy named Arnold Lang – he's missing. His car was found in Memphis. It had been wiped down. They'll run me out in a minute. Let me give it to you in order.

'Dolarhyde knew we were there. He gave us the slip at the plant and drove to a Servco Supreme station at Lindbergh and US 270. Arnold Lang worked there.

'Reba McClane said Dolarhyde had a tiff with a service-station attendant on Saturday before last. We think it was Lang.

'He snuffed Lang and took his body to the house. Then he went to Reba McClane's. She was in a clinch with Ralph Mandy at the door. He shot Mandy and dragged him into the hedge.'

The nurse came in.

'For God's sake, it's police business,' Crawford said. He talked fast as she pulled him by the coat sleeve to the door. 'He chloroformed Reba McClane and took her to the house. The body was there,' Crawford said from the hall.

Graham had to wait four hours to find out the rest.

'He gave her this and that, you know, "Will I kill you or not?"' Crawford said as he came in the door.

'You know the routine about the key hanging around his neck – that was to make sure she felt the body. So she could tell *us* she certainly did feel a body. All right, it's this way and that way. "I can't stand to see you burn," he says, and blows Lang's head off with a twelve-gauge.

'Lang was perfect. He didn't have any teeth anyway. Maybe Dolarhyde knew the maxillary arch survives fires a lot of times – who knows what he knew? Anyway, Lang didn't have any maxillary arch after Dolarhyde got through with him. He shot the head off Lang's body and he must have tipped a chair or something for the thud of the body falling. He'd hung the key around Lang's neck.

'Now Reba's scrambling around looking for the key. Dolarhyde's in the corner watching. Her ears are ringing from the shotgun. She won't hear his little noises.

'He's started a fire, but he hasn't put the gas to it yet. He's got gas in the room. She got out of the house okay. If she had panicked too much, run into a wall or something or frozen, I guess he'd have sapped her and dragged her outside. She wouldn't have known how she got out. But she had to get out for it to work. Oh hell, here comes that nurse.'

Graham wrote fast. 'How vehicle?'

'You have to admire this,' Crawford said. 'He knew he'd have to leave his van at the house. He couldn't drive two vehicles out there, and he needed a getaway piece.

'This is what he did: he made *Lang* hook up the service-station tow truck to his van. He snuffed Lang, locked the station, and towed his van out to his house. Then he left the tow truck on a dirt road back in the fields behind the house, got back in his van and went after Reba. When she got out of the house all right, he dragged out his dynamite, put the gasoline around the fire, and lammed out the back. He drove the tow truck *back to* the service station, left it and got Lang's car. No loose ends.

'It drove me crazy until we figured it out. I know it's right because he left a couple of prints on the tow bar.

'We probably met him in the road when we were going up there to the house . . . Yes, ma'am. I'm coming. Yes, ma'am.'

Graham wanted to ask a question, but it was too late.

Molly took the next five-minute visit.

Graham wrote 'I love you' on Crawford's pad.

She nodded and held his hand.

A minute later he wrote again. 'Willy okay?'

She nodded.

'Here?'

She looked up at him too quickly from the pad. She made a kiss with her mouth and pointed to the approaching nurse.

He tugged her thumb.

'*Where?*' he insisted, underlining twice.

'Oregon,' she said.

Crawford came a final time.

Graham was ready with his note. It said, 'Teeth?'

'His grandmother's,' Crawford said. 'The ones we found in the house were his grandmother's. St. Louis PD located one Ned Vogt – Dolarhyde's mother was Vogt's stepmother. Vogt saw Mrs Dolarhyde when he was a kid, and he never forgot the teeth.

'That's what I was calling you about when you ran into Dolarhyde. The Smithsonian had just called me. They finally had gotten the teeth from the Missouri authorities, just to examine for their own satisfaction. They noticed the upper part was made of vulcanite instead of acrylic like they use now. Nobody's made vulcanite plates in thirty-five years.

'Dolarhyde had a new acrylic pair just like them made to fit him. The new ones were on his body. Smithsonian looked at some features on them – the fluting, they said, and rugae. Chinese manufacture. The old ones were Swiss.

'He had a key on him too, for a locker in Miami. Big book in there. Kind of a diary – hell of a thing. I'll have it when you want to see it.

'Look, sport, I have to go back to Washington. I'll get back down here the weekend, if I can. You gonna be okay?'

Graham drew a question mark, then scratched it out and wrote 'sure.'

The nurse came after Crawford left. She shot some Demerol into his intravenous line and the clock grew fuzzy. He couldn't keep up with the second hand.

He wondered if Demerol would work on your feelings. He could hold Molly a while with his face. Until they finished fixing it anyway. That would be a cheap shot. Hold her for what? He was drifting off and he hoped he wouldn't dream.

He did drift between memory and dream, but it wasn't so bad. He didn't dream of Molly leaving, or of Dolarhyde. It was a long memory-dream of

Shiloh, interrupted by lights shone in his face and the gasp and hiss of the blood-pressure cuff . . .

It was spring, soon after he shot Garrett Jacob Hobbs, when Graham visited Shiloh.

On a soft April day he walked across the asphalt road to Bloody Pond. The new grass, still light green, grew down the slope to the water. The clear water had risen into the grass, and the grass was visible in the water, growing down, down, as though it covered the bottom of the pond.

Graham knew what had happened there in April 1862.

He sat down in the grass, felt the damp ground through his trousers.

A tourist's automobile went by and after it had passed, Graham saw movement behind it in the road. The car had broken a chicken snake's back. It slid in endless figure eights across itself in the center of the asphalt road, sometimes showing its black back, sometimes its pale belly.

Shiloh's awesome presence hooded him with cold, though he was sweating in the mild spring sun.

Graham got up off the grass, his trousers damp behind. He was light-headed.

The snake looped on itself. He stood over it, picked it up by the end of its smooth dry tail, and with a long fluid motion cracked it like a whip.

Its brains zinged into the pond. A bream rose to them.

He had thought Shiloh haunted, its beauty sinister like flags.

Now, drifting between memory and narcotic sleep, he saw that Shiloh was not sinister; it was indifferent. Beautiful Shiloh could witness anything. Its unforgivable beauty simply underscored the indifference of nature, the Green Machine. The loveliness of Shiloh mocked our plight.

He roused and watched the mindless clock, but he couldn't stop thinking:

In the Green Machine there is no mercy; we make mercy, manufacture it in the parts that have overgrown our basic reptile brain.

There is no murder. We make murder, and it matters only to us.

Graham knew too well that he contained all the elements to make murder; perhaps mercy too.

He understood murder uncomfortably well, though.

He wondered if, in the great body of humankind, in the minds of men set on civilization, the vicious urges we control in ourselves and the dark instinctive knowledge of those urges function like the crippled virus the body arms against.

He wondered if old, awful urges are the virus that makes vaccine.

Yes, he had been wrong about Shiloh. Shiloh isn't haunted – men are haunted.

Shiloh doesn't care.

And I gave my heart to know wisdom, and to
    know madness and folly:
I perceived that this also is vexation of spirit.
                    – ECCLESIASTES

THE SILENCE OF THE LAMBS

To the memory of my father

If after the manner of men I have fought
with beasts at Ephesus, what advantageth
it me, if the dead rise not?

– I Corinthians

Need I look upon a death's head in a
ring, that have one in my face?

– John Donne, 'Devotions'

Chapter One

Behavioral Science, the FBI section that deals with serial murder, is on the bottom floor of the Academy building at Quantico, half-buried in the earth. Clarice Starling reached it flushed after a fast walk from Hogan's Alley on the firing range. She had grass in her hair and grass stains on her FBI Academy windbreaker from diving to the ground under fire in an arrest problem on the range.

No one was in the outer office, so she fluffed briefly by her reflection in the glass doors. She knew she could look all right without primping. Her hands smelled of gunsmoke, but there was no time to wash – Section Chief Crawford's summons had said *now*.

She found Jack Crawford alone in the cluttered suite of offices. He was standing at someone else's desk talking on the telephone and she had a chance to look him over for the first time in a year. What she saw disturbed her.

Normally, Crawford looked like a fit, middle-aged engineer who might have paid his way through college playing baseball – a crafty catcher, tough when he blocked the plate. Now he was thin, his shirt collar was too big, and he had dark puffs under his reddened eyes. Everyone who could read the papers knew Behavioral Science section was catching hell. Starling hoped Crawford wasn't on the juice. That seemed most unlikely here.

Crawford ended his telephone conversation with a sharp 'No.' He took her file from under his arm and opened it.

'Starling, Clarice M., good morning,' he said.

'Hello.' Her smile was only polite.

'Nothing's wrong. I hope the call didn't spook you.'

'No.' *Not totally true,* Starling thought.

'Your instructors tell me you're doing well, top quarter of the class.'

'I hope so, they haven't posted anything.'

'I ask them from time to time.'

That surprised Starling; she had written Crawford off as a two-faced recruiting sergeant son of a bitch.

She had met Special Agent Crawford when he was a guest lecturer at the University of Virginia. The quality of his criminology seminars was a factor in her coming to the Bureau. She wrote him a note when she qualified for the Academy, but he never replied, and for the three months she had been a trainee at Quantico, he had ignored her.

Starling came from people who do not ask for favors or press for friendship, but she was puzzled and regretful at Crawford's behavior. Now, in his presence, she liked him again, she was sorry to note.

Clearly something was wrong with him. There was a peculiar cleverness in Crawford, aside from his intelligence, and Starling had first noticed it in his color sense and the textures of his clothing, even within the FBI-clone standards of agent dress. Now he was neat but drab, as though he were molting.

'A job came up and I thought about you,' he said. 'It's not really a job, it's more of an interesting errand. Push Berry's stuff off that chair and sit down. You put down here that you want to come directly to Behavioral Science when you get through with the Academy.'

'I do.'

'You have a lot of forensics, but no law enforcement background. We look for six years, minimum.'

'My father was a marshal, I know the life.'

Crawford smiled a little. 'What you *do* have is a double major in psychology and criminology, and how many summers working in a mental health center – two?'

'Two.'

'Your counselor's license, is it current?'

'It's good for two more years. I got it before you had the seminar at UVA – before I decided to do this.'

'You got stuck in the hiring freeze.'

Starling nodded. 'I was lucky though – I found out in time to qualify as a Forensic Fellow. Then I could work in the lab until the Academy had an opening.'

'You wrote to me about coming here, didn't you, and I don't think I answered – I know I didn't. I should have.'

'You've had plenty else to do.'

'Do you know about VI-CAP?'

'I know it's the Violent Criminal Apprehension Program. The *Law Enforcement Bulletin* says you're working on a database, but you aren't operational yet.'

Crawford nodded. 'We've developed a questionnaire. It applies to all the known serial murderers in modern times.' He handed her a thick sheaf of papers in a flimsy binding. 'There's a section for investigators, and one for

THE SILENCE OF THE LAMBS

surviving victims, if any. The blue is for the killer to answer if he will, and the pink is a series of questions an examiner asks the killer, getting his reactions as well as his answers. It's a lot of paperwork.'

Paperwork. Clarice Starling's self-interest snuffled ahead like a keen beagle. She smelled a job offer coming – probably the drudgery of feeding raw data into a new computer system. It was tempting to get into Behavioral Science in any capacity she could, but she knew what happens to a woman if she's ever pegged as a secretary – it sticks until the end of time. A choice was coming, and she wanted to choose well.

Crawford was waiting for something – he must have asked her a question. Starling had to scramble to recall it:

'What tests have you given? Minnesota Multiphasic, ever? Rorschach?'

'Yes MMPI, never Rorschach,' she said. 'I've done Thematic Apperception and I've given children Bender-Gestalt.'

'Do you spook easily, Starling?'

'Not yet.'

'See, we've tried to interview and examine all the thirty-two known serial murderers we have in custody, to build up a database for psychological profiling in unsolved cases. Most of them went along with it – I think they're driven to show off, a lot of them. Twenty-seven were willing to cooperate. Four on death row with appeals pending clammed up, understandably. But the one we want the most, we haven't been able to get. I want you to go after him tomorrow in the asylum.'

Clarice Starling felt a glad knocking in her chest and some apprehension too.

'Who's the subject?'

'The psychiatrist – Dr Hannibal Lecter,' Crawford said.

A brief silence follows the name, always, in any civilized gathering.

Starling looked at Crawford steadily, but she was too still. 'Hannibal the Cannibal,' she said.

'Yes.'

'Yes, well – Okay, right. I'm glad of the chance, but you have to know I'm wondering – why me?'

'Mainly because you're available,' Crawford said. 'I don't expect him to cooperate. He's already refused, but it was through an intermediary – the director of the hospital. I have to be able to say our qualified examiner went to him and asked him personally. There are reasons that don't concern you. I don't have anybody left in this section to do it.'

'You're jammed – Buffalo Bill – and the things in Nevada,' Starling said.

'You got it. It's the old story – not enough warm bodies.'

'You said tomorrow – you're in a hurry. Any bearing on a current case?'

'No. I wish there were.'

'If he balks on me, do you still want a psychological evaluation?'

'No. I'm waist-deep in inaccessible-patient evaluations of Dr Lecter and they're all different.'

Crawford shook two vitamin C tablets into his palm, and mixed an Alka-Seltzer at the water cooler to wash them down. 'It's ridiculous, you know; Lecter's a psychiatrist and he writes for the psychiatric journals himself – extraordinary stuff – but it's never about his own little anomalies. He pretended to go along with the hospital director, Chilton, once in some tests – sitting around with a bloodpressure cuff on his penis, looking at wreck pictures – then Lecter published first what he'd learned about Chilton and made a fool out of him. He responds to serious correspondence from psychiatric students in fields unrelated to his case, and that's all he does. If he won't talk to you, I just want straight reporting. How does he look, how does his cell look, what's he doing. Local color, so to speak. Watch out for the press going in and coming out. Not the real press, the supermarket press. They love Lecter even better than Prince Andrew.'

'Didn't a sleazo magazine offer him fifty thousand dollars for some recipes? I seem to remember that,' Starling said.

Crawford nodded. 'I'm pretty sure the *National Tattler* has bought somebody inside the hospital and they may know you're coming after I make the appointment.'

Crawford leaned forward until he faced her at a distance of two feet. She watched his half-glasses blur the bags under his eyes. He had gargled recently with Listerine.

'Now. I want your full attention, Starling. Are you listening to me?'

'Yes sir.'

'Be very careful with Hannibal Lecter. Dr Chilton, the head of the mental hospital, will go over the physical procedure you use to deal with him. Don't deviate from it. *Do not deviate from it one iota for any reason.* If Lecter talks to you at all, he'll just be trying to find out about you. It's the kind of curiosity that makes a snake look in a bird's nest. We both know you have to back-and-forth a little in interviews, but you tell him no specifics about yourself. You don't want any of your personal facts in his head. You know what he did to Will Graham.'

'I read about it when it happened.'

'He gutted Will with a linoleum knife when Will caught up with him. It's a wonder Will didn't die. Remember the Red Dragon? Lecter turned Francis Dolarhyde onto Will and his family. Will's face looks like damn Picasso drew him, thanks to Lecter. He tore a nurse up in the asylum. Do your job, just don't ever forget what he is.'

'And what's that? Do you know?'

'I know he's a monster. Beyond that, nobody can say for sure. Maybe you'll find out; I didn't pick you out of a hat, Starling. You asked me a couple of interesting questions when I was at UVA. The Director will see your own report over your signature – if it's clear and tight and organized. I decide that. And I *will* have it by 0900 Sunday. Okay, Starling, carry on in the prescribed manner.'

Crawford smiled at her, but his eyes were dead.

Chapter Two

Dr Frederick Chilton, fifty-eight, administrator of the Baltimore State Hospital for the Criminally Insane, has a long, wide desk upon which there are no hard or sharp objects. Some of the staff call it 'the moat.' Other staff members don't know what the word *moat* means. Dr Chilton remained seated behind his desk when Clarice Starling came into his office.

'We've had a lot of detectives here, but I can't remember one so attractive,' Chilton said without getting up.

Starling knew without thinking about it that the shine on his extended hand was lanolin from patting his hair. She let go before he did.

'It is *Miss* Sterling, isn't it?'

'It's *Starling*, Doctor, with an *a*. Thank you for your time.'

'So the FBI is going to the girls like everything else, ha, ha.' He added the tobacco smile he uses to separate his sentences.

'The Bureau's improving, Dr Chilton. It certainly is.'

'Will you be in Baltimore for several days? You know, you can have just as good a time here as you can in Washington or New York, if you know the town.'

She looked away to spare herself his smile and knew at once that he had registered her distaste. 'I'm sure it's a great town, but my instructions are to see Dr Lecter and report back this afternoon.'

'Is there someplace I could call you in Washington for a follow-up later on?'

'Of course. It's kind of you to think of it. Special Agent Jack Crawford's in charge of this project, and you can always reach me through him.'

'I see,' Chilton said. His cheeks, mottled with pink, clashed with the improbable red-brown of his coif. 'Give me your identification, please.' He let her remain standing through his leisurely examination of her ID card. Then he handed it back and rose. 'This won't take much time. Come along.'

'I understood you'd brief me, Dr Chilton,' Starling said.

'I can do that while we walk.' He came around his desk, looking at his watch. 'I have a lunch in half an hour.'

Dammit, she should have read him better, quicker. He might not be a total jerk. He might know something useful. It wouldn't have hurt her to simper once, even if she wasn't good at it.

'Dr Chilton, I have an appointment with you now. It was set at your convenience, when you could give me some time. Things could come up during the interview – I may need to go over some of his responses with you.'

'I really, really doubt it. Oh, I need to make a telephone call before we go. I'll catch up with you in the outer office.'

'I'd like to leave my coat and umbrella here.'

'Out there,' Chilton said. 'Give them to Alan in the outer office. He'll put them away.'

Alan wore the pajamalike garment issued to the inmates. He was wiping out ashtrays with the tail of his shirt.

He rolled his tongue around in his cheek as he took Starling's coat.

'Thank you,' she said.

'You're more than welcome. How often do you shit?' Alan asked.

'What did you say?'

'Does it come out lo-o-o-o-nnng?'

'I'll hang these somewhere myself.'

'You don't have anything in the way – you can bend over and watch it come out and see if it changes color when the air hits it, do you do that? Does it look like you have a big brown tail?' He wouldn't let go of the coat.

'Dr Chilton wants you in his office, right now,' Starling said.

'No I don't,' Dr Chilton said. 'Put the coat in the closet, Alan, and don't get it out while we're gone. *Do it.* I had a full-time office girl, but the cutbacks robbed me of her. Now the girl who let you in types three hours a day, and then I have Alan. Where are all the office girls, Miss Starling?' His spectacles flashed at her. 'Are you armed?'

'No, I'm not armed.'

'May I see your purse and briefcase?'

'You saw my credentials.'

'And they say you're a student. Let me see your things, please.'

Clarice Starling flinched as the first of the heavy steel gates clashed shut behind her and the bolt shot home. Chilton walked slightly ahead, down the green institutional corridor in an atmosphere of Lysol and distant slammings. Starling was angry at herself for letting Chilton put his hand in her purse and briefcase, and she stepped hard on the anger so that she could concentrate. It was all right. She felt her control solid beneath her, like a good gravel bottom in a fast current.

'Lecter's a considerable nuisance,' Chilton said over his shoulder. 'It takes an orderly at least ten minutes a day to remove the staples from the publications he receives. We tried to eliminate or reduce his subscriptions, but he wrote a brief and the court overruled us. The volume of his personal mail used to be enormous. Thankfully, it's dwindled since he's been overshadowed by other creatures in the news. For a while it seemed that every little student doing a master's thesis in psychology wanted something from Lecter in it. The medical journals still publish him, but it's just for the freak value of his byline.'

'He did a good piece on surgical addiction in the *Journal of Clinical Psychiatry*, I thought,' Starling said.

'You did, did you? *We* tried to study Lecter. We thought, "Here's an opportunity to make a landmark study" – it's so rare to get one alive.'

'One what?'

'A pure sociopath, that's obviously what he is. But he's impenetrable, much too sophisticated for the standard tests. And, my, does he hate us. He thinks I'm his nemesis. Crawford's very clever – isn't he? – using you on Lecter.'

'How do you mean, Dr Chilton?'

'A young woman to "turn him on," I believe you call it. I don't believe

Lecter's seen a woman in several years – he may have gotten a glimpse of one of the cleaning people. We generally keep women out of there. They're trouble in detention.'

Well fuck off, Chilton. 'I graduated from the University of Virginia with honors, Doctor. It's not a charm school.'

'Then you should be able to remember the rules: Do not reach through the bars, do not touch the bars. You pass him nothing but soft paper. No pens, no pencils. He has his own felt-tipped pens some of the time. The paper you pass him must be free of staples, paper clips or pins. Items come back out through the sliding food carrier. No exceptions. Do not accept anything he attempts to hold out to you through the barrier. Do you understand me?'

'I understand.'

They had passed through two more gates and left the natural light behind. Now they were beyond the wards where inmates can mix together, down in the region where there can be no windows and no mixing. The hallway lights are covered with heavy grids like the lights in the engine rooms of ships. Dr Chilton paused beneath one. When their footfalls stopped, Starling could hear somewhere beyond the wall the ragged end of a voice ruined by shouting.

'Lecter is never outside his cell without wearing full restraints and a mouthpiece,' Chilton said. 'I'm going to show you why. He was a model of cooperation for the first year after he was committed. Security around him was slightly relaxed – this was under the previous administration, you understand. On the afternoon of July 8, 1976, he complained of chest pain and he was taken to the dispensary. His restraints were removed to make it easier to give him an electrocardiogram. When the nurse bent over him, he did this to her.' Chilton handed Clarice Starling a dog-eared photograph. 'The doctors managed to save one of her eyes. Lecter was hooked up to the monitors the entire time. He broke her jaw to get at her tongue. His pulse never got over eighty-five, even when he swallowed it.'

Starling didn't know which was worse, the photograph or Chilton's attention as he gleaned her face with fast grabby eyes. She thought of a thirsty chicken pecking tears off her face.

'I keep him in here,' Chilton said, and pushed a button beside heavy double doors of security glass. A big orderly let them into the block beyond.

Starling made a tough decision and stopped just inside the doors. 'Dr

Chilton, we really need these test results. If Dr Lecter feels you're his enemy – if he's fixed on you, just as you've said – we might have more luck if I approached him by myself. What do you think?'

Chilton's cheek twitched. 'That's perfectly fine with me. You might have suggested that in my office. I could have sent an orderly with you and saved the time.'

'I could have suggested it there if you'd briefed me there.'

'I don't expect I'll see you again, Miss *Star*ling – Barney, when she's finished with Lecter, ring for someone to bring her out.'

Chilton left without looking at her again.

Now there was only the big impassive orderly and the soundless clock behind him and his wire mesh cabinet with the Mace and restraints, mouthpiece and tranquilizer gun. A wall rack held a long pipe device with a U on the end for pinioning the violent to the wall.

The orderly was looking at her. 'Dr Chilton told you, don't touch the bars?' His voice was both high and hoarse. She was reminded of Aldo Ray.

'Yes, he told me.'

'Okay. It's past the others, the last cell on the right. Stay toward the middle of the corridor as you go down, and don't mind anything. You can take him his mail, get off on the right foot.' The orderly seemed privately amused. 'You just put it in the tray and let it roll through. If the tray's inside, you can pull it back with the cord or he can send it back. He can't reach you where the tray stops outside.' The orderly gave her two magazines, their loose pages spilling out, three newspapers and several opened letters.

The corridor was about thirty yards long, with cells on both sides. Some were padded cells with an observation window, long and narrow like an archery slit, in the center of the door. Others were standard prison cells, with a wall of bars opening on the corridor. Clarice Starling was aware of figures in the cells, but she tried not to look at them. She was more than halfway down when a voice hissed, 'I can smell your cunt.' She gave no sign that she had heard it, and went on.

The lights were on in the last cell. She moved toward the left side of the corridor to see into it as she approached, knowing her heels announced her.

Chapter Three

Dr Lecter's cell is well beyond the others, facing only a closet across the corridor, and it is unique in other ways. The front is a wall of bars but within the bars, at a distance greater than the human reach, is a second barrier, a stout nylon net stretched from floor to ceiling and wall to wall. Behind the net Starling could see a table bolted to the floor and piled high with softcover books and papers, and a straight chair, also fastened down.

Dr Hannibal Lecter himself reclined on his bunk, perusing the Italian edition of *Vogue*. He held the loose pages in his right hand and put them beside him one by one with his left. Dr Lecter has six fingers on his left hand.

Clarice Starling stopped a little distance from the bars, about the length of a small foyer.

'Dr Lecter.' Her voice sounded all right to her.

He looked up from his reading.

For a steep second she thought his gaze hummed, but it was only her blood she heard.

'My name is Clarice Starling. May I talk with you?' Courtesy was implicit in her distance and her tone.

Dr Lecter considered his finger pressed against his pursed lips. Then he rose in his own time and came forward smoothly in his cage stopping short of the nylon web without looking at it as though he chose the distance.

She could see that he was small, sleek; in his hands and arms she saw wiry strength like her own.

'Good morning,' he said, as though he had answered the door. His cultured voice has a slight metallic rasp beneath it, possibly from disuse.

Dr Lecter's eyes are maroon and they reflect the light in pinpoints of red. Sometimes the points of light seem to fly like sparks to his center. His eyes held Starling whole.

She came a measured distance closer to the bars. The hair on her forearms rose and pressed against her sleeves.

'Doctor, we have a hard problem in psychological profiling. I want to ask you for your help.'

' "We" being Behavioral Science at Quantico. You're one of Jack Crawford's, I expect.'

'I am, yes.'

'May I see your credentials?'

She hadn't expected this. 'I showed them at the . . . office.'

'You mean you showed them to Frederick Chilton, PhD?'

'Yes.'

'Did you see *his* credentials?'

'No.'

'The academic ones don't make extensive reading, I can tell you. Did you meet Alan? Isn't he charming? Which of them had you rather talk with?'

'On the whole, I'd say Alan.'

'You could be a reporter Chilton let in for money. I think I'm entitled to see your credentials.'

'All right.' She held up her laminated ID card.

'I can't read it at this distance, send it through, please.'

'I can't.'

'Because it's hard.'

'Yes.'

'Ask Barney.'

The orderly came and considered. 'Dr Lecter, I'll let this come through. But if you don't return it when I ask you to – if we have to bother everybody and secure you to get it – then I'll be upset. If you upset me, you'll have to stay bundled up until I feel better toward you. Meals through the tube, dignity pants changed twice a day – the works. And I'll hold your mail for a week. Got it?'

'Certainly, Barney.'

The card rolled through on the tray and Dr Lecter held it to the light. 'A trainee? It says "trainee." Jack Crawford sent a *trainee* to interview me?' He tapped the card against his small white teeth and breathed in its smell.

'Dr Lecter,' Barney said.

'Of course.' He put the card back in the tray carrier and Barney pulled it to the outside.

'I'm still in training at the Academy, yes,' Starling said, 'but we're not discussing the FBI – we're talking about psychology. Can you decide for yourself if I'm qualified in what we talk about?'

'Ummmm,' Dr Lecter said. 'Actually . . . that's rather slippery of you. Barney, do you think Officer Starling might have a chair?'

'Dr Chilton didn't tell me anything about a chair.'

'What do your manners tell you, Barney?'

'Would you like a chair?' Barney asked her. 'We could have had one, but he never – well, usually nobody needs to stay that long.'

'Yes, thank you,' Starling said.

Barney brought a folding chair from the locked closet across the hall, set it up, and left them.

'Now,' Lecter said, sitting sideways at his table to face her, 'what did Miggs say to you?'

'Who?'

'Multiple Miggs, in the cell down there. He hissed at you. What did he say?'

'He said, "I can smell your cunt."'

'I see. I myself cannot. You use Evyan skin cream, and sometimes you wear L'Air du Temps, but not today. Today you are determinedly unperfumed. How do you feel about what Miggs said?'

'He's hostile for reasons I couldn't know. It's too bad. He's hostile to people, people are hostile to him. It's a loop.'

'Are you hostile to him?'

'I'm sorry he's disturbed. Beyond that, he's noise. How did you know about the perfume?'

'A puff from your bag when you got out your card. Your bag is lovely.'

'Thank you.'

'You brought your best bag, didn't you?'

'Yes.' It was true. She had saved for the classic casual handbag, and it was the best item she owned.

'It's much better than your shoes.'

'Maybe they'll catch up.'

'I have no doubt of it.'

'Did you do the drawings on your walls, Doctor?'

'Do you think I called in a decorator?'

'The one over the sink is a European city?'

'It's Florence. That's the Palazzo Vecchio and the Duomo, seen from the Belvedere.'

'Did you do it from memory, all the detail?'

'Memory, Officer Starling, is what I have instead of a view.'

'The other one is a crucifixion? The middle cross is empty.'

'It's Golgotha after the Deposition. Crayon and Magic Marker on butcher paper. It's what the thief who had been promised Paradise really got, when they took the paschal lamb away.'

'And what was that?'

'His legs broken of course, just like his companion who mocked Christ. Are you entirely innocent of the Gospel of St. John? Look at Duccio, then – he paints accurate crucifixions. How is Will Graham? How does he look?'

'I don't know Will Graham.'

'You know who he is. Jack Crawford's protégé. The one before you. How does his face look?'

'I've never seen him.'

'This is called "cutting up a few old touches," Officer Starling, you don't mind do you?'

Beats of silence and she plunged.

'Better than that, we could touch up a few old cuts here. I brought –'

'No. No, that's stupid and wrong. Never use wit in a segue. Listen, understanding a witticism and replying to it makes your subject perform a fast, detached scan that is inimical to mood. It is on the plank of mood that we proceed. You were doing fine, you'd been courteous and receptive to courtesy, you'd established trust by telling the embarrassing truth about Miggs, and then you come in with a ham-handed segue into your questionnaire. It won't do.'

'Dr Lecter, you're an experienced clinical psychiatrist. Do you think I'm dumb enough to try to run some kind of mood scam on you? Give me some credit. I'm asking you to respond to the questionnaire, and you will or you won't. Would it hurt to look at the thing?'

'Officer Starling, have you read any of the papers coming out of Behavioral Science recently?'

'Yes.

'So have I. The FBI stupidly refused to send me the *Law Enforcement Bulletin*, but I get it from secondhand dealers and I have the *News* from John Jay, and the psychiatric journals. They're dividing the people who practice serial murder into two groups – organized and disorganized. What do you think of that?'

'It's . . . fundamental, they evidently –'

'*Simplistic* is the word you want. In fact, most psychology is puerile, Officer Starling, and that practiced in Behavioral Science is on a level with phrenology. Psychology doesn't get very good material to start with. Go to any college psychology department and look at the students and faculty: ham radio enthusiasts and other personality-deficient buffs. Hardly the best brains on the campus. *Organized* and *disorganized* – a real bottom-feeder thought of that.'

'How would you change the classification?'

'I wouldn't.'

'Speaking of publications, I read your pieces on surgical addiction and left-side, right-side facial displays.'

'Yes, they were first-rate,' Dr Lecter said.

'I thought so, and so did Jack Crawford. He pointed them out to me. That's one reason he's anxious for you –'

'Crawford the Stoic is anxious? He must be busy if he's recruiting help from the student body.'

'He is, and he wants –'

'Busy with Buffalo Bill.'

'I expect so.'

'No. Not "I expect so." Officer Starling, you know perfectly well it's Buffalo Bill. I thought Jack Crawford might have sent you to ask me about that.'

'No.'

'Then you're not working around to it.'

'No. I came because we need your –'

'What do you know about Buffalo Bill?'

'Nobody knows much.'

'Has everything been in the papers?'

'I think so. Dr Lecter, I haven't seen any confidential material on that case, my job is –'

'How many women has Buffalo Bill used?'

'The police have found five.'

'All flayed?'

'Partially, yes.'

'The papers have never explained his name. Do you know why he's called Buffalo Bill?'

'Yes.'

'Tell me.'

'I'll tell you if you'll look at this questionnaire.'

'I'll look, that's all. Now, why?'

'It started as a bad joke in Kansas City homicide.'

'Yes . . . .?'

'They call him Buffalo Bill because he skins his humps.'

Starling discovered that she had traded feeling frightened for feeling cheap. Of the two, she preferred feeling frightened.

'Send through the questionnaire.'

Starling rolled the blue section through on the tray. She sat still while Lecter flipped through it.

He dropped it back in the carrier. 'Oh, Officer Starling, do you think you can dissect me with this blunt little tool?'

'No. I think you can provide some insight and advance this study.'

'And what possible reason could I have to do that?'

'Curiosity.'

'About what?'

'About why you're here. About what happened to you.'

'Nothing happened to me, Officer Starling. I happened. You can't reduce me to a set of influences. You've given up good and evil for behaviorism, Officer Starling. You've got everybody in moral dignity pants – nothing is ever anybody's fault. Look at me, Officer Starling. Can you stand to say I'm evil? Am I evil, Officer Starling?'

'I think you've been destructive. For me it's the same thing.'

'Evil's just destructive? Then *storms* are evil, if it's that simple. And we have *fire*, and then there's *hail*. Underwriters lump it all under "Acts of God." '

'Deliberate –'

'I collect church collapses, recreationally. Did you see the recent one in Sicily? Marvelous! The façade fell on sixty-five grandmothers at a special Mass. Was that evil? If so, who did it? If He's up there, He just loves it, Officer Starling. Typhoid and swans – it all comes from the same place.'

'I can't explain you. Doctor, but I know who can.'

He stopped her with his upraised hand. The hand was shapely, she noted, and the middle finger perfectly replicated. It is the rarest form of polydactyly.

When he spoke again, his tone was soft and pleasant. 'You'd like to quantify me Officer Starling. You're so ambitious, aren't you? Do you know what you look like to me, with your good bag and your cheap shoes? You look like a rube. You're a well-scrubbed, hustling rube with a little taste. Your eyes are like cheap birthstones – all surface shine when you stalk some little answer. And you're bright behind them, aren't you? Desperate not to be like your mother. Good nutrition has given you some length of bone, but you're not more than one generation out of the mines, *Officer* Starling. Is it the West Virginia Starlings or the Okie Starlings, Officer? It was a toss-up between college and the opportunities in the Women's Army

Corps, wasn't it? Let me tell you something specific about yourself, Student Starling. Back in your room, you have a string of gold add-a-beads and you feel an ugly little thump when you look at how tacky they are now, isn't that so? All those tedious thank-yous, permitting all that sincere fumbling, getting all sticky once for every bead. Tedious. Tedious. Bo-o-o-o-r-i-ing. Being smart spoils a lot of things, doesn't it? And taste isn't kind. When you think about this conversation, you'll remember the dumb animal hurt in his face when you got rid of him.

'If the add-a-beads got tacky, what else will as you go along? You wonder don't you, at night?' Dr Lecter asked in the kindest of tones.

Starling raised her head to face him. 'You see a lot, Dr Lecter. I won't deny anything you've said. But here's the question you're answering for me right now, whether you mean to or not: Are you strong enough to point that high-powered perception at yourself? It's hard to face. I've found that out in the last few minutes. How about it? Look at yourself and write down the truth. What more fit or complex subject could you find? Or maybe you're afraid of yourself.'

'You're tough, aren't you, Officer Starling?'

'Reasonably so, yes.'

'And you'd hate to think you were common. Wouldn't that sting? My! Well you're far from common, Officer Starling. All you have is fear of it. What are your add-a-beads, seven millimeter?'

' Seven. '

'Let me make a suggestion. Get some loose, drilled tiger's eyes and string them alternately with the gold beads. You might want to do two-and-three or one-and-two, however looks best to you. The tiger's eyes will pick up the color of your own eyes and the highlights in your hair. Has anyone ever sent you a Valentine?'

'Yep.'

'We're already into Lent. Valentine's Day is only a week away, hummmm, are you expecting some?'

'You never know.'

'No, you never do . . . I've been thinking about Valentine's Day. It reminds me of something funny. Now that I think of it, I could make you very happy on Valentine's Day, *Clarice* Starling.'

'How, Doctor Lecter?'

'By sending you a wonderful Valentine. I'll have to think about it. Now please excuse me. Good-bye, Officer Starling.'

'And the study?'

'A census taker tried to quantify me once. I ate his liver with some fava beans and a big Amarone. Go back to school, little Starling. '

Hannibal Lecter, polite to the last, did not give her his back. He stepped backward from the barrier before he turned to his cot again, and lying on it, became as remote from her as a stone crusader lying on a tomb.

Starling felt suddenly empty, as though she had given blood. She took longer than necessary to put the papers back in her briefcase because she didn't immediately trust her legs. Starling was soaked with the failure she detested. She folded her chair and leaned it against the utility closet door. She would have to pass Miggs again. Barney in the distance appeared to be reading. She could call him to come for her. Damn Miggs. It was no worse than passing construction crews or delivery louts every day in the city. She started back down the corridor.

Close beside her, Miggs' voice hissed, 'I bit my wrist so I can diiiieeeeeeeee – see how it bleeds?'

She should have called Barney but, startled, she looked into the cell, saw Miggs flick his fingers and felt the warm spatter on her cheek and shoulder before she could turn away.

She got away from him, registered that it was semen, not blood, and Lecter was calling to her, she could hear him. Dr Lecter's voice behind her, the cutting rasp in it more pronounced.

'Officer Starling.'

He was up and calling after her as she walked. She rummaged in her purse for tissues.

Behind her, 'Officer Starling.'

She was on the cold rails of her control now, making steady progress toward the gate.

'Officer Starling.' A new note in Lecter's voice.

She stopped. *What in God's name do I want this bad?* Miggs hissed something she didn't listen to.

She stood again in front of Lecter's cell and saw the rare spectacle of the doctor agitated. She knew that he could smell it on her. He could smell everything.

'I would not have had that happen to you. Discourtesy is unspeakably ugly to me.'

It was as though committing murders had purged him of lesser rudeness. Or perhaps, Starling thought, it excited him to see her marked in this particular way. She couldn't tell. The sparks in his eyes flew into his darkness like fireflies down a cave.

Whatever it is, use it, Jesus! She held up her briefcase. 'Please do this for me.'

Maybe she was too late; he was calm again.

'No. But I'll make you happy that you came. I'll give you something else. I'll give you what you love the most, Clarice Starling.'

'What's that, Dr Lecter?'

'Advancement, of course. It works out perfectly – I'm so glad. Valentine's Day made me think of it.' The smile over his small white teeth could have come for any reason. He spoke so softly she could barely hear. 'Look in Raspail's car for your Valentines. Did you hear me? Look in *Raspail's car* for your Valentines. You'd better go now; I don't think Miggs could manage again so soon, even if he *is* crazy, do you?'

Chapter Four

Clarice Startling was excited, depleted, running on her will. Some of the things Lecter had said about her were true, and some only clanged on the truth. For a few seconds she had felt an alien consciousness loose in her head, slapping things off the shelves like a bear in a camper.

She hated what he'd said about her mother and she had to get rid of the anger. This was business.

She sat in her old Pinto across the street from the hospital and breathed deeply. When the windows fogged she had a little privacy from the sidewalk.

Raspail. She remembered the name. He was a patient of Lecter's and one of his victims. She'd had only one evening with the Lecter background material. The file was vast and Raspail one of many victims. She needed to read the details.

Starling wanted to run with it, but she knew that the urgency was of her own manufacture. The Raspail case was closed years ago. No one was in danger. She had time. Better to be well informed and well advised before she went further.

Crawford might take it away from her and give it to someone else. She'd have to take that chance.

She tried to call him from a phone booth, but found he was budget-begging for the Justice Department before the House Subcommittee on Appropriations.

She could have gotten details of the case from the Baltimore Police Department's homicide division, but murder is not a federal crime and she knew they'd snatch it away from her immediately, no question.

She drove back to Quantico, back to Behavioral Science with its homey brown-checked curtains and its gray files full of hell. She sat there into the evening, after the last secretary had left, cranking through the Lecter microfilm. The contrary old viewer glowed like a jack-o'-lantern in the darkened room, the words and the negatives of pictures swarming across her intent face.

Raspail Benjamin René, WM, 46, was first flutist for the Baltimore Philharmonic Orchestra. He was a patient in Dr Hannibal Lecter's psychiatric practice.

On March 22, 1975, he failed to appear for a performance in Baltimore. On March 25 his body was discovered seated in a pew in a small rural church near Falls Church, Virginia, dressed only in a white tie and a tailcoat. Autopsy revealed that Raspail's heart was pierced and that he was short of his thymus and pancreas.

Clarice Starling, who from early life had known much more than she wished to know about meat processing, recognized the missing organs as the sweetbreads.

Baltimore Homicide believed that these items appeared on the menu of a dinner Lecter gave for the president and the conductor of the Baltimore Philharmonic on the evening following Raspail's disappearance.

Dr Hannibal Lecter professed to know nothing about these matters. The president and the conductor of the Philharmonic testified that they could not recall the fare at Dr Lecter's dinner, though Lecter was known for the excellence of his table and had contributed numerous articles to gourmet magazines.

The president of the Philharmonic subsequently was treated for anorexia and problems related to alcohol dependency at a holistic nerve sanitarium in Basel.

Raspail was Lecter's ninth known victim, according to the Baltimore police.

Raspail died intestate, and the lawsuits among his relatives over the estate were followed by the newspapers for a number of months before public interest flagged.

Raspail's relatives had also joined with the families of other victims in Lecter's practice in a successful lawsuit to have the errant psychiatrist's case files and tapes destroyed. There was no telling what embarrassing secrets he might blab, their reasoning went, and the files were documentation.

The court had appointed Raspail's lawyer, Everett Yow, to be executor of his estate.

Starling would have to apply to the lawyer to get at the car. The lawyer might be protective of Raspail's memory and, with enough advance notice, might destroy evidence to cover for his late client.

Starling preferred to pounce and she needed advice and authorization. She was alone in Behavioral Science and had the run of the place. She found Crawford's home number in the Rolodex.

She never heard the telephone ringing, but suddenly, his voice was there very quiet and even.

'Jack Crawford.'

'This is Clarice Starling. I hope you weren't eating dinner . . . She had to continue into silence. . . . Lecter told me something about the Raspail case today. I'm in the office following it up. He tells me there's something in Raspail's car. I'd have to get at it through his lawyer and since tomorrow's Saturday – no school – I wanted to ask you if –'

'Starling, do you have any recollection of what I told you to do with the Lecter information?' Crawford's voice was so terribly quiet.

'Give you a report by 0900 Sunday.'

'Do that, Starling. Do just exactly that.'

'Yes sir.'

The dial tone stung in her ear. The sting spread over her face and made her eyes burn.

'Well God fucking shit,' she said. You old creep. Creepo son of a bitch. Let Miggs squirt *you* and see how you like it.

Starling, scrubbed shiny and wearing the FBI Academy nightgown was working on the second draft of her report when her dormitory roommate, Ardelia Mapp, came in from the library. Mapp's broad, brown, eminently sane countenance was one of the more welcome sights of her day.

Ardelia Mapp saw the fatigue in her face.

'What did you do today, girl?' Mapp always asked questions as if the answers could make no possible difference.

'Wheedled a crazy man with come all over me.'

'I wish *I* had time for a social life – I don't know how you manage it, and school too.'

Starling found that she was laughing. Ardelia Mapp laughed with her, as much as the small joke was worth. Starling did not stop, and she heard herself from far away, laughing and laughing. Through Starling's tears Mapp looked strangely old and her smile had sadness in it.

Chapter Five

Jack Crawford, fifty-three, reads in a wing chair by a low lamp in the bedroom of his home. He faces two double beds both raised on blocks to hospital height. One is his own; in the other lies his wife Bella. Crawford can hear her breathing through her mouth. It has been two days since she last could stir or speak to him.

She misses a breath. Crawford looks up from his book over his half-glasses. He puts the book down. Bella breathes again, a flutter and then a full breath. He rises to put his hand on her, to take her blood pressure and her pulse. Over the months he has be come expert with the blood pressure cuff.

Because he will not leave her at night, he has installed a bed for himself beside her. Because he reaches out to her in the dark, his bed is high, like hers.

Except for the height of the beds and the minimal plumbing necessary for Bella's comfort, Crawford has managed to keep this from looking like a sickroom. There are flowers, but not too many. No pills are in sight – Crawford emptied a linen closet in the hall and filled it with her medicines and apparatus before he brought her home from the hospital. (It was the second time he had carried her across the threshold of that house and the thought nearly unmanned him.)

A warm front has come up from the south. The windows are open and the Virginia air is soft and fresh. Small frogs peep to one another in the dark.

The room is spotless, but the carpet has begun to nap – Crawford will not run the noisy vacuum cleaner in the room and uses a manual carpet sweeper that is not as good. He pads to the closet and turns on the light. Two clipboards hang on the inside of the door. On one he notes Bella's pulse and blood pressure. His figures and those of the day nurse alternate in a column that stretches over many yellow pages, many days and nights. On the other clipboard, the day-shift nurse has signed off Bella's medication.

Crawford is capable of giving any medication she may need in the night. Following a nurse's directions, he practiced injections on a lemon and then on his thighs before he brought her home.

Crawford stands over her for perhaps three minutes, looking down into her face. A lovely scarf of silk moiré covers her hair like a turban. She insisted on it, for as long as she could insist. Now he insists on it. He moistens her lips with glycerine and removes a speck from the corner of her eye with his broad thumb. She does not stir. It is not yet time to turn her.

At the mirror, Crawford assures himself that he is not sick, that he doesn't have to go into the ground with her, that he himself is well. He catches himself doing this and it shames him.

Back at his chair he cannot remember what he was reading. He feels the books beside him to find the one that is warm.

Chapter Six

On Monday morning, Clarice Starling found this message from Crawford in her mailbox:

> CS:
>
> Proceed on the Raspail car. On your own time. My office will provide you a credit card number for long distance calls. Ck with me before you contact estate or go anywhere. Report Wednesday 1600 hours.

The Director got your Lecter report over your signature. You did well.

JC
SAIC/Section 8

Starling felt pretty good. She knew Crawford was just giving her an exhausted mouse to bat around for practice. But he wanted to teach her. He wanted her to do well. For Starling, that beat courtesy every time.

Raspail had been dead for eight years. What evidence could have lasted in a car that long?

She knew from family experience that, because automobiles depreciate so rapidly, an appellate court will let survivors sell a car before probate, the money going into escrow. It seemed unlikely that even an estate as tangled and disputed as Raspail's would hold a car this long.

There was also the problem of time. Counting her lunch break, Starling had an hour and fifteen minutes a day free to use the telephone during business hours. She'd have to report to Crawford on Wednesday afternoon. So she had a total of three hours and forty-five minutes to trace the car, spread over three days, if she used her study periods and made up the study at night.

She had good notes from her Investigative Procedures classes, and she'd have a chance to ask general questions of her instructors.

During her Monday lunch, personnel at the Baltimore County Courthouse put Starling on hold and forgot her three times. During her study period she reached a friendly clerk at the courthouse who pulled the probate records on the Raspail estate.

The clerk confirmed that permission had been granted for sale of an auto and gave Starling the make and serial number of the car, and the name of a subsequent owner off the title transfer.

On Tuesday, she wasted half her lunch hour trying to chase down that name. It cost her the rest of her lunch period to find out that the Maryland Department of Motor Vehicles is not equipped to trace a vehicle by serial number, only by registration number or current tag number.

On Tuesday afternoon, a downpour drove the trainees in from the firing range. In a conference room steamy with damp clothing and sweat, John Brigham, the ex-Marine firearms instructor, chose to test Starling's hand strength in front of the class by seeing how many times she could pull the trigger on a Model 19 Smith & Wesson in sixty seconds.

She managed seventy-four with her left hand, puffed a strand of hair out of her eyes, and started over with her right while another student counted. She was in the Weaver stance, well braced, the front sight in sharp focus, the rear sight and her makeshift target properly blurred. Midway through her minute, she let her mind wander to get it off the pain. The target on the wall came into focus. It was a certificate of appreciation from the Interstate Commerce enforcement division made out to her instructor, John Brigham.

She questioned Brigham out of the side of her mouth while the other student counted the clicks of the revolver.

'How do you trace the current registration . . .'

'. . . *sixtyfivesixtysixsixtysevensixtyeightsixty* . . .'

'. . . of a car when you've only got the serial number . . .'

'. . . *seventyeightseventynineeightyeightyone* . . .'

'. . . and the make? You don't have a current tag number.'

'. . . *eightynineninety. Time.*'

'All right, you people,' the instructor said, 'I want you to take note of that. Hand strength's a major factor in steady combat shooting. Some of you gentlemen are worried I'll call on you next. Your worries would be justified – Starling is well above average with both hands. That's because she works at it. She works at it with the little squeezy things you all have access to. Most of you are not used to squeezing anything harder than your –' ever vigilant against his native Marine terminology, he groped for a polite simile – 'zits,' ' he said at last. 'Get serious, Starling, you're not good enough either. I want to see that left hand over ninety before you graduate. Pair up and time each other – chop-chop.

'Not you. Starling, come here. What else have you got on the car?'

'Just the serial number and make, that's it. One prior owner five years ago.'

'All right listen. Where most people f– fall into error is trying to leapfrog through the registrations from one owner to the next. You get fouled up between states. I mean, cops even do that sometimes. And registrations and tag numbers are all the computer's got. We're all accustomed to using tag numbers or registration numbers, not vehicle serial numbers.'

The clicking of the blue-handled practice revolvers was loud all over the room and he had to rumble in her ear.

'There's one way it's easy. R. L. Polk and Company, that publishes city directories – they also put out a list of current car registrations by make and consecutive serial number. It's the only place. Car dealers steer their advertising with them. How'd you know to ask me?'

'You were ICC enforcement, I figured you'd traced a lot of vehicles. Thanks.'

'Pay me back – get that left hand up where it ought to be and let's shame some of these lilyfingers.'

Back in her phone booth during study period, her hands trembled so that her notes were barely legible. Raspail's car was a Ford. There was a Ford dealer near the University of Virginia who for years had patiently done what he could with her Pinto. Now, just as patiently, the dealer poked through his Polk listings for her. He came back to the telephone with the name and address of the person who had last registered Benjamin Raspail's car.

Clarice is on a roll, Clarice has got control. Quit being silly and call the man up at his home in, lemme see, Number Nine Ditch, Arkansas. Jack Crawford will never let me go down there, but at least I can confirm who's got the ride.

No answer and again no answer. The ring sounded funny and far away, a double rump-rump like a party line. She tried at night and got no answer.

At Wednesday lunch period, a man answered Starling's call:

'WPOQ Plays the Oldies.'

'Hello, I' m calling to –'

'I wouldn't care for any aluminum siding and I don't want to live in no trailer court in Florida, what else you got?'

Starling heard a lot of the Arkansas hills in the man's voice. She could speak that with anybody when she wanted to, and her time was short.

'Yessir, if you could help me out I'd be much obliged. I'm trying to get ahold of Mr Lomax Bardwell? This is Clarice Starling?'

'It's Starling somebody,' the man yelled to the rest of his household. 'What do you want with Bardwell?'

'This is the Mid-South regional office of the Ford recall division? He's entitled to some warranty work on his LTD free of charge?'

'I'm Bardwell. I thought you was trying to sell me something on that cheap long distance. It's way too late for any adjustment, I need the whole thing. Me and the wife was in Little Rock, pulling out of the Southland Mall there?'

'Yessir.'

'Durn rod come out through the oil pan. Oil all over everywhere and that Orkin truck that's got the big bug on top of it? He hit that oil and got sideways.'

'Lord have mercy.'

'Knocked the Fotomat booth slap off the blocks and the glass fell out. Fotomat fella come wandering out addled. Had to keep him out of the road.'

'Well I'll be. What happened to it then?'

'What happened to what?'

'The car.'

'I told Buddy Sipper at the wrecking yard he could have it for fifty if he'd come get it. I expect he's parted it out.'

'Could you tell me what his telephone number is, Mr Bardwell?'

'What do you want with Sipper? If anybody gets something out of it, it ought to be me.'

'I understand that sir. I just do what they tell me till five o'clock, and they said find the car. Have you got that number, please?'

'I can't find my phone hook. It's been gone a good while now. You know how it is with these grandbabies. Central ought to give it to you, it's Sipper Salvage.'

'Much oblige, Mr Bardwell.'

The salvage yard confirmed that the automobile had been stripped and pressed into a cube to be recycled. The foreman read Starling the vehicle serial number from his records.

Shit House Mouse, thought Starling, not entirely out of the accent. Dead end. Some Valentine.

Starling rested her head against the cold coin box in the telephone booth. Ardelia Mapp, her books on her hip, pecked on the door of the booth and handed in an Orange Crush.

'Much oblige, Ardelia. I got to make one more call. If I can get done with that in time, I'll catch up with you in the cafeteria, okay?'

'I was *so* in hopes you'd overcome that ghastly dialect,' Mapp said. 'Books are available to help. I never use the colorful patois of my housing project anymore. You come talking that mushmouth, people say you eat up with the dumb-ass, girl.' Mapp closed the phone booth door.

Starling felt she had to try for more information from Lecter. If she already had the appointment, maybe Crawford would let her return to the asylum. She dialed Dr Chilton's number, but she never got past his secretary.

'Dr Chilton is with the coroner and the assistant district attorney,' the woman said. 'He's already spoken to your supervisor and he has nothing to say to you. Goodbye.'

Chapter Seven

'Your friend Miggs is dead,' Crawford said. 'Did you tell me everything, Starling?' Crawford's tired face was as sensitive to signals as the dished ruff of an owl, and as free of mercy.

'How?' She felt numb and she had to handle it.

'Swallowed his tongue sometime before daylight. Lecter suggested it to him, Chilton thinks. The overnight orderly heard Lecter talking softly to Miggs. Lecter knew a lot about Miggs. He talked to him for a little while, but the overnight couldn't hear what Lecter said. Miggs was crying for a while, and then he stopped. Did you tell me everything, Starling?'

'Yes sir. Between the report and my memo, there's everything, almost verbatim.'

'Chilton called up to complain about you . . .' Crawford waited, and seemed pleased when she wouldn't ask. 'I told him I found your behavior satisfactory. Chilton's trying to forestall a civil rights investigation.'

'Will there be one?'

'Sure, if Miggs' family want it. Civil Rights Division will do probably eight thousand this year. They'll be glad to add Miggs to the list.' Crawford studied her. 'You okay?'

'I don't know how to feel about it.'

'You don't have to feel any particular way about it. Lecter did it to amuse himself. He knows they can't really touch him for it, so why not? Chilton takes his books and his toilet seat for a while is all, and he doesn't get any Jell-O.' Crawford laced his fingers over his stomach and compared his thumbs. 'Lecter asked you about me didn't he?'

'He asked if you were busy. I said yes.'

'That's all? You didn't leave out anything personal because I wouldn't want to see it?'

'No. He said you were a Stoic, but I put that in.'

'Yes, you did. Nothing else?'

'No, I didn't leave anything out. You don't think I traded some kind of gossip, and that's why he talked to me?'

'No.'

'I don't know anything personal about you, and if I did I wouldn't discuss it. If you've got a problem believing that, let's get it straight now.'

'I'm satisfied. Next item.'

311

'You thought *something*, or –'

'Proceed to the next item, Starling.'

'Lecter's hint about Raspail's car is a dead end. It was mashed into a cube four months ago in Number Nine Ditch, Arkansas, and sold for recycling. Maybe if I go back in and talk to him, he'll tell me more.'

'You've exhausted the lead?'

'Yes.'

'Why do you think the car Raspail drove was his only car?'

'It was the only one registered, he was single, I assumed –'

'Aha, hold it.' Crawford's forefinger pointed to some principle invisible in the air between them. 'You assumed. You *assumed*, Starling. Look here.' Crawford wrote *assume* on a legal pad. Several of Starling's instructors had picked this up from Crawford and used it, but Starling didn't reveal that she'd seen it before.

Crawford began to underline. 'If you *assume* when I send you on a job, Starling, you can make an *ass* out of *u* and *me* both.' He leaned back, pleased. 'Raspail collected cars, did you know that?'

'No, does the estate still have them?'

'I don't know. Do you think you could manage to find out?'

'Yes, I can.'

'Where would you start?'

'His executor.'

'A lawyer in Baltimore, a Chinese, I seem to remember,' Crawford said.

'Everett Yow,' Starling said. 'He's in the Baltimore phone book.'

'Have you given any thought to the question of a warrant to search Raspail's car?'

Sometimes Crawford's tone reminded Starling of the know-it-all caterpillar in Lewis Carroll.

Starling didn't dare give it back, much. 'Since Raspail is deceased and not suspected of anything, if we have permission of his executor to search the car, then it is a valid search, and the fruit admissible evidence in other matters at law,' she recited.

'Precisely,' Crawford said. 'Tell you what: I'll advise the Baltimore field office you'll be up there. Saturday, Starling, on your own time. Go feel the fruit, if there is any.'

Crawford made a small, successful effort not to look after her as she left. From his wastebasket he lifted in the fork of his fingers a wad of heavy mauve notepaper. He spread it on his desk. It was about his wife and it said, in an engaging hand:

> O wrangling schools, that search what fire
> Shall burn this world, had none the wit
> Unto this knowledge to aspire
> That this her fever might be it?

I'm so sorry about Bella, Jack.

Hannibal Lecter

Chapter Eight

Everett Yow drove a black Buick with a De Paul University sticker on the back window. His weight gave the Buick a slight list to the left as Clarice Starling followed him out of Baltimore in the rain. It was almost dark; Starling's day as an investigator was nearly gone and she didn't have another day to replace it. She dealt with her impatience, tapping the wheel in time with the wipers as the traffic crawled down Route 301.

Yow was intelligent, fat, and had a breathing problem. Starling guessed his age at sixty. So far he was accommodating. The lost day was not his fault; returning in the late afternoon from a week-long business trip to Chicago, the Baltimore lawyer had come directly from the airport to his office to meet Starling.

Raspail's classic Packard had been stored since long before his death, Yow explained. It was unlicensed and never driven. Yow had seen it once, covered and in storage, to confirm its existence for the estate inventory he made shortly after his client's murder. If Investigator Starling would agree to 'frankly disclose at once' anything she found that might be damaging to his late client's interests, he would show her the automobile, he said. A warrant and the attendant stir would not be necessary.

Starling was enjoying the use for one day of an FBI motor pool Plymouth with a cellular telephone, and she had a new ID card provided by Crawford. It simply said FEDERAL INVESTIGATOR – and expired in a week, she noticed.

Their destination was Split City Mini-Storage, about four miles past the city limits. Creeping along with the traffic, Starling used her telephone to find out what she could about the storage facility. By the time she spotted the high orange sign, SPLIT CITY MINI-STORAGE – YOU KEEP THE KEY, she had learned a few facts.

Split City had an Interstate Commerce Commission freight-forwarder's license, in the name of Bernard Gary. A federal grand jury had barely missed Gary for interstate transportation of stolen goods three years ago, and his license was up for review.

Yow turned in beneath the sign and showed his keys to a spotty young man in uniform at the gate. The gatekeeper logged their license numbers, opened up and beckoned impatiently, as though he had more important things to do.

Split City is a bleak place the wind blows through. Like the Sunday divorce flight from La Guardia to Juárez, it is a service industry to the mindless Brownian movement in our population; most of its business is storing the sundered chattels of divorce. Its units are stacked with living room suites, breakfast ensembles, spotted mattresses, toys, and the photographs of things that didn't work out. It is widely believed among Baltimore County sheriff's officers that Split City also hides good and valuable consideration from the bankruptcy courts.

It resembles a military installation: thirty acres of long buildings divided by fire walls into units the size of a generous single garage, each with its roll-up overhead door. The rates are reasonable and some of the property has been there for years. Security is good. The place is surrounded by a double row of high hurricane fence, and dogs patrol between the fences twenty-four hours a day.

Six inches of sodden leaves, mixed with paper cups and small trash, had banked against the bottom of the door of Raspail's storage unit, number 31. A hefty padlock secured each side of the door. The left-side hasp also had a seal on it. Everett Yow bent stiffly over the seal. Starling held the umbrella and a flashlight in the early dark.

'It doesn't appear to have been opened since I was here five years ago,' he said. 'You see the impression of my notary seal here in the plastic. I had no idea at the time that the relatives would be so contentious and would drag out the probate for so many years.'

Yow held the flashlight and umbrella while Starling took a picture of the lock and seal.

'Mr Raspail had an office-studio in the city, which I closed down to save the estate from paying rent,' he said. 'I had the furnishings brought here and stored them with Raspail's car and other things that were already here. We brought an upright piano, books and music, a bed, I think.'

Yow tried a key. 'The locks may be frozen. At least this one's very stiff.' It was hard for him to bend over and breathe at the same time. When he tried to squat, his knees creaked.

Starling was glad to see that the padlocks were big chrome American Standards. They looked formidable, but she knew she could pop the brass cylinders out easily with a sheet metal screw and a claw hammer – her father had showed her how burglars do it when she was a child. The problem would be finding the hammer and screw; she did not even have the benefit of the resident junk in her Pinto.

She poked through her purse and found the de-icer spray she used on her Pinto's door locks.

'Want to rest a second in your car, Mr Yow? Why don't you warm up for a few minutes and I'll give this a try. Take the umbrella, it's only a drizzle now.'

Starling moved the FBI Plymouth up close to the door to use its headlights. She pulled the dipstick out of the car and dripped oil into the keyholes of the padlocks, then sprayed in de-icer to thin the oil. Mr Yow smiled and nodded from his car. Starling was glad Yow was an intelligent man; she could perform her task without alienating him.

It was dark now. She felt exposed in the glare of the Plymouth's headlights and the fan belt squealed in her ear as the car idled. She'd locked the car while it was running. Mr Yow appeared to be harmless, but she saw no reason to take a chance on being mashed against the door.

The padlock jumped like a frog in her hand and lay there open, heavy and greasy. The other lock, having soaked, was easier.

The door would not come up. Starling lifted on the handle until bright spots danced before her eyes. Yow came to help, but between the small, inadequate door handle and his hernia, they exerted little additional force.

'We might return next week, with my son, or with some workmen,' Mr Yow suggested. 'I would like very much to go home soon.'

Starling was not at all sure she'd ever get back to this place; it would be less trouble to Crawford if he just picked up the telephone and had the Baltimore field office handle it. 'Mr Yow, I'll hurry. Do you have a bumper jack in this car?'

With the jack under the handle of the door, Starling used her weight on top of the lug wrench that served as a jack handle. The door squealed horribly and went up a half-inch. It appeared to be bending upward in the center. The door went up another inch and another until she could slide the spare tire under it, to hold it up while she moved Mr Yow's jack and her own to the sides of the door placing them under the bottom edge, close to the tracks the door ran in.

Alternating at the jacks on each side, she inched the door up a foot and a half, where it jammed solidly and her full weight on the jack handles would not raise it.

Mr Yow came to peer under the door with her. He could only bend over for a few seconds at a time.

'It smells like mice in there,' he said. 'I was assured they used rodent poison here. I believe it is specified in the contract. Rodents are almost unknown, they said. But I hear them, do you?'

'I hear them,' Starling said. With her flashlight, she could pick out cardboard boxes and one big tire with a wide whitewall beneath the edge of a cloth cover. The tire was flat.

She backed the Plymouth up until part of the headlight pattern shone under the door, and she took out one of the rubber floor mats.

'You're going in there, Officer Starling?'

'I have to take a look, Mr Yow.'

He took out his handkerchief. 'May I suggest you tie your cuffs snugly around your ankles? To prevent mouse intrusion.'

'Thank you, sir, that's a very good idea. Mr Yow, if the door should come down, ha ha, or something else should occur, would you be kind enough to call this number? It's our Baltimore field office. They know I'm here with you right now, and they'll be alarmed if they don't hear from me in a little while, do you follow me?'

'Yes, of course. Absolutely, I do.' He gave her the key to the Packard.

Starling put the rubber mat on the wet ground in front of the door and lay down on it, her hand cupping a pack of plastic evidence bags over the lens of her camera and her cuffs tied snugly with Yow's han dkerchief and her own. A mist of rain fell in her face. and the smell of mold and mice was strong in her nose. What occurred to Starling was, absurdly, Latin.

Written on the blackboard by her forensics instructor on her first day in training, it was the motto of the Roman physician: *Primum non nocere*. First do no harm.

He didn't say that in a garage full of fucking mice.

And suddenly her father's voice, speaking to her with his hand on her brother's shoulder, 'If you can't play without squawling, Clarice, go on to the house.'

Starling fastened the collar button of her blouse, scrunched her shoulders up around her neck and slid under the door.

She was beneath the rear of the Packard. It was parked close to the left side of the storage room, almost touching the wall. Cardboard boxes were stacked high on the right side of the room, filling the space beside the car. Starling wriggled along on her back until her head was out in the narrow gap left between the car and the boxes. She shined her flashlight up the cliff face of boxes. Many spiders had spanned the narrow space with their webs. Orb weavers, mostly, the webs dotted with small shriveled carcasses tightly bound.

Well, a brown recluse spider is the only kind to worry about, and it wouldn't build out in the open, Starling said to herself. *The rest don't raise much of a welt.*

There would be space to stand beside the rear fender. She wriggled around until she was out from under the car, her face close beside the wide whitewall tire. It was hatched with dry rot. She could read the words GOODYEAR DOUBLE EAGLE on it. Careful of her head, she got to her feet in the narrow space, hand before her face to break the webs. Was this how it felt to wear a veil?

Mr Yow's voice from outside. 'Okay, Miss Starling?'

'Okay,' she said. There were small scurryings at the sound of her voice, and something inside a piano climbed over a few high notes. The car lights from outside lit her legs up to the calf.

'So you found the piano, Officer Starling,' Mr Yow called.

'That wasn't me.'

'Oh.'

The car was big, tall and long. A 1938 Packard limousine, according to Yow's inventory. It was covered with a rug, the plush side down. She played her flashlight over it.

'Did you cover the car with this rug, Mr Yow?'

'I found it that way and I never uncovered it,' Yow called under the door. 'I can't deal with a dusty rug. That's the way Raspail had it. I just made sure the car was there. My movers put the piano against the wall and covered it and stacked more boxes beside the car and left. I was paying them by the hour. The boxes are sheet music and books, mostly.'

The rug was thick and heavy and as she tugged at it, dust swarmed in the beam of her flashlight. She sneezed twice. Standing on tiptoe, she could fold the rug over to the midline of the tall old car. The curtains were drawn in the back windows. The door handle was covered with dust. She had to lean forward over cartons to reach it. Touching only the end of the handle, she tried to turn it downward. Locked. There was no keyhole in the rear door. She'd have to move a lot of boxes to get to the front door, and there was damn little place to put them. She could see a small gap between the curtain and the post of the rear window.

Starling leaned over boxes to put her eye close to the glass and shined her light through the crack. She could only see her reflection until she cupped her hand on top of the light. A splinter of the beam, diffused by the dusty glass, moved across the seat . An album lay open on the seat. The colors were poor in the bad light, but she could see Valentines pasted on the pages. Lacy old Valentines, fluffy on the page.

'Thanks a lot, Dr Lecter.' When she spoke, her breath stirred the fuzz of dust on the windowsill and fogged the glass. She didn't want to wipe it, so she had to wait for it to clear. The light moved on over a lap rug crumpled on the floor of the car and onto the dusty wink of a pair of man's patent leather evening shoes. Above the shoes, black socks and above the socks were tuxedo trousers with legs in them.

Nobodysbeeninthatdoorinfiveyears – easy, easy, hold it baby.

'Oh, Mr Yow. Say, Mr Yow?'

'Yes, Officer Starling?'

'Mr Yow, looks like somebody's sitting in this car.'

'Oh my. Maybe you better come out, Miss Starling.'

'Not quite yet, Mr Yow. Just wait there, if you will, please.'

Now is when it's important to think. Now is more important than all the crap you tell your pillow for the rest of your life. Suck it up and do this right. I don't want to destroy evidence. I do want some help. But most of all I don't want to cry wolf. If I scramble the Baltimore office and the cops out here for nothing, I've had it. I see what looks like some legs. Mr Yow would not have brought me here if he'd known there was a cool one in the car. She managed to smile at herself. 'Cool one' was bravado. *Nobody's been here since Yow's last visit. All right, that means the boxes were put here after whatever's in the car. And that means I can move the boxes without losing anything important.*

'All right, Mr Yow.'

'Yes. Do we have to call the police, or are you sufficient, Officer

Starling?'

'I've got to find that out. Just wait right there, please.'

The box problem was as maddening as Rubik's Cube. She tried to work with the flashlight under her arm, dropped it twice, and finally put it on top of the car. She had to put boxes behind her, and some of the shorter book cartons would slide under the car. Some kind of bite or splinter made the ball of her thumb itch.

Now she could see through the dusty glass of the front passenger's side window into the chauffeur's compartment. A spider had spun between the big steering wheel and the gearshift. The partition between the front and back compartments was closed.

She wished she had thought to oil the Packard key before she came under the door, but when she stuck it in the lock, it worked.

There was hardly room to open the door more than a third of the way in the narrow passage. It swung against the boxes with a thump that sent the mice scratching and brought additional notes from the piano. A stale smell of decay and chemicals came out of the car. It jogged her memory in a place she couldn't name.

She leaned inside, opened the partition behind the chauffeur's seat, and shined her flashlight into the rear compartment of the car. A formal shirt with studs was the bright thing the light found first, quickly up the shirtfront to the face, no face to see, and down again over glittering shirt studs and satin lapels to a lap with zipper open, and up again to the neat bow tie and the collar, where the white stub neck of a mannequin protruded. But above the neck, something else that reflected little light. Cloth, a black hood, where the head should be, big, as though it covered a parrot's cage. Velvet, Starling thought. It sat on a plywood shelf extending over the neck of the mannequin from the parcel shelf behind.

She took several pictures from the front seat, focusing with the flashlight and closing her eyes against the flash of the strobe. Then she straightened up outside the car. Standing in the dark, wet, with cobwebs on her, she considered what to do.

What she was *not* going to do was summon the special agent in charge of the Baltimore field office to look at a mannequin with its fly open and a book of Valentines.

Once she decided to get in the backseat and take the hood off the thing, she didn't want to think about it very long. She reached through the chauffeur's partition, unlocked the rear door, and rearranged some boxes to get it open. It all seemed to take a long time. The smell from the rear compartment was much stronger when she opened the door. She reached in and, carefully lifting the Valentine album by the corners, moved it onto an evidence bag on top of the car. She spread another evidence bag on the seat.

The car springs groaned as she got inside and the figure shifted a little when she sat down beside it. The right hand in its white glove slid off the thigh and lay on the seat. She touched the glove with her finger. The hand inside was hard. Gingerly she pushed the glove down from the wrist. The wrist was some white synthetic material. There was a lump in the trousers that for a silly instant reminded her of certain events in high school.

Small scrambling noises came from under the seat.

Gentle as a caress, her hand touching the hood. The cloth moved easily over something hard and slick beneath. When she felt the round knob on the top, she knew. She knew that it was a big laboratory specimen jar and she knew what would be in it. With dread, but little doubt, she pulled off the cover.

The head inside the jar had been severed neatly close beneath the jaw. It faced her, the eyes long burned milky by the alcohol that preserved it. The mouth was open and the tongue protruded slightly, very gray. Over the years, the alcohol had evaporated to the point that the head rested on the bottom of the jar, its crown protruding through the surface of the fluid in a cap of decay. Turned at an owlish angle to the body beneath, it gaped stupidly at Starling. Even in the play of light over the features, it remained dumb and dead.

Starling, in this moment, examined herself. She was pleased. She was exhilarated. She wondered for a second if those were worthy feelings. Now, at this moment, sitting in this old car with a head and some mice, she could think clearly, and she was proud of that.

'Well, Toto,' she said, 'we're not in Kansas anymore.' She'd always wanted to say that under stress, but doing it left her feeling phony, and she was glad nobody had heard. Work to do.

She sat back gingerly and looked around.

This was somebody's environment, chosen and created, a thousand light-years across the mind from the traffic crawling down Route 301.

Dried blossoms drooped from the cut-crystal bud vases on the pillars. The limousine's table was folded down and covered with a linen cloth. On it, a decanter gleamed through dust. A spider had built between the decanter and the short candlestick beside it.

She tried to picture Lecter, or someone, sitting here with her present companion and having a drink and trying to show him the Valentines. And what else? Working carefully, disturbing the figure as little as possible, she frisked it for identification. There was none. In a jacket pocket she found the bands of material left over from adjusting the length of the trousers – the dinner clothes were probably new when they were put on the figure.

Starling poked the lump in the trousers. Too hard, even for high school, she reflected. She spread the fly with her fingers and shined her light inside, on a dildo of polished, inlaid wood. Good-sized one, too. She wondered if she was depraved.

Carefully she turned the jar and examined the sides and back of the head for wounds. There were none visible. The name of a laboratory supply company was cast in the glass.

Considering the face again, she believed she learned something that would last her. Looking with purpose at this face, with its tongue changing color where it touched the glass, was not as bad as Miggs swallowing his tongue in her dreams. She felt she could look at anything, if she had something positive to do about it. Starling was young.

In the ten seconds after her WPIK-TV mobile news unit slid to a stop, Jonetta Johnson put in her earrings, powdered her beautiful brown face, and cased the situation. She and her news crew, monitoring the Baltimore County police radio, had arrived at Split City ahead of the patrol cars.

All the news crew saw in their headlights was Clarice Starling, standing in front of the garage door with her flashlight and her little laminated ID card, her hair plastered down by the drizzle.

Jonetta Johnson could spot a rookie every time. She climbed out with the camera crew behind her and approached Starling. The bright lights came on.

Mr Yow sank so far down in his Buick that only his hat was visible above the windowsill.

'Jonetta Johnson, WPIK news, did you report a homicide?'

Starling did not look like very much law and she knew it. 'I'm a federal officer, this is a crime scene. I have to secure it until the Baltimore authorities –'

The assistant cameraman had grabbed the bottom of the garage door and was trying to lift it.

'Hold it,' Starling said. 'I'm talking to *you*, sir. Hold it. Back off, please. I'm not kidding with you. Help me out here.' She wished hard for a badge, a uniform, anything.

'Okay, Harry,' the newswoman said. 'Ah, officer, we want to cooperate in every way. Frankly, this crew costs money and I just want to know whether to even keep them here until the other authorities arrive. Will you tell me if there's a body in there? Camera's off, just between us. Tell me and we'll wait. We'll be good, I promise. How about it?'

'I'd wait if I were you,' Starling said.

'Thanks, you won't be sorry,' Jonetta Johnson said. 'Look, I've got some information on Split City Mini-Storage that you could probably use. Would you shine your light on the clipboard? Let's see if I can find it here.'

'WEYE mobile unit just turned in at the gate, Joney,' the man Harry said.

'Let's see if I can find it here, Officer, here it is. There was a scandal about two years ago when they tried to prove this place was trucking and storing – was it fireworks?' Jonetta Johnson glanced over Starling's shoulder once too often.

Starling turned to see the cameraman on his back, his head and shoulders in the garage, the assistant squatting beside him, ready to pass the minicam under the door.

'Hey!' Starling said. She dropped to her knees on the wet ground beside him and tugged at his shirt. 'You can't go in there. Hey! I told you not to do that.'

And all the time the men were talking to her constantly, gently. 'We won't touch anything. We're pros, you don't have to worry. The cops will let us in anyway. It's all right, honey.'

Their cozening backseat manner put her over.

She ran to a bumper jack at the end of the door and pumped the handle. The door came down two inches, with a grinding screech. She pumped it again. Now the door was touching the man's chest. When he didn't come out she pulled the handle out of the socket and carried it back to the prone cameraman. There were other bright television lights now and in the glare of them she banged the door above him hard with the jack handle, showering dust and rust down on him.

'Give me your attention,' she said. 'You don't listen, do you? Come out of there. Now. You're one second from arrest for obstruction of justice.'

'Take it easy,' the assistant said. He put his hand on her. She turned on him. There were shouted questions from behind the glare and she heard sirens.

'Hands off and back off, buster.' She stood on the cameraman's ankle and faced the assistant, the jack handle hanging by her side. She did not raise the jack handle. It was just as well. She looked bad enough on television as it was.

Chapter Nine

The odors of the violent ward seemed more intense in the semidarkness. A TV set playing without sound in the corridor threw Starling's shadow on the bars of Dr Lecter's cage.

She could not see into the dark behind the bars , but she didn't ask the orderly to turn up the lights from his station. The whole ward would light at once and she knew the Baltimore County police had had the lights full on for hours while they shouted questions at Lecter. He had refused to speak but responded by folding for them an origami chicken that pecked when the tail was manipulated up and down. The senior officer, furious, had crushed the chicken in the lobby ashtray as he gestured for Starling to go in.

'Dr Lecter?' She heard her own breathing, and breathing down the hall, but from Miggs' empty cell, no breathing. Miggs' cell was vastly empty. She felt its silence like a draft.

Starling knew Lecter was watching her from the darkness. Two minutes passed. Her legs and back ached from her struggle with the garage door, and her clothes were damp. She sat on her coat on the floor, well back from the bars, her feet tucked under her, and lifted her wet, bedraggled hair over her collar to get it off her neck.

Behind her on the TV screen, an evangelist waved his arms.

'Dr Lecter, we both know what this is. They think you'll talk to me.'

Silence. Down the hall, someone whistled 'Over the Sea to Skye.'

After five minutes, she said, 'It was strange going in there. Sometime I'd like to talk to you about it.'

Starling jumped when the food carrier rolled out of Lecter's cell. There was a clean, folded towel in the tray. She hadn't heard him move.

She looked at it and, with a sense of falling, took it and toweled her hair.

'Thanks,' she said.

'Why don't you ask me about Buffalo Bill?' His voice was close, at her level. He must be sitting on the floor too.

'Do you know something about him?'

'I might if I saw the case.'

'I don't have the case,' Starling said.

'You won't have this one, either, when they're through using you.'

'I know.'

'You could get the files on Buffalo Bill. The reports and the pictures. I'd like to see it.'

I'll bet you would. 'Dr Lecter, you started this. Now please tell me about the person in the Packard.'

'You found an entire person? Odd. I only saw a head. Where do you suppose the rest came from?'

'All right. Whose *head* was it?'

'What can you tell?'

'They've only done the preliminary stuff. White male, about twenty-seven, both American and European dentistry. Who was he?'

'Raspail's lover. Raspail, of the gluey flute.'

'What were the circumstances – how did he die?'

'Circumlocution, Officer Starling?'

'No, I'll ask it later.'

'Let me save you some time. I didn't do it; Raspail did. Raspail liked sailors. This was a Scandinavian one named Klaus something. Raspail never told me the last name.'

Dr Lecter's voice moved lower. Maybe he was lying on the floor, Starling thought.

'Klaus was off a Swedish boat in San Diego. Raspail was out there teaching for a summer at the conservatory. He went berserk over the young man. The Swede saw a good thing and jumped his boat. They bought some kind of awful camper and sylphed through the woods naked. Raspail said the young man was unfaithful and he strangled him.'

'Raspail told you this?'

'Oh yes, under the confidential seal of therapy sessions. I think it was a lie. Raspail always embellished the facts. He wanted to seem dangerous and romantic. The Swede probably died in some banal erotic asphyxia transaction. Raspail was too flabby and weak to have strangled him. Notice how closely Klaus was trimmed under the jaw? Probably to remove a high ligature mark from hanging.'

'I see.'

'Raspail's dream of happiness was ruined. He put Klaus' head in a bowling bag and came back East.'

'What did he do with the rest?'

'Buried it in the hills.'

'He showed you the head in the car?'

'Oh yes, in the course of therapy he came to feel he could tell me anything. He went out to sit with Klaus quite often and showed him the Valentines.'

'And then Raspail himself . . . died. Why?'

'Frankly, I got sick and tired of his whining. Best thing for him, really. Therapy wasn't going anywhere. I expect most psychiatrists have a patient or two they'd like to refer to me. I've never discussed this before, and now I'm getting bored with it.'

'And your dinner for the orchestra officials.'

'Haven't you ever had people coming over and no time to shop? You have to make do with what's in the fridge, *Clarice*. May I call you Clarice?'

'Yes. I think I'll just call you –'

'Dr Lecter – that seems most appropriate to your age and station,' he said.

'Yes.'

'How did you feel when you went into the garage?'

'Apprehensive.'

'Why?'

'Mice and insects.'

'Do you have something you use when you want to get up your nerve?' Dr Lecter asked.

'Nothing I know of that works, except wanting what I'm after.'

'Do memories or tableaux occur to you then, whether you try for them or not?'

'Maybe. I haven't thought about it.'

'Things from your early life.'

'I'll have to watch and see.'

'How did you feel when you heard about my late neighbor, Miggs? You haven't asked me about it.'

'I was getting to it.'

'Weren't you *glad* when you heard?'

'No.'

'Were you *sad?*'

'No. Did you talk him into it?'

Dr Lecter laughed quietly. 'Are you asking me, Officer Starling, if I *suborned* Mr Miggs' felony suicide? Don't be silly. It has a certain pleasant symmetry, though, his swallowing that offensive tongue, don't you agree?'

'No.'

'Officer Starling, that was a lie. The first one you've told me. A *triste* occasion, Truman would say.'

'President Truman?'

'Never mind. Why do you think I helped you?'

'I don't know.'

'Jack Crawford likes you, doesn't he?'

'I don't know.'

'That's probably untrue. Would you like for him to like you? Tell me, do you feel an urge to please him and does it worry you? Are you *wary* of your urge to please him?'

'Everyone wants to be liked, Dr Lecter.'

'Not everyone. Do you think Jack Crawford wants you sexually? I'm sure he's very frustrated now. Do you think he visualizes . . . scenarios, transactions . . . fucking with you?'

'That's not a matter of curiosity to me, Dr Lecter, and it's the sort of thing Miggs would ask.'

'Not anymore.'

'Did you suggest to him that he swallow his tongue?'

'Your interrogative case often has that proper subjunctive in it. With your accent, it stinks of the lamp. Crawford clearly likes you and believes you competent. Surely the odd confluence of events hasn't escaped you, Clarice – you've had Crawford's help and you've had mine. You say you don't know why Crawford helps you – do you know why I did?'

'No, tell me.'

'Do you think it's because I like to look at you and think about eating you up – about how you would taste?'

'Is that it?'

'No. I want something Crawford can give me and I want to trade him for it. But he won't come to see me. He won't ask for my help with Buffalo Bill, even though he knows it means more young women will die.'

'I can't believe that, Dr Lecter.'

'I only want something very simple, and he could get it.' Lecter turned up the rheostat slowly in his cell. His books and drawings were gone. His toilet seat was gone. Chilton had stripped the cell to punish him for Miggs.

'I've been in this room eight years, Clarice. I know that they will never, ever let me out while I'm alive. What I want is a view. I want a window where I can see a tree, or even water.'

'Has your attorney petitioned –'

'Chilton put that television in the hall, set to a religious channel. As soon as you leave the orderly will turn the sound back up, and my attorney can't stop it, the way the court is inclined toward me now. I want to be in a federal institution and I want my books back and a view. I'll give good value for it. Crawford could do that. Ask him.'

'I can tell him what you've said.'

'He'll ignore it. And Buffalo Bill will go on and on. Wait until he scalps one and see how you like it. Ummmm . . . I'll tell you one thing about Buffalo Bill without ever seeing the case, and years from now when they catch him, if they ever do, you'll see that I was right and I could have helped. I could have saved lives. Clarice?'

'Yes?'

'Buffalo Bill has a two-storey house,' Dr Lecter said, and turned out his light.

He would not speak again.

Chapter Ten

Clarice Starling leaned against a dice table in the FBI's casino and tried to pay attention to a lecture on money-laundering in gambling. It had been thirty-six hours since the Baltimore County police took her deposition (via a chain-smoking two-finger typist: 'See if you can get that window open if the smoke bothers you') and dismissed her from its jurisdiction with a reminder that murder is not a federal crime.

The network news on Sunday night showed Starling's scrap with the television cameramen and she felt sure she was deep in the glue. Through it all, no word from Crawford or from the Baltimore field office. It was as though she had dropped her report down a hole.

The casino where she now stood was small – it had operated in a moving trailer truck until the FBI seized it and installed it in the school as a teaching aid. The narrow room was crowded with police from many jurisdictions; Starling had declined with thanks the chairs of two Texas Rangers and a Scotland Yard detective.

The rest of her class were down the hall in the Academy building, searching for hairs in the genuine motel carpet of the 'Sex-Crime Bedroom' and dusting the 'Anytown Bank' for fingerprints. Starling had spent so many hours on searches and fingerprints as a Forensic Fellow that she was sent instead to this lecture, part of a series for visiting lawmen.

She wondered if there was another reason she had been separated from the class: maybe they isolate you before you get the ax.

Starling rested her elbows on the pass line of the dice table and tried to concentrate on money-laundering in gambling. What she thought about instead was how much the FBI hates to see its agents on television, outside of official news conferences.

Dr Hannibal Lecter was catnip to the media, and the Baltimore police had happily supplied Starling's name to reporters. Over and over she saw herself on the Sunday-night network news. There was 'Starling of the FBI' in Baltimore, banging the jack handle against the garage door as the cameraman tried to slither under it. And here was 'Federal Agent Starling' turning on the assistant with the jack handle in her hand.

On the rival network, station WPIK, lacking film of its own, had announced a personal-injury lawsuit against 'Starling of the FBI' and the Bureau itself because the cameraman got dirt and rust particles in his eyes when Starling banged the door.

Jonetta Johnson of WPIK was on coast-to-coast with the revelation that Starling had found the remains in the garage through an 'eerie bonding with a man authorities have branded . . . a *monster!*' Clearly, WPIK had a source at the hospital.

BRIDE OF FRANKENSTEIN! ! screamed the *National Tattler* from its supermarket racks.

There was no public comment from the FBI, but there was plenty inside the Bureau, Starling was sure.

At breakfast, one of her classmates, a young man who wore a lot of Canoe after-shave, had referred to Starling as 'Melvin Pelvis,' a stupid play on the name of Melvin Purvis, Hoover's number one G-man in the thirties.

What Ardelia Mapp said to the young man made his face turn white, and he left his breakfast uneaten on the table.

Now Starling found herself in a curious state in which she could not be surprised. For a day and a night she'd felt suspended in a diver's ringing silence. She intended to defend herself, if she got the chance.

The lecturer spun the roulette wheel as he talked, but he never let the ball drop. Looking at him, Starling was convinced that he had never let the ball drop in his life. He was saying something now: 'Clarice Starling.' Why was he saying 'Clarice Starling'? *That's me.*

'Yes,' she said.

The lecturer pointed with his chin at the door behind her. Here it came. Her fate shied under her as she turned to see. But it was Brigham, the gunnery instructor, leaning into the room to point to her across the crowd. When she saw him, he beckoned.

For a second she thought they were throwing her out, but that wouldn't be Brigham's job.

'Saddle up, Starling. Where's your field gear?' he said in the hall.

'My room – C Wing.'

She had to walk fast then to keep up with him.

He was carrying the big fingerprint kit from the property room – the good one, not the play-school kit – and a small canvas bag.

'You go with Jack Crawford today. Take stuff for overnight. You may be back, but take it.'

'Where?'

'Some duck hunters in West Virginia found a body in the Elk River around daylight. In a Buffalo Bill-type situation. Deputies are bringing it out. It's real boonies, and Jack's not inclined to wait on those guys for details.' Brigham stopped at the door to C Wing. 'He needs somebody to help him that can print a floater, among other things. You were a grunt in the lab – you can do that, right?'

'Yeee, let me check the stuff.'

Brigham held the fingerprint kit open while Starling lifted out the trays. The fine hypodermics and the vials were there, but the camera wasn't.

'I need the one-to-one Polaroid, the CU-5, Mr Brigham, and film packs and batteries for it.'

'From property? You got it.'

He handed her the small canvas bag, and when she felt its weight, she realized why it was Brigham who had come for her.

'You don't have a duty piece yet, right?'

'No.'

'You gotta have full kit. This is the rig you've been wearing on the range. The gun is my own. It's the same K-frame Smith you're trained with, but the action's cleaned up. Dry-fire it in your room tonight when you get the chance. I'll be in a car behind C Wing in ten minutes flat with the camera. Listen, there's no head in the Blue Canoe. Go to the bathroom while you've got the chance is my advice. Chop-chop, Starling.'

She tried to ask him a question, but he was leaving her.

Has to be Buffalo Bill, if Crawford's going himself. What the hell is the Blue Canoe? But you have to think about packing when you pack. Starling packed fast and well.

'Is it –'

'That's okay,' Brigham interrupted as she got in the car. 'The butt prints against your jacket a little if somebody's looking for it, but it's okay for now.' She was wearing the snub-nosed revolver under her blazer in a pancake holster snug against her ribs, with a speedloader straddling her belt on the other side.

Brigham drove at precisely the base speed limit toward the Quantico airstrip.

He cleared his throat. 'One good thing about the range, Starling, is there's no politics out there.'

'No?'

'You were right to secure that garage up at Baltimore there. You worried about the TV?'

'Should I be?'

'We're talking just us, right?'

'Right.'

Brigham returned the greeting of a Marine directing traffic.

'Taking you along today, Jack's showing confidence in you where nobody can miss it,' he said. 'In case, say, somebody in the Office of Professional Responsibility has your jacket in front of him and his bowels in an uproar, understand what I'm telling you?'

'Ummm.'

'Crawford's a stand-up guy. He made it clear where it matters that you had to secure the scene. He let you go in there bare – that is, bare of all your visible symbols of authority, and he said that too. And the response time of the Baltimore cops was pretty slow. Also, Crawford needs the help today, and he'd have to wait an hour for Jimmy Price to get somebody here from the lab. So you got it cut out for you, Starling. A floater's no day at the beach, either. It's not punishment for you, but if somebody outside needed to see it that way, they could. See, Crawford is a very subtle guy, but he's not inclined to explain things, that's why I'm telling you . . . If you're working with Crawford, you should know what the deal is with him – do you know?'

'I really don't.'

'He's got a lot on his mind besides Buffalo Bill. His wife Bella's real sick. She's . . . in a terminal situation. He's keeping her at home. If it wasn't for Buffalo Bill, he'd have taken compassionate leave.'

'I didn't know that.'

'It's not discussed. Don't tell him you're sorry or anything, it doesn't help him . . . they had a good time.'

'I'm glad you told me.'

Brigham brightened as they reached the airstrip. 'I've got a couple of important speeches I give at the end of the firearms course, Starling, try not to miss them.' He took a shortcut between some hangars.

'I will.'

'Listen, what I teach is something you probably won't ever have to do. I hope you won't. But you've got some aptitude, Starling. If you have to shoot, you can shoot. Do your exercises.'

'Right.'

'Don't ever put it in your purse.'

'Right.'

'Pull it a few times in your room at night. Stay so you can find it.'

'I will.'

A venerable twin-engined Beechcraft stood on the taxiway at the Quantico airstrip with its beacons turning and the door open. One propeller was spinning, riffling the grass beside the tarmac.

'That wouldn't be the Blue Canoe,' Starling said.

'Yep.'

'It's little and it's old.'

'It *is* old,' Brigham said cheerfully. 'Drug Enforcement seized it in Florida a long time ago, when it flopped in the 'Glades. Mechanically sound now, though. I hope Gramm and Rudman don't find out we're using it – we're supposed to ride the bus.' He pulled up beside the airplane and got Starling's baggage out of the backseat. In some confusion of hands he managed to give her the stuff and shake her hand.

And then, without meaning to, Brigham said, 'Bless you, Starling.' The words felt odd in his Marine mouth. He didn't know where they came from and his face felt hot.

'Thanks . . . thank you, Mr Brigham.'

Crawford was in the copilot's seat, in shirtsleeves and sunglasses. He turned to Starling when he heard the pilot slam the door.

She couldn't see his eyes behind the dark glasses, and she felt she didn't know him. Crawford looked pale and tough, like a root a bulldozer pushes up.

'Take a pew and read,' is all he said.

A thick case file lay on the seat behind him. The cover said BUFFALO BILL. Starling hugged it tight as the Blue Canoe blatted and shuddered and began to roll.

Chapter Eleven

The edges of the runway blurred and fell away. To the east, a flash of morning sun off the Chesapeake Bay as the small plane turned out of traffic.

Clarice Starling could see the school down there, and the surrounding Marine base at Quantico. On the assault course, tiny figures of Marines scrambled and ran.

This was how it looked from above.

Once after a night-firing exercise, walking in the dark along the deserted Hogan's Alley, walking to think, she had heard airplanes roar over and then, in the new silence, voices calling in the black sky above her – airborne troops in a night jump calling to each other as they came down through the darkness. And she wondered how it felt to wait for the jump light at the aircraft door, how it felt to plunge into the bellowing dark.

Maybe it felt like this.

She opened the file.

He had done it five times that they knew of, had Bill. At least five times and probably more, over the past ten months he had abducted a woman, killed her and skinned her. (Starling's eye raced down the autopsy protocols to the free histamine tests to confirm that he killed them before he did the rest.)

He dumped each body in running water when he was through with it. Each was found in a different river, downstream from an interstate highway crossing, each in a different state. Everyone knew Buffalo Bill was a traveling man. That was all the law knew about him, absolutely all, except that he had at least one gun. It had six lands and grooves, left-hand twist – possibly a Colt revolver or a Colt clone. Skidmarks on recovered bullets indicated he preferred to fire .38 Specials in the longer chambers of a .357.

The rivers left no fingerprints, no trace evidence of hair or fiber.

He was almost certain to be a white male: white because serial murderers usually kill within their own ethnic group and all the victims were white; male because female serial murderers are almost unknown in our time.

Two big-city columnists had found a headline in e.e. cummings' deadly little poem, 'Buffalo Bill': . . . *how do you like your blueeyed boy Mister Death.*

Someone, maybe Crawford, had pasted the quotation inside the cover of the file.

There was no clear correlation between where Bill abducted the young women and where he dumped them.

In the cases where the bodies were found soon enough for an accurate determination of time of death, police learned another thing the killer did: Bill kept them for a while, alive. These victims did not die until a week to ten days after they were abducted. That meant he had to have a place to keep them and a place to work in privacy. It meant he wasn't a drifter. He was more of a trapdoor spider. With his own digs. Somewhere.

That horrified the public more than anything – his holding them for a week or more, knowing he would kill them.

Two were hanged, three shot. There was no evidence of rape or physical abuse prior to death, and the autopsy protocols recorded no evidence of 'specifically genital' disfigurement, though pathologists noted it would be almost impossible to determine these things in the more deteriorated bodies.

All were found naked. In two cases, articles of the victims' outer clothing were found beside the road near their homes, slit up the back like funeral suits.

Starling got through the photographs all right. Floaters are the worst kind of dead to deal with, physically. There is an absolute pathos about them, too, as there often is about homicide victims out of doors. The indignities the victim suffers, the exposure to the elements and to casual eyes, anger you if your job permits you anger.

Often, at indoor homicides, evidences of a victim's unpleasant personal practices, and the victim's own victims – beaten spouses, abused children – crowd around to whisper that the dead one had it coming, and many times he did.

But nobody had this coming. Here they had not even their skins as they lay on littered riverbanks amid the outboard-oil bottles and sandwich bags that are our common squalor. The cold-weather ones largely retained their faces. Starling reminded herself that their teeth were not bared in pain, that turtles and fish in the course of feeding had created that expression. Bill peeled the torsos and mostly left the limbs alone.

They wouldn't have been so hard to look at, Starling thought, if this airplane cabin wasn't so warm and if the damned plane didn't have this crawly yaw as one prop caught the air better than the other, and if the God damned sun didn't splinter so on the scratched windows and jab like a headache.

It's possible to catch him. Starling squeezed on that thought to help herself sit in this ever-smaller airplane cabin with her lap full of awful information. She could help stop him cold. Then they could put this slightly sticky, smooth-covered file back in the drawer and turn the key on it.

She stared at the back of Crawford's head. If she wanted to stop Buffalo Bill she was in the right crowd. Crawford had organized successful hunts for three serial murderers. But not without casualties. Will Graham, the keenest hound ever to run in Crawford's pack, was a legend at the Academy; he was also a drunk in Florida now with a face that was hard to look at, they said.

Maybe Crawford felt her staring at the back of his head. He climbed out of the co-pilot's seat. The pilot touched the trim wheel as Crawford came back to her and buckled in beside her. When he folded his sunglasses and put on his bifocals, she felt she knew him again.

When he looked from her face to the report and back again, something passed behind his face and was quickly gone. A more animated mug than Crawford's would have shown regret.

'I'm hot, are you hot?' he said. 'Bobby, it's too damned hot in here,' he called to the pilot. Bobby adjusted something and cold air came in. A few snowflakes formed in the moist cabin air and settled in Starling's hair.

Then it was Jack Crawford hunting, his eyes like a bright winter day.

He opened the file to a map of the Central and Eastern United States. Locations where bodies had been found were marked on the map – a scattering of dots as mute and crooked as Orion.

Crawford took a pen from his pocket and marked the newest location, their objective.

'Elk River? about six miles below US 79,' he said. 'We're lucky on this one. The body was snagged on a trotline – a fishing line set out in the river. They don't think she's been in the water all that long. They're bringing her to Potter, the county seat. I want to know who she is in a hurry so we can sweep for witnesses to the abduction. We'll send the prints back on a land line as soon as we get 'em.' Crawford tilted his head to look at Starling through the bottoms of his glasses. 'Jimmy Price says you can do a floater.'

'Actually, I never had an entire floater,' Starling said. 'I fingerprinted the hands Mr Price got in his mail every day. A good many of them were from floaters, though.'

Those who have never been under Jimmy Price's supervision believe him to be a lovable curmudgeon. Like most curmudgeons, he is really a mean old man. Jimmy Price is a supervisor in Latent Prints at the Washington lab. Starling did time with him as a Forensic Fellow.

'That Jimmy,' Crawford said fondly. 'What is it they call that job . . .'

'The position is called "lab wretch," or some people prefer "Igor" – that's what's printed on the rubber apron they give you.'

'That's it.'

'They tell you to pretend you're dissecting a frog.'

'I see –'

'Then they bring you a package from UPS. They're all watching – some of them hurry back from coffee, hoping you'll barf. I can print a floater very well. In fact –'

'Good, now look at this. His first victim that we know of was found in the Blackwater River in Missouri, outside of Lone Jack, last June. The Bimmel girl, she'd been reported missing in Belvedere, Ohio, on April 15, two months before. We couldn't tell a lot about it – it took another three months just to get her identified. The next one he grabbed in Chicago the third week in April. She was found in the Wabash in downtown Lafayette, Indiana, just ten days after she was taken, so we could tell what had happened to her. Next we've got a white female, early twenties, dumped in the Rolling Fork near I-65, about thirty-eight miles south of Louisville, Kentucky. She's never been identified. And the Varner woman, grabbed in Evansville, Indiana, and dropped in the Embarras just below Interstate 70 in eastern Illinois.

'Then he moved south and dumped one in the Conasauga below Damascus, Georgia, down from Interstate 75, that was this Kittridge girl from Pittsburgh – here's her graduation picture. His luck's ungodly – nobody's ever seen him make a snatch. Except for the dumps being near an Interstate, we haven't seen any pattern.'

'If you trace heaviest-traffic routes backward from the dump sites, do they converge at all?'

'No.'

'What if you . . . *postulate* . . . that he's making a dropoff and a new abduction on the same trip?' Starling asked, carefully avoiding the forbidden word *assume*. 'He'd drop off the body first, wouldn't he, in case he got in trouble grabbing the next one? Then, if he was caught grabbing somebody, he might get off for assault, plead it down to zip if he didn't have a body in his car. So how about drawing vectors backward from each abduction site through the previous dump site? You've tried it. '

'That's a good idea, but he had it too. If he is doing both things in one trip, he's zigging around. We've run computer simulations, first with him westbound on the Interstates, then eastbound, then various combinations with the best dates we can put on the dumps and abductions. You put it in the computer and smoke comes out. He lives in the East, it tells us. He's not in a moon cycle, it tells us. No convention dates in the cities correlate. Nothing but feathers. No, he's seen us coming, Starling.'

'You think he's too careful to be a suicide.'

Crawford nodded. 'Definitely too careful. He's found out how to have a meaningful relationship now, and he wants to do it a lot. I'm not getting my hopes up for a suicide.'

Crawford passed the pilot a cup of water from a thermos. He gave one to Starling and mixed himself an Alka-Seltzer.

Her stomach lifted as the airplane started down.

'Couple of things, Starling. I look for first-rate forensics from you, but I need more than that. You don't say much, and that's okay, neither do I. But don't ever feel you've got to have a new fact to tell me before you can bring something up. There aren't any silly questions. You'll see things that I won't, and I want to know what they are. Maybe you've got a knack for this. All of a sudden we've got this chance to see if you do.'

Listening to him, her stomach lifting and her expression properly rapt, Starling wondered how long Crawford had known he'd use her on this case, how hungry for a chance he had wanted her to be. He was a leader, with a leader's frank-and-open bullshit, all right.

'You think about him enough, you see where he's been, you get a feel for him,' Crawford went on. 'You don't even dislike him all the time, hard as that is to believe. Then, if you're lucky, out of the stuff you know, part of it plucks at you, tries to get your attention. Always tell me when something plucks, Starling.

'Listen to me, a crime is confusing enough without the investigation mixing it up. Don't let a herd of policemen confuse you. Live right behind your eyes. Listen to yourself. Keep the crime separate from what's going on around you now. Don't try to impose any pattern or symmetry on this guy. Stay open and let him show you.

'One other thing: an investigation like this is a zoo. It's spread out over a lot of jurisdictions, and a few are run by losers. We have to get along with them so they won't hold out on us. We're going to Potter, West Virginia. I don't know about these people we're going to. They may be fine or they may think we're the revenuers.'

The pilot lifted an earphone away from his head and spoke over his shoulder. 'Final approach, Jack. You staying back there?'

'Yeah,' Crawford said. 'School's out, Starling.'

Chapter Twelve

Now here is the Potter Funeral Home, the largest white frame house on Potter Street in Potter, West Virginia, serving as the morgue for Rankin County. The coroner is a family physician named Dr Akin. If he rules that a death is questionable, the body is sent on to Claxton Regional Medical Center in the neighboring county, where they have a trained pathologist.

Clarice Starling, riding into Potter from the airstrip in the back of a sheriff's department cruiser, had to lean up close to the prisoner screen to hear the deputy at the wheel as he explained these things to Jack Crawford.

A service was about to get under way at the mortuary. The mourners in their country Sunday best filed up the sidewalk between leggy boxwoods and bunched on the steps, waiting to get in. The freshly painted house and the steps had, each in its own direction, settled slightly out of plumb.

In the private parking lot behind the house, where the hearses waited, two young deputies and one old one stood with two state troopers under a bare elm. It was not cold enough for their breath to steam.

Starling looked at these men as the cruiser pulled into the lot, and at once she knew about them. She knew they came from houses that had chifforobes instead of closets and she knew pretty much what was in the chifforobes. She knew that these men had relatives who hung their clothes in suitbags on the walls of their trailers. She knew that the older deputy had grown up with a pump on the porch and had waded to the road in the muddy spring to catch the school bus with his shoes hanging around his neck by the laces, as her father had done. She knew they had carried their lunches to school in paper sacks with grease spots on them from being used over and over and that after lunch they folded the sacks and slipped them in the back pockets of their jeans.

She wondered how much Crawford knew about them.

There were no handles on the inside of the rear doors in the cruiser, as Starling discovered when the driver and Crawford got out and started toward the back of the funeral home. She had to bat on the glass until one of the deputies beneath the tree saw her, and the driver came back red-faced to let her out.

The deputies watched her sidelong as she passed. One said 'ma'am.' She gave them a nod and a smile of the correct dim wattage as she went to join Crawford on the back porch.

When she was far enough away, one of the younger deputies, a newlywed, scratched beneath his jaw and said, 'She don't look half as good as she thinks she does.'

'Well, if she just thinks she looks *pretty God damned good*, I'd have to agree with her, myself,' the other young deputy said. 'I'd put her on like a Mark Five gas mask.'

'I'd just as soon have a big watermelon, if it was cold,' the older deputy said, half to himself.

Crawford was already talking to the chief deputy, a small, taut man in steel-rimmed glasses and the kind of elastic-sided boots the catalogs call

'Romeos.'

They had moved into the funeral home's dim back corridor, where a Coke machine hummed and random odd objects stood against the wall – a treadle sewing machine, a tricycle, and a roll of artificial grass, a striped canvas awning wrapped around its poles. On the wall was a sepia print of Saint Cecilia at the keyboard. Her hair was braided around her head, and roses tumbled onto the keys out of thin air.

'I appreciate your letting us know so fast, Sheriff,' Crawford said.

The chief deputy wasn't having any. 'It was somebody from the district attorney's office called you,' he said. 'I know the sheriff didn't call you – Sheriff Perkins is on a guided tour of Hawaii at the present time with Mrs Perkins. I spoke to him on long distance this morning at eight o'clock, that's three A.M., Hawaii time. He'll get back to me later in the day, but he told me Job One is to find out if this is one of our local girls. It could be something that outside elements has just dumped on us. We'll tend to that before we do anything else. We've had 'em haul bodies here all the way from Phenix City, Alabama.'

'That's where we can help you, Sheriff. If –'

'I've been on the phone with the field services commander of the state troopers in Charleston. He's sending some officers from the Criminal Investigation Section – what's known as the CIS. They'll give us all the backup we need.' The corridor was filling with deputy sheriffs and troopers; the chief deputy had too much of an audience. 'We'll get around to you just as soon as we can, and extend you ever courtesy, work with you ever *way* we can, but right now –'

'Sheriff, this kind of a sex crime has some aspects that I'd rather say to you just between us men, you understand what I mean?' Crawford said, indicating Starling's presence with a small movement of his head. He hustled the smaller man into a cluttered office off the hall and closed the door. Starling was left to mask her umbrage before the gaggle of deputies. Her teeth hard together, she gazed on Saint Cecilia and returned the saint's ethereal smile while eavesdropping through the door. She could hear raised voices, then scraps of a telephone conversation. They were back out in the hall in less than four minutes.

The chief deputy's mouth was tight. 'Oscar, go out front and get Dr Akin. He's kind of obliged to attend those rites, but I don't think they've got started out there yet. Tell him we've got Claxton on the phone.'

The coroner, Dr Akin, came to the little office and stood with his foot on a chair, tapping his front teeth with a Good Shepherd fan while he had a brief telephone conference with the pathologist in Claxton. Then he agreed to everything.

So, in an embalming room with cabbage roses in the wallpaper and a picture molding beneath its high ceiling, in a white frame house of a type she understood, Clarice Starling met with her first direct evidence of Buffalo Bill.

The bright green body bag, tightly zipped, was the only modern object in the room. It lay on an old-fashioned porcelain embalming table reflected many times in the glass panes of cabinets holding trocars and packages of Rock-Hard Cavity Fluid.

Crawford went to the car for the fingerprint transmitter while Starling unpacked her equipment on the drainboard of a large double sink against the wall.

Too many people were in the room. Several deputies, the chief deputy, all had wandered in with them and showed no inclination to leave. It wasn't right. *Why didn't Crawford come on and get rid of them?*

The wallpaper billowed in a draft, billowed inward as the doctor turned on the big, dusty vent fan.

Clarice Starling, standing at the sink, needed now a prototype of courage more apt and powerful than any Marine parachute jump. The image came to her, and helped her, but it pierced her too:

Her mother, standing at the sink, washing blood out of her father's hat, running cold water over the hat, saying, 'We'll be all right, Clarice. Tell your brothers and sister to wash up and come to the table. We need to talk and then we'll fix our supper.'

Starling took off her scarf and tied it over her hair like a mountain midwife. She took a pair of surgical gloves out of her kit. When she opened her mouth for the first time in Potter, her voice had more than its normal twang and the force of it brought Crawford to the door to listen. 'Gentlemen. Gentlemen! You officers and gentlemen! Listen here a minute. Please. Now let me take care of her.' She held her hands before their faces as she pulled on the gloves. 'There's things we need to do for her. You brought her this far, and I know her folks would thank you if they could. Now please go on out and let me take care of her.'

Crawford saw them suddenly go quiet and respectful and urge each other out in whispers: 'Come on, Jess. Let's go out in the yard.' And Crawford saw that the atmosphere had changed here in the presence of the dead: that wherever this victim came from, whoever she was, the river had carried her into the country, and while she lay helpless in this room in the country, Clarice Starling had a special relationship to her. Crawford saw that in this place Starling was heir to the granny women, to the wise women, the herb healers, the stalwart country women who have always done the needful, who keep the watch and when the watch is over, wash and dress the country dead.

Then there were only Crawford and Starling and the doctor in the room with the victim, Dr Akin and Starling looking at each other with a kind of recognition. Both of them were oddly pleased, oddly abashed.

Crawford took a jar of Vicks VapoRub out of his pocket and offered it around. Starling watched to see what to do, and when Crawford and the doctor rubbed it around the rims of their nostrils, she did too.

She dug her cameras out of the equipment bag on the drainboard, her back to the room. Behind her she heard the zipper of the body bag go down.

Starling blinked at the cabbage roses on the wall, took a breath and let it out. She turned round and looked at the body on the table.

'They should have put paper bags on her hands,' she said. 'I'll bag them when we're through.' Carefully, overriding the automatic camera to bracket her exposures, Starling photographed the body.

The victim was a heavy-hipped young woman sixty-seven inches long by Starling's tape. The water had leached her gray where the skin was gone, but it had been cold water and she clearly hadn't been in it more than a few days. The body was flayed neatly from a clean line just below the breasts to the knees, about the area that would be covered by a bullfighter's pants and sash.

Her breasts were small and between them, over the sternum, was the apparent cause of death, a ragged, star-shaped wound a hand's breadth across.

Her round head was peeled to the skull from just above the eyebrows and ears to the nape.

'Dr Lecter said he'd start scalping,' Starling said.

Crawford stood with his arms folded while she took the pictures. 'Get her ears with the Polaroid,' was all he said.

He went so far as to purse his lips as he walked around the body. Starling peeled off her glove to trail her finger up the calf of the leg. A section of the trotline and treble fishhooks that had entangled and held the body in the moving river was still wrapped around the lower leg.

'What do you see, Starling?'

'Well, she's not a local – her ears are pierced three times each, and she wore glitter polish. Looks like town to me. She's got maybe two weeks' or so hair growth on her legs. And see how soft it's grown in? I think she got her legs waxed. Armpits too. Look how she bleached the fuzz on her upper lip. She was pretty careful about herself, but she hasn't been able to take care of it for a while.'

'What about the wound?'

I don't know,' Starling said. 'I would have said an exit gunshot wound except that looks like part of an abrasion collar and a muzzle stamp at the top there.'

'Good, Starling. It's a contact entrance wound over the sternum. The explosion gases expand between the bone and the skin and blow out the star around the hole.'

On the other side of the wall a pipe organ wheezed as the service got under way in the front of the funeral home.

'Wrongful death,' Dr Akins contributed, nodding his head. 'I've got to get in there for at least part of this service. The family always expects me to go the last mile. Lamar will be in here to help you as soon as he finishes playing the musical offering. I take you at your word on preserving evidence for the pathologist at Claxton, Mr Crawford.'

'She's got two nails broken off here on the left hand,' Starling said when the doctor was gone. 'They're broken back up in the quick and it looks like dirt or some hard particles driven up under some of the others. Can we take evidence?'

'Take samples of grit, take a couple of flakes of polish,' Crawford said. 'We'll tell 'em after we get the results.'

Lamar, a lean funeral home assistant with a whiskey bloom in the middle of his face, came in while she was doing it. 'You must of been a manicurist one time,' he said.

They were glad to see the young woman had no fingernail marks in her palms – an indication that, like the others, she had died before anything else was done to her.

'You want to print her facedown, Starling?' Crawford said.

'Be easier.'

'Let's do teeth first, and then Lamar can help us turn her over.'

'Just pictures, or a chart?' Starling attached the dental kit to the front of the fingerprint camera, privately relieved that all the parts were in the bag.

'Just pictures,' Crawford said. 'A chart can throw you off without rays. We can eliminate a couple of missing women with the pictures.'

Lamar was very gentle with his organist's hands, opening the young woman's mouth at Starling's direction and retracting her lips while Starling placed the one-to-one Polaroid against the face to get details of the front teeth. That part was easy, but she had to shoot the molars with a palatal reflector, watching from the side for the glow through the cheek to be sure the strobe around the lens was lighting the inside of the mouth. She had only seen it done in a forensics class.

Starling watched the first Polaroid print of the molars develop, adjusted the lightness control and tried again. This print was better. This one was very good.

'She's got something in her throat,' Starling said.

Crawford looked at the picture. It showed a dark cylindrical object just behind the soft palate. 'Give me the flashlight.'

'When a body comes out of the water, a lot of times there's like leaves and things in the mouth,' Lamar said, helping Crawford to look.

Starling took some forceps out of her bag. She looked at Crawford across the body. He nodded. It only took her a second to get it.

'What is it, some kind of seed pod?' Crawford said.

'Nawsir, that's a bug cocoon,' Lamar said. He was right.

Starling put it in a jar.

'You might want the county agent to look at that,' Lamar said.

Facedown , the body was easy to fingerprint. Starling had been prepared for the worst – but none of the tedious and delicate injection methods or finger stalls were necessary. She took the prints on thin card stock held in a device shaped like a shoehorn. She did a set of plantar prints as well, in case they had only baby footprints from a hospital for reference.

Two triangular pieces of skin were missing from high on the shoulders. Starling took pictures.

'Measure too,' Crawford said. 'He cut the girl from Akron when he slit her clothes off, not much more than a scratch, but it matched the cut up the back of her blouse when they found it beside the road. This is something new, though. I haven't seen this.'

'Looks like a burn across the back of her calf,' Starling said.

'Old people gets those a lot,' Lamar said.

'What?' Crawford said.

'*I SAID OLD PEOPLE GETS THOSE A LOT.*'

'I heard you fine, I want you to explain it. What about old people?'

'Old people pass away with a heating pad on them, and when they're dead it burns them, even when it's not all that hot. You burn under a heating pad when you're dead. No circulation under it.'

'We'll ask the pathologist at Claxton to test it, and see if it's postmortem,' Crawford said to Starling.

'Car muffler, most likely,' Lamar said.

'What?'

'*CAR MUFFL* – car muffler. One time Billy Petrie got shot to death and they dumped him in the trunk of his car? His wife drove the car around two or three days looking for him. When they brought him in here, the muffler had got hot under the car trunk and burned him just like that, only across his hip,' Lamar said. 'I can't put groceries in the trunk of my car for it melting the ice cream.'

'That's a good thought, Lamar, I wish you worked for me,' Crawford said. 'Do you know the fellows that found her in the river?'

'Jabbo Franklin and his brother, Bubba.'

'What do they do?'

'Fight at the Moose, make fun of people that's not bothering them – someone just comes in the Moose after a simple drink, worn out from looking at the bereaved all day, and it's "Set down there, Lamar, and play 'Filipino Baby.'" Make a person play "Filipino Baby" over and over on that sticky old bar piano. That's what Jabbo likes. "Well, make up some damn words if you don't know it," he says, "and make the damn thing rhyme this time." He gets a check from the Veterans and goes to dry out at the VA around Christmas. I been looking for him on this table for fifteen years.'

'We'll need serotonin tests on the fishhook punctures,' Crawford said. 'I'm sending the pathologist a note.'

'Them hooks are too close together,' Lamar said.

'What did you say?'

'The Franklins was running a trotline with the hooks too close together. It's a violation. That's prob'ly why they didn't call it in until this morning.'

'The sheriff said they were duck hunters.'

'I expect they did tell him that,' Lamar said. 'They'll tell you they wrestled Duke Keomuka in Honolulu one time too, tag team with Satellite Monroe. You can believe that too, if you feel like it. Grab a croaker sack and they'll take you on a snipe hunt too, if you favor snipe. Give you a glass of billiards with it.'

'What do you think happened, Lamar?'

'The Franklins was running this trotline, it's their trotline with these unlawful hooks, and they was pulling it up to see if they had any fish.'

'Why do you think so?'

'This lady's not near ready to float.'

'No.'

'Then if they hadna been pulling up on the trotline they never would have found her. They prob'ly went off scared and finally called in. I expect you'll want the game warden in on this.'

'I expect so,' Crawford said.

'Lots of times they've got a crank telephone behind the seat in their Ramcharger, that's a big fine right there, if you don't have to go to the pen.'

Crawford raised his eyebrows.

'To telephone fish with,' Starling said. 'Stun the fish with electric current when you hang the wires in the water and turn the crank. They come to the top and you just dip 'em out.'

'Right,' Lamar said, 'are you from around here?'

'They do it lots of places,' Starling said.

Starling felt the urge to say something before they zipped up the bag, to make a gesture or express some kind of commitment. In the end, she just shook her head and got busy packing the samples into her case.

It was different with the body and problem out of sight. In this slack moment, what she'd been doing came in on her. Starling stripped off her gloves and turned the water on in the sink. With her back to the room, she ran water over her wrists. The water in the pipes wasn't all that cool. Lamar, watching, disappeared into the hall. He came back from the Coke machine with an ice-cold can of soda, unopened, and offered it to her.

'No, thanks,' Starling said. 'I don't believe I'll have one.'

'No, hold it under your neck there,' Lamar said, 'and on that little bump at the back of your head. Cold'll make you feel better. It does me.'

By the time Starling had finished taping the memo to the pathologist across the zipper of the body bag, Crawford's fingerprint transmitter was clicking on the office desk.

Finding this victim so soon after the crime was a lucky break. Crawford was determined to identify her quickly and start a sweep around her home for witnesses to the abduction. His method was a lot of trouble to everyone, but it was fast.

Crawford carried a Litton Policefax fingerprint transmitter. Unlike federal-issue facsimile machines, the Policefax is compatible with most big-city police department systems. The fingerprint card Starling had assembled was barely dry.

'Load it, Starling, you've got the nimble fingers.'

Don't smear it was what he meant, and Starling didn't. It was hard, wrapping the glued-together composite card around the little drum while six wire rooms waited around the country.

Crawford was on the telephone to the FBI switchboard and wire room in Washington. 'Dorothy, is everybody on? Okay, gentlemen, we'll turn it down to one-twenty to keep it nice and sharp – check one-twenty, everybody? Atlanta, how about it? Okay, give me the picture wire . . . now.'

Then it was spinning at slow speed for clarity, sending the dead woman's prints simultaneously to the FBI wire room and major police department wire rooms in the East. If Chicago, Detroit, Atlanta, or any of the others got a hit on the fingerprints, a sweep would begin in minutes.

Next Crawford sent pictures of the victim's teeth and photos of her face, the head draped by Starling with a towel in the event the supermarket press got hold of the photographs.

Three officers of the West Virginia State Police Criminal Investigation Section arrived from Charleston as they were leaving. Crawford did a lot of handshaking, passing out cards with the National Crime Information Center hotline number. Starling was interested to see how fast he got them into a male bonding mode. They sure would call up with anything they got, they sure would. You betcha and much oblige. Maybe it wasn't male bonding, she decided; it worked on her too.

Lamar waved with his fingers from the porch as Crawford and Starling rode away with the deputy toward the Elk River. The Coke was still pretty cold. Lamar took it into the storeroom and fixed a refreshing beverage for himself.

Chapter Thirteen

'Drop me at the lab, Jeff,' Crawford told the driver. 'Then I want you to wait for Officer Starling at the Smithsonian. She'll go on from there to

Quantico'.

'Yes, sir.'

They were crossing the Potomac River against the after-dinner traffic, coming into downtown Washington from National Airport.

The young man at the wheel seemed in awe of Crawford and drove with excessive caution, Starling thought. She didn't blame him; it was an article of faith at the Academy that the last agent who'd committed a Full Fuck-Up in Crawford's command now investigated pilfering at DEW-line installations along the Arctic Circle.

Crawford was not in a good humor. Nine hours had passed since he transmitted the fingerprints and pictures of the victim, and she remained unidentified. Along with the West Virginia troopers, he and Starling had worked the bridge and the river bank until dark without result.

Starling had heard him on the phone from the airplane, arranging for an evening nurse at home.

The FBI plain-jane sedan seemed wonderfully quiet after the Blue Canoe, and talking was easier.

'I'll post the hotline and the Latent Descriptor Index when I take your prints up to ID,' Crawford said. 'You draft me an insert for the file. An insert, not a 302 – do you know how to do it?'

'I know how.'

'Say I'm the Index, tell me what's new.'

It took her a second to get it together – she was glad Crawford seemed interested in the scaffolding on the Jefferson Memorial as they passed by.

The Latent Descriptor Index in the Identification Section's computer compares the characteristics of a crime under investigation to the known proclivities of criminals on file. When it finds pronounced similarities, it suggests suspects and produces their fingerprints. Then a human operator compares the file fingerprints with latent prints found at the scene. There were no prints yet on Buffalo Bill, but Crawford wanted to be ready.

The system requires brief, concise statements. Starling tried to come up wlth some.

'White female, late teens or early twenties, shot to death, lower torso and thighs flayed –'

'Starling, the Index already knows he kills young white women and skins their torsos – use "skinned," by the way, "flayed" is an uncommon term another officer might not use, and you can't be sure the damned thing will read a synonym. It already knows he dumps them in rivers. It doesn't know what's *new* here. What's new here, Starling?'

'This is the sixth victim, the first one scalped, the first one with triangular patches taken from the back of the shoulders, the first one shot in the chest, the first one with a cocoon in her throat.'

'You forgot broken fingernails.'

'No sir, she's the second one with broken fingernails.'

'You're right. Listen, in your insert for the file, note that the cocoon is confidential. We'll use it to eliminate false confessions.'

'I'm wondering if he's done that before – placed a cocoon or an insect,' Starling said. 'It would be easy to miss in an autopsy, especially with a floater. You know, the medical examiner sees an obvious cause of death, it's hot in there, and they want to get through . . . can we check back on that?'

'If we have to. You can count on the pathologists to say they didn't miss anything, naturally. The Cincinnati Jane Doe's still in the freezer out there. I'll ask them to look at her, but the other four are in the ground. Exhumation orders stir people up. We had to do it with four patients who passed away under Dr Lecter's care, just to make sure what killed them. Let me tell you, it's a lot of trouble and it upsets the relatives. I'll do it if I have to, but we'll see what you find out at the Smithsonian before I decide.'

'Scalping . . . that's rare, isn't it?'

'Uncommon, yes,' Crawford said.

'But Dr Lecter said Buffalo Bill would do it. How did he know that?'

'He didn't know it.'

'He said it, though.'

'It's not a big surprise, Starling. I wasn't surprised to see that. I should have said that it was rare until the Mengel case, remember that? Scalped the woman? There were two or three copycats after that. The papers, when they were playing around with the Buffalo Bill tag, they emphasized more than once that this killer doesn't take scalps. It's no surprise after that – he probably follows his press. Lecter was guessing. He didn't say *when* it would happen, so he could never be wrong. If we caught Bill and there was no scalping, Lecter could say we got him just *before* he did it.'

'Dr Lecter also said Buffalo Bill lives in a two-story house. We never got into that. Why do you suppose he said it?'

'That's not a guess. He's very likely right, and he could have told you why, but he wanted to tease you with it. It's the only weakness I ever saw in him – he has to look smart, smarter than anybody. He's been doing it for years.'

'You said ask if I don't know – well, I have to ask you to explain that.'

'Okay, two of the victims were hanged, right? High ligature marks, cervical displacement, definite hanging. As Dr Lecter knows from personal experience, Starling, it's very hard for one person to hang another against his will. People hang *themselves* from doorknobs all the time. They hang themselves sitting down, it's easy. But it's hard to hang somebody else – even when they're bound up, they manage to get their feet under them, if there's any support to find with their feet. A ladder's threatening. Victims won't climb it blindfolded and they sure won't climb it if they can see the noose. The way it's done is in a stairwell. Stairs are familiar. Tell them you're taking them up to use the bathroom, whatever, walk them up with a hood on, slip the noose on, and boot them off the top step with the rope fastened to the landing railing. It's the only good way in a house. Fellow in California popularized it. If Bill didn't have a stairwell, he'd kill them another way. Now give me those names, the senior deputy from Potter and the state police guy, the ranking officer.'

Starling found them in her notepad, reading by a penlight held in her teeth.

'Good,' Crawford said. 'When you're posting a hotline, Starling, always credit the cops by name. They hear their own names, they get more friendly to the hotline. Fame helps them remember to call us if they get something. What does the burn on her leg say to you?'

'Depends if it's postmortem.'

'If it is?'

'Then he's got a closed truck or a van or a station wagon, something long.'

'Why?'

'Because the burn's across the back of her calf.'

They were at Tenth and Pennsylvania, in front of the new FBI headquarters that nobody ever refers to as the J. Edgar Hoover Building.

'Jeff you can let me out here,' Crawford said. 'Right here, don't go underneath. Stay in the car, Jeff, just pop the trunk. Come show me, Starling.'

She got out with Crawford while he retrieved his datafax and briefcase from the luggage compartment.

'He hauled the body in something big enough for the body to be stretched out on its back,' Starling said. 'That's the only way the back of her calf would rest on the floor over the exhaust pipe. In a car trunk like this, she'd be curled up on her side and –'

'Yeah, that's how I see it,' Crawford said.

She realized then that he'd gotten her out of the car so he could speak with her privately.

'When I told that deputy he and I shouldn't talk in front of a woman, that burned you, didn't it?'

'Sure.'

'It was just smoke. I wanted to get him by himself.'

'I know that.'

'Okay.' Crawford slammed the trunk and turned away.

Starling couldn't let it go.

'It matters, Mr Crawford.'

He was turning back to her, laden with his fax machine and briefcase, and she had his full attention.

'Those cops know who you are,' she said. 'They look at you to see how to act. She stood steady, shrugged her shoulders, opened her palms. There it was, it was true.

'Crawford performed a measurement on his cold scales.

'Duly noted, Starling. Now get on with the bug.'

'Yes sir.'

She watched him walk away, a middle-aged man laden with cases and rumpled from flying, his cuffs muddy from the riverbank, going home to what he did at home.

She would have killed for him then. That was one of Crawford's great talents.

Chapter Fourteen

The Smithsonian's National Museum of Natural History had been closed for hours, but Crawford had called ahead and a guard waited to let Clarice Starling in the Constitution Avenue entrance.

The lights were dimmed in the closed museum and the air was still. Only the colossal figure of a South Seas chieftain facing the entrance stood tall enough for the weak ceiling light to shine on his face.

Starling's guide was a big black man in the neat turnout of the Smithsonian guards. She thought he resembled the chieftain as he raised his face to the elevator lights. There was a moment's relief in her idle fancy, like rubbing a cramp.

The second level above the great stuffed elephant, a vast floor closed to the public, is shared by the departments of Anthropology and Entomology. The anthropologists call it the fourth floor. The entomologists contend it is the third. A few scientists from Agriculture say they have proof that it is the sixth. Each faction has a case in the old building with its additions and subdivisions.

Starling followed the guard into a dim maze of corridors walled high with wooden cases of anthropological specimens. Only the small labels revealed their contents.

'Thousands of people in these boxes,' the guard said. 'Forty thousand specimens.'

He found office numbers with his flashlight and trailed the light over the labels as they went along.

Dyak baby carriers and ceremonial skulls gave way to Aphids, and they left Man for the older and more orderly world of Insects. Now the corridor was walled with big metal boxes painted pale green.

'Thirty million insects – and the spiders on top of that. Don't lump the spiders in with the insects,' the guard advised. 'Spider people jump all over you about that. There, the office that's lit. Don't try to come out by yourself. If they don't say they'll bring you down, call me at this extension, it's the guard office. I'll come get you.' He gave her a card and left her.

She was in the heart of Entomology, on a rotunda gallery high above the great stuffed elephant. There was the office with the lights on and the door open.

'Time, Pilch!' A man's voice, shrill with excitement. 'Let's go here. Time!'

Starling stopped in the doorway. Two men sat at a laboratory table playing chess. Both were about thirty, one black-haired and lean, the other pudgy with wiry red hair. They appeared to be engrossed in the chessboard. If they noticed Starling, they gave no sign. If they noticed the enormous rhinoceros beetle slowly making its way across the board, weaving among the chessmen, they gave no sign of that either.

Then the beetle crossed the edge of the board.

'Time, Roden,' the lean one said instantly.

The pudgy one moved his bishop and immediately turned the beetle around and started it trudging back the other way.

'If the beetle just cuts across the corner, is time up then?' Starling asked.

'Of course time's up then,' the pudgy one said loudly, without looking up. 'Of *course* it's up then. How do *you* play? Do you make him cross the whole board? Who do you play against, a sloth?'

'I have the specimen Special Agent Crawford called about.'

'I can't imagine why we didn't hear your siren,' the pudgy one said. 'We're waiting all night here to identify a *bug* for the FBI. Bugs're all we do. Nobody said anything about Special Agent Crawford's *specimen*. He should show his *specimen* privately to his family doctor. Time, Pilch!'

'I'd love to catch your whole routine another time,' Starling said, 'but this is urgent, so let's do it now. Time, Pilch.'

The black-haired one looked around at her, saw her leaning against the doorframe with her briefcase. He put the beetle on some rotten wood in a box and covered it with a lettuce leaf.

When he got up, he was tall.

'I'm Noble Pilcher,' he said. 'That's Albert Roden. You need an insect identified? We're happy to help you.' Pilcher had a long friendly face, but his black eyes were a little witchy and too close together, and one of them had a slight cast that made it catch the light independently. He did not offer to shake hands. 'You are . . . ?'

'Clarice Starling.'

'Let's see what you've got.'

Pilcher held the small jar to the light.

Roden came to look. 'Where did you find it? Did you kill it with your *gun*? Did you see its *mommy*?'

It occurred to Starling how much Roden would benefit from an elbow smash in the hinge of his jaw.

'Shhh,' Pilcher said. 'Tell us where you found it. Was it attached to anything – a twig or a leaf – or was it in the soil?'

'I see,' Starling said. 'Nobody's talked to you.'

'The Chairman asked us to stay late and identify a bug for the FBI,' Pilcher said.

' *Told* us,' Roden said. '*Told* us to stay late.'

'We do it all the time for Customs and the Department of Agriculture,' Pilcher said.

'But not in the middle of the night,' Roden said.

'I need to tell you a couple of things involving a criminal case,' Starling said. 'I'm allowed to do that if you'll keep it in confidence until the case is resolved. It's important. It means some lives, and I'm not just saying that. Dr Roden, can you tell me seriously that you'll respect a confidence?'

'I'm not a doctor. Do I have to sign anything?'

'Not if your word's any good. You'll have to sign for the specimen if you need to keep it, that's all.'

'Of course I'll help you. I'm not *uncaring*.'

'Dr Pilcher?'

'That's true,' Pilcher said. 'He's not uncaring.'

'Confidence?'

'I won't tell.'

'Pilch isn't a doctor yet either,' Roden said. 'We're on an equal educational footing. But notice how he *allowed* you to call him that.' Roden placed the tip of his forefinger against his chin, as though pointing to his judicious expression. 'Give us all the details. What might seem irrelevant to *you* could be vital information to an expert.'

'This insect was found lodged behind the soft palate of a murder victim. I don't know how it got there. Her body was in the Elk River in West Virginia, and she hadn't been dead more than a few days.'

'It's Buffalo Bill, I heard it on the radio,' Roden said.

'You didn't hear about the insect on the radio, did you?' Starling said.

'No, but they said Elk River – are you coming in from that today, is that why you're so late?'

'Yes,' Starling said.

'You must be tired, do you want some coffee?' Roden said.

'No, thank you.'

'Water?'

'No.'

'A Coke?'

'I don't believe so. We want to know where this woman was held captive and where she was killed. We're hoping this bug has some specialized habitat, or it's limited in range, you know, or it only sleeps on some kind of tree – we want to know where this insect is from. I'm asking for your confidence because – if the perpetrator put the insect there deliberately – then only he would know that fact and we could use it to eliminate false confessions and save time. He's killed six at least. Time's eating us up.'

'Do you think he's holding another woman right this minute, while we're looking at his bug?' Roden asked in her face. His eyes were wide and his mouth open. She could see into his mouth, and she flashed for a second on something else.

'*I don't know.*' A little shrill, that. 'I don't know,' she said again, to take the edge off it. 'He'll do it again as soon as he can.'

'So we'll do this as soon as we can,' Pilcher said. 'Don't worry, we're good at this. You couldn't be in better hands.' He removed the brown object from the jar with a slender forceps and placed it on a sheet of white paper beneath the light. He swung a magnifying glass on a flexible arm over it.

The insect was long and it looked like a mummy. It was sheathed in a semitransparent cover that followed its general outlines like a sarcophagus. The appendages were bound so tightly against the body, they might have been carved in low relief. The little face looked wise.

'In the first place, it's not anything that would normally infest a body outdoors and it wouldn't be in the water except by accident,' Pilcher said. I don't know how familiar you are with insects or how much you want to hear.'

'Let's say I don't know diddly. I want you to tell me the whole thing.'

'Okay, this is a pupa, an immature insect, in a chrysalis – that's the cocoon that holds it while it transforms itself from a larva into an adult,' Pilcher said.

'Obtect pupa, Pilch?' Roden wrinkled his nose to hold his glasses up.

'Yeah, I think so. You want to pull down Chu on the immature insects? Okay, this is the pupal stage of a large insect. Most of the more advanced insects have a pupal stage. A lot of them spend the winter this way.'

'Book or look, Pilch?' Roden said.

'I'll look.' Pilcher moved the specimen to the stage of a microscope and hunched over it with a dental probe in his hand. 'Here we go: No distinct respiratory organs on the dorsocephalic region, spiracles on the mesothorax and some abdominals, let's start with that.'

'Ummhumm,' Roden said, turning pages in a small manual. 'Functional mandibles?'

'Nope.'

'Paired galeae of maxillae on the ventro meson?'

'Yep, yep.'

'Where are the antennae?'

'Adjacent to the mesal margin of the wings. Two pairs of wings, the inside pair are completely covered up. Only the bottom three abdominal segments are free. Little pointy cremaster – I'd say Lepidoptera.'

'That's what it says here,' Roden said.

'It's the family that includes the butterflies and moths. Covers a lot of territory,' Pilcher said.

'It's gonna be tough if the wings are soaked. I'll pull the references,' Roden said. 'I guess there's no way I can keep you from talking about me while I'm gone.'

'I guess not,' Pilcher said. 'Roden's all right,' he told Starling as soon as Roden left the room.

'I'm sure he is.'

Are you now?' Pilcher seemed amused. 'We were undergraduates together, working and glomming any kind of fellowship we could. He got one where he had to sit down in a coal mine waiting for proton decay. He just stayed in the dark too long. He's all right. Just don't mention proton decay.'

'I'll try to talk around it.'

Pilcher turned away from the bright light. 'It's a big family, Lepidoptera. Maybe thirty thousand butterflies and a hundred thirty thousand moths. I'd like to take it out of the chrysalis – I'll have to if we're going to narrow it down.'

'Okay. Can you do it in one piece?'

'I think so. See, this one had started out on its own power before it died. It had started an irregular fracture in the chrysalis right here. This may take a little while.'

Pilcher spread the natural split in the case and eased the insect out. The bunched wings were soaked. Spreading them was like working with a wet, wadded facial tissue. No pattern was visible.

Roden was back with the books.

'Ready?' Pilcher said. 'Okay, the prothoracic femur is concealed.'

'What about pilifers?'

'No pilifers,' Pilcher said. 'Would you turn out the light, Officer Starling?'

She waited by the wall switch until Pilcher's penlight came on. He stood back from the table and shined it on the specimen. The insect's eyes glowed in the dark, reflecting the narrow beam.

'Owlet,' Roden said.

'Probably, but which one?' Pilcher said. 'Give us the lights, please. It's a Noctuid, Officer Starling – a night moth. How many Noctuids are there,

Roden?'

'Twenty-six hundred and . . . about twenty-six hundred have been described.'

'Not many this big, though. Okay, let's see you shine, my man.'

Roden's wiry red head covered the microscope.

'We have to go to chaetaxy now – studying the skin of the insect to narrow it down to one species,' Pilcher said. 'Roden's the best at it.'

Starling had the sense that a kindness had passed in the room.

Roden responded by starting a fierce argument with Pilcher over whether the specimen's larval warts were arranged in circles or not. It raged on through the arrangement of the hairs on the abdomen.

'*Erebus odora,*' Roden said at last.

'Let's go look,' Pilcher said.

They took the specimen with them, down in the elevator to the level just above the great stuffed elephant and back into an enormous quad filled with pale green boxes. What was formerly a great hall had been split into two levels with decks to provide more storage for the Smithsonian's insects. They were in Neo-tropical now, moving into Noctuids. Pilcher consulted his notepad and stopped at a box chest-high in the great wall stack.

'You have to be careful with these things,' he said, sliding the heavy metal door off the box and setting it on the floor. 'You drop one on your foot and you hop for weeks.'

He ran his finger down the stacked drawers, selected one, and pulled it out.

In the tray Starling saw the tiny preserved eggs, the caterpillar in a tube of alcohol, a cocoon peeled away from a specimen very similar to hers, and the adult – a big brown-black moth with a wingspan of nearly six inches, a furry body, and slender antennae.

'*Erebus odora,*' Pilcher said. 'The Black Witch Moth.'

Roden was already turning pages. '"A tropical species sometimes straying up to Canada in the fall,"' he read. '"The larvae eat acacia, catclaw, and similar plants. Indigenous West Indies, Southern US, considered a pest in Hawaii."'

Fuckola, Starling thought. 'Nuts,' she said aloud. 'They're all over.'

'But they're not all over all the time.' Pilcher's head was down. He pulled at his chin. 'Do they double-brood, Roden?'

'Wait a second . . . yeah, in extreme south Florida and south Texas.'

'When?'

'May and August.'

'I was just thinking,' Pilcher said. 'Your specimen's a little better developed than the one we have, and it's fresh. It had started fracturing its cocoon to come out. In the West Indies or Hawaii, maybe, I could understand it, but it's winter here. In this country it would wait three months to come out. Unless it happened accidentally in a greenhouse, or somebody raised it.'

'Raised it how?'

'In a cage, in a warm place, with some acacia leaves for the larvae to eat until they're ready to button up in their cocoons. It's not hard to do.'

'Is it a popular hobby? Outside professional study, do a lot of people do it?'

'No, primarily it's entomologists trying to get a perfect specimen, maybe a few collectors. There's the silk industry too, they raise moths, but not this kind.'

'Entomologists must have periodicals, professional journals, people that sell equipment,' Starling said.

'Sure, and most of the publications come here.'

'Let me make you a bundle,' Roden said. 'A couple of people here subscribe privately to the smaller newsletters – keep 'em locked up and make you give them a quarter just to look at the stupid things. I'll have to get those in the morning.'

'I'll see they're picked up, thank you, Mr Roden.'

Pilcher photocopied the references on *Erebus odora* and gave them to her, along with the insect. 'I'll take you down,' he said.

They waited for the elevator. 'Most people love butterflies and hate moths,' he said. 'But moths are more – interesting, engaging.'

'They're destructive.'

'Some are, a lot are, but they live in all kinds of ways. Just like we do.' Silence for one floor. 'There's a moth, more than one in fact, that lives only on tears,' he offered. 'That's all they eat or drink.'

'What kind of tears? Whose tears?'

'The tears of large land mammals, about our size. The old definition of moth was "anything that gradually, silently eats, consumes, or wastes any other thing." It was a verb for destruction too . . . Is this what you do all the time – hunt Buffalo Bill?'

'I do it all I can.'

Pilcher polished his teeth, his tongue moving behind his lips like a cat beneath the covers. 'Do you ever go out for cheeseburgers and beer or the' amusing house wine?'

'Not lately.'

'Will you go for some with me now? It's not far.'

'No, but I'll treat when this is over – and Mr Roden can go too, naturally.'

'There's nothing natural about that,' Pilcher said. And at the door, 'I hope you're through with this soon, Officer Starling.'

She hurried to the waiting car.

Ardelia Mapp had left Starling's mail and half a Mounds candy har on her bed. Mapp was asleep.

Starling carried her portable typewriter down to the laundry room, put it on the clothes-folding shelf and cranked in a carbon set. She had organized her notes on *Erebus odora* in her head on the ride back to Quantico, and she covered that quickly.

Then she ate the Mounds and wrote a memo to Crawford suggesting they cross-check the entomology publications' computerized mailing lists against the FBI's known offender files and the files in the cities closest to the abductions, plus felon and sex-offender files of Metro Dade, San Antonio, and Houston, the areas where the moths were most plentiful.

There was another thing, too, that she had to bring up for a second time: *Let's ask Dr Lecter why he thought the perpetrator would start taking scalps.*

She delivered the paper to the night duty officer and fell into her grateful bed, the voices of the day still whispering, softer than Mapp's breathing across the room. On the swarming dark she saw the moth's wise little face. Those glowing eyes had looked at Buffalo Bill.

Out of the cosmic hangover the Smithsonian leaves came her last thought and a coda for her day: *Over this odd world, this half of the world that's dark now, I have to hunt a thing that lives on tears.*

Chapter Fifteen

In East Memphis, Tennessee, Catherine Baker Martin and her best boyfriend were watching a late movie on television in his apartment and having a few hits off a bong pipe loaded with hashish. The commercial breaks grew longer and more frequent.

'I've got the munchies, want some popcorn?' she said.

'I'll go get it, give me your keys.'

'Sit still. I need to see if Mom called, anyway.'

She got up from the couch, a tall young woman, big-boned and well fleshed, nearly heavy, with a handsome face and a lot of clean hair. She found her shoes under the coffee table and went outside.

The February evening was more raw than cold. A light fog off the Mississippi River hung breast-high over the big parking area. Directly overhead she could see the dying moon, pale and thin as a bone fishhook. Looking up made her a little dizzy. She started across the parking field, navigating steadily toward her own front door a hundred yards away.

The brown panel truck was parked near her apartment, among some motor homes and boats on trailers. She noticed it because it resembled the parcel delivery trucks which often brought presents from her mother.

As she passed near the truck, a lamp came on in the fog. It was a floor lamp with a shade. standing on the asphalt behind the truck. Beneath the lamp was an overstuffed armchair in red-flowered chintz, the big red flowers blooming in the fog. The two items were like a furniture grouping in a showroom.

Catherine Baker Martin blinked several times and kept going. She thought the word *surreal* and blamed the bong. She was all right. Somebody was moving in or moving out. In. Out. Somebody was always moving at the Stonehinge Villas. The curtain stirred in her apartment and she saw her cat on the sill, arching and pressing his side against the glass.

She had her key ready, and before she used it she looked back. A man climbed out of the back of the truck. She could see by the lamplight that he had a cast on his hand and his arm was in a sling. She went inside and locked the door behind her.

Catherine Baker Martin peeped around the curtain and saw the man trying to put the chair into the back of the truck. He gripped it with his good hand and tried to boost it with his knee. The chair fell over. He righted it, licked his finger and rubbed at a spot of parking-lot grime on the chintz.

She went outside.

'Help you with that.' She got the tone just right – helpful and that's all.

'Would you? Thanks.' An odd, strained voice. Not a local accent.

The floor lamp lit his face from below, distorting his features, but she could see his body plainly. He had on pressed khaki trousers and some kind of chamois shirt, unbuttoned over a freckled chest. His chin and cheeks were hairless, as smooth as a woman's, and his eyes only pinpoint gleams above his cheekbones in the shadows of the lamp.

He looked at her too, and she was sensitive to that. Men were often surprised at her size when she got close to them and some concealed it better than others.

'Good,' he said.

There was an unpleasant odor about the man, and she noticed with distaste that his chamois shirt still had hairs on it, curly ones across the shoulders and beneath the arms.

It was easy lifting the chair onto the low floor of the truck.

'Let's slide it to the front, do you mind?' He climbed inside and moved some clutter, the big flat pans you can slide under a vehicle to drain the oil, and a small hand winch called a coffin hoist.

They pushed the chair forward until it was just behind the seats.

'Are you about a fourteen?' he said.

'What?'

'Would you hand me that rope? It's just at your feet.'

When she bent to look, he brought the plaster cast down on the back of her head. She thought she'd bumped her head and she raised her hand to it as the cast came down again, smashing her fingers against her skull, and down again, this time behind her ear, a succession of blows, none of them too hard, as she slumped over the chair. She slid to the floor of the truck and lay on her side.

The man watched her for a second, then pulled off his cast and the arm sling. Quickly he brought the lamp into the truck and closed the rear doors.

He pulled her collar back and, with a flashlight, read the size tag on her blouse.

'Good,' he said.

He slit the blouse up the back with a pair of bandage scissors, pulled the blouse off, and handcuffed her hands behind her. Spreading a mover's pad on the floor of the truck, he rolled her onto her back.

She was not wearing a brassiere. He prodded her big breasts with his fingers and felt their weight and resilience.

'Good,' he said.

There was a pink suck mark on her left breast. He licked his finger to rub it as he had done the chintz and nodded when the lividity went away with light pressure. He rolled her onto her face and checked her scalp, parting her thick hair with his fingers. The padded cast hadn't cut her.

He checked her pulse with two fingers on the side of her neck and found it strong.

'Gooood,' he said. He had a long way to drive to his two-story house and he'd rather not field-dress her here.

Catherine Baker Martin's cat watched out the window as the truck pulled away, the taillights getting closer and closer together.

Behind the cat the telephone was ringing. The machine in the bedroom answered, its red light blinking in the dark.

The caller was Catherine's mother, the junior US Senator from Tennessee.

Chapter Sixteen

In the 1980s, the Golden Age of Terrorism, procedures were in place to deal with a kidnapping affecting a member of Congress:

At 2:45 A.M. the special agent in charge of the Memphis FBI office reported to headquarters in Washington that Senator Ruth Martin's only daughter had disappeared.

At 3:00 A.M. two unmarked vans pulled out of the damp basement garage at the Washington field office, Buzzard's Point. One van went to the Senate Office Building, where technicians placed monitoring and recording equipment on the telephones in Senator Martin's office and put a Title 3 wiretap on the pay phones closest to the Senator's office. The Justice Department woke the most junior member of the Senate Select Intelligence Committee to provide the obligatory notice of the tap.

The other vehicle, an 'eyeball van' with one-way glass and surveillance equipment, was parked on Virginia Avenue to cover the front of the Watergate West, Senator Martin's Washington residence. Two of the van's occupants went inside to install monitoring equipment on the Senator's home telephones.

Bell Atlantic estimated the mean trace time at seventy seconds on any ransom call placed from a domestic digital switching system.

The Reactive Squad at Buzzard's Point went to double shifts in the event of a ransom drop in the Washington area. Their radio procedure changed to mandatory encryption to protect any possible ransom drop from intrusion by news helicoptors – that kind of irresponsibility on the part of the news business was rare, but it had happened.

The Hostage Rescue Team went to an alert status one level short of airborne.

Everyone hoped Catherine Baker Martin's disappearance was a professional kidnapping for ransom; that possibility offered the best chance for her survival.

Nobody mentioned the worst possibility of all.

Then, shortly before dawn in Memphis, a city patrolman investigating a prowler complaint on Winchester Avenue stopped an elderly man collecting aluminum cans and junk along the shoulder of the road. In his cart the patrolman found a woman's blouse, still buttoned in front. The blouse was slit up the back like a funeral suit. The laundry mark was Catherine Baker Martin's.

Jack Crawford was driving south from his home in Arlington at 6:30 A.M. when the telephone in his car beeped for the second time in two minutes.

'Nine twenty-two forty.'

'Forty stand by for Alpha 4.'

Crawford spotted a rest area, pulled in, and stopped to give his full attention to the telephone. Alpha 4 is the Director of the FBI.

'Jack – you up on Catherine Martin?'

'The night duty officer called me just now.'

'Then you know about the blouse. Talk to me.'

'Buzzard's Point went to kidnap alert,' Crawford said. 'I'd prefer they didn't stand down yet. When they do stand down I'd like to keep the phone surveillance. Slit blouse or not, we don't know for sure it's Bill. If it's a copycat he might call for ransom. Who's doing taps and traces in Tennessee, us or them?'

'Them. The state police. They're pretty good. Phil Adler called from the White House to tell me about the President's "intense interest." We could use a win here, Jack.'

'That had occurred to me. Where's the Senator?'

'En route to Memphis. She got me at home a minute ago. You can imagine. '

'Yes.' Crawford knew Senator Martin from budget hearings.

'She's coming down with all the weight she's got.'

'I don't blame her.'

'Neither do I,' the Director said. 'I've told her we're going flat-out just as we've done all along. She is . . . she's aware of your personal situation and she's offered you a company Lear. Use it – come home at night if you can.'

'Good. The Senator's tough, Tommy. If she tries to run it we'll butt heads.'

'I know. Do a set-pick off me if you have to. What have we got at the best – six or seven days, Jack?'

'I don't know. If he panics when he finds out who she is – he might just do her and dump her.'

'Where are you?'

'Two miles from Quantico.'

'Will the strip at Quantico take a Lear?'

'Yes.'

'Twenty minutes.'

'Yes sir.'

Crawford punched numbers into his phone and pulled back into the traffic.

Chapter Seventeen

Sore from a troubled sleep, Clarice Starling stood in her bathrobe and bunny slippers, towel over her shoulder waiting to get in the bathroom she and Mapp shared with the students next door. The news from Memphis on the radio froze her for half a breath.

'Oh God,' she said. 'Oh boy. ALL RIGHT IN THERE! THIS BATHROOM IS SEIZED. COME OUT WITH YOUR PANTS UP. THIS IS NOT A DRILL!' She climbed into the shower with a startled nextdoor neighbor. 'Ooch over, Gracie, and would you pass me that soap.'

Ear cocked to the telephone, she packed for overnight and set her forensic kit by the door. She made sure the switchboard knew she was in her room and gave up breakfast to stick by the phone. At ten minutes to class time, with no word, she hurried down to Behavioral Science with her equipment.

'Mr Crawford left for Memphis forty-five minutes ago,' the secretary told her sweetly. 'Burroughs went, and Stafford from the lab left from National.'

'I put a report here for him last night. Did he leave any message for me? I'm Clarice Starling.'

'Yes. I know who you are. I have three copies of your telephone number right here, and there are several more on his desk, I believe. No. he didn't leave a thing for you, Clarice.' The woman looked at Starling's luggage. 'Would you like me to tell him something when he calls in?'

'Did he leave a Memphis phone number on his three-card?'

'No, he'll call with it. Don't you have classes today, Clarice? You're still in school, aren't you?'

'Yes. Yes, I am.'

Starling's entry, late, into the classroom was not eased by Gracie Pitman, the young woman she had displaced in the shower. Gracie Pitman sat directly behind Starling. It seemed a long way to her seat. Gracie Pitman's tongue had time to make two full revolutions in her downy cheek before Starling could submerge into the class.

With no breakfast she sat through two hours of 'The Good-Faith Warrant Exception to the Exclusionary Rule in Search and Seizure,' before she could get to the vending machine and chug a Coke.

She checked her box for a message at noon and there was nothing. It occurred to her then, as it had on a few other occasions in her life, that intense frustration tastes very much like the patent medicine called Fleet's that she'd had to take as a child.

Some days you wake up changed. This was one for Starling, she could tell. What she had seen yesterday at the Potter Funeral Home had caused in her a small tectonic shift.

Starling had studied psychology and criminology in a good school. In her life she had seen some of the hideously offhand ways in which the world breaks things. But she hadn't really *known* and now she knew: sometimes the family of man produces, behind a human face, a mind whose pleasure is what lay on the porcelain table at Potter, West Virginia, in the room with the cabbage roses. Starling's first apprehension of that mind was worse than anything she could see on the autopsy scales. The knowledge would lie against her skin forever, and she knew she had to form a callus or it would wear her through.

The school routine didn't help her. All day she had the feeling that things were going on just over the horizon. She seemed to hear a vast murmur of events, like the sound from a distant stadium. Suggestions of movement unsettled her, groups passing in the hallway, cloud shadows moving over, the sound of an airplane.

After class Starling ran too many laps and then she swam. She swam until she thought about the floaters and then she didn't want the water on her anymore.

She watched the seven o'clock news with Mapp and a dozen other students in the recreation room. The abduction of Senator Martin's daughter was not the lead item, but it was first after the Geneva arms talks.

There was film from Memphis, starting with the sign of the Stonehinge Villas shot across the revolving light of a patrol car. The media was blitzing the story and, with little new to report, reporters interviewed each other in the parking lot at Stonehinge.

Memphis and Shelby County authorities ducked their heads to unaccustomed banks of microphones. In a jostling, squealing hell of lens flare and audio feedback, they listed the things they didn't know. Still-photographers stooped and darted, backpedaling into the TV minicams whenever investigators entered or left Catherine Baker Martin's apartment.

A brief, ironic cheer went up in the Academy recreation room when Crawford's face appeared briefly in the apartment window. Starling smiled on one side of her mouth.

She wondered if Buffalo Bill was watching. She wondered what he thought of Crawford's face or if he even knew who Crawford was.

Others seemed to think Bill might be watching, too.

There was Senator Martin, on television live with Peter Jennings. She stood alone in her child's bedroom, a Southwestern University pennant and posters favoring Wile E. Coyote and the Equal Rights Amendment on the wall behind her.

She was a tall woman with a strong, plain face.

'I'm speaking now to the person who is holding my daughter,' she said. She walked closer to the camera, causing an unscheduled refocus, and spoke as she never would have spoken to a terrorist.

'You have the power to let my daughter go unharmed. Her name is Catherine. She's very gentle and understanding. Please let my daughter go, please release her unharmed. You have control of this situation. You have the power. You are in charge. I know you can feel love and compassion. You can protect her against anything that might want to harm her. You now have a wonderful chance to show the whole world that you are capable of great kindness, that you are big enough to treat others better than the world has treated you. Her name is Catherine.'

Senator Martin's eyes cut away from the camera as the picture switched to a home movie of a toddler helping herself walk by hanging on to the mane of a large collie.

The Senator's voice went on: 'The film you're seeing now is Catherine as a little child. Release Catherine. Release her unharmed anywhere in this country and you'll have my help and my friendship.'

Now a series of still photographs – Catherine Martin at eight, holding the tiller of a sailboat. The boat was up on blocks and her father was painting the hull. Two recent photographs of the young woman, a full shot and a close-up of her face.

Now back to the Senator in close-up: 'I promise you in front of this entire country, you'll have my unstinting aid whenever you need it. I'm well equipped to help you. I am a United States Senator. I serve on the Armed Services Committee. I am deeply involved in the Strategic Defense Initiative, the space weapons systems which everyone calls "Star Wars." If you have enemies I will fight them. If anyone interferes with you, I can stop them. You can call me at any time, day or night. Catherine is my daughter's name. Please show us your strength,' Senator Martin said in closing, 'release Catherine unharmed.'

'Boy, is that smart,' Starling said. She was trembling like a terrier. 'Jesus, that's smart.'

'What, the Star Wars?' Mapp said. 'If the aliens are trying to control Buffalo Bill's thoughts from another planet, Senator Martin can protect him – is that the pitch?'

Starling nodded. 'A lot of paranoid schizophrenics have that specific hallucination – alien control. If that's the way Bill's wired, maybe this approach could bring him out. It's a damn good shot, though, and she stood up there and fired it, didn't she? At the least it might buy Catherine a few more days. They may have time to work on Bill a little. Or they may not; Crawford thinks his period may be getting shorter. They can *try* this, they can try other things.'

'Nothing I *wouldn't* try if he had one of mine. Why did she keep saying "Catherine," why the name all the time?'

'She's trying to make Buffalo Bill see Catherine as a person. They're thinking he'll have to depersonalize her, he'll have to see her as an object before he can tear her up. Serial murderers talk about that in prison interviews, some of them. They say it's like working on a doll.'

'Do you see Crawford behind Senator Martin's statement?'

'Maybe, or maybe Dr Bloom – there he is,' Starling said. On the screen was an interview taped several weeks earlier with Dr Alan Bloom of the University of Chicago on the subject of serial murder.

Dr Bloom refused to compare Buffalo Bill with Francis Dolarhyde or Garrett Hobbs, or any of the others in his experience. He refused to use the term 'Buffalo Bill.' In fact he didn't say much at all, but he was known to be an expert, probably *the* expert on the subject, and the network wanted to show his face.

They used his final statement for the snapper at the end of the report: 'There's nothing we can threaten him with that's more terrible than what he faces every day. What we *can* do is ask him to come to us. We can promise him kind treatment and relief, and we can mean it absolutely and sincerely.'

'Couldn't we all use some relief,' Mapp said. 'Damn if I couldn't use some relief myself. Slick obfuscation and facile bullshit, I love it. He didn't tell them anything, but then he probably didn't stir Bill up much either.'

'I can stop thinking about that kid in West Virginia for a while,' Starling said, 'it goes away for, say, a half an hour at a time, and then it pokes me in the throat. Glitter polish on her nails – let me not get into it.'

Mapp, rummaging among her many enthusiasms, lightened Starling's gloom at dinner and fascinated eavesdroppers by comparing slant-rhymes in the works of Stevie Wonder and Emily Dickinson.

On the way back to the room, Starling snatched a message out of her box and read this: *Please call Albert Roden,* and a telephone number.

'That just proves my theory,' she told Mapp as they flopped on their beds with their books.

'What's that?'

'You meet two guys, right? The wrong one'll call you every God damned time.'

'I *been* knowing that.'

The telephone rang.

Mapp touched the end of her nose with her pencil. 'If that's Hot Bobby Lowrance, would you tell him I'm in the library?' Mapp said. 'I'll call him tomorrow, tell him.'

It was Crawford calling from an airplane, his voice scratchy on the phone. 'Starling, pack for two nights and meet me in an hour.'

She thought he was gone, there was only a hollow humming on the telephone, then the voice came back abruptly ' – won't need the kit, just clothes.'

'Meet you where?'

'The Smithsonian.' He started talking to someone else before he punched off.

'Jack Crawford,' Starling said, flipping her bag on the bed.

Mapp appeared over the top of her *Federal Code of Criminal Procedure*. She watched Starling pack, an eyelid dropping over one of her great dark eyes.

'I don't want to put anything on your mind,' she said.

'Yes you do,' Starling said. She knew what was coming.

Mapp had made the Law Review at the University of Maryland while working at night. Her academic standing at the Academy was number two in the class, her attitude toward the books was pure banzai.

'You're supposed to take the Criminal Code exam tomorrow and the PE test in two days. You make sure Supremo Crawford knows you could get recycled if he's not careful. Soon as he says, "Good work, Trainee Starling," don't you say, "The pleasure was mine." You get right in his old Easter Island face and say, "I'm counting on you to see to it *yourself* that I'm not recycled for missing school." Understand what I'm saying?'

'I can get a makeup on the Code,' Starling said, opening a barrette with her teeth.

'Right, and you fail it with no time to study, you think they won't recycle you? Are you kidding me? Girl, they'll sail you off the back steps like a dead Easter chick. Gratitude's got a short half-life, Clarice. Make him say *no recycle*. You've got good grades – make him say it. I never would find another roommate that can iron as fast as you can at one minute to class.'

Starling had her old Pinto moving up the four-lane at a steady lope, one mile an hour below the speed where the shimmy sets in. The smells of hot oil and mildew, the rattles underneath, the transmission's whine resonated faintly with memories of her father's pickup truck, her memories of riding beside him with her squirming brothers and sister.

She was doing the driving now, driving at night, the white dashes passing under blip blip blip. She had time to think. Her fears breathed on her from close behind her neck; other, recent memories squirmed beside her.

Starling was very much afraid Catherine Baker Martin's body had been found. When Buffalo Bill found out who she was, he might have panicked. He might have killed her and dumped her body with a bug in the throat.

Maybe Crawford was bringing the bug to be identified. Why else would he want her at the Smithsonian? But any agent could carry a bug into the Smithsonian, an FBI messenger could do it for that matter. And he told her to pack for two days.

She could understand Crawford not explaining it to her over an unsecured radio link, but it was maddening to wonder.

She found an all-news station on the radio and waited through the weather report. When the news came, it was no help. The story from Memphis was a rehash of the seven o'clock news. Senator Martin's daughter was missing. Her blouse had been found slit up the back in the style of Buffalo Bill. No witnesses. The victim found in West Virginia remained unidentified.

West Virginia. Among Clarice Starling's memories of the Potter Funeral Home was something hard and valuable. Something durable, shining apart from the dark revelations. Something to keep. She deliberately recalled it now and found that she could squeeze it like a talisman. In the Potter Funeral Home, standing at the sink, she had found strength from a source that surprised and pleased her – the memory of her mother. Starling was a seasoned survivor on hand-me-down grace from her late father through her brothers; she was surprised and moved by this bounty she had found.

She parked the Pinto beneath FBI headquarters at Tenth and Pennsylvania. Two television crews were set up on the sidewalk, reporters looking over-groomed in the lights. They were intoning standup reports with the J. Edgar Hoover Building in the background. Starling skirted the lights and walked the two blocks to the Smithsonian's National Museum of Natural History.

She could see a few lighted windows high in the old building. A Baltimore County Police van was parked in the semicircular drive. Crawford's driver, Jeff, waited at the wheel of a new surveillance van behind it. When he saw Starling coming, he spoke into a handheld radio.

Chapter Eighteen

The guard took Clarice Starling to the second level above the Smithsonian's great stuffed elephant. The elevator door opened onto that vast dim floor and Crawford was waiting there alone, his hands in the pockets of his raincoat.

'Evening, Starling.'

'Hello,' she said.

Crawford spoke over her shoulder to the guard. 'We can make it from here by ourselves, Officer, thank you.'

Crawford and Starling walked side by side along a corridor in the stacked trays and cases of anthropological specimens. A few ceiling lights were on, not many. As she fell with him into the hunched, reflective attitude of a campus stroll, Starling became aware that Crawford wanted to put his hand on her shoulder, that he would have done it if it were possible for him to touch her.

She waited for him to say something. Finally she stopped, put her hands in her pockets too, and they faced each other across the passage in the silence of the bones.

Crawford leaned his head back against the cases and took a deep breath through his nose. 'Catherine Martin's probably still alive' he said.

Starling nodded, kept her head down after the last nod. Maybe he would find it easier to talk if she didn't look at him. He was steady, but something had hold of him. Starling wondered for a second if his wife had died. Or maybe spending all day with Catherine's grieving mother had done it.

'Memphis was pretty much of a wipe,' he said. 'He got her on the parking lot, I think. Nobody saw it. She went in her apartment and then she came back out for some reason. She didn't mean to stay out long – she left the door ajar and flipped the deadbolt so it wouldn't lock behind her. Her keys were on top of the TV. Nothing disturbed inside. I don't think she was in the apartment long. She never got as far as her answering machine in the bedroom. The message light was still blinking when her yo-yo boyfriend finally called the police.' Crawford idly let his hand fall into a tray of bones, and quickly took it out again.

'So now he's got her, Starling. The networks agreed not to do a countdown on the evening news – Dr Bloom thinks it eggs him on. A couple of the tabloids'll do it anyway.'

In one previous abduction clothing slit up the back had been found soon enough to identify a Buffalo Bill victim while she was still being held alive. Starling remembered the black-bordered countdown on the front pages of the trash papers. It reached eighteen days before the body floated.

'So Catherine Baker Martin's waiting in Bill's green room, Starling, and we have maybe a week. That's at the outside – Bloom thinks his period's getting shorter.'

This seemed like a lot of talk for Crawford. The theatrical 'green room' reference smacked of bullshit. Starling waited for him to get to the point, and then he did.

'But this time, Starling, *this* time we may have a little break.'

She looked up at him beneath her brows, hopeful and watchful too.

'We've got another insect. Your fellows, Pilcher and that . . . other one.'

'Roden.'

'They're working on it.'

'Where was it – Cincinnati? – the girl in the freezer?'

'No. Come on and I'll show you. Let's see what you think about it.'

'Entomology's the other way, Mr Crawford.'

'I know,' he said.

They rounded the corner to the door of Anthropology. Light and voices came through the frosted glass. She went in.

Three men in laboratory coats worked at a table in the center of the room beneath a brilliant light. Starling couldn't see what they were doing. Jerry Burroughs from Behavioral Science was looking over their shoulders taking notes on a clipboard. There was a familiar odor in the room.

Then one of the men in white moved to put something in the sink and she could see all right.

In a stainless-steel tray on the workbench was 'Klaus,' the head she had found in the Split City Mini-Storage.

'Klaus had the bug in his throat,' Crawford said. 'Hold on a minute, Starling. Jerry, are you talking to the wire room?'

Burroughs was reading from his clipboard into the telephone. He put his hand over the mouthpiece. 'Yeah, Jack, they're drying the art on Klaus.'

Crawford took the receiver from him. 'Bobby, don't wait for the Interpol split. Get a picture wire and transmit the photographs now along with the medical. Scandinavian countries, West Germany, the Netherlands. Be sure to say Klaus could be a merchant sailor that jumped ship. Mention that their National Health may have a claim for the cheek bone fracture. Call it the what, the zygomatic arch. Make sure you move both dental charts, the universal and the Fédération Dentaire. They're coming with an age, but emphasize that it's a rough estimate – you can't depend on skull sutures for that.' He gave the phone back to Burroughs. 'Where's your gear, Starling?'

'The guard office downstairs.'

'Johns Hopkins found the insect,' Crawford said as they waited for the elevator. 'They were doing the head for the Baltimore County police. It was in the throat, just like the girl in West Virginia.'

'Just like West Virginia.'

'You clucked. Johns Hopkins found it about seven tonight. The Baltimore district attorney called me on the plane. They sent the whole thing over, Klaus and all, so we could see it *in situ.* They also wanted an opinion from Dr Angel on Klaus's age and how old he was when he fractured his cheekbone. They consult the Smithsonian just like we do.'

'I have to deal with this a second. You're saying maybe Buffalo Bill killed *Klaus?* Years ago?'

'Does it seem farfetched. too much of a coincidence?'

'Right this second it does.'

'Let it cook a minute.'

'Dr Lecter told me where to find Klaus,' Starling said.

'Yes, he did.'

'Dr Lecter told me his patient, Benjamin Raspail, claimed to have killed Klaus. But Lecter said he believed it was probably accidental erotic asphyxia.'

'That's what he said.'

'You think maybe Dr Lecter knows exactly how Klaus died, and it wasn't Raspail, and it wasn't erotic asphyxia?'

'Klaus had a bug in his throat, the girl in West Virginia had a bug in her throat. I never saw that anywhere else. Never read about it, never heard of it. What do you think?'

'I think you told me to pack for two days. You want me to ask Dr Lecter? don't you?'

'You're the one he talks to, Starling.' Crawford looked so sad when he said, 'I figure you're game.'

She nodded.

'We'll talk on the way to the asylum,' he said.

Chapter Nineteen

'Dr Lecter had a big psychiatric practice for years before we caught him for the murders,' Crawford said. 'He did a slew of psychiatric evaluations for the Maryland and Virginia courts and some others up and down the East Coast. He's seen a lot of the criminally insane. Who knows what he turned loose, just for fun? That's one way he could know. Also, he knew Raspail socially and Raspail told him things in therapy. Maybe Raspail told him who killed Klaus.'

Crawford and Starling faced each other in swivel chairs in the back of the surveillance van, whizzing north on US 95 toward Baltimore, thirty-seven miles away. Jeff, in the driver's compartment, clearly had orders to step on it.

'Lecter offered to help, and I had no part of him. I've had his help before. He gave us nothing useful and he helped Will Graham get a knife jammed through his face last time. For fun.

'But a bug in Klaus's throat, a bug in the girl's throat in West Virginia, I can't ignore that. Alan Bloom's never heard of that specific act before, and neither have I. Have you ever run across it before. Starling? You've read the literature since I have.'

'Never. Inserting other objects, yes, but never an insect.'

'Two things to begin with. First, we go on the premise that Dr Lecter really knows something concrete. Second, we remember that Lecter looks only for the fun. Never forget fun. He has to want Buffalo Bill caught while Catherine Martin's still alive. All the fun and benefits have to lie in that direction. We've got nothing to threaten him with – he's lost his commode seat and his books already. That cleans him out.'

'What would happen if we just told him the situation and offered him something – a cell with a view. That's what he asked for when he offered to help.'

'He offered to *help*, Starling. He didn't offer to snitch. Snitching wouldn't give him enough of a chance to show off. You're doubtful. You favor the truth. Lister, Lecter's in no hurry. He's followed this like it was baseball. We ask him to snitch, he'll wait. He won't do it right away.'

'Even for a reward? Something he won't get if Catherine Martin dies?'

'Say we tell him we *know* he's got information and we want him to snitch. He'd have the most fun by waiting and acting like he's trying to remember week after week, getting Senator Martin's hopes up and letting Catherine die, and then tormenting the next mother and the next, getting their hopes up, always just about to remember – that would be better than having a view. It's the kind of thing he lives on. It's his nourishment.'

'I'm not sure you get wiser as you get older, Starling, but you do learn to dodge a certain amount of hell. We can dodge some right there.'

'So Dr Lecter has to think we're coming to him strictly for theory and insight,' Starling said.

'Correct.'

'Why did you tell me? Why didn't you just send me in to ask him that way?'

'I level with you. You'll do the same when you have a command. Nothing else works for long.'

'So there's no mention of the insect in Klaus's throat, no connection between Klaus and Buffalo Bill.'

'No. You came back to him because you were so impressed that he could predict Buffalo Bill would start scalping. I'm on the record dismissing him and so is Alan Bloom. But I'm letting you fool with it. You have an offer for some privileges – stuff that only somebody as powerful as Senator Martin could get for him. He has to believe he should hurry because the offer ends if Catherine dies. The Senator totally loses interest in him if that happens. And if he fails, it's because he's not smart and knowledgeable enough to do what he said he could do – it's not because he's holding out to spite us.'

'*Will* the Senator lose interest?'

'Better you should be able to say under oath that you never knew the answer to that question.'

'I see.' So Senator Martin hadn't been told. That took some nerve. Clearly, Crawford was afraid of interference, afraid the Senator might make the mistake of appealing to Dr Lecter.

'*Do* you see?'

'Yes. How can he be specific enough to steer us to Buffalo Bill without showing he's got special knowledge? How can he do that with just theory and insight?'

'I don't know, Starling. He's had a long time to think about it. He's waited through six victims.'

The scrambler phone in the van buzzed and blinked with the first of a series of calls Crawford had placed with the FBI switchboard.

Over the next twenty minutes he talked to officers he knew in the Dutch

State Police and Royal Marechausee, an *Overstelojtnant* in the Swedish Technical Police who had studied at Quantico, a personal acquaintance who was assistant to the *Rigspolitichef* of the Danish governmental police, and he surprised Starling by breaking into French with the night command desk of the Belgian Police Criminelle. Always he stressed the need for speed in identifying Klaus and his associates. Each jurisdiction would already have the request on its Interpol telex but, with the old-boy network buzzing, the request wouldn't hang from the machine for hours.

Starling could see that Crawford had chosen the van for its communications – it had the new Voice Privacy system – but the job would have been easier from his office. Here he had to juggle his notebooks on the tiny desk in marginal light, and they bounced each time the tires hit a tar strip. Starling's field experience was small, but she knew how unusual it was for a section chief to be booming along in a van on an errand like this. He could have briefed her over the radio telephone. She was glad he had not.

Starling had the feeling that the quiet and calm in this van, the time allowed for this mission to proceed in an orderly way, had been purchased at a high price. Listening to Crawford on the phone confirmed it.

He was speaking with the Director at home now. 'No sir. Did they roll over for it? . . . How long? No sir. No. No wire. Tommy, that's my recommendation, I stand on it. I *do not* want her to wear a wire. Dr Bloom says the same thing. He's fogged in at O'Hare. He'll come as soon as it clears. Right.'

Then Crawford had a cryptic telephone conversation with the night nurse at his house. When he had finished, he looked out the one way window of the van for perhaps a minute, his glasses held on his knee in the crook of his finger, his face looking naked as the oncoming lights crawled across it. Then he put the glasses on and turned back to Starling.

'We have Lecter for three days. If we don't get any results, Baltimore sweats him until the court pulls them off.'

'Sweating him didn't work last time. Dr Lecter doesn't sweat much.'

'What did he give them after all that, a paper chicken?'

'A chicken, yes.' The crumpled origami chicken was still in Starling's purse. She smoothed it out on the little desk and made it peck.

'I don't blame the Baltimore cops. He's their prisoner. If Catherine floats, they have to be able to tell Senator Martin they tried it all.'

'How is Senator Martin?'

'Game but hurting. She's a smart, tough woman with a lot of sense, Starling. You'd probably like her.'

'Will Johns Hopkins and Baltimore County homicide keep quiet about the bug in Klaus's throat? Can we keep it out of the papers?'

'For three days at least.'

'That took some doing.'

'We can't trust Frederick Chilton, or anybody else at the hospital,' Crawford said. 'If Chilton knows, the world knows. Chilton has to know you're there, but it's simply a favor you're doing Baltimore Homicide, trying to close the Klaus case – it has nothing to do with Buffalo Bill.'

'And I'm doing this late at night?'

'That's the only time I'd give you. I should tell you, the business about the bug in West Virginia will be in the morning papers. The Cincinnati coroner's office spilled it, so that's no secret anymore. It's an inside detail that Lecter can get from you and it doesn't matter really, as long as he doesn't know we found one in Klaus too.'

'What have we got to trade him?'

'I'm working on it,' Crawford said, and turned back to his telephones.

Chapter Twenty

A big bathroom, all white tile and skylights and sleek Italian fixtures standing against exposed old brick. An elaborate vanity flanked by tall plants and loaded with cosmetics, the mirror beaded by the steam the shower made. From the shower came humming in a key too high for the unearthly voice. The song was Fats Waller's 'Cash for Your Trash,' from the musical *Ain't Misbehavin'* . Sometimes the voice broke into the words:

'Save up all your old newsPA-PERS.
Save and pile 'em like a high skySCRAPER
DAH DAHDAHDAH DAH DAH DAHDAH DAH
DAH . . .'

Whenever there were words, a small dog scratched at the bathroom door.

In the shower was Jame Gumb, white male, thirty-four, six feet one inch, 205 pounds, brown and blue, no distinguishing marks. He pronounces his first name like *James* without the *s*, Jame. He insists on it.

After his first rinse, Gumb applied Friction des Bains, rubbing it over his chest and buttocks with his hands and using a dishmop on the parts he did not like to touch. His legs and feet were a little stubbly, but he decided they would do.

Gumb toweled himself pink and applied a good skin emollient. His full-length mirror had a shower curtain on a bar in front of it.

Gumb used the dishmop to tuck his penis and testicles back between his legs. He whipped the shower curtain aside and stood before the mirror, hitting a hipshot pose despite the grinding it caused in his private parts.

'Do something *for* me, honey. Do something for me SOON.' He used the upper range of his naturally deep voice, and he believed he was getting better at it. The hormones he'd taken – Premarin for a while and then diethylstilbestrol orally – couldn't do anything for his voice but they had thinned the hair a little across his slightly budding breasts. A lot of electrolysis had removed Gumb's beard and shaped his hairline into a widow's peak but he did not look like a woman. He looked like a man inclined to fight with his nails as well as his fists and feet.

Whether his behavior was an earnest, inept attempt to swish or a hateful mocking would be hard to say on short acquaintance and short acquaintances were the only kind he had.

'Whatcha gonna do for meeee?'

The dog scratched on the door at the sound of his voice. Gumb put on his robe and let the dog in. He picked up the little champagne-colored poodle and kissed her plump back.

'Ye-e-e-e-s. Are you *famished*, Precious? I am too.'

He switched the little dog from one arm to the other to open the bedroom door. She squirmed to get down.

'Just a mo', sweetheart.' With his free hand he picked up a Mini-14 carbine from the floor beside the bed and laid it across the pillows. 'Now. Now, then. We'll have our supper in a minute. He put the little dog on the floor while he found his nightclothes. She trailed him eagerly downstairs to the kitchen.

Jame Gumb took three TV dinners from his microwave oven. There were two Hungry Man dinners for himself and one Lean Cuisine for the poodle.

The poodle greedily ate her entrée and the dessert, leaving the vegetable.

Jame Gumb left only the bones on his two trays.

He let the little dog out the back door and clutching his robe closed against the chill. He watched her squat in the narrow strip of light from the doorway.

'You haven't done Number Two-ooo. All right, I won't watch.'

But he took a sly peek between his fingers. 'Oh, *super*, you little baggage, aren't you a perfect lady? Come on, let's go to bed.'

Mr Gumb liked to go to bed. He did it several times a night. He liked to get up too, and sit in one or another of his many rooms without turning on the light, or work for a little while in the night, when he was hot with something creative.

He started to turn out the kitchen light, but paused, his lips in a judicious pout as he considered the litter of supper. He gathered up the three TV trays and wiped off the table.

A switch at the head of the stairs turned on the lights in the basement. Jame Gumb started down, carrying the trays. The little dog cried in the kitchen and nosed open the door behind him.

'All right, Silly Billy.' He scooped up the poodle and carried her down. She wriggled and nosed at the trays in his other hand. 'No you don't, you've had enough.' He put her down and she followed close beside him through the rambling, multilevel basement.

In a basement room directly beneath the kitchen was a well, long dry. Its stone rim, reinforced with modern well rings and cement, rose two feet above the sandy floor. The original wooden safety cover, too heavy for a child to lift, was still in place. There was a trap in the lid big enough to lower a bucket through. The trap was open and Jame Gumb scraped his trays and the dog's tray into it.

The bones and bits of vegetable winked out of sight into the absolute blackness of the well. The little dog sat up and begged.

'No, no, all gone,' Gumb said. 'You're too fat as it is.'

He climbed the basement stairs, whispering 'Fatty Bread, Fatty Bread' to his little dog. He gave no sign if he heard the cry, still fairly strong and sane that echoed up from the black hole:

'*PLEEASE.*'

Chapter Twenty-one

Clarice Starling entered the Baltimore State Hospital for the Criminally Insane at a little after 10 P.M. She was alone. Starling had hoped Dr Frederick Chilton wouldn't be there, but he was waiting for her in his office.

Chilton wore an English-cut sportscoat in windowpane check. The double vent and skirts gave it a peplum effect, Starling thought. She hoped to God he hadn't dressed for her.

The room was bare in front of his desk, except for a straight chair screwed to the floor. Starling stood beside it while her greeting hung in the air. She could smell the cold, rank pipes in the rack beside Chilton's humidor.

Dr Chilton finished examining his collection of Franklin Mint locomotives and turned to her.

'Would you like a cup of decaf?'

'No, thanks. I'm sorry to interrupt your evening.'

'You're still trying to find out something about that head business,' Dr Chilton said.

'Yes. The Baltimore district attorney's office told me they'd made the arrangements with you, Doctor?'

'Oh yes. I work *very* closely with the authorities here, Miss Starling. Are you doing an article or a thesis, by the way?'

'No.'

'Have you ever been published in any of the professional journals?'

'No, I never have. This is just an errand the US Attorney's office asked me to do for Baltimore County Homicide. We left them with an open case and we're just helping them tidy up the loose ends.' Starling found her distaste for Chilton made the lying easier.

'Are you wired, Miss Starling?'

'Am I – '

'Are you wearing a microphone device to record what Dr Lecter says? The police term is "wired," I'm sure you've heard it.'

'No.'

Dr Chilton took a small Pearlcoder from his desk and popped a cassette into it. 'Then put this in your purse. I'll have it transcribed and forward you a copy. You can use it to augment your notes.'

'No, I can't do that, Dr Chilton.'

'Why on earth not? The Baltimore authorities have asked me all along for my analysis of anything Lecter says about this Klaus business.'

Get around Chilton if you can Crawford told her. *We can step on him in a minute with a court order but Lecter will smell it. He can see through Chilton like a CAT scan.*

'The US Attorney thought we'd try an informal approach first. If I recorded Dr Lecter without his knowledge, and he found out, it would really, it would be the end of any kind of working atmosphere we had. I'm sure you'd agree with that.'

'How would he find out?'

He'd read it in the newspaper with everything else you know, you fucking jerk. She didn't answer. 'If this should go anywhere and he has to depose you'd be the first one to see the material and I'm sure you'd be invited to serve as expert witness. We're just trying to get a lead out of him now.'

'Do you know why he talks to you, Miss Starling?'

'No, Dr Chilton.'

He looked at each item in the claque of certificates and diplomas on the walls behind his desk as though he were conducting a poll. Now a slow turn to Starling. 'Do you *really* feel you know what you're doing?'

'Sure I do.' *Lot of 'do 's' there.* Starling's legs were shaky from too much exercise. She didn't want to fight with Chilton. She had to have something left when she got to Lecter.

'What you're doing is coming into my hospital to conduct an interview and refusing to share information with me.'

'I'm acting on my instructions, Dr Chilton. I have the US Attorney's night number here. Now please, either discuss it with him or let me do my job.'

'I'm not a turnkey here, Miss Starling. I don't come running down here at night just to let people in and out. I had a ticket to *Holiday on Ice.*'

He realized he'd said *a* ticket. In that instant Starling saw his life, and he knew it.

She saw his bleak refrigerator, the crumbs on the TV tray where he ate alone, the still piles his things stayed in for months until he moved them – she felt the ache of his whole yellow-smiling Sen-Sen lonesome life – and switchblade-quick she knew not to spare him, not to talk on or look away. She stared into his face, and with the smallest tilt of her head, she gave him her good looks and bored her knowledge in, speared him with it, knowing he couldn't stand for the conversation to go on.

He sent her with an orderly named Alonzo.

Chapter Twenty-two

Descending through the asylum with Alonzo toward the final keep, Starling managed to shut out much of the slammings and the screaming, though she felt them shiver the air against her skin. Pressure built on her as though she sank through water, down and down.

The proximity of madmen – the thought of Catherine Martin bound and alone, with one of them snuffling her, patting his pockets for his tools – braced Starling for her job. But she needed more than resolution. She needed to be calm, to be still, to be the keenest instrument. She had to use patience in the face of the awful need to hurry. If Dr Lecter knew the answer, she'd have to find it down among the tendrils of his thought.

Starling found she thought of Catherine Baker Martin as the child she'd seen in the film on the news, the little girl in the sailboat.

Alonzo pushed the buzzer at the last heavy door.

'Teach us to care and not to care, teach us to be still.'

'Pardon me?' Alonzo said, and Starling realized she had spoken aloud.

He left her with the big orderly who opened the door. As Alonzo turned away, she saw him cross himself.

'Welcome back,' the orderly said, and shot the bolts home behind her.

'Hello, Barney.'

A paperback book was wrapped around Barney's massive index finger as he held his place. It was Jane Austen's *Sense and Sensibility*; Starling was set to notice everything.

'How do you want the lights?' he said.

The corridor between the cells was dim. Near the far end she could see bright light from the last cell shining on the corridor floor.

'Dr Lecter's awake.'

'At night, always – even when his lights are off.'

'Let's leave them like they are.'

'Stay in the middle going down, don't touch the bars, right?'

'I want to shut that TV off.' The television had been moved. It was at the far end, facing up the center of the corridor. Some inmates could see it by leaning their heads against the bars.

'Sure, turn the sound off, but leave the picture if you don't mind. Some of 'em like to look at it. The chair's right there if you want it.'

Starling went down the dim corridor alone. She did not look into the cells on either side. Her footfalls seemed loud to her. The only other sounds were wet snoring from one cell, maybe two, and a low chuckle from another.

The late Miggs' cell had a new occupant. She could see long legs outstretched on the floor, the top of a head resting against the bars. She looked as she passed. A man sat on the cell floor in a litter of shredded construction paper. His face was vacant. The television was reflected in his eyes and a shiny thread of spit connected the corner of his mouth and his shoulder.

She didn't want to look into Dr Lecter's cell until she was sure he had seen her. She passed it, feeling itchy between the shoulders, went to the television and turned off the sound.

Dr Lecter wore the white asylum pajamas in his white cell. The only colors in the cell were his hair and eyes and his red mouth, in a face so long out of the sun it leached into the surrounding whiteness; his features seemed suspended above the collar of his shirt. He sat at his table behind the nylon net that kept him back from the bars. He was sketching on butcher paper, using his hand for a model. As she watched he turned his hand over and, flexing his fingers to great tension, drew the inside of the forearm. He used his little finger as a shading stump to modify a charcoal line.

She came a little closer to the bars, and he looked up. For Starling every shadow in the cell flew into his eyes and widow's peak.

'Good evening, Dr Lecter.'

The tip of his tongue appeared, with his lips equally red. It touched his upper lip in the exact center and went back in again.

'Clarice.'

She heard the slight metallic rasp beneath his voice and wondered how long it had been since last he spoke. Beats of silence . . .

'You're up late for a school night,' he said.

'This is night school,' she said, wishing her voice were stronger. 'Yesterday I was in West Virginia –'

'Did you hurt yourself?'

'No, I –'

'You have on a fresh Band-Aid, Clarice.'

Then she remembered. 'I got a scrape on the side of the pool, swimming today.' The Band-Aid was out of sight, on her calf beneath her trousers. He must smell it. 'I was in West Virginia yesterday. They found a body over there, Buffalo Bill's latest.'

'Not quite his *latest*, Clarice.'

'His next-to-latest.'

'Yes.'

'She was scalped. Just as you said she would be.'

'Do you mind if I go on sketching while we talk?'

'No, please.'

'You viewed the remains?'

'Yes.'

'Had you seen his earlier efforts?'

'No. Only pictures.'

'How did you feel?'

'Apprehensive. Then I was busy.'

'And after?'

'Shaken.'

'Could you function all right?' Dr Lecter rubbed his charcoal on the edge of his butcher paper to refine the point.

'Very well. I functioned very well.'

' For Jack Crawford? Or does he still make house calls?'

'He was there.'

'Indulge me a moment, Clarice. Would you let your head hang forward, just let it hang forward as though you were asleep. A second more. Thank you, I've got it now. Have a seat, if you like. You had told Jack Crawford what I said before they found her?'

'Yes. He pretty much pooh-poohed it.'

'And after he saw the body in West Virginia?'

'He talked to his main authority, from the University of –'

'Alan Bloom.'

'That's right. Dr Bloom said Buffalo Bill was fulfilling a persona the newspapers created, the Buffalo Bill scalp-taking business the tabloids were playing with. Dr Bloom said anybody could see that was coming.'

'Dr Bloom saw that coming?'

'He said he did.'

'He saw it coming, but he kept it to himself. I see. What do you think, Clarice?'

'I'm not sure.'

'You have some psychology, some forensics. Where the two flow together you fish, don't you? Catching anything, Clarice?'

'It's pretty slow so far.'

'What do your two disciplines tell you about Buffalo Bill?'

'By the book, he's a sadist.'

'Life's too slippery for books, Clarice; anger appears as lust, lupus presents as hives.' Dr Lecter finished sketching his left hand with his right, switched the charcoal and began to sketch his right with his left, and just as well. 'Do you mean Dr Bloom's book?'

'Yes.'

'You looked me up in it, didn't you?'

Yes.'

'How did he describe me?'

'A pure sociopath.'

'Would you say Dr Bloom is always right?'

'I'm still waiting for the shallowness of affect.'

Dr Lecter's smile revealed his small white teeth. 'We have experts at every hand, Clarice. Dr Chilton says Sammie, behind you there, is a hebephrenic schizoid and irretrievably lost. He put Sammie in Miggs' old cell, because he thinks Sammie's said bye-bye . Do you know how hebephrenics usually go? Don't worry, he won't hear you.'

'They're the hardest to treat,' she said. 'Usually they go into terminal withdrawal and personality disintegration.'

Dr Lecter took something from between his sheets of butcher paper and put it in the sliding food carrier. Starling pulled it through.

'Only yesterday Sammie sent that across with my supper,' he said.

It was a scrap of construction paper with writing in crayon.

Starling read:

I WAN TOO GO TO JESA
I WAN TOO GO WIV CRIEZ
I CAN GO WIV JESA
EF I AC RELL NIZE

SAMMIE

Starling looked back over her right shoulder. Sammie sat vacant faced against the wall of his cell, his head leaning against the bars.

'Would you read it aloud? He won't hear you.'

Starling began. '"I want to go to Jesus, I want to go with Christ, I can go with Jesus if I act real nice." '

'No, no. Get a more assertive "Pease porridge hot" quality into it. The meter varies but the intensity is the same.' Lecter clapped time softly, 'Pease porridge *in* the pot *nine days old*. Intensely, you see. Fervently. "I *wan* to go to Jesa, I *wan* to go wiv Criez."'

'I see,' Starling said, putting the paper back in the carrier.

'No, you don't see anything at all.' Dr Lecter bounded to his feet, his lithe body suddenly grotesque, bent in a gnomish squat, and he was bouncing, clapping time, his voice ringing like sonar, 'I *wan* to go to Jesa –'

Sammie's voice boomed behind her sudden as a leopard's cough, louder than a howler monkey, Sammie up and mashing his face into the bars, livid and straining, the cords standing out in his neck:

'I *WAN* TOO GO TO JESA
I *WAN* TOO GO WIV *CRIEZ*
I CAN *GO* WIV JESA *EF I AC RELL NIIIZE.* '

Silence. Starling found that she was standing and her folding chair was over backwards. Her papers had spilled from her lap.

'Please,' Dr Lecter said erect and graceful as a dancer once again inviting her to sit. He dropped easily into his seat and rested his chin on his hand. 'You don't see at all,' he said again. 'Sammie is intensely religious. He's simply disappointed because Jesus is so late. May I tell Clarice why you're here, Sammie?'

Sammie grabbed the lower part of his face and halted its movement.

'Please?' Dr Lecter said.

'Eaaah,' Sammie said between his fingers.

'Sammie put his mother's head in the collection plate at the Highway Baptist Church in Trune. They were singing "Give of Your Best to the Master" and it was the nicest thing he had.' Lecter spoke over her shoulder. 'Thank you, Sammie. It's perfectly all right. Watch television.'

The tall man subsided to the floor with his head against the bars, just as before, the images from the television worming on his pupils, three streaks of silver on his face now, spit and tears.

'Now. See if you can apply yourself to his problem and perhaps I'll apply myself to yours. Quid pro quo. He's not listening.'

Starling had to bear down hard. 'The verse changes from "go to Jesus" to "go with Christ,"' she said. 'That's a reasoned sequence: going to, arriving at, going with.'

'Yes. It's a linear progression. I'm particularly pleased that he knows "Jesa" and "Criez" are the same. That's progress. The idea of a single Godhead also being a Trinity is hard to reconcile, particularly for Sammie, who's not positive how many people he is himself. Eldridge Cleaver gives us the parable of the 3-in-One Oil, and we find that useful.'

'He sees a causal relationship between his behavior and his aims, that's structured thinking,' Starling said. 'So is the management of a rhyme. He's not blunted – he's crying. You believe he's a catatonic schizoid?'

'Yes. Can you smell his sweat? That peculiar goatish odor is trans-3-methyl-2 hexenoic acid. Remember it, it's the smell of schizophrenia.'

'And you believe he's treatable?'

'Particularly now, when he's coming out of a stuporous phase. How his cheeks shine!'

'Dr Lecter, why do you say Buffalo Bill's not a sadist?'

'Because the newspapers have reported the bodies had ligature marks on the wrists, but not the ankles. Did you see any on the person's ankles in West Virginia?'

'No.'

'Clarice, recreational flayings are always conducted with the victim inverted, so that blood pressure is maintained longer in the head and chest and the subject remains conscious. Didn't you know that?'

'No.'

'When you're back in Washington, go to the National Gallery and look at Titian's *Flaying of Marsyas* before they send it back to Czechoslovakia. Wonderful for details, Titian – look at helpful Pan, bringing the bucket of water.'

'Dr Lecter, we have some extraordinary circumstances here and some unusual opportunities.'

'For whom?'

'For you, if we save this one. Did you see Senator Martin on television?'

'Yes, I saw the news.'

'What did you think of the statement?'

'Misguided but harmless. She's badly advised.'

'She's very powerful, Senator Martin. And determined.'

'Let's have it.'

'I think you have extraordinary insight. Senator Martin has indicated that if you help us get Catherine Baker Martin back alive and unharmed, she'll help you get transferred to a federal institution, and if there's a view available, you'll get it. You may also be asked to review written psychiatric evaluations of incoming patients – a job, in other words. No relaxing of security restrictions.'

'I don't believe that, Clarice.'

'You should.'

'Oh, I believe you. But there are more things you don't know about human behavior than how a proper flaying is conducted. Would you say that for a United States Senator, you're an odd choice of messenger?'

'I was your choice, Dr Lecter. You chose to speak to me. Would you prefer someone else now? Or maybe you don't think you could help.'

'That is both impudent and untrue, Clarice. I don't believe Jack Crawford would allow any compensation ever to reach me . . . Possibly I'll tell you one thing you can tell the Senator, but I operate strictly COD. Maybe I'll trade for a piece of information about you. Yes or no?'

'Let's hear the question.'

'Yes or no? Catherine's waiting, isn't she? Listening to the whetstone? What do you think she'd ask you to do?'

'Let's hear the question.'

'What's your worst memory of childhood?'

Starling took a deep breath.

'Quicker than that,' Dr Lecter said. 'I'm not interested in your worst *invention*.'

'The death of my father,'Starling said.

'Tell me.'

'He was a town marshal. One night he surprised two burglars, addicts coming out of the back of the drugstore. As he was getting out of his pickup he short-shucked a pump shotgun and they shot him.'

'Short-shucked?'

'He didn't work the slide fully. It was an old pump gun, a Remington 870, and the shell hung up in the shell carrier. When it happens the gun won't shoot and you have to take it down to clear it. I think he must have hit the slide on the door getting out.'

'Was he killed outright?'

'No. He was strong. He lasted a month.'

'Did you see him in the hospital?'

'Dr Lecter – yes.'

'Tell me a detail you remember from the hospital.'

Starling closed her eyes. 'A neighbor came, an older woman, a single lady, and she recited the end of "Thanatopsis" to him. I guess that was all she knew to say. That's it. We've traded.'

'Yes we have. You've been very frank, Clarice. I always know. I think it would be quite something to know you in private life.'

'Quid pro quo.'

'In life, was the girl in West Virginia very attractive physically, do you think?'

'She was well-groomed.'

'Don't waste my time with loyalty.'

'She was heavy.'

'Large?'

'Yes.'

'Shot in the chest.'

'Yes.

'Flat-chested I expect.'

'For her size, yes.'

'But big through the hips. Roomy.'

'She was, yes.'

'What else?'

'She had an insect deliberately inserted in her throat – that hasn't been made public.'

'Was it a butterfly?'

Her breath stopped for a moment. She hoped he didn't hear it. 'It was a moth,' she said. 'Please tell me how you anticipated that.'

'Clarice, I'm going to tell you what Buffalo Bill wants Catherine Baker Martin for, and then good night. This is my last word under the current terms. You can tell the Senator what he wants with Catherine and she can come up with a more interesting offer for me . . . or she can wait until Catherine bobs to the surface and see that I was right.'

'What does he want her for, Dr Lecter?'

'He wants a vest with tits on it,' Dr Lecter said.

Chapter Twenty-three

Catherine Baker Martin lay seventeen feet below the cellar floor. The darkness was loud with her breathing, loud with her heart. Sometimes the fear stood on her chest the way a trapper kills a fox. Sometimes she could think: she knew she was kidnapped, but she didn't know by whom. She knew she wasn't dreaming; in the absolute dark she could hear the tiny clicks her eyes made when she blinked.

She was better now than when she first regained consciousness. Much of the awful vertigo was gone, and she knew there was enough air. She could tell *down* from *up* and she had some sense of her body's position.

Her shoulder, hip, and knee hurt from being pressed against the cement floor where she lay. That side was *down. Up* was the rough futon she had crawled beneath during the last interval of blazing, blinding light. The throbbing in her head had subsided now and her only real pain was in the fingers of her left hand. The ring finger was broken, she knew.

She wore a quilted jumpsuit that was strange to her. It was clean and smelled of fabric softener. The floor was clean too, except for the chicken bones and bits of vegetable her captor had raked into the hole. The only other objects with her were the futon and a plastic sanitation bucket with a thin string tied to the handle. It felt like cotton kitchen string and it led up into the darkness as far as she could reach.

Catherine Martin was free to move around, but there was no place to go. The floor she lay on was oval, about eight by ten feet, with a small drain in the center. It was the bottom of a deep covered pit. The smooth cement walls sloped gently inward as they rose.

Sounds from above now or was it her heart? Sounds from above. Sounds came clearly to her from overhead. The oubliette that held her was in the part of the basement directly beneath the kitchen. Footsteps now across the kitchen floor, and running water. The scratching of dog claws on linoleum. Nothing then until a weak disc of yellow light through the open trap above as the basement lights came on. Then blazing light in the pit, and this time she sat up into the light, the futon across her legs, determined to look around, trying to peer through her fingers as her eyes adjusted, her shadow swaying around her as a flood-lamp lowered into the pit swung on its cord high above.

She flinched as her toilet bucket moved, lifted, swayed upward on its flimsy string, twisting slowly as it rose toward the light. She tried to swallow down her fear, got too much air with it, but managed to speak.

'My family will pay,' she said. 'Cash. My mother will pay it now, no questions asked. This is her private – *oh!*' a flapping shadow down on her, only a towel. 'This is her private number. It's 202 –'

'Wash yourself.'

It was the same unearthly voice she'd heard talking to the dog.

Another bucket coming down on a thin cord. She smelled hot, soapy water.

'Take it off and wash yourself all over, or you'll get the hose.' And an aside to the dog as the voice faded, 'Yes it will get the hose, won't it, Darlingheart, yes it *will!*'

Catherine Martin heard the footsteps and the claws on the floor above the basement. The double vision she'd had the first time the lights went on was gone now. She could see. How high was the top, was the floodlight on a strong cord? Could she snag it with the jumpsuit, catch something with the towel? Do *something*, hell. The walls were so smooth, a smooth tube upward.

A crack in the cement a foot above her reach, the only blemish she could see. She rolled the futon as tightly as she could and tied the roll with the towel. Standing on it, wobbly, reaching for the crack, she got her fingernails in it for balance and peered up into the light. Squinting into the glare. It's a floodlight with a shade, hanging just a foot down into the pit, almost ten feet above her upstretched hand, it might as well be the moon, and he was coming, the futon was wobbling, she scrabbling at the crack in the wall for balance, hopping down, something, a flake falling past her face.

Something coming down past the light, a hose. A single spatter of icy water, a threat.

'Wash yourself. All over.'

There was a washcloth in the bucket and floating in the water was a plastic bottle of an expensive foreign skin emollient.

She did it, goosebumps on her arms and thighs, nipples sore and shriveled in the cool air, she squatted beside the bucket of warm water as close to the wall as she could get and washed.

'Now dry off and rub the cream all over. Rub it all over.'

The cream was warm from the bath water. Its moisture made the jumpsuit stick to her skin.

'Now pick up your litter and wash the floor.'

She did that too, gathering the chicken bones and picking up the English peas. She put them in the bucket, and dabbed the little spots of grease on the cement. Something else here, near the wall. The flake that had fluttered down from the crack above. It was a human fingernail, covered with glitter polish and torn off far back in the quick.

The bucket was pulled aloft.

'My mother will pay,' Catherine Martin said. 'No questions asked. She'll pay enough for you all to be rich. If it's a cause, Iran or Palestine, or Black Liberation, she'll give the money for that. All you have to do –'

The lights went out. Sudden and total darkness.

She flinched and went 'Uhhhhhh!' when her sanitation bucket settled beside her on its string. She sat on the futon, her mind racing. She believed now that her captor was alone, that he was a white American. She'd tried to give the impression she had no idea what he was, what color or how many, that her memory of the parking lot was wiped out by the blows on her head. She hoped that he believed he could safely let her go. Her mind was working, working, and at last it worked too well:

The fingernail, someone else was here. A woman, a girl was here. Where was she now? What did he do to her?

Except for shock and disorientation, it would not have been so long in coming to her. As it was, the skin emollient did it. Skin. She knew who had her then. The knowledge fell on her like every scalding awful thing on earth and she was screaming, screaming, under the futon, up and climbing, clawing at the wall, screaming until she was coughing something warm and salty in her mouth, hands to her face, drying sticky on the backs of her hands and she lay rigid on the futon, arching off the floor from head to heels, her hands clenched in her hair.

Chapter Twenty-four

Clarice Starling's quarter bonged down through the telephone in the shabby orderlies' lounge. She dialed the van.

'Crawford.'

'I'm at a pay phone outside the maximum security ward,' Starling said.

'Dr Lecter asked me if the insect in West Virginia was a butterfly. He wouldn't elaborate. He said Buffalo Bill needs Catherine Martin because, I'm quoting, "He wants a vest with tits on it." Dr Lecter wants to trade. He wants a "more interesting" offer from the Senator.'

'Did he break it off?'

'Yes.'

'How soon do you think he'll talk again?'

'I think he'd like to do this over the next few days, but I'd rather hit him again now, if I can have some kind of urgent offer from the Senator.'

'Urgent is right. We got an ID on the girl in West Virginia, Starling. A missing-person fingerprint card from Detroit rang the cherries in ID section about a half hour ago. Kimberly Jane Emberg, twenty-two, missing from Detroit since February seventh. We're canvassing her neighborhood for witnesses. The Charlottesville medical examiner says she died not later than February eleventh, and possibly the day before, the tenth.'

'He only kept her alive three days,' Starling said.

'His period's getting shorter. I don't think anybody's surprised.' Crawford's voice was even. 'He's had Catherine Martin about twenty-six hours. I think if Lecter can deliver, he'd better do it in your next conversation. I'm set up in the Baltimore field office, the van patched you through. I have a room for you in the HoJo two blocks from the hospital if you need a catnap later on.'

'He's leery, Mr Crawford, he's not sure you'd let him have anything good. What he said about Buffalo Bill, he traded for personal information about me. I don't think there's any textual correlation between his questions and the case . . . Do you want to know the questions?'

'No.'

'That's why you didn't make me wear a wire, isn't it? You thought it'd be easier for me, I'd be more likely to tell him stuff and please him if nobody else could hear.'

'Here's another possibility for you: What if I trusted your judgment, Starling? What if I thought you were my best shot, and I wanted to keep a lot of second-guessers off your back? Would I have you wear a wire then?'

'No sir.' *You're famous for handling agents, aren't you, Mr Crawfish?* 'What can we offer Dr Lecter?'

'A couple of things I'm sending over. It'll be there in five minutes, unless you want to rest a little first.'

'I'd rather do it now,' Starling said. 'Tell them to ask for Alonzo. Tell

Alonzo I'll meet him in the corridor outside Section 8.'

'Five minutes,' Crawford said.

Starling walked up and down the linoleum of the shabby lounge far underground. She was the only brightness in the room.

We rarely get to prepare ourselves in meadows or on graveled walks; we do it on short notice in places without windows, hospital corridors, rooms like this lounge with its cracked plastic sofa and Cinzano ashtrays, where the café curtains cover blank concrete. In rooms like this, with so little time, we prepare our gestures, get them by heart so we can do them when we're frightened in the face of Doom. Starling was old enough to know that; she didn't let the room affect her.

Starling walked up and down. She gestured to the air. 'Hold on, girl,' she said aloud. She said it to Catherine Martin and she said it to herself. 'We're better than this room. We're better than this fucking place,' she said aloud. 'We're better than wherever he's got you. Help me. Help me. Help me.' She thought for an instant of her late parents. She wondered if they would be ashamed of her now – just that question, not its pertinence, no qualifications – the way we always ask it. The answer was no, they would not be ashamed of her.

She washed her face and went out into the hall.

The orderly Alonzo was in the corridor with a sealed package from Crawford. It contained a map and instructions. She read them quickly by the corridor light and pushed the button for Barney to let her in.

Chapter Twenty-five

Dr Lecter was at his table, examining his correspondence. Starling found it easier to approach the cage when he wasn't looking at her.

'Doctor.'

He held up a finger for silence. When he had finished reading his letter, he sat musing, the thumb of his six-fingered hand beneath his chin, his index finger beside his nose. 'What do you make of this?' he said, putting the document in to the food carrier .

It was a letter from the US Patent Office.

'This is about my crucifixion watch,' Dr Lecter said. 'They won't give me a patent, but they advise me to copyright the face. Look here.' He put a drawing the size of a dinner napkin in the carrier and Starling pulled it through. 'You may have noticed that in most crucifixions the hands point to, say, a quarter to three, or ten till two at the earliest, while the feet are at six. On this watch face, Jesus is on the cross, as you see there, and the arms revolve to indicate the time, just like the arms on the popular Disney watches. The feet remain at six and at the top a small second hand revolves in the halo. What do you think?'

The quality of the anatomical sketching was very good. The head was hers.

'You'll lose a lot of detail when it's reduced to watch size,' Starling said.

'True, unfortunately, but think of the clocks. Do you think this is safe without a patent?'

'You'd be buying quartz watch movements – wouldn't you? – and they're already under patent. I'm not sure, but I think patents only apply to unique mechanical devices and copyright applies to design.'

'But you're not a lawyer, are you? They don't require that in the FBI anymore.'

'I have a proposal for you,' Starling said, opening her briefcase.

Barney was coming. She closed the briefcase again. She envied Barney's enormous calm. His eyes read negative for dope and there was considerable intelligence behind them.

'Excuse me,' Barney said. 'If you've got a lot of papers to wrestle, there's a one-armed desk, a school desk, in the closet here that the shrinks use. Want it?'

School image. Yes or no?

'May we talk now, Dr Lecter?'

The doctor held up an open palm.

'Yes, Barney. Thank you.'

Seated now and Barney safely away.

'Dr Lecter, the Senator has a remarkable offer.'

'I'll decide that. You spoke to her so soon?'

'Yes. She's not holding anything back. This is all she's got, so it's not a matter for bargaining. This is it, everything, one offer.' She glanced up from her briefcase.

Dr Lecter, murderer of nine, had his fingers steepled beneath his nose and he was watching her. Behind his eyes was endless night.

'If you help us find Buffalo Bill in time to save Catherine Martin unharmed, you get the following: transfer to the Veterans' Administration hospital at Oneida Park, New York, to a cell with a view of the woods around the hospital. Maximum security measures still apply. You'll be asked to help evaluate written psychological tests on some federal inmates, though not necessarily those sharing your own institution. You'll do the evaluations blind. No identities. You'll have reasonable access to books.' She glanced up.

Silence can mock.

'The best thing, the remarkable thing: one week a year, you will leave the hospital and go here.' She put a map in the food carrier. Dr Lecter did not pull it through.

'Plum Island,' she continued. 'Every afternoon of that week you can walk on the beach or swim in the ocean with no surveillance closer than seventy-five yards, but it'll be SWAT surveillance. That's it.'

'If I decline?'

'Maybe you could hang some café curtains in there. It might help. We don't have anything to threaten you with, Dr Lecter. What I've got is a way for you to see the daylight.'

She didn't look at him. She didn't want to match stares now. This was not a confrontation.

'Will Catherine Martin come and talk to me – only about her captor – if I decide to publish? Talk *exclusively* to me?'

'Yes. You can take that as a given.'

'How do you know? *Given* by whom?'

'I'll bring her myself.'

'If she'll come.'

'We'll have to ask her first, won't we?'

He pulled the carrier through. 'Plum Island.'

'Look off the tip of Long Island, the north finger there.'

'Plum Island. "The Plum Island Animal Disease Center. (Federal, hoof and mouth disease research)," it says. Sounds charming.'

'That's just part of the island. It has a nice beach and good quarters. The terns nest there in the spring.'

'Terns.' Dr Lecter sighed. He cocked his head slightly and touched the center of his red lip with his red tongue. 'If we talk about this, Clarice, I have to have something on account. Quid pro quo. I tell you things, and you tell me.'

'Go,' Starling said.

She had to wait a full minute before he said, 'A caterpillar becomes a pupa in a chrysalis. Then it emerges, comes out of its secret changing room as the beautiful imago. Do you know what an imago is, Clarice?'

'An adult winged insect.'

'But what else?'

She shook her head.

'It's a term from the dead religion of psychoanalysis. An imago is an image of the parent buried in the unconscious from infancy and bound with infantile affect. The word comes from the wax portrait busts of their ancestors the ancient Romans carried in funeral processions . . . Even the phlegmatic Crawford must see some significance in the insect chrysalis.'

'Nothing to jump on except checking the entomology journals' subscription lists against known sex offenders in the descriptor index.'

'First, let's drop Buffalo Bill. It's a misleading term and has nothing to do with the person you want. For convenience we'll call him Billy. I'll give you a precis of what I think. Ready?'

'Ready. '

'The significance of the chrysalis is change. Worm into butterfly, or moth. Billy thinks he wants to change. He's making himself a girl suit out of real girls. Hence the large victims – he has to have things that fit. The number of victims suggests he may see it as a series of molts. He's doing this in a two-story house, did you find out why two stories?'

'For a while he was hanging them on the stairs.'

'Correct.'

'Dr Lecter, there's no correlation that I ever saw between transsexualism and violence – transsexuals are passive types, usually.'

'That's true, Clarice. Sometimes you see a tendency to surgical addiction – cosmetically, transsexuals are hard to satisfy – but that's about all. Billy's not a real transsexual. You're very close, Clarice, to the way you're going to catch him, do you realize that?'

'No, Dr Lecter.'

'Good. Then you won't mind telling me what happened to you after your father's death.'

Starling looked at the scarred top of the school desk.

'I don't imagine the answer's in your papers, Clarice.'

'My mother kept us together for more than two years.'

'Doing what?'

'Working as a motel maid in the daytime, cooking at a café at night.'

'And then?'

'I went to my mother's cousin and her husband in Montana.'

'Just you?'

'I was the oldest.'

'The town did nothing for your family?'

'A check for five hundred dollars.'

'Curious there was no insurance. Clarice, you said your father hit the shotgun slide on the door of his pickup.'

'Yes.'

'He didn't have a patrol car?'

'No .'

'It happened at night.'

'Yes.'

'Didn't he have a pistol?'

'No.'

'Clarice, he was working at night in a pickup truck, armed only with a shotgun . . . Tell me, did he wear a time clock on his belt by any chance? One of those things where they have keys screwed to posts all over town and you have to drive to them and stick them in your clock? So the town fathers know you weren't asleep. Tell me if he wore one, Clarice.'

'Yes.'

'He was a night watchman, wasn't he, Clarice, he wasn't a marshal at all. I'll know if you lie.'

'The job description said night marshal.'

'What happened to it?'

'What happened to what?'

'The time clock. What happened to it after your father was shot?'

'I don't remember.'

'If you do remember, will you tell me?'

'Yes. Wait – the mayor came to the hospital and asked my mother for the clock and the badge.' She hadn't known she knew that. The mayor in his leisure suit and Navy surplus shoes. The cocksucker. 'Quid pro quo, Dr Lecter.'

'Did you think for a second you'd made that up? No, if you'd made it up, it wouldn't sting. We were talking about transsexuals. You said violence and destructive aberrant behavior are not statistical correlatives of transsexualism. True. Do you remember what we said about anger expressed as lust, and lupus presenting as hives? Billy's not a transsexual, Clarice, but he thinks he is, he tries to be. He's tried to be a lot of things, I expect.'

'You said that was close to the way we'd catch him.'

'There are three major centers for transsexual surgery: Johns Hopkins, the University of Minnesota, and Columbus Medical Center. I wouldn't be surprised if he's applied for sex reassignment at one or all of them and been denied.'

'On what basis would they reject him, what would show up?'

'You're very quick, Clarice. The first reason would be criminal record. That disqualifies an applicant, unless the crime is relatively harmless and related to the gender-identity problem. Cross-dressing in public, something like that. If he lied successfully about a serious criminal record, then the personality inventories would get him.'

'How?'

'You have to know how in order to sieve them, don't you?'

'Yes.'

'Why don't you ask Dr Bloom?'

'I'd rather ask you.'

'What will you get out of this, Clarice, a promotion and a raise? What are you, a G-9? What do little G-9s get nowadays?'

'A key to the front door, for one thing. How would he show up on the diagnostics?'

'How did you like Montana, Clarice?'

'Montana's fine.'

'How did you like your mother's cousin's husband?'

'We were different.'

'How were they?'

'Worn out from work.'

'Were there other children?'

'No.'

'Where did you live?'

'On a ranch.'

'A sheep ranch?'

'Sheep and horses.'

'How long were you there?'

'Seven months.'

'How old were you?'

'Ten.'

'Where did you go from there?'

'The Lutheran Home in Bozeman.'

'Tell me the truth.'

'I am telling you the truth.'

'You're hopping around the truth. If you're tired, we could talk toward the end of the week. I'm rather bored myself. Or had you rather talk now?'

'Now, Dr Lecter.'

'All right. A child is sent away from her mother to a ranch in Montana. A sheep and horse ranch. Missing the mother, excited by the animals . . .' Dr Lecter invited Starling with his open hands.

'It was great. I had my own room with an Indian rug on the floor. They let me ride a horse – they led me around on this horse – she couldn't see very well. There was something wrong with all the horses. Lame or sick. Some of them had been raised with children and they would, you know, nicker at me in the mornings when I went out to the school bus.'

'But then?'

'I found something strange in the barn. They had a little tack room out there. I thought this thing was some kind of old helmet. When I got it down it was stamped "W. W. Greener's Humane Horse Killer." It was sort of a bell-shaped metal cap and it had a place in the top to chamber a cartridge. Looked like about a .32.'

'Did they feed out slaughter horses on this ranch, Clarice?'

'Yes, they did.'

'Did they kill them at the ranch?'

'The glue and fertilizer ones they did. You can stack six in a truck if they're dead. The ones for dog food they hauled away alive.'

'The one you rode around the yard?'

'We ran away together.'

'How far did you get?'

'I got about as far as I'm going until you break down the diagnostics for me.'

'Do you know the procedure for testing male applicants for transsexual surgery?'

'No.'

'It may help if you bring me a copy of the regimen from any of the centers, but to begin: the battery of tests usually includes Wechsler Adult Intelligence Scale, House-Tree-Person, Rorschach, Drawing of Self-Concept, Thematic Apperception, MMPI, of course, and a couple of others – the Jenkins, I think, that NYU developed. You need something you can see quickly, don't you? Don't you, Clarice?'

'That would be the best, something quick.'

'Let's see . . . our hypothesis is we're looking for a male who will test differently from the way a true transsexual would test. All right – on House-Tree-Person, look for someone who didn't draw the female figure first. Male transsexuals almost always draw the female first and, typically, they pay a lot of attention to adornments on the females they draw. Their male figures are simple stereotypes – there are some notable exceptions where they draw Mr America – but not much in between.

'Look for a house drawing without the rosy-future embellishments – no baby carriage outside, no curtains, no flowers in the yard.

'You get two kinds of trees with real transsexuals – flowing, copious willows and castration themes. The trees that are cut off by the edge of the drawing or the edge of the paper, the castration images, are full of life in the drawings of true transsexuals. Flowering and fruitful stumps. That's an important distinction. They're very unlike the frightened, dead, mutilated trees you see in drawings by people with mental disturbances. That's a good one – Billy's tree will be frightful. Am I going too fast?'

'No, Dr Lecter.'

'On his drawing of himself, a transsexual will almost never draw himself naked. Don't be misled by a certain amount of paranoid ideation in the TAT cards – that's fairly common among transsexual subjects who cross-dress a lot; often times they've had bad experiences with the authorities. Shall I summarize?'

'Yes. I'd like a summary.'

'You should try to obtain a list of people rejected from all three gender-reassignment centers. Check first the ones rejected for criminal record – and among those look hard at the burglars. Among those who tried to conceal criminal records, look for severe childhood disturbances associated with violence. Possibly internment in childhood. Then go to the tests. You're looking for a white male, probably under thirty-five and sizable. He's not a transsexual, Clarice. He just thinks he is, and he's puzzled and angry because they won't help him. That's all I want to say, I think, until I've read the case. You *will* leave it with me.'

'Yes.'

'And the pictures.'

'They're included.'

'Then you'd better run with what you have, Clarice, and we'll see how you do.'

'I need to know how you –'

'No. Don't be grabby or we'll discuss it next week. Come back when you've made some progress. Or not. And Clarice?'

'Yes.'

'Next time you'll tell me two things. What happened with the horse is one. The other thing I wonder is . . . how do you manage your rage?'

Alonzo came for her. She held her notes against her chest, walking head bent, trying to hold it all in her mind. Eager for the outside air, she didn't even glance toward Chilton's office as she hurried out of the hospital.

Dr Chilton's light was on. You could see it under the door.

Chapter Twenty-six

Far beneath the rusty Baltimore dawn, stirrings in the maximum security ward. Down where it is never dark the tormented sense beginning day as oysters in a barrel open to their lost tide. God's creatures who cried themselves to sleep stirred to cry again and the ravers cleared their throats.

Dr Hannibal Lecter stood stiffly upright at the end of the corridor, his face a foot from the wall. Heavy canvas webbing bound him tightly to a mover's tall hand truck as though he were a grandfather clock. Beneath the webbing he wore a straitjacket and leg restraints. A hockey mask over his face precluded biting; it was as effective as a mouthpiece, and not so wet for the orderlies to handle.

Behind Dr Lecter, a small, round-shouldered orderly mopped Lecter's cage. Barney supervised the thrice-weekly cleaning and searched for contraband at the same time. Moppers tended to hurry, finding it spooky in Dr Lecter's quarters. Barney checked behind them. He checked everything and he neglected nothing.

Only Barney supervised the handling of Dr Lecter, because Barney never forgot what he was dealing with. His two assistants watched taped hockey highlights on television.

Dr Lecter amused himself – he has extensive internal resources and can entertain himself for years at a time. His thoughts were no more bound by fear or kindness than Milton's were by physics. He was free in his head.

His inner world has intense colors and smells, and not much sound. In fact, he had to strain a bit to hear the voice of the late Benjamin Raspail. Dr Lecter was musing on how he would give Jame Gumb to Clarice Starling, and it was useful to remember Raspail. Here was the fat flutist on the last day of his life, lying on Lecter's therapy couch, telling him about Jame Gumb:

'Jame had the most atrocious room imaginable in this San Francisco flophouse, sort of aubergine walls with smears of psychedelic Day-Glo here and there from the hippie years, terribly battered everything.

'Jame – you know it's actually spelled that way on his birth certificate, that's where he got it and you have to pronounce it "Jame," like "name," or he gets livid, even though it was a mistake at the hospital – they were hiring cheap help even then that couldn't even get a name right. It's even worse today, it's worth your life to go in a hospital. Anyway, here was Jame sitting on his bed with his head in his hands in that awful room, and he'd been fired from the curio store and he'd done the bad thing again.

'I'd told him I simply couldn't put up with his behavior, and Klaus had just come into my life, of course. Jame is not really gay,you know, it's just something he picked up in jail. He's not anything, really, just a sort of total lack that he wants to fill, and so angry. You always felt the room was a little emptier when he came in. I mean he killed his grandparents when he was twelve, you'd think a person that volatile would have some presence, wouldn't you?

'And here he was, no job, he'd done the bad thing again to some luckless bag person. I was gone. He'd gone by the post office and picked up his former employer's mail, hoping there was something he could sell. And there was a package from Malaysia, or somewhere over there. He eagerly opened it up and it was a suitcase full of dead butterflies, just in there loose.

'His boss sent money to postmasters on all those islands and they sent him boxes and boxes of dead butterflies. He set them in Lucite and made the tackiest ornaments imaginable – and he had the gall to call them objets. The butterflies were useless to Jame and he dug his hands in them thinking there might be jewellery underneath – sometimes they got bracelets from Bali – and he got *butterfly powder on his fingers. Nothing. He sat on the bed with his head in his hands, butterfly colors on his hands and face and he was at the bottom, just as we've all been, and he was crying. He heard a little noise and it was a butterfly in the open suitcase. It was struggling out of a cocoon that had been thrown in with the butterflies and it climbed out. There was dust in the air from the butterflies and dust in the sun from the window – you know how terribly vivid it all is when somebody's describing it to you stoned. He watched it pump up its wings. It was a big one, he said. Green. And he opened the window and it flew away and he felt so light, he said, and he knew what to do.*

'Jame found the little beach house Klaus and I were using, and when I came home from rehearsal, there he was. But I didn't see Klaus. Klaus wasn't there. I said where 's Klaus and he said swimming. I knew that was a lie. Klaus never swam, the Pacific's much too crashy-bangy. And when I opened the refrigerator, well, you know what I found. Klaus's head looking out from behind the orange juice. Jame had made himself an apron too, you know, from Klaus, and he put it on and asked me how I liked him now. I know you must be appalled that I'd ever have anything else to do with Jame – he was even more unstable when you met him, I think he was just astounded that you weren't afraid of him.'

And then, the last words Raspail ever said: 'I wonder why my parents didn't kill me before I was old enough to fool them.'

The slender handle of the stiletto wiggled as Raspail's spiked heart tried to keep beating, and Dr Lecter said, 'Looks like a straw down a doodlebug hole, doesn't it?' but it was too late for Raspail to answer.

Dr Lecter could remember every word, and much more too. Pleasant thoughts to pass the time while they cleaned his cell.

Clarice Starling was astute, the doctor mused. She might get Jame Gumb with what he had told her, but it was a long shot. To get him in time, she would need more specifics. Dr Lecter felt sure that when he read the details of the crimes, hints would suggest themselves – possibly having to do with Gumb's job training in the juvenile correction facility after he killed his grandparents. He'd give her Jame Gumb tomorrow, and make it clear enough so that even Jack Crawford couldn't miss it. Tomorrow should see it done.

Behind him, Dr Lecter heard footsteps and the television was turned off. He felt the hand truck tilt back. Now would begin the long, tedious process of freeing him within the cell. It was always done the same way. First Barney and his helpers laid him gently on his cot, facedown. Then Barney tied his ankles to the bar at the foot of the cot with towels, removed the leg restraints, and, covered by his two helpers armed with Mace and riot batons, undid the buckles on the back of the straitjacket and backed out of the cell, locking the net and the barred door in place, and leaving Dr Lecter to work his way out of his bonds. Then the doctor traded the equipment for his breakfast. The procedure had been in effect ever since Dr Lecter savaged the nurse, and it worked out nicely for everyone.

Today the process was interrupted.

Chapter Twenty-seven

A slight bump as the hand truck carrying Dr Lecter rolled over the threshold of the cage. And here was Dr Chilton, sitting on the cot, looking through Dr Lecter's private correspondence. Chilton had his tie and coat off. Dr Lecter could see some kind of medal hanging from his neck.

'Stand him up beside the toilet, Barney,' Dr Chilton said without looking up. 'You and the others wait at your station.'

Dr Chilton finished reading Dr Lecter's most recent exchange with the General Archives of Psychiatry. He tossed the letters on the cot and went outside the cell. A glint from behind the hockey mask as Dr Lecter's eyes tracked him, but Lecter's head didn't move.

Chilton went to the school desk in the hall and, bending stiffly, removed a small listening device from beneath the seat.

He waggled it in front of the eye holes in Dr Lecter's mask and resumed his seat on the cot.

'I thought she might be looking for a civil rights violation in Miggs' death, so I listened,' Chilton said. 'I hadn't heard your voice in years – I suppose the last time was when you gave me all the misleading answers in my interviews and then ridiculed me in your *Journal* articles. It's hard to believe an inmate's opinions could count for anything in the professional community, isn't it? But I'm still here. And so are you.'

Dr Lecter said nothing.

'Years of silence, and then Jack Crawford sends down his girl and you just went to jelly, didn't you? What was it that got you, Hannibal? Was it those good, hard ankles? The way her hair shines? She's glorious, isn't she? Remote and glorious. A winter sunset of a girl, that's the way I think of her. I know it's been some time since you've seen a winter sunset, but take my word for it.

'You only get one more day with her. Then Baltimore Homicide takes over the interrogation. They're screwing a chair to the floor for you in the electroshock therapy room. The chair has a commode seat for your convenience, and for their convenience when they attach the wires. I won't know a thing.

'Do you get it yet? They *know*, Hannibal. They know that you know exactly who Buffalo Bill is. They think you probably treated him. When I heard Miss Starling ask about Buffalo Bill, I was puzzled. I called a friend at Baltimore Homicide. They found an insect in Klaus's throat, Hannibal. They know Buffalo Bill killed him. Crawford's letting you think you're smart. I don't think you know how much Crawford hates you for cutting up his protégé. He's got you now. Do you feel *smart* now?'

Dr Lecter watched Chilton's eyes moving over the straps that held on the mask. Clearly Chilton wanted to remove it so he could watch Lecter's face. Lecter wondered if Chilton would do it the safe way, from behind. If he did it from the front, he'd have to reach around Dr Lecter's head, with the blue-veined insides of his forearms close to Lecter's face. Come, Doctor. Come close. No, he's decided against it.

'Do you still think you're going someplace with a window? Do you think you'll walk on the beach and see the birds? I don't think so. I called Senator Ruth Martin and she never heard of any deal with you. I had to remind her who you were. She never heard of Clarice Starling, either. It's a scam. We have to expect *small* dishonesties in a woman, but that's a shocker, wouldn't you say?

'When they get through milking you, Hannibal, Crawford's charging you with misprision of a felony. You'll duck it on *M'Naghten*, of course, but the judge won't like it. You sat through six deaths. The judge won't take such interest in your welfare anymore.

'No window, Hannibal. You'll spend the rest of your life sitting on the floor in a state institution watching the diaper cart go by. Your teeth will go and your strength and nobody will be afraid of you anymore and you'll be out in the ward at someplace like Flendauer. The young ones will just push you around and use you for sex when they feel like it. All you'll get to read is what you write on the wall. You think the court will care? You've seen the old ones. They cry when they don't like the stewed apricots.

'Jack Crawford and his fluff. They'll get together openly after his wife dies. He'll dress younger and take up some sport they can enjoy together. They've been intimate ever since Bella Crawford got sick, they're certainly not fooling anybody about that. They'll get their promotions and they won't think about you once a year. Crawford probably wants to come personally at the end to tell you what *you're* getting. Up the booty. I'm sure he has a speech all prepared.

'Hannibal, he doesn't know you as well as I do. He thought if he asked you for the information, you'd just torment the mother with it.'

Quite right, too, Dr Lecter reflected. *How wise of Jack – that obtuse Scotch-Irish mien is misleading. His face is all scars if you know how to look. Well, possibly there's room for a few more.*

'I know what you're afraid of. It's not pain, or solitude. It's *indignity* you can't stand, Hannibal, you're like a cat that way. I'm on my honor to look after you, Hannibal, and I do it. No personal considerations have ever entered into our relationship, from my end. And I'm looking after you now.

'There never was a deal for you with Senator Martin, but there is now. Or there could be. I've been on the phone for hours on your behalf and for the sake of that girl. I'm going to tell you the first condition: you speak only through me. I alone publish a professional account of this, my successful interview with you. You publish nothing. I have exclusive access to any material from Catherine Martin, if she should be saved.

'That condition is non-negotiable. You'll answer me now. Do you accept that condition?'

Dr Lecter smiled to himself.

'You'd better answer me now or you can answer Baltimore Homicide. This is what you get: If you identify Buffalo Bill and the girl is found in time, Senator Martin – and she'll confirm this by telephone – Senator Martin will have you installed in Brushy Mountain State Prison in Tennessee, out of the reach of the Maryland authorities. You'll be in her bailiwick, away from Jack Crawford. You'll be in a maximum-security cell with a view of the woods. You get books. Any outdoor exercise, the details will have to be worked out, but she's amenable. Name him and you can go at once. The Tennessee State Police will take custody of you at the airport, the governor has agreed.'

At last Dr Chilton has said something interesting, and he doesn't even know what it is. Dr Lecter pursed his red lips behind the mask. *The custody of police. Police are not as wise as Barney. Police are accustomed to handling criminals. They're inclined to use leg irons and handcuffs. Handcuffs and leg irons open with a handcuff key. Like mine.*

'His first name is Billy,' Dr Lecter said. 'I'll tell the rest to the Senator. In Tennessee.'

Chapter Twenty-eight

Jack Crawford declined Dr Danielson's coffee, but took the cup to mix himself an Alka-Seltzer at the stainless-steel sink behind the nursing station. Everything was stainless-steel, the cup dispenser, the counter, the waste bin, the rims of Dr Danielson's spectacles. The bright metal suggested the wink of instruments and gave Crawford a distinct twinge in the area of his inguinal ring.

He and the doctor were alone in the little gallery.

'Not without a court order, you don't,' Dr Danielson said again. He was brusque this time, to counter the hospitality he'd shown with the coffee.

Danielson was head of the Gender Identity Clinic at Johns Hopkins and he had agreed to meet Crawford at first light, long before morning rounds. 'You'll have to show me a separate court order for each specific case and we'll fight every one. What did Columbus and Minnesota tell you – same thing, am I right?'

'The Justice Department's asking them right now. We have to do this fast, Doctor. If the girl's not dead already, he'll kill her soon – tonight or tomorrow. Then he'll pick the next one,' Crawford said.

'To even mention Buffalo Bill in the same breath with the problems we treat here is ignorant and unfair and dangerous, Mr Crawford. It makes my hair stand on end. It's taken years – we're not through yet – showing the public that transsexuals aren't crazy, they aren't perverts, they aren't *queers*, whatever that is –'

'I agree with you –'

'Hold on. The incidence of violence among transsexuals is a lot lower than in the general population. These are decent people with a real problem – a famously intransigent problem. They deserve help and we can give it.

I'm not having a witch hunt here. We've never violated a patient's confidence, and we never will. Better start from there, Mr Crawford.'

For months now in his private life, Crawford had been cultivating his wife's doctors and nurses, trying to weasel every minute advantage for her. He was pretty sick of doctors. But this was not his private life. This was Baltimore and it was business. Be nice now.

'Then I haven't made myself clear, Doctor. My fault – it's early, I'm not a morning person. The whole idea is, the man we want is *not your patient*. It would be someone you *refused* because you recognized that he was *not a transsexual*. We're not flying blind here – I'll show you some specific ways he'd deviate from typical transsexual patterns in your personality inventories. Here's a short list of things your staff could look for among your rejects.'

Dr Danielson rubbed the side of his nose with his finger as he read. He handed the paper back. 'That's original, Mr Crawford. In fact it's extremely bizarre, and that's a word I don't use very often. May I ask who provided you with that piece of . . . conjecture?'

I don't think you'd like to know that, Dr Danielson. 'The Behavioral Science staff,' Crawford said, 'in consultation with Dr Alan Bloom at the University of Chicago.'

'Alan Bloom endorsed that?'

'And we don't just depend on the tests. There's another way Buffalo Bill's likely to stand out in your records – he probably tried to conceal a record of criminal violence, or falsified other background material. Show me the ones you turned away, Doctor.'

Danielson was shaking his head the whole time. 'Examination and interview materials are confidential.'

'Dr Danielson, how can fraud and misrepresentation be confidential? How does a criminal's real name and real background fall under the doctor-patient relationship when he never told it to you, you had to find it out for yourself? I know how thorough Johns Hopkins is. You've got cases like that, I'm sure of it. Surgical addicts apply every place surgery's performed. It's no reflection on the institution or the legitimate patients. You think nuts don't apply to the FBI? We get 'em all the time. A man in a Moe hairpiece applied in St Louis last week. He had a bazooka, two rockets, and a bearskin shako in his golf bag.'

'Did you hire him?'

'Help me, Dr Danielson. Time's eating us up. While we're standing here,

Buffalo Bill may be turning Catherine Martin into one of these.' Crawford put a photograph on the gleaming counter.

'Don't even do that,' Dr Danielson said. 'That's a childish, bullying thing to do. I was a battle surgeon, Mr Crawford. Put your picture back in your pocket.'

'Sure, a surgeon can stand to look at a mutilated body,' Crawford said, crumpling his cup and stepping on the pedal of the covered wastebasket. 'But I don't think a doctor can stand to see a life wasted.' He dropped in his cup and the lid of the wastebasket came down with a satisfactory clang. 'Here's my best offer: I won't ask you for patient information, only application information selected by you, with reference to these guidelines. You and your psychiatric review board can handle your rejected applications a lot faster than I can. If we find Buffalo Bill through your information, I'll suppress that fact. I'll find another way we could have done it and we'll walk through it that way, for the record.'

'Could Johns Hopkins be a protected witness, Mr Crawford? Could we have a new identity? Move us to Bob Jones College, say? I doubt very much that the FBI or any other government agency can keep a secret very long.'

'You'd be surprised.'

'I doubt it. Trying to crawl out from under an inept bureaucratic lie would be more damaging than just telling the truth. Please don't ever protect us that way, thank you very much.'

'Thank *you*, Dr Danielson, for your humorous remarks. They're very helpful to me – I'll show you how in a minute. You like the truth – try this. He kidnaps young women and rips their skins off. He puts on these skins and capers around in them. We don't want him to do that anymore. If you don't help me as fast as you can, this is what I'll do to you: this morning the Justice Department will ask publicly for a court order, saying you've refused to help. We'll ask twice a day, in plenty of time for the A.M. and P.M. news cycles. Every news release from Justice about this case will say how we're coming along with Dr Danielson at Johns Hopkins, trying to get him to pitch in. Every time there's news in the Buffalo Bill case – when Catherine Martin floats, when the next one floats, and the next one floats – we'll issue a news release right away about how we're doing with Dr Danielson at Johns Hopkins, complete with your humorous comments about Bob Jones College. One more thing, Doctor. You know, Health and Human Services is right here in Baltimore. My thoughts are running to the Office of Eligibility, Police, and I expect *your* thoughts got there first, didn't they? What if Senator Martin, sometime after her daughter's funeral, asked the fellows over at Eligibility this question: Should the sex-change operations you perform here be considered cosmetic surgery? Maybe they'll scratch their heads and decide, "Why, you know, Senator Martin's *right*. Yes. We think it's cosmetic surgery," then this program won't qualify for federal assistance any more than a nose-job clinic.'

'That's insulting.'

'No, it's just the truth.'

'You don t frighten me, you don't intimidate me –'

'Good. I don't want to do either one, Doctor. I just want you to know I'm serious. Help me, Doctor. Please.'

'You said you're working with Alan Bloom.'

'Yes. The University of Chicago –'

'I know Alan Bloom, and I'd rather discuss this on a professional level. Tell him I'll be in touch with him this morning. I'll tell you what I've decided before noon. I do care about the young woman, Mr Crawford. And the others. But there's a lot at stake here, and I don't think it's as important to you as it ought to be. . . . Mr Crawford, have you had your blood pressure checked recently ?'

'I do it myself.'

'And do you prescribe for yourself?'

'That's against the law, Dr Danielson.'

'But you have a doctor.'

'Yes.'

'Share your findings with him, Mr Crawford. What a loss to us all if you dropped dead. You'll hear from me later in the morning.'

'How much later, Doctor? How about an hour?'

'An hour.'

Crawford's beeper sounded as he got off the elevator at the groundfloor. His driver, Jeff, was beckoning as Crawford trotted to the van. *She's dead and they found her*, Crawford thought as he grabbed the phone. It was the Director calling. The news wasn't as bad as it could get but it was bad enough: Chilton had butted into the case and now Senator Martin was stepping in. The attorney general of the State of Maryland, on instructions from the governor, had authorized the extradition to Tennessee of Dr Hannibal Lecter. It would take all the muscle of the Federal Court, District of Maryland, to prevent or delay the move. The Director wanted a judgment call from Crawford and he wanted it now.

'Hold on,' Crawford said. He held the receiver on his thigh and looked out the van window. There wasn't much color in February for the first light to find. All gray. So bleak.

Jeff started to say something and Crawford hushed him with a motion of his hand.

Lecter's monster ego. Chilton's ambition. Senator Martin's terror for her child. Catherine Martin's life. Call it.

'Let them go,' he said into the phone.

Chapter Twenty-nine

Dr Chilton and three well-pressed Tennessee state troopers stood close together on the windy tarmac at sunrise, raising their voices over a wash of radio traffic from the open door of the Grumman Gulfstream and from the ambulance idling beside the airplane.

The trooper captain in charge handed Dr Chilton a pen. The papers blew over the end of the clipboard and the policeman had to smooth them down.

'Can't we do this in the air?' Chilton asked.

'Sir, we have to do the documentation at the moment of physical transfer. That's my instructions.'

The copilot finished clamping the ramp over the airplane steps. 'Okay,' he called.

The troopers gathered with Dr Chilton at the back of the ambulance. When he opened the back doors, they tensed as though they expected something to jump out.

Dr Hannibal Lecter stood upright on his hand truck, wrapped in canvas webbing and wearing his hockey mask. He was relieving his bladder while Barney held the urinal.

One of the troopers snorted. The other two looked away.

'Sorry,' Barney said to Dr Lecter, and closed the doors again.

'That's all right, Barney,' Dr Lecter said. 'I'm quite finished, thank you.'

Barney rearranged Lecter's clothing and rolled him to the back of the ambulance.

'Barney?'

'Yes, Dr Lecter?'

'You've been decent to me for a long time. Thank you.'

'You're welcome.'

'Next time Sammie's at himself, would you say goodbye for me.

'Sure.'

'Goodbye, Barney.'

The big orderly pushed open the doors and called to the troopers. 'You want to catch the bottom there, fellows? Take it on both sides. We'll set him on the ground. Easy.'

Barney rolled Dr Lecter up the ramp and into the airplane. Three seats had been removed on the craft's right side. The copilot lashed the hand truck to the seat brackets in the floor.

'He's gonna fly laying down?' one trooper asked. 'Has he got rubber britches on?'

'You'll just have to hold your water to Memphis, buddy ruff,' the other trooper said.

'Doctor Chilton, could I speak to you?' Barney said.

They stood outside the airplane while the wind made little twisters of dust and trash around them.

'These fellows don't know anything,' Barney said.

'I'll have some help on the other end – experienced psychiatric orderlies. He's their responsibility now.'

'You think they'll treat him all right? You know how he is – you have to threaten him with boredom. That's all he's afraid of. Slapping him around's no good.'

'I'd never allow that, Barney.'

'You'll be there when they question him?'

'Yes.' *And you won't*, Chilton added privately.

'I could get him settled on the other end and be back here just a couple of hours behind my shift,' Barney said.

'He's not your job anymore, Barney. I'll be there. I'll show them how to manage him, every step.'

'They better pay attention,' Barney said. '*He* will.'

Chapter Thirty

Clarice Starling sat on the side of her motel bed and stared at the black telephone for almost a minute after Crawford hung up. Her hair was tousled and she had twisted her FBI Academy nightgown about her, tossing in her short sleep. She felt like she had been kicked in the stomach.

It had only been three hours since she left Dr Lecter, and two hours since she and Crawford finished working out the sheet of characteristics to check against applications at the medical centers. In that short time, while she slept, Dr Frederick Chilton had managed to screw it up.

Crawford was coming for her. She needed to get ready, had to think about getting ready.

God dammit. God DAMMIT. GOD DAMMIT. You've killed her, Dr Chilton. You've killed her, Dr Fuck Face. Lecter knew some more and I could have gotten it. All gone, all gone, now. All for nothing. When Catherine Martin floats, I'll see that you have to look at her, I swear I will. You took it away from me. I really have to have something useful to do. Right now. What can I do right now, what can I do this minute? Get clean.

In the bathroom, a little basket of paper-wrapped soaps, tubes of shampoo and lotion, a little sewing kit, the favors you get at a good motel.

Stepping into the shower, Starling saw in a flash herself at eight, bringing in the towels and the shampoo and paper-wrapped soap to her mother when her mother cleaned motel rooms. When she was eight, there was a crow, one of a flock on the gritty wind of that sour town, and this crow liked to steal from the motel cleaning carts. It took anything bright. The crow would wait for its chance, and then rummage among the many housekeeping items on the cart. Sometimes, in an emergency takeoff, it crapped on the clean linens. One of the other cleaning women threw bleach at it, to no effect except to mottle its feathers with snow-white patches. The black-and-white crow was always watching for Clarice to leave the cart, to take things to her mother, who was scrubbing bathrooms. Her mother was standing in the door of a motel bathroom when she told Starling she would have to go away, to live in Montana. Her mother put down the towels she was holding and sat down on the side of the motel bed and held her. Starling still dreamed about the crow, saw it now with no time to think why. Her hand came up in a shooing motion and then, as though it needed to excuse the gesture, her hand continued to her forehead to slick back the wet hair.

She dressed quickly. Slacks, blouse, and a light sweater vest, the snub-nosed revolver tucked tight against her ribs in the pancake holster, the speedloader straddling her belt on the other side. Her blazer needed a little work. A seam in the lining was fraying over the speedloader. She was determined to be busy, be busy, until she cooled off. She got the motel's little paper sewing kit and tacked the lining down. Some agents sewed washers into the tail of the jacket so it would swing away cleanly, she'd have to do that. . . .

Crawford was knocking on the door.

Chapter Thirty-one

In Crawford's experience, anger made women look tacky. Rage made their hair stick out behind and played hell with their color and they forgot to zip. Any unattractive feature was magnified. Starling looked herself when she opened the door of her motel room, but she was mad all right.

Crawford knew he might learn a large new truth about her now.

Fragrance of soap and steamy air puffed at him as she stood in the doorway. The covers on the bed behind her had been pulled up over the pillow.

'What do you *say*, Starling?'

'I say God dammit, Mr Crawford, what do *you* say?'

He beckoned with his head. 'Drugstore's open on the corner already. We'll get some coffee.'

It was a mild morning for February. The sun, still low in the east, shone red on the front of the asylum as they walked past. Jeff trailed them slowly in the van, the radios crackling. Once he handed a phone out the window to Crawford for a brief conversation.

'Can I file obstruction of justice on Chilton?'

Starling was walking slightly ahead. Crawford could see her jaw muscles bunch after she asked.

'No, it wouldn't stick.'

'What if he's wasted her, what if Catherine dies because of him? I really want to get in his face . . . Let me stay with this, Mr Crawford. Don't send me back to school.'

'Two things. If I keep you, it won't be to get in Chilton's face, that comes later. Second, if I keep you much longer, you'll be recycled. Cost you some months. The Academy cuts nobody any slack. I can guarantee you get back in, but that's all – there'll be a place for you, I can tell you that.'

She leaned her head far back, then put it down again, walking. 'Maybe this isn't a polite question to ask the boss, but are you in the glue? Can Senator Martin do anything to you?'

'Starling, I have to retire in two years. If I find Jimmy Hoffa and the Tylenol killer I still have to hang it up. It's not a consideration.'

Crawford, ever wary of desire, knew how badly he wanted to be wise. He knew that a middle-aged man can be so desperate for wisdom he may try to make some up, and how deadly that can be to a youngster who believes him. So he spoke carefully, and only of things he knew.

What Crawford told her on that mean street in Baltimore he had learned in a succession of freezing dawns in Korea, in a war before she was born. He left the Korea part out, since he didn't need it for authority.

'This is the hardest time, Starling. Use this time and it'll temper you. Now's the hardest test – not letting rage and frustration keep you from thinking. It's the core of whether you can command or not. Waste and stupidity get you the worst. Chilton's a God damned fool and he may have cost Catherine Martin her life. But maybe not. We're her chance. Starling, how cold is liquid nitrogen in the lab?'

'What? Ah, liquid nitrogen . . . minus two hundred degrees Centigrade, about. It boils at a little more than that.'

'Did you ever freeze stuff with it?'

'Sure. '

'I want you to freeze something now. Freeze the business with Chilton. Keep the information you got from Lecter and freeze the feelings. I want you to keep your eyes on the prize, Starling. That's all that matters. You worked for some information, paid for it, got it, now we'll use it. It's just as good – or as worthless – as it was before Chilton messed in this. We just won't get any more from Lecter, probably. Take the knowledge of Buffalo Bill you got from Lecter and keep fit. Freeze the rest. The waste, the loss, your anger, Chilton. Freeze it. When we have time, we'll kick Chilton's butt up between his shoulder blades. Freeze it now and slide it aside. So you can see past it to the prize, Starling. Catherine Martin's life. And Buffalo Bill's hide on the barn door. Keep your eyes on the prize. If you can do that, I need you.'

'To work with the medical records?'

They were in front of the drugstore now.

'Not unless the clinics stonewall us and we have to take the records. I want you in Memphis. We have to hope Lecter tells Senator Martin something useful. But I want you to be close by, just in case – if he gets tired of toying with her, maybe he'll talk to you. In the meantime, I want you to try to get a feel for Catherine, how Bill might have spotted her. You're not a lot older than Catherine, and her friends might tell you things they wouldn't tell somebody that looks more like a cop.

'We've still got the other things going. Interpol's working on identifying Klaus. With an ID on Klaus we can take a look at his associates in Europe and in California where he had his romance with Benjamin Raspail. I'm going to the University of Minnesota – we got off on the wrong foot up there – and I'll be in Washington tonight. I'll get the coffee now. Whistle up Jeff and the van. You're on a plane in forty minutes.'

The red sun had reached three-quarters of the way down the telephone poles. The sidewalks were still violet. Starling could reach up into the light as she waved for Jeff.

She felt lighter, better. Crawford really was very good. She knew that his little nitrogen question was a nod to her forensic background, meant to please her and to trigger ingrained habits of disciplined thinking. She wondered if men actually regard that kind of manipulation as subtle. Curious how things can work on you even when you recognize them. Curious how the gift of leadership is often a coarse gift.

Across the street, a figure coming down the steps of the Baltimore State Hospital for the Criminally Insane. It was Barney, looking even larger in his lumber jacket. He was carrying his lunchpail.

Starling mouthed 'Five minutes' to Jeff waiting in the van. She caught Barney as he was unlocking his old Studebaker.

'Barney.'

He turned to face her, expressionless. His eyes may have been a bit wider than usual. He had his weight on both feet.

'Did Dr Chilton tell you you'd be all right from this?'

'What else would he tell me?'

'You believe it?'

The corner of his mouth turned down. He didn't say yes or no.

'I want you to do something for me. I want you to do it now, with no questions. I'll ask you nicely – we'll start with that. What's left in Lecter's cell?'

'A couple of books – *Joy of Cooking*, medical journals. They took his court papers.'

'The stuff on the walls, the drawings?'

'It's still there.'

'I want it all and I'm in a hell of a hurry.'

He considered her for a second. 'Hold on,' he said and trotted back up the steps, lightly for such a big man.

Crawford was waiting for her in the van when Barney came back out with rolled drawings and the papers and books in a shopping bag.

'You sure I knew the bug was in that desk I brought you?' Barney said as he handed her the stuff.

'I have to give that some thought. Here's a pen, write your phone numbers on the bag. Barney, you think they can *handle* Dr Lecter?'

'I got my doubts and I said so to Dr Chilton. Remember I told you that, in case it slips his mind. You're all right, Officer Starling. Listen, when you get Buffalo Bill?'

'Yeah?'

'Don't bring him to me just because I got a vacancy, all right?' He smiled. Barney had little baby teeth.

Starling grinned at him in spite of herself. She flapped a wave back over her shoulder as she ran to the van.

Crawford was pleased.

Chapter Thirty-two

The Grumman Gulfstream carrying Dr Hannibal Lecter touched down in Memphis with two puffs of blue tire smoke. Following directions from the tower, it taxied fast toward the Air National Guard hangars, away from the passenger terminal. An Emergency Service ambulance and a limousine waited inside the first hangar.

Senator Ruth Martin watched through the smoked glass of the limousine as the state troopers rolled Dr Lecter out of the airplane. She wanted to run up to the bound and masked figure and tear the information out of him, but she was smarter than that.

Senator Martin's telephone beeped. Her assistant, Brian Gossage, reached it from the jump seat.

'It's the FBI – Jack Crawford,' Gossage said.

Senator Martin held out her hand for the phone without taking her eyes off Dr Lecter.

'Why didn't you tell me about Dr Lecter, Mr Crawford?'

'I was afraid you'd do just what you're doing, Senator.'

'I'm not fighting you, Mr Crawford. If you fight me, you'll be sorry.'

'Where's Lecter now?'

'I'm looking at him.'

'Can he hear you?'

'No.'

'Senator Martin, listen to me. You want to make personal guarantees to Lecter – all right, fine. But do this for me. Let Dr Alan Bloom brief you before you go up against Lecter. Bloom can help you, believe me.'

'I've got professional advice.'

'Better than Chilton, I hope.'

Dr Chilton was pecking on the window of the limousine. Senator Martin sent Brian Gossage out to take care of him.

'Infighting wastes time, Mr Crawford. You sent a green recruit to Lecter with a phony offer. I can do better than that. Dr Chilton says Lecter's capable of responding to a straight offer and I'm giving him one – no red tape, no personalities, no questions of credit. If we get Catherine back safe, everybody smells like a rose, you included. If she . . . dies, I don't give a God damn about excuses.'

'*Use* us then, Senator Martin.'

She heard no anger in his voice, only a professional, cut-your-losses cool that she recognized. She responded to it. 'Go on.'

'If you get something, let us act on it. Make sure we have everything. Make sure the local police share. Don't let them think they'll please you by cutting us out.'

'Paul Krendler from Justice is coming. He'll see to it.'

'Who's your ranking officer there now?'

'Major Bachman from the Tennessee Bureau of Investigation.'

'Good. If it's not too late, try for a media blackout. You better threaten Chilton about that – he likes attention. We don't want Buffalo Bill to know anything. When we find him, we want to use the Hostage Rescue Team. We want to hit him fast and avoid a standoff. You mean to question Lecter yourself?'

'Yes.'

'Will you talk to Clarice Starling first? She's on the way.'

'To what purpose? Dr Chilton's summarized that material for me. We've fooled around enough.'

Chilton was pecking on the window again, mouthing words through the glass. Brian Gossage put a hand on his wrist and shook his head.

'I want access to Lecter after you've talked to him,' Crawford said.

'Mr Crawford, he's promised he'll name Buffalo Bill in exchange for privileges – amenities, really. If he doesn't do that, you can have him forever.'

'Senator Martin, I know this is sensitive, but I have to say it to you: whatever you do, don't beg him.'

'Right, Mr Crawford. I really can't talk right now.' She hung up the phone. 'If I'm wrong, she won't be any deader than the last six you handled,' she said under her breath, and waved Gossage and Chilton into the car.

Dr Chilton had requested an office setting in Memphis for Senator Martin's interview with Hannibal Lecter. To save time, an Air National Guard briefing room in the hangar had been rearranged hastily for the meeting.

Senator Martin had to wait out in the hangar while Dr Chilton got Lecter settled in the office. She couldn't stand to stay in the car. She paced in a small circle beneath the great roof of the hangar, looking up at the high, latticed rafters and down again at the painted stripes on the floor. Once she stopped beside an old Phantom F-4 and rested her head against its cold side where the stencil said NO STEP. *This airplane must be older than Catherine. Sweet Jesus, come on.*

'Senator Martin.' Major Bachman was calling her. Chilton beckoned from the door.

There was a desk for Chilton in the room, and chairs for Senator Martin and her assistant and for Major Bachman. A video cameraman was ready to record the meeting. Chilton claimed it was one of Lecter's requirements.

Senator Martin went in looking good. Her navy suit breathed power. She had put some starch in Gossage too.

Dr Hannibal Lecter sat alone in the middle of the room in a stout oak armchair bolted to the floor. A blanket covered his straitjacket and leg restraints and concealed the fact that he was chained to the chair. But he still wore the hockey mask that kept him from biting.

Why? the Senator wondered – the idea had been to permit Dr Lecter some dignity in an office setting. Senator Martin gave Chilton a look and turned to Gossage for papers.

Chilton went behind Dr Lecter and, with a glance at the camera, undid the straps and removed the mask with a flourish.

'Senator Martin, meet Dr Hannibal Lecter.'

Seeing what Dr Chilton had done for showmanship frightened Senator Martin as much as anything that had happened since her daughter disappeared. Any confidence she might have had in Chilton's judgment was replaced with the cold fear that he was a fool.

She'd have to wing it.

A lock of Dr Lecter's hair fell between his maroon eyes. He was as pale as the mask. Senator Martin and Hannibal Lecter considered each other, one extremely bright and the other not measurable by any means known to man.

Dr Chilton returned to his desk, looked around at everyone, and began:

'Dr Lecter has indicated to me, Senator, that he wants to contribute to the investigation some special knowledge, in return for considerations regarding the conditions of his confinement.'

Senator Martin held up a document. 'Dr Lecter, this is an affidavit which I'll now sign. It says I'll help you. Want to read it?'

She thought he wasn't going to reply and turned to the desk to sign, when he said:

'I won't waste your time and Catherine's time bargaining for petty privileges. Career climbers have wasted enough already. Let me help you now, and I'll trust you to help me when it's over.'

'You can count on it. Brian?'

Gossage raised his pad.

'Buffalo Bill's name is William Rubin. He goes by Billy Rubin. He was referred to me in April or May 1975, by my patient Benjamin Raspail. He said he lived in Philadelphia, I can't remember an address, but he was staying with Raspail in Baltimore.'

'Where are your records?' Major Bachman broke in.

'My records were destroyed by court order shortly after –'

'What did he look like?' Major Bachman said.

'Do you *mind*, Major? Senator Martin, the only –'

'Give me an age and a physical description, anything else you can remember,' Major Bachman said.

Dr Lecter simply went away. He thought about something else – Géricault's anatomical studies for *The Raft of the Medusa* – and if he heard the questions that followed, he didn't show it.

When Senator Martin regained his attention, they were alone in the room. She had Gossage's pad.

Dr Lecter's eyes focused on her. 'That flag smells like cigars,' he said. 'Did you nurse Catherine?'

'Pardon me? Did I . . .'

'Did you breast-feed her?'

'Yes.'

'Thirsty work, isn't it . . .?'

When her pupils darkened, Dr Lecter took a single sip of her pain and found it exquisite. That was enough for today. He went on: 'William Rubin is about six feet one, and would be thirty-five years old now. He's strongly built – about one hundred ninety pounds when I knew him and he's gained since then, I expect. He has brown hair and pale blue eyes. Give them that much, and then we'll go on.'

'Yes, I'll do that,' Senator Martin said. She passed her notes out the door.

'I only saw him once. He made another appointment, but he never came again.'

'Why do you think he's Buffalo Bill?'

'He was murdering people then, and doing some similar things with them, anatomically. He said he wanted some help to stop, but actually he just wanted to schmooze about it. To *rap*.'

'And you didn't – he was sure you wouldn't turn him in?'

'He didn't think I would, and he likes to takes chances. I had honored the confidences of his friend Raspail.'

'*Raspail* knew he was doing this?'

'Raspail's appetites ran to the louche – he was covered with scars.

'Billy Rubin told me he had a criminal record, but no details. I took a brief medical history. It was unexceptional, except for one thing: Rubin told me he once suffered from elephant ivory anthrax. That's all I remember, Senator Martin, and I expect you're anxious to go. If anything else occurs to me, I'll send you word.'

'Did Billy Rubin kill the person whose head was in the car?'

'I believe so.'

'Do you know who that is?'

'No. Raspail called him Klaus.'

'Were the other things you told the FBI true?'

'At least as true as what the FBI told *me*, Senator Martin.'

'I've made some temporary arrangements for you here in Memphis. We'll talk about your situation and you'll go on to Brushy Mountain when this is . . . when we've got it settled.'

'Thank you. I'd like a telephone, if I think of something . . .'

'You'll have it.'

'And music. Glenn Gould, the *Goldberg Variations*? Would that be too much?'

'Fine.'

'Senator Martin, don't entrust any lead solely to the FBI. Jack Crawford never plays fair with the other agencies. It's such a game with those people. He's determined to have the arrest himself. A "collar," they call it.'

'Thank you, Dr Lecter.'

'Love your suit,' he said as she went out the door.

Chapter Thirty-three

Room into room, Jame Gumb's basement rambles like the maze that thwarts us in dreams. When he was still shy, lives and lives ago, Mr Gumb took his pleasure in the rooms most hidden, far from the stairs. There are rooms in the farthest corners, rooms from other lives, that Gumb hasn't opened in years. Some of them are still occupied, so to speak, though the sounds from behind the doors peaked and trailed off to silence long ago.

The levels of the floors vary from room to room by as much as a foot. There are thresholds to step over, lintels to duck. Loads are impossible to roll and difficult to drag. To march something ahead of you – it stumbling and crying, begging, banging its dazed head – is difficult, dangerous even.

As he grew in wisdom and in confidence, Mr Gumb no longer felt he had to meet his needs in the hidden parts of the basement. He now uses a suite of basement rooms around the stairs, large rooms with running water and electricity.

The basement is in total darkness now.

Beneath the sand-floored room, in the oubliette, Catherine Martin is quiet.

Mr Gumb is here in the basement, but he is not in this chamber.

The room beyond the stairs is black to human vision, but it is full of small sounds. Water trickles here and small pumps hum. In little echoes the room sounds large. The air is moist and cool. Smell the greenery. A flutter of wings against the cheek, a few clicks across the air. A low nasal sound of pleasure, a human sound.

The room has none of the wavelengths of light the human eye can use, but Mr Gumb is here and he can see very well, though he sees everything in shades and intensities of green. He's wearing an excellent pair of infrared goggles (Israeli military surplus, less than four hundred dollars) and he directs the beam of an infrared flashlight on the wire cage in front of him. He is sitting on the edge of a straight chair, rapt, watching an insect climb a plant in the screen cage. The young imago has just emerged from a split chrysalis in the moist earth of the cage floor. She climbs carefully on a stalk of nightshade, seeking space to unfurl the damp new wings still wadded on her back. She selects a horizontal twig.

Mr Gumb must tilt his head to see. Little by little the wings are pumped full of blood and air. They are still stuck together over the insect's back.

Two hours pass. Mr Gumb has hardly moved. He turns the infrared flashlight on and off to surprise himself with the progress the insect has made. To pass the time he plays the light over the rest of the room – over his big aquariums full of vegetable tanning solution. On forms and stretchers in the tanks, his recent acquisitions stand like broken classic statuary green beneath the sea. His light moves over the big galvanized worktable with its metal pillow block and backsplash and drains, touches the hoist above it. Against the wall, his long industrial sinks. All in the green images of filtered infrared. Flutters, streaks of phosphorescence cross his vision, little comet trails of moths free in the room.

He switches back to the cage just in time. The big insect's wings are held above her back, hiding and distorting her markings. Now she brings down her wings to cloak her body and the famous design is clear. A human skull, wonderfully executed in the furlike scales, stares from the back of the moth. Under the shaded dome of the skull are the black eye holes and prominent cheekbones. Beneath them darkness lies like a gag across the face above the jaw. The skull rests on a marking flared like the top of a pelvis.

A skull stacked upon a pelvis, all drawn on the back of a moth by an accident of nature.

Mr Gumb feels so good and light inside. He leans forward, puffs soft air across the moth. She raises her sharp proboscis and squeaks angrily.

He walks quietly with his light into the oubliette room. He opens his mouth to quiet his breathing. He doesn't want to spoil his mood with a lot of noise from the pit. The lenses of his goggles on their small protruding barrels look like crab eyes on stalks. Mr Gumb knows the goggles aren't the least bit attractive, but he has had some great times with them in the black basement, playing basement g ames.

He leans over and shines his invisible light down the shaft.

The material is lying on her side, curled like a shrimp. She seems to be asleep. Her waste bucket stands beside her. She has not foolishly broken the string again, trying to pull herself up the sheer walls. In her sleep, she clutches the corner of the futon against her face and sucks her thumb.

Watching Catherine, playing the infrared flashlight up and down her, Mr Gumb prepares himself for the very real problems ahead.

The human skin is fiendishly difficult to deal with if your standards are as high as Mr Gumb's. There are fundamental structural decisions to make, and the first one is where to put the zipper.

He moves the beam down Catherine's back. Normally he would put the closure in the back, but then how could he do it alone? It won't be the sort of thing he can ask someone to help him with, exciting as that prospect might be. He knows of places, circles, where his efforts would be much admired – there are certain yachts where he could preen – but that will have to wait. He must have things he can use alone. To split the center front would be sacrilege – he puts that right out of his mind.

Mr Gumb can tell nothing of Catherine's color by infrared, but she looks thinner. He believes she may have been dieting when he took her.

Experience has taught him to wait from four days to a week before harvesting the hide. Sudden weight loss makes the hide looser and easier to remove. In addition, starvation takes much of his subjects' strength and makes them more manageable. More docile. A stuporous resignation comes over some of them. At the same time, it's necessary to provide a few rations to prevent despair and destructive tantrums that might damage the skin.

It definitely has lost weight. This one is so special, so central to what he is doing, he can't stand to wait long, and he doesn't have to. Tomorrow afternoon, he can do it, or tomorrow night. The next day at the latest. Soon.

Chapter Thirty-four

Clarice Starling recognized the Stonehinge Villas sign from television news. The East Memphis housing complex, a mix of flats and town houses, formed a large U around a parking field.

Starling parked her rented Chevrolet Celebrity in the middle of the big lot. Well-paid blue-collar workers and bottom-echelon executives lived here – the Trans-Ams and IROC-Z Camaros told her that. Motor homes for the weekends and ski boats bright with glitter paint were parked in their own section of the lot.

Stonehinge Villas – the spelling grated on Starling every time she looked at it. Probably the apartments were full of white wicker and peach shag. Snapshots under the glass of the coffee table. The *Dinner for Two Cookbook* and *Fondue on the Menu*. Starling, whose only residence was a dormitory room at the FBI Academy, was a severe critic of these things.

She needed to know Catherine Baker Martin, and this seemed an odd place for a senator's daughter to live. Starling had read the brief biographical material the FBI had gathered, and it showed Catherine Martin to be a bright underachiever. She'd failed at Farmington and had two unhappy years at Middlebury. Now she was a student at Southwestern and a practice teacher.

Starling could easily have pictured her as a self-absorbed, blunted, boarding-school kid, one of those people who never listen. Starling knew she had to be careful here because she had her own prejudices and resentments. Starling had done her time in boarding schools, living on scholarships, her grades much better than her clothes. She had seen a lot of kids from rich, troubled families, with too much boarding-school time. She didn't give a damn about some of them, but she had grown to learn that inattention can be a stratagem to avoid pain, and that it is often misread as shallowness and indifference.

Better to think of Catherine as a child sailing with her father, as she was in the film they showed with Senator Martin's plea on television.

She wondered if Catherine tried to please her father when she was little. She wondered what Catherine was doing when they came and told her that her father was dead of a heart attack at forty-two. Starling was positive Catherine missed him. Missing your father, the common wound, made Starling feel close to this young woman.

Starling found it essential to like Catherine Martin because it helped her to bear down.

Starling could see where Catherine's apartment was located – two Tennessee Highway Patrol cruisers were parked in front of it. There were spots of white powder on the parking lot in the area closest to the apartment. The Tennessee Bureau of Investigation must have been lifting oil stains with pumice or some other inert powder. Crawford said the TBI was pretty good.

Starling walked over to the recreational vehicles and boats parked in the special section of the lot in front of the apartment. This is where Buffalo Bill got her. Close enough to her door so that she left it unlocked when she came out. Something tempted her out. It must have been a harmless-looking setup.

Starling knew the Memphis police had done exhaustive door-to-door interviews and nobody had seen anything, so maybe it happened among the tall motor homes. He must have watched from here. Sitting in some kind of vehicle, had to be. But Buffalo Bill *knew* Catherine was here. He must have spotted her somewhere and stalked her, waiting for his chance. Girls the size of Catherine aren't common. He didn't just sit around at random locations until a woman of the right size came by. He could sit for days and not see one.

All the victims were big. All of them were big. Some were fat, but all were big. 'So he can get something that will fit.' Remembering Dr Lecter's words, Starling shuddered. Dr Lecter, the new Memphian.

Starling took a deep breath, puffed up her cheeks and let the air out slowly. *Let's see what we can tell about Catherine.*

A Tennessee state trooper wearing his Smokey the Bear hat answered the door of Catherine Martin's apartment. When Starling showed him her credentials, he motioned her inside.

'Officer, I need to look over the premises here.' *Premises* seemed a good word to use to a man who had his hat on in the house.

He nodded. 'If the phone rings, leave it alone. I'll answer it.'

On the counter in the open kitchen Starling could see a tape recorder attached to the telephone. Beside it were two new telephones. One had no dial – a direct line to Southern Bell security, the mid-South tracing facility.

'Can I help you any way?' the young officer asked.

'Are the police through in here?'

'The apartment's been released to the family. I'm just here for the telephone. You can touch stuff, if that's what you want to know.'

'Good, I'll look around then.'

'Okay.' The young policeman retrieved the newspaper he had stuffed beneath the couch and resumed his seat.

Starling wanted to concentrate. She wished she were alone in the apartment, but she knew she was lucky the place wasn't full of cops.

She started in the kitchen. It was not equipped by a serious cook. Catherine had come for popcorn, the boyfriend had told police. Starling opened the freezer. There were two boxes of microwave popcorn. You couldn't see the parking lot from the kitchen.

'Where you from?'

Starling didn't register the question the first time.

'Where you from?'

The trooper on the couch was watching her over his newspaper.

'Washington,' she said.

Under the sink – yep, scratches on the pipe joint, they'd taken the trap out and examined it. Good for the TBI. The knives were not sharp. The dishwasher had been run, but not emptied. The refrigerator was devoted to cottage cheese and deli fruit salad. Catherine Martin shopped for fast-food groceries, probably had a regular place, a drive-in she used close by. Maybe somebody cruised the store. That's worth checking.

'You with the Attorney General?'

'No, the FBI.'

'The Attorney General's coming. That's what I heard at turnout. How long you been in the FBI?'

Starling looked at the young policeman.

'Officer, tell you what. I'll probably need to ask you a couple of things after I've finished looking around here. Maybe you could help me out then.'

'Sure. If I can –'

'Good, okay. Let's wait and talk then. I have to think about this right now.'

'No problem, there.'

The bedroom was bright, with a sunny, drowsy quality Starling liked. It was done with better fabrics and better furnishings than most young women could afford. There were a Coromandel screen, two pieces of cloisonné on the shelves, and a good secretary in burled walnut. Twin beds. Starling lifted the edge of the coverlets. Rollers were locked on the left bed, but not on the right-hand one. *Catherine must push them together when it suits her. May have a lover the boyfriend doesn't know about. Or maybe they stay over here sometimes. There's no remote beeper on her answering machine. She may need to be here when her mom calls.*

The answering machine was like her own, the basic Phone-Mate. She opened the top panel. Both incoming and outgoing tapes were gone. In their place was a note, TAPES TBI PROPERTY #6.

The room was reasonably neat but it had the ruffled appearance left by searchers with big hands, men who try to put things back exactly, but miss just a little bit. Starling would have known the place had been searched even without the traces of fingerprint powder on all the smooth surfaces.

Starling didn't believe that any part of the crime had happened in the bedroom. Crawford probably was right, Catherine had been grabbed in the parking lot. But Starling wanted to know her, and this is where she lived. *Lives*, Starling corrected herself. She *lives* here.

In the cabinet of the nightstand were a telephone book, Kleenex, a box of grooming items and, behind the box, a Polaroid SX-70 camera with a cable release and a short tripod folded beside it. Ummmm. Intent as a lizard, Starling looked at the camera. She blinked as a lizard blinks and didn't touch it.

The closet interested Starling most. Catherine Baker Martin, laundry mark C-B-M, had a lot of clothes and some of them were very good. Starling recognized many of the labels, including Garfinkel's and Britches in Washington. *Presents from Mommy*, Starling said to herself. Catherine had fine, classic clothes in two sizes, made to fit her at about 145 and 165 pounds, Starling guessed, and there were a few pairs of crisis fat pants and pullovers from the Statuesque Shop. In a hanging rack were twenty-three pairs of shoes. Seven pairs were Ferragamos in 10C, and there were some Reeboks and run-over loafers. A light backpack and a tennis racket were on the top shelf.

The belongings of a privileged kid, a student and practice teacher who lived better than most.

Lots of letters in the secretary. Loopy backhand notes from former classmates in the East. Stamps, mailing labels. Gift wrapping paper in the bottom drawer, a sheaf in various colors and patterns. Starling's fingers walked through it. She was thinking about questioning the clerks at the local drive-in market when her fingers found a sheet in the stack of gift wrap that was too thick and stiff. Her fingers went past it, walked back to it. She was trained to register anomalies and she had it half pulled out when she looked at it. The sheet was blue, of a material similar to a lightweight blotter, and the pattern printed on it was a crude imitation of the cartoon dog Pluto. The little rows of dogs all looked like Pluto, they were the proper yellow, but they weren't exactly right in their proportions.

'Catherine, Catherine,' Starling said. She took some tweezers from her bag and used them to slide the sheet of colored paper into a plastic envelope. She placed it on the bed for the time being.

The jewelry box on the dresser was a stamped-leather affair, the kind you see in every girl's dormitory room. The two drawers in front and the tiered lid contained costume jewelry, no valuable pieces. Starling wondered if the best things had been in the rubber cabbage in the refrigerator, and if so, who took them.

She hooked her finger under the side of the lid and released the secret drawer in the back of the jewelry box. The secret drawer was empty. She wondered whom these drawers were a secret from – certainly not burglars. She was reaching behind the jewelry box, pushing the drawer back in, when her fingers touched the envelope taped to the underside of the secret drawer.

Starling pulled on a pair of cotton gloves and turned the jewelry box around. She took out the empty drawer and inverted it. A brown envelope was taped to the bottom of the drawer with masking tape. The flap was just tucked in, not sealed. She held the paper close to her nose. The envelope had not been fumed for fingerprints. Starling used the tweezers to open it and extract the contents. There were five Polaroid pictures in the envelope and she took them out one by one. The pictures were of a man and a woman coupling. No heads or faces appeared. Two of the pictures were taken by the woman, two by the man, and one appeared to have been shot from the tripod set up on the nightstand.

It was hard to judge scale in a photograph, but with that spectacular 145 pounds on a long frame, the woman had to be Catherine Martin. The man wore what appeared to be a carved ivory ring on his penis. The resolution of the photograph was not sharp enough to reveal the details of it. The man had had his appendix out. Starling bagged the photographs, each in a sandwich bag, and put them in her own brown envelope. She returned the drawer to the jewelry box.

'I have the good stuff in my pocketbook,' said a voice behind her. 'I don't think anything was taken.'

Starling looked in the mirror. Senator Ruth Martin stood in the bedroom door. She looked drained.

Starling turned around. 'Hello, Senator Martin. Would you like to lie down? I'm almost finished.'

Even exhausted, Senator Martin had a lot of presence. Under her careful finish, Starling saw a scrapper.

'Who are you, please? I thought the police were through in here.'

'I'm Clarice Starling, FBI. Did you talk to Dr Lecter, Senator?'

'He gave me a name.' Senator Martin lit a cigarette and looked Starling up and down. 'We'll see what it's worth. And what did you find in the jewelry box, Officer Starling? What's *it* worth?'

'Some documentation we can check out in just a few minutes,' was the best Starling could do.

'In my daughter's jewelry box? Let's see it.'

Starling heard voices in the next room and hoped for an interruption. 'Is Mr Copley with you, the Memphis special agent in –'

'No, he's not and that's not an answer. No offense, Officer, but I'll see what you got out of my daughter's jewelry box.' She turned her head and called over her shoulder. 'Paul. Paul, would you come in here? Officer Starling, you may know Mr Krendler from the Department of Justice. Paul, this is the girl Jack Crawford sent in to Lecter.'

Krendler's bald spot was tanned and he looked fit at forty.

'Mr Krendler, I know who you are. Hello.' Starling said. *Dee Jay Criminal Division congressional liaison, troubleshooter, at least an Assistant Deputy Attorney General, Jesus God, save my bod.*

'Officer Starling found something in my daughter's jewelry box and she put it in her brown envelope. I think we'd better see what it is, don't you?'

'Officer,' Krendler said.

'May I speak to you, Mr Krendler?'

'Of course you can. Later.' He held out his hand.

Starling's face was hot. She knew Senator Martin was not herself, but she would never forgive Krendler for the doubt in his face. Never.

'You got it,' Starling said. She handed him the envelope.

Krendler looked in at the first picture and had closed the flap again when Senator Martin took the envelope out of his hands.

It was painful to watch her examine the pictures. When she finished, she went to the window and stood with her face turned up to the overcast sky, her eyes closed. She looked old in the daylight and her hand trembled when she tried to smoke.

'Senator, I –' Krendler began.

'The police searched this room,' Senator Martin said. 'I'm sure they found those pictures and had sense enough to put them back and keep their mouths shut.'

'No they did *not*,' Starling said. The woman was wounded but, hell. 'Mrs Martin, we need to know who this man is, you can see that. If it's the boyfriend, fine. I can find that out in five minutes. Nobody else needs to see the pictures and Catherine never needs to know.'

'I'll tend to it.' Senator Martin put the envelope in her purse, and Krendler let her do it.

'Senator, did you take the jewelry out of the rubber cabbage in the kitchen?' Starling asked.

Senator Martin's aide, Brian Gossage, stuck his head in the door. 'Excuse me, Senator, they've got the terminal set up. We can watch them search the William Rubin name at the FBI.'

'Go ahead, Senator Martin,' Krendler said. 'I'll be out in a second.'

Ruth Martin left the room without answering Starling's question.

Starling had a chance to look Krendler over as he was closing the bedroom door. His suit was a triumph of single-needle tailoring and he was not armed. The shine was buffed off the bottom half inch of his heels from walking on much deep carpet, and the edges of the heels were sharp.

He stood for a moment with his hand on the doorknob, his head down.

'That was a good search,' he said when he turned around.

Starling couldn't be had that cheap. She looked back at him.

'They turn out good rummagers at Quantico,' Krendler said.

'They don't turn out thieves.'

'I know that,' he said.

'Hard to tell.'

'Drop it.'

'We'll follow up on the pictures and the rubber cabbage, right?' she said.

'Yes.'

'What's the "William Rubin" name, Mr Krendler?'

'Lecter says that's Buffalo Bill's name. Here's our transmission to ID section and NCIC. Look at this.' He gave her a transcript of the Lecter interview with Senator Martin, blurry copy from a dot-matrix printer.

'Any thoughts?' he said when she finished reading.

'There's nothing here he'll ever have to eat,' Starling said. 'He says it's a white male named Billy Rubin who had elephant ivory anthrax. You couldn't catch him in a lie here, no matter what happens. At the worst he'd just be mistaken. I hope this is true. But he could be having fun with her. Mr Krendler, he's perfectly capable of that. Have you ever . . . met him?'

Krendler shook his head and snorted air from his nose.

'Dr Lecter killed nine people we know of. He's not walking, no matter – he could raise the dead and they wouldn't let him out. So all that's left for him is *fun*. That's why we were playing him –'

'I know how you were playing him. I heard Chilton's tape. I'm not saying it was wrong – I'm saying it's over. Behavioral Science can follow up what you got – the transsexual angle – for what it's worth. And you'll be back in school at Quantico tomorrow.'

Oh boy. 'I found something else.'

The sheet of colored paper had lain on the bed unnoticed. She gave it to him.

'What is it?'

'Looks like a sheet of Plutos.' She made him ask the rest.

He beckoned for the information with his hand.

'I'm pretty sure it's blotter acid. LSD. From maybe the middle seventies or before. It's a curiosity now. It's worth finding out where she got it. We should test it to be sure.'

'You can take it back to Washington and give it to the lab. You'll be going in a few minutes.'

'If you don't want to wait, we can do it now with a field kit. If the police've got a standard Narcotics Identification Kit, it's test J, take two seconds, we can –'

'Back to Washington, back to school,' he said, opening the door.

'Mr Crawford instructed me –'

'Your *instructions* are what I'm telling you. You're not under Jack Crawford's direction now. You're back under the same supervision as any other trainee forthwith, and your business is at Quantico, do you understand me? There's a plane at two-ten. Be on it.'

'Mr Krendler, Dr Lecter talked to me after he refused to talk to the

Baltimore police. He might do that again. Mr Crawford thought –'

Krendler closed the door again, harder than he had to. 'Officer Starling, I don't have to explain myself to you, but listen to me. Behavioral Science's brief is advisory, always has been. It's going back to that. Jack Crawford should be on compassionate leave anyway. I'm surprised he's been able to perform as well as he has. He took a foolish chance with this, keeping it from Senator Martin, and he got his butt sawed off. With his record, this close to retirement, even *she* can't hurt him that much. So I wouldn't worry about his pension, if I were you.'

Starling lost it a little. 'You've got somebody else who's caught three serial murderers? You know anybody else who's caught one? You shouldn't let her run this, Mr Krendler.'

'You must be a bright kid, or Crawford wouldn't bother with you, so I'll tell you one time: do something about that mouth or it'll put you in the typing pool. Don't you understand – the only reason you were ever sent to Lecter in the first place was to get some news for your Director to use on Capitol Hill. Harmless stuff on major crimes, the "inside scoop" on Dr Lecter, he hands that stuff out like pocket candy while he's trying to get the budget through. Congressmen eat it up, they dine out on it. You're out of line, Officer Starling, and you're out of this case. I know you got supplementary ID. Let's have it.'

'I need the ID to fly with the gun. The gun belongs at Quantico.'

'Gun. *Jesus.* Turn in the ID as soon as you get back.'

Senator Martin, Gossage, a technician, and several policemen were gathered around a video display terminal with a modem connected to the telephone. The National Crime Information Center's hotline kept a running account of progress as Dr Lecter's information was processed in Washington. Here was news from the National Center for Disease Control in Atlanta: Elephant ivory anthrax is contracted by breathing dust from grinding African ivory, usually for decorative handles. In the United States it is a disease of knifemakers.

At the word 'knifemakers', Senator Martin closed her eyes. They were hot and dry. She squeezed the Kleenex in her hand.

The young trooper who had let Starling into the apartment was bringing the Senator a cup of coffee. He still had on his hat.

Starling was damned if she'd slink out. She stopped before the woman and said, 'Good luck, Senator. I hope Catherine's all right.'

Senator Martin nodded without looking at her. Krendler urged Starling out.

'I didn't know she wasn't s'posed to be in here,' the young trooper said as she left the room.

Krendler stepped outside with her. 'I have nothing but respect for Jack Crawford,' he said. 'Please tell him how sorry we all are about . . . Bella's problem, all that. Now let's get back to school and get busy, all right?'

'Goodbye, Mr Krendler.'

Then she was alone on the parking lot, with the unsteady feeling that she understood nothing at all in this world.

She watched a pigeon walk around beneath the motor homes and boats. It picked up a peanut hull and put it back down. The damp wind ruffled its feathers.

Starling wished she could talk to Crawford. *Waste and stupidity get you the worst*, that's what he said. *Use this time and it'll temper you. Now's the hardest test – not letting rage and frustration keep you from thinking. It's the core of whether you can command or not.*

She didn't give a damn about commanding. She found she didn't give a damn, or a shit for that matter, about being Special Agent Starling. Not if you play this way.

She thought about the poor, fat, sad, dead girl she saw on the table in the funeral home at Potter, West Virginia. *Painted her nails with glitter just like these God damned redneck ski boats.*

What was her name? Kimberly.

Damn if these assholes are gonna see me cry.

Jesus, everybody was named Kimberly, four in her class. Three guys named Sean. Kimberly with her soap opera name tried to fix herself, punched all those holes in her ears trying to look pretty, trying to decorate herself. And Buffalo Bill looked at her sad flat tits and stuck the muzzle of a gun between them and blew a starfish on her chest.

Kimberly, her sad, fat sister who waxed her legs. No wonder – judging from her face and her arms and legs, her skin was her best feature. *Kimberly, are you angry somewhere?* No senators looking out for her. No jets to carry crazy men around. *Crazy* was a word she wasn't supposed to use. Lot of stuff she wasn't supposed to do. *Crazy men.*

Starling looked at her watch. She had an hour and a half before the plane, and there was one small thing she could do. She wanted to look in Dr Lecter's face when he said 'Billy Rubin.' If she could stand to meet those strange maroon eyes for long enough, if she looked deeply where the dark sucks in the sparks, she might see something useful. She thought she might see glee.

Thank God I've still got the ID.
She laid twelve feet of rubber pulling out of the parking lot.

Chapter Thirty-five

Clarice Starling driving in a hurry through the perilous Memphis traffic, two tears of anger dried stiff on her cheeks. She felt oddly floaty and free now. An unnatural clarity in her vision warned her that she was inclined to fight, so she was careful of herself.

She had passed the old courthouse earlier on her way from the airport, and she found it again without trouble.

The Tennessee authorities were taking no chances with Hannibal Lecter. They were determined to hold him securely without exposing him to the dangers of the city jail.

Their answer was the former courthouse and jail, a massive Gothic-style structure built of granite back when labor was free. It was a city office building now, somewhat over-restored in this prosperous, history-conscious town.

Today it looked like a medieval stronghold surrounded by police.

A mix of law-enforcement cruisers – highway patrol, Shelby County Sheriff's Department, Tennessee Bureau of Investigation, and Department of Corrections – crowded the parking lot. There was a police post to pass before Starling even could get in to park her rented car.

Dr Lecter presented an additional security problem from outside. Threatening calls had been coming in ever since the mid-morning newscasts reported his whereabouts; his victims had many friends and relatives who would love to see him dead.

Starling hoped the resident FBI agent, Copley, wasn't here. She didn't want to get him in trouble.

She saw the back of Chilton's head in a knot of reporters on the grass beside the main steps. There were two television minicams in the crowd. Starling wished her head were covered. She turned her face away as she approached the entrance to the tower.

A state trooper stationed in front of the door examined her ID card before she could go into the foyer. The foyer of the tower looked like a guardroom now. A city policeman was stationed at the single tower elevator, and another at the stairs. State troopers, the relief for the patrol units stationed around the building, read the *Commercial Appeal* on the couches where the public could not see them.

A sergeant manned the desk opposite the elevator. His name tag said TATE, C.L.

'No press,' Sergeant Tate said when he saw Starling.

'No,' she said.

'You with the Attorney General's people?' he said when he looked at her card.

'Deputy Assistant Attorney General Krendler,' she said. 'I just left him.'

He nodded. 'We've had every kind of cop in West Tennessee in here wanting to look at Dr Lecter. Don't see something like that very often, thank God. You'll need to talk to Dr Chilton before you go up.'

'I saw him outside,' Starling said. 'We were working on this in Baltimore earlier today. Is this where I log in, Sergeant Tate?'

The sergeant briefly checked a molar with his tongue. 'Right there,' he said. 'Detention rules, miss. Visitors check weapons, cops or not.'

Starling nodded. She dumped the cartridges from her revolver, the sergeant glad to watch her hands move on the gun. She gave it to him butt first, and he locked it in his drawer.

'Vernon, take her up.' He dialed three digits and spoke her name into the phone.

The elevator, an addition from the 1920s, creaked up to the top floor. It opened onto a stair landing and a short corridor.

'Right straight across, ma'am,' the trooper said.

Painted on the frosted glass of the door was SHELBY COUNTY HISTORICAL SOCIETY.

Almost all the top floor of the tower was one octagonal room painted white, with a floor and moldings of polished oak. It smelled of wax and library paste. With its few furnishings, the room had a spare, Congregational feeling. It looked better now than it ever had as a bailiff's office.

Two men in the uniform of the Tennessee Department of Corrections were on duty. The small one stood up at his desk when Starling came in. The bigger one sat in a folding chair at the far end of the room, facing the door of a cell. He was the suicide watch.

'You're authorized to talk with the prisoner, ma'am?' the officer at the desk said. His nameplate read PEMBRY, T.W. and his desk set included a telephone, two riot batons, and Chemical Mace. A long pinion stood in the corner behind him.

'Yes, I am,' Starling said. 'I've questioned him before.'

'You know the rules? Don't pass the barrier.'

'Absolutely.'

The only color in the room was the police traffic barrier, a brightly striped sawhorse in orange and yellow mounted with round yellow flashers, now turned off. It stood on the polished floor five feet in front of the cell door. On a coat tree nearby hung the doctor's things – the hockey mask and something Starling had never seen before, a Kansas gallows vest. Made of heavy leather, with double-locking wrist shackles at the waist and buckles in the back, it may be the most infallible restraint garment in the world. The mask and the black vest suspended by its nape from the coat tree made a disturbing composition against the white wall.

Starling could see Dr Lecter as she approached the cell. He was reading at a small table bolted to the floor. His back was to the door. He had a number of books and the copy of the running file on Buffalo Bill she had given him in Baltimore. A small cassette player was chained to the table leg. How strange to see him outside the asylum.

Starling had seen cells like this before, as a child. They were prefabricated by a St Louis company around the turn of the century, and no one has ever built them better – a tempered steel modular cage that turns any room into a cell. The floor was sheet steel laid over bars, and the walls and ceiling of cold-forged bars completely lined the room. There was no window. The cell was spotlessly white and brightly lit. A flimsy paper screen stood in front of the toilet.

These white bars ribbed the walls. Dr Lecter had a sleek dark head.

He's a cemetery mink. He lives down in a ribcage in the dry leaves of a heart.

She blinked it away.

'Good morning, Clarice,' he said without turning around. He finished his page, marked his place and spun in his chair to face her, his forearms on the chair back, his chin resting on them. 'Dumas tells us that the addition of a crow to bouillon in the fall, when the crow has fattened on juniper berries, greatly improves the color and flavor of stock. How do you like it in the soup, Clarice?'

'I thought you might want your drawings, the stuff from your cell, just until you get your view.'

'How thoughtful. Dr Chilton's euphoric about you and Jack Crawford being put off the case. Or did they send you in for one last wheedle?'

The officer on suicide watch had strolled back to talk to Officer Pembry at the desk. Starling hoped they couldn't hear.

'They didn't send me. I just came.'

'People will say we're in love. Don't you want to ask about Billy Rubin, Clarice?'

'Dr Lecter, without in any way . . . impugning what you've told Senator Martin, would you advise me to go on with your idea about –'

'*Impugning* – I love it. I wouldn't advise you at all. You tried to fool me, Clarice. Do you think I'm playing with these people?'

'I think you were telling me the truth.'

'Pity you tried to fool me, isn't it?' Dr Lecter's face sank behind his arms until only his eyes were visible. 'Pity Catherine Martin won't ever see the sun again. The sun's a mattress fire her God died in, Clarice.'

'Pity you have to pander now and lick a few tears when you can,' Starling said. 'It's a pity we didn't get to finish what we were talking about. Your idea of the imago, the structure of it, had a kind of . . . elegance that's hard to get away from. Now it's like a ruin, half an arch standing there.'

'Half an arch won't stand. Speaking of arches, will they still let you pound a beat, Clarice? Did they take your badge?'

'No.'

'What's that under your jacket, a watchman's clock just like Dad's?'

'No, that's a speedloader.'

'So you go around armed?'

'Yes.'

'Then you should let your jacket out. Do you sew at all?'

'Yes.'

'Did you make that costume?'

'No. Dr Lecter, you find out everything. You couldn't have talked intimately with this "Billy Rubin" and come out knowing so little about him.'

'You think not?'

'If you met him, you know *everything*. But today you happened to remember just one detail. He'd had elephant ivory anthrax. You should have seen them jump when Atlanta said it's a disease of knifemakers. They ate it up, just like you knew they would. You should have gotten a suite at the Peabody for that. Dr Lecter, if you met him you know about him. I think maybe you didn't meet him and Raspail told you about him. Secondhand stuff wouldn't sell as well to Senator Martin, would it?'

Starling took a quick look over her shoulder. One of the officers was showing the other something in *Guns & Ammo* magazine. 'You had more to tell me in Baltimore, Dr Lecter. I believe that stuff was valid. Tell me the rest.'

'I've read the cases, Clarice, have you? Everything you need to know to find him is right there, if you're paying attention. Even Inspector Emeritus Crawford should have figured it out. Incidentally, did you read Crawford's *stupefying* speech last year to the National Police Academy? Spouting Marcus Aurelius on duty and honor and fortitude – we'll see what kind of a Stoic Crawford is when Bella bites the big one. He copies his philosophy out of *Bartlett's Familiar*, I think. If he understood Marcus Aurelius, he might solve his case.'

'Tell me how.'

'When you show the odd flash of contextual intelligence, I forget your generation can't read, Clarice. The Emperor counsels simplicity. First principles. Of each particular thing, ask: What is it in itself, in its own constitution? What is its causal nature?'

'That doesn't mean anything to me.'

'What does he do, the man you want?'

'He kills –'

'Ah –' he said sharply, averting his face for a moment from her wrongheadedness. 'That's incidental. What is the first and principal thing he does, what need does he serve by killing?'

'Anger, social resentment, sexual frus –'

'What, then?'

'He covets. In fact, he covets being the very thing you are. It's his nature to covet. How do we begin to covet, Clarice? Do we seek out things to covet? Make an effort at an answer.'

'No. We just –'

'No. Precisely so. We begin by coveting what we see every day. Don't you feel eyes moving over you every day, Clarice, in chance encounters? I hardly see how you could not. And don't your eyes move over things?'

'All right, then tell me how –'

'It's your turn to tell *me*, Clarice. You don't have any beach vacations at the Hoof and Mouth Disease Station to offer me anymore. It's strictly quid pro quo from here on out. I have to be careful doing business with you. Tell me, Clarice.'

'Tell you what?'

'The two things you owe me from before. What happened to you and the horse, and what you do with your anger.'

'Dr Lecter, when there's time I'll –'

'We don't reckon time the same way, Clarice. This is all the time you'll ever have.'

'Later, listen, I'll –'

'I'll *listen now*. Two years after your father's death, your mother sent you to live with her cousin and her husband on a ranch in Montana. You were ten years old. You discovered they fed out slaughter horses. You ran away with a horse that couldn't see very well. And?'

'– It was summer and we could sleep out. We got as far as Bozeman by a back road.'

'Did the horse have a name?'

'Probably, but they don't – you don't find that out when you're feeding out slaughter horses. I called her Hannah, that seemed like a good name.'

'Were you leading her or riding?'

'Some of both. I had to lead her up beside a fence to climb on.'

'You rode and walked to Bozeman.'

'There was a livery stable, dude ranch, riding academy sort of thing just outside of town. I tried to see about them keeping her. It was twenty dollars a week in the corral. More for a stall. They could tell right off she couldn't see. I said okay, I'll lead her around. Little kids can sit on her and I'll lead her around while their parents are, you know, regular riding. I can stay right here and muck out stalls. One of them, the man, agreed to everything I said while his wife called the sheriff.'

'The sheriff was a policeman, like your father.'

'That didn't keep me from being scared of him, at first. He had a big red face. The sheriff finally put up twenty dollars for a week's board while he "straightened things out." He said there was no use going for the stall in warm weather. The papers picked it up. There was a flap. My mother's cousin agreed to let me go. I wound up going to the Lutheran Home in Bozeman.'

'It's an orphanage?'

'Yes.'

'And Hannah?'

'She went too. A big Lutheran rancher put up the hay. They already had a barn at the orphanage. We plowed the garden with her. You had to watch where she was going, though. She'd walk through the butterbean trellises and step on any kind of plant that was too short for her to feel it against her legs. And we led her around pulling kids in a cart.'

'She died though.'

'Well, yes.'

'Tell me about that.'

'It was last year, they wrote me at school. They think she was about twenty-two. Pulled a cart full of kids the last day she lived, and died in her sleep.'

Dr Lecter seemed disappointed. 'How heartwarming,' he said. 'Did your foster father in Montana fuck you, Clarice?'

'No.'

'Did he try?'

'No.'

'What made you run away with the horse?'

'They were going to kill her.'

'Did you know when?'

'Not exactly. I worried about it all the time. She was getting pretty fat.'

'What triggered you then? What set you off on that particular day?'

'I don't know.'

'I think you do.'

'I had worried about it all the time.'

'What set you off, Clarice? You started what time?'

'Early. Still dark.'

'Then something woke you. What woke you up? Did you dream? What was it?'

'I woke up and heard the lambs screaming. I woke up in the dark and the lambs were screaming.'

'They were slaughtering the spring lambs?'

'Yes.'

'What did you do?'

'I couldn't do anything for them. I was just a –'

'What did you do with the *horse*?'

'I got dressed without turning on the light and went outside. She was scared. All the horses in the pen were scared and milling around. I blew in her nose and she knew it was me. Finally she'd put her nose in my hand.

The lights were on in the barn and in the shed by the sheep pen. Bare bulbs, big shadows. The refrigerator truck had come and it was idling, roaring. I led her away.'

'Did you saddle her?'

'No. I didn't take their saddle. Just a rope hackamore was all.'

'As you went off in the dark, could you hear the lambs back where the lights were?'

'Not long. There weren't but twelve.'

'You still wake up sometimes, don't you? Wake up in the iron dark with the lambs screaming?'

'Sometimes.'

'Do you think if you caught Buffalo Bill yourself and if you made Catherine all right, you could make the lambs stop screaming, do you think they'd be all right too and you wouldn't wake up again in the dark and hear the lambs screaming? Clarice?'

'Yes. I don't know. Maybe.'

'Thank you, Clarice.' Dr Lecter seemed oddly at peace.

'Tell me his name, Dr Lecter,' Starling said.

'Dr Chilton,' Lecter said, 'I believe you know each other.'

For an instant, Starling didn't realize Chilton was behind her. Then he took her elbow.

She took it back. Officer Pembry and his big partner were with Chilton.

'In the elevator,' Chilton said. His face was mottled red.

'Did you know Dr Chilton has no medical degree?' Dr Lecter said. 'Please bear that in mind later on.'

'Let's go,' Chilton said.

'You're not in charge here, Dr Chilton,' Starling said.

Officer Pembry came around Chilton. 'No, ma'am, but I am. He called my boss and your boss both. I'm sorry, but I've got orders to see you out. Come on with me, now.'

'Goodbye, Clarice. Will you let me know if ever the lambs stop screaming?'

'Yes.'

Pembry was taking her arm. It was go or fight him.

'Yes,' she said. 'I'll tell you.'

'Do you promise?'

'Yes.'

'Then why not finish the arch? Take your case file with you, Clarice, I won't need it anymore. ' He held it at arm's length through the bars, his forefinger along the spine. She reached across the barrier and took it. For an instant the tip of her forefinger touched Dr Lecter's. The touch crackled in his eyes.

'Thank you, Clarice.'

'Thank you, Dr Lecter.'

And that is how he remained in Starling's mind. Caught in the instant when he did not mock. Standing in his white cell, arched like a dancer, his hands clasped in front of him and his head slightly to the side.

She went over a speed bump at the airport fast enough to bang her head on the roof of the car, and had to run for the airplane Krendler had ordered her to catch.

Chapter Thirty-six

Officers Pembry and Boyle were experienced men brought especially from Brushy Mountain State Prison to be Dr Lecter's warders. They were calm and careful and did not feel they needed their job explained to them by Dr Chilton.

They had arrived in Memphis ahead of Lecter and examined the cell minutely. When Dr Lecter was brought to the old courthouse, they examined him as well. He was subjected to an internal body search by a male nurse while he was still in restraints. His clothing was searched thoroughly and a metal detector run over the seams.

Boyle and Pembry came to an understanding with him, speaking in low, civil tones close to his ears as he was examined.

'Dr Lecter, we can get along just fine. We'll treat you just as good as you treat us. Act like a gentleman and you get the Eskimo Pie. But we're not pussyfooting around with you, buddy. Try to bite, and we'll leave you smooth-mouthed. Looks like you got something good going here. You don't want to fuck it up, do you?'

Dr Lecter crinkled his eyes at them in a friendly fashion. If he had been inclined to reply he would have been prevented by the wooden peg between his molars as the nurse shone a flashlight in his mouth and ran a gloved finger into his cheeks.

The metal detector beeped at his cheeks.

'What's that?' the nurse asked.

'Fillings,' Pembry said. 'Pull his lip back there. You've put some miles on them back ones, haven't you Doc?'

'Strikes me he's pretty much of a broke-dick,' Boyle confided to Pembry after they had Dr Lecter secure in his cell. 'He won't be no trouble if he don't flip out.'

The cell, while secure and strong, lacked a rolling food carrier. At lunchtime, in the unpleasant atmosphere that followed Starling's visit, Dr Chilton inconvenienced everyone, making Boyle and Pembry go through the long process of securing the compliant Dr Lecter in the straitjacket and leg restraints as he stood with his back to the bars, Chilton poised with the Mace, before they opened the door to carry in his tray.

Chilton refused to use Boyle's and Pembry's names, though they wore nameplates, and addressed them indiscriminately as 'you there.'

For their part, after the warders heard Chilton was not a real M.D., Boyle observed to Pembry that he was just 'some kind of a God damned schoolteacher.'

Pembry tried once to explain to Chilton that Starling's visit had been approved not by them but by the desk downstairs, and saw that in Chilton's anger it didn't matter.

Dr Chilton was absent at supper and, with Dr Lecter's bemused cooperation, Boyle and Pembry used their own method to take in his tray. It worked very well.

'Dr Lecter, you not gonna be needing your dinner jacket tonight,' Pembry said. 'I'll ask you to sit on the floor and scoot backwards till you can just stick your hands out through the bars, arms extended backward. There you go. Scoot up a little and straighten 'em out more behind you, elbows straight.' Pembry handcuffed Dr Lecter tightly outside the bars, with a bar between his arms, and a low crossbar above them. 'That hurts just a little bit, don't it? I know it does and they won't be on there but a minute, save us both a lot of trouble.'

Dr Lecter could not rise, even to a squat, and with his legs straight in front of him on the floor, he couldn't kick.

Only when Dr Lecter was pinioned did Pembry return to the desk for the key to the cell door. Pembry slid his riot baton in the ring at his wrist, put a canister of Mace in his pocket, and returned to the cell. He opened the door while Boyle took in the tray. When the door was secured, Pembry took the key back to the desk before he took the cuffs off Dr Lecter. At no time was he near the bars with the key while the doctor was free in the cell.

'Now that was pretty easy, wasn't it?' Pembry said.

'It was very convenient, thank you, Officer,' Dr Lecter said. 'You know, I'm just trying to get by.'

'We all are, brother,' Pembry said.

Dr Lecter toyed with his food while he wrote and drew and doodled on his pad with a felt-tipped pen. He flipped over the cassette in the tape player chained to the table leg and punched the play button. Glenn Gould playing Bach's *Goldberg Variations* on the piano. The music, beautiful beyond plight and time, filled the bright cage and the room where the warders sat.

For Dr Lecter, sitting still at the table, time slowed and spread as it does in action. For him the notes of music moved apart without losing tempo. Even Bach's silver pounces were discrete notes glittering off the steel around him. Dr Lecter rose, his expression abstracted, and watched his paper napkin slide off his thighs to the floor. The napkin was in the air a long time, brushed the table leg, flared, sideslipped, stalled and turned over before it came to rest on the steel floor. He made no effort to pick it up, but took a stroll across his cell, went behind the paper screen and sat on the lid of his toilet, his only private place. Listening to the music, he leaned sideways on the sink, his chin in his hand, his strange maroon eyes half-closed. The *Goldberg Variations* interested him structurally. Here it came again, the bass progression from the saraband repeated, repeated. He nodded along, his tongue moving over the edges of his teeth. All the way around on top, all the way around on the bottom. It was a long and interesting trip for his tongue, like a good walk in the Alps.

He did his gums now, sliding his tongue high in the crevice between his cheek and gum and moving it slowly around as some men do when ruminating. His gums were cooler than his tongue. It was cool up in the crevice. When his tongue got to the little metal tube, it stopped.

Over the music he heard the elevator clank and whir as it started up. Many notes of music later, the elevator door opened and a voice he did not know said, 'I'm s'posed to get the tray.'

Dr Lecter heard the smaller one coming, Pembry. He could see through the crack between the panels in his screen. Pembry was at the bars.

'Dr Lecter. Come sit on the floor with your back to the bars like we did before.'

'Officer Pembry, would you mind if I just finish up here? I'm afraid my trip's gotten my digestion a little out of sorts.' It took a very long time to say.

'All right.' Pembry calling down the room, 'We'll call down when we got it.'

'Can I look at him?'

'We'll call you.'

The elevator again and then only the music.

Dr Lecter took the tube from his mouth and dried it on a piece of toilet tissue. His hands were steady, his palms perfectly dry.

In his years of detention, with his unending curiosity, Dr Lecter had learned many of the secret prison crafts. In all the years after he savaged the nurse in the Baltimore asylum, there had been only two lapses in the security around him, both on Barney's days off. Once a psychiatric researcher loaned him a ballpoint pen and then forgot it. Before the man was out of the ward, Dr Lecter had broken up the plastic barrel of the pen and flushed it down his toilet. The metal ink tube went in the rolled seam edging his mattress.

The only sharp edge in his cell at the asylum was a burr on the head of a bolt holding his cot to the wall. It was enough. In two months of rubbing, Dr Lecter cut the required two incisions, parallel and a quarter-inch long, running along the tube from its open end. Then he cut the ink tube in two pieces one inch from the open end and flushed the long piece with the point down the toilet. Barney did not spot the calluses on his fingers from the nights of rubbing.

Six months later, an orderly left a heavy-duty paper clip on some documents sent to Dr Lecter by his attorney. One inch of the steel clip went inside the tube and the rest went down the toilet. The little tube, smooth and short, was easy to conceal in seams of clothing, between the cheek and gum, in the rectum.

Now, behind his paper screen, Dr Lecter tapped the little metal tube on his thumbnail until the wire inside it slipped out. The wire was a tool and this was the difficult part. Dr Lecter stuck the wire halfway into the little tube and with infinite care used it as a lever to bend down the strip of metal between the two incisions. Sometimes they break. Carefully, with his powerful hands, he bent the metal and it was coming. Now. The minute strip of metal was at right angles to the tube. Now he had a handcuff key.

Dr Lecter put his hands behind him and passed the key back and forth between them fifteen times. He put the key back in his mouth while he washed his hands and meticulously dried them. Then, with his tongue, he hid the key between the fingers of his right hand, knowing Pembry would stare at his strange left hand when it was behind his back.

'I'm ready when you are, Officer Pembry,' Dr Lecter said. He sat on the floor of the cell and stretched his arms behind him, his hands and wrists through the bars. 'Thank you for waiting.' It seemed a long speech, but it was leavened by the music.

He heard Pembry behind him now. Pembry felt his wrist to see if he had soaped it. Pembry felt his other wrist to see if he had soaped it. Pembry put the cuffs on tight. He went back to the desk for the key to the cell. Over the piano, Dr Lecter heard the clink of the key ring as Pembry took it from the desk drawer. Now he was coming back, walking through the notes, parting the air that swarmed with crystal notes. This time Boyle came back with him. Dr Lecter could hear the holes they made in the echoes of the music.

Pembry checked the cuffs again. Dr Lecter could smell Pembry's breath behind him. Now Pembry unlocked the cell and swung the door open. Boyle came in. Dr Lecter turned his head, the cell moving by his vision at a rate that seemed slow to him, the details wonderfully sharp – Boyle at the table gathering the scattered supper things onto the tray with a clatter of annoyance at the mess. The tape player with its reels turning, the napkin on the floor beside the bolted-down leg of the table. Through the bars, Dr Lecter saw in the corner of his eye the back of Pembry's knee, the tip of the baton hanging from his belt as he stood outside the cell holding the door.

Dr Lecter found the keyhole in his left cuff, inserted the key and turned it. He felt the cuff spring loose on his wrist. He passed the key to his left hand, found the keyhole, put in the key and turned it.

Boyle bent for the napkin on the floor. Fast as a snapping turtle the handcuff closed on Boyle's wrist and as he turned his rolling eye to Lecter the other cuff locked around the fixed leg of the table. Dr Lecter's legs under him now, driving to the door, Pembry trying to come from behind it and Lecter's shoulder drove the iron door into him, Pembry going for the Mace in his belt, his arm mashed to his body by the door. Lecter grabbed the long end of the baton and lifted. With the leverage twisting Pembry's belt tight around him, he hit Pembry in the throat with his elbow and sank his teeth in Pembry's face. Pembry trying to claw at Lecter, his nose and upper lip caught between the tearing teeth. Lecter shook his head like a rat-killing dog and pulled the riot baton from Pembry's belt. In the cell Boyle bellowing now, sitting on the floor, digging desperately in his pocket for his handcuff key, fumbling, dropping it, finding it again. Lecter drove the end of the baton into Pembry's stomach and throat and he went to his knees. Boyle got the key in a lock of the handcuffs, he was bellowing, Lecter coming to him now. Lecter shut Boyle up with a shot of the Mace and as he wheezed, cracked his upstretched arm with two blows of the baton. Boyle tried to get under the table, but blinded by the Mace he crawled the wrong way and it was easy, with five judicious blows, to beat him to death.

Pembry had managed to sit up and he was crying. Dr Lecter looked down at him with his red smile. 'I'm ready if you are, Officer Pembry,' he said.

The baton, whistling in a flat arc, caught Pembry *pock* on the back of the head and he shivered out straight like a clubbed fish.

Dr Lecter's pulse was elevated to more than one hundred by the exercise, but quickly slowed to normal. He turned off the music and listened.

He went to the stairs and listened again. He turned out Pembry's pockets, got the desk key and opened all its drawers. In the bottom drawer were Boyle's and Pembry's duty weapons, a pair of .38 Special revolvers. Even better, in Boyle's pocket he found a pocket knife.

Chapter Thirty-seven

The lobby was full of policemen. It was 6:30 P.M. and the police at the outside guard posts had just been relieved at their regular two-hour interval. The men coming into the lobby from the raw evening warmed their hands at several electric heaters. Some of them had money down on the Memphis State basketball game in progress and were anxious to know how it was going.

Sergeant Tate would not allow a radio to be played aloud in the lobby, but one officer had a Walkman plugged in his ear. He reported the score often, but not often enough to suit the bettors.

In all there were fifteen armed policemen in the lobby plus two Corrections officers to relieve Pembry and Boyle at 7:00 P.M. Sergeant Tate himself was looking forward to going off duty with the eleven-to-seven shift.

All posts reported quiet. None of the nut calls threatening Lecter had come to anything.

At 6:45, Tate heard the elevator start up. He saw the bronze arrow above the door begin to crawl around the dial. It stopped at five.

Tate looked around the lobby. 'Did Sweeney go up for the tray?'

'Naw, I'm here, Sarge. You mind calling, see if they're through? I need to get going.'

Sergeant Tate dialed three digits and listened. 'Phone's busy,' he said. 'Go ahead up and see.' He turned back to the log he was completing for the eleven-to-seven shift.

'Had to have *lamb chops* tonight, rare,' Sweeney said. 'What you reckon he'll want for breakfast, some fucking thing from the zoo? And who'll have to catch it for him? Sweeney.'

The bronze arrow above the door stayed on five.

Sweeney waited another minute. 'What *is* this shit?' he said.

The .38 boomed somewhere above them, the reports echoing down the stone stairs, two fast shots and then a third.

Sergeant Tate, on his feet at the third one, microphone in his hand. 'CP, shots fired upstairs at the tower. Outside posts look sharp. We're going up.'

Yelling, milling in the lobby.

Tate saw the bronze arrow of the elevator moving then. It was already down to four. Tate roared over the racket, 'Hold it! Guard mount double up at your outside posts, first squad stays with me. Berry and Howard cover that fucking elevator if it comes –' The needle stopped at three. 'First squad, here we go. Don't pass a door without checking it. Bobby, outside – get a shotgun and the vests and bring 'em up.'

Tate's mind was racing on the first flight of stairs. Caution fought with the terrible need to help the officers upstairs. *God don't let him be out. Nobody wearing vests, shit. Fucking Corrections screws.*

The offices on two, three and four were supposed to be empty and locked. You could get from the tower to the main building on those floors, if you went through the offices. You couldn't on five.

Tate had been to the excellent Tennessee SWAT school and he knew how to do it. He went first and took the young ones in hand. Fast and careful they took the stairs, covering each other from landing to landing.

'You turn your back on a door before you check it, I'll ream your ass.'

The doors off the second-floor landing were dark and locked.

Up to three now, the little corridor dim. One rectangle of light on the floor from the open elevator car. Tate moved down the wall opposite the open elevator, no mirrors in the car to help him. With two pounds' pressure on a nine-pound trigger, he looked inside the car. Empty.

Tate yelled up the stairs, 'Boyle! Pembry! Shit.' He posted a man on three and moved up.

Four was flooded with the music of the piano coming from above. The door into the offices opened at a push. Beyond the offices, the beam of the long flashlight shone on a door open wide into the great dark building beyond.

'Boyle! Pembry!' He left two on the landing. 'Cover the door. Vests are coming. Don't show your ass in that doorway.'

Tate climbed the stone stairs into the music. At the top of the tower now, the fifth-floor landing, light dim in the short corridor. Bright light through the frosted glass that said SHELBY COUNTY HISTORICAL SOCIETY.

Tate moved low beneath the door glass to the side opposite the hinges. He nodded to Jacobs on the other side, turned the knob and shoved hard, the door swinging all the way back hard enough for the glass to shatter, Tate inside fast and out of the doorframe, covering the room over the wide sights of his revolver.

Tate had seen many things. He had seen accidents beyond reckoning, fights, murders. He had seen six dead policemen in his time. But he thought that what lay at his feet was the worst thing he had ever seen happen to an officer. The meat above the uniform collar no longer resembled a face. The front and top of the head were a slick of blood peaked with torn flesh and a single eye was stuck beside the nostrils, the sockets full of blood.

Jacobs passed Tate, slipping on the bloody floor as he went in to the cell. He bent over Boyle, still handcuffed to the table leg. Boyle, partly eviscerated, his face hacked to pieces, seemed to have exploded blood in the cell, the walls and the stripped cot covered with gouts and splashes.

Jacobs put his fingers on the neck. 'This one's dead,' he called over the music. 'Sarge?'

Tate, back at himself, ashamed of a second's lapse, and he was talking into his radio. 'Command post, two officers down. Repeat, two officers down. Prisoner is missing. Lecter is missing. Outside posts watch the windows, subject has stripped the bed, he may be making a rope. Confirm ambulances en route.'

'Pembry dead, Sarge?' Jacobs shut the music off.

Tate knelt and as he reached for the neck to feel, the awful thing on the floor groaned and blew a bloody bubble.

'Pembry's alive.' Tate didn't want to put his mouth in the bloody mess, knew he would if he had to to help Pembry breathe, knew he wouldn't make one of the patrolmen do it. Better if Pembry died, but he would help him breathe. But there was a heartbeat, he found it, there was breathing. It was ragged and gurgling but it was breathing. The ruin was breathing on its own.

Tate's radio crackled. A patrol lieutenant set up on the lot outside took command and wanted news. Tate had to talk.

'Come here, Murray,' Tate called to a young patrolman. 'Get down here with Pembry and take ahold of him where he can feel your hands on him. Talk to him.'

'What's his name, Sarge?' Murray was green.

'It's Pembry, now talk to him, God dammit.' Tate on the radio. 'Two officers down, Boyle's dead and Pembry's bad hurt. Lecter's missing and armed – he took their guns. Belts and holsters are on the desk.'

The lieutenant's voice was scratchy through the thick walls. 'Can you confirm the stairway clear for stretchers?'

'Yes sir. Call up to four before they pass. I have men on every landing.'

'Roger, Sergeant. Post Eight out here thought he saw some movement behind the windows in the main building on four. We've got the exits covered, he's not getting out. Hold your positions on the landings. SWAT's rolling. We're gonna let SWAT flush him out. Confirm.'

'I understand. SWAT's play.'

'What's he got?'

'Two pistols and a knife, Lieutenant – Jacobs, see if there's any ammo in the gunbelts.'

'Dump pouches,' the patrolman said. 'Pembry's still full, Boyle's too. Dumb shit didn't take the extra rounds.'

'What are they?'

'Thirty-eight + Ps JHP.'

Tate was back on the radio. 'Lieutenant, it looks like he's got two six-shot .38s. We heard three rounds fired and the dump pouches on the gunbelts are still full, so he may just have nine left. Advise SWAT it's + Ps jacketed hollowpoints. This guy favors the face.'

Plus Ps were hot rounds, but they would not penetrate SWAT's body armor. A hit in the face would very likely be fatal, a hit on a limb would maim.

'Stretchers coming up, Tate.'

The ambulances were there amazingly fast, but it did not seem fast enough to Tate, listening to the pitiful thing at his feet. Young Murray was trying to hold the groaning, jerking body, trying to talk reassuringly and not look at him, and he was saying, 'You're just fine Pembry, looking good,' over and over in the same sick tone.

As soon as he saw the ambulance attendants on the landing, Tate yelled, 'Corpsman!' as he had in war.

He got Murray by the shoulder and moved him out of the way. The ambulance attendants worked fast, expertly securing the clenched, blood-slick fists under the belt, getting an airway in and peeling a nonstick surgical bandage to get some pressure on the bloody face and head. One of them popped an intravenous plasma pack, but the other, taking blood pressure and pulse, shook his head and said, 'Downstairs.'

Orders on the radio now. 'Tate, I want you to clear the offices in the tower and seal it off. Secure the doors from the main building. Then cover from the landings. I'm sending up vests and shotguns. We'll get him alive if he wants to come, but we take no special risks to preserve his life. Understand me?'

'I got it, Lieutenant.'

'I want SWAT and nobody but SWAT in the main building. Let me have that back.'

Tate repeated the order.

Tate was a good sergeant and he showed it now as he and Jacobs shrugged into their heavy armored vests and followed the gurney as the orderlies carried it down the stairs to the ambulance. A second crew followed with Boyle. The men on the landings were angry, seeing the gurneys pass, and Tate had a word of wisdom for them: 'Don't let your temper get your ass shot off.'

As the sirens wailed outside, Tate, backed by the veteran Jacobs, carefully cleared the offices and sealed off the tower.

A cool draft blew down the hall on four. Beyond the door, in the vast dark spaces of the main building, the telephones were ringing. In dark offices all over the building, buttons on telephones were winking like fireflies, the bells sounding over and over.

The word was out that Dr Lecter was 'barricaded' in the building, and radio and television reporters were calling, dialing fast with their modems, trying to get live interviews with the monster. To avoid this, SWAT usually has the telephones shut off, except for one that the negotiator uses. This building was too big, the offices too many.

Tate closed and locked the door on the rooms of blinking telephones. His chest and back were wet and itching under the hardshell vest.

He took his radio off his belt. 'CP, this is Tate, the tower's clear, over.'

'Roger, Tate. Captain wants you at the CP.'

'Ten-four. Tower lobby, you there?'

'Here, Sarge.'

'It's me on the elevator, I'm bringing it down.'

'Gotcha, Sarge.'

Jacobs and Tate were in the elevator riding down to the lobby when a drop of blood fell on Tate's shoulder. Another hit his shoe.

He looked at the ceiling of the car, touched Jacobs, motioning for silence.

Blood was dripping from the crack around the service hatch in the top of the car. It seemed a long ride down to the lobby. Tate and Jacobs stepped off backwards, guns pointed at the ceiling of the elevator. Tate reached back in and locked the car.

'Shhhh,' Tate said in the lobby. Quietly, 'Berry, Howard, he's on the roof of the elevator. Keep it covered.'

Tate went outside. The black SWAT van was on the lot. SWAT always had a variety of elevator keys.

They were set up in moments, two SWAT officers in black body armor and headsets climbing the stairs to the third-floor landing. With Tate in the lobby were two more, their assault rifles pointed at the elevator ceiling.

Like the big ants that fight, Tate thought.

The SWAT commander was talking into his headset. 'Okay, Johnny.'

On the third floor, high above the elevator, Officer Johnny Peterson turned his key in the lock and the elevator door slid open. The shaft was dark. Lying on his back in the corridor, he took a stun grenade from his tactical vest and put it on the floor beside him. 'Okay, I'll take a look now.'

He took out his mirror with its long handle and stuck it over the edge while his partner shined a powerful flashlight down the shaft.

'I see him. He's on top of the elevator. I see a weapon beside him. He's not moving.'

The question in Peterson's earphone, 'Can you see his hands?'

'I see one hand, the other one's under him. He's got the sheets around him.'

'Tell him.'

'PUT YOUR HANDS ON TOP OF YOUR HEAD AND FREEZE,' Peterson yelled down the shaft. 'He didn't move, Lieutenant . . . Right.

'IF YOU DON'T PUT YOUR HANDS ON TOP OF YOUR HEAD I'LL DROP A STUN GRENADE ON YOU. I'LL GIVE YOU THREE SECONDS,' Peterson called. He took from his vest one of the doorstops every SWAT officer carries. 'OKAY, GUYS, WATCH OUT DOWN THERE – HERE COMES THE GRENADE.' He dropped the doorstop over the edge, saw it bounce on the figure. 'He didn't move, Lieutenant.'

'Okay, Johnny, we're gonna push the hatch up with a pole from outside the car. Can you get the drop?'

Peterson rolled over. His 10 mm Colt, cocked and locked, pointed straight down at the figure. 'Got the drop,' he said.

Looking down the elevator shaft, Peterson could see the crack of light appear below as the officers in the foyer pushed up on the hatch with a SWAT boathook. The still figure was partly over the hatch and one of the arms moved as the officers pushed from below.

Peterson's thumb pressed a shade harder on the safety of the Colt. 'His arm moved, Lieutenant, but I think it's just the hatch moving it.'

'Roger. Heave.'

The hatch banged backward and lay against the wall of the elevator shaft. It was hard for Peterson to look down into the light. 'He hasn't moved. His hand's *not* on the weapon.'

The calm voice in his ear, 'Okay, Johnny, hold up. We're coming into the car, so watch with the mirror for movement. Any fire will come from us. Affirm?'

'Got it.'

In the lobby, Tate watched them go into the car. A rifleman loaded with armor-piercing aimed his weapon at the ceiling of the elevator. A second officer climbed on a ladder. He was armed with a large automatic pistol with a flashlight clamped beneath it. A mirror and the pistol-light went up through the hatch. Then the officer's head and shoulders. He handed down a .38 revolver. 'He's dead,' the officer called down.

Tate wondered if the death of Dr Lecter meant Catherine Martin would die too, all the information lost when the lights went out in that monster mind.

The officers were pulling him down now, the body coming upside down through the elevator hatch, eased down into many arms, an odd deposition in a lighted box. The lobby was filling up, policemen crowding up to see.

A corrections officer pushed forward, looked at the body's outflung tattooed arms.

'That's Pembry,' he said.

Chapter Thirty-eight

In the back of the howling ambulance, the young attendant braced himself against the sway and turned to his radio to report to his emergency room supervisor, talking loud above the siren.

'He's comatose but the vital signs are good. He's got good pressure. One-thirty over ninety. Yeah, ninety. Pulse eighty-five. He's got severe facial cuts with elevated flaps, one eye enucleated. I've got pressure on the face and an airway in place. Possible gunshot in the head, I can't tell.'

Behind him on the stretcher, the balled and bloody fists relax inside the waistband. The right hand slides out, finds the buckle on the strap across the chest.

'I'm scared to put much pressure on the head – he showed some convulsive movement before we put him on the gurney. Yeah, got him in the Fowler position.'

Behind the young man, the hand gripped the surgical bandage and wiped out the eyes.

The attendant heard the airway hiss close behind him, turned and saw the bloody face in his, did not see the pistol descending and it caught him hard over the ear.

The ambulance slowing to a stop in traffic on the six-lane freeway, drivers behind it confused and honking, hesitant to pull around an emergency vehicle. Two small pops like backfires in the traffic and the ambulance started up again, weaving, straightening out, moving to the right lane.

The airport exit coming up. The ambulance piddled along in the right lane, various emergency lights going on and off on the outside of it, wipers on and off, then the siren wailing down, starting up, wailing down to silence and the flashing lights going off. The ambulance proceeding quietly, taking the exit to Memphis International Airport, the beautiful building floodlit in the winter evening. It took the curving drive as far as the automated gates to the vast underground parking field. A bloody hand came out to take a ticket. And the ambulance disappeared down the tunnel to the parking field beneath the ground.

Chapter Thirty-nine

Normally, Clarice Starling would have been curious to see Crawford's house in Arlington, but the bulletin on the car radio about Dr Lecter's escape knocked all that out of her.

Lips numb and scalp prickling, she drove by rote, saw the neat 1950s ranch house without looking at it, and only wondered dimly if the lit curtained windows on the left were where Bella was lying. The doorbell seemed too loud.

Crawford opened the door on the second ring. He wore a baggy cardigan and he was talking on a wireless phone. 'Copley in Memphis,' he said. Motioning for her to follow, he led her through the house, grunting into the telephone as he went.

In the kitchen, a nurse took a tiny bottle from the refrigerator and held it to the light. When Crawford raised his eyebrows to the nurse, she shook her head, she didn't need him.

He took Starling to his study, down three steps into what was clearly a converted double garage. There was good space here, a sofa and chairs, and on the cluttered desk a computer terminal glowed green beside an antique astrolabe. The rug felt as though it was laid on concrete. Crawford waved her to a seat.

He put his hand over the receiver. 'Starling, this is baloney, but did you hand Lecter anything at all in Memphis?'

'No.'

'No object.'

'Nothing.'

'You took him the drawings and stuff from his cell.'

'I never gave it to him. The stuff's still in my bag. He gave me the file. That's all that passed between us.'

Crawford tucked the phone under his jowl. 'Copley, that's unmitigated bullshit. I want you to step on that bastard and do it now. Straight to the chief, straight to the TBI. See the hotline's posted with the rest. Burroughs is on it. Yes.' He turned off the phone and stuffed it in his pocket.

'Want some coffee, Starling? Coke?'

'What was that about handing things to Dr Lecter?'

'Chilton's saying you must have given Lecter something he used to slip the ratchet on the cuffs. You didn't do it on purpose, he says – it was just ignorance.' Sometimes Crawford had angry little turtle-eyes. He watched how she took it. 'Did Chilton try to snap your garters, Starling? Is that what's the matter with him?'

'Maybe. I'll take black with sugar, please.'

While he was in the kitchen, she took deep breaths and looked around the room. If you live in a dormitory or a barracks, it's comforting to be in a home. Even with the ground shaking under Starling, her sense of the Crawfords' lives in this house helped her.

Crawford was coming, careful down the steps in his bifocals, carrying the cups. He was half an inch shorter in his moccasins. When Starling stood to take her coffee, their eyes were almost level. He smelled like soap, and his hair looked fluffy and gray.

'Copley said they haven't found the ambulance yet. Police barracks are turning out all over the South.'

She shook her head. 'I don't know any details. The radio just had the bulletin – Dr Lecter killed two policemen and got away.'

'Two corrections officers.' Crawford punched up the crawling text on his computer screen. 'Names were Boyle and Pembry. You deal with them?'

She nodded. 'They . . . put me out of the lockup. They were okay about it.' *Pembry coming around Chilton, uncomfortable, determined, but country-courteous. Come on with me, now, he said. He had liver spots on his hands and forehead. Dead now, pale beneath his spots.*

Suddenly Starling had to put her coffee down. She filled her lungs deep and looked at the ceiling for a moment. 'How'd he do it?'

'He got away in an ambulance, Copley said. We'll go into it. How did you make out with the blotter acid?'

Starling had spent the late afternoon and early evening walking the sheet of Plutos through Scientific Analysis on Krendler's orders. 'Nothing. They're trying the DEA files for a batch-match, but the stuff's ten years old. Documents may do better with the printing than DEA can do with the dope.'

'But it *was* blotter acid.'

'Yes. How'd he do it, Mr Crawford?'

'Want to know?'

She nodded.

'Then I'll tell you. They loaded Lecter into an ambulance by mistake. They thought he was Pembry, badly injured.'

'Did he have on Pembry's uniform? They were about the same size.'

'He put on Pembry's uniform and part of Pembry's face. And about a pound off Boyle, too. He wrapped Pembry's body in the waterproof mattress cover and the sheets from his cell to keep it from dripping and stuffed it on top of the elevator. He put on the uniform, got himself fixed up, laid on the floor and fired shots into the ceiling to start the stampede. I don't know what he did with the gun, stuffed it down the back of his pants, maybe. The ambulance comes, cops everywhere with their guns out. The ambulance crew came in fast and did what they're trained to do under fire – they stuffed in an airway, slapped a bandage over the worst of it, pressure to stop bleeding, and hauled out of there. They did their job. The ambulance never made it to the hospital. The police are still looking for it. I don't feel good about those medics. Copley said they're playing the dispatcher's tapes. The ambulances were called a couple of times. They think Lecter called the ambulances himself before he fired the shots, so he wouldn't have to lie around too long. *Dr Lecter likes his fun.*'

Starling had never heard the bitter snarl in Crawford's voice before. Because she associated bitter with weak, it frightened her.

'This escape doesn't mean Dr Lecter was lying,' Starling said. 'Sure, he was lying to somebody – us or Senator Martin – but maybe he wasn't lying to both of us. He told Senator Martin it was Billy Rubin and claimed that's all he knew. He told me it was somebody with delusions of being a transsexual. About the last thing he said to me was, "Why not finish the arch?" He was talking about following the sex-change theory that –'

'I know, I saw your summary. There's nowhere to go with that until we get names from the clinics. Alan Bloom's gone personally to the department heads. They say they're looking. I have to believe it.'

'Mr Crawford, are you in the glue?'

'I'm directed to take compassionate leave,' Crawford said. 'There's a new task force of FBI, DEA, and "additional elements" from the Attorney General's office – meaning Krendler.'

'Who's boss?'

'Officially, FBI Assistant Director John Golby. Let's say he and I are in close consultation. John's a good man. What about you, are you in the glue?'

'Krendler told me to turn in my ID and the roscoe and report back to school.'

'That was all he did *before* your visit to Lecter. Starling, he sent a rocket this afternoon to the Office of Professional Responsibility. It was a request "without prejudice" that the Academy suspend you pending a reevaluation of your fitness for the service . It's a chickenshit backshot. The Chief Gunny, John Brigham, saw it in the faculty meeting at Quantico a little while ago. He gave 'em an earful and got on the horn to me.'

'How bad is that?'

'You're entitled to a hearing. I'll vouch for your fitness and that'll be enough. But if you spend any more time away, you'll definitely be recycled, regardless of any finding at a hearing. Do you know what happens when you're recycled?'

'Sure, you're sent back to the regional office that recruited you. You get to file reports and make coffee until you get another spot in a class.'

'I can promise you a place in a later class, but I can't keep them from recycling you if you miss the time.'

'So I go back to school and stop working on this, or . . .'

'Yeah.'

'What do you want me to do?'

'Your job was Lecter. You did it. I'm not asking you to take a recycle. It could cost you, maybe half a year, maybe more.'

'What about Catherine Martin?'

'He's had her almost forty-eight hours – be forty-eight hours at midnight. If we don't catch him he'll probably do her tomorrow or the next day, if it's like last time.'

'Lecter's not all we had.'

'They got six William Rubins so far, all with priors of one kind or another. None of 'em look like much. No Billy Rubins on the bug journal subscription lists. The Knifemakers Guild knows about five cases of ivory anthrax in the last ten years. We've got a couple of those left to check. What else? Klaus hasn't been identified – yet. Interpol reports a fugitive warrant outstanding in Marseilles for a Norwegian merchant seaman, a "Klaus Bjetland," however you say it. Norway's looking for his dental records to send. If we get anything from the clinics, and you've got the time, you can help with it. Starling?'

'Yes, Mr Crawford?'

'Go back to school.'

'If you didn't want me to chase him you shouldn't have taken me in that funeral home, Mr Crawford.'

'No,' Crawford said. 'I suppose I shouldn't. But then we wouldn't have the insect. You don't turn in your roscoe. Quantico's safe enough, but you'll be armed any time you're off the base at Quantico until Lecter's caught or dead.'

'What about you? He hates you. I mean he's given this some thought.'

'Lot of people have, Starling, in a lot of jails. One of these days he might get around to it, but he's way too busy now. It's sweet to be out and he's not ready to waste it that way. And this place is safer than it looks.'

The phone in Crawford's pocket buzzed. The one on the desk purred and blinked. He listened for a few moments, said 'Okay,' and hung up.

'They found the ambulance in the underground garage at the Memphis airport.' He shook his head. 'No good. Crew was in the back. Dead, both of them.' Crawford took off his glasses, rummaged for his handkerchief to polish them.

'Starling, the Smithsonian called Burroughs asking for you. The Pilcher fellow. They're pretty close to finishing up on the bug. I want you to write a 302 on that and sign it for the permanent file. You found the bug and followed up on it and I want the record to say so. You up to it?'

Starling was as tired as she had ever been. 'Sure,' she said.

'Leave your car at the garage, and Jeff'll drive you back to Quantico when you're through.'

On the steps she turned her face toward the lighted, curtained windows where the nurse kept watch, and then looked back at Crawford.

'I'm thinking about you both, Mr Crawford.'

'Thank you, Starling,' he said.

Chapter Forty

'Officer Starling, Dr Pilcher said he'd meet you in the Insect Zoo. I'll take you over there,' the guard said.

To reach the Insect Zoo from the Constitution Avenue side of the museum, you must take the elevator one level above the great stuffed elephant and cross a vast floor devoted to the study of man.

Tiers of skulls were first, rising and spreading, representing the explosion of human population since the time of Christ.

Starling and the guard moved in a dim landscape peopled with figures illustrating human origin and variation. Here were displays of ritual – tattoos, bound feet, tooth modification, Peruvian surgery, mummification.

'Did you ever see Wilhelm von Ellenbogen?' the guard asked, shining his light into a case.

'I don't believe I have,' Starling said without slowing her pace.

'You should come sometime when the lights are up and take a look at him. Buried him in Philadelphia in the eighteenth century? Turned right to soap when the ground water hit him.'

The Insect Zoo is a large room, dim now and loud with chirps and whirs. Cages and cases of live insects fill it. Children particularly like the zoo and troop through it all day. At night, left to themselves, the insects are busy. A few of the cases were lit with red, and the fire exit signs burned fiercely red in the dim room.

'Dr Pilcher?' the guard called from the door.

'Here,' Pilcher said, holding a penlight up as a beacon.

'Will you bring this lady out?'

'Yes, thank you, Officer.'

Starling took her own small flashlight out of her purse and found the switch already on, the batteries dead. The flash of anger she felt reminded her that she was tired and she had to bear down.

'Hello, Officer Starling.'

'Dr Pilcher.'

'How about "Professor Pilcher"?'

'Are you a professor?'

'No, but I'm not a doctor either. What I *am* is glad to see you. Want to look at some bugs?'

'Sure. Where's Dr Roden?'

'He made most of the progress over the last two nights with chaetaxy and finally he had to crash. Did you see the bug before we started on it?'

'No.'

'It was just mush, really.'

'But you got it, you figured it out.'

'Yep. Just now.' He stopped at a mesh cage. 'First let me show you a moth like the one you brought in Monday. This is not exactly the same as yours, but the same family, an owlet.' The beam of his flashlight found the large sheeny blue moth sitting on a small branch, its wings folded. Pilcher blew air at it and instantly the fierce face of an owl appeared as the moth flared the undersides of its wings at them, the eye-spots on the wings glaring like the last sight a rat ever sees. 'This one's *Caligo beltrao* – fairly common. But with this Klaus specimen, you're talking some heavy moths. Come on.'

At the end of the room was a case set back in a niche with a rail in front of it. The case was beyond the reach of children and it was covered with a cloth. A small humidifier hummed beside it.

'We keep it behind glass to protect people's fingers – it can fight. It likes the damp too, and glass keeps the humidity in.' Pilcher lifted the cage carefully by its handles and moved it to the front of the niche. He lifted off the cover and turned on a small light above the cage.

'This is the Death's-head Moth,' he said. 'That's nightshade she's sitting on – we're hoping she'll lay.'

The moth was wonderful and terrible to see, its large brownblack wings tented like a cloak, and on its wide furry back, the signature device that has struck fear in men for as long as men have come upon it suddenly in their happy gardens. The domed skull, a skull that is both skull and face, watching from its dark eyes, the cheekbones, the zygomatic arch traced exquisitely beside the eyes.

'*Acherontia styx*,' Pilcher said. 'It's named for two rivers in Hell. Your man, he drops the bodies in a river every time – did I read that?'

'Yes,' Starling said. 'Is it rare?'

'In this part of the world it is. There aren't any at all in nature.'

'Where's it from?' Starling leaned her face close to the mesh roof of the case. Her breath stirred the fur on the moth's back. She jerked back when it squeaked and fiercely flapped its wings. She could feel the tiny breeze it made.

'Malaysia. There's a European type too, called *atropos*, but this one and the one in Klaus's mouth are Malaysian.'

'So somebody raised it.'

Pilcher nodded. 'Yes,' he said when she didn't look at him. 'It had to be shipped from Malaysia as an egg or more likely as a pupa. Nobody's ever been able to get them to lay eggs in captivity. They mate, but no eggs. The hard part is finding the caterpillar in the jungle. After that, they're not hard to raise.'

'You said they can fight.'

'The proboscis is sharp and stout, and they'll jam it in your finger if you fool with them. It's an unusual weapon and alcohol doesn't affect it in preserved specimens. That helped us narrow the field so we could identify it so fast.' Pilcher seemed suddenly embarrassed, as though he had boasted. 'They're tough too,' he hurried on to say. 'They go in beehives and Bogart honey. One time we were collecting in Sabah, Borneo, and they'd come to the light behind the youth hostel. It was weird to hear them, we'd be –'

'Where did this one come from?'

'A swap with the Malaysian government. I don't know what we traded. It was funny, there we were in the dark, waiting with this cyanide bucket, when –'

'What kind of customs declaration came with this one? Do you have records of that? Do they have to be cleared out of Malaysia? Who would have that?'

'You're in a hurry. Look, I've written down all the stuff we have and the places to put ads if you want to do that kind of thing. Come on, I'll take you out.'

They crossed the vast floor in silence. In the light of the elevator, Starling could see that Pilcher was as tired as she was.

'You stayed up with this,' she said. 'That was a good thing to do. I didn't mean to be abrupt before, I just –'

'I hope they get him. I hope you're through with this soon,' he said. 'I put down a couple of chemicals he might be buying if he's putting up soft specimens . . . Officer Starling, I'd like to get to know you.'

'Maybe I should call you when I can.'

'You definitely should, absolutely, I'd like that,' Pilcher said.

The elevator closed and Pilcher and Starling were gone. The floor devoted to man was still and no human figure moved, not the tattooed, not the mummified, the bound feet didn't stir.

The fire lights glowed red in the Insect Zoo, reflected in ten thousand active eyes of the older phylum. The humidifier hummed and hissed. Beneath the cover, in the black cage, the Death's-head Moth climbed down the nightshade. She moved across the floor, her wings trailing like a cape, and found the bit of honeycomb in her dish. Grasping the honeycomb in her powerful front legs, she uncoiled her sharp proboscis and plunged it through the wax cap of a honey cell. Now she sat sucking quietly while all around her in the dark the chirps and whirs resumed, and with them the tiny tillings and killings.

Chapter Forty-one

Catherine Baker Martin down in the hateful dark. Dark swarmed behind her eyelids and, in jerky seconds of sleep, she dreamed the dark came into her. Dark came insidious, up her nose and into her ears, damp fingers of dark proposed themselves to each of her body openings. She put her hand over her mouth and nose, put her other hand over her vagina, clenched her buttocks, turned one ear to the mattress and sacrificed the other ear to the intrusion of the dark. With the dark came a sound, and she jerked awake. A familiar busy sound, a sewing machine. Variable speed. Slow, now fast.

Up in the basement the lights were on – she could see a feeble disc of yellow high above her where the small hatch in the well lid stood open. The poodle barked a couple of times and the unearthly voice was talking to it, muffled.

Sewing. Sewing was so wrong down here. Sewing belongs to the light. The sunny sewing room of Catherine's childhood flashed so welcome in her mind . . . the housekeeper, dear Bea Love, at the machine . . . her little cat batted at the blowing curtain.

The voice blew it all away, fussing at the poodle.

'Precious, put that *down*. You'll stick yourself with a pin and *then* where will we be? I'm almost done. Yes, Darlingheart. You get a Chew-wy *when we get through-y*, you get a Chew-wy *doody doody doo*.'

Catherine did not know how long she had been captive. She knew that she had washed twice – the last time she had stood up in the light, wanting him to see her body, not sure if he was looking down from behind the blinding light. Catherine Baker Martin naked was a show-stopper, a girl and a half in all directions, and she knew it. She wanted him to see. She wanted out of the pit. Close enough to fuck is close enough to fight – she said it silently to herself over and over as she washed. She was getting very little to eat and she knew she'd better do it while she had her strength. She knew she would fight him. She knew she could fight. Would it be better to fuck him first, fuck him as many times as he could do it and wear him out? She knew if she could ever get her legs around his neck she could send him home to Jesus in about a second and a half. *Can I stand to do that? You're damned right I can. Balls and eyes, balls and eyes, ballsandeyes.* But there had been no sound from above as she finished washing and put on the fresh jumpsuit. There was no reply to her offers as the bath bucket swayed up on its flimsy string and was replaced by her toilet bucket.

She waited now, hours later, listening to the sewing machine. She did not call out to him. In time, maybe a thousand breaths, she heard him going up the stairs, talking to the dog, saying something, '– breakfast when I get back.' He left the basement light on. Sometimes he did that.

Toenails and footsteps on the kitchen floor above. The dog whining. She believed her captor was leaving. Sometimes he went away for a long time.

Breaths went by. The little dog walked around in the kitchen above, whining, rattling something along the floor, bonging something along the floor, maybe its bowl. Scratching, scratching above. And barking again, short sharp barks, this time not as clear as the sounds had been when the dog was above her in the kitchen. Because the little dog was not in the kitchen. It had nosed the door open and it was down in the basement chasing mice, as it had done before when he was out.

Down in the dark, Catherine Martin felt beneath her mattress. She found the piece of chicken bone and sniffed it. It was hard not to eat the little shreds of meat and gristle on it. She put it in her mouth to get it warm. She stood up now, swaying a little in the dizzy dark. With her in the sheer pit was nothing but her futon, the jumpsuit she was wearing, the plastic toilet bucket – and its flimsy cotton string stretching upward toward the pale yellow light.

She had thought about it in every interval when she could think. Catherine stretched as high as she could and grasped the string. Better to jerk or to pull? She had thought about it through thousands of breaths. Better to pull steadily.

The cotton string stretched more than she expected. She got a new grip as high as she could and pulled, swinging her arm from side to side, hoping the string was fraying where it passed over the wooden lip of the opening above her. She frayed until her shoulder ached. She pulled, the string stretching, now not stretching, no more stretch. Please break high. Pop, and it fell, hanks of it across her face.

Squatting on the floor, the string lying on her head and shoulder, not enough light from the hole far above to see the string piled on her. She didn't know how much she had. Must not tangle. Carefully she laid the string out on the floor in bights, measuring them on her forearm. She counted fourteen forearms. The string had broken at the lip of the well.

She tied the chicken bone with its shredded morsels of flesh securely into the line where it attached to the bucket handle.

Now the harder part.

Work carefully. She was in her heavy-weather mind-set. It was like taking care of yourself in a small boat in heavy weather.

She tied the broken end of the string to her wrist, tightening the knot with her teeth.

She stood as clear of the string as possible. Holding the bucket by the handle, she swung it in a big circle and threw it straight upward at the faint disc of light above her. The plastic bucket missed the open hatch, hit the underside of the lid and fell back, hitting her in the face and shoulder. The little dog barked louder.

She took the time to lay out the line and threw again, and again. On the third throw, the bucket hit her broken finger when it fell and she had to lean against the in-sloping wall and breathe until the nausea went away. Throw four banged down on her, but five did not. It was out. The bucket was somewhere on the wooden cover of the well beside the open trap. How far from the hole? Get steady. Gently she pulled. She twitched the string to hear the bucket handle rattle against the wood above her.

The little dog barked louder.

She mustn't pull the bucket over the edge of the hole, but she must pull it close. She pulled it close.

The little dog among the mirrors and the mannequins in a nearby basement room. Sniffing at the threads and shreds beneath the sewing machine. Nosing around the great black armoire. Looking toward the end of the basement where the sounds were coming from. Dashing toward the gloomy section to bark and dash back again.

Now a voice, echoing faintly through the basement.

'Preeeee-cious.'

The little dog barked and jumped in place. Its fat little body quivered with the barks.

Now a wet kissing sound.

The dog looked up at the kitchen floor above, but that wasn't where the sound came from.

A smack-smack sound like eating. 'Come on, Precious. Come on, Sweetheart.'

On its tiptoes, ears up, the dog went into the gloom.

Slurp-slurp. 'Come on, Sweetums, come on, Precious.'

The poodle could smell the chicken bone tied to the bucket handle. It scratched at the side of the well and whined.

Smack-smack-smack.

The small poodle jumped up onto the wooden cover of the well. The smell was over here, between the bucket and the hole. The little dog barked at the bucket, whined in indecision. The chicken bone twitched ever so slightly.

The poodle crouched with its nose between its front paws, behind in the air, wagging furiously. It barked twice and pounced on the chicken bone, gripping it with its teeth. The bucket seemed to be trying to nose the little dog away from the chicken. The poodle growled at the bucket and held on, straddling the handle, teeth firmly clamped on the bone. Suddenly the bucket bumped the poodle over, off its feet, pushed it, it struggled to get up, bumped again, it struggled with the bucket, a back foot and haunch went off in the hole, its claws scrabbled frantically at the wood, the bucket sliding, wedging in the hole with the dog's hindquarters and the little dog pulled free, the bucket slipping over the edge and plunging, the bucket escaping down the hole with the chicken bone. The poodle barked angrily down the hole, barks ringing down in the well. Then it stopped barking and cocked its head at a sound only it could hear. It scrambled off the top of the well and went up the stairs yipping as a door slammed somewhere upstairs.

Catherine Baker Martin's tears spread hot on her cheeks and fell, plucking at the front of her jumpsuit, soaking through, warm on her breasts, and she believed that she would surely die.

Chapter Forty-two

Crawford stood alone in the center of his study with his hands jammed deep in his pockets. He stood there from 12:30 A.M. to 12:33, demanding an idea. Then he telexed the California Department of Motor Vehicles requesting a trace on the motor home Dr Lecter said Raspail had bought in California, the one Raspail used in his romance with Klaus. Crawford asked the DMV to check for traffic tickets issued to any driver other than Benjamin Raspail.

Then he sat on the sofa with a clipboard and worked out a proactive personal ad to run in the major papers:

> Junoesque creamy passion flower, 21, model, seeks man who appreciates quality AND quantity. Hand and cosmetic model, you've seen me in the magazine ads, now I'd like to see you. Send pix first letter.

Crawford considered for a moment, scratched out 'Junoesque,' and substituted 'full-figured.'

His head dipped and he dozed. The green screen of the computer terminal made tiny squares in the lenses of his glasses. Movement on the screen now, the lines crawling upward, moving on Crawford's lenses. In his sleep he shook his head as though the image tickled him.

The message was:

> MEMPHIS POX RECOVERED 2 ITEMS IN SEARCH OF LECTER'S CELL.

> (I) IMPROVISED HANDCUFF KEY MADE FROM BALLPOINT TUBE. INCISIONS BY ABRASION, BALTIMORE REQUESTED TO CHECK HOSPITAL CELL FOR TRACES OF MANUFACTURE, AUTH COPLEY, SAC MEMPHIS .

2) SHEET OF NOTEPAPER LEFT FLOATING IN TOILET BY FUGITIVE. ORIGINAL EN ROUTE TO WX DOCUMENT SECTION/LAB. GRAPHIC OF WRITING FOLLOWS. GRAPHIC SPLIT TO LANGLEY, ATTN: BENSON – CRYPTOGRAPHY.

When the graphic appeared, rising like something peeping over the bottom edge of the screen, it was this:

$$C_{33}H_{36}I \; L \; T \; O_6 \; N_4$$

The soft double beep of the computer terminal did not wake Crawford, but three minutes later the telephone did. It was Jerry Burroughs at the National Crime Information Center hotline.

'See your screen, Jack?'

'Just a second,' Crawford said. 'Yeah, okay.'

'The lab's got it already, Jack. The drawing Lecter left in the john. The numbers between the letters in Chilton's name, it's biochemistry – $C_{33}H_{36}N_4O_4$– it's the formula for a pigment in human bile called bilirubin. Lab advises it's a chief coloring agent in shit.'

'Balls.'

'You were right about Lecter, Jack. He was just jerking them around. Too bad for Senator Martin. Lab says bilirubin's just about exactly the color of Chilton's hair. Asylum humor, they call it. Did you see Chilton on the six o'clock news?'

'No.'

'Marilyn Sutter saw it upstairs. Chilton was blowing off about "The Search for Billy Rubin." Then he went to dinner with a television reporter. That's where he was when Lecter took a walk. What a pluperfect asshole.'

'Lecter told Starling to "bear in mind" that Chilton didn't have a medical degree,' Crawford said.

'Yeah I saw it in the summary. I think Chilton tried to fuck Starling's what I think, and she sawed him off at the knees. He may be dumb but he ain't blind. How is the kid?'

'Okay, I think. Worn down.'

'Think Lecter was jerking her off too?'

'Maybe. We'll stay with it, though. I don't know what the clinics are doing, I keep thinking I should've gone after the records in court. I hate to have to depend on them. Midmorning, if we haven't heard anything, we'll go the court route.'

'Say, Jack . . . you got some people outside that know what Lecter looks like, right?'

'Sure.'

'Don't you know he's laughing somewhere.'

'Maybe not for long,' Crawford said.

Chapter Forty-three

Dr Hannibal Lecter stood at the registration desk of the elegant Marcus Hotel in St Louis. He wore a brown hat and a raincoat buttoned to the neck. A neat surgical bandage covered his nose and cheeks.

He signed the register 'Lloyd Wyman,' a signature he had practiced in Wyman's car.

'How will you be paying, Mr Wyman?' the clerk said.

'American Express.' Dr Lecter handed the man Lloyd Wyman's credit card.

Soft piano music came from the lounge. At the bar Dr Lecter could see two people with bandages across their noses. A middleaged couple crossed to the elevators, humming a Cole Porter tune. The woman wore a gauze patch over her eye.

The clerk finished making the credit card impression. 'You do know, Mr Wyman, you're entitled to use the hospital garage.'

'Yes, thank you,' Dr Lecter said. He had already parked Wyman's car in the garage, with Wyman in the trunk.

The bellman who carried Wyman's bags to the small suite got one of Wyman's five-dollar bills in compensation.

Dr Lecter ordered a drink and a sandwich and relaxed with a long shower.

The suite seemed enormous to Dr Lecter after his long confinement. He enjoyed going to and fro in his suite and walking up and down in it.

From his windows he could see across the street the Myron and Sadie Fleischer Pavilion of St Louis City Hospital, housing one of the world's foremost centers for craniofacial surgery.

Dr Lecter's visage was too well known for him to be able to take advantage of the plastic surgeons here, but it was one place in the world where he could walk around with a bandage on his face without exciting interest.

He had stayed here once before, years ago, when he was doing psychiatric research in the superb Robert J. Brockman Memorial Library.

Heady to have a window, several windows. He stood at his windows in the dark, watching the car lights move across the MacArthur Bridge and savoring his drink. He was pleasantly fatigued by the five-hour drive from Memphis.

The only real rush of the evening had been in the underground garage at Memphis International Airport. Cleaning up with cotton pads and alcohol and distilled water in the back of the parked ambulance was not at all convenient. Once he was in the attendant's whites, it was just a matter of catching a single traveler in a deserted aisle of long-term parking in the great garage. The man obligingly leaned into the trunk of his car for his sample case, and never saw Dr Lecter come up behind him.

Dr Lecter wondered if the police believed he was fool enough to fly from the airport.

The only problem on the drive to St Louis was finding the lights, the dimmers, and the wipers in the foreign car, as Dr Lecter was unfamiliar with stalk controls beside the steering wheel.

Tomorrow he would shop for things he needed, hair bleach, barbering supplies, a sunlamp, and there were other, prescription, items that he would obtain to make some immediate changes in his appearance. When it was convenient, he would move on.

There was no reason to hurry.

Chapter Forty-four

Ardelia Mapp was in her usual position, propped up in bed with a book. She was listening to all-news radio. She turned it off when Clarice Starling trudged in. Looking into Starling's drawn face, blessedly she didn't ask anything except, 'Want some tea?'

When she was studying, Mapp drank a beverage she brewed of mixed loose leaves her grandmother sent her, which she called 'Smart People's Tea.'

Of the two brightest people Starling knew, one was also the steadiest person she knew and the other was the most frightening. Starling hoped that gave her some balance in her acquaintance.

'You were lucky to miss today,' Mapp said. 'That damn Kim Won ran us right into the *ground*. I'm not lying. I believe they must have more gravity in Korea than we do. Then they come over here and get *light*, see, get jobs teaching PE because it's not any work for them . . . John Brigham came by.'

'When?'

'Tonight, a little while ago. Wanted to know if you were back yet. He had his hair slicked down . Shifted around like a freshman in the lobby. We had a little talk. He said if you're behind and we need to jam instead of shoot during the range period the next couple of days, he'll open up the range this weekend and let us make it up. I said I'd let him know. He's a nice man.'

'Yeah, he is.'

'Did you know he wants you to shoot against the DEA and Customs in the interservice match?'

'Nope.'

'Not the Women's. The Open. Next question: Do you know the Fourth Amendment stuff for Friday?'

'A lot of it I do.'

'Okay, what's *Chimel versus California?*'

'Searches in secondary schools.'

'What *about* school searches?'

'I don't know. '

'It's the "immediate reach" concept. Who was *Schneckloth?*'

'Hell, I don't know.'

'*Schneckloth versus Bustamonte.*'

'Is it the reasonable expectation of privacy?'

'Boo to you. Expectation of privacy is the *Katz* principle. *Sckneckloth is* consent to search. I can see we've got to jam on the books, my girl. I've got the notes.'

'Not tonight.'

'No. But tomorrow you'll wake up with your mind fertile and ignorant, and then we'll begin to plant the harvest for Friday. Starling, Brigham said – he's not supposed to tell, so I promised – he said you'll beat the hearing. He thinks that signifying son of a bitch Krendler won't remember you two days from now. Your grades are good, we'll knock this stuff out easy.' Mapp studied Starling's tired face. 'You did the best anybody could for that poor soul, Starling. You stuck your neck out for her and you got your butt kicked for her and you moved things along. You deserve a chance yourself. Why don't you go ahead and crash? I'm fixing to shut this down myself.'

'Ardelia. Thanks.'

And after the lights were out.

'Starling?'

'Yeah?'

'Who do you think's prettiest, Brigham or Hot Bobby Lowrance?'

'That's a hard one.'

'Brigham's got a tattoo on his shoulder, I could see it through his shirt. What does it say?'

'I wouldn't have any idea.'

'Will you let me know soon as you find out?'

'Probably not.'

'I told you about Hot Bobby's python briefs.'

'You just saw 'em through the window when he was lifting weights.'

'Did Gracie tell you that? That girl's mouth is gonna –'

Starling was asleep.

Chapter Forty-five

Shortly before 3:00 A.M., Crawford, dozing beside his wife, came awake. There was a catch in Bella's breathing and she had stirred on her bed. He sat up and took her hand.

'Bella?'

She took a deep breath and let it out. Her eyes were open for the first time in days. Crawford put his face close before hers, but he didn't think she could see him.

'Bella, I love you, kid,' he said in case she could hear.

Fear brushed the walls of his chest, circling inside him like a bat in a house. Then he got hold of it.

He wanted to get something for her, anything, but he did not want her to feel him let go of her hand.

He put his ear to her chest. He heard a soft beat, a flutter, and then her heart stopped. There was nothing to hear, there was only a curious cool rushing. He didn't know if the sound was in her chest or only in his ears.

'God bless you and keep you with Him . . . and with your folks,' Crawford said, words he wanted to be true.

He gathered her to him on the bed, sitting against the headboard, held her to his chest while her brain died. His chin pushed back the scarf from the remnants of her hair. He did not cry. He had done all that.

Crawford changed her into her favorite, her best bed gown and sat for a while beside the high bed, holding her hand against his cheek. It was a square, clever hand, marked with a lifetime of gardening, marked by IV needles now.

When she came in from the garden, her hands smelled like thyme.

('Think about it like egg white on your fingers,' the girls at school had counseled Bella about sex. She and Crawford had joked about it in bed, years ago, years later, last year. Don't think about that, think about the good stuff, the pure stuff. That *was* the pure stuff. She wore a round hat and white gloves and going up in the elevator the first time he whistled a dramatic arrangement of 'Begin the Beguine.' In the room she teased him that he had the cluttered pockets of a boy.)

Crawford tried going into the next room – he still could turn when he wanted to and see her through the open door, composed in the warm light of the bedside lamp. He was waiting for her body to become a ceremonial object apart from him, separate from the person he had held upon the bed and separate from the life's companion he held now in his mind. So he could call them to come for her.

His empty hands hanging palms forward at his sides, he stood at the window looking to the empty east. He did not look for dawn; east was only the way the window faced.

Chapter Forty-six

'Ready, Precious?'

Jame Gumb was propped against the headboard of his bed and very comfortable, the little dog curled up warm on his tummy.

Mr Gumb had just washed his hair and he had a towel wrapped around his head. He rummaged in the sheets, found the remote control for his VCR, and pushed the play button.

He had composed his program from two pieces of videotape copied onto one cassette. He watched it every day when he was making vital preparations, and he always watched it just before he harvested a hide.

The first tape was from scratchy film of Movietone News, a black-and-white newsreel from 1948. It was the quarter-finals of the Miss Sacramento contest, a preliminary event on the long road to the Miss America pageant in Atlantic City.

This was the swimsuit competition, and all the girls carried flowers as they came in a file to the stairs and mounted to the stage.

Mr Gumb's poodle had been through this many times and she squinted her eyes when she heard the music, knowing she'd be squeezed.

The beauty contestants looked very World War II. They wore Rose Marie Reid swimsuits, and some of the faces were lovely. Their legs were nicely shaped too, some of them, but they lacked muscle tone and seemed to lap a little at the knee.

Gumb squeezed the poodle.

'Precious, here she comes, hereshecomes hereshecomes!'

And here she came, approaching the stairs in her white swimsuit, with a radiant smile for the young man who assisted at the stairs, then quick on her high heels away, the camera following the backs of her thighs: Mom. There was Mom.

Mr Gumb didn't have to touch his remote control, he'd done it all when he dubbed this copy. In reverse, here she came backward, backward down the stairs, took back her smile from the young man, backed up the aisle, now forward again, and back and forward, forward and back.

When she smiled at the young man, Gumb smiled too.

There was one more shot of her in a group, but it always blurred in freeze-frame. Better just to run it at speed and get the glimpse. Mom was with the other girls, congratulating the winners.

The next item he'd taped off cable television in a motel in Chicago – he'd had to rush out and buy a VCR and stay an extra night to get it. This was the loop film they run on seedy cable channels late at night as background for the sex ads that crawl up the screen in print. The loops are made of junk film, fairly innocuous naughty movies from the forties and fifties, and there was nudist camp volleyball and the less explicit parts of thirties sex movies where the male actors wore false noses and still had their socks on. The sound was any music at all. Right now it was 'The Look of Love,' totally out of sync with the sprightly action.

There was nothing Mr Gumb could do about the ads crawling up the screen. He just had to put up with them.

Here it is, an outdoor pool – in California, judging from the foliage. Good pool furniture, everything very fifties. Naked swimming, some graceful girls. A few of them might have appeared in a couple of B-pictures. Sprightly and bouncing, they climbed out of the pool and ran, much faster than the music, to the ladder of a water slide, climbed up – down they came, Wheeee! Breasts lifting as they plunged down the slide, laughing, legs out straight, Splash!

Here came Mom. Here she came, climbing out of the pool behind the girl with the curly hair. Her face was partly covered by a crawl ad from Sinderella, a sex boutique, but here you saw her going away, and there she went up the ladder all shiny and wet, wonderfully buxom and supple, with a small cesarean scar, and down the slide, Wheeee! So beautiful, and even if he couldn't see her face, Mr Gumb knew in his heart it was Mom, filmed after the last time in his life that he ever got to really see her. Except in his mind, of course.

The scene switched to a filmed ad for a marital aid and abruptly ended.

The poodle squinted her eyes two seconds before Mr Gumb hugged her tight.

'Oh, Precious. Come here to Mommy. Mommy's gonna be *so* beautiful.'

Much to do, much to do, much to do to get ready for tomorrow.

He could never hear it from the kitchen even at the top of its voice, thank goodness, but he could hear it on the stairs as he went down to the basement. He had hoped it would be quiet and asleep. The poodle, riding beneath his arm, growled back at the sounds from the pit.

'*You've* been raised better than that,' he said into the fur on the back of her head.

The oubliette room is through a door to the left at the bottom of the stairs. He didn't spare it a glance, nor did he listen to the words from the pit – as far as he was concerned, they bore not the slightest resemblance to English.

Mr Gumb turned right into the workroom, put the poodle down and turned on the lights. A few moths fluttered and lit harmlessly on the wire mesh covering the ceiling lights.

Mr Gumb was meticulous in the workroom. He always mixed his fresh solutions in stainless steel, never in aluminum.

He had learned to do everything well ahead of time. As he worked he admonished himself:

You have to be orderly, you have to be precise, you have to be expeditious, because the problems are formidable.

The human skin is heavy – sixteen to eighteen percent of body weight – and slippery. An entire hide is hard to handle and easy to drop when it's still wet. Time is important too; skin begins to shrink immediately after it has been harvested, most notably from young adults, whose skin is tightest to begin with.

Add to that the fact that the skin is not perfectly elastic, even in the young. If you stretch it, it never regains its original proportions. Stitch something perfectly smooth, then pull it too hard over a tailor's ham, and it bulges and puckers. Sitting at the machine and crying your eyes out won't remove one pucker. Then there are the cleavage lines, and you'd better know where they are. Skin doesn't stretch the same amount in all directions before the collagen bundles deform and the fibers tear; pull the wrong way, and you get a stretch mark.

Green material is simply impossible to work with. Much experimentation went into this, along with much heartbreak, before Mr Gumb got it right.

In the end he found the old ways were best. His procedures were these: First he soaked his items in the aquariums, in vegetable extracts developed by the Native Americans – all-natural substances that contain no mineral salts whatsoever. Then he used the method that produced the matchless butter-soft buckskin of the New World – classic brain tanning. The Native Americans believed that each animal has just enough brains to tan its own hide. Mr Gumb knew that this was not true and long ago had quit trying it, even with the largest-brained primate. He had a freezer full of beef brains now, so he never ran short.

The problems of processing the material he could manage; practice had made him near perfect.

Difficult structural problems remained, but he was especially well qualified to solve them, too.

The workroom opened into a basement corridor leading to a disused bath where Mr Gumb stored his hoisting tackle and his timepiece, and on to the studio and the vast black warren beyond.

He opened his studio door to brilliant light – floodlights and incandescent tubes, color-corrected to daylight, were fastened to ceiling beams. Mannequins posed on a raised floor of pickled oak. All were partly clad, some in leather and some in muslin patterns for leather garments. Eight mannequins were doubled in the two mirrored walls – good plate mirror too, not tiles. A makeup table held cosmetics, several wig forms, and wigs. This was the brightest of studios, all white and blond oak.

The mannequins wore commercial work in progress, dramatic Armani knockoffs mostly, in fine black cabretta leather, all rollpleats and pointed shoulders and breastplates.

The third wall was taken up by a large worktable, two commercial sewing machines, two dressmaker's forms, and a tailor's form cast from the very torso of Jame Gumb.

Against the fourth wall, dominating this bright room, was a great black armoire in Chinese lacquer that rose almost to the eight-foot ceiling. It was old and the designs on it had faded; a few gold scales remained where a dragon was, his white eye still clear and staring, and here was the red tongue of another dragon whose body had faded away. The lacquer beneath them remained intact, though it was crackled.

The armoire, immense and deep, had nothing to do with commercial work. It contained on forms and hangers the Special Things, and its doors were closed.

The little dog lapped from her water bowl in the corner and lay down between the feet of a mannequin, her eyes on Mr Gumb.

He had been working on a leather jacket. He needed to finish it – he'd meant to get everything out of the way, but he was in a creative fever now and his own muslin fitting garment didn't satisfy him yet.

Mr Gumb had progressed in tailoring far beyond what the California Department of Corrections had taught him in his youth, but this was a true challenge. Even working delicate cabretta leather does not prepare you for really fine work.

Here he had two muslin fitting garments, like white waistcoats, one his exact size and one he had made from measurements he took while Catherine Baker Martin was still unconscious. When he put the smaller one on his tailor's form, the problems were apparent. She was a big girl, and wonderfully proportioned, but she wasn't as big as Mr Gumb, and not nearly so broad across the back.

His ideal was a seamless garment. This was not possible. He was determined, though, that the bodice front be absolutely seamless and without blemish. This meant all figure corrections had to be made on the back. Very difficult. He'd already discarded one fitting muslin and started over. With judicious stretching, he could get by with two underarm darts – not French darts, but vertical inset darts, apexes down. Two waist darts also in the back, just inside his kidneys. He was used to working with only a tiny seam allowance.

His considerations went beyond the visual aspects to the tactile; it was not inconceivable that an attractive person might be hugged.

Mr Gumb sprinkled talc lightly on his hands and embraced the tailor's form of his body in a natural, comfortable hug.

'Give me a kiss,' he said playfully to the empty air where the head should be. 'Not *you*, silly,' he told the little dog, when she raised her ears.

Gumb caressed the back of the form at the natural reach of his arms. Then he walked behind it to consider the powder marks. Nobody wanted to feel a seam. In an embrace, though, the hands lap over the center of the back. Also, he reasoned, we are accustomed to the center line of a spine. It is not as jarring as an asymmetry in our bodies. Shoulder seams were definitely out, then. A center dart at the top was the answer, apex a little above the center of the shoulder blades. He could use the same seam to anchor the stout yoke built into the lining to provide support. Lycra panels beneath plackets on both sides – he must remember to get the Lycra – and a Velcro closure beneath the placket on the right. He thought about those marvelous Charles James gowns where the seams were staggered to lie perfectly flat.

The dart in back would be covered by his hair, or rather the hair he would have soon.

Mr Gumb slipped the muslin off the dressmaker's form and started to work.

The sewing machine was old and finely made, an ornate foot treadle machine that had been converted to electricity perhaps forty years ago. On the arm of the machine was painted in gold-leaf scroll 'I Never Tire, I

Serve.' The foot treadle remained operative, and Gumb started the machine with it for each series of stitches. For fine stitching, he preferred to work barefoot, rocking the treadle delicately with his meaty foot, gripping the front edge of it with his painted toes to prevent overruns. For a while there were only the sounds of the machine, and the little dog snoring, and the hiss of the steam pipes in the warm basement.

When he had finished inserting the darts in the muslin pattern garment, he tried it on in front of the mirrors. The little dog watched from the corner, her head cocked.

He needed to ease it a little under the arm holes. There were a few remaining problems with facings and interfacings. Otherwise it was so nice. It was supple, pliant, bouncy. He could see himself just running up the ladder of a water slide as fast as you please.

Mr Gumb played with the lights and his wigs for some dramatic effects and he tried a wonderful choker necklace of shells over the collar line. It would be stunning when he wore a décolleté gown or hostess pajamas over his new thorax.

It was so tempting to just go on with it now, to really get busy, but his eyes were tired. He wanted his hands to be absolutely steady, too, and he just wasn't up for the noise. Patiently he picked out the stitches and laid out the pieces. A perfect pattern to cut by.

'Tomorrow, Precious,' he told the little dog as he set the beef brains out to thaw. 'We'll do it first thing tomooooooorooow. Mommy's gonna be so *beautiful* !'

Chapter Forty-seven

Starling slept hard for five hours and woke in the pit of the night, driven awake by fear of the dream. She bit the corner of the sheet and pressed her palms over her ears, waiting to find out if she was truly awake and away from it. Silence and no lambs screaming. When she knew she was awake her heart slowed, but her feet would not stay still beneath the covers. In a moment her mind would race, she knew it.

It was a relief when a flush of hot anger rather than fear shot through her.

'Nuts,' she said, and put a foot out in the air.

In all the long day, when she had been disrupted by Chilton, insulted by Senator Martin, abandoned, and rebuked by Krendler, taunted by Dr Lecter and sickened by his bloody escape, and put off the job by Jack Crawford, there was one thing that stung the worst: being called a thief.

Senator Martin was a mother under extreme duress, and she was sick of policemen pawing her daughter's things. She hadn't meant it.

Still, the accusation stuck in Starling like a hot needle.

As a small child, Starling had been taught that thieving is the cheapest, most despicable act short of rape and murder for money. Some kinds of manslaughter were preferable to theft.

As a child in institutions where there were few prizes and many hungers, she had learned to hate a thief.

Lying in the dark, she faced another reason Senator Martin's implication bothered her so.

Starling knew what the malicious Dr Lecter would say, and it was true: she was afraid there was something tacky that Senator Martin saw in her, something cheap, something thieflike that Senator Martin reacted to. That Vanderbilt bitch.

Dr Lecter would relish pointing out that class resentment, the buried anger that comes with mother's milk, was a factor too. Starling gave away nothing to any Martin in education, intelligence, drive, and certainly physical appearance, but still it was there and she knew it.

Starling was an isolated member of a fierce tribe with no formal genealogy but the honors list and the penal register. Dispossessed in Scotland, starved out of Ireland, a lot of them were inclined to the dangerous trades. Many generic Starlings had been used up this way, had thumped on the bottom of narrow holes or slid off planks with a shot at their feet or were commended to glory with a cracked 'Taps' in the cold when everyone wanted to go home. A few may have been recalled tearily by the officers on regimental mess nights, the way a man in drink remembers a good bird dog. Faded names in a Bible.

None of them had been very smart, as far as Starling could tell, except for a great-aunt who wrote wonderfully in her diary until she got 'brain fever.'

They didn't steal, though.

School was the thing in America, don't you know, and the Starlings caught on to that. One of Starling's uncles had his junior college degree cut on his tombstone.

Starling had lived by schools, her weapon the competitive exam, for all the years when there was no place else for her to go.

She knew she could pull out of this. She could be what she had always been, ever since she'd learned how it works: she could be near the top of her class, approved, included, chosen, and not sent away.

It was a matter of working hard and being careful. Her grades would be good. The Korean couldn't kill her in PE. Her name would be engraved on the big plaque in the lobby, the 'Possible Board,' for extraordinary performance on the range.

In four weeks she would be a special agent of the Federal Bureau of Investigation.

Would she have to watch out for that fucking Krendler for the rest of her life?

In the presence of the Senator, he had wanted to wash his hands of her. Every time Starling thought about it, it stung. He wasn't positive that he would find evidence in the envelope. That was shocking. Picturing Krendler now in her mind, she saw him wearing Navy oxfords on his feet like the mayor, her father's boss, coming to collect the watchman's clock.

Worse, Jack Crawford in her mind seemed diminished. The man was under more strain than anyone should have to bear. He had sent her in to check out Raspail's car with no support or evidence of authority. Okay, she had asked to go under those terms – the trouble was a fluke. But Crawford had to know there'd be trouble when Senator Martin saw her in Memphis; there would have been trouble even if she hadn't found the fuck pictures.

Catherine Baker Martin lay in this same darkness that held her now. Starling had forgotten it for a moment while she thought about her own best interests.

Pictures of the past few days punished Starling for the lapse, flashed on her in sudden color, too much color, shocking color, the color that leaps out of black when lightning strikes at night.

It was Kimberly that haunted her now. Fat dead Kimberly who had her ears pierced trying to look pretty and saved to have her legs waxed. Kimberly with her hair gone. Kimberly her sister. Starling did not think Catherine Baker Martin would have much time for Kimberly. Now they were sisters under the skin. Kimberly lying in a funeral home full of state trooper buckaroos.

Starling couldn't look at it anymore. She tried to turn her face away as a swimmer turns to breathe.

All of Buffalo Bill's victims were women, his obsession was women, he lived to hunt women. Not one woman was hunting him full time. Not one woman investigator had looked at every one of his crimes.

Starling wondered if Crawford would have the nerve to use her as a technician when he had to go look at Catherine Martin. Bill would 'do her tomorrow,' Crawford predicted. *Do her. Do her. Do her.*

'*Fuck* this,' Starling said aloud and put her feet on the floor.

'You're over there corrupting a moron, aren't you, Starling?' Ardelia Mapp said. 'Sneaked him in here while I was asleep and now you're giving him instructions – don't think I don't hear you.'

'Sorry, Ardelia, I didn't –'

'You've got to be a lot more specific with 'em than that, Starling. You can't just say what *you* said. Corrupting morons is just like journalism, you've got to tell 'em *What, When, Where,* and *How.* I think *Why* gets self-explanatory as you go along.'

'Have you got any laundry?'

'I thought you said did I have any laundry.'

'Yep, I think I'll run a load. Whatcha got?'

'Just those sweats on the back of the door.'

'Okay. Shut your eyes, I'm gonna turn on the light for just a second.'

It was not the Fourth Amendment notes for her upcoming exam that she piled on top of the clothes basket and lugged down the hall to the laundry room.

She took the Buffalo Bill file, a four-inch-thick pile of hell and pain in a buff cover printed with ink the color of blood. With it was a hotline printout of her report on the Death's-head moth.

She'd have to give the file back tomorrow and, if she wanted this copy to be complete, sooner or later she had to insert her report. In the warm laundry room, in the washing machine's comforting chug, sh e took off the rubber bands that held the file together. She laid out the papers on the clothes-folding shelf and tried to do the insert without seeing any of the pictures, without thinking of what pictures might be added soon. The map was on top, that was fine. But there was handwriting on the map.

Dr Lecter's elegant script ran across the Great Lakes, and it said:

Clarice, does this *random* scattering of sites seem overdone to you? Doesn't it seem *desperately* random? Random past all possible convenience? Does it suggest to you the elaborations of a bad liar?

Ta,

Hannibal Lecter

P.S. Don't bother to flip through, there isn't anything else.

It took twenty minutes of page-turning to be sure there wasn't anything else.

Starling called the hotline from the pay phone in the hall and read the message to Burroughs. She wondered when Burroughs slept.

'I have to tell you, Starling, the market in Lecter information is way down,' Burroughs said. 'Did Jack call you about Billy Rubin?'

'No.'

She leaned against the wall with her eyes closed while he described Dr Lecter's joke.

'I don't know,' he said at last. 'Jack says they'll go on with the sex-change clinics, but how hard? If you look at the information in the computer, the way the field entries are styled, you can see that all the Lecter information, yours and the stuff from Memphis, has special prefixes. All the Baltimore stuff or all the Memphis stuff or both can be knocked out of consideration with one button. I think Justice wants to push the button on all of it. I got a memo here suggesting the bug in Klaus's throat was, let's see, "flotsam."'

'You'll punch this up for Mr Crawford, though,' Starling said.

'Sure, I'll put it on his screen, but we're not calling him right now. You shouldn't either. Bella died a little while ago.'

'Oh,' Starling said.

'Listen, on the bright side, our guys in Baltimore took a look at Lecter's cell in the asylum. That orderly, Barney, helped out. They got brass grindings off a bolt head in Lecter's cot where he made his handcuff key. Hang in there, kid. You're gonna come out smelling like a rose.'

'Thank you, Mr Burroughs. Good night.'

Smelling like a rose. Putting Vicks VapoRub under her nostrils.

Daylight coming on the last day of Catherine Martin's life.

What could Dr Lecter mean?

There was no knowing what Dr Lecter knew. When she first gave him the file, she expected him to enjoy the pictures and use the file as a prop while he told her what he already knew about Buffalo Bill.

Maybe he was always lying to her, just as he lied to Senator Martin.

Maybe he didn't know or understand anything about Buffalo Bill.

He sees very clearly – he damn sure sees through me. It's hard to accept that someone can understand you without wishing you well. At Starling's age it hadn't happened to her much.

Desperately random, Dr Lecter said.

Starling and Crawford and everyone else had stared at the map with its dots marking the abductions and body dumps. It had looked to Starling like a black constellation with a date beside each star, and she knew Behavioral Science had once tried imposing zodiac signs on the map without result.

If Dr Lecter was reading for recreation, why would he fool with the map? She could see him flipping through the report making fun of the prose style of some of the contributors.

There was no pattern in the abductions and body dumps, no relationships of convenience, no coordination in time with any known business conventions, any spate of burglaries or clothes-line thefts or other fetish-oriented crimes.

Back in the laundry room, with the dryer spinning, Starling walked her fingers over the map. Here an abduction, there the dump. Here the second abduction, there the dump. Here the third and – But are these dates backward or, no, the second body was discovered first.

That fact was recorded, unremarked, in smudged ink beside the location on the map. The body of the second woman abducted was found first, floating in the Wabash River in downtown Lafayette, Indiana, just below Interstate 65.

The first young woman reported missing was taken from Belvedere, Ohio, near Columbus, and found much later in the Blackwater River in Missouri, outside of Lone Jack. The body was weighted. No others were weighted.

The body of the first victim was sunk in water in a remote area. The second was dumped in a river upstream from a city, where quick discovery was certain.

Why?

The one he started with was well hidden, the second one, not.

Why?

What does 'desperately random' mean?

The first, first. What did Dr Lecter say about 'first'? What did anything mean that Dr Lecter said?

Starling looked at the notes she had scribbled on the airplane from Memphis.

Dr Lecter said there was enough in the file to locate the killer. 'Simplicity,' he said. What about 'first,' where was first? Here – 'First Principles' were important. 'First Principles' sounded like pretentious bullshit when he said it.

What does he do, Clarice? What is the first and principal thing he does, what need does he serve by killing? He covets. How do we begin to covet? We begin by coveting what we see every day.

It was easier to think about Dr Lecter's statements when she wasn't feeling his eyes on her skin. It was easier here in the safe heart of Quantico.

If we begin to covet by coveting what we see every day, did Buffalo Bill surprise himself when he killed the first one? Did he do someone close around him? Is that why he hid the first body well, and the second one poorly? Did he abduct the second one far from home and dump her where she'd be found quickly because he wanted to establish early the belief that the abduction sites were random?

When Starling thought of the victims, Kimberly Emberg came first to mind because she had seen Kimberly dead and, in a sense, had taken Kimberly's part.

Here was the first one. Fredrica Bimmel, twenty-two, Belvedere, Ohio. There were two photos. In her yearbook picture she looked large and plain, with good thick hair and a good complexion. In the second photo, taken at the Kansas City morgue, she looked like nothing human.

Starling called Burroughs again. He was sounding a little hoarse by now, but he listened.

'So what are you saying, Starling?'

'Maybe he lives in Belvedere, Ohio, where the first victim lived. Maybe he saw her every day, and he killed her sort of spontaneously. Maybe he just meant to . . . give her a 7-Up and talk about the choir. So he did a good job of hiding the body and then he grabbed another one far from home. He didn't hide that one very well, so it would be found first and the attention would be directed away from him. You know how much attention a missing-person report gets, it gets zip until the body's found.'

'Starling, the return's better where the trail is fresh, people remember better, witnesses –'

'That's what I'm saying. He *knows* that.'

'For instance, you won't be able to sneeze today without spraying a cop in that last one's hometown – Kimberly Emberg from Detroit. Lot of interest in Kimberly Emberg all of a sudden since little Martin disappeared. All of a sudden they're working the hell out of it. You never heard me say that.'

'Will you put it up for Mr Crawford, about the first town?'

'Sure. Hell, I'll put it on the hotline for everybody. I'm not saying it's bad thinking, Starling, but the town was picked over pretty good as soon as the woman – what's her name, Bimmel, is it? – as soon as Bimmel was identified. The Columbus office worked Belvedere, and so did a lot of locals. You've got it all there. You're not gonna raise much interest in Belvedere or any other theory of Dr Lecter's this morning.'

'All he –'

'Starling, we're sending a gift to UNICEF for Bella. You want in, I'll put your name on the card.'

'Sure, thanks, Mr Burroughs.'

Starling got the clothes out of the dryer. The warm laundry felt good and smelled good. She hugged the warm laundry close to her chest.

Her mother with an armload of sheets.

Today is the last day of Catherine's life.

The black-and-white crow stole from the cart. She couldn't be outside to shoo it and in the room too.

Today is the last day of Catherine's life.

Her father used an arm signal instead of the blinkers when he turned his pickup into the driveway. Playing in the yard, she thought with his big arm he showed the pickup where to turn, grandly directed it to turn.

When Starling decided what she would do, a few tears came. She put her face in the warm laundry.

Chapter Forty-eight

Crawford came out of the funeral home and looked up and down the street for Jeff with the car. Instead he saw Clarice Starling waiting under the awning, dressed in a dark suit, looking real in the light.

'Send me,' she said.

Crawford had just picked out his wife's coffin and he carried in a paper sack a pair of her shoes he had mistakenly brought. He collected himself.

'Forgive me,' Starling said. 'I wouldn't come now if there were any other time. Send me.'

Crawford jammed his hands in his pockets, turned his neck in his collar until it popped. His eyes were bright, maybe dangerous. 'Send you where?'

'You sent me to get a feel for Catherine Martin – let me go to the others. All we've got left is to find out how he hunts. How he finds them, how he picks them. I'm as good as anybody you've got at the cop stuff, better at some things. The victims are all women and there aren't any women working this. I can walk in a woman's room and know three times as much about her as a man would know, and *you* know that's a fact. Send me.'

'You ready to accept a recycle?'

'Yes.'

'Six months of your life, probably.'

She didn't say anything.

Crawford stubbed at the grass with his toe. He looked up at her, at the prairie distance in her eyes. She had backbone, like Bella. 'Who would you start with?'

'The first one, Fredrica Bimmel, Belvedere, Ohio.'

'Not Kimberly Emberg, the one you saw?'

'*He* didn't start with her.' *Mention Lecter? No. He'd see it on the hotline.*

'Emberg would be the *emotional* choice, wouldn't she, Starling? Travel's by reimbursement. Got any money?' The banks wouldn't open for an hour.

'I've got some left on my Visa.'

Crawford dug in his pockets. He gave her three hundred dollars cash and a personal check.

'Go, Starling. Just to the first one. Post the hotline. Call me.'

She raised her hand to him. She didn't touch his face or his hand, there didn't seem to be any place to touch, and she turned and ran for the Pinto.

Crawford patted his pockets as she drove away. He had given her the last cent he had with him.

'Baby needs a new pair of shoes,' he said. 'My baby doesn't need any shoes.' He was crying in the middle of the sidewalk, sheets of tears on his face, a Section Chief of the FBI, silly now.

Jeff from the car saw his cheeks shine and backed into an alley where Crawford couldn't see him. Jeff got out of the car. He lit a cigarette and smoked furiously. As his gift to Crawford he would dawdle until Crawford was dried off and pissed off and justified in chewing him out.

Chapter Forty-nine

On the morning of the fourth day, Mr Gumb was ready to harvest the hide.

He came in from shopping with the last things he needed, and it was hard to keep from running down the basement stairs. In the studio he unpacked his shopping bags, new bias seam-binding, panels of stretchy Lycra to go under the plackets, a box of kosher salt. He had forgotten nothing.

In the workroom, he laid out his knives on a clean towel beside the long sinks. The knives were four: a sway-backed skinning-knife, a delicate drop-point caper that perfectly followed the curve of the index finger in close places, a scalpel for the closest work, and a World War 1-era bayonet. The rolled edge of the bayonet is the finest tool for fleshing a hide without tearing it.

In addition he had a Strycker autopsy saw, which he hardly ever used and regretted buying.

Now he greased the head of a wig stand, packed coarse salt over the grease and set the stand in a shallow drip pan. Playfully he tweaked the nose on the face of the wig stand and blew it a kiss.

It was hard to behave in a responsible manner – he wanted to fly about the room like Danny Kaye. He laughed and blew a moth away from his face with a gentle puff of air.

Time to start the aquarium pumps in his fresh tanks of solution. Oh, was there a nice chrysalis buried in the humus in the cage? He poked with his finger. Yes, there was.

The pistol, now.

The problem of killing this one had perplexed Mr Gumb for days. Hanging her was out because he didn't want the pectoral mottling, and besides, he couldn't risk the knot tearing her behind the ear.

Mr Gumb had learned from each of his previous efforts, sometimes painfully. He was determined to avoid some of the nightmares he'd gone through before. One cardinal principle: no matter how weak from hunger or faint with fright, they always fought you when they saw the apparatus.

He had in the past hunted young women through the blacked-out basement using his infrared goggles and light, and it was wonderful to do, watching them feel their way around, seeing them try to scrunch into corners. He liked to hunt them with the pistol. He liked to use the pistol. Always they became disoriented, lost their balance, ran into things. He could stand in absolute darkness with his goggles on, wait until they took their hands down from their faces, and shoot them right in the head. Or in the legs first, below the knee so they could still crawl.

That was childish and a waste. They were useless afterward and he had quit doing it altogether.

In his current project, he had offered showers upstairs to the first three, before he booted them down the staircase with a noose around their necks – no problem. But the fourth had been a disaster. He'd had to use the pistol in the bathroom and it had taken an hour to clean up. He thought about the girl, wet, goosebumps on her, and how she shivered when he cocked the pistol. He liked to cock it, snick snick, one big bang and no more racket.

He liked his pistol, and well he should, because it was a very handsome piece, a stainless steel Colt Python with a six-inch barrel. All Python actions are tuned at the Colt custom shop, and this one was a pleasure to feel. He cocked it now and squeezed it off, catching the hammer with his thumb. He loaded the Python and put it on the workroom counter.

Mr Gumb wanted very much to offer this one a shampoo, because he wanted to watch it comb out the hair. He could learn much for his own grooming about how the hair lay on the head. But this one was tall and probably strong. This one was too rare to risk having to waste the whole thing with gunshot wounds.

No, he'd get his hoisting tackle from the bathroom, offer her a bath, and when she had put herself securely in the hoisting sling he'd bring her halfway up the shaft of the oubliette and shoot her several times low in the spine. When she lost consciousness he could do the rest with chloroform.

That's it. He'd go upstairs now and get out of his clothes. He'd wake up Precious and watch his video with her and then go to work, naked in the warm basement, naked as the day he was born.

He felt almost giddy going up the stairs. Quickly out of his clothes and into his robe. He plugged in his videocassette.

'Precious, come on, Precious. Busybusy day. Come on, Sweetheart.' He'd have to shut her up here in the upstairs bedroom while he got through with the noisy part in the basement – she hated the noise and got terribly upset. To keep her occupied, he'd gotten her a whole box of Chew-eez while he was out shopping.

'Precious.' When she didn't come, he called in the hall, 'Precious!' and then in the kitchen, and in the basement, 'Precious!' When he called at the door of the oubliette room, he got an answer:

'She's down here, you son of a bitch,' Catherine Martin said.

Mr Gumb sickened all over in a plunge of fear for Precious. Then rage tightened him again and, fists against the sides of his head, he pressed his forehead into the doorframe and tried to get hold of himself. One sound between a retch and a groan escaped him and the little dog answered with a yip.

He went to the workroom and got his pistol.

The string to the sanitation bucket was broken. He still wasn't sure how she'd done it. Last time the string was broken, he'd assumed she'd broken it in an absurd attempt to climb. They had tried to climb it before – they had done every fool thing imaginable.

He leaned over the opening, his voice carefully controlled.

'Precious, are you all right? Answer me.'

Catherine pinched the dog's plump behind. It yipped and paid her back with a nip on the arm.

'How's that?' Catherine said.

It seemed very unnatural to Mr Gumb to speak to Catherine in this way, but he overcame his distaste.

'I'll lower a basket. You'll put her in it.'

'You'll lower a telephone or I'll have to break her neck. I don't want to hurt you, I don't want to hurt this little dog. Just give me the telephone.'

Mr Gumb brought the pistol up. Catherine saw the muzzle extending past the light. She crouched, holding the dog above her, weaving it between her and the gun. She heard him cock the pistol.

'You shoot motherfucker you better kill me quick or I'll break her fucking neck. I swear to God.'

She put the dog under her arm, put her hand around its muzzle, raised its head. 'Back off, you son of a bitch.' The little dog whined. The gun withdrew.

Catherine brushed the hair back from her wet forehead with her free hand. 'I didn't mean to insult you,' she said. 'Just lower me a phone. I want a live phone. You can go away, I don't care about you, I never saw you. I'll take good care of Precious.'

'No.'

'I'll see she has everything. Think about her welfare, not just yourself. You shoot in here, she'll be deaf whatever happens. All I want's a live telephone. Get a long extension, get five or six and clip them together – they come with the connections on the ends and lower it down here. I'd air-freight you the dog anywhere. My family has dogs. My mother loves dogs. You can run, I don't care what you do.'

'You won't get any more water, you've had your last water.'

'She won't get any either, and I won't give her any from my water bottle. I'm sorry to tell you, I think her leg's broken.' This was a lie – the little dog, along with the baited bucket, had fallen onto Catherine and it was Catherine who suffered a scratched cheek from the dog's scrabbling claws. She couldn't put it down or he'd see it didn't limp. 'She's in pain. Her leg's all crooked and she's trying to lick it. It just makes me sick,' Catherine lied. 'I've got to get her to a vet.'

Mr Gumb's groan of rage and anguish made the little dog cry. 'You think *she's* in pain,' Mr Gumb said. 'You don't know what pain is. You hurt her and I'll scald you.'

When she heard him pounding up the stairs Catherine Martin sat down, shaken by gross jerks in her arms and legs. She couldn't hold the dog, she couldn't hold her water, she couldn't hold anything.

When the little dog climbed into her lap she hugged it, grateful for the warmth.

Chapter Fifty

Feathers rode on the thick brown water, curled feathers blown from the coops, carried on breaths of air that shivered the skin of the river.

The houses on Fell Street, Fredrica Bimmel's street, were termed waterfront on the weathered realtors' signs because their backyards ended at a slough, a backwater of the Licking River in Belvedere, Ohio, a Rust Belt town of 112,000, east of Columbus.

It was a shabby neighborhood of big, old houses. A few of them had been bought cheap by young couples and renovated with Sears Best enamel, making the rest of the houses look worse. The Bimmel house had not been renovated.

Clarice Starling stood for a moment in Fredrica's backyard looking at the feathers on the water, her hands deep in the pockets of her trenchcoat. There was some rotten snow in the reeds, blue beneath the blue sky on this mild winter day.

Behind her Starling could hear Fredrica's father hammering in the city of pigeon coops, the Orvieto of pigeon coops rising from the water's edge and reaching almost to the house. She hadn't seen Mr Bimmel yet. The neighbors said he was there. Their faces were closed when they said it.

Starling was having some trouble with herself. At that moment in the night when she knew she had to leave the Academy to hunt Buffalo Bill, a lot of extraneous noises had stopped. She felt a pure new silence in the center of her mind, and a calm there. In a different place, down the front of her, she felt in flashes that she was a truant and a fool.

The petty annoyances of the morning hadn't touched her – not the gymnasium stink of the airplane to Columbus, not the confusion and ineptitude at the rental-car counter. She'd snapped at the car clerk to make him move, but she hadn't felt anything.

Starling had paid a high price for this time and she meant to use it as she thought best. Her time could be up at any moment, if Crawford was overruled and they pulled her credentials.

She should hurry, but to think about why, to dwell on Catherine's plight on this final day, would be to waste the day entirely. To think of her in real time, being processed at this moment as Kimberly Emberg and Fredrica Bimmel had been processed, would jam all other thought.

The breeze fell off, the water still as death. Near her feet a curled feather spun on the surface tension. Hang on, Catherine.

Starling caught her lip between her teeth. If he shot her, she hoped he'd do a competent job of it.

Teach us to care and not to care.

Teach us to be still.

She turned to the leaning stack of coops and followed a path of boards laid on the mud between them, toward the sound of hammering. The hundreds of pigeons were of all sizes and colors; there were tall knock-kneed ones and pouters with their chests stuck out. Eyes bright, heads jerking as they paced, the birds spread their wings in the pale sun and made pleasant sounds as she passed.

Fredrica's father, Gustav Bimmel, was a tall man, flat and wide-hipped with red-rimmed eyes of watery blue. A knit cap was pulled down to his eyebrows. He was building another coop on sawhorses in front of his work shed. Starling smelled vodka on his breath as he squinted at her identification.

'I don't know nothing new to tell you,' he said. 'The policemen come back here night before last. They went back over my statement with me again. Read it back to me. "Is that right? Is that right?" I told him, I said hell yes, if that wasn't right I wouldn't have told you in the first place.'

'I'm trying to get an idea where the – get an idea where the kidnapper might have seen Fredrica, Mr Bimmel. Where he might have spotted her and decided to take her away.'

'She went into Columbus on the bus to see about a job at that store there. The police said she got to the interview all right. She never came home. We don't know where else she went that day. The FBI got her Master Charge slips, but there wasn't nothing for that day. You know all that, don't you?'

'About the credit card, yes sir, I do. Mr Bimmel, do you have Fredrica's things, are they here?'

'Her room's in the top of the house.'

'May I see?'

It took him a moment to decide where to lay down his hammer. 'All right,' he said, 'come along.'

Chapter Fifty-one

Jack Crawford's office in the FBI's Washington Headquarters was painted an oppressive gray, but it had big windows.

Crawford stood at these windows with his clipboard held to the light, peering at a list off a God damned fuzzy dot-matrix printer that he'd told them to get rid of.

He'd come here from the funeral home and worked all morning, tweaking the Norwegians to hurry with their dental records on the missing seaman named Klaus, jerking San Diego's chain to check Benjamin

Raspail's familiars at the Conservatory where he had taught, and stirring up Customs, which was supposed to be checking for import violations involving living insects.

Within five minutes of Crawford's arrival, FBI Assistant Director John Golby, head of the new interservice task force, stuck his head in the office for a moment to say 'Jack, we're all thinking about you. Everybody appreciates you coming in. Has the service been set yet?'

'The wake's tomorrow evening. Service is Saturday at eleven o'clock.'

Golby nodded. 'There's a UNICEF memorial, Jack, a fund. You want it to read Phyllis or Bella, we'll do it any way you like.'

'Bella, John. Let's make it Bella.'

'Can I do anything for you, Jack?'

Crawford shook his head. 'I'm just working. I'm just gonna work now.'

'Right,' Golby said. He waited the decent interval. 'Frederick Chilton asked for federal protective custody.'

'Grand. John, is somebody in Baltimore talking to Everett Yow, Raspail's lawyer? I mentioned him to you. He might know something about Raspail's friends.'

'Yeah, they're on it this morning. I just sent Burroughs my memo on it. The Director's putting Lecter on the Most Wanted. Jack, if you need anything . . . Golby raised his eyebrows and his hand and backed out of sight.

If you need anything.

Crawford turned to the windows. He had a fine view from his office. There was the handsome old Post Office building where he'd done some of his training. To the left was the old FBI headquarters. At graduation, he'd filed through J. Edgar Hoover's office with the others. Hoover stood on a little box and shook their hands in turn. That was the only time Crawford ever met the man. The next day he married Bella.

They had met in Livorno, Italy. He was Army, she NATO staff, and she was Phyllis then. They walked on the quays and a boatman called 'Bella' across the glittering water and she was always Bella to him after that. She was only Phyllis when they disagreed.

Bella's dead. That should change the view from these windows. It wasn't right this view stayed the same. Had to fucking *die* on me. Jesus, kid. I knew it was coming but it *smarts*.

What do they say about forced retirement at fifty-five? You fall in love with the Bureau, but it doesn't fall in love with you. He'd seen it.

Thank God, Bella had saved him from that. He hoped she was somewhere today and that she was comfortable at last. He hoped she could see in his heart.

The phone was buzzing its intraoffice buzz.

'Mr Crawford, a Dr Danielson from –'

'Right.' Punch. 'Jack Crawford, Doctor.'

'Is this line secure, Mr Crawford?'

'Yes. On this end it is.'

'You're not taping, are you?'

'No, Dr Danielson. Tell me what's on your mind.'

'I want to make it clear this has nothing to do with anybody who was ever a patient at Johns Hopkins.'

'Understood.'

'If anything comes of it, I want you to make it clear to the public he's not a transsexual, he had nothing to do with this institution.'

'Fine. You got it. Absolutely.' *Come on, you stuffy bastard.* Crawford would have said anything.

'He shoved Dr Purvis down.'

'Who, Dr Danielson?'

'He applied to the program three years ago as John Grant of Harrisburg, Pennsylvania.'

'Description?'

'Caucasian male, he was thirty-one. Six feet one, a hundred and ninety pounds. He came to be tested and did very well on the Wechsler intelligence scale – bright normal – but the psychological testing and the interviews were another story. In fact, his House Tree-Person and his TAT were spot-on with the sheet you gave me. You let me think Alan Bloom authored that little theory, but it was Hannibal Lecter, wasn't it?'

'Go on with Grant, Doctor.'

'The board would have turned him down anyway, but by the time we met to discuss it, the question was moot because the background checks got him.'

'Got him how?'

'We routinely check with the police in an applicant's hometown. The Harrisburg police were after him for two assaults on homosexual men. The last one nearly died. He'd given us an address that turned out to be a boarding house he stayed in from time to time. The police got his fingerprints there and a credit-card gas receipt with his license number on it. His name wasn't John Grant at all, he'd just told us that. About a week later he waited outside the building here and shoved Dr Purvis down, just for spite.'

'What was his name, Dr Danielson?'

'I'd better spell it for you, it's J-A-M-E G-U-M-B.'

Chapter Fifty-two

Fredrica Bimmel's house was three stories tall and gaunt, covered with asphalt shingles stained rusty where the gutters had spilled over. Volunteer maples growing in the gutters had stood up to the winter pretty well. The windows on the north side were covered with sheet plastic. In a small parlor, very warm from a space heater, a middle-aged woman sat on a rug, playing with an infant.

'My wife,' Bimmel said as they passed through the room. 'We just got married Christmas.'

'Hello,' Starling said. The woman smiled vaguely in her direction. Cold in the hall again and everywhere boxes stacked waist-high filling the rooms, passageways among them, cardboard cartons filled with lampshades and canning lids, picnic hampers, back numbers of the *Reader's Digest* and *National Geographic*, thick old tennis rackets, bed linens, a case of dartboards, fiber car-seat covers in a fifties plaid with the intense smell of mouse pee.

'We're moving pretty soon,' Mr Bimmel said.

The stuff near the windows was bleached by the sun, the boxes stacked for years and bellied with age, the random rugs worn bare in the paths through the rooms.

Sunlight dappled the bannister as Starling climbed the stairs behind Fredrica's father. His clothes smelled stale in the cold air. She could see sunlight coming through the sagging ceiling at the top of the stairwell. The cartons stacked on the landing were covered with plastic.

Fredrica's room was small, under the eaves on the third floor.

'You want me anymore?'

'Later, I'd like to talk to you, Mr Bimmel. What about Fredrica's mother?' The file said 'deceased,' it didn't say when.

'What do you mean, what about her? She died when Fredrica was twelve.'

'I see.'

'Did you think that was Fredrica's mother downstairs? After I told you we just been married since Christmas? That what you thought is it? I guess the law's used to handling a different class of people, missy. She never knew Fredrica at all.'

'Mr Bimmel, is the room pretty much like Fredrica left it?'

The anger wandered somewhere else in him.

'Yah,' he said softly. 'We just left it alone. Nobody much could wear her stuff. Plug in the heater if you want it. Remember and unplug it before you come down.'

He didn't want to see the room. He left her on the landing.

Starling stood for a moment with her hand on the cold porcelain knob. She needed to organize a little, before her head was full of Fredrica's things.

Okay, the premise is Buffalo Bill did Fredrica first, weighted her and hid her well, in a river far from home. He hid her better than the others – she was the only one weighted – because he wanted the later ones found first. He wanted the idea of random selection of victims in widely scattered towns well established before Fredrica, of Belvedere, was found. It was important to take attention away from Belvedere. Because he lives here, or maybe in Columbus.

He started with Fredrica because he coveted her hide. We don't begin to covet with imagined things. Coveting is a very literal sin – we begin to covet with tangibles, we begin with what we see every day. He saw Fredrica in the course of his daily life. He saw her in the course of her daily life.

What was the course of Fredrica's daily life? All right . . .

Starling pushed the door open. Here it was, this still room smelling of mildew in the cold. On the wall, last year's calendar was forever turned to April. Fredrica had been dead ten months.

Cat food, hard and black, was in a saucer in the corner.

Starling, veteran yard-sale decorator, stood in the center of the room and turned slowly around. Fredrica had done a pretty good job with what she had. There were curtains of flowered chintz. Judging from the piped edges, she had recycled some slipcovers to make the curtains.

There was a bulletin board with a sash pinned to it. BHS BAND was printed on the sash in glitter. A poster of the performer Madonna was on the wall, and another of Deborah Harry and Blondie. On a shelf above the desk, Starling could see a roll of the bright self-adhesive wallpaper Fredrica had used to cover her walls. It was not a great job of papering, but better than her own first effort, Starling thought.

In an average home, Fredrica's room would have been cheerful. In this bleak house it was shrill; there was an echo of desperation in it.

Fredrica did not display photographs of herself in the room.

Starling found one in the school yearbook on the small bookcase. Glee Club, Home-Ec Club, Sew n' Sew, Band, 4-H Club – maybe the pigeons served as her 4-H project.

Fredrica's school annual had some signatures. 'To a great pal,' and a 'great gal' and 'my chemistry buddy,' and 'Remember the bake sale?!!'

Could Fredrica bring her friends up here? Did she have a friend good enough to bring up those stairs beneath the drip? There was an umbrella beside the door.

Look at this picture of Fredrica, here she's in the front row of the band. Fredrica is wide and fat, but her uniform fits better than the others. She's big and she has beautiful skin. Her irregular features combine to make a pleasant face, but she is not attractive looking by conventional standards.

Kimberly Emberg wasn't what you would call fetching either, not to the mindless gape of high school, and neither were a couple of the others.

Catherine Martin, though, would be attractive to anybody, a big, good-looking young woman who would have to fight the fat when she was thirty.

Remember, he doesn't look at women as a man looks at them. Conventionally attractive doesn't count. They just have to be smooth and roomy.

Starling wondered if he thought of women as 'skins,' the way some cretins call them 'cunts.'

She became aware of her own hand tracing the line of credits beneath the yearbook picture, became aware of her entire body, the space she filled, her figure and her face, their effect, the power in them, her breasts above the book, her hard belly against it, her legs below it. What of her experience applied?

Starling saw herself in the full-length mirror on the end wall and was glad to be different from Fredrica. But she knew the difference was a matrix in her thinking. What might it keep her from seeing?

How did Fredrica want to appear? What was she hungry for, where did she seek it? What did she try to do about herself?

Here were a couple of diet plans, the Fruit Juice Diet, the Rice Diet, and a crackpot plan where you don't eat and drink at the same sitting.

Organized diet groups – did Buffalo Bill watch them to find big girls? Hard to check. Starling knew from the file that two of the victims had belonged to diet groups and that the membership rosters had been compared. An agent from the Kansas City office, the FBI's traditional Fat Boys' Bureau, and some over-weight police were sent around to work out at Slenderella, and Diet Center, and join Weight Watchers and other diet denominations in the victims' towns. She didn't know if Catherine Martin belonged to a diet group. Money would have been a problem for Fredrica in organized dieting.

Fredrica had several issues of *Big Beautiful Girl*, a magazine for large women. Here she was advised to 'come to New York City, where you can meet newcomers from parts of the world where your size is considered a prized asset.' Right. Alternatively, 'you could travel to Italy or Germany, where you won't be alone after the first day.' You bet. Here's what to do if your toes hang out over the ends of your shoes. Jesus! All Fredrica needed was to meet Buffalo Bill, who considered her size a 'prized asset.'

How did Fredrica manage? She had some makeup, a lot of skin stuff. Good for you, *use* that asset. Starling found herself rooting for Fredrica as though it mattered anymore.

She had some junk jewelry in a White Owl cigar box. Here was a gold-filled circle pin that most likely had belonged to her late mother. She'd tried to cut the fingers off some old gloves of machine lace, to wear them Madonna-style, but they'd raveled on her.

She had some music, a single-shot Decca record player from the fifties with a jackknife attached to the tone arm with rubber bands for weight. Yard-sale records. Love themes by Zamfir, Master of the Pan Flute.

When she pulled the string to light the closet, Starling was surprised at Fredrica's wardrobe. She had nice clothes, not a great many, but plenty for school, enough to get along in a fairly formal office or even a dressy retail job. A quick look inside them, and Starling saw the reason. Fredrica made her own, and made them well, the seams were bound with a serger, the facings carefully fitted. Stacks of patterns were on a shelf at the back of the closet. Most of them were Simplicity, but there were a couple of Vogues that looked hard.

She probably wore her best thing to the job interview. What had she worn? Starling flipped through her file. Here: last seen wearing a green outfit. Come on, Officer, what the hell is a 'green outfit'?

Fredrica suffered from the Achilles' heel of the budget wardrobe – she was short on shoes – and at her weight she was hard on the shoes she had. Her loafers were strained into ovals. She wore Odor-Eaters in her sandals. The eyelets were stretched in her running shoes.

Maybe Fredrica exercised a little – she had some outsized warmups.

They were made by Juno.

Catherine Martin also had some fat pants made by Juno.

Starling backed out of the closet. She sat on the foot of the bed with her arms folded and stared into the lighted closet.

Juno was a common brand, sold in a lot of places that handle outsizes, but it raised the question of clothing. Every town of any size has at least one store specializing in clothes for fat people.

Did Buffalo Bill watch fat stores, select a customer and follow her?

Did he go into oversize shops in drag and look around? Every oversize shop in a city gets both transvestites and drag queens as customers.

The idea of Buffalo Bill trying to cross over sexually had just been applied to the investigation very recently, since Dr Lecter gave Starling his theory. What about his clothes?

All of the victims must have shopped in fat stores – Catherine Martin would wear a twelve, but the others couldn't, and Catherine must have shopped in an oversize store to buy the big Juno sweats.

Catherine Martin could wear a twelve. She was the smallest of the victims. Fredrica, the first victim, was largest. How was Buffalo Bill managing to down-size with the choice of Catherine Martin? Catherine was plenty buxom, but she wasn't that big around. Had he lost weight himself? Might he have joined a diet group lately? Kimberly Emberg was sort of in-between, big, but with a good waist indention . . .

Starling had specifically avoided thinking about Kimberly Emberg, but now the memory swamped her for a second. Starling saw Kimberly on the slab in Potter. Buffalo Bill hadn't cared about her waxed legs, her carefully glittered fingernails: he looked at Kimberly's flat bosom and it wasn't good enough and he took his pistol and blew a starfish in her chest.

The door to the room pushed open a few inches. Starling felt the movement in her heart before she knew what it was. A cat came in, a large tortoiseshell cat with one eye gold, the other blue. It hopped up on the bed and rubbed against her. Looking for Fredrica.

Loneliness. Big lonesome girls trying to satisfy somebody.

The police had eliminated lonely-hearts clubs early. Did Buffalo Bill have another way to take advantage of loneliness? Nothing makes us more vulnerable than loneliness except greed.

Loneliness might have permitted Buffalo Bill an opening with Fredrica, but not with Catherine. Catherine wasn't lonesome.

Kimberly was lonesome. *Don't start this.* Kimberly, obedient and limp, past rigor mortis, being rolled over on the mortician's table so Starling could fingerprint her. *Stop it. Can't stop it.* Kimberly lonesome, anxious to please, had Kimberly ever rolled over obediently for someone, just to feel his heart beat against her back? She wondered if Kimberly had felt whiskers grating between her shoulder blades.

Staring into the lighted closet, Starling remembered Kimberly's plump back, the triangular patches of skin missing from her shoulders.

Staring into the lighted closet, Starling saw the triangles on Kimberly's shoulders outlined in the blue dashes of a dressmaking pattern. The idea swam away and circled and came again, came close enough for her to grab it this time and she did with a fierce pulse of joy: THEY'RE DARTS – HE TOOK THOSE TRIANGLES TO MAKE DARTS SO HE COULD LET OUT HER WAIST. MOTHERFUCKER CAN SEW. BUFFALO BILL'S TRAINED TO SERIOUSLY SEW – HE'S NOT JUST PICKING OUT READY-TO-WEAR.

What did Dr Lecter say? 'He's making himself a girl suit out of real girls.' What did he say to me? 'Do you sew, Clarice?' Damn straight I do.

Starling put her head back, closed her eyes for one second. Problem-solving is hunting; it is savage pleasure and we are born to it.

She'd seen a telephone in the parlor. She started downstairs to use it but Mrs Bimmel's reedy voice was calling up to her already, calling her to the phone.

Chapter Fifty-three

Mrs Bimmel gave Starling the telephone and picked up the fretting baby. She didn't leave the parlor. 'Clarice Starling.'

'Jerry Burroughs, Starling –'

'Good, Jerry, listen I think Buffalo Bill can sew. He cut the triangles – just a sec – Mrs Bimmel, could I ask you to take the baby in the kitchen? I need to talk here. Thank you . . . Jerry, he can sew. He took –'

'Starling –'

'He took those triangles off of Kimberly Emberg to make darts, dressmaking darts, do you know what I'm saying? He's skilled, he's not just making caveman stuff. ID Section can search Known Offenders for tailors, sailmakers, drapers, upholsterers – run a scan on the Distinguishing Marks field for a tailor's notch in his teeth –'

'Right, right, right, I'm punching up a line now to ID. Now listen up – I may have to get off the phone here. Jack wanted me to brief you. We got a name and a place that looks not bad. The Hostage Rescue Team's airborne from Andrews. Jack's briefing them on the scrambler.'

'Going where?'

'Calumet City, edge of Chicago. Subject's Jame, like "Name" with a J, last name Gumb, a.k.a. John Grant, WM, thirty-four, one-ninety, brown and blue. Jack got a beep from Johns Hopkins. Your thing – your profile on how he'd be different from a transsexual – it rang the cherries at Johns Hopkins. Guy applied for sex reassignment three years ago. Roughed up a doctor after they turned him down. Hopkins had the Grant alias and a flop address in Harrisburg, Pennsylvania. The cops had a gas receipt with his tag number and we went from there. Big jacket in California as a juvenile – he killed his grandparents when he was twelve and did six years in Tulare Psychiatric. The state let him out sixteen years ago when they shut down the asylum. He disappeared a long time. He's a fag-basher. Had a couple of scrapes in Harrisburg and faded out again.'

'Chicago, you said. How do you know Chicago?'

'Customs. They had some paper on the John Grant alias. Customs stopped a suitcase at LAX a couple of years ago shipped from Surinam with live "pupae" – is that how you say it? – insects anyway, moths, in it. The addressee was John Grant, care of a business in Calumet called – get this – called "Mr Hide." Leather goods. Maybe the sewing fits with that; I'm relaying the sewing to Chicago and Calumet. No home address yet on Grant, or Gumb – the business is closed, but we're close.'

'Any pictures?'

'Just the juveniles from Sacramento PD so far. They're not much use – he was twelve. Looked like Beaver Cleaver. The wire room's faxing them around anyway.'

'Can I go?'

'No. Jack said you'd ask. They've got two female marshals from Chicago and a nurse to take charge of Martin if they get her. You'd never be in time anyway, Starling.'

'What if he's barricaded? It could take –'

'There won't be any standoff. They find him – they fall on him Crawford's authorized an explosive entry. Special problems with this guy, Starling, he's been in a hostage situation before. His juvenile homicides, they got him in a barricade situation in Sacramento with his grandmother as hostage – he'd already killed his grandfather – and it came out gruesome, let me tell you. He walked her out in front of the cops, they had this preacher talking to him. He's a kid, nobody took the shot. He was behind her and he did her kidneys. Medical attention no avail. At twelve, he did this. So this time no negotiations, no warning. Martin's probably dead already, but say we're lucky. Say he had a lot on his mind, one thing and another he didn't get around to it yet. If he sees us coming, he'll do her right in our faces for spite. Costs him nothing, right? So they find him and – Boom! – the door's down.'

The room was too damned hot and it smelled of baby ammonia.

Burroughs was still talking. 'We're looking for both names on the entomology magazine subscription lists, Knifemakers Guild, known offenders, the works – nobody stands down until it's over. You're doing Bimmel's acquaintances, right?'

'Right.'

'Justice says it's a tricky case to make if we don't catch him dirty. We need him with Martin or with something identifiable – something with teeth or fingers, frankly. Goes without saying, if he's dumped Martin already, we need witnesses to put him with a victim before the fact. We can use your stuff from Bimmel regardless . . . Starling, I wish to God this had happened yesterday for more reasons than the Martin kid. They throw the switch on you at Quantico?'

'I think so. They put in somebody else that was waiting out a recycle – that's what they tell me.'

'If we get him in Chicago, you made a lot of contribution here. They're hardasses at Quantico like they're supposed to be, but they have to see *that*. Wait a minute.'

Starling could hear Burroughs barking, away from the phone. Then he was back again.

'Nothing – they can deploy in Calumet City in forty to fifty-five, depends on the winds aloft. Chicago SWAT's deputized in case they find him sooner. Calumet Power and Light's come up with four possible addresses. Starling, watch for anything they can use up there to narrow it down. You see anything about Chicago or Calumet, get to me fast.'

'Righto.'

'Now listen – this and I gotta go. If it happens, if we get him in Calumet City, you fall in at Quantico 0800 *mañana* with your Mary Janes shined. Jack's going before the board with you. So is the chief gunny, Brigham. It don't hurt to ask.'

'Jerry, one other thing: Fredrica Bimmel had some warmups made by Juno, it's a brand of fat clothes. Catherine Martin had some too, for what it's worth. He might watch fat stores to find large victims. We could ask Memphis, Akron, the other places.'

'Got it. Keep smiling.'

Starling walked out in the junky yard in Belvedere, Ohio, 380 long miles from the action in Chicago. The cold air felt good on her face. She threw a small punch in the air, rooting hard for the Hostage Rescue Team. At the same time, she felt a little trembly in her chin and cheeks. What the hell was this? What the hell would she have done if she'd found anything? She'd have called the cavalry, the Cleveland field office, and Columbus SWAT, the Belvedere PD too.

Saving the young woman, saving the daughter of Senator Fuck-You Martin and the ones that might come after – truly, that was what mattered. If they did it, everybody was right.

If they weren't in time, if they found something awful, please God they got Buffa – got Jame Gumb or Mr Hide or whatever they wanted to call the damned thing.

Still, to be so close, to get a hand on the rump of it, to have a good idea a day late and wind up far from the arrest, busted out of school, it all smacked of losing. Starling had long suspected, guiltily, that the Starlings' luck had been sour for a couple of hundred years now – that all the Starlings had been wandering around pissed off and confused back through the mists of time. That if you could find the tracks of the first Starling, they would lead in a circle. This was classic loser thinking, and she was damned if she'd entertain it.

If they caught him because of the profile she'd gotten from Dr Lecter, it had to help her with the Department of Justice. Starling had to think about that a little; her career hopes were twitching like a phantom limb.

Whatever happened, having the flash on the dressmaking pattern had felt nearly as good as anything ever had. There was stuff to keep here. She'd found courage in the memory of her mother as well as her father. She'd earned and kept Crawford's confidence. These were things to keep in her own White Owl cigar box.

Her job, her duty, was to think about Fredrica and how Gumb might have gotten her. A criminal prosecution of Buffalo Bill would require all the facts.

Think about Fredrica, stuck here all her young life. Where would she look for the exit? Did her longings resonate with Buffalo Bill's? Did that draw them together? Awful thought, that he might have understood her out of his own experience, empathized even, and still helped himself to her skin.

Starling stood at the edge of the water.

Almost every place has a moment of the day, an angle and intensity of light, in which it looks its best. When you're stuck someplace, you learn that time and you look forward to it. This, midafternoon, was probably the time for the Licking River behind Fell Street. Was this the Bimmel girl's time to dream? The pale sun raised enough vapor off the water to blur the old refrigerators and ranges dumped in the brush on the far side of the backwater. The northeast wind, opposite the light, pushed the cattails toward the sun.

A piece of white PVC pipe led from Mr Bimmel's shed toward the river. It gurgled and a brief rush of bloody water came out, staining the old snow. Bimmel came out into the sun. The front of his trousers was flecked with blood and he carried some pink and gray lumps in a plastic food bag.

'Squab,' he said, when he saw Starling looking. 'Ever eat squab?'

'No,' Starling said, turning back to the water, 'I've eaten doves.'

'Never have to worry about biting on a shot in these.'

'Mr Bimmel, did Fredrica know anybody from Calumet City or the Chicago area?'

He shrugged and shook his head.

'Had she ever been to Chicago, to your knowledge?'

'What do you mean, "to my knowledge"? You think a girl of mine's going off to Chicago and I don't know it? She didn't go to *Columbus* I didn't know it.'

'Did she know any men that sew, tailors or sailmakers?'

'She sewed for everybody. She could sew like her mother. I don't know of any men. She sewed for stores, for ladies, I don't know who.'

'Who was her best friend, Mr Bimmel? Who did she hang out with?' *Didn't mean to say 'hang.' Good, it didn't stick him – he's just pissed off.*

'She didn't hang out like the good-for-nothings. She always had some work. God didn't make her pretty, he made her busy.'

'Who would you say was her best friend?'

'Stacy Hubka, I guess, since they were little. Fredrica's mother used to say Stacy went around with Fredrica just to have somebody to wait on her, I don't know.'

'Do you know where I could get in touch with her?'

'Stacy worked at the insurance, I guess she still does. The Franklin Insurance.'

Starling walked to her car across the rutted yard, her head down, hands deep in her pockets. Fredrica's cat watched her from the high window.

Chapter Fifty-four

FBI Credentials get a snappier response the farther west you go. Starling's ID, which might have raised one bored eyebrow on a Washington functionary, got the undivided attention of Stacy Hubka's boss at the Franklin Insurance Agency in Belvedere, Ohio. He relieved Stacy Hubka at the counter and the telephones himself, and offered Starling the privacy of his cubicle for the interview.

Stacy Hubka had a round, downy face and stood five-four in heels. She wore her hair in frosted wings and used a Cher Bono move to brush them back from her face. She looked Starling up and down whenever Starling wasn't facing her.

'Stacy – may I call you Stacy?'

'Sure.'

'I'd like you to tell me, Stacy, how you think this might have happened to Fredrica Bimmel – where this man might have spotted Fredrica.'

'Freaked me *out*. Get your *skin* peeled off, is that a bummer? Did you see her? They said she was just like *rags*, like somebody let the air out of –'

'Stacy, did she ever mention anybody from Chicago or Calumet City?'

Calumet City. The clock above Stacy Hubka's head worried Starling. If the Hostage Rescue Team makes it in forty minutes, they're just ten minutes from touchdown. Did they have a hard address? Tend to your business.

'Chicago?' Stacy said. 'No, we marched at Chicago one time in the Thanksgiving parade.'

'When?'

'Eighth grade, that would be what? – nine years ago. The band just went there and back on the bus.'

'What did you think last spring when she first disappeared?'

'I just didn't know.'

'Remember where you were when you first found it out? When you got the news? What did you think then?'

'That first night she was gone, Skip and me went to the show and then we went to Mr Toad's for a drink and Pam and them, Pam Malavesi, came in and said Fredrica had disappeared, and Skip goes, *Houdini* couldn't make Fredrica disappear. And then he's got to tell everybody who Houdini was, he's always showing off how much he knows, and we just sort of blew it off. I thought she was just mad at her dad. Did you *see* her house? Is *that* the pits? I mean, wherever she is, I know she's embarrassed you saw it. Wouldn't *you* run away?'

'Did you think maybe she'd run away *with* somebody, did anybody pop into your mind – even if it was wrong?'

'Skip said maybe she'd found her a chubby-chaser. But no, she never had anybody like that. She had one boyfriend, but that's like ancient history. He was in the band in the tenth grade, I say "boyfriend" but they just talked and giggled like a couple of girls and did homework. He was a big sissy though, wore one of these little Greek fisherman's caps? Skip thought he was a, you know, a queer. She got kidded about going out with a queer. Him and his sister got killed in a car wreck though, and she never got anybody else.'

'What did you think when she didn't come back?'

'Pam thought maybe it was some Moonies got her, I didn't know, I was scared every time I thought about it. I wouldn't any more go out at night without Skip, I told him, I said uh-uh, buddy, when the sun goes down, *we* go out.'

'Did you ever hear her mention anybody named Jame Gumb? Or John Grant?'

'Ummmm . . . no.'

'Do you think she could have had a friend you didn't know about? Were there gaps in time, days when you didn't see her?'

'No. She had a guy, I'd of known, believe me. She never had a guy.'

'Do you think it might be just possible, let's say, she could have had a friend and didn't say anything about it?'

'Why wouldn't she?'

'Scared she'd get kidded, maybe?'

'Kidded by us? What are you saying, because of the other time? The sissy kid in high school?' Stacy reddened. 'No. No way we would hurt her. I just mentioned that together. She didn't . . . everybody was like, *kind* to her after he died.'

'Did you work with Fredrica, Stacy?'

'Me and her and Pam Malavesi and Jaronda Askew all worked down at the Bargain Center summers in high school. Then Pam and me went to Richards' to see could we get on, it's real nice clothes, and they hired me and then Pam, so Pam says to Fredrica come on they need another girl and she came, but Mrs Burdine – the merchandising manager? – she goes, "Well, Fred*rica*, we need somebody that, you know, people can relate to, that they come in and say I want to look like *her*, and you can give them advice how they look in this and stuff. And if you get yourself together and lose your weight I want you to come right back here and see me," she says. "But right now, if you want to take over some of our alterations I'll try you at that, I'll put in a word with Mrs Lippman." Mrs Burdine talked in this sweety voice but she turned out to be a bitch really, but I didn't know it right at first.'

'So Fredrica did alterations for Richards', the store where you worked?'

'It hurt her feelings, but sure. Old Mrs Lippman did everybody's alterations. She had the business and she had more than she could do, and Fredrica worked for her. She did them for old Mrs Lippman. Mrs Lippman sewed for everybody, made dresses. After Mrs Lippman retired, her kid or whatever didn't want to do it and Fredrica got it all and just kept sewing for everybody. That's all she did. She'd meet me and Pam, we'd go to Pam's house on lunch and watch "The Young and the Restless" and she'd bring something and be working in her lap the whole time.'

'Did Fredrica ever work at the store, taking measurements? Did she meet customers or the wholesale people?'

'Sometimes, not much. I didn't work every day.'

'Did Mrs Burdine work every day, would she know?'

'Yeah, I guess.'

'Did Fredrica ever mention sewing for a company called Mr Hide in Chicago or Calumet City, maybe lining leather goods?'

'I don't know, Mrs Lippman might have.'

'Did you ever see the Mr Hide brand? Did Richards' ever carry it, or one of the boutiques?'

'No.'

'Do you know where Mrs Lippman is? I'd like to talk to her.'

'She died. She went to Florida to retire and she died down there, Fredrica said. I never did know her, me and Skip just picked up Fredrica over there sometimes when she had a bunch of clothes. You might could talk to her family or something. I'll write it down for you.'

This was extremely tedious, when what Starling wanted was news from Calumet City. Forty minutes was up. The Hostage Rescue Team ought to be on the ground. She shifted so she didn't have to look at the clock, and pressed on.

'Stacy, where did Fredrica buy clothes, where did she get those oversize Juno workout clothes, the sweats?'

'She made just about everything. I expect she got the sweats at Richards', you know, when everybody started wearing them real big, so they came down over tights like that? A lot of places carried them then. She got a discount at Richards' because she sewed for them.'

'Did she ever shop at an oversize store?'

'We went in every place to look, you know how you do. We'd go in Personality Plus and she'd look for ideas, you know, flattering patterns for big sizes.'

'Did anybody ever come up and bug you around an oversize store, or did Fredrica ever feel somebody had his eye on her?'

Stacy looked at the ceiling for a second and shook her head.

'Stacy, did transvestites ever come into Richards', or men buying large dresses, did you ever run into that?'

'No. Me and Skip saw some at a bar in Columbus one time.'

'Was Fredrica with you?'

'Not *hardly*. We'd gone, like, for the weekend.'

'Would you write down the oversize places you went with Fredrica, do you think you could remember all of them?'

'Just here, or here and Columbus?'

'Here and Columbus. And Richards' too, I want to talk to Mrs Burdine.'

'Okay. Is it a pretty good job, being a FBI agent?'

'I think it is.'

'You get to travel around and stuff? I mean places better than this.'

'Sometimes you do.'

'Got to look good every day, right?'

'Well, yeah. You have to try to look businesslike.'

'How do you get into that, being a FBI agent?'

'You have to go to college first, Stacy.'

'That's tough to pay for.'

'Yeah, it is. Sometimes there are grants and fellowships that help out, though. Would you like me to send you some stuff?'

'Yeah. I was just thinking, Fredrica was so *happy* for me when I got this job. She really got her rocks off – she never had a real office job – she thought this was getting somewhere. *This* – cardboard files and Barry Manilow on the speakers all day – she thought it was hot shit. What did she know, big dummy.' Tears stood in Stacy Hubka's eyes. She opened them wide and held her head back to keep from having to do her eyes over.

'How about my list now?'

'I better do it at my desk, I got my word processor and I need my phone book and stuff.' She went out with her head back, navigating by the ceiling.

It was the telephone that was tantalizing Starling. The moment Stacy Hubka was out of the cubicle, Starling called Washington collect to get the news.

Chapter Fifty-five

At that moment, over the southern tip of Lake Michigan, a twenty-four-passenger business jet with civilian markings came off maximum cruise and began the long curve down to Calumet City, Illinois.

The twelve men of the Hostage Rescue Team felt the lift in their stomachs. There were a few elaborately casual tension yawns up and down the aisle.

Team commander Joel Randall, at the front of the passenger compartment, took off the headset and glanced over his notes before he got up to talk. He believed he had the best-trained SWAT team in the world, and he may have been right. Several of them had never been shot at, but as far as simulations and tests could tell, these were the best of the best.

Randall had spent a lot of time in airplane aisles, and kept his balance easily in the bumpy descent.

'Gentlemen, our ground transportation's courtesy of DEA undercover. They've got a florist's truck and a plumbing van. So Vernon, Eddie, into your long handles and your civvies. If we go in behind stun grenades, remember you've got no flash protection on your faces.'

Vernon muttered to Eddie, 'Make sure you cover up your cheeks.'

'Did he say don't moon? I thought he said don't flash,' Eddie murmured back.

Vernon and Eddie, who would make the initial approach to the door, had to wear thin ballistic armor beneath civilian clothes. The rest could go in hardshell armor, proof against rifle fire.

'Bobby, make sure and put one of your handsets in each van for the driver, so we don't get fucked up talking to those DEA guys,' Randall said.

The Drug Enforcement Administration uses UHF radios in raids, while the FBI has VHF. There had been problems in the past.

They were equipped for most eventualities, day or night: for walls they had basic rappelling equipment, to listen they had Wolf's Ears and a VanSleek Farfoon, to see they had night-vision devices. The weapons with night scopes looked like band instruments in their bulging cases.

This was to be a precise surgical operation and the weapons reflected it – there was nothing that fired from an open bolt.

The team shrugged into their web gear as the flaps went down.

Randall got news from Calumet on his headset. He covered the microphone and spoke to the team again. 'Guys, they got it down to two addresses. We take the best one and Chicago SWAT's on the other.'

The field was Lansing Municipal, the closest to Calumet on the southeast side of Chicago. The plane was cleared straight in. The pilot brought it to a stop in a stink of brakes beside two vehicles idling at the end of the field farthest from the terminal.

There were quick greetings beside the florist's truck. The DEA commander handed Randall what looked like a tall flower arrangement. It was a twelve-pound door-buster sledgehammer, the head wrapped in colored foil like a flowerpot, foliage attached to the handle.

'You might want to deliver this,' he said. 'Welcome to Chicago.'

Chapter Fifty-six

Mr Gumb went ahead with it in the late afternoon. With dangerous steady tears standing in his eyes, he'd watched his video again and again and again. On the small screen, Mom climbed the waterslide and whee down into the pool, whee down into the pool. Tears blurred Jame Gumb's vision as though he were in the pool himself.

On his middle a hot-water bottle gurgled, as the little dog's stomach had gurgled when she lay on him.

He couldn't stand it any longer – what he had in the basement holding Precious prisoner, threatening her. Precious was in pain, he knew she was. He wasn't sure he could kill it before it fatally injured Precious, but he had to try. Right now.

He took off his clothes and put on the robe – he always finished a harvest naked and bloody as a newborn.

From his vast medicine cabinet he took the salve he had used on Precious when the cat scratched her. He got out some little Band-Aids and Q-tips and the plastic 'Elizabethan collar' the vet gave him to keep her from worrying a sore place with her teeth. He had tongue depressors in the basement to use for splints on her little broken leg, and a tube of Sting-Eez to take the hurt away if the stupid thing scratched her thrashing around before it died.

A careful head shot, and he'd just sacrifice the hair. Precious was worth more to him than the hair. The hair was a sacrifice, an offering for her safety.

Quietly down the stairs now, to the kitchen. Out of his slippers and down the dark basement stairs, staying close to the wall to keep the stairs from creaking.

He didn't turn on the light. At the bottom of the stairs, he took a right into the workroom, moving by touch in the familiar dark, feeling the floor change under his feet.

His sleeve brushed the cage and he heard the soft angry chirp of a brood moth. Here was the cabinet. He found his infrared light and slipped the goggles on his head. Now the world glowed green. He stood for a moment in the comforting burble of the tanks, in the warm hiss of the steam pipes. Master of the dark, queen of the dark.

Moths free in the air left green trails of fluorescence across his vision, faint breaths across his face as their downy wings brushed the darkness.

He checked the Python. It was loaded with .38 Special lead wadcutters. They would slam into the skull and expand for an instant kill. If it was standing when he shot, if he shot down into the top of the head, the bullet was less likely than a Magnum load to exit the lower jaw and tear the bosom.

Quiet, quiet he crept, knees bent, painted toes gripping the old boards. Silent on the sand floor of the oubliette room. Quiet but not too slow. He didn't want his scent to have time to reach the little dog in the bottom of the well.

The top of the oubliette glowed green, the stones and mortar distinct, the grain of the wooden cover sharp in his vision. Hold the light and lean over. There they were. It was on its side like a giant shrimp. Perhaps asleep. Precious was curled up close against its body, surely sleeping, oh please not dead.

The head was exposed. A neck shot was tempting – save the hair. Too risky.

Mr Gumb leaned over the hole, the stalk-eyes of his goggles peering down. The Python has a good, muzzle-heavy feel, wonderfully pointable it is. Have to hold it in the beam of infrared. He lined up the sights on the side of its head, just where the hair was damp against the temple.

Noise or smell, he never knew – but Precious up and yipping, jumping straight up in the dark, Catherine Baker Martin doubling around the little dog and pulling the futon over them. Just lumps moving under the futon, he couldn't tell what was dog and what was Catherine. Looking down in infrared, his depth perception was impaired. He couldn't tell which lumps were Catherine.

But he had seen Precious jump. He knew her leg was all right, and at once he knew something more: Catherine Baker Martin wouldn't hurt the dog, any more than he would. Oh, sweet relief. Because of their shared feeling, he could shoot her in the God damned legs and when she clutched her legs, blow her fucking head off. No caution necessary.

He turned on the lights, all the damned lights in the basement, and got the floodlight from the storeroom. He had control of himself, he was reasoning well – on his way through the workroom he remembered to run a little water in the sinks so nothing would clot in the traps.

As he hurried past the stairs, ready to go, carrying the floodlight, the doorbell rang.

The doorbell grating, rasping, he had to stop and think about what it was. He hadn't heard it in years, hadn't even known whether it worked. Mounted in the stairway so it could be heard upstairs and down, clanging now, black metal tit covered with dust. As he looked at it, it rang again, kept ringing, dust flying off it. Someone was at the front, pushing the old button marked SUPERINTENDENT.

They would go away.

He rigged the floodlight.

They didn't go away.

Down in the well, it said something he paid no attention to. The bell was clanging, grating, they were just leaning on the button.

Better go upstairs and peek out the front. The long-barreled Python wouldn't go in the pocket of his robe. He put it on the workroom counter.

He was halfway up the stairs when the bell stopped ringing. He waited a few moments halfway up. Silence. He decided to look anyway. As he went through the kitchen a heavy knock on the back door made him jump. In the pantry near the back door was a pump shotgun. He knew it was loaded.

With the door closed to the basement stairs, nobody could hear it yelling down there, even at the top of its voice, he was sure of that.

Banging again. He opened the door a crack on the chain.

'I tried the front but nobody came,' Clarice Starling said. 'I'm looking for Mrs Lippman's family, could you help me?'

'They don't live here,' Mr Gumb said, and closed the door. He had started for the stairs again when the banging resumed, louder this time.

He opened the door on the chain.

The young woman held an ID close to the crack. It said Federal Bureau of Investigation. 'Excuse me, but I need to talk to you. I want to find the family of Mrs Lippman. I know she lived here. I want you to help me, please.'

'Mrs Lippman's been dead for ages. She didn't have any relatives that I know of.'

'What about a lawyer, or an accountant? Somebody who'd have her business records? Did you know Mrs Lippman?'

'Just briefly. What's the problem?'

'I'm investigating the death of Fredrica Bimmel. Who are you, please?'

'Jack Gordon.'

'Did you know Fredrica Bimmel when she worked for Mrs Lippman?'

'No. Was she a great, fat person? I may have seen her, I'm not sure. I didn't mean to be rude – I was sleeping . . . Mrs Lippman had a lawyer, I may have his card somewhere, I'll see if I can find it. Do you mind stepping in? I'm freezing and my cat will *streak* through here in a second. She'll be outside like a shot before I can catch her.'

He went to a rolltop desk in the far corner of the kitchen, raised the top and looked in a couple of pigeonholes. Starling stepped inside the door and took her notebook out of her purse.

'That horrible business,' he said, rummaging the desk. 'I shiver every time I think about it. Are they close to catching somebody, do you think?'

'Not yet, but we're working. Mr Gordon, did you take over this place after Mrs Lippman died?'

'Yes.' Gumb bent over the desk, his back to Starling. He opened a drawer and poked around in it.

'Were there any records left here? Business records?'

'No, nothing at all. Does the FBI have any ideas? The police here don't seem to know the first thing. Do they have a description, or fingerprints?'

Out of the folds in the back of Mr Gumb's robe crawled a Death's-head Moth. It stopped in the center of his back, about where his heart would be, and adjusted its wings.

Starling dropped her notebook into the bag.

Mister Gumb. Thank God my coat's open. Talk out of here, go to a phone. No. He knows I'm FBI, I let him out of my sight he'll kill her. Do her kidneys. They find him, they fall on him. His phone. Don't see it. Not in here, ask for his phone. Get the connection, then throw down on him. Make him lie facedown, wait for the cops. That's it, do it. He's turning around.

'Here's the number,' he said. He had a business card.

Take it? No.

'Good, thank you. Mr Gordon, do you have a telephone I could use?'

As he put the card on the table, the moth flew. It came from behind him, past his head and lit between them, on a cabinet above the sink.

He looked at it. When she didn't look at it, when her eyes never left his face, he knew.

Their eyes met and they knew each other.

Mr Gumb tilted his head a little to the side. He smiled. 'I have a cordless phone in the pantry, I'll get it for you.'

No! Do it. She went for the gun, one smooth move she'd done four thousand times and it was right where it was supposed to be, good two-hand hold, her world the front sight and the center of his chest. 'Freeze.'

He pursed his lips.

'Now. Slowly. Put up your hands.'

Move him outside, keep the table between us. Walk him to the front. Facedown in the middle of the street and hold up the badge.

'Mr Gub – Mr Gumb, you're under arrest. I want you to walk slowly outside for me.'

Instead, he walked out of the room. If he had reached for his pocket, reached behind him, if she'd seen a weapon, she could have fired. He just walked out of the room.

She heard him go down the basement stairs fast, she around the table and to the door at the top of the stairwell. He was gone, the stairwell brightly lit and empty. *Trap.* Be a sitting duck on the stairs.

From the basement then a thin paper cut of a scream.

She didn't like the stairs, didn't like the stairs, Clarice Starling in the quick where you give it or you don't.

Catherine Martin screamed again, he's killing her and Starling went down them anyway, one hand on the bannister, gun arm out, the gun just under her line of vision, floor below bounding over the gunsight, gun arm swinging with her head as she tried to cover the two facing doors open at the bottom of the staircase.

Lights blazing in the basement, she couldn't go through one door without turning her back on the other, do it quick then, to the left toward the scream. Into the sand-floored oubliette room, clearing the doorframe fast, eyes wider than they had ever been. Only place to hide was behind the well, she sliding sideways around the wall, both hands on the gun, arms out straight, a little pressure on the trigger, on around the well and nobody behind it.

A small scream rising from the well like thin smoke. Yipping now, a dog. She approached the well, eyes on the door, got to the rim, looked over the edge. Saw the girl, looked up again, down again, said what she was trained to say, calm the hostage:

'FBI, you're safe.'

'Safe SHIT, he's got a gun. Getmeout. GETMEOUT.'

'Catherine, you'll be all right. Shut up. Do you know where he is?'

'GETMEOUT, I DON'T GIVE A SHIT WHERE HE IS, GETMEOUT.'

'I'll get you out. Be quiet. Help me. Be quiet so I can hear. Try and shut that dog up.'

Braced behind the well, covering the door, her heart pounded and her breath blew dust off the stone. She could not leave Catherine Martin to get help when she didn't know where Gumb was. She moved up to the door and took cover behind the frame. She could see across the foot of the stairs and into part of the workroom beyond.

Either she found Gumb, or she made sure he'd fled, or she took Catherine out with her, those were the only choices.

A quick look over her shoulder, around the oubliette room.

'Catherine. Catherine. Is there is a ladder?'

'I don't know, I woke up down here. He let the bucket down on strings.'

Bolted to a wall beam was a small hand winch. There was no line on the drum of the winch.

'Catherine, I have to find something to get you out with. Can you walk?'

'Yes. Don't leave me.'

'I have to leave the room for just a minute.'

'You fucking bitch don't you leave me down here, my mother will tear your goddamn shit brains out –'

'Catherine shut up. I want you to be quiet so I can hear. To *save* yourself be quiet, do you understand?' Then, louder, 'The other officers will be here any minute, now shut up. We won't leave you down there.'

He had to have a rope. Where was it? Go see.

Starling moved across the stairwell in one rush, to the door of the workroom, door's the worst place, in fast, back and forth along the near wall until she had seen all the room, familiar shapes swimming in the glass tanks, she too alert to be startled. Quickly through the room, past the tanks, the sinks, past the cage, a few big moths flying. She ignored them.

Approaching the corridor beyond, it blazing with light. The refrigerator turned on behind her and she spun in a crouch, hammer lifting off the frame of the Magnum, eased the pressure off. On to the corridor. She wasn't taught to peek. Head and gun at once, but low.

The corridor empty. The studio blazing with light at the end of it. Fast along it, gambling past the closed door, on to the studio door. The room all white and blond oak. Hell to clear from the doorway. Make sure every mannequin is a mannequin, every reflection is a mannequin. Only movement in the mirrors your movement.

The great armoire stood open and empty. The far door open onto darkness, the basement beyond. No rope, no ladder anywhere. No lights beyond the studio. She closed the door into the dark part of the basement, pushed a chair under the knob, and pushed a sewing machine against it. If she could be positive he wasn't in this part of the basement, she'd risk going upstairs for a moment to find a phone.

Back down the corridor, one door she'd passed.

Get on the side opposite the hinges. All the way open in one move. The door slammed back, nobody behind it. An old bathroom. In it, rope, hooks, a sling. Get Catherine or go for the phone? In the bottom of the well Catherine wouldn't get shot by accident.

But if Starling got killed, Catherine was dead too. Take Catherine with her to the phone.

Starling didn't want to stay in the bathroom long. He could come to the door and hose her. She looked both ways and ducked inside for the rope. There was a big bath tub in the room. The tub was almost filled with hard red-purple plaster. A hand and wrist stuck up from the plaster, the hand turned dark and shriveled, the fingernails painted pink. On the wrist was a dainty watch. Starling was seeing everything at once, the rope, the tub, the hand, the watch.

The tiny insect-crawl of the second-hand was the last thing she saw before the lights went out.

Her heart knocked hard enough to shake her chest and arms. Dizzy dark, need to touch something, the edge of the tub. The bathroom. Get out of the bathroom. If he can find the door he can hose this room, nothing to get behind. Oh dear Jesus go out. Go out down low and out in the hall. Every light out? Every light. He must have done it at the fuse box, pulled the lever, where would it be? Where would the fuse box be? Near the stairs. Lot of times near the stairs. If it is, he'll come from that way. But he's between me and Catherine.

Catherine Martin was keening again.

Wait here? Wait forever? Maybe he's gone. He can't be sure no backup's coming. Yes he can. But soon I'll be missed. Tonight. The stairs are in the direction of the screams. Solve it now.

She moved, quietly, her shoulder barely brushing the wall, brushing it too lightly for sound, one hand extended ahead, the gun at waist level, close to her in the confined hallway. Out into the workroom now. Feel the space opening up. Open room. In the crouch in the open room, arms out, both hands on the gun. You know exactly where the gun is, it's just below eye level. Stop, listen. Head and body and arms turning together like a turret. Stop, listen.

In absolute black the hiss of steam pipes, trickle of water.

Heavy in her nostrils the smell of the goat.

Catherine keening.

Against the wall stood Mr Gumb with his goggles on. There was no danger she'd bump into him – there was an equipment table between them. He played his infrared light up and down her. She was too slender to be of great utility to him. He remembered her hair though, from the kitchen, and it was glorious, and that would only take a minute. He could slip it right off. Put it on himself. He could lean over the well wearing it and tell that thing 'Surprise!'

It was fun to watch her trying to sneak along. She had her hip against the sinks now, creeping toward the screams with her gun stuck out. It would have been fun to hunt her for a long time – he'd never hunted one armed before. He would have *thoroughly* enjoyed it. No time for that. Pity.

A shot in the face would be fine and easy at eight feet. Now.

He cocked the Python as he brought it up snick snick and the figure blurred, bloomed, bloomed green in his vision and his gun bucked in his hand and the floor hit him hard in the back and his light was on and he saw the ceiling. Starling on the floor, flashblind, ears ringing, deafened by the blast of the guns. She worked in the dark while neither could hear, dump the empties, tip it, feel to see they're all out, in with the speedloader, feel it, tip it down, twist, drop it, close the cylinder. She'd fired four. Two shots and two shots. He'd fired once. She found the two good cartridges she'd dumped. Put them where? In the speedloader pouch. She lay still. Move before he can hear?

The sound of a revolver being cocked is like no other. She'd fired at the sound, seen nothing past the great muzzle flashes of the guns. She hoped he'd fire now in the wrong direction, give her the muzzle flash to shoot at. Her hearing was coming back, her ears still rang, but she could hear.

What was that sound? Whistling? Like a teakettle, but interrupted. What was it? Like breathing. Is it me? No. Her breath blew warm off the floor, back in her face. Careful, don't get dust, don't sneeze. It's breathing. It's a sucking chest wound. He's hit in the chest. They'd taught her how to seal one, to put something over it, a rain slicker, a plastic bag, something airtight, strap it tight. Reinflate the lung. She'd hit him in the chest, then. What to do? Wait. Let him stiffen up and bleed. Wait.

Starling's cheek stung. She didn't touch it, if it was bleeding she didn't want her hands slick.

The moaning from the well came again, Catherine talking, crying.

Starling had to wait. She couldn't answer Catherine. She couldn't say anything or move.

Mr Gumb's invisible light played on the ceiling. He tried to move it and he couldn't, any more than he could move his head. A great Malaysian Luna Moth passing close beneath the ceiling picked up the infrared and came down, circled, lit on the light. The pulsing shadows of its wings, enormous on the ceiling, were visible only to Mr Gumb.

Over the sucking in the dark, Starling heard Mr Gumb's ghastly voice, choking: 'How . . . does . . . it feel . . . to be . . . so beautiful?'

And then another sound. A gurgle, a rattle and the whistling stopped.

Starling knew that sound too. She'd heard it once before, at the hospital when her father died.

She felt for the edge of the table and got to her feet. Feeling her way along, going toward the sound of Catherine, she found the stairwell and climbed the stairs in the dark.

It seemed to take a long time. There was a candle in the kitchen drawer. With it she found the fuse box beside the stairs, jumped when the lights came on. To get to the fuse box and shut off the lights, he must have left the basement another way and come down again behind her.

Starling had to be positive he was dead. She waited until her eyes were well adjusted to the light before she went back in the workroom, and then she was careful. She could see his naked feet and legs sticking out from under the worktable. She kept her eyes on the hand beside the gun until she kicked the gun away. His eyes were open. He was dead, shot through the right side of the chest, thick blood under him. He had put on some of his things from the armoire and she couldn't look at him long.

She went to the sink, put the Magnum on the drainboard and ran cold water on her wrists, wiped her face with her wet hand. No blood. Moths batted at the mesh around the lights. She had to step around the body to retrieve the Python.

At the well she said, 'Catherine, he's dead. He can't hurt you. I'm going upstairs and call –'

'No! GET ME OUT. GET ME OUT. GET ME OUT.'

'Look here. He's dead. This is his gun. Remember it? I'm going to call the police and the fire department. I'm afraid to hoist you out myself, you might fall. Soon as I call them I'll come back down and wait with you. Okay? Okay. Try to shut that dog up. Okay? Okay.'

The local television crews arrived just after the fire department and before the Belvedere police. The fire captain, angered at the glare from the lights, drove the television crews back up the stairs and out of the basement while he rigged a pipe frame to hoist out Catherine Martin, not trusting Mr Gumb's hook in the ceiling joist. A fireman went down into the well and put her in the rescue chair. Catherine came out holding the dog, kept the dog in the ambulance.

They drew the line on dogs at the hospital and wouldn't let the dog in. A fireman, instructed to drop it off at the animal shelter, took it home with him instead.

Chapter Fifty-seven

There were about fifty people at National Airport in Washington, meeting the red-eye flight from Columbus, Ohio. Most of them were meeting relatives and they looked sleepy and grumpy enough, with their shirttails sticking out below their jackets.

From the crowd, Ardelia Mapp had a chance to look Starling over as she came off the plane. Starling was pasty, dark under the eyes. Some black grains of gunpowder were in her cheek. Starling spotted Mapp and they hugged.

'Hey, Sport,' Mapp said. 'You check anything?'

Starling shook her head.

'Jeff's outside in the van. Let's go home.'

Jack Crawford was outside too, his car parked behind the van in the limousine lane. He'd had Bella's relatives all night.

'I . . .' he started. 'You know what you did. You hit a home run, kid.' He touched her cheek. 'What's this?'

'Burnt gunpowder. The doctor said it'll work out by itself in a couple of days – better than digging for it.'

Crawford took her to him and held her very tight for a moment, just a moment, and then put her away from him and kissed her on the forehead. 'You know what you did,' he said again. 'Go home. Go to sleep. Sleep in. I'll talk to you tomorrow.'

The new surveillance van was comfortable, designed for long stakeouts. Starling and Mapp rode in the big chairs in the back.

Without Jack Crawford in the van, Jeff drove a little harder. They made good time toward Quantico.

Starling rode with her eyes closed. After a couple of miles, Mapp nudged her knee. Mapp had opened two short-bottle Cokes. She handed Starling a Coke and took a half-pint of Jack Daniel's out of her purse.

They each took a swig out of their Cokes and poured in a shot of sour mash. Then they stuck their thumbs in the necks of the bottles, shook them, and shot the foam in their mouths.

'Ahhh,' Starling said.

'Don't spill that in here,' Jeff said.

'Don't worry, Jeff,' Mapp said. Quietly to Starling, 'You should have seen my man Jeff waiting for me outside the liquor store. He looked like he was passing peach seeds.' When Mapp saw the whiskey start to work a little, when Starling sank a little deeper in her chair, Mapp said, 'How you doing, Starling?'

'Ardelia, I'm damned if I know.'

'You don't have to go back, do you?'

'Maybe for one day next week, but I hope not. The US Attorney came over from Columbus to talk to the Belvedere cops. I did depositions out the wazoo.'

'Couple of good things,' Mapp said. 'Senator Martin's been on the phone all evening from Bethesda – you knew they took Catherine to Bethesda? Well, she's okay. He didn't mess her up in any physical way. Emotional damage, they don't know, they have to watch. Don't worry about school. Crawford and Brigham both called. The hearing's canceled. Krendler asked for his memo back. These people have got a heart like a greasy BB, Starling – you get no slack. You don't have to take the Search-and-Seizure exam at 0800 tomorrow, but you take it Monday, and the PE test right after. We'll jam over the weekend.'

They finished the half-pint just north of Quantico and dumped the evidence in a barrel at a roadside park.

'That Pilcher, Doctor Pilcher at the Smithsonian, called three times. Made me promise to tell you he called.'

'He's not a doctor.'

'You think you might do something about him?'

'Maybe. I don't know yet.'

'He sounds like he's pretty funny. I've about decided funny's the best thing in men, I'm talking about *aside* from money and your basic manageability.'

'Yeah, and manners too, you can't leave that out.'

'Right. Give me a son of a bitch with some manners every time.'

Starling went like a zombie from the shower to the bed.

Mapp kept her reading light on for a while, until Starling's breathing was regular. Starling jerked in her sleep, a muscle in her cheek twitched, and once her eyes opened wide.

Mapp woke sometime before daylight, the room feeling empty. Mapp turned on her light. Starling was not in her bed. Both of their laundry bags were missing, so Mapp knew where to look.

She found Starling in the warm laundry room, dozing against the slow rump-rump of a washing machine in the smell of bleach and soap and fabric softener. Starling had the psychology background – Mapp's was law – yet it was Mapp who knew that the washing machine's rhythm was like a great heartbeat and the rush of its waters was what the unborn hear – our last memory of peace.

Chapter Fifty-eight

Jack Crawford woke early on the sofa in his study and heard the snoring of his in-laws in his house. In the free moments before the weight of the day came on him, he remembered not Bella's death, but the last thing she'd said to him, her eyes clear and calm: 'What's going on in the yard?'

He took Bella's grain scoop and, in his bathrobe, went out and fed the birds as he had promised to do. Leaving a note for his sleeping in-laws, he eased out of the house before sunrise. Crawford had always gotten along with Bella's relatives, more or less, and it helped to have the noise in the house, but he was glad to get away to Quantico.

He was going through the overnight telex traffic and watching the early news in his office when Starling pressed her nose to the glass of the door. He dumped some reports out of a chair for her and they watched the news together without saying anything. Here it came.

The outside of Jame Gumb's old building in Belvedere with its empty storefront and soaped windows covered with heavy gates. Starling hardly recognized it.

'Dungeon of Horrors,' the news reader called it.

Harsh, jostled pictures of the well and the basement, still cameras held up before the television camera, and angry firemen waving the photographers back. Moths crazed by the television lights, flying into the lights, a moth on the floor on its back, wings beating down to a final tremor.

Catherine Martin refusing a stretcher and walking to the ambulance with a policeman's coat around her, the dog sticking its face out between the lapels.

A side view of Starling walking fast to a car, her head down, hands in the pockets of her coat.

The film was edited to exclude some of the more grisly objects. In the far reaches of the basement, the cameras could show only the low, lime-sprinkled thresholds of the chambers holding Gumb's tableaux. The body count in that part of the basement stood at six so far.

Twice Crawford heard Starling expel air through her nose. The news went to a commercial break.

'Good morning, Starling.'

'Hello,' she said, as though it were later in the day.

'The US Attorney in Columbus faxed me your depositions overnight. You'll have to sign some copies for him . . . So you went from Fredrica Bimmel's house to Stacy Hubka, and then to the Burdine woman at the store Bimmel sewed for, Richards' Fashions, and Mrs Burdine gave you Mrs Lippman's old address, the building there.'

Starling nodded. 'Stacy Hubka had been by the place a couple of times to pick up Fredrica, but Stacy's boyfriend was driving and her directions were vague. Mrs Burdine had the address.'

'Mrs Burdine never mentioned a man at Mrs Lippman's?'

'No.'

The television news had film from Bethesda Naval Hospital. Senator Ruth Martin's face framed in a limousine window.

'Catherine was rational last night, yes. She's sleeping, she's sedated right now. We're counting our blessings. No, as I said before, she's suffering from shock, but she's rational. Just bruises, and her finger is broken. And she's dehydrated as well. Thank you.' She poked her chauffeur in the back.

'Thank you. No, she mentioned the dog to me last night, I don't know what we'll do about it, we already *have* two dogs.'

The story closed with a nothing quote from a stress specialist who would be talking with Catherine Martin later in the day to assess emotional damage.

Crawford shut it off.

'How're you hittin' 'em, Starling?'

'Kind of numb . . . you too?'

Crawford nodded, quickly moved along. 'Senator Martin's been on the phone overnight. She wants to come see you. Catherine does too, as soon as she can travel.'

'I'm always home.'

'Krendler too, he wants to come down here. He asked for his memo back.'

'Come to think of it, I'm not always home.'

'Here's some free advice. Use Senator Martin. Let her tell you how grateful she is, let her hand you the markers. Do it soon. Gratitude has a short half-life. You'll need her one of these days, the way you act.'

'That's what Ardelia says.'

'Your roomie, Mapp? The Superintendent told me Mapp's set to cram you for your makeup exams on Monday. She just pulled a point and a half ahead of her archrival, Stringfellow, he tells me.'

'For valedictorian?'

'He's tough, though, Stringfellow – he's saying she can't hold him off.'

'He best bring his lunch.'

In the clutter on Crawford's desk was the origami chicken Dr Lecter had folded. Crawford worked the tail up and down. The chicken pecked. 'Lecter's gone platinum – he's at the top of everybody's Most Wanted list,' he said. 'Still, he could be out for a while. Off the post, you need some good habits.'

She nodded.

'He's busy now,' Crawford said, 'but when he's not busy, he'll entertain himself. We need to be clear on this: You know he'd do it to you, just like he'd do anybody else.'

'I don't think he'd ever bushwhack me – it's rude, and he wouldn't get to ask any questions that way. Sure he'd do it as soon as I bored him.'

'Maintain good habits is all I'm saying. When you go off the post, flag your three-card – no phone queries on your whereabouts without positive

ID. I want to put a trace-alert on your telephone, if you don't mind. It'll be private unless you push the button.'

'I don't look for him to come after me, Mr Crawford.'

'But you heard what I said.'

'I did. I did hear.'

'Take these depositions and look 'em over. Add if you want to. We'll witness your signatures here when you're ready. Starling, I'm proud of you. So is Brigham, so is the Director.' It sounded stiff, not like he wanted it to sound.

He went to his office door. She was going away from him, down the deserted hall. He managed to hail her from his berg of grief: 'Starling, your father sees you.'

Chapter Fifty-nine

Jame Gumb was news for weeks after he was lowered into his final hole.

Reporters pieced together his history, beginning with the records of Sacramento County:

His mother had been carrying him a month when she failed to place in the Miss Sacramento Contest in 1948. The 'Jame' on his birth certificate apparently was a clerical error that no one bothered to correct.

When her acting career failed to materialize, his mother went into an alcoholic decline; Gumb was two when Los Angeles County placed him in a foster home.

At least two scholarly journals explained that this unhappy childhood was the reason he killed women in his basement for their skins. The words *crazy* and *evil* do not appear in either article.

The film of the beauty contest that Jame Gumb watched as an adult was real footage of his mother, but the woman in the swimming pool film was not his mother, comparative measurements revealed.

Gumb's grandparents retrieved him from an unsatisfactory foster home when he was ten, and he killed them two years later.

Tulare Vocational Rehabilitation taught Gumb to be a tailor during his years at the psychiatric hospital. He demonstrated definite aptitude for the work.

Gumb's employment record is broken and incomplete. Reporters found at least two restaurants where he worked off the books, and he worked sporadically in the clothing business. It has not been proven that he killed during this period, but Benjamin Raspail said he did.

He was working at the curio store where the butterfly ornaments were made when he met Raspail, and he lived off the musician for some time. It was then that Gumb became obsessed with moths and butterflies and the changes they go through.

After Raspail left him, Gumb killed Raspail's next lover, Klaus, beheaded and partially flayed him.

Later he dropped in on Raspail in the East. Raspail, ever thrilled by bad boys, introduced him to Dr Lecter.

This was proven in the week after Gumb's death when the FBI seized from Raspail's next of kin the tapes of Raspail's therapy sessions with Dr Lecter.

Years ago, when Dr Lecter was declared insane, the therapy session tapes had been turned over to the families of the victims to be destroyed. But Raspail's wrangling relatives kept the tapes, hoping to use them to attack Raspail's will. They had lost interest listening to the early tapes, which are only Raspail's boring reminiscences of school life. After the news coverage of Jame Gumb, the Raspail family listened to the rest. When the relatives called the lawyer Everett Yow and threatened to use the tapes in a renewed assault on Raspail's will, Yow called Clarice Starling.

The tapes include the final session, when Lecter killed Raspail. More important, they reveal how much Raspail told Lecter about Jame Gumb:

Raspail told Dr Lecter that Gumb was obsessed with moths, that he had flayed people in the past, that he had killed Klaus, that he had a job with the Mr Hide leather-goods company in Calumet City, but was taking money from an old lady in Belvedere, Ohio, who had made linings for Mr Hide, Inc. One day Gumb would take everything the old lady had, Raspail predicted.

'When Lecter read that the first victim was from Belvedere and she was flayed, he knew who was doing it,' Crawford told Starling as they listened together to the tape. 'He'd have given you Gumb and looked like a genius if Chilton had stayed out of it.'

'He hinted to me by writing in the file that the sites were too random,' Starling said. 'And in Memphis he asked me if I sew. What did he want to happen?'

'He wanted to amuse himself,' Crawford said. 'He's been amusing himself for a long, long time.'

No tape of Jame Gumb was ever found, and his activities in the years after Raspail's death were established piecemeal through business correspondence, gas receipts, interviews with boutique owners.

When Mrs Lippman died on a trip to Florida with Gumb, he inherited everything – the old building with its living quarters and empty storefront and vast basement, and a comfortable amount of money. He stopped working for Mr Hide, but maintained an apartment in Calumet City for a while, and used the business address to receive packages in the John Grant name. He kept favored customers, and continued to travel to boutiques around the country, as he had for Mr Hide, measuring for custom garments he made in Belvedere. He used his trips to scout for victims and to dump them when they were used up – the brown van droning for hours on the Interstate with finished leather garments swaying on racks in the back above the rubberized body bag on the floor.

He had the wonderful freedom of the basement.

Room to work and play. At first it was only games – hunting young women through the black warren, creating amusing tableaux in remote rooms and sealing them up, opening the doors again only to throw in a little lime.

Fredrica Bimmel began to help Mrs Lippman in the last year of the old lady's life. Fredrica was picking up sewing at Mrs Lippman's when she met Jame Gumb. Fredrica Bimmel was not the first young woman he killed, but she was the first one he killed for her skin.

Fredrica Bimmel's letters to Gumb were found among his things.

Starling could hardly read the letters, because of the hope in them, because of the dreadful need in them, because of the endearments from Gumb that were implied in her responses: 'Dearest Secret Friend in my Breast, I love you! – I didn't *ever* think I'd get to say that, and it is best of all to get to say it *back*.'

When did he reveal himself? Had she discovered the basement? How did her face look when he changed, how long did he keep her alive?

Worst, Fredrica and Gumb truly were friends to the last; she wrote him a note from the pit.

The tabloids changed Gumb's nickname to Mr Hide and, sick because they hadn't thought of the name themselves, virtually started over with the story.

Safe in the heart of Quantico, Starling did not have to deal with the press, but the tabloid press dealt with her.

From Dr Frederick Chilton, the *National Tattler* bought the tapes of Starling's interview with Dr Hannibal Lecter. The *Tattler* expanded on their conversations for their 'Bride of Dracula' series and implied that Starling had made frank sexual revelations to Lecter in exchange for information, spurring an offer to Starling from *Velvet Talks: The Journal of Telephone Sex*.

People magazine did a short, pleasant item on Starling, using yearbook pictures from the University of Virginia and from the Lutheran Home at Bozeman. The best picture was of the horse, Hannah, in her later years, drawing a cart full of children.

Starling cut out the picture of Hannah and put it in her wallet. It was the only thing she saved.

She was healing.

Chapter Sixty

Ardelia Mapp was a great tutor – she could spot a test question in a lecture farther than a leopard can see a limp – but she was not much of a runner. She told Starling it was because she was so weighted with facts.

She had fallen behind Starling on the jogging trail and caught up at the old DC-6 the FBI uses for hijack simulations. It was Sunday morning. They had been on the books for two days, and the pale sun felt good.

'So what did Pilcher say on the phone?' Mapp said, leaning against the landing gear.

'He and his sister have this place on the Chesapeake.'

'Yeah, and?'

'His sister's there with her kids and dogs and maybe her husband.'

'So?'

'They're in one end of the house – it's a big old dump on the water they inherited from his grandmother.'

'Cut to the chase.'

'Pilch has the other end of the house. Next weekend, he wants us to go. Lots of rooms, he says. "As many rooms as anybody might need," I believe is the way he put it. His sister would call and invite me, he said.'

'No kidding. I didn't know people did that anymore.'

'He did this nice scenario – no hassles, bundle up and walk on the beach, come in and there's a fire going, dogs jump all over you with their big sandy paws.'

'Idyllic, umm-humm, big sandy paws, go on.'

'It's kind of much, considering we've never had a date, even. He claims it's best to sleep with two or three big dogs when it gets really cold. He says they've got enough dogs for everybody to have a couple.'

'Pilcher's setting you up for the old dog-suit trick, you snapped to that didn't you?'

'He claims to be a good cook. His sister says he is.'

'Oh, she called already.'

'Yep.'

'How'd she sound?'

'Okay. Sounded like she was in the other end of the house.'

'What did you tell her.'

'I said, "Yes, thank you very much," is what I said.'

'Good,' Mapp said. 'That's very good. Eat some crabs. Grab Pilcher and smooch him on his face, go wild.'

Chapter Sixty-one

Down the deep carpet in the corridor of the Marcus Hotel, a room-service waiter trundled a cart.

At the door of suite 91, he stopped and rapped softly on the door with his gloved knuckle. He cocked his head and rapped again to be heard above the music from within – Bach, *Two- and Three-Part Inventions*, Glenn Gould at the piano.

'Come.'

The gentleman with the bandage across his nose was in a dressing gown, writing at the desk.

'Put it by the windows. May I see the wine?'

The waiter brought it. The gentleman held it under the light of his desk lamp, touched the neck to his cheek.

'Open it, but leave it off the ice,' he said, and wrote a generous tip across the bottom of the bill. 'I won't taste it now.'

He did not want the waiter handing him wine to taste – he found the smell of the man's watchband objectionable.

Dr Lecter was in an excellent humor. His week had gone well. His appearance was coming right along, and as soon as a few small discolorations cleared, he could take off his bandages and pose for passport photos.

The actual work he was doing himself – minor injections of silicon in his nose. The silicon gel was not a prescription item, but the hypodermics and the Novocaine were. He got around this difficulty by pinching a prescription off the counter of a busy pharmacy near the hospital. He blanked out the chicken scratches of the legitimate physician with typist's correction fluid and photocopied the blank prescription form. The first prescription he wrote was a copy of the one he stole, and he returned it to the pharmacy, so nothing was missing.

The palooka effect in his fine features was not pleasing, and he knew the silicon would move around if he wasn't careful, but the job would do until he got to Rio.

When his hobbies began to absorb him – long before his first arrest – Dr Lecter had made provisions for a time when he might be a fugitive. In the wall of a vacation cottage on the banks of the Susquehanna River were money and the credentials of another identity, including a passport and the cosmetic aids he'd worn in the passport photos. The passport would have expired by now, but it could be renewed very quickly.

Preferring to be herded through customs with a big tour badge on his chest, he'd already signed up for a ghastly sounding tour called 'South American Splendor' that would take him as far as Rio.

He reminded himself to write a check on the late Lloyd Wyman for the hotel bill and get the extra five days' lead while the check plodded through the bank, rather than sending an Amex charge into the computer.

This evening he was catching up on his correspondence, which he would have to send through a remailing service in London.

First, he sent to Barney a generous tip and a thank-you note for his many courtesies at the asylum.

Next, he dropped a note to Dr Frederick Chilton in federal protective custody, suggesting that he would be paying Dr Chilton a visit in the near future. After this visit, he wrote, it would make sense for the hospital to tattoo feeding instructions on Chilton's forehead to save paperwork.

Last, he poured himself a glass of the excellent Batard-Montrachet and addressed Clarice Starling:

Well, Clarice, have the lambs stopped screaming?

You owe me a piece of information, you know, and that's what I'd like.

An ad in the national edition of the *Times* and in the *International Herald-Tribune* on the first of any month will be fine. Better put it in the *China Mail* as well.

I won't be surprised if the answer is yes and no. The lambs will stop for now. But, Clarice, you judge yourself with all the mercy of the dungeon scales at Threave; you'll have to earn it again and again, the blessed silence. Because it's the plight that drives you, seeing the plight, and the plight will not end, ever.

I have no plans to call on you, Clarice, the world being more interesting with you in it. Be sure you extend me the same courtesy.

Dr Lecter touched his pen to his lips. He looked out at the night sky and smiled.

I have windows.

Orion is above the horizon now, and near it Jupiter, brighter than it will ever be again before the year 2000. (I have no intention of telling you the time and how high it is.) But I expect you can see it too. Some of our stars are the same.

Clarice.

Hannibal Lecter

Far to the east, on the Chesapeake shore, Orion stood high in the clear night, above a big old house, and a room where a fire is banked for the night, its light pulsing gently with the wind above the chimneys. On a large bed there are many quilts and on the quilts and under them are several large dogs. Additional mounds beneath the covers may or may not be Noble Pilcher, it is impossible to determine in the ambient light. But the face on the pillow, rosy in the firelight, is certainly that of Clarice Starling, and she sleeps deeply, sweetly, in the silence of the lambs.

In his note of condolence to Jack Crawford, Dr Lecter quotes from 'The Fever' without troubling to credit John Donne.

Clarice Starling's memory alters lines from T. S. Eliot's 'Ash Wednesday' to suit her.

T.H.